Executive Reprieve

By

Philip Childs

PublishAmerica
Baltimore

First printing

ISBN: 1-4241-4353-5
PUBLISHED BY PUBLISHAMERICA, LLLP
www.publishamerica.com
Baltimore

Printed in the United States of America

Dedicated to Dr. R for telling me to write something
And to LO for telling me I actually could write.

My thanks also to PublishAmerica for all their help

John
Sorry there is no golf in this

Chapter 1

"All clear sir," the man said as he began packing up his electronic gear.

"Fine, thank you. Clean up as quickly as you can. Will anyone know you've been here?" asked the portly man behind a large mahogany desk.

"No sir. The CO thinks I'm having the gear calibrated"

"What if he checks?" came the worried question.

"No sweat sir, the tech is one of us. I gave him a heads up, so everything's cool" came the measured reply as the Sergeant picked up his case and left the office.

Twenty seconds later the phone rang.

"Yes," the man answered

"Your one o'clock is here sir," his secretary told him.

"Send him in," he ordered, getting up from behind the desk and walking to the door.

He arrived just in time to meet his guest as he entered. The two made a striking contrast. The man coming through the door was tall, trim and athletic with hair graying at the temples. He looked ten years younger than the fifty-two he was.

By comparison his host was just under 5'7" tall, noticeably overweight, and almost totally bald. He looked every day of his sixty-four years. The only difference between them was physical, however. Both men had extremely sharp minds and were both driven to the same goal.

"Jack so good of you to see me on such short notice." The tall man said to his shorter host warmly embracing him.

"My pleasure sir," Jack replied. "Please have a seat."

The two men moved over to the side of the office wear a pair of leather easy chairs fronted a coffee table holding a steaming pot of Columbian coffee and two cups.

"Coffee sir?" Jack asked his visitor.

" Jack, Jack. How many times do I have to tell you to call me Chris when we're alone?"

"Sorry sir, but I feel that it is appropriate to be formal at all times. After all we wouldn't want anyone to think we know each other better than we've let on."

"As always Jack, you're right. Now tell me, have you found him?"

"Yes we have sir," he answered, his voice low and filled with excitement. "He's everything we've been waiting for, and more."

Jack poured them each a cup of coffee and handed one to Chris.

" So, tell me," he said taking a sip of his coffee and sighing with pleasure at the taste.

"Yes sir. As you know we've had teams scouting for the last few years. Everyone we've found has had ties that could be traced so we discarded them as usable. Now, however, we've found someone that is perfect. He has no ties, born an only child, and his parents died in a car crash when he was seventeen. His closest living relatives are more than a thousand miles away from him. No one will ever miss him."

" That's great Jack, but…"

"As I said, all that we've been waiting for….and more." Jack said getting up and moving to his desk. He unlocked the bottom drawer and removed a file folder taking it back to Chris and handing it to him. "Read this, here if you have a few minutes to do so. I would prefer that this doesn't leave this room."

Chris raised his eyebrow, "Could you just tell me what it says?"

"I'd rather you read it sir."

Chris sat up looking worried. "I thought you had this room swept…."

"Yes….yes I did just moments before you came in. However, sir I feel that some things should remain unspoken."

Chris opened the file and quickly read through it. The contents outlined the life of Charles Watkins, starting with his grandfather who was a WW2 hero in the British army who immigrated to Canada after the war. The man started a construction firm that was very successful and who died when

Charles was thirteen. His estate went to Charles's father who sold the business and retired. Then a few years later on a vacation, both parents were killed in an auto accident leaving everything to Charles including a very large insurance policy adding to the already considerable wealth of the young man. After his parents death the boy took up big bore rifle shooting and had become an extremely good shot managing to get himself and invitation to the National Championship.

"You've got to be joking!" he exclaimed slamming the file closed. "This is fantastic. Is all of this true?"

"Absolutely sir," Jack said, taking the file back to his desk and locking the file back in the desk. "I should let you get back to your day sir. Once again thank you for meeting with me. I felt you should know about this."

Chris virtually jumped to his feet " Not a problem Jack, not a problem. For news like this I'd take a whole day off. However if we are done I will be heading back to my office. We wouldn't want MY boss wondering where I was now would we."

"No sir," Jack answered, opening the door and escorting him out.

SIX MONTHS EARLIER

The target was tiny, even through the 9X rifle scope. At 500 meters the bull's eye was a mere speck surrounded by a small patch of white. The shooter slowly exhaled and then drew in half a breath and held it. His brain sent a message to his finger to squeeze the trigger and send the 148-grain bullet on its way. By now his actions were automatic. The trigger broke at exactly 4.5 pounds of pressure sending the firing pin into the cartridge, which shot the bullet on its way to the target.

"Bull's eye!" the spotter yelled a second later.

The shooter stood up from the bench rest he had been shooting from and slowly began to take his rifle apart. He was the last competitor of the day and now all that was left was to announce the winner.

The crowd of spectators began milling about and murmuring. The young man taking apart and cleaning his rifle had been a last minute entry into the competition, literally. He had shown up just seconds before the entry admissions office had closed stating that his late arrival was the result of a hold up at US customs. A Canadian carrying a rifle into the US was a bit of a rarity. This wasn't the most surprising thing though; the most surprising thing was his skill with that rifle. After his last shot several other shooters had started congratulating him on what they felt was a sure victory. The only competitor not sure was the locale favorite who thought that He was the winner

"Damn kid!" he exclaimed. "Look at all those fools trampin' around tryin' to shake his hand like he's some kind of famous sniper or something."

"Now Billy, don't be like that." His wife told him. "You know that the first time you entered folks 'round here was congratulatin' you on your shootin' too. You know how these boys love to see a fine marksman. You're just sore that he beat you."

"He did nothin' of the kind!" Bill yelled. "You just..."

"Don't you go yellin' at me William Jefferson Allen." His wife told him calmly. " There ain't nothin' wrong with my eyes, and I can see plain as day that that boy done better than you. You'd see it too if you weren't so stubborn. Now you swallow your pride and go on over there and shake his hand."

Knowing better than to argue to the woman he'd married almost forty years ago Bill took a deep breath and slowly started towards the still growing crowd around the young man. People seeing him coming moved out of his way as if by common consent letting him walk straight up to the young shooter.

"That was some damn fine shootin' there son. Name's William but folks call me Bill," he said, sticking his hand out.

The young man smiled and took the pro-offered hand. "Charles but everyone generally calls me Charley. I'm glad to meet you. I was told that if I wanted to win here you'd be the man to beat. I can see that I was told right."

Bill seemed to stand a bit straighter. "Folks actually told you I was the man to beat?" he asked with a touch of pride in his voice.

"Yes sir."

"Now don't you go callin' me sir. I told ya it's Billy to those that know me. And anyone that can shoot like you just did it'd would be my privilege to know."

Charley relaxed a bit and went back to cleaning and packing the rifle.

"I'm glad to hear that. Usually when I come to a shoot, the local competitors aren't too happy to see me. Seems that lots of people don't feel a Canadian belongs at these things"

"Now that's nonsense boy. Where you come from doesn't mean a thing to me. I judge people by how they treat others. So far you seem to be a respectable man and ya got manners too. Truth is if I was mad it'd be because you beat me and nothing else, and up until a minute ago that's how I felt. But my wife is a lot smarter than I am and pointed out to me that I got beat fair and square so I got no call to be mad."

"Thank you Bill, but I wouldn't declare any winners yet. The judges are still looking at the targets."

Billy glared at the young man. "Now don't you go acting stupid after I made up my mind that you're a smart lad. Any one with a set of eyes can see that you beat everyone here. The judges are just going to confirm what we all know."

Charlie's face cracked into a small grin. "Well again I thank you for the kindness, but I was always taught not to take things for granted. Until the judges say it, I haven't won."

Just then a loud speaker boomed out "Will all contestants please proceed to the judges tent."

"Well I guess they're about to let us know." Bill stated, heading to find his wife before going to the judges tent. A few minutes later the contestants and spectators were crowded around in front of the tent that had been set up for the people that would judge the event. There were five judges in all and they now stood in front of the tent holding the targets used by the finalists.

"After reviewing all the targets and tallying up the shots we are ready to announce the winners." one of the judges stated, talking into a microphone attached to a portable amp. "In third place, from Boston Mass, is Sam Wilson" the judge paused for the polite applause. In second place, from right here in our very own hometown, is Bill Allen." The applause was louder and a bit longer with a few shouts and whistles tossed in.

"And the winner is...From some place in Canada called Port Williams, where I thought they didn't even have guns, Charles Watkins." The crowd applauded loudly and with enthusiasm and a few laughs mixed in for the judges comments.

After receiving his prize and spending an hour answering questions from the curious crowd, Charles loaded his rifle into his pickup and headed back to the motel he was staying in. His thoughts were of the contest and how pleased he was that he had done so well. It was his first shooting competition in the United States and he'd won. Even thought it was only a small local competition it had given him the exposure to shooting with crowds watching, that he needed. More importantly it was a step to a regional final and the chance to break into the competitive shooting world that he wanted so badly. Even as a boy learning to shoot he'd had a natural talent for hitting his targets, no matter what they were. He was expert with any hunting rifle made but his first large rifle had been a 30-06 and that was still his favorite caliber.

Charley suddenly realized that there were lights flashing behind him. He checked his rearview mirror and saw the Police car directly behind him. He slowed down and pulled to the shoulder of the highway, wondering why he was being stopped. He was wearing his seatbelt, not even sure if that was required in this state, and he'd been driving below the speed limit. Maybe one of his taillights wasn't working. The police car stopped behind him and two officers stepped out and slowly approved his car, their hands on their guns. Charley, having two rifle cases sitting in the cab beside him visible to the police officers, sat still with his hands on the steering wheel so that he wouldn't do anything to make the officers nervous.

When the driver of the police car tapped on his window Charley rolled it down. "Yes sir, how can I help you?" he asked.

"May I see your license and vehicle registration sir?" the officer asked.

"Yes sir. The papers are in the glove box," Charley announced, sensing that the policeman was nervous. He removed them and handed them out the window.

The cop scanned the papers quickly. "Are those gun cases there beside you Mr. Watkins?"

"Yes sir. I just competed in the local rifle shoot. I'm heading back to my motel now."

"That's nice," came the curt reply. "Your license and registration are both from Canada. Is this your current address sir?"

"Yes sir," Charley answered, deciding to keep everything brief.

The other officer had moved up to the passenger side window and was standing with his hand on his gun starring intently at the two rifle cases.

"The reason we pulled you over Mr. Watkins is that there's a report of a shooting in the area and the suspect in the incident matches your description. It was also reported that the suspect was driving a pickup with out of state plates on it and a rifle case could be seen in the cab with him. Would you mind stepping out of your vehicle sir?" the officer asked, moving back from the side of the pickup and placing his hand on his gun. The officer on the other side pulled his handgun out of the holster but stopped short of pointing it at Charley.

Charley, nervous but not worrying, slowly got out of his truck making sure that the two saw his hands at all times. He knew that his biggest enemy wasn't the police, but surprise. Doing anything to startle the two could result in his getting shot. As he got out the officer grabbed his arm and pulled him around until he was facing his truck and pushed until he was leaning against it. The officer held him there with one hand and started searching him with the other one. As this was happening to him the second officer took the two can cases out of his truck and opened them. He removed the rifles from the cases and sniffed the end of the barrels.

"This one's been fired and cleaned recently," he stated matter-of-factly.

Charley was now worried. "Yes it has. That's the one I used to shoot in the competition with. If you look in the bag on the seat you'll see the check and the first place trophy I won."

"Quiet!" the one frisking him ordered. "We'll check your story out but for right now I'm afraid you'll have to come with us."

Charley felt cold steel on his wrists, as he was hand cuffed. Now he was scared. Even though it was an obvious misunderstanding, the sensation of being arrested was an unpleasant one.

The ride to the local police station was a quiet one as neither officer said a word. Charley, in no mood to talk anyway, never bothered trying to get any information from them. After arriving at the station Charley was placed in a windowless room and left alone for twenty minutes. The only thing in the room was a table, bolted to the floor, and a folding chair that he was sitting in. Unlike in the movies there was no two-way mirror that allowed the police to watch him.

When the door facing him finally opened, three men in suits walked through the door carrying chairs similar to the Charley was sitting in. They set the chairs up in a line on the opposite side of the table from him and sat down. None of them bothered to introduce themselves and Charley was too nervous to ask their names.

They could have been brothers they looked so much alike. All three were wearing dark suits with white shirts and dark colored ties. All were clean-shaven around six feet in height and athletic looking. Their hair was cut short, above the collars, but not a crew cut. To any familiar with the look, they screamed lawyer or government. A few years back Charley had seen a lot of both attending to the burial of his parents.

All three men sat down and opened a file folder and began reading from it. Several minutes passed before any words were spoken.

"Good evening Mr. Watkins," the man in the middle said. "My name is Mr. Cooper, to my left is Mr. Jackson, and to my right is Mr. Wallace. We'd like to ask you a few questions if you don't mind."

The tone he used told Charley that even if he did mind they would be asking him questions. Not sure what the problem was, he was sure that it could be cleared up by talking with the people from the competition and he could be on his way.

"Ummm…sure whatever you need to know." He answered hesitantly but eager to clear this matter up. "But if you just call the guys that put on the competition they'll tell you that I was there all day. I was on my way back to my motel straight from there so whatever is going on I couldn't have been any part of it."

The three men never looked up, never acknowledged what he had said. Charley was beginning to sweat. "Excuse me sir? Mr. Cooper? I'm not sure what the problem is but I'm telling you I was at that competition all day. Just ask and they'll tell you I was."

Mr. Cooper looked up, eyed Charley slowly and deliberately then quietly asked, "Would you please stand up and face the wall Mr. Watkins?"

Charley stood up and did as ordered. The three men huddled together in whispered conversation and when he started to turn to face them a steely voice commanded. "Do not turn around Mr. Watkins!"

The sweat was gathering in Charlie's armpits and the small of his back as he strained to hear the whispered conversation going on behind him. Suddenly the whispers ended and the three quickly closed the folders, gathered up the chairs and headed for the door

"You may sit down now and we'll be talking to you after the trial Mr. Watkins" he was told by Wallace as they left the room.

The door had no sooner closed than it was opened again and a harried looking woman entered struggling with a chair and a briefcase. She put the chair behind the table, opened the briefcase and removed a file folder, placed it on the table and sat down.

"Hi I'm Martha, Martha Little. I'm from the Public Defenders office and I'll be your counsel for the trial," she said, extending her hand to Charley.

"WHAT TRIAL?" he yelled in shock ignoring her outstretched hand. "I haven't done anything!"

"Have you been told why you're here?" she asked.

"No. No I haven't," answered a stunned Charley.

"Oh. Well…. I see then." She looked down at the file in front of her. "You are being charged with murder. The district attorney will be filling the charge in the morning and a grand jury will be convened to hear the evidence and see if a trial is warranted. They are accusing you of killing a U.S. deputy marshal."

Charley was shocked into total silence.

After several moments the woman continued: "I think we should talk about your case. The evidence the police have is that it was a hunting accident. You panicked and fled the scene after discovering that you had killed a man. Is there anything you'd like to tell me at this time?"

Charley sat still in stunned silence. There had to be a mistake. This couldn't be happening to him. He had been at the competition all day, there was no way he could have done what they were saying. All anyone had to do was ask the judges from the competition and they could verify his whereabouts for the whole day.

"Excuse me, Mr. Watkins? Are you all right?" the voice slowly penetrated Charlie's mind.

Would you like cup of coffee or something?" she persisted.

"Lady look..." Charley began.

"Martha Little," she interrupted "I can understand your confusion but we really need to discuss this"

"Yes we do. See there's been a mistake. I was at a shooting competition all day. I won the thing. Just make some calls and anyone can tell you I was there all day. I couldn't have shot anyone. I didn't have time to go hunting. I never left the range at all day today."

Martha looked at Charley intently. "Did you tell the police this?" her voice full of surprise.

"Yes, yes of course I did."

Martha sat quietly a smile slowly forming on her face. As a public defender she rarely ever got handed a case that was winnable. If what this young man had told her was true it looked as if she had a slam dunk on her hands. "I'll check into this immediately for you. If I can get a verification of where you were I can have you out of here by morning."

"Thank you," Charley whispered, relieved that someone would be trying to clear this whole mess up.

"Just relax Charley. I'm on your side and I'll do everything I can for you," Martha told him as she packed up her papers, getting ready to leave. "I know some of the folks that were at that competition so I'll make some phone calls and be back here first thing in the morning. This will all be over soon."

Martha left and a police officer came in to the room and re-handcuffed Charley. He was led down to the basement of the station and put into one of the cells. Charley noticed that he was the only one there; all the other cells were empty. It was obvious that these were only temporary holding cells as there were only benches bolted along the walls. They're no beds or toilets in any of the cells. Charley laid down on one of the benches and covered his eyes with his arm, trying to sleep so the night would go by faster.

He had no idea what time it was when he heard the noise of several people coming down the hall. By the sounds being made several of them were drunk and an argument was in full swing. He heard another voice yelling for quiet and eventually the sounds subsided into quiet muttering and footsteps. A few seconds later four large and obviously drunken men were stopped in front of the holding cell by three police officers. One of the officers unlocked the cell door and the other two herded the men inside. After the door was shut and locked the men were told to put their hands through the slot in the door one at a time so the handcuffs could be removed. As soon as this was done the 3 officers left, one wishing Charley a good night.

Charley was now sitting up and wondering why the men had been put in his cell when there was an empty one right across the hall from him. He watched the four slowly wander around the cell looking at him. All four were wearing dirty jeans and t-shirts and hadn't shaved or bathed in several days. The smell of body odor and alcohol was overpowering. Charley said nothing, just watched the men move to the back of the cell and stretch out on the bench there. He had an odd feeling about three of them they looked familiar. Charley stole a glance every few minutes trying to place the men. It was just at the edge of his memory. Somewhere he had seen them before. All except the very large one that had been staring at him since he sat down on the bench. He had noticed every one of Charley's glances.

"Boy, why do you keep looking at us?" the large man asked loudly. "You think we're pretty or something?" He got up and slowly walked toward Charley.

"No sir," Charley answered quietly. "I just had a feeling that I've met you gentlemen some where before.

The big man started to laugh loudly while the other three stared impassively at Charley.

"Hear that? The boy thinks he's seen us before. Well let me tell you something boy, I don't think you ever would have seen us before cause we don't hang out in them gay bars you'd be going to," he yelled at Charley.

The man was now looming over Charley, hands on his hips looking down at him. He stood there daring Charley to look at him. "Well boy, what do you think now?"

Charley kept his head down, "I'm sorry I was mistaken. I didn't mean anything by it."

"Oh you're sorry now are you? Well that may be the only right thing you've said so far. You are a sorry sight."

The big man swung his fist from the hip with no warning. He caught

Charley flush on the side of the face, slamming his head into the wall behind him. Charley slumped flat on the bench, rolling off it to the floor without making a sound. He was out cold.

The other three men moved quickly to Charley, one checking for a pulse the other two lying him out straight on the floor checking the damage done to him. There was blood pouring out of a gash in his head where it had hit the wall and a large bruise was beginning to show on the cheek that the big man had landed his punch. It looked like there may be some loose teeth but if the head wound weren't too serious then Charley would be fine.

"His pulse is weak and thready," Stated the man taking Charley's pulse. He took a handkerchief from his pocket and applied pressure to the cut on the head to slow the bleeding down. One of the men stood up and calmly speared the big man in the throat with his thumb.

"You were told to knock him out without causing too much damage," he said to the man now holding his throat and choking. "If he has a head injury that affects his vision or motor skills he's no good to us. If that happens I'll kill you."

He knelt back down to help the other two with Charley dismissing the man from his mind. The three men began removing medical supplies from pouches they had taped to the back of their calves. They removed gauze pads, antibiotic cream, alcohol pads, tape, a bottle of clear liquid and a needle. They filled the needle with liquid from the bottle and swabbed Charley's arm. After giving him the shot they put the cream on his wound and bandaged his head to stop the bleeding. When they finished one of the men took a cell phone from his packet and dialed a number.

"We need to move now. The subject was injured a little more then was planned." He said and hung up the phone not waiting for a reply. All three removed their jackets and covered the unconscious Charley to keep him warm. Finally having regained normal breathing, the big man also removed his jacket and handed it to one of the men squatting near Charley. They put it under his feet to elevate them and help reduce the risk of shock.

Two minutes later they heard the sound of people moving down the hallway toward their cell. A stretcher with a paramedic at each end was stopped in front of the cell door as a police officer unlocked it. Charley was quickly loaded onto the stretcher and one of the paramedics immediately started an IV going. Charley was taken outside and placed in an ambulance and driven off. The four men headed away from the police station as soon as the ambulance was out of site.

"You will rendezvous at the clinic and keep the subject under observation until he is medically cleared to begin training, is that clear?" The big man was ordered.

He turned and headed in the opposite direction never saying a word. The three stood for a moment watching him and then began walking away from the police station, already thinking ahead to the next phase of their plan.

Charley arrived at the clinic and was taken straight to an MRI room and was checked to determine the extent of his head injury. After several scans and x-rays were taken they placed him in the ICU ward and a large silent man sat and watched over him. The doctors and nurses knew better then to question why the man was there or who he was. They didn't even know the name of the patient. All they did know was that the company that funded their clinic occasionally called them and sent over a patient with orders to treat him and keep no records. These patients were always accompanied by someone else, usually a very large someone else. The clinic staff assumed it was to keep them in line and make sure the orders were not challenged. They never once thought that the man might be there to watch the patient.

In the morning another man showed up and with out saying a word took the place of the one watching Charley. The staff was used to this happening and took the silent exchange in stride. As the watchers switch was occurring the ICU nurse was taking Charley's vital signs. As she was finishing with his blood pressure the doctor entered to examine him. While he was dilating the pupils Charley began to stir.

"Can you hear me?" the doctor asked several times in a slow steady voice. He was gently squeezing Charley's hands as he was trying to get the patient to respond to his voice.

The watcher stood and moved near the bed to get a closer look. As soon as the patient was awake he was to call in and report it.

Charley opened his eyes and looked around slowly trying to focus. His head hurt and everything was blurry.

The watcher left the room and dialed his cell phone, speaking quietly into it when the ringing stopped "The subject is awake sir."

"Have the doctor ensure there is no sign of lasting trauma and then have him sedated. A transport team will be there in twenty minutes."

The watcher hung up and headed back to the ICU to speak with the doctor and get the patient ready to move.

Chapter 2

Slowly the realization hit him that he wasn't where he should have been. It was a distant fuzzy thing in his memory. What had he been doing? Where had he been? Whatever and wherever, he was sure it wasn't where he now found himself. After all, lying face down in a damp ditch, the smell of musty earth filling his nostrils would be something he would remember. At least he thought he should remember. Perhaps he had been drunk the night before and had lost consciousness, falling into the ditch. He thought about this for a second, trying to recall how he had felt the last time he had awoken after a night of drinking. The pounding headache was present as was the body aches associated with sleeping in a very uncomfortable position in a comatose state. But, and this was a key ingredient, his mouth didn't feel as if it was full of sawdust and there was no raging thirst. If he had been drinking the night before he would be thirsty, very thirsty. That ruled out a drunken stupor. He was suddenly hit by the thought that maybe he should try to move. He could be injured, that could be the answer to his current problem. He was driving home, got into an accident and was thrown from the vehicle hitting his head. His brain sized on this as the answer. To back up his theory he gingerly moved head, rocking it side-to-side less than an inch just to see how much pain there was. None. No pain at all. Feeling surer of his physical condition he attempted to push himself to a sitting position, taking note of any spasms of pain or discomfort along the way. He reached a sitting position with out trouble and the only event of any note was a mild dizziness that seemed to fade almost as soon as it started.

Have succeeded in rising to a sitting position he felt brave enough to attempt standing. Moving slowly, just in case there was something wrong he pushed himself to his feet. As his head came above the level of the ditch he had been lying in several things caught his attention at once. He had assumed that the ditch would be beside a road, yet he saw no roadway. He smelled wood smoke and heard the sound of wood crackling in a fire. But the item that most caught his attention was the elderly man pointing a rifle in his direction. Suddenly he was no longer worried about any harm that had already happened to him, he was more concerned about harm that might happen to him.

"Morning!" the man greeted him heartily. "Step up out of the ditch and join me for a cup of coffee."

Charley didn't move. Even though the voice had been friendly and the invitation sounded sincere, the rifle pointed straight at him was something he wasn't about to make a mistake about. Moving slowly and cautiously he stepped up out of the ditch and moved towards the man and the small campfire at his feet.

"Don't be shy son, have a seat. There's a cup next to the fire, pour your self some coffee and have a seat. I do hope you like it black though, I forgot to bring milk or sugar."

The voice had curious sound to it, as if he used to speak with an accent but over the years it had almost faded away, but not quite entirely. Charley quietly sat down and poured coffee into a battered enamel cup. It smelled great. He had never been a coffee drinker but he thought this morning he would make an exception, if only to keep the man in front of him relaxed and friendly. Taking a sip, he found it tasted surprisingly good.

"I can see that you were in doubt of my coffee brewing skills," the man commented. Charley looked up sharply.

"One must learn how to read his opponent in situations like this," the man continued. "I also see that you are a little bewildered as to where you are and what's going on. Let me try to fill in the blanks for you. You will obviously have some questions so ask away and I'll answer as best I can."

Charley took another tentative sip of the coffee and tried to think of where to start. Knowing that to get out of this alive he would need to play dumb, and although he didn't really believe he'd get any truthful answers what did he have to lose by asking questions.

"Well, I suppose the most logical question to ask first is who are you?"

"Ah yes, that would be logical. I apologize for my rudeness. My name is Sean Miller. Pleased to make your acquaintance. And you are?"

Charley eyed him warily. "I'm Charles Watkins." He replied, sure that Sean already knew who he was.

"Well, then Charley, do you mind if I call you Charley?" Sean went on without waiting for an answer. "It would seem as if you and I are to spend some time together, assuming of course you are agreeable to the arrangement."

Charley put the cup down. "What are you talking about?"

"Another excellent question, but let's leave that one for a little farther on in our discussion shall we? Instead let's talk about where we are. Do you know where we are, Charley?

"I have no idea where we are. Why don't you tell me?

"I'm afraid I can't do that. You see the object of this particular exercise is for you to learn."

"I see. What is it I'm supposed to be learning, or am I not allowed to know that either?"

"It's all very simple, young Charley. You have been chosen to work for the organization I'm employed with. As a senior instructor it's my job to impart to you the various skills that my superiors feel you will be required to use."

"I see. Do I have a choice in this?" Charley asked sarcastically.

"But of course you do. Simply tell me to leave and I'll be on my way," Sean answered with a chuckle.

Charley had been watching the man in front of him, slowly taking note of everything he could see. Sean's age appeared to be somewhere in the late forties or early fifties. His hair was shot through with gray but had been a dark brown at one time. He looked extremely fit with good muscle tone but the physique of a runner rather than a weight lifter. The most important thing Charley had noticed was that throughout their conversation the barrel of the rifle had been pointed solidly at his midsection, never wavering. Even now the rifle was rock solid and didn't so much as tremble when Sean had chuckled. This man, even though much older than Charley, was a very capable and dangerous person. Charley was very skeptical that he was going to be allowed to simply leave if he asked to. Still the only way to find out for sure was to ask. "Okay then. Would you be so kind as to leave?"

"As you wish," Sean replied casually. He stood up effortlessly still keeping the rifle pointed at Charley. With an economy of one-handed motion he emptied the coffee pot rinsed it with water from canteen that had been lying near him and put it into a backpack that he had been using as a seat. Hoisting the pack to his shoulders, still with one hand, he smiled at Charley and started to back away from the campfire. "I trust you can look after the fire and put it out before you leave?" He asked

"Sure thing," Charley replied, stunned that Sean was actually leaving. "Just one more question, how do I get out of here?"

"Why you walk of course. Good luck" With that Sean turned and began walking towards the forest that was about 100 yards away.

Charley sat there and watched him walk into the forest and disappear out of site. He looked at his wrist for the time and discovered his watch was gone. He began counting under his breath and when he reached 300, judged that five minutes had passed. He scanned the tree line for some sign of Sean but found nothing. He held his breath and listened turning his head left and right to see if he could hear anything. Beside a gentle breeze blowing and the distant sounds of birdcalls, there was nothing out of the ordinary.

Charley stood up and kicked dirt on the fire to put it out. When there was nothing left but smoldering coals he walked over to the ditch and examined it a little closer. He could see the faded marks of an excavator meaning that the ditch was man made. If this were the case then it would stand to reason that there was a purpose for it and it had to lead somewhere. That being the case he could follow it and find his way to a phone. The sun was at a 45-degree angle in the sky. Charley reasoned that since he had just woken up it made sense to assume it was morning. If this was the case then the ditch was running in an east west direction. He turned toward the east and began walking.

After a few minutes the thought suddenly came to him that he could be in serious trouble. Charley stopped to take stock of his situation. Checking his pockets he discovered that he had absolutely nothing on him. No identification, no money, nothing at all. No food, no water, he didn't know where he was or how long it would take him to get somewhere that had food or water. And even though the bottom of the ditch was damp and muddy in places Charley was fairly sure that if he did find water in the ditch it wouldn't be fit to drink. The last thing he remembered was his prison cell and someone throwing something through the cell bars at him. He had a hazy memory of a doctor but he couldn't be sure of it. Between the punch in the head in jail and waking up in this ditch he wasn't sure what had happened or how much time had passed. He'd been so preoccupied with Sean and his rifle that he hadn't taken the time to find out what had happened to him. What had Sean meant when he said Charley had been chosen to work with the organization. Had this whole thing been some sort of setup to recruit him into some type of criminal outfit? If it had been, would they be inclined to let him simply walk away? He didn't think so. Perhaps this was the way they, whoever they were, intended to get rid of him. Dump in the middle of nowhere and let him starve to death.

Having grown up in a rural area Charley was very familiar with the outdoors and the forest. He had spent more than a few school vacations camping and was comfortable in the forest. Looking at the trees he could see that most of them were pine or spruce and the rest of the plants around indicated that he was in a temperate zone. It was a warm day but not hot. The air smelled clean and clear with no hint of any of the smells that he associated with towns or cities. There were insects and birds around so he knew that he would find some source of water if he looked hard enough. The realization dawned on him that a more immediate problem than finding a phone was finding food, water and shelter. He could be several days walk from any type of settlement and if that was the case he would be dead before he got any help.

Charley headed to the tree line, scouting the ground as he went looking for anything useful. He picked up and examined rocks along the way hoping to find one that had an edge to it that could be used for cutting or scraping. Even though he had spent time in the forest he was unfamiliar with the plants that were edible. Like most people he knew the common berries that could be eaten but not all of them. He saw several mushrooms but he had no idea if they were edible or not and Charley was aware that the wrong type of mushroom could kill him, or at the very least incapacitate him which would also result in his death.

He reached the tree line and started looking for a branch to use as a walking stick and to double as a club. He saw a few dead ones lying on the ground and picked them up one by one. In each instance they were too dead or rotten to be of any use and broke with ease when he tested them. Searching the lower branches of the trees near him he saw a few that looked as if they would be a good choice. He tested a couple and selecting one began bending back and forth to break it free of the tree. After several minutes of bending and twisting it broke off. Charley started pulling the leaves off of it and working on it to get it to a usable shape and length. At the end of his task he had a stick around four feet in length and one inch round at one end tapering to a half inch around at the other end. Feeling a little better now with his club in hand he started heading east again along the edge of the forest once again scouting for anything that could be of use to him.

His work to get his stick had left him hot and sweaty, and he realized, very thirsty. He remembered once reading an article that had mentioned putting a pebble in your mouth if you were thirsty but had no water. He couldn't remember what if anything it was supposed to do but for some reason it stuck in his mind. Searching the ground he found several pebbles and searched for a smooth one. Wiping it free of dirt he popped it into his mouth and started sucking on it as he continued along. After a few minutes he noticed with a bit of surprise that he wasn't as thirsty. That would hold him for a little while but he was going to have to find a source of water and soon.

Sean walked into the trees, turned and stopped. He squatted down and watched the boy to see what he would do. He had read the dossier on Charley and knew that he was an orphan and a crack shot. The rest of his background was a little thin. No one knew what type of survival skills he had. Would he panic at being dumped in the middle of nowhere and just sit there waiting? Would he start walking and simply travel in circles or follow the ditch until he was exhausted? He had intended to leave Charley alone to test his resourcefulness but thought he would need to abandon him in the middle of the night. He would have preferred to have done it that way as it would have let him see how the young man handled the panic of waking up to find himself alone. This way there was no panic, Charley had time to adjust and adapt. No matter, it would still show Sean how the boy looked after himself and how much work Sean had ahead of him. His orders had been specific: train Charley in outdoor survival, tracking and shooting skills. He meant to do that but first wanted to know how much work was ahead of him.

Sean had been recruited almost forty years ago. He looked much younger than he was, nearing his 62nd birthday. He had hoped to retire but knew that the people he worked for would never let him do that. The best he could hope for was to die peacefully in his sleep. The worst, was to be shot from behind one day by one of his co-workers. He knew that this was a real possibility, he had been ordered to do the same thing to several of his co-workers in the years he had been with the organization. He had assured him that he was too valuable for this to happen to and that the men that had been "retired" had become "untrustworthy".

In Seans mind this simply meant that they had outlived their usefulness to the organization. Sean knew that when this happened to him, he too would be "retired". The organization was so secretive that they operated without a name. He doubted that anyone ever had been allowed to leave or ever would be allowed to leave. You were recruited for life. Even the word recruited was a euphemism members were blackmailed into joining. Even after accepting the invitation they would let you know that the blackmail was always there. Most blackmail involved a faked murder charge, as was the case with Charley. With no statute of limitation on murder, the case could always be re-opened should the employee forget who was in charge or decide that retirement looked good. Sometimes, as in Sean's case, the organization visited prisons looking for talent. Three men who had promised a parole and pardon should he choose to work for them had interviewed him. No mention of what type of work or whom he worked for was ever made, it was simply hinted that he would be working for the government. In his youth and eagerness to escape from prison life he accepted without asking enough questions, not that they would have been answered truthfully. It was only after he had completed his training that he fully realized that he had sold his soul for the illusion of freedom. While there were no bars around him anymore he was still as effectively in prison as he had been almost forty years ago. The difference was that in prison he would have been released someday.

As Charley began walking Sean stalked him from inside the tree line. The forest was an old one with little undergrowth, so the walking was easy. As most of the trees had needles instead of leaves the footing was soft and quiet, mostly moss with very little leaf clutter underfoot. Adding to the ease of walking was the fact that Sean was well trained in woodcraft and trailing someone had become second nature to him. He was equally at home in a forest as he was in a city. He had been trained to blend in and move with an economy of motion. Trailing Charley was easy and effortless for him.

He was becoming more and more impressed with Charley as he followed him. The boy didn't panic or get excited and the trick with the pebble was an interesting one, Sean would have to try it himself sometime. Sean had assumed that he would simply follow the ditch until he feel down from exhaustion but Charley's action surprised him. The boy showed a lot of promise. He was steady and used his brain. Sean watched him search for a stick to use as a weapon and smiled to himself when the lad found one. Finally, someone he was looking forward to training.

Charley kept moving slowly along the edge of the forest, constantly on the look out for things he could use. He had picked up dozens of rocks, none of them useful to him. He spotted a flash of red just inside ahead and quickly moved to investigate it. He found a bunch of brambles and a very large clump of raspberries. At first he started grabbing them and stuffing them into his mouth as fast as he could pull them from the branches, but he found that in his haste he was dropping half of what he was picking. He took off his jacket and laid it on the ground and slowly started picking berries and dropping them onto the open coat. After fifteen minutes he had a decent sized mound of berries and he moved into the shade of the trees and sat down to feast on them. When he finished he went back to the berries and began filling the pockets of his coat so as to have some for later. He tied his jacket around his waist, picked up his stick and resumed his trek. Every so often he stopped and turned to survey the trail behind him and to mark in his mind the location of the raspberry bushes, in case he needed to come back to them.

He had no watch and no concept of how much time had passed but he assumed it had been several hours since the breakfast of berries and once again his thirst had returned. Even the pebble trick did little to help this time. He had also started to sweat, as the day grew warmer. He thought about sitting down to rest and save his energy during the hottest part of the day but knew that he couldn't. His mind would not allow him to rest so he kept walking. He guessed that he had covered a few miles but had no way to know for sure. It was hard no knowing where he was or where he was going, and suddenly he realized that the ditch was no longer there. He was standing at the edge of a forest looking at a meadow with trees on the other side. Where there had been a ditch running down the center there was now just flat land. He had no idea when the ditch had stopped, having been concentrating on the forests edge and scouting for food and water. He wondered if the disappearance of the ditch was good or bad. Not being able to do anything about it, and not curious enough to go back to see where it had ended, Charley shrugged his shoulder and continued on.

Sean thought about having a few of the raspberries himself but though better of it deciding that if Charley doubled back he might notice that there were fewer berries than before. With most people Sean would have thought that it would go unnoticed but with Charley he wasn't about to take a chance. The lad had so far shown a pretty keen mind and Sean wasn't about to test his powers of observation just for a few berries. While Charley feasted on fresh berries Sean took the time to eat himself. He opened his pack and dug out a stick of beef jerky and popped it into his mouth slowly chewing on the leathery beef. A quick swallow of water from his canteen finished his snack and he patiently waited for Charley to finish up and move on.

The longer he followed Charley the more impressed he became. With most new trainees, he had by this time "rescued" them and explained the facts of life to them. Seven hours after leaving him Charley was still moving along at a steady clip. There was a brief moment of concern when Charley stopped suddenly and made what appeared to be a panicked circle looking for something. It took Sean a few seconds to figure out that Charley had just noticed that the ditch had petered out. He waited with a bit of anxiety to see what Charley would do and was relieved when he shrugged and moved on. It had looked for a second like Charley would backtrack to find the ditch. Sean was glad he hadn't done that, as it would have meant either hiding while Charley walked past him, or moving quickly to avoid him, two activities Sean wanted to avoid. The human eye was naturally attracted to fast movements as the brain registered them as potential threats. Sean had no doubt that young Charley's eye would notice any quick movements in the forest and draw his attention to it.

Charley felt like his feet were on fire. With no way to tell time other then the sun he wasn't entirely sure how long he'd been walking. When he started the sun had be at a 45-degree angle in front of him and was now behind his shoulder. Unless the forest had curved around it was now mid afternoon. He thought he had been walking in a more or less straight line but the was no sure way to tell.

Exhausted and sore he looked for a good spot to rest and sat down under the branches of a pine tree. It was cool in the shade and relaxing. Charley removed his shoes and socks to give his feet a chance to air out and dry off the sweat. He sat there slowly rubbing his feet dreaming of a tall glass of water, cold enough to have condensation forming on the outside. His thirst was overpowering and he imagined that he could here the gurgle of water running. He shook his head to clear it and leaned back against the tree to take a quick nap. As he lay there trying to relax the sound of running water played more and more on his mind. He shook his head again and furrowed his brow in concentration to try and get rid of the sound. No matter how hard he tried he couldn't get the sound out of his head. Charley wondered if he was becoming delirious from thirst. He wasn't sure if that could happen or not. Never having been this thirsty in his life he was sure that as his body craved fluid more and more there would be some kind of effect on his mind. Rather than try and fight it anymore he laid flat on the ground and let the sound in his head lull him to sleep.

Charley woke up rested but still very thirsty. His feet had swollen a bit and it made getting his shoes back on a little hard. The sound of running water was even more pronounced now that he was rested. Suddenly, Charley sat bolt upright, very still and held his breath.

He turned his head slightly back and forth. The sound of running water increased or decreased very slightly depending on which way his head was pointing. The realization hit him like a brick; there actually was running water somewhere close. Trying hard not to let his excitement overpower him he finished tying his shoes up and began to move in a zigzag pattern.

When Charley sat down under the tree for a break Sean took the time to rest him self. The longer he followed Charley the more impressed he became. It was four in the afternoon and Charley had been moving at a steady pace all day. He didn't panic or run, he just kept walking in a measured step, eating up the miles. Sean estimated that they had covered fifteen miles so far. The fact that Charley was able to do this on only some raspberries said a lot about his strength and conditioning. Sean had stopped twice to eat some jerky and drink from his canteen. He was in great shape himself and was used to walking long distances. Having the added benefit of knowing exactly where he was gave him the peace of mind to actually enjoy the day.

Sean had one moment of anxiety. When the young man jumped up and started moving in a zigzag Sean slowly crouched down moving a tree between his line of sight. He was a considerable distance back and didn't think Charley would see him but why take the risk. Sean guessed that the lad was scouting for water, knowing that there was a stream close by. Had he heard the sound of water running? Had he smelled it? Sean had heard stories of people that had a sense of smell keen enough to detect water the way an animal would and was curious if Charley could be one of them. Sean himself could hear nothing other then Charley moving through the forest and the occasional sound of a bird or insect. He did know however that there was a stream nearby. He had been planning on refilling his canteen from it, knowing it to be a clean water supply.

As Charley moved out of sight Sean silently followed him, moving in a casual manner from tree to tree always keeping something between himself and Charley. Sean was almost totally silent in his movements with nothing other then the whisper of his clothes moving to betray his presence. He was wearing soft-soled shoes and before putting his weight on a foot he felt the ground under it to feel for small twigs that could snap and give him away. He moved this way out of habit without giving it a second thought. It was as natural to him as walking down a sidewalk was for people in a city. All of his attention was focused on stalking Charley, even though this was not at all difficult. Charley moved with no thought to what he was stepping on. Sean could have followed him just by sound alone. It seemed that he stepped on twigs and dries leaves at every other footstep. Charley broke branches off trees as he went by them, taking a direct route no matter how noisy it was.

Charley caught a glimpse of sunlight flashing in the distance and assumed it was reflecting off of water. He rushed toward the spot, his thirst suddenly raging. He flopped onto his stomach on the bank and plunged his head into the cold water, gulping it down. Charley pushed his head under the water, feeling flow around and over him. He sat up and shook his head vigorously, drops of water flying in all directions. He was still thirsty but he knew that drinking too much too fast could make him sick. He cupped his hands and used them to splash water over his head and shoulders feeling the coolness take away the heat of his body. He sprawled on the bank next to the stream enjoying the sensations around him. The feeling of the sun flashing through the trees, the sound of the stream gurgling, the sound of insects buzzing around him, birds chirping in the distance. Charley stopped breathing as his ears picked up a sound that shouldn't have been there. He lay perfectly still, concentrating on listening to hear the sounds around him. One by one he identified natural sounds and then blocked them out. Moving his head side to side he kept blocking out sounds until he was left with the intermittent whisper of something at the very edge of his hearing. Suddenly it disappeared. Not abruptly, but fading quickly like the sound of an animal settling to rest.

Keeping his head frozen in the position he had last heard the noise Charley searched him memory for the hunting lessons he had learned as a boy. Animals tended to move in sudden movements interspersed with moments of stillness to watch for either predators or prey. Charley listened for this, frozen in place. Then faintly he heard a whisper of sound. What ever was out there was no animal. When it did move, it moved slowly and steadily in a straight line, as if going from tree to tree looking for the best cover. Exactly the type of thing a man would do if he were stalking and animal, or another man. Charley rolled over onto his stomach and pushed himself to his feet. In a crouched position he moved away from the water towards a large oak tree behind him. Charley moved around the tree placing it between himself and the direction of the noise, and laid down flat on the ground peering around the tree with one eye toward the stream. He could no longer hear anything other than the sound of the stream and natural sounds of the forest. Rather then trying to move to hear better he swallowed his impatience and forced himself to lie still and wait. With no way to tell time he had no idea how long he lay there waiting. Suddenly he saw movement out of the corner of his eye. He forced his will to over-ride the instinct to turn and look, knowing that movement attracts attention. If he was being stalked, safety lay in staying totally motionless. Whatever was moving disappeared behind a tree. He took a second to adjust his vision and froze just as a leg appeared from behind the tree he was watching. Slowly the man who had introduced himself as Sean Miller eased into view. Charley noticed he was moving with every footstep measured and sure, the foot being placed just so before he moved weight onto it. Sean's head never stopped moving, looking left and right with the same measured pace he was using to walk. He was totally alert and in tune with his surroundings. It was just luck that Charley had heard him at all and had the patience to hide and wait.

Sean moved forward cautiously. The sound of the water and forest was all he could hear now. All day he had been listening to the sounds Charley made as he walked along or moved through the forest. Those sounds had been gone now for more than an hour. This meant that the lad was either no longer moving or had somehow managed to lose him. Having supreme confidence in his stalking skills, Sean doubted the boy's ability to lose him. This meant that he had stopped moving. Knowing how long Charley had been without water Sean assumed that he had found the stream, drank his fill of water and fallen asleep next to the stream. Sean didn't make the mistake of completely believing this however. Making an assumption that the person you were stalking was asleep was a very fast way to become the one being stalked. Even though he was armed with a firearm and Charley wasn't, a club to the back of the head could soon turn the tables. Sean stopped and took stock of his situation. He could now catch glimpse of the stream through the trees but saw no signs of Charley. Sean suddenly had another thought, what if somehow Charley had become aware that he was being followed and had hidden himself to catch the follower. A long shot to be sure, but Sean believed that even long shots were possible. He froze in place and after a moments hesitation lowered himself to the ground.

Sean could now make out a clearing by the stream and if Charley had found the stream and fallen asleep beside it after drinking his fill then the logical place for him to be was right there. Sean slowly reached into his pocket and removed and miniature spotting scope and began slowly scanning the small clearing. There was no sign of Charley, but Sean could see several small birds hunting for insects, something he would not see if there were a human in the cleaning. That meant Charley was somewhere else, but was he close or not.

Not wanting to take the risk that he would be seen Sean laid prone and slow crawled away from the stream. Once he had placed a tree between him and the stream he stood up and debated his next move. He had several choices open to him, he could wait in the area to see if he heard sounds of movement that he was sure Charley would make or he could circle around in an arc and try to pick up Charley's trail, assuming he had moved off.

Charley realized he was being followed, but for what reason? Was Sean planning to kill him? That didn't make sense. If Sean wanted him dead he could have killed him this morning. Unless he wanted to make it look accidental. Dying from starvation would look accidental. And all Sean had to do was follow him to make sure that Mother Nature did the work for him and no one would ever know. But why go to all that trouble? He had almost been killed in prison and if they had wanted him dead that would have been the place to do it. His death would have become just one more statistic and then forgotten. He had no family and his friends had no idea where he was so there would be no one to ever question his disappearance. No, he was missing something, something simple. He thought back to this morning and what Sean had told him. He was supposed to be training Charley for some organization. But training for what?

Sean put his pack down and slung his rifle across his back. Reaching into the tree above him he slowly pulled himself up into the tree branches. He worked his way up the tree gaining height to get a better view of the area. He climbed about twenty-five feet up the tree and took a mini-monocle from his jacket. With one arm wrapped around the tree he scanned the clearing by the stream looking for Charley or a sign that he had been there. Sean noticed some scuffed ground by the edge of the stream indicating that someone or something had laid there drinking water. After fifteen minutes of careful search, this was the only thing out of the ordinary that he saw. Putting the monocle back in his pocket, Sean climbed back down to the ground.

Charley was getting more and more nervous. Should he wait to see what happened? Should he try to sneak away? Should he just walk over to where Sean was? Suddenly movement in a tree across the clearing caught his eye. Charley carefully raised his head and stared intently at the tree. Something large was perched on a branch on third of the way up. The shape formed into Sean. After watching Sean search the area and climb back down the tree Charley stood up and walked towards the tree he had seen Sean climb down from. When he was halfway there he called out to Sean

"Sean, I know your following me so if your going to kill me I'd like to get it over with."

Sean froze in place behind the tree. Charley's voice caught him unprepared, his rifle was slung across his shoulder and he was crouched over opening his backpack. With a nimbleness that belied his age he leapt from behind the tree rolling onto his shoulders and back using the momentum of his jump to swing his rifle off his shoulder and into his hands, and then following the role back onto his knees to face Charley with the rifle pointing at his midsection and Sean in a crouched position ready to fire.

It was Charley's turn to freeze. Slowly raising his hands to shoulder height he stood quietly waiting for Sean to make up his mind about shooting. Charley was still very unsure of why he was being followed. He didn't really think Sean was going to shoot him. After all he could have done that anytime throughout the day. No, if he was supposed to be dead it would have happened already.

Sean slowly stood up and then, seeming to think about it for half a minute, slung the rifle back over his shoulder. He retrieved his pack from behind the tree and casually walked to the stream. He dug his coffee pot out and dipped it into the stream to fill it with water.

"If you'd like some coffee you'll need to help me gather some firewood," Sean said, putting the pot down and looking around for some sticks to start a fire with. For the next few minutes the two gather the material to make a campfire. Neither said a word until they came together by the stream and set the wood down they had gathered.

Sean sat back and looked at Charley, a slight smile on his face. "Well boy you've done great so far. Do you think you could make a fire for us?'

Charley looked at him carefully "And just how would I do that without any matches or a lighter?'

"Do you read lad? Have you ever read a book about someone that's been shipwrecked? Perhaps you saw the movie *Castaway* with Tom Hanks? How did he start a fire without matches or a lighter?"

Charley thought for a second, he had seen the movie. How did Tom Hanks start his fire? Suddenly the scene came to him and he started gathering up some small twigs and dried moss to make tinder with. He found a relatively flat piece of wood and set it flat on the ground pointing away from him. He piled his tinder at the far end and searched through his firewood looking for a stick that was round and blunt at one end. Finding one he began to rub it against the flat stick back and forth in a rapid motion trying to create enough friction to generate a spark and ignite the tinder.

Charley worked steadily for almost an hour without even getting a whiff of smoke from his two sticks. Through this Sean sat quietly watching his efforts.

Exhausted, Charley abandoned his efforts and flopped onto his back panting.

"Okay so we know I can't start a fire by rubbing two sticks together. What do we do now? Can you start a fire that way?" he said between pants.

Sean laughed. "I'm not even going to try to do that."

Charley sat up, his face red "Then why did you have me try it?" he asked angrily.

"To show you how hard it is to start a fire with two sticks, of course. Also to point out that you didn't think it through before you began trying to start the fire. You remembered seeing something in a movie and tried to copy it. Did you take the time to think about what you were trying to do? Did you think about how to accomplish your task? No you didn't, you simply tried to copy a movie scene."

Charley though for a moment, "But you were the one that mentioned the movie to me. If you knew it wasn't going to work why did you tell me to try it?"

"I didn't say to try it, I asked you how he did it in the movie. And I didn't say it wouldn't work, I told you I wasn't going to try it. There are many ways to start a fire. But the smart way is to think about what you need to do and take stock of the supplies you have at hand. You did none of those things. Now I want you to think about how to start a fire and take stock of what you have at hand. Let me know when you're ready to try again and we'll see how you do. In the meantime, I'm hungry and I'd love a cup of coffee so I'll get a fire going."

Sean picked up the tinder Charley had prepared and lit it with a lighter. In two minutes he had a small comfortable fire going and the coffee pot on to boil. Reaching into his pack he took out some coffee and some beef jerky along with biscuits and trail mix. He split the jerky, biscuits and trail mix in two and passed half to Charley. He dropped the coffee grounds into the now boiling water in the coffee pot and popped a piece of the jerky into his mouth.

"Eat up boy, coffee will be done soon."

Charley had watched with rapt attention Sean while he prepared the food and coffee. Never having been much of a coffee drinker, he was curious as to how Sean was going to make it.

"So you just boil the coffee in the water?" Charley asked. "How do you filter it?"

Sean smiled "Do you drink coffee?"

"No, I never really got a taste for it."

"Ah, I see. Well when you are camping with out the usual amenities that one would normally have, you try to make do. I normally prefer to drip filter my coffee but as you can see I find myself without the means to do this. So in light of our primitive surroundings I must either make the best of the situation or go without my coffee. And as I truly enjoy a cup of coffee I choose not to go without."

Sean removed the coffee pot from the fire and pored half a cup of cold water into the boiling coffee. He watched the contents of the pot for another few moments and then slowly poured two cups of the black steaming liquid and passed one to Charley. He took the cup and raised it to his mouth. It smelled like coffee and looked like coffee. He tasted it and was surprised to find that it wasn't as bitter as he thought it would be. He was also expecting to taste the grit from the coffee grounds but didn't. Over all it was pretty good, considering how it had been made.

"How come I don't have coffee grounds in here?" Charley asked. "You boiled them in the water and they should be all through it."

"That's why I dropped the cold water in," Sean answered. "It stops the boiling and settles the grounds to the bottom of the pot. If you pour it carefully and don't try to drink the last inch or so you avoid the grounds. It's an old trick. I believe the old west cowboys did the same thing. Just one of the many little bits of knowledge I've acquired over the years."

"Well it's a neat trick and it doesn't taste bad either."

"Well you are obviously not a coffee drinker because this tastes like absolute shit, but it's better than going without. Now about that fire you're going to start?"

"But you've already got a fire going," protested Charley "Why do you want me to start another one?"

"So you'll know how to in the future," Sean answered casually. "This time before you try, take stock of what you have available to help you. Think hard about what you have to do and different ways you can do it. Use all the tools at hand to complete the job."

Charley looked around carefully and examined the clearing next to the stream. He gathered up twigs and dried moss and dead branches to make the fire with. Now that he had the material he needed a way to start a fire. He tried to think of all the ways he had seen or read about starting a fire without matches. He had tried the rubbing two sticks together and while he was sure that would work he wasn't about to attempt it again. If he had a flint and steel he could strike them together to make sparks but none of the rocks around looked like it could be substituted for either flint or steel and he had no idea if banging two rocks together would make sparks. No way to find out other then doing it to see. Charley scouted the entire clearing looking over all the rocks in view until he found two that were of decent size to hold in his hands. Setting himself he struck them together as hard as he could. The only result was a stinging sensation in his hands causing him to drop the rocks.

"You're certainly no geologist," Sean commented dryly.

Charley stood shaking his hands grinning stupidly at Sean. "Well the only way I was going to know if I could get sparks from banging two rocks together was to try it. I was thinking about what happens when you strike flint and steel and wondered if rocks would work too."

"I see, well at least you're using your brain this time and experimenting," Sean commented. "However let me assure you that no rock around here is going to help you produce sparks so you can give up on that idea."

Charley nodded his understanding and began checking the clearing once more hoping for other ideas. He stumbled over a root and looked down at the ground to see what had tripped him. He looked at his shoe and the site of the lace gave him an idea. Walking into the trees he began looking for a branch that was sturdy but flexible enough to be bent into a half moon shape so he could make a crude bow from it. Finding one that looked suitable he began twisting it to break it from the tree. Charley headed back to the clearing stripping the leaves and smaller branches as he walked. He had the stick mostly cleaned off except for a few pieces that he couldn't get a grip on to tear them off. He dropped the stick near the pile of twigs and went to the stream to see if he could find a stone with a sharp edge that he could use to scrape the stick smooth and make groves in it. After sifting through a dozen or so stones he found one that he liked and took it back to his pile of tinder. Using the stone he scrapped the stick clean of bark and notched both ends. Then he removed the laces from both shoes and braided them together to make it stronger and used it for the string on his bow. Looping the string around another stick he place the stick against a flat piece of bark and put the bark on top of a piece of dead wood holding it in place by putting the rock on top of the stick and pressing down. With the dead moss and dries twigs piled around the stick Charley began to move the bow back and forth in a sawing motion causing the end of the stick to spin against the bark creating friction. After a few moments of vigorous sawing he began to see a tiny wisp of smoke float up from the pile of tinder. He dropped the bow and blew gently on the tinder, getting rewarded with more tendrils of smoke. A few more breaths and suddenly a small flame burst into life. Charley shielded this with his hand and fed more tinder to the growing fire. Within ten minutes had a decent fire going and he looked up proudly to see Sean smiling at him

"Excellent. Sean praised him. "See the difference between trying to copy Hollywood and using your own intelligence? Now think about this question before you answer it. Look around and tell me if there is anything here that could have helped you start that fire any faster, save my lighter of course."

Charley looked around studying everything in his view. He had dismissed Sean's rifle out of hand until he realized that the cartridges in it contained gunpowder. "Yes there is. I could have taken the powder from one of your rifle cartridges and used it to speed things up."

"That's correct, and if the tinder was wet you can use the gunpowder to kick-start the fire and dry the tinder out so it will burn for you. Learn to see everything and think if there is a way you can use it in whatever task you are working on."

Charley realized the wisdom of Sean's words. He had never before had to truly look at his surroundings before, accustomed as he was to living in a world where if you didn't have what you needed you simply went to a store and bought it. He made up his mind that no matter what else happened he would listen and learn from Sean, it could save his life in the future. The decision was all the easier since he still had no idea what Sean was going to do with him.

Sean stood, picked up his rifle and told Charley he was going to look around and then headed off.

Charley got the impression that they would be camping there for the night and though that he should try to find something that would make the stay a little less uncomfortable then just lying on the bare ground. He began scouting around the area stripping small branches off the pine and fir trees. Careful not to take anything to big or too many from one he soon had a double armload of small pine and fir boughs and started arranging them into two groups near the fire. Charley built a rectangular box of two rows of branches about six feet long. He placed the branches on the ground with the needles in the middle and the ends of the branches on facing out. In this way he soon had a rudimentary bed of needles to lie on. When the first was finished he began working on the second. He was half completed when Sean appeared back by the fire.

"Very nice work." He said quietly, startling Charley. "However there are two things you've done wrong. First you were so engrossed in your work that you didn't hear me return. Second you've set the beds too close to the water. If you can help it, never camp close to the only source of water around you. If there are other people around they will naturally be drawn to the water, as will all the animals in the area. If you are hunting, camping close to the water scares off the game. If you are not hunting it just keeps the animals from getting a drink and there's no reason to be cruel now is there?"

Charley though about what Sean had said and was astounded by the simplicity of it. It was perfectly clear now that he was thinking about it. Take what you need and move away to allow others to have their share. Also if you were hunting something or someone, this would be a good time to set an ambush. It would also be a good time for someone to ambush you. Charley's education was coming along very quickly once his mind began to work. Kicking out both fires, he gathered up the boughs he had laid out for the beds and followed Sean away from the stream into grove of trees that were growing closely together.

"I see that you thought of using the coniferous tree branches for a base to lie on. Excellent thinking. I even noticed that you were careful not to take to many from one tree. That shows you do have a mind and can use it when prodded in the right direction. Something else that happened quite by accident is that all the branches were collected away from where we are actually spending the night. They only error you made, and I'm sure it's only because you haven't yet grown as paranoid as I am, is that you collected the branches around the clearing near the water. An astute observer such as myself would notice this and then become aware that there are others nearby. Even though it's only you and I out here, always assume that there are, or could be others. When doing anything, make sure it will leave no mark of your presence. This one of the many lessons I will be teaching you."

Charley took this moment to ask the questions foremost in his mind. "How long will this take and why me?"

Sean looked carefully at Charley. "Normally I would tell you that that's not something you need to know but in this case the truth can't hurt anyone at all. The answer to both questions is I simply don't know. Whenever my employer, and yours too now for that matter, decide that we've had enough fun and rest they will contact us and tell us what we are to do next.

"So what is it you actually do?"

"You mean aside from wandering around playing Davey Crockett in the wilderness? Well I do lots of different things, but don't worry, all will be reveled in time. For now let's just focus on your education. One of the most important life lessons is always be aware for your surroundings. Use what ever you see around you to your advantage. Can you tell me why I dragged you into this tiny cramped clump of trees?"

Charley thought for a moment. “It makes us hard to see if anyone comes near the stream.”

“Yes it does but also and more importantly, the trees are very close together so we can use them to form a shelter. We simply tie the upper branches together and while not completely waterproof it will provide much more protection from the elements then simply lying on the ground. Any other reasons you can think of?

Charley sat and thought for a moment putting his mind to the problem in earnest. “Once we leave all we need to do is untie the branches and move the bedding and no one will ever know we were here.”

“Excellent and 100% correct,” Sean exclaimed happily. He removed a role of twine from his pocket and tossed it to Charley, “let’s see how your tree tying skills are then, shall we?”

Charley began bending the trees in to form a cone over the area he and Sean had been sitting in. The trees were close packed and not overly tall so he was able to weave and tie together the branches of 5 trees to form a nice tight shelter for the two of them to sleep under. The trees also created a wind break should a breeze spring up overnight. While Charley was doing that Sean took the boughs Charley had gathered and quickly but expertly created two beds for them to sleep in. This was the first time Charley had seen him put his rifle down, even though it was never more than three feet from him at any one time.

“Starting to trust me a little?” Charley asked nodding to where the rifle lay next to Sean.

“I trust no one.” Sean answered calmly. “But I can’t hold it forever and I need both hands for this. I’m simply counting on your common sense to know that with out me to get you out of here you’ll die should you get my rifle and shoot me with it.”

“How do you know that I couldn’t find my way our of here with out you? If you’re dead I’ll have that backpack of yours and everything in it. That should be enough to get me home.”

Sean turned and picked up the rifle and handed it to Charley. “So take it and shoot me then.”

“Is this some kind of a trick?” Charley asked backing up a step.

“No this is were I see if I’m as good a judge of character as I once was. You seem to be a sincere, kind young man. I don’t think you would shoot me even if you have the opportunity. At some point in all our training I will need to decide that you’ve either accepted working with me or that you haven’t. I may as well know now and get it over with because I intend to get a good nights sleep, not sit up guarding you. Now take the damn rifle and let's see how good you are at getting out of here without me. Just remember what it took to get your fire going."

Charley took the rifle from Sean and, out of long habit, checked to see if the was a round in the chamber and make sure the safety was on. He then moved to the bed Sean had made for himself and laid the rifle down on it. "I don't think you'd be that easy to kill. And truth is I'm a little curious as to why someone has gone to all this trouble for me," Charley said, lying down on his pine branch bed and trying to get comfortable.

"Don't get comfortable lad, we aren't staying here. It's just a little after five and there is a lot of daylight left. We are going to keep moving for a while yet," Sean said as he began untying the trees.

"If we aren't staying here why did we make the beds and tie the trees together?" Charley asked puzzled over the wasted effort.

"Well to start with you were the one that started making the beds while I was gone. I never said anything about staying for the night or setting up a camp. You simply assumed we would be doing that after we finished our food and coffee. Now let's go back to where the fires were and make sure they are completely dead. We'll also scatter the ashes a bit better before we leave. We can't completely mask the fires, I'll show you how to do that later."

With that Sean stuffed the twine back into his pockets, went back to their campfires and spent a few minutes scattering the ashes and dropping dead leaves and dirt over them to try and mask the site. It didn't do a very good job, but it did show Charley how to go about doing it. Once done Sean hitched up his pack, shouldered his rifle and stuck off through the forest more or less following the stream.

Several hours later, near dark, he stopped near the stream. "Okay Lad, have a drink and then find us a place to spend the night."

Charley dropped down next to the water and greedily slurped up the cool refreshing liquid. Once his thirst was slaked he jumped up and began looking for place to make camp. The two men repeated the earlier exercise, finding a small grove of trees and tying the tops together. Then moving around they both stripped enough branches to make a sleeping pad to lie on and settled in for the night.

"A good first day lad, you have the making of a first class woodsmen. One thing though, when getting a drink, kneel down, cup your hand into the water and bring it to your mouth. Never lie down to get a drink, leaves you too vulnerable," Sean said casually adding one more lesson to the day and then rolling over on his side. "Have a good sleep lad."

"Good night," Charley answered, trying to get as comfortable as possible himself and in time drifting off to sleep. He noticed the ease with which Sean had settled in and heard the regular even deep breaths of the man signifying he was asleep.

When Charley woke up Sean was already gone. For a moment he was worried then his fears went away with the knowledge once again that someone had gone to too much trouble to leave him here alone. Even if Sean wasn't around, Charley was sure that he would be following to make sure nothing happened to his new student. Charley crawled out from the rude shelter of trees and stretched to work out some of the kinks in his back. Sleeping on the pine boughs had only been slightly better than sleeping on the bare ground in his opinion. He wandered toward the stream to get a drink of water and saw Sean in the clearing next to a small fire shaving.

"Morning lad. Finally up I see. Do you always sleep this late?" Sean said with a smile on his face.

Charley looked at the older man. "And just what makes you so cheery this morning?" he asked with a touch of bitterness in his voice.

"I can assume, by the fact that you didn't attack me in my sleep and either murder me or take all my belongings and leave that you have accepted your fate and are now willing to learn from me." Sean replied going back to his shaving. "That means that over the next few weeks I get to drag you around in gods backyard, the great outdoors, doing what I love to do most in this world. Live off the land. The fact that I get to teach you, is merely a bonus, for like all natural teachers I am happiest when I imparting my considerable wisdom to those poor ignorant soles that have net yet reached the level of appreciation that I have for mother nature.

"Do I sense a little bit of ego in that rather long winded speech you just gave?" Charley asked sitting down next to Sean.

He watched a Sean deftly using one of the cups rinsed his razor and shook it to get the water and soap off of it. Done with his shaving he rinsed out the cup and wrapped his razor and a small bar of soap up in what looked like a piece of leather, and put it in his backpack. Sean then took out a small bundle and tossed it to Charley.

"Here, go clean yourself up a bit. I'm going to see about breakfast.

Charlie's stomach rumbled at the though of food and he suddenly realized how hungry he was. He opened the bundle and saw a disposable razor, a washcloth, hand towel and a stainless steel mirror. Wrapped up in a piece of plastic was a small bar of soap, the type used by most hotel chains. He picked up the cup Sean had been using and went to the stream to get some water. Following Sean's example he cleaned himself up and rather than sit around bored he began gathering up wood to make a fire. He wasn't sure what Sean had meant by breakfast but he was fairly sure coffee would be included and that meant they needed a fire. Repeating his efforts of yesterday he gathered the makings and with his newfound confidence had a small fire going in a short while.

When Sean returned he was please to see a small stack of wood and a fire going with Charley, cleaned up and shaved sitting next to it.

"Excellent. I see you are using you head this morning. Got a fire going without having to either ask or be told. I knew you were a bright lad." Sean said. "Now do you know how to clean and cook fish?" he asked throwing four trout on the ground next to Charley.

"I've cleaned them before but never cooked them without a stove so I'll be a little lost there," Charley answered.

"We'll start with the cleaning then and educate you on how to cook after that."

Sean pulled a thin bladed skinning knife from his pack and handed it to Charley. "You start, I need to find some good straight branches," he told Charley and then headed into the woods. Charley noticed he didn't take his rifle with him this time.

By the time Sean came back carrying two long relatively straight branches Charley had the fish cleaned. Sean took two of them and cut a slit in the tail and one in the head them slid one of the branches through the two slits skewering the fish. He did the same to the other two and the second branch. He then dug a small hole on either side of the fire and jammed the ends of the branches in the hole forming two spits to cook the fish over the fire with.

Sean dusted of his hands on his pants and looked at Charley "Think about this before you answer. If you didn't have a branch to use to roast them over the fire, how else could you cook them? Again look around and see what's at hand that could help."

Charley took his time studying everything in his view. He saw some rocks that looked as if they may have been big enough to use to cook the fish on but nothing other then more tree branches. He mentioned this to Sean.

"What if there are no rocks or trees around, just the stream and grass and brush for the fire? Sean asked quietly. "What do you do then?"

Charley thought for a few more minutes. "I honestly don't know," he finally replied.

Sean nodded "At least you thought about it. Another way would be to cover them in mud and put them back in the coals; the mud will act as an oven and bake the fish. It will also work with potatoes and other food as well. The hard part is knowing when the food is done, which is why I only use mud as a last resort."

Charley watched the fish roasting while he thought about what he had just learned. It made sense and it was something he never would have thought of. He had done a lot of camping and had cooked over his share of campfires but it had always been with a pot or a frying pan. Charley had never thought about cooking any other way.

For the next two weeks Sean lead Charley in a large circle. Everything they did and saw was treated as an exercise or lesson like a school field trip. Sean taught him how to make a fire that could be completely hidden when done. How to find water by following game trails and watching the patterns of animals. The proper way to make a deadfall to trap small game, and how to build a fish trap to catch fish. He showed Charley how to recognize plants that could be eaten. The two seemed to be on one long camping trip where the learning never stopped. They lived off the land with nothing other then what Sean had in his small backpack. Although Charley was certain that there were others around. Every second day Charley would wake up to find Sean gone. He would appear an hour after Charley had gotten up with fresh fish and his supply of coffee and beef jerky never ran out. It was the coffee that made Charley think. The pack Sean carried wasn't that big and yet there was always coffee and beef jerky in the pack. Charley figured that over the last two weeks they had consumed several pounds of each and there was no way there could have been that much in the backpack. Charley didn't say anything, however, figuring that if Sean wanted Charley to think they were alone, he had a good reason.

As they complete the circle back to the clearing that they had first started camping in Charley suddenly realized where they were.

"Well it took you long enough to figure that out" Sean commented dryly seeing the look on the Lads face. " Didn't you notice the position of the sun every morning when you woke up?"

"No I didn't". Charley answered honestly. "I always figured you knew where we were going so I never gave it any thought."

"Well lad you had best start thinking about it now. The fun training is almost over."

Sean looked at the sky and back at Charley, "How much daylight is left?"

Charley glanced up, and then around, looking at the shadows being cast by the trees. "I'd say about three, three and a half hours before sunset. Why?"

"I've got to go and get some items I cached so that we can move on to the next step of your training. I want you to catch some fish, get a fire going and make a shelter while I'm gone. I should be back just before sunset but If I'm a little late don't worry."

"Okay I'll see you when you get back." Charley said and watch Sean turn and head into the forest.

As if he had been doing it his whole life, Charley stripped several trees of the tender supple young branches and wove a fish trap with them. He used a large rock to anchor it to the bottom of the stream and baited it with some worms then went to gather firewood. Using the same location as the last time he and Sean used the clearing he quickly had a fire going and the built a shelter in the small grove of trees. Moving back to the stream he saw that there was three fish in the trap and decided that that would be enough for now; he could reset the trap later if he wanted. Charley cleaned the fish and skewered them on branches to roast them over the fire, but set them to the side. It was too early to start cooking them yet; Sean would be gone for anther hour at least. Charley was proud of the new skills he had learned. He had always thought himself a good woodsman, but compared to what he had learned in the last two weeks he had known nothing about living off the land before. He realized that being a hunter is not the same as being able to survive in the wilderness.

Gauging the sun to be about thirty minutes from setting, Charley set the fish to cook and watched them as the sun slowly set.

The fish were done shortly after the sun set. Charley took them off the fire and started to eat one wondering how much longer Sean would be. As he took the first bite of the fish he heard the sound of movement in the woods behind him.

"Sean the fish are done," Charley yelled. He was taking another bite when there seemed to be a bright light going off in his head

Charley opened his eyes and noticed pain. A lot of pain. Mostly in his head, but also in his left arm and shoulder, and the left side of his face. He was lying on his left side but couldn't remember going to bed. Even funnier he realized that he wasn't in bed but lying on the ground next to the fire. He had trouble focusing his eyes but he was finally able to see Sean sitting across from him drinking coffee. He was puzzled by this because he knew he hadn't made any coffee. Slowly sitting up he wondered what had happened. He reached up and touched the back of his head and felt a large bump that was very tender.

Sean sat starring at him with an amused look on his face. "Now it's time for part two of your training. First lesson: when you hear a noise never assume who it is and never, ever let anyone know where you are by yelling. As you by now know if I was someone looking to kill you, you would be dead."

"You hit me?" asked a still stunned Charley. "Why would you do that?"

"You've grown complacent with your surroundings lad. Always be wary, no matter where you are. Even if you are sure you're alone, never let your guard down."

"I don't understand."

"Up until now I've been teaching you how to survive off the land. Now I'm going to start teaching you how to survive around people."

Sean stood up and picked up a backpack he had been sitting on and tossed it to Charley. "Open that up and take everything out."

Charley began emptying the pack moving slowly so he wouldn't aggravate the throbbing in his head. "What did you hit me with, a boulder?"

Sean chuckled. "No, I hit you with a home made blackjack. You'll be learning how to make and use one of those in the near future."

"Great, do I get to practice on your head?"

"Absolutely. All you have to do is sneak up behind me and hit me without me catching you. Of course if I catch you I get to hit you again."

"Yeah right," Charley said sarcastically.

"That will be just one of the many things I'll be teaching you next. But first, could you pick up that large leather wrapped bundle you have just so casually tossed to the ground. I think we'll start with the basics.

Charley picked up the object Sean was referring to and began unwrapping it. As the leather fell away he found a holster containing a very large pistol. "What the hell is this?" he asked, opening the holster and removing the weapon.

"That is a .45 ACP Double action Colt M1911 Pistol. Once the standard sidearm of the US military," Sean answered as he removed a matching gun from his own pack. "Tell me what you know about handguns lad."

"Not very much at all. I'm a rifle and shotgun fan. Hard to hit a target 500 yards away with a handgun. And remember I'm Canadian; handguns aren't too popular where I'm from. If you own a handgun in Canada the only place you can use it is at a gun club and you need to get special permits just to take from your house to the club and back. For me they are too much of a pain in the ass to have around. Too many restrictions on them."

"Well you are going to become very familiar with the one you're holding. First a little back ground...."

"Wait!" Charley cut him off. "Why do I need to know about handguns?"

Sean sighed. "Stop asking so many questions. Just pay attention and learn. When the time is right you'll be told all you need to know."

"Fine, whatever you say. So back to the gun."

"Right, a little background." Sean held up the gun and proceeded to dismantle it. "The .45 ACP fires a large, subsonic round. This is important because even though the report of the firing is loud the bullet does not break the sound barrier so there is no sonic boom. As a result of this if you silence the report of the round being fired the weapon is almost totally silent. This is why it was so popular with the military for so long. It's also why gangsters liked it as well. Today however most people are using the 9MM because it has more than double the cartridge capacity, or it comes in a very compact size, thus making it easy to conceal. And as silenced rounds aren't in as much demand the noise issue isn't as important. I however still like the older .45 for one very large reason. When you hit something with a 240-grain bullet it usually falls down. I've seen people shot with a 9MM keep moving like nothing had happened."

Sean placed the disassembled gun on a piece of leather stretched out on the ground in front of him. Piece by piece he went over it with Charley and several times reassembled and dis-assembled the firearm, showing Charley how fast it could be done. He had Charley strip his .45 and then put it back together several times to get a feel for doing it.

"We are just starting with the .45 but we will eventually be going over a large range of handguns." Sean told him. I know you can shoot with a rifle so we'll start your target training with handguns first." He pulled a box of bullets out of his pack and tossed them over to Charley.

Sean watched Charley load a clip and then insert it into the gun and chamber a round. He was quietly please when Charley automatically put the safety on, it showed that the young man was safety conscious. After putting up some targets on the other side of the clearing, Sean paced it off at roughly fifty feet. Charley fired a few rounds to get the feel of the handgun. He hit the target every time but they were all high and to the right. Charley started getting the feel of the .45 and his shots were getting closer to the center. After changing the targets Charley was consistently hitting the center ring of the targets. By this time Charley had fired about twenty-five shots.

"Well that's rather impressive," Sean commented. "Half a box and you're hitting the center ring."

Charley smiled and unloaded the gun.

Chapter 3

The three men quietly filed into Carters office. They stood across the desk waiting patiently for Carter to finish reading the report in front of him. They already knew its contents, having been the ones that had written the report.

Carter finished reading and looked up "Any problems so far?"

"No sir," Agent Smith answered. "Everything is going as planned."

"Where is he now?" None of the three answered, looking around the room nervously.

"The room has been swept this morning by one of ours," Carter told them. "Please speak freely

"Yes sir. He is with Agent Miller, undergoing field survival training. I believe the plan in place to bring him back to the Factory and begin training in tactics and advanced field craft. If everything stays on our current timetables he should be ready to deploy by the project target date. If there is any problem with his training schedule, the failsafe is to have agent Miller make the shot and have the evidence point to Mr Watkins. At that time we will become expendable and will be left at the site to take the fall for the shooting."

"Didn't we stage his demise so as to bring him into the fold?"

"That was the original plan sir," Agent Johnson answered. "However as a backup plan it was felt that leaving him listed as an escaped fugitive would give the organization more options in the future."

"How did we work this?"

"After staging the injury to get him transferred to a medical facility, an accident was arranged to disable the ambulance. During the accident several operatives removed Mr Watkins from the ambulance, leaving evidence to indicate he had broken free on his own. The operatives kept Mr Watkins in a state of unconsciousness and then delivered him to the training area for Mr Miller."

"Very good. Have you been keeping tabs on him since then?"

"We are in contact with agent Miller every two to three days," Agent Wheeler replied. "He slips away from the subject early in the morning and meets with one of our surveillance team. He updates us on the training and requests supplies that he may need. Until the last meeting he has only requested coffee beans and beef jerky. All of his reports indicate that the training is exceeding expectations and can be accelerated. Agent Miller had planned on two full months of survival training but now feels that this is unnecessary and he has requested additional items to begin parts of the field craft training. We have approved this request and the items he needs are being left at the latest drop site."

"Thank you gentleman, you may go," Carter said, dismissing them. He turned back to the report and read it through again for the third time. For some reason he was feeling uneasy about this latest recruit. He couldn't quite put his finger on what it was that bothered him. They had been extremely lucky to find Charley when they did. The fact that he was not a US citizen didn't bother him at all. That was actually a very large bonus. The organization preferred non-Americans as operatives for the wet work, that way if they were ever caught they could be denied. Not that this had ever happened while he had been a director, one of three that ran the organization. The operations they undertook were very well planned and to date had all been complete successes. The three men that had just left his office were assistants, they looked after the day to day running of the organization leaving him and his fellow directors free to focus on strategy, along with working in the government jobs that had taken them years to obtain.

Putting the report in his private safe he went back to his official work putting the matter completely out of his mind. The three assistants went from Carters office directly to a rundown warehouse on the outskirts of the city next to the river. From the outside, the building looked as rundown as the rest or the neighborhood with broken windows covered with plastic, paint peeling off the woodwork, and the tin roof rusting. The parking lot was unpaved and overgrown with weeds, giving the entire place a look of being abandoned. The only part of the property that was not run down was the chain link fence topped with barbed wire surrounding it.

Using a remote control Johnson opened the fence gate, then the door in the side of the warehouse and drove inside the building. All three waited until the gate and the door had closed before getting out of the car. The plastic covered windows let in light but obscured any clear view of the interior of the building if anyone tried to look through them. If anyone did manage to get a glimpse of the inside all they would have seen was an empty structure with offices running down one side. Every office looked as abandoned as the rest of the building. Some were empty, others had a desk and a couple of chairs, all but one were covered in a layer of dust. That office had a massive six-drawer file cabinet. It would take a vary careful observer to see that this was not a file cabinet. Miller took a key from his pocket and unlocked the second drawer from the bottom and then pulled on the handle of the third drawer from the top and the front of the cabinet opened to reveal an elevator. The three men got on and closed the fake file cabinet behind them. As soon as the door shut the elevator started to descend dropping 200 feet. When the elevator stopped they were facing a man holding a machine pistol and standing behind a bulletproof lexan shield with a hole to point the machine pistol through. In front of the shield was a magnetic card reader. As the elevator stopped the guard trained his weapon on the three men and even thought every single man was known to the guard he still, in a firm but respectful tone, asked them to swipe their access cards through the reader. One at a time they swiped their cards, each swipe being rewarded with a single beep and a green access light going on.

"Thank you gentleman" the guard said respectfully lowering his weapon and standing at ease.

The three men walked past the guard and opened the steel door behind him. Behind the door was a four-acre room with a forty-foot high ceiling that was the training area of the organization. Along the walls were enclosed rooms lined with steel and bulletproof plastic. The rooms were testing labs for various firearms or other projectile weapons. There were also soundproof rooms for other experiments and one section was simply office space with secure computer terminals connected to their own server and isolated from the outside. Most of the large room was open and divided into training areas with a running track circling the training areas. Here hand-to-hand combat was taught and agents worked out to stay in shape. There was also a mock up of a house and a small office building for other training purposes. There was no connection to the outside world in any way. The walls, floor and ceiling were all lead lined to block any electronic signal and the power came from a small nuclear reactor on site. There were no telephones or internet connection and the only way in or out of the facility was by way of the elevator. The air came through the elevator shaft as well being filtered in the process and passing through an electromagnetic screen and air conditioner unit meant to filter any outside signals as well as filter the air.

The three walked straight to the opposite wall to another steel door. Opening this door they entered a hallway with wooden doors along both sides and an open doorway at the end. These were the living quarters for the people working and training at the facility. Each door lead to a four-bed dorm room with a shower and toilet in it. There were twenty rooms in all, enough to accommodate eighty people at any one time.

One half was in use for the staff permanently assigned to the facility. The rest of the dorms were for new recruits and transient members of the organization. Once trained the new agents were sent out into the field and did not come back to the factory as it was called. Only trainers, security, and administration staff were regulars here. Movement in and out of the factory was controlled so as to keep the illusion of the warehouse cover being unused and rundown. All permanent staff and most agents were single with no family or at least no family close. The organization preferred its members that way; it kept questions about agent's activities to a minimum.

The three went to their dorm, they lived in the same room, and changed into sweat suits and running shoes and headed to the training area to work out. Staying in shape was of paramount importance in the organization and the only people exempt were the senior people or those under deep cover. The 3 ran on the track, lifted weights and engaged in hand to hand sparring with the unarmed combat instructors for a few hours then showered and went to their offices to check up on the various projects that were ongoing. Once in the field every agent was assigned to a handler, and each handler had two encrypted hand held computers to record notes and updates from the agents on the various projects they were involved with. Once a week one of the hand held computers was sent to the facility so the data could be downloaded to the server and the files updated. Once downloaded the computer was returned to the handler to be used again. These were the files the three men were now going over. Each deep cover agent used dead drops to leave information for the organization to collect. The notes were scanned into one of the handhelds and then destroyed. Other methods were emails or bulletin boards that were controlled by the organization. This info was also copied to one of the handhelds and then erased so as to cover the trail of the deep cover people. The organization also used the tried and true method of recruiting everyday people to spy for them. These spies were never told the true nature of the organization they were giving the information too. The end result was that each day more information was added to the secure servers in the underground complex. The three men sitting at the terminals were the only ones with total access to the servers.

The organization was controlled by three men in top government jobs. They were known as the board of directors or simply the board. The factory staff called them the three wise men. As a result of their government jobs they were unable to be involved with the day to day running of the organization. They each employed an administrator to act in their behalf. These administrators always traveled together and worked together. No one of them saw or did anything that the other two did not see. When the board was updated once a week the updates were given by all three men. In this way it was assured that one person did not gain control of the organization. The factory staff called the three administrators the three stooges as they took all their direction from the three wise men.

The administrators were selected directly by the board members, each member picking one administrator. They were selected from the ranks of the organization staff and all were chosen for their physical and mental abilities as well as their loyalty to the organization. The three were a team and when one was disabled or could no longer perform his duties all three were replaced. Once replaced the former administrators went to work in the facility. They were never allowed into the field again as they were considered a security risk. The current three had been the administrators for more then ten years. They were the best the organization had ever produced and had never failed in any of the projects they started.

The three stooges checked over the updates and updated the project files accordingly. Once done, the information was downloaded to their handhelds for briefing the board. They didn't need to do this as each was able to recite the files from memory but the board liked to have files to look over at their leisure.

Done with the office work they went back to the training area to talk to the trainers and keep up to the day-to-day needs of the facility.

Chapter 4

" I believe it's time to move on to the next step in your training," Sean said, taking the gun from Charley.

"And that would be?" Charley asked letting the question hang in the air.

Sean just smiled and began packing up the camp and cleaning the area to remove signs of their presence. Realizing he wasn't going to get an answer, Charley helped him pack and clean the campsite. As soon as they were done Sean hitched up his pack and headed out of the forest towards the open field, Charley following him as always. After several hours of walking Sean stop and dropped the pack on the ground. He squatted beside it and took out a small black case that looked like a transistor radio. He turned it on and a small green light started to blink. Sean sat down using the pack for a cushion and smiled at Charley.

"Sit down lad, it'll be a while before our ride gets here."

Charley stood looking at Sean for a few moments, then finally sat down. He desperately wanted to know where he was going but knew asking would be a waste of time. He was unsure of how much time actually passed, but it felt like a little more then an hour, when he heard the sound of a helicopter in the distance steadily getting louder. A minute later he could see it coming towards them. Sean and Charley sat quietly and watched the chopper land twenty meters away. Sean stood up as soon as the chopper was settled and walked towards the rear door. He pulled it opened and tossed his pack inside and was handed something by the copilot. Sean turned around extended his arm and calmly shot Charley.

The young man stared at the dart sticking out of his leg and had enough time to wonder what was going on before the drug took effect and knocked him out. Sean walked over and picked Charley up, put him in the helicopter then climbed in himself. He put on a set of headphones and told the pilot they were all loaded and ready to go.

For the second time, Charley woke up with a vicious headache to find Sean sitting with a cup of coffee in his hand, starring at him. This time Charley was lying in a bed and there was no rifle pointed at him. Sean picked up another cup of coffee and handed it to him.

"What no gun this time?" Charley asked taking the cup and sipping from it.

"I didn't think I'd need it this time what with us being old friends."

"You shot me!" Charley suddenly yelled. "You didn't think I might be a little pissed about that?"

Sean smiled "Well there were only two options lad. One was to tie you up and blindfold you and the other was to knock you out. I thought the nap would be the better of the two choices and didn't feel the need to burden you with making a decision."

"Next time burden me. I'm tired of the headaches I get from whatever it is you people shoot me full of."

"Drink the coffee lad and you'll feel better. All will be explained soon. Through that rear door you'll find a shower and everything you need to clean yourself up. There are some clothes in the closet next to your bed so get cleaned and dressed we've got a lot of work to do." Sean got up and opened the door to leave. "When you're done, out this door and to your left. Through the door at the end of the hall and then just ask someone for me." He closed the door leaving Charley alone.

After the first shower and clean clothes in several weeks Charley finally felt clean himself. He had gotten so used to the dirt of living in the forest he had forgotten how nice it was to have something as simple as fresh socks on. Once ready he followed Sean's directions and found himself in what he assumed was a large warehouse with no windows. He had no idea of where he was. He strained to hear something beyond the sounds of the building but it was a waste of time. He shrugged his shoulders and headed toward a group of people he could see that appeared to be doing martial arts. One of the group spotted Charley heading towards them and moved to meet him.

"Mr Watkins?" the man asked.

"Yes I am," Charley told him.

"Follow me please," he said heading towards the left side of the facility.

He dropped Charley off at an office telling him to wait until a doctor came for him.

When the doctor arrived Charley was given a through physical and blood was taken, as well, his eyes and reflexes were checked. After a clean bill of health Charley was given a personal fitness trainer named Paul.

Within a few days Charley learned that training was all that went on in the warehouse. On the first day the Paul and Charley spent the rest of day after his physical doing mostly light calisthenics and running, with some free weights to break up the day. Each day thereafter the workout got a little bit more difficult. Paul was slowly building up Charley's strength and stamina. On the second week Charley met Lee the martial arts and unarmed combat instructor and an hour a day was now devoted to learning hand to hand combat. At the start of the third week He was introduced to Walter and began learning computers and electronics. His days were now starting at 5 AM with two hours of exercising. He then had breakfast for an hour and then spent the next four hours with Paul and Lee. He was given a one-hour break for lunch and in the afternoon studied in a classroom setting with Walter. After an hour break for dinner Paul would collect him again for some running and then some sports with other members of the facility. As there was no TV reception, recreation consisted of games such as Floor Hockey, Basketball, or Ping Pong. There was a TV and VCR and movies were supplied but the recruits were encouraged to stay active and play sports. Charley went to bed at ten. By the end of the first month he was running several miles a day and working out several hours a day. He was in excellent physical condition, and getting stronger every day. His eye hand co-ordination had improved and he was quickly becoming an excellent fighter.

Charley woke up and showered and headed to the kitchen to get a bagel and some juice. Finished with his light breakfast he headed to the training area to start his morning workout. He was surprised to see Sean waiting for him.

"Morning lad," Sean greeted him. "Paul, Lee and Walter tell me you're doing fine with your training. Are you enjoying yourself?"

"Well given the alternative is death I don't see that I have much choice in being here. But to answer your question, yes I'm enjoying myself. The workouts are fun and the computer and electronics stuff is great."

"Well that's nice to hear."

"So why are you here?" Charley asked

"I'm here to finish your training and prepare you for the real work. Today we're going to add to your training. Paul has told me you can work on your own So do a quick work out and then see Lee for an hour and come to room 210, I'll be waiting for you."

Sean headed across the facility leaving the young man to stretch and warm up on his own.

After his session with Lee, Charley took a quick shower and went to room 210. Sean was sitting at a desk reading when he walked in.

"Hello lad," Sean greeted him. "Ready to learn your new job?"

Charley looked around the room seeing nothing other then the desk Sean was sitting at and an extra chair in front of the desk. "Sure, why not. What is it I'm supposed to do anyway?"

"You have been recruited to work as an undercover operative for the Government of the United States," Sean said in his best official voice. " You will be working on your own with no support from the government and you will not have any contact with any other US government employee. In effect you are what is called a NOC. It stands for no operational cover."

Charley was puzzled. "Well I enjoy your term 'recruited'. So much better then kidnapped and blackmailed isn't it? But why would they want me?"

"That's simple, you can shoot. And at very long ranges. A good sniper is hard to find so when they do find a good one that has no family and no apparent ties to anyone they see this as an opportunity to recruit them."

"Maybe I'm jumping to conclusions here, but if my prime asset is my ability to shoot a rifle from a long range it sounds as if you people want me to be a killer for you," Charley said with an edge to his voice. "Is that what you're planning for me? If so forget it, I'm not a murderer, and I don't plan to be."

"First of all, when you work for a government it's not killing or murder. It's called termination or a sanction. And it's not random. You won't be sent out to shoot people willy-nilly all over the place. But yes, part of your job will be to remove from society those individuals that have proven that they cannot be trusted to abide by the rules. And trust me this will be a last resort. The reason you were recruited in the manner you were is so that you are completely deniable if caught."

"But the US government doesn't work this way. No democratic government works this way."

"Don't kid yourself lad, they all do it. Every single country on earth, some just hide it better then others."

"I don't understand Sean. Why does it have to be done this way?"

"It's simple, the government has laws and they can't be seen as breaking their own laws. The problem is that some of the citizens of the country don't share the same view. They break the law and use the courts to get away with it. That's why you always see the mafia bosses getting nailed for tax evasion. We can't get them for the real crimes so we get them for ones that will hold up in court. With you it's a little different. You'll be asked to remove the real scum. The guys that use lawyers to cover their tracks and buy politicians and judges. The reason it's done this way is so that it can be done. If you get caught you're already a criminal on the loose. So what's one more crime? Nothing at all and there is no way to tie you back to the government."

"So I do their dirty work and if I ever get caught I'm left hanging for it? That seems fair, after I was blackmailed into it in the first place."

"If you get caught you surrender peacefully to the police and go to jail, yes. That's how it works. And then, as before, some night you'll go to sleep and wake up in a different place, ready to go back to work. We never leave our own hanging. We get you out. Always remember that even though they won't admit it, you work for the government."

"How often will I have to kill people?"

"We don't call it that." Sean said flatly. "Here it's known as a removal. You'll be working with me and the most removals I've ever done in a year was four. Some years I don't do any. Not all will be done with a rifle from long range though so that's why you will need to learn other skills. Most of the time you will be doing surveillance work. Shadowing people, finding information, things like that. The beauty of your job is that you don't need to worry about the rule of law. You won't need a search warrant and you can use a wiretap on anyone you feel like. You will also learn how to hack into computer systems or by pass alarms to break into buildings. You will be known as a black bag man. Once your loyalty to the organization has been proven you will be free to roam around the country and occasionally go to other countries to get the job done. There will be some periods of inactivity and the management will view these as your vacation time so you won't actually be entitled to vacation. When you leave here you will be on call 24/7 and expected to answer at all times. You will have false identity papers and credit cards to use and nothing will ever be traced back to your real identity. For the time being you will be partnered with me and all of your activities will be closely monitored."

Charley relaxed a bit after hearing this information. "I still don't know if I can…remove someone," he said haltingly.

Sean smiled at him. "We'll worry about that when the time comes. For right now we need to concentrate on your education. First thing we'll learn about is alarms.

Sean stood and walked to the back wall of the room and flipped a switch. Part of the wall opened to reveal a hidden room inside that seemed filled with equipment. For the rest of the day Sean taught Charley about alarms and how to defeat them. They started with basic alarms on doors and moved onto motion detectors, heat sensors, and laser and infrared beams. The next few days followed the routine of morning workouts followed by an hour with Walter and his computer then off to the alarm room for the rest of the day. After a week of this Charley had mastered most of the common commercial alarm systems and knew enough to defeat almost any system.

When finished with alarm system Sean moved the training on to surveillance equipment. He showed Charley the latest in minicams, tracking devices, and listening bugs. Sean taught him how to install and monitor the devices that were supplied by the organization. He also showed Charley how to make less sophisticated bugs with parts from retail electronics stores. Sean also began working out with Charley in the mornings. Charley quickly adapted to the new routine and was an excellent pupil. He soaked up all the information he was given and whenever he was tested he scored perfect marks. Slowly they were turning Charley into a first class agent for the organization.

The weeks flew by for Charley and for a while he forgot why he was there and immersed him self in the learning. He was learning things that he would never have had the chance to before coming to the organization. He hardly believed that some of what he learned was even possible. Under the direction of Walter he had learned how to hack into secure systems and while he had never had the chance to try it for real yet he was sure it would work. His fighting skills had improved to the point that the only person in the complex that could beat him all the time was Lee the instructor. When sparring with anyone else it was an even contest. Even Lee admitted that Charley's progress was remarkable. His eye hand coordination was near perfect along with his reflexes. His strength had grown thanks to the training as well.

As each week passed Sean would add to Charley's training. He had been at the complex for two months and was further along in his training that anyone had thought he would be. It was assumed that he would resist training but he had accepted everything eagerly.

The three stooges met weekly with Sean to assess the training to make sure Charley would be prepared with in the time frame that had been set. They were pleased at the rapid progress and told Sean to increase the training.

The following Monday Sean met Charley for breakfast, a rare occurrence; they normally met on the training floor for a work out before heading to a classroom.

Charley raised his eyebrows as Sean sat down across from him with a tray of eggs and toast. "What's the special occasion? I didn't think you ate breakfast."

"Normally I don't. A cup of coffee usually suffices, but as your training regimen will be changing today I thought it better to met you for breakfast."

Charley was surprised. "Changing? What's changing mean?"

"It means my young protégé that you and I will be leaving this wonderful place and join the real world once again. There are certain things I need to teach you that can only be done outside of here."

Charley was shocked to hear this. He had assumed that he would be here for a much longer period of time. Not just for the training but also to ensure the higher ups that he could be trusted not to run back to Canada and escape them.

Almost as if Sean was reading his mind he said. "Now once we leave, let's have no silly notions about trying to get back home, all right. Just accept that you are now an employee of the organization and enjoy the new job. If you run we will find you and you will go back to prison. The difference is that you will face a trial and the organization will not get you out a second time. And yes it's blackmail, but that's the way it is. In time you'll find it's not so bad. You will have a lot of free time to do with as you please. In fact we already have a cover for you. It seems the higher ups think it would be good if you went back to school. We will be enrolling you in a university, of your choice, and you can study what you like."

"University?" Charley asked. "How are you going to manage that, I'm an escaped prisoner."

"I've learned over the years not to questions how things are done. I get my orders and I carry them out, you would be wise to do the same lad. If the three stooges say you go to university then off you go. And what the hell, it beats working."

Charley eyes him suspiciously. "There's a catch there somewhere isn't there?"

Sean smiled, happy that his protégé was catching on. "Yes there is a catch.

You have to choose a school in the northeast. The powers that be want you in that area. And they want you to take something that missing classes won't be a problem with."

Charley looked puzzled and Sean explained further. "You are to chose a university in New York or New England. You do know where those places are, don't you?"

"Of course I do, I'm from Nova Scotia. Everyone there knows about New England, it's only a few hours drive to Maine. What I'm wondering is why they would let me get so close to home?"

"Simple lad, to show you that you can't go home and they know it. If you run we'll catch you and toss you back in jail," Sean told him matter-of-factly. "Now enough about your former home, let's talk about schools. Any idea where you want to go?"

Charley though for a moment, not really knowing much about university. He finally picked the first school he knew the Name of. "MIT, I guess. I've heard lots of good things about it. Might was well try there."

Sean slowly shook his head. "No lad you don't understand. This is just a cover for you. We need you going someplace that doesn't care if you're in class or not. MIT would not be a good cover for you. It's very technical and you would need to be in class all the time. Think more along the line of history or English. Maybe learn poetry or something along those lines. A course heavy in written work without much in the way of class learning. Keep thinking on it."

Chapter 5

The young woman sat down at her terminal, booted it up and typed in her user ID and password to log into the network. Many of her co-workers hated their jobs, but even after three years she was as eager to work as the day she started. The team she was assigned to all worked in the basement of the NSA building in Fort Meade, Maryland. They worked in the internet section of the building and their specific job was to search the internet looking for information that could be of value to the United States. Everyone had a small cubical with a desk and a computer terminal, the workstations separated with the use of standard movable four-foot tall walls. At one end of the room there was a raised section that was glassed off floor to ceiling, where the supervisors had their offices and where a small boardroom was located. When sitting, no one could see over the walls into the next workstation so it gave the illusion of privacy. However, anyone standing at the end of the room on the raised platform would have a clear view of all the workers.

It was for this reason most of the analysts hated their job. They felt like drones, sitting in front of a computer screen in a windowless air-conditioned room all day long. For Holly it was the challenge of searching the internet for those small pieces of information that pushed her. She had been recruited her fourth year at university. She was a brilliant student and had won a full academic scholarship in high school. That the scholarship came from a small local university was unimportant; she was getting a degree in Computer Science and it was free.

She had been playing with computers since Grade 8 in junior high. Having been a late bloomer and somewhat tall for her age, her circle of friends was limited and as a result she had turned to computers to occupy her time. By the time she was a senior, she was tall, athletic, and very good looking with long auburn hair, but the internet was now her playground. Online she could be the equal of anyone else she met and she was judged on her mind not her looks. The fact that men now chased her because of her looks, was something that she had never gotten used to as a result of her early high school experiences.

In her first year at Middlebury College she had written a program that allowed her to search the internet for key words, and ran in the background of her system. It continuously generated reports that were outputted to a text file once every four hours. This worked the same as any other search engine on the internet with the exception that she had inadvertently written a program that would also search secured and restricted files and databases. Her search did all this without tripping any alarms of the secure sites it scanned. She used this for her own personal use only, but not because she felt she was doing anything wrong. In fact she had no idea she was searching secure and restricted sites, she only new that most of her friends were using Yahoo or Google for their searches. She thought they would have made fun of her for wasting the time to write the code for something as simple as an internet search program. She wrote just to see how hard it was to do and she had to admit that it wasn't that easy. It had taken her three weeks to get something that worked well and most of the first term to get the program she now had. But the program when finished turned up astonishing information. She was at first puzzled that some of the information seemed to come from sites that she couldn't access with her internet browser program, but after a while she stopped thinking about it and ignored the occasional access denied or page not found error she saw. Because of it's uncanny ability to always find the right information on the internet she called the program spock, after one of her favorite TV characters.

What finally got her into trouble was an email. A small insignificant little note to an email address that was noted at the bottom of one of the pages Spock had brought up. It was her final year and she was doing her last term paper for her honors program in preparation for a masters. She was writing the paper on computers and their use in helping terrorists created nuclear weapons. She was trying to argue that the increase in computing power had gone so far that the average desktop computer could now be used for calculations in the construction of atomic weapons. His search engine had found an article written by a professor at the University of California that concurred with her. His email address was listed at the bottom and she had emailed him to ask him if she could quote his work in her paper.

She returned to her dorm room the next day after classes to find two men in suits outside her room and several people in her dorm room systematically taking it apart. The two men were with the FBI and they arrested her on the spot for suspicion of espionage. The following two weeks were a blur of questions and threats to make her tell the government whom she was working for. They wanted to know how she had gained access to top-secret government papers. When they searched the computer they found the search results, which included information from sites that were thought to have been totally secure. With out knowing that she had done it, Holly Rebecca McClare had broken into 18 US government databases that were labeled top secret or above. The email she had sent had been the alias of one of the top weapons engineers at the Los Alamos national Laboratory.

After a thorough investigation the FBI came to the conclusion that she was telling the truth. She had, however broken the law and she was charged with hacking the databases. It was the NSA that came up with the solution to what was very quickly becoming an embarrassing problem. The government did not want the world to know that a collage student had hacked into their most secure sites and a trial would certainly make that fact known. The FBI was persuaded to drop the charges and Holly was offered a position with the NSA to do what she already seemed so good at, finding secure information. As an employee of the government she would have to sign the official secrets act, which prevented her from ever talking about the search program she had written. She went back to school finished her Masters program and then moved to Maryland to begin work as an analyst for the NSA. Her program was classified black and all records of her as the author were destroyed.

Once at the NSA she had even had the chance to enhance Spock, and it now worked it's magic for the government. What she had programmed in less than three months had taken the top government programmers almost a year to crack, and program a protection against. As soon as they certified that her search engine was no longer able to hack into the secure sites her boss had her see if she could once again get around the new security. It took her two weeks to have the program running like it did before. The side benefit of this work was that now the tool searched email servers as well. If it was sent or stored electronically, Spock could find it.

Spock was now highly classified and in use by less than a handful of US intelligence analyst who had no idea where the program had come from or who had written it. In fact less then 30 people in total knew about Spock and its author, Holly McClare, and they were all bound by the official secrets act as well. The last thing that the government wanted known was that their own databases could be hacked into.

Before starting work at the NSA Holly had been given a polygraph test and had agreed to be questioned under the influence of drugs. She wanted there to be no questions that she was not working for any one other then her own government. Even with this, the FBI was doubtful and kept a close watch on her. They had bugged her apartment and had put trace programs on all her phone data lines and internet connections. This eventually caused problems because one day at work Holly typed her own name in her search engine and found the files on her detailing the surveillance she was under. She had gone to her boss with this and quit on the spot telling him that she was not going to be trusted then she wasn't going to work there.

Five minutes later her boss had called Lieutenant General Donavan, the head of the NSA, and explained that their star hacker was about to walk out the door and why. Donovan called the Secretary of defense who in turn called the president. It had been a total of twenty-one minutes since Holly had quit and she was cleaning up her desk when her phone rang.

She hesitated then answered. "Miss McClare, how can I help you?"

"Hello Miss McClare. My name is Sally and I'm calling from the Federal Bureau of investigations. Could you please hold one moment so I can connect you to the Directors office." Said a voice that sounded like it was used to getting it's own way.

Holly was irritated that the question sounded more that an order. She had already quit so she didn't have to hold for anyone. "No I won't," she said firmly. "If the FBI wants to talk to me they can call me at home and record the conversation to play to the director at his convenience." She hung up the phone leaving a stunned Sally trying to understand how anyone could be so bold as to ignore a call from the director of the FBI.

The phone rang just seconds later. Holly picked it up and answered very differently this time. "Listen to me carefully. I don't care who you are or what you want. I don't care how important the director's time is. If that sneaky bastard wants to talk to me he can call me at home because I no longer work for the government of the United States. That way he can listen to the smug sound of his own voice when he replays the tapes of my phone calls."

"That sounds fair," said the man on the other end of the phone. "What time will be convenient for you this evening Miss McClare?"

Holly had been expecting a woman and was momentarily distracted by hearing a man. "Who is this?" She asked, afraid of the answer.

"I believe you called me a sneaky bastard but most people call me Director Gates. Please feel free to call me Peter, and no, I'm no relation to Bill." He chuckled at his own joke

Holly was silent with just the sound of her breathing being heard over the phone.

"I know you don't care about my time but I really do have quite a bit of work to do. I can call you at your home anytime you'd like but it would help if you could tell me when would be best for you," Director Gates said.

Holly found her voice. "What did you want to talk about?"

"I would like to discuss the information you found about our surveillance on you. I'd like the chance to explain myself. I've been ordered by the president to apologize but to be honest I find that distasteful. It would be insincere and if given the change I think I can tell you why I don't feel that it's needed."

"Well I have some time right now, seeing as how I'm unemployed, so we might as well get this over with. But I have one question, why did you call me?

"I called because I was told to by the president," Gates told her truthfully. "I've also been ordered to suspend all surveillance of you as well. It seems that the White House considers your work very valuable and they don't want you to leave. I believe there is also the little matter of the fact that nothing stored electronically is secure from you and should you become upset, certain people feel you may cause some harm to us. I don't believe that would happen but at the same time if you were to be kidnapped by a terrorist group or an unfriendly foreign power and they managed to get you to work for them we'd all be in trouble."

"I signed the non disclosure paper and I know what would happen if I told anyone what I used to do here and the penalties if I do so there's no way I'd risk that," Holly said hotly.

"I know Miss McClare. And I believe you. The reason I ordered surveillance on you is not because we don't trust you but because we can't afford to lose you. You have no idea how much someone hostile to the US would pay for your abilities Are you aware that you have been declared a national security risk Miss McClare?"

"WHAT?" Holly yelled into the phone. "When did that happen, and why?"

"It happened the second you quit your job and I did it. The reason for it should be obvious. I have a suggestion, why don't you and I meet in person. I'd really like to talk to you and explain everything, and it would be faster if we talked face to face. Are you agreeable to that?"

Holly thought for a moment. "All right, that sounds fair. When and were would you like me to meet you?"

"If it's not a problem for you I could send a car over and we could have lunch together. We have a very good executive dinning room at the Hoover building and to be perfectly honest I'd feel better about talking to you here where I can be certain it is secure."

"That sounds fine." Holly told him. "I'll be ready to go at 12:30. I have some things I need to finish up here."

"Excellent Miss McClare. My driver will identify himself as Agent Boles and he'll be alone. I'll see you this afternoon for lunch." With that he hung up.

Holly called security to have her belongings checked and get escorted from the building. This was standard procedure when leaving to insure that a person only took what belonged to them. She thought it was actually a very good rule and protected her more then the agency. Later on she could not be accused of theft, or worse, espionage. The security guard showed up two minutes later and Holly was surprised to see the head of the NSA with him. Even more surprising was the invitation to join him in the boardroom for a private chat.

"General Donavan, what are you doing here?"

"Miss McClare I'm here to ask you to reconsider." The General told her truthfully. "The government keeps tabs on all it's employees that have security clearances as high as you do. You know that. So why did you blow a gasket when you saw your file."

Holly had at first been flattered that the head of the NSA would personally ask her to stay but his condescending tone of voice made her angry. "Of course I know that my actions are occasionally monitored, I had no problem with that. What I object to was the 24-hour a day watch the FBI has had on me since I was caught with my program. I passed the polygraphs and you people still don't trust me."

The General sighed. "You know I'm not used to dealing with civilians and God knows that with young women I am especially bad mannered. So please bear with me, and just listen for a second, and yes I'm asking even though it sounds more like an order. Look at it from the FBI's point of view; you hacked into every secure site in the US. If people found out you could do that, then what's to stop someone from kidnapping you and forcing you to do that for them. Think what a windfall you would be for a foreign government or a criminal organization. What about a terrorist? There is just a chance that the surveillance was for your protection rather then monitoring you."

"General have you ever ordered surveillance on me?"

The General looked embarrassed for a split second then remembered who he was and what he was tasked with doing. "Yes I have. And if you stay with the NSA I'll do it again. Hell young lady even if you don't stay I'll order surveillance on you. You have a very unique talent and one that I am not about to let run around free. Whether you like it or not you are a security risk and that has to be taken seriously by someone. This may be news to you but the fact that you are the author of Spock is a more closely held secret than the program itself."

His honest answer shocked her just a bit. She thought about it and from the government's point of view she had to admit that she was indeed a security risk. If information was stored electronically and hooked to a network she could find it. Until the general had said it she had never considered her work that way. Suddenly she had much more to think about.

"General please, be honest with me, if I was declared a national security risk what would happen to me?"

"There is a strong possibility you would be detained by the government until such time as what ever risk you posed no longer existed. At the very least you would be placed under constant surveillance and your travel limited to with in the continental United States. You would never be allowed to travel abroad," he told her flatly.

"And in your mind do I constitute a national security risk?"

"You, no. But your ability to retrieve information, yes."

She sat down at her desk for a second, thinking about what she had to do next. She turned the possibilities over in her mind finally coming to a decision. She would stay but first she had to find something out.

"General I don't like the fact that Spock can do what it does. I also don't like the implications that it has created for me personally. I like the work I do, but I hate the fact that I am living under a microscope. If I stay, the FBI is going to keep me watched 24/7 simply because they don't trust me. If I leave I'll probably be arrested and held for my own protection. I seem to be screwed here don't I?"

The general smiled at her choice of words, not exactly politically correct or very ladylike, but direct and to the point. "Do you mind if we sit and talk for a few minutes? See if we can't sort something out that will work for both of us?"

"I'd like that a lot sir"

The general pulled up a chair at the other side of the meeting table and sat down. "You have a couple of options available. During World War Two, the scientists working on the Manhattan Project, and the people working as code breakers in the UK, were all moved to secure locations and housed there. These people were very good at their jobs but they were mostly civilians, not used to security and the risk associated with it. As such they were all declared security assets and put under guard. It became quickly apparent that this was not going to work. The people stopped working and demanded to be given their freedom. To get things back on track a compromise was worked out. They lived in a closed military compound but had the freedom to come and go with in limits. There were always security personnel close to them no matter where they went but they were allowed to move freely. As I remember you were offered the option of joining the military and you declined, correct?"

"That's right I did. But what has the little history lesson got to do with that?"

"That was the first option given to those men and women too and they also declined. Here is an option for you, we move you onto a military base where you live and work. This way your security can be monitored with out your apartment having to be monitored. On a base you'd be checked in and out so we would always know when you were home and that would be that. I won't hide the fact that some times you will be followed when you are off base and I will order your car rigged with a tracking device so that you can be followed by satellite. These security measures should satisfy everyone including yourself and the FBI. I'm sure you will understand the need for you to do a little compromising about your movements. It will be as unobtrusive as we can make it but it will always be there. At least until we can find a way to stop Spock."

Holly took less than ten seconds to decide. She did like her work and even though it was no fault of her own she was a security risk simply because of Spock. If the result of having a good job and access to any information she cared to search for was the compromise the General was suggesting, then it was still much better then her other options. "Deal General. When do I move?"

"It will be taken care of this afternoon. I can set it all up for you if you are in agreement and get you moved today. You won't have to do anything other then stay here at work. If you will give your keys to the security desk at the front door they will take car of your car and getting it rigged up and I promise the devices will be for tracking only, no listening at all. If there is nothing else I'll get back to work and let you do the same."

"Oh sir? I am supposed to have lunch with the Director of the FBI, he is sending a car for me."

The General stopped. "Director Gates? When were you talking with him?"

Just before you showed up, sir. He heard I was leaving the NSA and wanted to speak with me. Now that I'm not, I guess I don't need to have lunch with him."

"Miss McClare I'll call Director Gates and tell him you're staying with the NSA and I'll detail the new security arrangements for him. That should ease his mind."

"Thank you sir."

Vermont was an excellent choice, full of small towns and villages and people that enjoyed their privacy. There were also a lot of excellent collages that offered just the kind of programs Charley needed. He and Sean had rented a small house just outside Burlington, Vermont, close to the University of Vermont where he would attend. They had found the place through a local real estate agent and taken it based solely on the fact that the house was on four acres of land and wooded. Sean felt that this would give them a good degree of privacy to continue their training. Every morning they went for a five-mile run and then did twenty minutes of calisthenics. Sean followed this with a sparring session to keep their fighting skills honed to a keen edge. Since moving to Vermont Sean had been introducing his young partner to the dirty tricks of fighting, adding to his knowledge. It was good to be trained in a martial art and be proficient at it, but having a back up in the more unorthodox skill of street fighting could save his life. Sean also built a gun range for target practice. Charley was an expert shot now with both the rifle and handguns. The range was just to keep the skill up, and Sean enjoyed shooting. Just to be sure that no one complained about the noise, Sean used silencers on all the weapons, which changed the feel and balance of them and it would be good for Charley to learn as well.

Over the last several weeks the two had started working with knives and the garrote, two very difficult but highly efficient ways to kill silently and close up. At first Charley had shied away from these. Finally Sean had explained that he needed to know how to kill with them to defend against them. With this logic in place Charley had agreed and gone on with the training. Sean was finding out that Charley was quickly becoming a first class assassin. He had mastered every weapon he had been trained on.

Charley woke up at 6 AM, what had become his usual time, and had a glass of orange juice before heading outside for his run. As usual Sean was waiting for him, stretching and warming up in the driveway.

"Morning lad. I see you're finally up and about."

Charley just grinned at what had become a routine greeting from his teacher. The two started out the driveway at a slow jog, warming their muscles up and getting into the rhythm of the run. The first mile was a hard fast five-minute mile and then the slowed to a steady pace for the rest of the run. When they returned to the house the two completed their morning work out and went in for a shower and breakfast.

"So have you though about your courses at the university?" Sean asked between forkfuls of eggs.

Charley took a sip of orange juice to clear his mouth. "Definitely history. I like the past and people can learn from it. Maybe I can go into teaching afterward, who knows?" he said forgetting for a second that his future was to be dictated by someone else.

After breakfast they went into town to check for mail; Sean received orders through a blind mailbox that they had rented to begin scouting the city of Boston for a possible shooting assignment. The information was carefully vague and was written to sound like a photographic assignment more than anything else. Sean's traditional cover was that of a photojournalist so it made sense to issue his orders in this manner. The assignment included the area they were to cover and the safe distances out from them. Sean could tell that it wouldn't be easy as the safe distance started at 1,500 meters.

"Charley, do you think you could hit a man sized target at 2,000 meters?" he asked in a low voice as they left the mailbox.

Charley thought for a moment. "That's a hell of a long shot but theoretically it can be done with the right rifle. Why?"

"We've been told to scout out Boston for a possible shot and the inside safe distance is listed as 1,500 meters. What would you need to make a shot like that?"

Reality hit Charley. After six months of training he was being put to work. Until know it had all been more like a big game and he had kidded himself that he would be able to get away before actually needing to kill someone for the organization. He stopped dead in his tracks and looked at Sean with genuine fear in his eyes.

"W-w-who is it?" Charley asked with a shaky voice.

"Who is what?"

"W-w-who are we going to kill?"

"Keep your voice down Lad. No one has said anything about killing anyone yet. All we are going to do is take a drive down to Boston and tour around the city for a few days and see about some shooting sites. They may have someone else take the shot and all we are doing is the leg work." It was lie and Sean knew it, but he wanted to calm the young man down.

Charley relaxed a bit, certain Sean was lying, but in the end he wanted it to be true. "Okay, so when do we go?"

"We'll leave on Thursday. What do you want for supper?" He asked changing the subject.

Chapter 6

Adam studied the personal file of one Andrea Drake, noting all the remarks from the training staff. Words like outstanding, exemplary, superb and dedicated were all over the fitness reports. She had a law degree from Northwestern and had been accepted into the FBI, graduating first in her class from Quantico. She had run the second fastest time ever in the obstacle course and had perfect scores in marksmanship. She was a marathon runner and had entered and done well in both the New York City and Boston marathons. After graduation she had her choice of field assignments and had chosen New York. There, she had worked in counter espionage and had cracked a middle eastern terror cell that had been in the process of trying to buy portable anti-aircraft missiles. This brought her to the attention of the secret service and they recruited her. Andrea accepted the offer and after two years of diplomatic protection, had been tasked to the Presidential security detail's advance party. While there she worked harder than any other agent and as a result was being promoted to the Presidents personal security detail. The head of the presidential detail had forwarded her file on to Adam as a heads up and to let the president know. Andrea had just finished her meeting with the Head of the Presidential detail Corey Campbell informing her of her promotion.

Adam got up from his desk and walked through the adjoining door knocking politely as he did so.

"Mr President, have you got a second?"

President Mills looked up from his desk at his Chief of Staff Adam Myles. He was the youngest chief of staff in the history of the white house. Many said that he got the job only because the President was his godfather and the best friend of his grandfather. The true reason he got the position was carefully hidden. Adam Myles was a genius with an IQ off the scale. This alone would have been reason enough but when coupled with his photographic memory it made him the perfect person for the job. Only a handful of people, the President being one of them, knew of Adams phenomenal mind. He had a PhD in economics from Glasgow, a PhD in history from Oxford and an MBA in business from Cambridge. He finished his last degree at the age of twenty and had been schooled entirely in the United Kingdom to avoid the media hype that would have followed an eleven-year-old attending university in the US. The President considered him the most qualified man he had ever met for the job of running both his day and the White House.

"What's up Adam?"

"Corey just sent up a file on a new agent he's putting on your detail. Her name is Andrea and she's been on the advance team for a few months now. Corey thinks it's a good idea to have a woman on the team and she's good, damn good. I was wondering if you have any problems with a female being your body guard."

The President smiled at his godson. "Should I have a problem with a woman being a bodyguard? I know you think of me as old fashioned Adam but this is the 21st century we live in and as long as she is qualified to do the job why should it matter that she's a woman?"

Adam looked at the floor as his face turned red. "You're absolutely right sir. My apologies," he said in a quiet voice.

"How about we meet this new agent," the president said. "Find out where this lady is and get her in here. I do have the time, don't I?"

Adam memorized the Presidents schedule each morning and knew exactly what was going on each minute of the day. It was rare for the President to have any free time, but Adam made sure that there was an hour set aside each day for reading right after lunch. They were half way through this reading hour now

"I'll find her and have her here before your two o'clock sir" Adam said as he headed back to his office.

He got back to his desk and picked up the phone. "Find agent Drake and send her up please." he ordered his assistant.

Two minutes later there was a discreet knock on his door and Mary his assistant opened the door and showed agent drake in. Adam got us from his desk and moved around it extending his hand. "Nice to meet you agent drake." He said politely as they shook hands.

He took two seconds to study the new agent. She was about 5'5" and looked around 125 pounds with shoulder length light reddish brown hair and intense dark brown eyes. Her smile was sincere and lit up her face which Adam classed as very pretty. As they shook hands he rethought her weight, her grip was extremely strong and muscle was heavy so he added ten to fifteen pounds to his guess.

"Thanks for coming up. We have a little tradition with new agents of introducing them to the Boss. He likes to meet all the new people," he explained, turning and heading to the door leading directly to the Oval Office.

Andrea followed the chief of staff her heart pounding loudly enough she was sure he heard it. She knew she would be on the Presidents protection detail but she didn't think she would actually meet him. As she entered the Oval Office she saw the man she was assigned to protect. This was the man she had swore to die for if needed. He looked like any other executive of a large company. He was just getting up from behind the large desk smiling at her as she entered. He was a good looking man of average height and trim, looking to be in excellent physical condition for a man in his early sixties. The collar of his shirt was open and his tie was off. The desk, she noticed was covered with papers and books. She had never thought of the desk of the most powerful man in the world as being messy. The President, a very observant man, caught her glance at his desk as he extended his arm to shake her hand.

"The only time I'm allowed to feel at home in this office is my reading hour," he commented dryly. "At 1:55 PM exactly, two of my assistance come in and sterilize my office so no one will know my secret."

Andrea was caught off guard by the comment. And for a brief second she was unsure what to do. "I don't understand sir," she finally said.

The president smiled and leaned in close and whispered, "My secret is that I'm a slob. I prefer my desk cluttered and messy. The Chief of Staff however doesn't feel that it would be proper to show this to the world. Adam thinks that looking organized and neat presents a better view of the President. What do you think?"

"Sir, I'm not sure that I'm allowed to have an opinion. My duties are to observe and protect. I'm not the right person to even comment sir."

The President smiled. "Perfect agent response. I've asked that question to every agent I've met and you all say the same thing. Is it something they train you to say? No never mind, forget I asked. I'm sure you wouldn't answer me anyway. Well on to why you're here. As I'm sure Adam has told you I meet all the new agents. The reason I do this is I like to know the people around me. You have the worst job of any one in the white house. You are supposed to keep me alive even at the cost of your own. I don't think that's right but as I've been told I have no say over this. Every agent on my detail has my permission to cancel an event or hold up a procession for any reason. I trust your instincts; more to the point lives depend on them. If at any time you have a feeling that something is not right, stop things. Don't worry about chain of command. I've told this to the service director, who by the way works for my treasury secretary, and to Corey the head of the detail. I don't think they like this but I don't care. If you ever feel the need to take action do it and the Oval Office will back you 100%. Not just me, but the office and everyone in it. While I'm here there will be no favoritism, all agents will get treated the same. My vacation time will be spent at my home or Camp David. I do not intend to put lives at risk or make your life harder by making a surprise visit to a friend. The only time you'll find a problem with me is when I go boating. I sail my own boat and I do it alone with just my friends and family. Adam has a way around this though; he has me do my sailing with one of the fleets that's exercising near Puerto Rico. During this time you and the rest of the detail will either be on another sailboat following or one of the navy ships. If you get seasick you don't have to go. I guess that about covers my pep talk and welcome speech. Welcome aboard Agent Drake.

They shook hands one more time and then Adam took Andrea and left the President to his reading.

"You've been on the advanced detail for a few months but have you had any time in the White House?" Adam asked when they were back in his office

"No sir. The advance team works out of the old executive building. We brief and prep there."

"Okay, you've had your meeting with Corey when did he tell you to start."

"My first shift is this evening. I have the afternoon to move my things to the detail office and get ready for my shift, sir"

Adam smiled. "We're pretty informal around here. Please call me Adam. You only have to sir the President and your supervisors. Is it okay if we call you Andrea?"

Andrea returned the smile "That would be fine. But I'm afraid the sir is habit. I'm not sure Mr Campbell would approve of his detail agents being on a first name basis with the senior staff. After all we're supposed to be seen but not heard."

Adam picked up his phone. "Mary do me a favor and ask Corey if he's got a few seconds free, please."

The phone rang thirty seconds later. "Yes?" Adam answered, "No we'll go to him, thanks Mary."

Adam headed for the door. "Come on I'll give you the grand tour."

Adam lead Andrea around the mansion showing her the different rooms, and giving a quick tour guide speech. They ended up in Corey's office about five minutes later.

"Hey guy." Adam greeted Corey grabbing the outstretched hand and shaking it. "So when you were giving the welcome spiel how come you missed the part about us being all the same except for the boss?" Adam asked, referring to the President.

Corey grinned mischievously. "Well I remember how unsettled I was when I met everyone including the boss. It's unusual to meet a group of people that want the secret service around and actually try to include them in the day-to-day conversations. Usually no one wants us around and I don't remember the last time someone asked me to address them by their first name. I just thought Andrea should hear it from you."

"Thanks that was nice of you. I think I scared her. She doesn't believe me though so please update her on house rules." With that Adam headed back to his office leaving Andrea with her supervisor.

"So what do you think so far?" Corey asked Andrea indicating her to take a seat. "Not exactly what you would expect from politicians is it? Did you get the presidents welcome aboard talk?"

"sir what is going on? Is all this to make me fell at home? Am I getting some sort of special treatment because I'm the only woman on the president's detail?"

"No you're not Agent Drake. The people you've met are that way all the time. This house is frank and friendly. The current people in power see everyone that works inside the white house to all be on an equal footing. The only person that we need to sir is the President. Every other person you meet is going to give you their first name and ask you yours. You'll find out that these people like an informal work environment. It took me two months to get used to it myself. Some agents asked to be transferred out simply because they were uncomfortable with the laid back approach these folks have. How about you, any problems with the laid back style?"

"No sir, no problems. I'd just like to know the guidelines I'm to work with in," Andrea stated confidently.

Corey smiled. "That's the easy part. When on duty your job is to observe and protect. Nothing that's said around you is to be repeated, as per normal. Address people as they ask you to address them, with one exception. The president will ask you to call him by his first name when no one is around. He is always the president, remember that. When off duty, act normal. The president's staff gets together several times a month and they enjoy asking off duty White house staff to join them. If asked it's your choice to go or not. One of the president's standing rules is all persons working in the White House are invited to his get togethers. Helps him feel like a normal boss, or so he says. Anything else?"

"No sir," Andrea said as she stood up to leave. "I'll finish moving my things in and find my desk. I'll check the duty rosters for code words and get ready for my shift."

"Fine. Before you start find Sam Grey, he'll be your partner for your first few weeks her to show you the routine. And from now on call me Corey. It's easier that way. The only sir in this house is the Boss in the Oval Office."

Andrea headed to the staff parking area to get her things from her car. She was back at her desk five minutes later and getting settled in. She picked an empty desk at the back of the room and began putting her things away and organizing her desk. Each desk had a network cable to plug in a laptop for the internal network and access to the internet. As soon as Andrea had things as she wanted them she plugged in her laptop and booted it up. She logged into the secret service network and read up on the day's memos and advisories. The president received hundreds of death threats a year and each one was investigated. Every investigation was detailed and followed until it was assured that there was no actual threat to the president. All agents on security details read these updates daily to keep informed and to be aware of extra potential threats.

After catching up on all the security memos Andrea logged onto the internet and began searching bulletin boards and websites of known hate groups. This was a common practice among agents to keep tabs on the leanings of the groups. Most were disorganized and plagued with infighting. The website for these groups reflected this with the discussion threads full of hate and threats. The violence was directed at other members of the groups as much as it was at people outside the groups. Occasionally someone in a discussion thread mentioned something they shouldn't and it helped an investigation. The secret service didn't need to do this as both the FBI and NSA routinely monitored these sites as well as doing more in-depth searches for possible security problems. Any information that related to threats on the president, or any member of the government, was forwarded to the secret service. The internet was a breeding ground for this type of thing. It was also a way for false information to be feed to the hate groups to distract them, which the FBI routinely did as well.

Andrea checked her watch and noticed that she had fifteen minutes before starting her shift. She logged off and shut down her laptop and checked her pistol to be sure everything was proper. With just the hint of a smile on her face she headed for the sift supervisors station to receive her post assignment for the evening and meet her new partner to officially with the president's detail.

Chapter 7

Sean came home to find Charley in the basement working on the computer. Since they had installed a broadband connection Charley spent more and more time on the Internet. He was become very adept at breaking into secure sites. Charley had built the computer system himself and had installed Linux as the operating system rather then the more traditional Windows. He had told Sean that it made it harder for people to hack into him and was immune to the viruses infecting the Windows OS and email software. Sean looked over the young mans shoulder to see that he had hacked into the database of National Reconnaissance Office and was downloading satellite images. The old man was still not comfortable with the internet, preferring more traditional means to get the things he needed such as breaking into an office and stealing it. Charley had pointed out that this carried the risk of getting caught. Sean had countered that hackers were routinely caught all the time so the risks seemed to be about the same. The two were from different times and from their respective points of view the others method of getting information was risky. In truth the risks were about the same. If a person was very careful, both hacking a network and breaking into a building were no more risky than driving your car on the interstate.

"Are you packed and ready to go lad?"

"Are you sure we need to do this Sean?"

"Do what Lad, we're just scouting the city for a possible action later on.

The key word here is possible, so relax and let's go and enjoy the trip."

"How many times have you scouted and area that you didn't go through with the 'action' as you so lightly describe murder?" Charley asked sarcastically.

Sean was getting more and more worried about his young protégé's attitude. He had become very fond of the boy and was hoping he could adjust to the life. Not everyone did and once recruited there was no leaving. If Charley couldn't make the shot then his life was over.

"Charley, just do your job. The higher ups make the decisions, not you. You just pull the trigger." Sean explained patiently. "If you don't do it then someone else will. And the price for failure with the organization is not something you want to contemplate. Trust me Charley, you need to do this."

"Sean you can't tell me this is right, you can't tell me this is justified. How can you follow an order like this?"

Sean sighed deeply. "This is just a scouting mission, that's all. We go, we look around, we come home and we report. All very simple, and easy. Now are you ready to go?

"You know we're going to have to kill someone don't you? You know that this is going to happen." He was almost shouting now.

"Charley, just for the sake of argument let's say we get orders to do the job. If you don't pull the trigger then I have to, and then I have to tell the three stooges that you were unable to do your job. You know what happens then, they give you to the cops and you're left holding the bag anyway." Sean did not tell him that what would really happen is he would be dead ten seconds after he refused to take the shot, then left with evidence next to his body pointing to him as the assassin.

Charley saw the pain in Sean's eyes and knew there was something that he was not being told. He wanted to push Sean to get more information but knew that would be a waste of time. Still he had the feeling that if he failed to do the job the consequences would be more sever than simply going back to prison. Charley suddenly knew that if he didn't kill he would end up being killed for his failure. In mid argument he changed tactics.

"Have you ever thought of leaving? Just heading off for a job, and never coming back? A man with your talent should be able to pull that off."

Sean stared at Charley for moment. "How do you think we pay for everything?"

Charley was puzzled, what did that have to do with anything. "I guess right now you are paying the bills. No one ever talked to me about money and I never asked. I guess I should start asking. How much do we get paid anyway?"

Sean chuckled. "Not hard to tell you don't obsess about money. You never asked anyone how you were going to live after your training?"

"I got a lot of money form the life insurance from my parents deaths and never had to worry about it. And I just figured that when the training was finished I start receiving a paycheck to live on."

"The organization doesn't pay its agents," Sean explained. "Each agent is given three credit cards with which to live. These cards are rotated every few months so that our movement is hard to track. Hard to track for everyone but the organization, that is. By using credit cards the organization can track us all the time. They also know we can't run because we have no money to run with."

"But what about a cash advance?"

"The cards are limited to $50 a day. Hard to get enough money to live on that way."

"So along with the threat of prison, they keep us a slave by not giving us any money, is that what you're saying?" Charley asked in a hard voice.

"Did you think that after training you to be an efficient and lethal killer, they would just let you walk out the door and risk you disappearing?"

"Isn't that what the prison threat is all about? To keep us from trying to run?"

"Yes it is and yet here you are trying to find a way to run before you even start working for them. So it would seem that they have thought of this and taken steps to prevent just that." Sean answered him dryly.

"So you're saying that in all your time with these people you have never once tried to run?"

"Where would I run to? No money, no place to call home, no way to get there if I did have a home. And to what end? They have a criminal charge against me so they could just turn the matter over to the police and forget about me. And if you make them really angry the organization would just send someone like me after you."

"Well I guess we better be heading to Boston then." Charley said with resignation in his voice.

Sean had decided to drive rather then fly, as Boston was only a few hours away. This had the added benefit of giving them a car while they were there. It also avoided the risk of trying to take a gun through airport security. The two men packed a small duffel bag each and put them in the back seat of the car rather then the trunk. Just before leaving Sean checked to see if Charley was armed.

"Lad, are you carrying?"

Charley was surprised by the question. "No I'm not, should I be?"

"From this moment on you are working for the organization. You should always be armed. And if you remember anything I taught you you'll carry a back up as well."

Charley headed back into the house and down to the basement. He opened the arms locker and took out a Ruger .357 revolver. It was an older GP-100 model with a four-inch barrel but it had quickly become one of his favorites on the target range. It had been fitted to use a silencer, and even though revolvers could not be silenced as effectively as a pistol due to the chamber being separate from the barrel, it still made it hard to hear the shot past thirty feet. He could have used a pistol just as easily, but he used the revolver just to be different from his mentor and he knew it drove the old man crazy.

Sean knew that a firearm was an individual thing for all shooters. Each person had a reason for the particular gun they used; his favorite was the Colt 1911 in .45ACP. He liked the heavy bullet and the fact that the round was very easily silenced due to already being subsonic. He had tried to influence Charley to using the .45 but the lad liked the feel and stability of the revolver and Sean respected this. In their line of work the handgun was usually reserved for self-defense and in cases such as this silence wasn't the paramount importance, stopping power was. The .357 magnum in the hands of an experienced shooter was an excellent stopping tool.

Charley slipped into a shoulder holster and snapped the revolver into place. He picked up a couple of speed loaders and a box of rounds. At the last second he also grabbed the silencer and put it in his pocket.

Sean drove the car and headed towards I-89 to take them south to Boston. Once on the interstate Charley took out the speed loaders and the box of shells and, one by one, loaded the speed loaders with rounds.

"Pistols with magazines are faster to reload you know," Sean said in a teasing tone.

Charley smiled at the good-natured jib. "Yes but once you run out of mags you have to reload them before you can reload the pistol. I don't need the speed loaders, I just like to play with them," he countered.

Sean chuckled and turned on the radio. After finishing with the speed loaders Charley emptied the rest of the rounds in his coat pocket and put the empty cartridge box in the glove compartment. He put the seat back and within minutes he was asleep.

Charley woke up as they were entering the outskirts of Boston. "So what's the plan?"

Sean turned off the radio. "First we need to find a nice obscure motel out near the airport. After that we'll catch the bus into downtown and walk around for a bit."

"Why don't we just get a place in the city? That'll cut out the need to use the bus and we can walk around all we want."

"It would seem that it's time to start you on your urban education. Now think carefully, why would anyone want to stay near an airport? Remember this is not the wilderness so the rules are a little different here."

Charley thought for a second. "Motels near the airport would get a greater turn over of guests. We'd be just one more face in the crowd."

"Very good lad. Soon you won't need me along as your nursemaid." Sean said, very please with the answer.

"But a large hotel in the city would see the same turnover rate and it would be unexpected for us to do something like that. Most law enforcement people would think to check the motels near the airport for just the type of people looking for anonymity such us."

Sean was impressed with Charley's logic. He had a point. Throughout his long career, if it could be called that, he had always stayed at the out of the way places. Staying at a downtown hotel was no more or less risky than a motel by the airport. If they chose a large hotel they could just blend in with the rest of the guests. The more he thought about the more he liked the idea.

"Would you have any other reasoning behind staying at a large hotel in the city?" Sean asked the lad.

"Sure is. The cops don't usually look for trouble at the higher priced places. Normally, troublemakers stay in the dives so they can use cash without spending a lot. You probably wouldn't see that much as you have spent most of your life in the US but as a Canadian traveling down here I can tell you that money buys you respect. If you act like you belong, then you do. And rich people don't cause trouble, or so the police believe. The truth is that as long as you have money you can pay people to look the other way. And the rich break more laws then the poor, it's just they can afford the fines. And since the organization is paying for our expenses, but won't pay us a salary, then what the hell, we might as well enjoy our hotel stay and let them worry about the cost."

Sean had never, in all the time he had worked for the organization, wasted money. He had lived as cheaply as he could, always thinking that this was the way he was supposed to work. He spent a few minutes thinking about what Charley had just said and realized that the lad was right. They weren't getting paid. They had no savings to take a vacation with, even if they had been allowed to have a vacation. They were on call twenty-four hours a day, seven days a week. Why shouldn't they enjoy a few nights at an expensive hotel? After all this was just a scouting mission, not the real operation. Sean made up his mind and watched for an information center at one of the many rest areas along the interstate. Seeing a sign indicating an information booth at the next rest area he pulled. Both men got out of the car, Charley heading for the restroom, and Sean heading to the information center. He picked up all the brochures for the luxury hotels and took them back to the car to read. Charley joined him a few minutes later and they looked over their options.

"I think this is a good choice," Charley said, picking out the Boston Harbor Hotel.

Sean read over the brochure and noted the $400 dollar a night room price. "Sounds good to me." He agreed feeling strangely pleased to be spending so much of the organizations money for a change.

"We may need to do a little shopping to fit in," the young man said with a huge grin on his face. "After all we wouldn't want to stand out in jeans and t-shirts."

Sean matched the grin on his partners face and thought how much fun it would be to go on a spending spree courtesy of the organization. He wondered just how much he could spend on the credit cards, he had never been told what the actual limit was. He pulled back onto the interstate and headed for Boston.

When they arrived at the hotel Sean walked up the front desk, and in his most courteous voice asked the desk clerk. "Excuse me, but would you be able to help my young associate and I? We had a bit of trouble with our travel arrangements and it seems our luggage has been lost. We were wondering if you would have a room available and if you could direct us to a decent clothing establishment."

The clerk looked at the two in front of him for a second, he was used to seeing all types of people come into the hotel, and he judged them on their manner of speaking rather then their dress. With the bubble and bust of the tech sector in recent years millionaires in jeans, t-shirts, and windbreakers were as common as millionaires in suits. It was how one addressed him that mattered the most. The gentleman in front of him was well spoken and polite. He almost seemed to be embarrassed by his attire and in the clerks mind this made him the type of guest that the hotel preferred.

"Certainly sir. We have several rooms available and there may even be some suites left, if you would prefer a little more privacy for you and your associate."

Sean thought for a second. "A suite would be perfect, however I would be grateful for whatever you have seeing as how we have arrived with no reservation."

The desk clerk smiled at the obvious class of the gentleman and checked the computer for a suite. "We have a suite on the 5th floor overlooking the Harbor. Not our best unfortunately but it is still quit nice. I hope it will meet your needs sir."

"That would be wonderful, we'll take it," Sean said enthusiastically handing the clerk his credit card.

The clerk accepted the credit card and ran it through the computer checking to ensure it was valid and finding that it had unlimited credit available. He immediately became more subservient as he knew he was now dealing with a man of considerable wealth "Very good sir. With regard to new attire, if you would be so kind as to give our Concierge your sizes, we have arraignments with several of the finest establishments to deliver. We can request an assortment of clothes be brought over if this would be more convenient for you."

"You are too kind sir. That would be most helpful to us." Sean signed the register and was handed back his card.

The concierge came over to escort them to their suite. "Will you be needing any specific clothes for your stay in Boston, Gentleman?" He asked guiding them onto the elevator

Sean pretended to think for a moment. "Most of our trip is purely recreation so casual would be the best, but we will be dining out and would like to look presentable. I'm a forty-four regular with a thirty-two-inch inseam. My associate is a thirty-eight regular with the same inseam."

"Very good sir. If you would care to relax in your room I'll have someone send up several choices for you to take a look at."

They arrived at the suite and Sean tipped the concierge as he was leaving and asked one more question. "I was wondering if you could make a reservation for us to dine somewhere tonight? I'll leave the choice up to you."

"It would be my pleasure sir. Would 7 PM be all right?"

"That would be perfect."

Sean closed the door and sighed contentedly. This was becoming fun. He looked for Charley and saw him at one of the windows watching the harbor.

"Lad this was a wonderful idea. I do believe I'm going to enjoy this trip. The stooges are going to have a complete fit about the money we are wasting but as you so eloquently pointed out, we aren't getting paid for this."

Charley turned from the window. "Where did you learn to act so upper class?"

Sean looked surprised. "Excuse me?"

"At the front desk, you were very proper and acted as if you were embarrassed to be seen in jeans. What was that all about?"

Sean chuckled. "That was all about blending in. The desk clerk heard a gentleman talking to him and so that is what were are, gentlemen. The only thing he is going to remember about us is that we had some trouble with our luggage. We will now be just one more face in the crowd, as soon as we get some new clothes. It's the same as blending-in in the forest. Here you just do it differently. If you are around rich folks act as if you are rich yourself. You'll learn to do it as well."

"In the car you were all set to stay at a dive motel and since we got here you act like you've never stayed at anything less than a four-star hotel in your life. I'm just surprised by the change is all."

"So you assumed that just because I was always wearing jeans and I lived cheaply I had no manners?" Sean asked with a little edge to his voice.

"I'm not sure." Charley answered truthfully. "I don't really know you."

This stopped the older man cold. "How well can you judge people Charley?"

"Not very well apparently."

"That is something we are going to have to work on. Tonight we'll go to dinner and we can spend the evening watching people. Being able to judge people is going to be very important in your future."

"Why is that?"

"Nevermind for now, lad. I'm going to have a shower and clean up. Let me know when the clothes arrive." Sean said heading to the larger of the two bedrooms.

Forty minutes later two sales people arrived with several garment bags of clothes. Sean and Charley spent the next hour trying them on and picking the ones they liked best. There were also measured for suits that would be altered to the correct fit and delivered by 5 PM so they could have a formal supper. At the end of the fitting both men had four new outfits and a new dark blue pinstripe suit. Sean never even looked at the bill as he signed it. The two changed into one of their new outfits and headed out to explore the town. Sean took with him his 35 MM Camera with a large telephoto lens attached.

The two flagged a taxi and asked if the driver would be willing to play tour guide and show them the city. A price was agreed on and for the next hour the cabbie drove them around explaining the history of Boston. Twice they drove past the area that would have the speaker's platform set up in two months time. Sean took seven rolls of film, shooting all the streets and buildings he could find. When the tour was done they had the cab drop them off near their hotel and then walked back to the area they were scouting.

The cabbie had been a great source of information and had shown them the fastest ways in and out of downtown Boston. There was a lot of construction going on in the area and the immediate area where the speakers would be was to be closed off two days prior to the event. Sean had noticed several cranes in the area that might be useful, along with a few buildings. As they neared the site itself the older man dismissed the cranes, they would be obvious choices and no doubt the police would search them.

Sean was becoming more and more concerned with this job; he couldn't see a good spot to shoot from at all. All of the buildings in sight that had a good view would be under close watch for just what he wanted to do. As he was thinking what to do next Charley moved down to the next intersection and looked up the street.

"There's the place Sean," Charley called out.

Sean moved down next to him and looked up the street to the building Charley pointed at. He moved back to where the speakers would be and checked the building again. He couldn't see it.

"Lad, have you lost your mind? You can't see a thing."

Charley smiled. "Come here and take a closer look." He was still at the corner.

Sean walked back to him and closely examined the building. From the angle he was looking he could see the edge of the building was barely hidden buy the one in front of it.

"So what are you thinking lad?"

"Well I was thinking that they usually set up a platform or stage that's six to ten feet high. Once that is done that building will have a line of sight right to anyone speaking at a podium in the middle of it. But it looks to be the best part of 2,000 yards away and from ground level you can't even see it so the logical thought is going to be that it's not a threat."

Sean smiled at his young companion. "And you think you can make a shot from there? A bit cocky don't you think?"

"I can make the shot from there with the right rifle. How hard will that be to get?" the young man said, radiating confidence as he applied his mind to a familiar shooting problem.

"The hardware will be no problem at all lad."

"Okay all I need to do is get to the top of that building and take a look and then I'm done," Charley said confidently.

Sean was both happy and very surprised that his young disciple was beginning to accept his new life. He knew it was hard but the alternative was worse. And after all they were just following orders, not making the decisions. He took a few shots with the camera to look at later and then pulled what looked like a telescope out of his pocket. It was a small laser range finder and he used it to check the distance.

"1,871 meters," he whispered to Charley as he put the range finder back in his pocket. "Are you sure you can make that shot? That's farther then I've ever even tried before."

It was Charley's turn to smile. "You get me the right gear and I'll make it, no problems. Let's go see the waterfront. I hear the historic section is very nice." His mind was making his mentor believe he could make the shot. In truth he was actually wondering himself if he could make a shot like that, not that he ever planned on finding out.

The two turned and headed toward the harbor to do a little real sight seeing. Charley had other reasons for wanting to see the harbor. They wandered around for an hour and in that time Charley managed to get five minutes alone to find out what he needed. The day was cool but with the sun shining and only the tiniest of breezes, it was a very pleasant day. The two headed back to the building they had picked as the shooting platform to take a closer look. It was your standard city office building with several different companies renting space. Sean made a mental note of the address and motioned to Charley to go inside the lobby and look around. Charley spent four minutes inside, taking note of the layout of the building and where the elevators were situated. He also noticed that like most big city buildings, this one had security guards at a desk in the lobby. Charley walked past the desk on his way out to check for video monitors. He saw four that were displaying random shots of the building interior, and seemed to be changing every ten seconds or so.

He rejoined Sean on the street, heading back toward the hotel. "The elevators are clustered in the center of the building, four in all. They have the standard rent a cop security and video cameras. We'll need to get a layout of the building and the plans to make sure we can get to the roof," he told Sean.

"Okay we'll start with the lay out first. You go back tomorrow and check the building again. Take the elevator to the top and see what kind of access there is and then take the stairs down. Also check the stairwell for roof access. I'll start looking for building plans and see what I can find out about security. Did you notice any company name on the guards' uniforms?"

"There was a shoulder patch with Eagle Security on it."

"I'll check into them as well." Sean checked his watch seeing that it was just after 5PM. "Let's head back and have some dinner and see what kind of fun we can have for the evening."

After returning to the hotel the two changed for dinner and took a cab to the restaurant that the concierge had booked them reservations at where they enjoyed an excellent meal. Once again Sean got a perverse amount of pleasure out of signing the credit card bill and rounding it up to $250 with the tip. The accountants were going to have a fit over this scouting trip. After the meal they headed back to the room and picked a movie from the pay list, while enjoying a drink from the mini bar.

The next morning Sean ordered breakfast from room service, which arrived while his young partner was just getting out of the shower. The two ate while going over their day one more time. Charley was at first leery of checking out the building on his own but as Sean pointed out, he was the one capable of taking the shot so the final decision on the site would rest with him. With this in mind the young man left the hotel and spent the morning walking around checking angles and sight lines from the ground. He then went to the building, took the elevator to the top floor and looked for a window that he could see out of, in the direction that the speech would be. He was able to find one saw immediately that it wouldn't tell him if the sight line was workable. To know if the building would work he really had to get to the roof. Charley went to the stair well and found the roof access door, which was locked and alarmed. He would need some help getting on to the roof. Getting back to the lobby using the stairs he noticed motion detectors stationed at every other floor. The security was simple and adequate for the building but not airtight. It looked as if one only needed to bypass motion detectors and the door to access the roof from the stairwell. The must be other ways as well.

After sending his partner off to scout the building, Sean spent some time making phone calls. The organization had phone lines set up for all its operatives in the field to use for requesting information. Sean called two of them explained what he needed and leaving a phone number that he could be reached at with the information. In the case of his requests he was looking for plans so he wouldn't be getting the information back in a phone call. He requested a dead drop be used for this. Sean wasn't sure how long it would take but he had attached a priority to his request so he knew he would have the answer before the day was over. That was one good point about working for the organization; they got you what you needed in a very short amount of time. For now there was nothing to do but wait, so he turned on the TV and watched CNN to catch up on the news.

Charley walked through the door at the same time the phone rang. Sean picked up the phone with a pen and pad in his hand ready to write down the directions. The voice on the other end informed him that the items he requested would be couriered to his hotel and to expect them no later then 3 PM. Once again room service was ordered after which they relaxed watching CNN while waiting for the information to arrive.

At 2:30 the front desk called informing them that a gentleman was there with a package for them. Did they wish the desk to take it or should they send the gentleman up. Sean had them send the man up. Charley opened the door to the loud knock and was handed three-foot long tube. The courier left without even asking for a signature or waiting for a tip. The package had the building plans and schematics, a map of the sewer system, along with all the security information from Eagle Security. Charley was amazed at the speed with which the information showed up, he had figured they wouldn't get it until they were back in Vermont, saying so out loud to himself.

Sean chuckled, "Lad when you need something in the field the organization gets it to you. They expect results and also fully support their men, now let's see what we have here."

They spent two hours going over the plans looking for all the ways in and out of the building, including from the sewers, and places to hid while there. One thing Charley noticed right away was that the roof house an elevated AC unit that was on the side of the building they would need to shoot from, and that the elevators had a rooftop shed housing the motors, winches, and cables.

While Charley looked at the plans of the top Sean checked over the basement. He would need to scout it to be sure but it looked as if they would be able to access the basement through the storm sewers. He cross referenced the security plans and found that the basement was free of alarms with the exception of sensors on the doors. There were no motion detectors or pressure pads to worry about, which removed a lot of work in regard to getting into the building. He noticed that the elevator shafts could be accessed from the basement for maintenance. Another cross reference with the alarm system showed that the elevator doors were alarmed but not the shafts proper. A notation in the security plans stated that the elevators were locked out of service between 10 PM and 6 AM. This left an eight-hour window to use the shafts with out fears of the elevators moving. They had found their way in, along with a shooting perch if the sight line panned out.

The old man checked the phone book for outdoor outfitting stores in the city and found several that carried mountain climbing gear. He and Charley took a cab to the nearest one and picked up ropes, harnesses and the rest of the gear Sean thought they would need and packed everything in a couple of duffel bags. After stops at a few more sporting goods stores they headed back to the hotel with the new purchases. When they returned to their room both men laid down to catch some sleep for what was bound to be a long night.

"Andrea!" Her boss yelled, as she was about to get into her car. "Have you got a sec?"

She opened her door and dropped her handbag on the drivers seat before turning to face Corey. "Sure, what's up?"

"We need a favor from you. I know you were bumped up to the bosses' team because of your great work on the advance teams, but I was wondering if you could take charge of one of the advance teams for a few days and scout Boston. Now don't worry this is not a demotion." He quickly said to mollify any anger she might have at going back to the advance team. "You're still on the boss' detail. This request came right from the director's office. He wants one of sailors detail to go up four days before sailor does and take over the advance team at the speech site. Your name was the one that he gave. You'll be in total charge for four days until I get there, then you go back into your regular rotation. And I'll make sure you're on the podium during the speech so no one thinks you're taking a step down for any reason."

Andrea smiled at the length Corey had gone to ensure her that she wasn't being sent back to the advance teams. For every security agent, the Presidential detail was the place to be. The advance team was for the agents that were good but not quite ready or those that had been on the detail but were slowing down. Others would see her going back to the advance team after only a few months on the Bosses detail as a punishment; no matter what was official said. This was why they were going to let her be on the podium during the speech. As the most junior agent she would normally be on the crowd during the speech. Having her on the podium would erase any hint of blemish that sending her back to the advance team may put on her.

"Sure thing Corey. I'd be happy to go up early," she told him, becoming the total team player. "It'll give me a chance to see old friends for a few days."

"Great, I'll have the details on your desk first thing in the morning. And again thanks." Corey headed back into the White House while Andrea got in her car and headed home.

She had a small place in Rockville and as she was heading home she saw a van parked facing the wrong way on her street. She drove by her apartment and looped back towards Washington driving into Chevy Chase Village. She parked at a convenience store and walked four blocks to the post office, checking box 121 when she got there. Inside the box was a plain white envelope, which she placed in her purse. Going back to the store she went inside and picked some vegetables for her supper and than retraced her steps back to her apartment.

Andrea made a stir-fry with the fresh veggies she had just bought and had a glass of wine along with it. After doing up her dishes, she took her handbag and went into the bathroom. The bathroom was on the inside of the apartment building and as a result had no window. She closed the door, placing a towel along the bottom of the door to block any light from entering. She removed the envelope and a small black light flashlight from her purse then turned off the bathroom light. The light from the flashlight barely let her see what she was doing but was essential for her to read the message on the photosensitive paper enclosed in the envelope. She memorized the message, placed it in the sink and, closing her eyes, turned on the light. The magnesium coating on the paper flashed as soon as the light hit it, incinerating the message in an instant, turning it to charred powder. Andrea washed the powder down the drain and went into the living room to watch the news on CNN.

The phone's soft chirping had Sean awake before the first ring finished. "Yes?" he answered simply.

"Your wake up call sir. Would you like anything from room service?" the desk clerk asked.

"Send up a pot of coffee please, thank you." He hung the phone up and went to wake Charley. "Get up lad it's time to go to work."

The two began getting ready for their night of scouting, going through the items they had purchased all over the city earlier in the day. Each had a backpack, and into these they put the equipment they would need later. Everything they had bought was black or a dark color, including two sets of coveralls in dark navy blue. Each had a pair of skintight leather gloves and a pair of heavy work gloves. Sean had also picked up a few pair of surgical latex gloves as well, in case they needed a fine touch for something. There were ropes and screwdrivers, pliers and bolt cutters, even a GPS unit and a map of the city. Sean also had his lock pick tools as well. The coffee arrived as they were about halfway through packing and Sean went out into the hall to sign for the pot. He explained to the room attendant that his friend was sleeping on the couch and did not want to disturb him, adding a generous tip to the bill to help the attendant forget this odd behavior.

They drank the coffee as they finished packing, with the final touch being a canteen of water and the ever-ready packet of beef jerky topping off the list.

"Let's go lad," Sean said hitching his pack onto his back and heading out the door.

It was a six-block walk to the nearest sewer access point that they could use without being seen but once in the system they were able to move directly to the building to scout it. The storm system was large enough that they could walk upright and there was only about an inch of water on the floor of the tunnel so it wasn't that bad. The worst part of the walk was the damp musty smell but they got over that fairly quickly. Making their way through the storm sewers they headed toward the building they had chosen. Several wrong turns later Charley stumbled across the access to the basement of the building the needed to get into. Security was ridiculously light under the assumption no one would every use the storm sewers to break into the basement of an office tower. There was a simple grate over a floor drain that was secured with a padlock, which Sean was able to pick in seconds. Lifting the grate he eased his way onto the floor looking for security cameras or motion detectors, aside from the padlock, there was nothing at all in the way of other security measures.

Using the building plans they made their way to the basement maintenance access to the elevator shafts. Opening the door the two climbed inside and closed it after them. The elevators were a few floors above them being parked at the lobby level for the night and they were in the sub basement. Up both sides of the shaft were ladders bolted into the walls for maintenance workers to climb from floor to floor should anything go wrong with the equipment in the shaft. There was also a rail next to the ladders that had a mount every ten feet to clip a climbing harness too. As you climbed you re-clipped the harness every ten feet as a safety measure. The climbing harnesses Sean and Charley had purchased had two clips on them so at no time would they ever be unclipped from the safety rail. In this way if one did fall, it would only be ten feet before the safety rope would stop them.

It took over an hour to climb to the top of the shaft; once there the two stopped for a break to drink water and chew on some jerky. Both were tired from the climb but no more so then if they had gone on a five-mile run. Charley had scouted the shaft on the way up and had seen several side shafts that were used for ventilation that could be of use. He filed them away in his mind saying nothing to Sean about them for now. Finished resting and with a schedule to keep, Sean checked the roof access door and found an alarm on it as well as a lock. He defeated both in under five minutes opening the door and stepping out into the cool night air. Charley followed him out, surprised at how clear the view was from the top of the building with the lights of the city mostly below them.

Sean used his camera, shooting off roll after roll of the rooftop and the view it gave him. Happy with the pictures he moved back inside the shaft housing and again took more pictures.

"I think this will do nicely lad, what do you think?"

"I agree. This will work just fine."

Happy that the scouting had been a success Charley made ready to begin the long climb back down the shaft ladders. Sean stopped him with a soft chuckle. "I think we'll take the express way down lad. I'll set up a rappelling line" And with that he opened his pack and removed several very long ropes from it. Tying the ends of two together he looped it over a steel cross-member, then tied the other ends together as well using a large knot them dropped it down the shaft.

"Ah Sean? This is not something I've done before," the young man said in a low voice.

"It's easy lad," Sean reassured him. "I'll go first and when I'm down I'll call up for you to come down just watch me and I'll show you how to rig the rope so you can control the speed as you slide down at."

Sean clipped the rope to the harness then showed Charley what to do when it was his turn. With that done he simply stepped off the platform and disappeared down the shaft. Five minutes later his voice floated up telling Charley it was his turn. Copying what he had seen the older man do he clipped himself up to the rope and with his heart in his throat stepped off the platform. It took several minutes for him to become comfortable with the decent and just as he was beginning to even enjoy it he saw the roof of the elevators come into view with Sean standing on one of them.

Helping Charley unclip from the rope he motioned him to climb down the ladder beside the elevator cars. Once the Lad was out of the way Sean untied the ends of the rope and began pulling on one of them. As he pulled on one side the other went up sliding over the support at the top. It took several minutes for him to get to the point where the side he was pulling on had enough weight to continue on it's own but eventually the rope was heavy enough that it was pulling it's self over the beam. Sean jumped to the ladder and climbed down beside Charley to avoid the rope landing on him as it came free of the beam and fell down the shaft. It took several more seconds but there was a loud thud as the rope hit the top of the elevator car after falling free of the beam and down the shaft. Sean climbed back onto the car and coiled up the rope stuffing it back into his backpack. When he was done they retraced their steps through the basement to the storm sewer followed. An hour later the two were back in their hotel room showering and getting ready for bed.

The ringing phone woke both men, but Sean was the quicker of the two, picking it up. "Hello?"

"Your wake up call sir. Check out is in two hours, would you like anything from room service?"

"Send up a pot of strong black coffee please." Sean hung up the phone and got out of bed. "Rise and shine Lad, time to head home, our work here is done. Coffee is on the way up."

Charley reluctantly got up after only a few hours of sleep trying to get the grit out of his eyes. After getting dressed he began packing and was nearly done by the time he heard the light tap on the door. Sean let in the room service attendant and tipped them five dollars for bringing the coffee. Pouring two cups he handed one to the young man and took a sip of his own, sighing with contentment. The coffee was excellent, and even Charley who normally didn't drink it thought it tasted good. Done packing they finished off the coffee and watched CNN for a few moments to see if there was anything-momentous going on around them. There was news of both the Pope and the President visiting Boston soon and that seemed to be the lead story at the top of the hour. Charley suddenly had an uneasy feeling but dismissed it. No one was that crazy, were they?

Taking their new luggage down to the desk Sean settled the bill while a valet brought their car around to the front door. As he left Sean thought that this was by far one of the best assignments he had ever been on, but knew he would hear it from the organization for the wasted money.

The trip home was uneventful with both taking turns at the wheel, one driving and the other sleeping the entire trip. As soon as they were home Sean headed for the darkroom he had built to develop the films he had taken. They would need to report to the organization right away and he needed to be sure that he could report a successful mission.

They both poured over the pictures, looking at the building from every angle. There would be no way for them to know for sure if a stage was going to be used for the event or not. If no stage was used then the rooftop was worthless as the targets would be too low. Sean still wasn't sure about the location, being uncomfortable with the distance from where the targets would be.

"Charley are you sure that you can hit a target the size of a man at that distance?"

"What's the matter, not sure you could do it?"

The comment was closer to the truth then the young man knew. The distance was much further then Sean had ever shot before. It certainly wasn't the maximum distance on record for a confirmed kill but it was well beyond the capability of any commercial hunting rifle on the market today and Sean knew it. "So tell me then lad, what are you going to need to make that shot?" he asked avoiding the young man's question

"I'll need a 50-cal rifle to even think about it. There are several companies that make a fifty, the most well known being Barrett. However I'd like to build one from parts, do you think you can get the parts for me?"

"That will depend on the parts. If they are available then you'll have them. But why don't you want a Barrett? I would have thought that to be the perfect choice being a proven weapon."

"First off the Barrett comes standard with a 32-inch barrel and I want a 36-inch so we'll need to order a new barrel anyway. Second, I always do a little custom work to my rifles; I want to bed the barrel into the stock myself. If I order a Barrett the second it gets here I'll strip it and rework it. Why not just skip the middle step and order the parts and put it together the way I want from the start."

Sean had never been in a rifle competition and wasn't into the fine-tuning of rifles that the competition crowd was. He was an excellent shot with any firearm and as such left it at that. To him the rifle was just another tool of his trade, nothing more. For young Charley it was a different matter altogether, so Sean just nodded his head in agreement. "Well lad if that's what you'd prefer to do, get a list together and I'll get it to the organization. We'll have an answer on the availability in two days. The question is are you able to put it together with what tools you already have?"

"It's a straight assembly job, the parts will be main components that are already finished and just need to be mated to the rest of the components. I already have the list of what we need, along with the places to get them. They won't even have to look, just call and order them. The only item that could be a problem is a reflex suppressor, I'll need that to hide the muzzle flash and buying one of those will get some questions asked." Charley handed a piece of paper to Sean with his parts list on it.

"I'll pass this along, anything else?"

Charley thought for a moment "I'll need to load my own bullets so I'm going to need all the reloading gear to make that happen. I think I can get that off the net though so let me check first and if we need to have the organization order it I can do that later. Is that okay?"

"As long as everything is ready to go in thirty days."

Sean read through the list and again nodded his head, this time in approval. His young trainee seemed to be coming along nicely, finally accepting his new role. He had trained a lot of agents for the assassination role but this was the first time he ever had regrets about his job. Charley was still just a boy really, with the promise of a full life ahead of him. With the organization, all Charley had to look forward to was a lifetime of killing and dirty tricks for a group of men that would have him killed at the first hint of trouble or failure. It wasn't fair, but there was no other option. If he failed it would mean his life too. Putting on his coat the old man left to set the wheels in motion to get the rifle parts for the job.

When Sean left Charley began to surf the net to find the things he needed. He found all of the reloading tools and dies he would need and was able to order them online. To make sure that he obscured what he really needed he bought a universal set that came with eight different caliber reloading dies, the largest being the 50 BMG. He also ordered the gunpowder and several different calibers of brass and bullets so as not to draw attention to the real reason for the orders. He had all the items mailed to a general delivery box in Burlington Vermont and left under the assumed name the organization had provided him with.

Sean returned an hour later to find his partner still in front of the computer. "That can't be good for your eyes, come on it's time to do something else. Let's go work out in the back yard." Charley logged off the computer and followed Sean outside with a deep sigh of the young trying to show tolerance for the stubbornness of his elders.

The two men worked on the plan between their normal daily routines of exercise and training. Charley was now Sean's equal in almost every way. He was an expert shot with any type of rifle or handgun, he was deadly with a knife or garrote, and his hand to hand skill would make any military combat instructor green with envy. They had also been working in Burlington on his abilities to tail people and lose a tail. When the two used each other for practice neither could follow the other for more than three blocks before the exercise was over. To make it more interesting, Sean had Charley tail police officers to see if he would be noticed. The lad moved like a ghost in the city, blending in with crowds and never once even came close to being caught by any of the officers he was following.

Sean had left the final learning process for the last, how to break into building and be an expert thief. The Lad had already been taught to defeat alarms so the only thing missing was practical application of the training. Sean decided to wait until after the Boston mission so that Charley had proven himself to the organization. It was also an unnecessary risk so close to a real job. He was pleased with his latest trainee; this was the best student he had ever had. It was a shame to have the organization take the boy's future away from him but there was nothing that could be done now other then give Charley the skills he would need to stay alive. The only thing he hadn't trained the lad in was automatic weapons and assault tactics. Seeing as how the boy's job was that of stealth he hardly thought it was needed training at this stage of his recruitment, there would be time for it later.

The rifle parts began arriving from the organization two days later by UPS, disguised as items other than what they really were, and over the span of a week, Charley had everything he needed. The rifle was built in the bullpup configuration to keep the overall length down. Charley used a pistol grip on the trigger mechanism for comfort. He had wanted a bolt action because he was more comfortable with it but with the receiver close to the shoulder throwing a bolt would mean moving from a shooting position and then trying to get settled again. Knowing he may have to take two shots he had opted for semi auto with a six or ten round magazine. He spent eight days assembling and tuning the rifle, making sure the Hart barrel mated just so, to the receiver. The trigger was taken apart no less than 6 times before he got the right pull weight he wanted. The scope was adjusted more times than Sean could count and bore sighted each and every time Charley moved it the slightest amount.

Miller had never seen anyone be so picky over a gun in his life before. Finally the rifle was assembled to Charley's satisfaction, the only thing left to do was sight it in and test fire it. To do the test firing they would need an open area that was free of people, Charley wanted to take no chance that he might be seen with the rifle. He asked Sean to arrange for a place to test the rifle, adding that it needed to be as soon as possible in case there were modifications that needed to be made.

Sean again left to make contact with the organization to pass on the request for a suitable shooting range for the big gun. The answer came that afternoon in the form of a taxi pulling up to the door and the driver knocking on it.

Sean slipped a .45 behind his belt at the small of his back and answered the door. He was sure that the man was from the organization, but he hadn't stayed alive all this time by trusting his assumptions.

"Hello," Sean said politely opening the door halfway.

"The cab you ordered to the airport is here. Can I load your luggage for you?" the man said pleasantly.

Sean knew instantly the man was from the organization and that a shooting range had been set up that they would need to fly to. "I'm sorry I thought you were coming later, we aren't quite ready to go yet. How much time before the flight departs?"

"As always sir you have a chartered plane, it will leave when you are onboard."

"Thank you, I'll get my partner and we'll be out in a few minutes, you can wait in the car, we'll carry our own luggage."

Sean closed the door without waiting for an answer and went to get Charley to tell him to pack up the rifle and get ready for a trip. As always the young man had questions, which Sean as usual ignored. The old man didn't really know anything himself, however he enjoyed the discomfort his silence caused the young man. He was used to the way the organization operated and the lad was not, yet. The two were packed in thirty minutes; the rifle was disassembled and placed in a large aluminum carry case that had been bought and refitted for it. Charley insisted on carrying the rifle himself and wouldn't put it in the trunk. He carried it in his lap the entire way to the airport.

The cab drove them to private hanger where a twin-engine jet waited the cab driving them right up to the planes door. As soon as they and their gear were aboard, the pilot started engines and requested permission to taxi from the tower. Several minutes after that they were in the air heading southwest at over 400 knots, with only the pilot knowing the destination. Charley and Sean talked for a few minutes then both nodded off to sleep out of boredom. Both men dozed for the entire flight waking only when the plane started to descend, the change in the engine noise waking them up. Looking out the window to see if they could spot any recognizable features, nothing looked familiar. There were a few houses to be seen but mostly flat land around. They had to be somewhere in the Midwest but where was the airport?

"Sean do you see an airport anywhere?"

"No lad I don't, it looks like we are landing on a private strip."

The pilot announced over the intercom what was already apparent, they were landing, and asked them to fasten their seatbelts, which both did. They were still looking out the window but there was nothing at all to give them any indication of where they were. The plane was on the ground and stopped fifteen minutes later. The door was opened from the outside and a man stuck his head in asking them to get out. Even though it was phrased as a request, both knew it was an order so they undid their seatbelts and stepped off the plane, Charley still carrying his rifle case. The young man looked around seeing a house and huge barn in the distance as well as a long strip of pavement that the plane had landed on. Other than that there was nothing in view. Their gear was unloaded and placed by the edge of the strip; to be picked up later they were told.

The man who had met them, didn't offer his name or ask theirs, but did offer to take the rifle case which Charley politely refused, the stranger then lead the way to the house several hundred yards away while the plane started the engines back up, turned around and took off again. Charley watched the plane climb until Sean called out to him to hurry up. Charley was unhappy about not knowing where he was or who the strange man was but his mentor seemed to be okay with things so he simply followed Sean not knowing what else he could do.

After being shown to the room they would share the two were told that their things would be brought up and that everything they needed was in the barn. They were given the run of the house and barn but told that could not leave the surrounding area. The stranger told them that there were targets in the barn that they could use and that they were twenty miles form the nearest house so they didn't need to concern themselves with the sound of rifle fire, no one would be complaining. As soon as the door was closed Sean motioned the lad to unpack his rifle. By use of hand gestures Sean indicated to the Lad that he was going to search the room but not to make any indication of what was going on. So while Sean circled the room checking things over Charley opened the case and carefully assembled the big rifle checking each part over to ensure a perfect fit.

"So lad do you think this place will do?" Sean asked after his examination was done.

"If there is no one around for twenty miles I certainly have the range to test the rifle with. All I really need is 3,000 yards. Can we go check out the barn and see what they have for us?"

"Let's go lad," Sean said leading the way out of the room.

With the exception of the man that met them at the plane, who was now in the kitchen, Sean and Charley didn't see another person around. The barn was on a north south axis, with doors at both ends, which were open. When they walked inside they saw several shooting ranges already set up. Along the east side of the structure there were several elaborate shooting ranges constructed using mechanical moving targets to assist in simulating combat shooting. Along the west side was a van and a four-wheel drive Pick-up truck. As well there were several ATVs and a snowmobile for use in the winter. None of the ranges would work for what Charley needed so they walked to the other end of the barn toward the door open there as well. Set up just inside the door way was shooting bench for a rifle to rest on, facing south. On the bench were sandbags along with a large spotting scope to check the targets being shot at. Charley looked south seeing several metal frames that could hold paper targets for shooting. He judged the farthest away at 1,000 yards, only a third of the distance he needed, however, there was plenty of distance to move the frames back to add more range.

"What do you think lad? Will this work for you?" Sean asked him

"It should work fine. I'll need to move the targets back to get more range. The only thing I wish I had was the same height that I'll be shooting from, but I can use ballistics charts to calculate the drop. The important thing is going to get a feel for the distance and see what the drop is going to be on the flight path along with the bullet travel time."

Both men headed back to the house to see about their gear, but the lone occupant of the place was nowhere to be found. Going up their room they found their gear had already been delivered and was sitting next to the door in a pile. Charley went through the bags grabbing the one with his ammunition in it and opening it to check on the rounds. He had brought 250 rounds with him, 200 rounds were factory made, and had been supplied by the organization; the other fifty were ones that he had hand loaded himself. Sean had never hand loaded a cartridge in his life, always using whatever bullets were supplied or that he could buy at a sporting goods store. He was amused at the amount of time Charley had fussed over the bullets and brass. The young man had taken a fine file and worked on the primer holes doing what he called de-burring, before inserting the primers, seating them just so. Then Charley had taken each piece of brass and worked on the neck where the bullet would be seated, doing what he called neck-turning, he told Sean this was to get a better joining of the bullet the lad was doing but as long as it made him happy he left it alone. Each hand loaded round had exactly the same amount of powder, measured out in a jewelers scale, and all of them had been polished until they gleamed. Each round had taken over an hour to produce, which Sean felt was a huge waste of time that could be better spent on training.

Charley separated the rounds into fifty round lots with ten of his hand loads going into each group. Next he striped the rifle down cleaned it and fully assembled it, bore sighting it to make sure the telescopic sights hadn't been thrown off by the trip. Everything looked fine and the only thing left to do was test fire the big rifle. Looking out the window and seeing it was late in the day, he decided to wait until tomorrow. He wanted the sun high in the sky so the shadows would be smaller. With nothing else to do he and Sean went down to the kitchen to see about getting something to eat.

No one was around when they entered the kitchen so they began looking through the cupboards and refrigerator to see what there was to eat. They found canned vegetables, potatoes, and in the fridge, two good-looking steaks on a platter with the note on top that said help yourself, so they did. The two split up the cooking with one prepping the steak and the other getting the vegetables ready. After the meal they washed the dishes and put them away then went outside for a walk. Throughout the entire meal they hadn't seen anything of the man that greeted them when they arrived. Charley thought this strange, but Sean was used to the ways of the organization. Everything was compartmentalized and the other agent didn't need to know anything about his two guests other then the fact they were there to test fire a rifle and needed a lot of range to do it.

With nothing else to do Sean decided that they might as well exercise so he led Charley on a light run down the shooting range out to the 3,000 yard mark and back. After that the two engaged in a hand-to-hand sparring session, both for the work out and to hone their fighting skills. Then came a shower and off to bed early so they could be up early the next day. Their host was still nowhere to be found when they went to bed. While Charley still found this very strange, to Sean, it was normal behavior in another agent of the organization.

The rising sun peeking through the window woke both men with in seconds of each other. They lay still for a moment listening to the surroundings for any sound out of the ordinary. With nothing to alarm them they got up, put on shorts and t-shirts and went outside for a morning run. Just like the day before, Sean led the two down the shooting range, out to the 3,000 yard mark, and back for a light run. Then they again spent thirty minutes sparring. After a shower, they headed to the kitchen for something to eat. This time their host was there with coffee brewing and cooking omelets for all three of them. There was also fresh fruit and juice and all three ate their fill almost in complete silence. It was as if their host wanted nothing to do with his two guests and was going out of his way to avoid them. As soon as they were done eating, he told them to just stack the dishes in the sink and he would do them later then he left.

Charley could stand it no longer, once they were out of the house he looked at his partner. “What the hell is wrong with that guy?”

“What do you mean Lad?”

“Well he’s about as unfriendly as I’ve ever seen, he hasn’t even told us his name or asked ours. It’s like he doesn’t want us around at all, he avoids us.”

“Charley that’s not him, that’s the organization. His orders are to give us a place to target practice with a long-range rifle and to leave us alone. He avoids us because he was told to. As for the no names bit, that’s standard operating procedure for the organization as well. You notice I didn’t ask or volunteer my name either. Now enough about that let’s go set up some targets and try this rifle of yours.”

“Hell of a way to run an outfit,” Charley muttered, heading back into the house.

After retrieving the rifle and gear from the room he headed back out to the barn where Sean had set up one of the ATV’s with a small utility trailer to move the targets around with. With the engine warmed up and running smoothly he hopped on and headed out to the range to set up the targets at 500, 1,000, 2,000, and 3,000 yards. While he did that Charley set up the bench to his satisfaction and did one last bore sight of the rifle to make sure the scope was properly aligned. Satisfied that it was as correct as it could be before he fired it, he set everything down to wait for Sean to finish with the targets and get back to the bench.

Done with the targets Sean returned to the barn and sat down at the bench behind the spotting scope while Charley loaded two, six round clips with five of the factory rounds each. Checking the wind with a hand-held wind gauge it showed almost no breeze at all, perfect for shooting. Snapping the clip into the receiver he loaded the rifle, put on shooting glasses and ear protectors, checked to make sure Sean had done the same thing, and sighted on the 500-yard target. Setting his breathing into a rhythm he let his mind go and began taking up the slack in the trigger. With out conscience thought his mind willed his finger to squeeze until the trigger broke at exactly six pounds of pressure and the firing pin snapped forward to strike the primer. The big 50-cal fired, hitting the target high and to the left.

Sean called the round and Charley adjusted the scope two clicks to the right but left the elevation alone. Sighting again he lowered his point of aim and went into the familiar, comfortable pattern of shooting. Control the breathing, take up the slack, and let the unconscious mind tell the finger when to squeeze the trigger. Another round hit the paper this time only an inch above the center and just slightly to the left. He moved the scope one more click, then fired another round and this time was in the x ring. The last two shots went with in two inches of the third one.

Swapping clips he sighted on the 1000-yard target and fired through the clip to get the feel of the big gun. The rounds were all inside the target ring but the grouping was ragged and all over the place. Sean glanced over at the young man to see a look of joy on his face. He was having a blast sitting at a bench with the big rifle in his hands. Concentrating on the moment he was at one with the rifle, striving to get the best performance from it and loving the challenge

Charley let the rifle cool down then broke it down to check the receiver and barrel. Using a small magnifying glass he looked over the entire action of the big rifle then ran a cleaning swab through the barrel to examine the powder residue left there from the ten rounds. Everything looked fine, and he reassembled the rifle then began loading two ten round clips again using the factory ammo. While he had been checking the rifle over Sean had used the ATV to drive out and switch targets bringing the old ones back.

With the new targets in place Charley loaded a clip sighted on the 1000-yard target and squeezed off all ten rounds in a controlled spaced out manner, then quickly swapped clips and rapid fired the second one. Checking the target he could see two clusters of holes, one to the left of the center and one to the right of the center of the target, each group where he had been aiming.

Sean looked through the spotting scope noting that the groups seemed to be in diameters of about 5 inches each, very good for the range. He was impressed with both the shooting of his young partner and the performance of the big rifle.

Charley fired off several more clips at both the 500 and 1,000 yard targets then again let the rifle cool down after which he began to strip it down to inspect it. Going over everything with the magnifying glass once again showed no problems with the rifle. He cleaned, inspected, and oiled it again before assembling it once more. Sean had gone and replaced the targets and then sat there watching the care and attention being shown the rifle.

"Just out of curiosity lad, when are you going to take a shot at the 3,000 yard target?" Sean asked as the young man finished loading the rifle.

"Right now." Came the answer as Charley sighted through the scope and settled into position and looking for the spot-weld that made a solid connection between him and the rifle. Once there his unconscious mind took over once more and he began methodically sending rounds out to the farthest target. Firing five rounds he changed clips and fired five more then set the rifle down to look through the spotting scope On either side of the center of the target exactly where he had aimed there were two distinct groups of holes. Loading a clip with five of his hand-loads he again picked up the big 50, loaded it, and settled into the bench carefully aiming. Five more times the loud bark rang out and this time looking through the spotting scope it showed the exact center of the target gone.

Sean hopped on the ATV and ran down to retrieve the target. Taking it down he was amazed at the shooting ability of the young man. He had hit the bull's-eye 5 times at a range Sean wouldn't even have thought possible. The lad's skill with a rifle was beyond belief.

Charley was done sighting in the rifle, he had it zeroed in exactly the way he wanted. He spent two more hours firing the rifle testing the factory loads against the handloads, shooting with the barrel cold and hot, getting the feel of the big gun. As Sean was replacing the targets for the last set of rounds Charley loaded a clip with the last five hand loads, all special rounds he had made on a hunch. He waited till the barrel was completely cold then one last time carefully sighted on the small speck of paper 3,000 yards away. This time, after each round was fired, he used the spotting scope himself to check the target. He was high on the target with the first round, with each round after moving closer to the bulls-eye. The last two rounds punched holes in the paper that could have been covered with a quarter. The young man was satisfied that his crazy idea would work. Smiling to himself he broke the big rifle down for the last time, carefully inspecting and cleaning each piece before packing it all away.

Sean went down the range one last time retrieving the targets and stands and returning everything to the barn. Looking at the last target he was surprised to see three shots out of the bulls eye. He also noticed the holes were smaller then in the other targets. These seemed more in line with .308 rounds then .50 caliber rounds.

The lad was cleaning his rifle so Sean folded up all the targets then began picking up all the spent brass. Charley would reload the brass later when they got home. Before heading back to the house Sean carefully burned the paper targets and then kicked the ashes around.

Back in the house the two looked for their host to tell him they were done but couldn't find him. With nothing else to do Sean started making a late lunch. Just in case, he made enough for three and as he was serving it up the nameless host walked in. Sean dished out the food for all of them and they sat down to eat. The meal was quiet with no one talking and when they were done Sean informed his quiet host that they were done and could leave anytime. The man told Sean that the plane would arrive later that afternoon and then left the room.

Sean and Charley cleaned up the dishes then went upstairs to take a nap and wait for the plane. It was three hours later when the sound of a plane landing told them it was time to go. Their gear was already packed and they started carrying it downstairs when the host showed up to let them know the plane was waiting for them. Helping them with their gear the three moved everything to the plane and as soon as it was all loaded the nameless man simply turned and headed back to the house without a second glance at either his two former guests, or the plane.

For their part Sean and Charley closed the plane door and belted themselves in for the take off. The trip home was a carbon copy of the trip out, with nothing-uneventful taking place. Landing back in Vermont the same cab that had picked them up was waiting to take them home. Charley was totally amazed that he had just taken a trip where he had not learned the name of one single person he had met. The organization he worked for was indeed a very strange group of people. But the rifle was ready and he was set. The scope was dialed in for the shot, all that had to happen now was the order to take it. And even though he had loved the thrill of building the big gun and zeroing it in, he was becoming more and more uneasy by the second.

Somehow he had to find a way out of this mess, not just for him but for his new mentor too.

The next morning Charley went to the reloading bench to reload the used brass from the day before. Using 30-caliber, 168-grain boat tail bullets, he fashioned several sabot rounds using plastic collars to hold the smaller bullet into the larger brass case. These were the same as the last five rounds he had test fired. Being much lighter then the .50 cal rounds they had a much higher muzzle velocity and as a result were a flatter shooting bullet. This was why the first three had hit higher then the .50 cal rounds had. He had expected them to drop faster but they didn't which was a surprise to the young man. One thing he would need to watch for would be crosswind. Being lighter they would be far more susceptible to being blow on course by a breeze. Well that was something he would need to research using ballistic tables. His reloading work done, he hid the sabot rounds and went to find Sean to see what they were doing next.

For the rest of the day Sean worked the lad in hand-to-hand combat and then simply ran ten miles for exercise. It was his idea of a light workout, a heavy workout involved loaded packs and running twenty miles over rough terrain. When they were done for the day Sean told Charley to start supper while he went to check the mail. Looking at the dead drop he found the orders he had been waiting for. They told him the time and place and what he was supposed to do. Now to break the bad news to Charley, he was going to have to kill two people, he would keep the identity of the targets to himself for now, no use upsetting the lad even further. His easygoing life truly was over. He went to tell his young protégé to pack for the trip; they would leave in a week's time. Sean had planned everything out when they were in Boston and had all the gear ready, now it was time to use it.

Chapter 8

The return trip to Boston was done late in the day to arrive at night. Sean parked on a quiet side street and together he and Charley lowered all the gear down a storm drain into the sewer system. Even this had been planned out in advance. Once the gear was all down, the two packed it onto two folding carts to tow behind them in the sewer. Charley would pull the carts to the building entrance while Sean drove to the airport and parked their car in the long-term storage area. The airport shuttle would get him back to the downtown. From there he would rejoin Charley in the sewer. It was 1 am by the time they were in the bottom of the elevator shaft. Sean nodded to himself; they would be at the top of the shaft with all their gear long before the building opened for the business in the morning.

Sean and Charley had been hiding at the top of the elevator shaft for four days now. They had come prepared with food, water, blankets, and a portable chemical toilet. Sean had known that in the post 9-11 world, security for a speech of this type would be extreme. The secret service, the FBI, state and city police, would all be at the height of alertness. The city core was virtually shut down to allow the teams of experts with their chemical sniffers and dogs to scour every building car and person within a 2,000-yard radius of where the speech platform would be located. No official word had been given on the exact location, but based on the number of police in the area everyone had a pretty good guess of where it would be.

The top of the shaft was actually a machinery shed on the roof of the building that housed the pulley's, cables, and motors needed to run the elevators. The elevator shaft doubled as the ventilation shaft for the building so there was good airflow for the two men. Sean was worried that a maintenance man might come up and check the elevator equipment but according to the information obtained by the organization, routine maintenance on the elevators and gear was carried out by a contractor on a monthly basis. This was always the beginning of the month and had already been done this month. If this information was accurate then there was no reason for anyone to check the machinery shed for another two weeks

Except for the smell of their unwashed bodies they were quite comfortable. The only complaint Charley had was with the food and water situation. Not being able to cook anything they were forced to resort to MRE's they had purchased at the local army surplus store. Charley found the selection a little on the thin side. Sean supplemented his MRE's with a good supply of his ever-present beef jerky. They had lots of water to drink but it was at room temperature and tasted like the five-gallon plastic container they carried it in. Their hideaway gave them enough room to move around in, and they had a great view from the vents in the side of the housing. During the day it was noisy being right next to the AC unit on the roof but at night the AC was shut down and it became very quiet.

The access door to the roof was with in ten feet of the AC housing unit and there was a crawl space under the AC unit itself. When they had scouted the building two months before, the plan was to set up a shooting nest under the AC unit on the side closest to the edge of the building. This would give them a decent line of site to the podium but keep them in the shadows, making them hard to spot. All of the equipment they had, including their clothes was colored a flat black to avoid reflecting any light.

Security had begun patrolling the city with helicopters two days before the event and Sean had tried to time them to a pattern but they were too random. On the second day the two noted, that even thought there was no pattern to the flyovers, the closet interval between the flyovers was never less then four minutes. They would have no problems moving from the shaft housing to under the AC unit. It would be only a matter of seconds to cross the ten feet of space. All they needed to do was wait until thirty seconds after a patrolling helicopter had flown over the building and make their move then. Sean planned on moving to the shooting nest at sunrise, when the natural patterns of shadows would give them even more cover. Charley had wanted to go out during the night but Sean had killed that idea fast. The security teams in the helicopters would be using thermal sensors and infrared scanners to search rooftops with. The two would stand out brightly against the cold of the roof. Hidden inside the shaft housing the rising heat of the building would mask them.

Waiting as long as he could Sean finally told the young man who the targets were the night before the job, there were two of them. The information shocked Charley and he exploded in rage refusing to do it. The argument went on most of the night until Sean finally explained that either Charley took the shot or he would be framed for it and left for the authorities to find. But the two men were going to die and that was final. The young man retreated to a corner at that point and sat quietly not moving or talking at all. As the dawn was breaking the two checked over the equipment one more time. Sean looked at Charley and noticed his mounting nervousness.

"Relax lad, we're almost there. Once we set up it's a matter of waiting till the right time, squeeze off the shot and then pop back into the shaft for a nap. As soon as the searching dies down we drop to the basement and head home."

Charley smiled as his mentor's easy statement. The lad wasn't actually worried about the shot itself. He was worried about something far more deadly, he was worried about Sean. He watched his friend open the door and peek out to check for the helicopters. As soon as he was occupied Charley reached for the small of his back and removed the gun from his waistband. He shot his partner twice in the back and then dropped the gun preparing to defend himself. Sean felt the two hits and turned to face Charley, he had time to see the young man ready himself for a fight before his vision clouded over and he dropped to the floor. Charley was surprised that the tranquilizer darts had worked so fast.

He moved Sean to a comfortable spot and tied him up with duct tape, taking care not to cut off the blood flow to his hands or feet. Once he was confident that Sean would not be able to escape he gathered up the gear and moved to the door. He judged the time and jumped onto the roof, sprinting the ten feet to the AC unit and diving underneath it. He was back in the shadows and lay there for five minutes while his pounding heart slowed down. The outside temperature was cool in the early morning but Charley was sweating as if he had just finished his usual morning run.

With his pulse back to normal he opened the duffel bag and slowly removed a foam pad and spread it out. Careful to stay in the shadow and not move too fast he rolled onto the pad and began to take his equipment from the bag. He first removed a 50x spotting scope mounted on a small tripod. He used this to carefully scan the city, looking for any signs that one of the security men had spotted movement on his rooftop. Seeing nothing to indicate he had been detected, Charley began to assemble his rifle.

Once he had the rifle assembled and mounted on the tripod he folded the empty duffel bag and used it as a pillow to lie on. Charley once again scanned the city, this time through the 36x scope mounted on his rifle. He could see the security teams with dogs checking and rechecking the area around the podium. Every car in the area was being checked and sniffed by dogs, people were being checked to make sure they had the right to be there. All across the roof tops he could see armed riflemen, part of the counter sniper teams, setting up and searching through high-powered scopes. Suddenly he was aware of a helicopter flying over his hiding place. Before he had time to even flinch the aircraft was past him. Charley rolled onto his back and checked behind him to see if the helicopter was turning around and coming back for a better look. He held his breath waiting for a full minute and then slowly let it out, as he realized that he was still safe.

He checked his watch and discovered that eight minutes had passed since he left the Shaft housing. It was early morning and the event wasn't scheduled to begin until 3 PM. It was going to be a long, stress filled day.

Taking the rifle off the tripod and laying it on the pad next to him, he pulled a piece of black camouflage netting over him and his gear and set the vibrating alarm in his watch for 2 PM then settled in to try and sleep. He knew it would be along day and the best way to pass it would be sleeping through it. After being up all night sleep came easily to him.

A tingling in his wrist woke him. He was surprised that he had been able to fall asleep as wired up as he had been. Slowly he tensed and relaxed his muscles starting with his legs, to loosen his body up. He slowly pulled the netting back and took a careful look around. He could see the helicopters still circling the city but did not notice anything out of place on his roof. He could hear the normal city sounds of traffic, but no sirens were going off. He set up the spotting scope again and took a careful look around. The security was even tighter than it had been in the morning. Dozens of rooftops had men on them and in windows he could see more armed men, some with rifles others with what could only be machine pistols. They were taking security very serious.

Charley finally scanned the platform. There were lots of police around the stage area. The back and side were roped off to allow no one with in fifty feet.

He could not see the front of the stage but that didn't matter, he could see the podium set up in the middle of the stage and was within his line of sight, meaning he had a clear shot. Much more important were the four men with sniper rifles on the roof of the building directly in his line of fire. In all the planning he had not thought about men being on the roof between him and the target. Although why he didn't, completely escaped him. It was a natural building to place a counter sniper on. Having a direct line of tight to the podium made it an obvious choice. Charley set the BMG back on the tripod and lifted his eye to the scope. As long as no one moved too much he would still have a clear shot. If they did move then that would be too bad for them. He was going to take his shot and that was that.

Over the next hour Charley watched more and more people arrive. It seemed that each time a new person in a suit arrived there was a flurry of security men converging on the suit and then they scattered after about two minutes. If he hadn't been watching the men through the scope of the most powerful rifle on the commercial market Charley would have thought all the running around funny. Considering what he was holding he realized how justified their paranoia was. They were worried about an assassination attempt, which is exactly what he was in the perfect position to do. And unless the police got very lucky in the next few moments there was nothing anyone could do to stop him.

Time slowed down for Charley. He could feel each second tick by with the beating of his heart. He could see the people on the stage moving one at a time to the podium to address the crowd for a few moments each. The sound from the public address system was muted to a background noise across the 1,800 meters that separated them. He could, however hear the roar and clapping of the crowd every time something was said that they approved off. Speaker after speaker came to the mike and had his or her say to the clapping, yelling approval of the crowd. This was a big day for the city of Boston and every politician in the state wanted a little piece of the glory. Charley checked his watch after what seemed like an eternity only to find that the time was 3:12 PM. Time moved so slow for him. He took off his watch and placed it in his pocket and concentrated on the rifle and the scope.

He had felt his heart speeding up and concentrated on his breathing to slow it down. In for a count of two, hold for a count of two, out for a count of two. Over and over he let his mind work on his breathing while his eyes watched the stage. The roar of the crowd grew and reached a new peak. At that moment, a new group of people moved into view. Surrounded by Secret

Service and his aides, the President of the United States came out of the building and moved up the stairs onto the stage. He waved to the crowd basking in the cheering and clapping. As he moved to the mike the crowd got louder still and finally quit only after he started to speak. He had to repeat his first two lines four times before the audience was finally quiet enough for him to be heard.

Charley placed the scope on the President. It was a clean shot, all he needed to do was apply four pounds of pressure to the trigger and the 165 grain boat-tail bullet would be on it's way to rip out the heart of the leader of the United States. Charley shifted his aim and scanned the rest of the stage area. He had no idea what he was looking for but he knew he would recognize it when he saw it. When the crowd began roaring again he shifted his aim again to the building behind the stage. There he saw emerging into the crowd, the Pope.

The Pontiff moved up the stairs with two cardinals escorting him, one on either side. He stopped at the top of the stairs and made the sign of the cross, blessing the President. For his part the President moved his gaze to the ground and bowed his head to accept the Catholic leaders benediction. The two met at the center of the stage and then faced the crowd one waving and the other making the sign of the cross in the air. After several minutes an aid moved in to reposition the microphone near the two men. The president motioned the crowd for silence and began speaking. This was the moment that Charley had been waiting for. The two men he was supposed to kill were together and in the open. A perfect shot.

Scanning the stage again he noticed one of the security detail. While every other agent was scanning the crowd in a slow deliberate motion, one lone female was standing looking straight at the rooftop Charley was on. He could tell she was part of the secret service by the sunglasses she wore and the dark suit that was open with her hand right hand near the open edge of her suit jacket, the standard look of a secret service agent. What was different was that the head wasn't moving. In that second he knew that she was part of the organization, placed there to make sure his job was completed. There to make sure that both the Pope and the president died on the stage.

Without any conscience thought his brain willed his finger to take up the slack on the trigger and begin the slow steady pull needed to fire the rifle. The sound of the heavy gun going off was almost a surprise it happened so naturally. He knew that his bullet would hit it's mark and without needing anymore time to watch, shifted his point of aim and fired the other five rounds as rapidly as possible. Charley was dead on target.

Andrea blended in with the other agents on the podium, scanning the crowd, looking for problems. As the President took the stage the cheering increased to a deafening level, making it hard to hear agent reports on her earphone. Her gaze kept going back to the building top she had been briefed to expect the shot to come from. Once the pope took the stage with the President she could expect the shot anytime. Her job was to misdirect the Secret Service, make sure they looked elsewhere for the assassin, leaving the agent time to escape. If he was captured she was to report this right away so that steps could be taken to ensure the security of the organization. As the two men embraced on the podium she watched the distant rooftop waiting for the muzzle flash. Just as her mind was beginning to nag at her that there was a problem, something smashed into her upper right leg throwing her to the floor of the stage. As she hit the stage she heard the yelling of other agents and her earphone came alive with reports of gunshots. Her brain commanded her to stand up and check the President and the Pope but her body would not respond. Then the pain hit.

She grabbed her leg and felt warm wetness. She lifted her hand and saw it covered with blood. She was trying to figure out why there was blood on her hand and why her leg hurt so much when she was picked up by several other agents and carried from the stage. She was placed on a stretcher and a medic was talking to her, telling her that she had been shot in the leg and checking her wound. Her brain grasped what was happening at the some time she felt the prick of a needle enter her arm. As she slipped into unconsciousness she realized that the shooter had hit her.

Pandemonium erupted with security men rushing the two leaders and carrying them off the stage and into the building directly behind the stage. No one stopped until both men were safely back in the room that had been selected as the safe base prior to the speeches. The security team all had weapons drawn and tensions were high. The president tried to get up to find out what was going on only to be pushed back down onto a couch by Corey, the head of his security detail.

"Sorry, sir, please don't move. We have the marines on route to evacuate you and his Holiness. Please relax so the doctor can look you over," Corey told the president.

With out waiting for a reply the doctor began removing the president's tie and jacket. The security agents helped and with in seconds the doctor was taking the president's pulse and checking his vital signs. On the other side of the room the Pope was receiving the same examination from his own personal physician that traveled with him. The personal guard of the pontiff was also very much in evidence with weapons out; while the liaison agents between the two security details were communicating each assuring the other that everything was okay with their respective charges. Slowly the tension drained from the room as the realization that both men were healthy and safe. Outside was a totally different matter.

After firing the last round Charley rolled his gear into a long tube, with the pad keeping everything together, and rammed it back into the duffel bag. All across the rooftops the riflemen were scanning windows to find out where the shots had come from. It had taken him just six seconds to pack his gear and another five to get back inside the elevator shaft housing. He moved to the edge of the shaft and secured the bag to a rope. Once tied on, he checked the shaft to make sure the elevator car was below the level he was planning on descending to then tripped the circuit breaker on the pulley motor to stop anyone from using the elevator until it the breaker was reset. Knowing it was now safe he tossed the bag down the shaft watching it disappear into the darkness. He had rigged the rope to play out for half the length of the shaft then the fall was stopped by a twenty foot section of bungee cord that was tied to one end of the rope and the other end to an over head cross member. He quickly rounded up the rest of the gear and did the same with all of it, until all the gear was suspended eleven floors below.

Charley moved over to were he had tied up Sean to check on him. Sean was awake with his eyes open and a look of pure rage on his face. Charley slipped a climbing harness on his partner and snapped it to a bungee cord of the same type used by the adventure seekers to jump off bridges.

"Sorry Sean, I hate to do this but I don't think untying you right now would be in my best interests." He explained as he levered the man toward the shaft

As gently as he could he got Sean over the side and let him go. He watched hoping nothing would go wrong and helpless to prevent it if it did. Sean stopped after several pendulum swings up and down close to the spot Charley had planned on. The drop had not been painless, as he had watched the man hit the side of the shaft several times. To his credit Sean made no sound at all even though it must have been painful. With everything now hanging in the taken care up Charley rigged a final rope, checked the area to make sure no signs of their stay were evident, and repelled down the shaft to the level of Sean and their gear. Here was the central cooling duct and it was a four-foot by four-foot shaft that ran through the center of the building, branching off as it went.

Charley climbed into the shaft and pulled in his gear and then Sean. He moved down the shaft for twenty feet coming to the first side branch. He stashed his gear and went back for Sean. With Sean in place he began unpacking the gear one more time. He strung the foam pad across the junction of the branch and the main shaft plunging him and Sean into total darkness. He turned on one of the battery-powered lamps he had brought with him and then moved back into the main shaft to check for light showing past the pad. He didn't want to take a chance on anyone examining the elevator shaft and seeing light in the shaft they were hiding in. Satisfied that their hiding place was secure Charley went back and finished setting up their new camping area.

With everything set up he moved Sean onto his sleeping pad to make him more comfortable. "Old friend I have some bad news for you. I missed the president and the Pope."

Sean started struggling trying to rip the tape that had him tied up. As he struggled he quietly cursed the young man interspersing his swearing with threats of great bodily harm and death.

"Relax, relax, you'll hurt yourself. Let me explain." Sean relaxed to give Charley time to speak. "First let me say that there is no way you will ever convince me that shooting the President would be anything other than murder. No matter what the man may have done there is no good reason to kill him and no rational government would ever sanction the murder of it's own leader. Add in the order to kill the Pope and I knew that this was not a government action. I'm young not stupid. Something your bosses failed to tell you, if they ever even knew, is that my IQ is in the near genius range. I don't think we work for the government at all."

Charley saw the fire start to leave Sean's eyes. "Now here's the thing, I'm going to need your help to get out of the mess we are both in. We can both walk away from this organization of yours and get on with our lives but it's going to take the two of us to do it. I started the ball rolling by failing to finish the job and from what you say they'll kill you as well as me for failure, am I right on that?

Sean slowly nodded his head.

"Great, well no, not really but it will be."

"Okay boy wonder, tell me what the hell you've done."

"Well for starters I changed our after action plan as you can see. Rather than running right after the shooting, I am hiding us in the center of the building for a few days. Both the police and the organization will make the assumption that we are on the run, or so I'm hoping. I figure if we stay here a few days when we do leave we can walk out like normal people and catch a bus to somewhere."

"Perhaps you've forgotten that we don't have any money to run with. All we have is credit cards, which by now will be flagged to alert the three stooges as soon as we try and use them. There is no where we can go that we will be safe." Sean said with resignation in his voice. "You can untie me lad. Killing you won't save my life now. For better or worse we are a team and need each other to survive."

Charley thought for a moment and decided that he had to trust Sean some time might as well make it now and get it over with. If Sean were going to kill him, waiting wouldn't change anything. And he could keep him tied up forever. Charley cut the tape holding his hands and feet together and sat down on his sleeping bag. Sean pulled the rest of the tape off cursing as it pulled out hair coming off.

As soon as his hands were free he hammer Charley once in the center of his chest, just to get rid of a little of his frustration. "Do you have any idea how much that hurts when you pull it off? You're a sadistic son-of-a-bitch aren't you. And I now know what you mean about the headaches you get with that tranquilizer. Gets to really pounding, doesn't it. But why the hell did you shoot me twice?"

Charley smiled rubbing his chest which hurt like hell. "I've never drugged anyone before and I wasn't sure how fast it would take. The last thing I needed was a fight with you at the top of an elevator shaft. As for the headache, I owed you that. You shot me on two separate occasions I only shot you on one occasion. I'm surprised you weren't out for longer though."

"Just doubling the dose doesn't double the length of time you'll be out. It does speed up knocking you out though. And I hope that it doubles up the pain of the headache, because if you got a headache this bad twice I am deeply sorry for the pain I cause you."

Charley chuckled "Yeah it really hurts. Now either you're with me on trying to get out or you're going to kill me and turn me in to the three stooges to prove your loyalty to them. One way or the other it's time to find out. So do you feel like eating?"

"No but I'd love some coffee, and then we can discuss our future and how to make it last longer than next week."

Sean rubbed his wrists and stretched out his arms and legs working the stiffness out of them. He ignored the coffee and went straight to the chemical toilet. When he was finished he picked up the coffee. "Lad you made the choice for both of us when you tied me up and missed that shot. They'll kill us now because we both failed. By the way how did you know?"

Charley looked at him puzzled, "How did I know what?"

"How did you know that if you didn't take the shot I was supposed to kill you and take the shot myself?"

Charley almost dropped his coffee. "I didn't, not for sure. I thought you were supposed to take the shot and leave me to take the fall. But I wasn't about to take a chance on either one happening"

"I don't know how much time we've got but we need to start running and do it now," Sean said, starting to pack up his things.

"Relax old man, we've got time."

"Don't be a fool lad, you don't think the organization is going to leave you alive to tell the world what you know do you. Don't be so stupid. Now come on and get ready to go, we'll leave most of this here and take only what we need."

"They aren't really a government agency are they?" Charley asked.

"To be truthful Lad I have no idea what they are. All I know is they are very powerful and have people everywhere, including in the government so they may as well be a government agency." Sean said in a tired voice. "Now can we get going?"

"What's the rush to get out of here?" Charley asked leaning back against the wall "Are the accommodations no longer to your liking?"

"Son, have you lost your mind? Everyone in the US is going to be hunting us. You just took a shot at the President of the United States. The government tends to frown on that type of thing you know. And the organization is going to want you dead because you missed. Not that it matters, I'm sure whatever backup plan was in place covered your miss and the president is dead by now. One way or the other you're going to be hunted for killing the man."

"Nope," Charley said quietly with a smirk on his face.

"Excuse me?"

"The president is very much alive and well, or at least he was when he was being dragged to safety. And I don't think the back up plan was too well thought out."

Sean leaned against the opposite wall with a puzzled look on his face. "Perhaps you should fill me in on what you did."

Charley smiled smugly. "I knew that there was no way anyone was going to trust that I would take the shot so I figured there would be a backup plan. And I know you're a good shot but let's face it, if you could have taken the shot yourself I wouldn't have been needed. So that meant, in my mind, that there would need to be another plan in case I wouldn't, and you couldn't do the job. So I simply looked for someone out of place. And you know what? There on the stage, was a female secret service agent starring right at me. It's almost as if she knew I was there and was waiting for the muzzle flash. Even stranger was the fact that she was completely oblivious to what was happening around her. Everyone else was watching the crowd or the president and Pope, but not her. No she knew something was going to happen. So I shot her then shot up the stage a little. Right after that the shit hit the fan and I bolted back to get you and hide. So here we are, safe and sound."

Sean was amazed at Charley's thinking. He didn't know about the secret service agent but it didn't surprise him. Sean lowered his head. "There's something else you should know. You were chosen not only for your skill with a rifle but also that you were expendable; they could throw you away at any time. If the search got to close you would have been sacrificed."

"Well that's no surprise."

"You guessed that too?"

"Sean, with all the talent in the military the only reason to go to the amount of trouble they went to with me is to get someone that is not going to be missed. It doesn't take a rocket scientist to figure out that as soon as your usefulness is up, they're going to get rid of you, I just didn't think it would be you doing the job. I've been trying to find a way out of this mess since those guys shanghaied me. I wasn't quite ready but I couldn't take that shot so it had to be now. I knew if I killed either the president or the Pope, my life was over for good."

"So you've been planning to try and get out all the time?"

"What did you think I was doing on the internet all the time, surfing for porn?"

Sean laughed, "Yes I did. That's why I kept trying to get you off the computer. So what were you doing?"

"Setting up an escape plan for us, see..."

"For us?" Sean interrupted him. "How did you know I'd go along?"

"I didn't but I thought I'd give you a choice in the matter if you wanted to come along."

Sean was stunned. This was the first time since his childhood that anyone had thought about helping him.

Charley went on, "See I knew we'd need money if we were going to get free. That's the beauty of the internet. If you know what you're doing it's an anonymous way to make money. I opened a Paypal account with one of the credit cards and used it to buy some things online. I then canceled that account since the organization would know about it, and opened another one using the refund of the leftover money in the original account. This is where it got a bit tricky; I knew, since I didn't have receipts to show I had spent all the money in the original account, I would have to come up with the refund cash so that the bean counters wouldn't get suspicious. So I did some quick day trading to get the money, which I used to purchase a wire transfer online that was sent to our post office box looking as a refund from the original Paypal account. I gave that to you and I was in the clear. I just kept on with the day trading after that. I was always careful to stash the money at the end of a session in a stock that was safe."

"So how much do you have?"

"Not me, we, and we have a little over $9,000 in the bank."

Sean was again stunned with what Charley had done. "Nine thousand dollars? Where is it?"

"Right here in Boston. And I've got a bank card for the account so now we've got the cash to run with."

Sean thought for a moment. "That's not going to last long on the run Charley. But since you've planned this far, tell me what you think we should do now?"

"I don't plan to run forever, Sean. I don't care what I've been told there is no way this organization is a legit government operation. That means they're hiding too. If I want peace I need to expose them and clear my name, so that's what I plan to do. I haven't figured out how to do that yet, that's why I was really hoping you would join me."

"Jesus lad, you've got balls I'll say that much for you. You want the two of us to take on an organization that has been around for who knows how long? How about another plan, you and I take your money and buy some good rifles and gear and head into the Rocky Mountains for a few years. We live off the land and wait until we're forgotten and then find a small out of the way place to live in. Should only take six or seven years."

"Don't you want to be a free man, Sean? Make your own choices, live where you want and do what you want to do?"

"I'm sixty years old, it's been forty years since I had any free will. And what the hell am I supposed to do; all I know how to do is be a criminal. Most people my age are looking forward to retirement; I'm just trying to stay alive. No matter what happens I don't see any chance for me to live a free life anymore. But if we can get you out of this then I'll be happy."

Charley smiled at his mentor. "Well let's play it by ear shall we. Here's what I was thinking; we hold here for a week and then we go to the waterfront. We charter a sailboat and head out to sea. Nova Scotia is three or four days away, we can sink the boat and swim ashore. I've got a place there where we can rest and make some better plans."

"Lad one of the first places they'll keep a watch on is your home. Going there will be same as walking right into a bullet. We might as well shot ourselves."

"Not this place, Sean. No one knows about it. I've never told anyone about it and as far as official records go it's a woodlot that was left to me by my grandfather. It's safe, I promise."

"Lad anything that has your name on it will be checked out, even a woodlot. They know you are trained to live off the land, believe me they'll check it out."

Charley had a Cheshire cat grin on his face. "Sean I'm counting on them to check out the woodlot. Once they do you and I are in the clear. So what do you feel like for breakfast?" Charley started going through the MRE's.

When Andrea woke up she was in a bed, attached to several tubes, and a nurse watching her. As soon as she opened her yes the nurse began checking her pulse and eye response by flashing a little light at her. Andrea tried to wave her away so that she could figure out what was happening, when her boss stepped into view.

"Andrea, can you hear me?"

She looked up at the voice to see a familiar face. She knew she should know him but couldn't remember his name.

"I know you, don't I?" she asked in a low tone.

"It's Corey, Andrea. Do you know where you are?"

"Corey? I know that name but I can't remember why. Where am I?"

Corey looked questioningly at the nurse, who explained, "It the anesthetic, sir. She was in the OR for two hours so she'll be a little groggy for a while. Her vitals are all fine and the doctor reported it was a clean wound; the bullet didn't strike the bone. She will make a full recovery. Give her another two hours and she can answer your questions.

"Thank you ma'am," Corey replied. "Two of my men will be her at all times. I know this is against policy but this patient is a federal witness and one of our own."

The nurse smiled. "I saw the news and I understand completely. We have orders to cooperate fully so your men will be no problem. I'll see that they are comfortable. Miss Drake is the only patient in this ward, keeping an eye on her will be simple. There is coffee at the nurse's station just outside and I'll have the orderly bring in some chairs for the men. Is there anything else I can do?"

Corey shook his head. "No thank you. I'll be on my way." Corey motioned to two men in the hall to come in. "One of you stay with her at all times, no exceptions, but don't get in the way of the medical staff. The nurse her will let you know where you can sit. Notify me the second she is able to give a statement."

"Yes sir," the two replied in unison.

Corey left the hospital to head back to the local treasury office that his security detail had set up a command post in. The president and his guest the Pope had left for Washington right after the shooting but Corey had stayed behind to take charge of the investigation and because one of his detail had been wounded. The FBI and US Marshals service had both sent over 100 agents each to supplement the more than 200 secret service agents already in the area, to help with the search. The doctors had recovered the bullet from Agent Drakes lag and the preliminary report was that is was a 30-caliber round. It had been sent to the local FBI lab for ballistics testing, and a report should be coming anytime now. Not that this would matter if they didn't find a rifle, however the caliber of the bullet told them the range and gave them an area to search based on simple mathematics. They had thrown up a roadblock perimeter around the suspected area. And anyone going in or out was being searched and their identity thoroughly checked. They would begin a room-to-room search of every building in the suspect area as soon as the rest of the FBI and US Marshals showed up. To help with the roadblocks the National Guard had been called out and the first of those troops were now beginning to man the barricades as well. By the end of the day Corey would have more than 1000 people to assist in finding the shooter.

The first thing Andrea noticed was the smell. It was unmistakable, all hospitals had it. That antiseptic sick smell that was the signature of healing centers the world over. Her mind was still fuzzy as she tried to work out the puzzle of why she would be in a hospital. A few seconds later the answer came from her leg in the form of a dull throbbing ache. Realizing she had been shot she sat bolt upright in bed. The sudden movement caused her head to spin and she fell back as the nurse came running in who immediately called a doctor that showed up thirty seconds later. The two secret service agents were at the foot of the bed watching the nurse and doctor check vital signs and waiting.

"What's your name?" the doc asked quietly.

"Andrea Drake, is the president okay?"

The two agents smiled to themselves, this would make great PR, the only person shot and her first question is about the President. The boss would love that. "He's fine Agent Drake," one of them told her. "When you feel up to it we'll do the debrief and fill you in"

"I'm fine now," Andrea said, trying to sit up. "Someone get me my clothes and..."

She fell back to the bed, her head spinning.

The doctor immediately checked her pupils and then took her pulse and blood pressure again. "I don't think you're going anywhere for a while. Agent Drake you need rest. Gentleman please tell your boss she'll be up to be up to answering questions in about thirty minutes."

Andrea looked at the doctor, "How long before I can get back to work?"

"You are the most amazing patient I've ever had. You ask about the president before yourself, you want to leave right away and now you're wondering how long before you can return to work. You haven't even asked where you were wounded or how bad it is. Are you even curious?"

"I know I was shot in the leg because it hurts, but how bad is it? When will I be able to leave?"

"You were shot in the upper thigh, the bullet lodged in the back of the leg just under the skin, missing the bone and major arteries. We removed it for your ballistics team. The damage was limited mostly to muscle tissue, and with the exception of a nice scar, you will make a full recover. I want you to stay overnight for observation, but if your vital signs are fine in the morning you can leave. You will of course need to stay off the leg for a few days and see your own doctor when you get home. The stitches can come out in a few weeks."

"Thank you doctor."

"Your welcome, now please take it easy and get some rest."

One of the agents went to get some coffee while the second agent sat just inside the door of Andrea's room making sure that she was not disturbed.

Fifteen minutes later a nurse came in pulled the curtain around the bed and once again took Andreas vital signs. She hurried through the procedure marking the information down on the chart them leaned close to Andrea and whispered to her. "I'm placing a micro-recorder under your pillow. When you are debriefed make sure it is on and I'll collect it later for the organization. They have not made contact with the other agent and are anxious to know what happened."

The nurse left before Andrea had time to ask her anything. Reaching under the pillow she found a small but powerful tape recorder of a type she was familiar with. It had four hours of recording time and was ultra quiet making no sound at all. She placed it under the sheet next to her good leg. Tucking it close to her body to hide it but have it close to hand, then lay back to relax. Suddenly she was being gently nudged awake by a nurse with no memory of falling asleep.

At the foot of the bed were her boss and the doctor. "If it's all right with you I'd like to ask her a few questions now," Corey told the doc.

She checked with the nurse who nodded that the vitals were fine. "That will be fine, but try not to take more than an hour if you can avoid it and if Agent Drake gets tired you'll need to stop and come back."

"Thank you doctor. Andrea, how are you feeling?"

"My leg hurts and I'm tired, but other then that I'm feeling fine."

"I hate to have to do this now but you understand the drill, we need to debrief you and anything you can remember, no matter how insignificant may help us. I'd like you to go over the events of the day as clearly as you can remember them."

Andrea sat up a little straighter in her bed and slowly started to recite the events of the day she had been shot. "I was on with the team that did the prelim stage check and we verified that there were no reasons to stop the event. As the speakers took the stage I was scanning the crowd and I detected nothing unusual. Once I heard the crowd get louder I surmised that the boss was coming on stage, which was confirmed a moment later when he took the podium. Once the boss was on stage my post was to scan the windows and roof line, which I was doing when suddenly I felt something hard slam into my upper leg. Someone yelled gun and I tried to move to the boss to get him to cover but I couldn't stand. That was when I realized I had been shot. Once the boss was secure the medics got me stable and moved me to the hospital. I've been replaying the scene in my head ever since and I can't remember any telltales of a rifle shot. I didn't see a muzzle flash, I didn't hear anything at all."

Corey thought for a moment "One of the crowd detail reported that just before you were hit you were starring up and seemed to be fixed on a spot or rooftop, do you have any recollection of that?"

Andrea shook her head. "I was scanning the roof lines just before being hit but there was nothing that caught my eye. Aside from counter-sniper squads, there was nothing unusual. Did we get the shooter yet?"

"At this time we haven't located the where the shooter operated from, we where hoping you could help out with that. Is there anything from at all that sticks out in your mind?"

Andrea shook her head.

"Okay well let you get some rest, once you're discharged we will do the formal debrief back at the house.

Sean and Charley two spent 5 more days in the air ducts sleeping most of the time. During the time they were there, no sound of any investigation came their way. The building had been searched, including the elevator shafts, but no one had taken the time to examine the duct work. They debated taking everything with them or just leaving most of it there. As Sean pointed out if the left the gear no one was likely to find it until the duct work failed or the building was torn down. And it would only get them into trouble if they took it with them and were caught with it. They took their clothes and wrapped the rest up in duffel bags sealing it all with duct tape to leave in the shaft.

By 10 PM the building was empty save for the cleaning crew. They rappelled down the elevator shaft to the basement and left the way they had come in with no one ever knowing they had been there. They were dirty and smelly and needed cleaning up in the worst way. Walking until they found and ATM Charley withdrew $1000 from his hidden account. Sean then had them look around for a hooker. At first Charley was confused thinking that this was the last thing they should be doing but as Sean explained it they couldn't get a hotel room themselves without attracting some attention. They would find a hooker and have her get a room for them. She would only think it was two guys out for some fun. Charley still had the tranquilizer gun so they could drug her, and when she woke up they would be gone. Since prostitution was illegal it was unlikely she would go to the police.

Sean went to seven different women working the street before he found one willing to talk to him as prospective customer. He assured the woman that he had cash and played Charley as his son. Pretending that he had no idea how he smelled the woman agreed for $500 along with the requirement that both of them shower first. Sean looked puzzled at the demand for cleanliness but told her that would be no problem at all.

The women lead them to seedy hotel where the night clerk was sitting behind bulletproof glass. She registered and paid for the room with money given her by Sean. She met the two, seemingly eager men on the first floor as agreed; they had come in the back way to avoid drawing attention, again the hooker's idea. Stepping through the door to the room she pointed out the bathroom and asked which one was going first. Charley stepped through the doorway last closing the door, turned and shot her in the thigh. Sean slapped his hand over her mouth so that she would make no noise while the drug took effect. The women slumped in his arms, going slack in seconds. Sean carried her to the bed and laid her out on it. He didn't bother tying her up as they were only going to be there long enough to shower and change clothes. He let Charley go first to the bathroom as he sorted through their things digging out their clean clothes.

An hour later they were done and Sean wiped down the room to remove their fingerprints. Charley left $200 on the dresser and turned out the lights as they left the room. Sean wasn't sure about leaving the money but as Charley pointed out, leaving money lowered the chances of the woman complaining even further. After turning out the lights they closed and locked the door leaving the woman as comfortable as they could make her on the bed. Turning left they walked down an alley next to the Hotel to the street behind and began looking for a cab, fifteen minutes later they flagged one down

"How much to go to Marblehead?" Charley asked as he and Sean climbed in.

Holly began searching the internet as soon as news of the assassination attempt made the news. The traffic on the web relating to it was incredible. Everyone in every political chat room had a theory on why it had happened and just keeping track of those would have required a room full of IT specialists. After thirty minutes her senses were completely overwhelmed but just trying to keep up. She stopped surfing and opened her search tool and programmed it to look for websites of anyone taking claim for the attempt. The search showed a few claims already but as she investigated they all turned out to be fake. By the time she was officially ordered to begin searching she had been on the job for forty-five minutes, which earned her a huge smile from her boss.

Widening the search she began looking for groups with websites that had a record of threatening to kill the president and then after that programmed the search to look for groups with a motive to kill the president. She took the results of those two searches and began looking for possibilities to see if any of the groups reported actually had the means to carry out the attempt. The list of results was copied to an email, which she sent to the Secret service and carbon copied to her boss. This had taken her a mere ninety minutes and had resulted in 144 names, all US citizens. With that done she widened her search to the rest of the world, focusing on extremist groups. While the results were large when she began looking for confirmation that any of the groups had operatives in the US she came up empty. This didn't mean they couldn't be in the US, it just meant that there were no positive indicators listed on the world wide web.

With the initial website search over she once again widened the parameters of the search and started looking at news groups and bulletin boards to see what she could find there. All she found was a massive amount of conspiracy theorists, the two most common being that it was once again the work of either the government or a lone gunman gone nuts. At the end of the day she printed out a hard copy of her results and marked them to be sent to her boss for possible forwarding to the Secret Service. She shut off her monitor but left the computer running to keep the search going, and went home for the night. The news was nothing but coverage of the attempt with the usual litany of so called experts on TV offering up their theories of what happened. She eventually shut off the TV certain that whoever it was that had pulled the trigger would be in custody when she woke up in the morning, and went to bed.

The alarm buzzing her ear woke Holly at her usual time of 5:30. She was out of bed and dressed for her morning jog in five minutes. Heading out her door she noticed other people also heading out for morning PT as it was called in the army. As she was not part of a platoon she did not follow the standard morning calisthenics that the infantry soldiers performed instead opting to jog five miles every morning for her exercise. When the run was finished she showered and had one boiled egg with whole-wheat toast and orange juice for breakfast then hopped in her car for the drive to the office. As the trip was only four minutes she didn't bother to even turn on the radio, she normally caught her morning news off the CNN website.

Sitting down at her desk she first checked on the search results then checked to see who the attempted assassin was, as she was sure he had been caught by now. Checking the US page of CNN showed that no one had been caught yet and that the president and the Pope were both unharmed and fine, the only casualty was a female agent shot in the leg and expected to make a full recovery. The story quoted the White House Chief of Staff as saying that the two men would conclude the official visit at Camp David and that there would be no photo opportunities in light of the recent events. The story did not mention any suspects or any hint of a possible conspiracy, they were fairly certain however that the target was the president and not the Pope, even though this could not be confirmed.

Holly was surprised that there were no named suspects yet and once again renewed her search on the internet. There was no new information on possible groups, although there were now several more groups and even a few individuals claiming they were behind the plot. One man even claimed to be the shooter stating that he missed only due to a sudden gust of wind. Holly logged all of these to pass on but most were known to be habitual in their claiming responsibility for terrorist acts and were already on a watch list. Those not on a watch list would be thoroughly investigated she was sure.

She worked steadily through the morning taking a twenty-minute break for lunch and then right back at it until 6 PM, when it was past time to quit for the day. Once again she left her computer on to keep the search running. This routine continued for two weeks with her boss stopping by daily for updates. The only news was that there was no news. Whoever had pulled the trigger had managed to do the impossible and simply disappear. The president and the Pope had gone back to their respective lives and duties. Even many of the police agencies initially involved had handed over their files to the FBI and Secret Service and given up the search. All the possibilities Holly had found had been investigated ruthlessly; even involving the CIA in the overseas suspects and none had turned up the guilty party. It was quickly becoming a black hole for information.

Then a strange thing happened, her searches began to find references to two renegades on news groups and bulletin boards. At first she wrote it off as an anomaly of the search and rewrote the parameters but unless she left out the word Boston, the infrequent hits concerning the subject of two renegades kept happening. Finally, more out of curiosity and boredom than anything else, she did a full-blown search using the phrase "two renegades". The results were rather startling. There were over 500 hits. She did some in-depth digging but the identities of the posters was impossible to pin down as all the posts seemed to come from public IP addresses. This meant that in every case the person posting or replying to the post was at a public access computer like a library. To make matters even more confusing the forums were always located on a free hosting site that did not point to anyone at all. She finally decided to make a report about it and let the higher ups decide if it was important or not.

Chapter 9

They arrived at the woodlot at 3 AM to avoid being seen. Sean wanted to make sure that no one knew they were even in Canada, let alone in Charley's hometown. The standard operating procedures of the organization were to stake out the known places of any agent that attempts to leave. Having done this many times himself, Sean was confident that there would be agents watching for them to show up. Charley however was sure that they would be safe and no matter how many times they discussed it the young man kept insisting that everything would be fine.

Sean insisted on scouting the area before entering the woodlot, he was looking for any signs of other people around. It would only take one agent spotting them to alert the organization of their presence and bring the hunters down on them. If that happened they would need to run hard and fast, and even then Sean rated their chances at no better then 30%. Charley was far more optimistic about things though. Smiling with the confidence of a man that knows something others do not, he allowed Sean to scout out the area. After forty-five minutes of crawling along the ditch he finally felt secure enough to enter the woodlot and moved across the road to the trees. As soon as they were inside the tree line Charley took over and lead them straight to the center of the property. There in a small clearing were two lean-tos; one that had signs of an old campfire in front of it and another that covered a pile of split wood.

"So where do we hide out lad?" asked Sean in an anxious voice. "We can't stay in the open like this, they could spot us from the air in a small plane."

Charley smiled and walked to the lean-to covering the wood. He began moving the wood over to one side and eventually uncovered the wooden floor of the lean-to. When a big enough piece of the floor was exposed he took his knife from his pocket and levered up the back edge of the flooring. It moved up a few inches, enough for him to get his hand under it and pull it up a trap-door to reveal a ladder going down into the ground. He spent a few minutes re-stacking the wood and tying a string onto a couple of the pieces. Once he was happy with the woodpile he motioned Sean to head down the ladder.

"Were going to stay in a hole under a lean-to? Have you lost your mind? And what are you planning to do with that string?" Sean asked.

"Relax and get down there please. When you get to the bottom you'll find a candle on a shelf behind the ladder, light it up please." Charley instructed his confused partner.

Sean started down the ladder followed by his young friend. He looked up to see the door almost closed and watched closely as Charley gave the string a hard yank. The trapdoor slammed shut with the sound of wood hitting it; they were plunged into total darkness. With no other option open to him, now that the trapdoor was covered with wood, Sean started down the ladder again carefully feeling each rung. The climb down lasted twenty feet and when he was standing back on solid ground he felt behind the ladder and there, as promised was the ledge with the candle. He felt around and found a box of matches; striking one he help it to the candle lighting up the ladder and the area around it. He was standing in an open area that was about five feet square with a tunnel going up twenty feet. The ceiling of the tunnel was the floor of the lean-to and looked to be made out of planks that were about four inches thick. There were only two things of interest in the small room, the shelf behind the ladder and a metal door opposite the ladder.

Charley jumped the last few rungs to the ground and moved over to the door. "Having fun yet, old man?" he asked with a mischievous grin on his face.

"Now that you ask, no I'm not. Please tell me what the hell you are doing and why you felt it necessary to trap us down here."

Charley was pacing off steps from the corner of the door back to the ladder. Getting to a certain spot he knelt down and started digging at the dirt of the floor. Buried a few inches down was what looked like a rusty key. Using this, he unlocked the door and opened it to reveal a large underground chamber. In the dim light of the candle it was hard to see the objects inside the room, in fact Sean couldn't even tell how big the room was. Charley moved into the room and searched around on his left for something. As Sean followed him inside he could see that the lad had picked up a propane lantern and was getting it ready for lighting. Once it was going Sean could see the room better in the stronger light. He noticed that for being underground the room was very large, around twenty feet by twenty-five feet with a seven foot ceiling, and there were other doorways. There was a table and chairs in the center and along the walls were benches and shelves along with bunk beds at the back of the room, but the strangest thing of all were the lights hanging from the ceiling. They were obviously electric lights but he had seen no signs of wiring coming into the wood lot from the road.

"So are you planning on filling me in here or do you intend to make me guess what all of this is?" Sean asked

"This is where we are going to hide while we figure out how to get ourselves free. This was built by my grandfather in the 60's when the whole bomb shelter craze was going on. He did all the work himself and it's all made from concrete and rebar. He owned his own construction firm so he had the equipment to build it, but he had to do it in secret so the government wouldn't know. Never really sure why he did that but I'm certainly glad now that he did, Anyway, it took him years to finish and by the time it was done the threat of an actual nuclear war was almost gone. Rather then fill it all back in or just forget about it he turned it into a combination workshop slash weekend retreat. The first time I saw the place I was five years old. That ladder is terrifying for a five-year-old but I got down here and I fell in love with the place. You're only the third person to ever see this, not even my parents were told about this. It was my grandfather's little secret, he didn't want people to think he was nuts."

"So how big is this place? And what's here?"

"It has seven rooms in total but there are four tunnels, one to each corner of the property, so it sprawls over most of the lot but in actual size this is the largest room. Come on and I'll give you the grand tour."

Charley lead him around the underground complex showing him the other rooms which all opened off the main room. There was an armory containing his considerable collection of firearms all well oiled and locked up in metal cases. There was a complete workshop for working on the firearms and Sean even noticed a barrel lathe for making barrels. In the corner of the workshop he thought he noticed blanks for making barrels from but he didn't have time to make sure. The next room was a welding shop with both an ARC welder and MIG welder along with cutting gear. After that came a woodworking shop with all the tools needed to make almost any thing you could think of out of wood. The storeroom contained dried and canned foodstuffs stacked along shelves along with sealed bins that had flour and sugar written on them. The two real surprises were the bathroom complete with a hot tub and the machinery room that answered his question as to how all of the power tools worked.

There, twenty feet under ground, was an electrical generator that was half the size of a small car. The generator sat in a housing in the middle of the room with two pipes running from either side of it and electrical wires leading out from the top of it to a fuse panel in the corner. The pipes both had what looked like a water valve on the parts closest to the housing. He walked all around it looking for an engine to run the generator but couldn't see one. He had no idea how this could provide power without someway to turn it. Charley walked over to the panel with a smirk on his face and threw the main breaker to turn on the power. He then opened the valves on both of the pipes and the sound of water flowing could clearly be heard, followed by the noise of a turbine spooling up, slowly at first but gaining speed as the water in the pipe spun it faster and faster.

The overhead lights began to glow dimly gaining brightness as the turbine came up to operating speed. Even at full speed the generator was quiet enough that they could carry on a conversation in the room.

"My god that's the most amazing thing I've seen in a long time. How did you ever get a hydroelectric generator to work down here? Where does the water come from, and where does it go?" Sean asked closely examining the generator

"It's hard to see from outside because the lot is so big, but the ground slopes down over 50 feet from the north side of the property to the south side. There is a stream along the north side of the lot, so we ran a pipe from the stream down to the generator. Most of the pipe is only 3 feet underground and then forty feet from this room it drops to add speed to the flow and then comes into the generator. It then runs along the floor of one of the tunnels, to the southwest edge of the property. It empties into a small pond I built there that is stocked with bass and trout. The hard part was getting the generator set down here. The rest was built on site. My grandfather started running the pipe just to have running water in the place. The pipes also supply the bathroom and kitchen with water. For drinking water I have a reverse osmosis water purifier."

"How long did all this take? Who did the work? This is amazing, is there anything else down here?" Sean asked his mind overflowing with questions

Charley chuckled. "As I said most of the work was done by my grandfather. I started helping him when I was ten and he died when I was fifteen. All the rooms were built by granddad, the generator was set up by the both of us and I did the fish pond. I use one of the tunnels for a shooting range to test the work I do on my rifles. See one of the other things that the organization didn't know about is that granddad was a master gunsmith and he started teaching me about firearms when I was a kid. By the time I was twelve I could strip and repair almost any rifle on the planet."

Sean looked at Charley in a new light. "So tell me lad what other surprises are you hiding from me? Aside from all this that is."

Charley had a smirk on his face. "For the next surprise let's go take a look at the armory, I think you'll find that I know more about weapons than I was letting on."

"Oh?" Sean remarked following the lad back to the first room they opened.

Charley began opening the locked cabinets one by one and displaying the contents to his mentor. There were four cabinets in all holding a wide variety of firearms. Sean looked at the array of weaponry displayed and noticed two very striking things at the same time. Most of the guns were of World War Two vintage and there were several of them that looked to be machine guns. Talking a closer looked he recognized several of the guns as being bipod mounted machine guns or submachine guns. They were all together in one of the cabinets, in two others were rifles grouped by the different types of actions and the last cabinet held shotguns. All together there were over 100 weapons in the room.

"Are those real?" Sean asked pointing to the automatic weapons.

"Yes they are, each and every one of them. They are all WW2 vintage but they are in perfect working order."

"Where did you ever get them, lad? I know collectors that don't have some of the guns you have."

Sean reached into the case and removed one of the bipod mounted machine guns. "Is this a German MG-42?"

"No that's the MG-34. They are very close but the 34 was a bit better made. That one has been re-chambered for the 7.62 Nato round. The original rounds are too hard to get."

Sean put it back and picked up and assault rifle that look very familiar but he was sure it couldn't be an AK-47. "Lad this looks like the Soviet AK-47 but they didn't have those in WW2. Are you sure these are all WW2 vintage?"

Charley smiled again at the comment. "My grandfather brought all of these back from Europe with him in '46. They are all WW2 vintage. It took him six months to get them all over here. When he did he hid them in his basement. When he built this bunker he moved them all over here. That piece you're holding is the world's first true assault rifle the STG-44 also known as the MP-44. It was built by the Germans and fired a 7.92 MM round. Granddad was going to re-chamber it for the 7.62 but wanted to keep it authentic so he left it alone. The only thing Granddad didn't collect was handguns, he could never shoot them very well so he had no use for them."

Sean gazed over the guns, several of each with different variations, Sten, Stirling, Thompson, M3, MP40, MG-34, Bren, and a few others of Russian design. He picked up one of the Sterlings with an unusually fat barrel and examined it.

"Is this a built in silencer?"

"Yes it is. There are a few there that I have silencers for, that Stirling, the Thompson and the M3. They all work too. I have the M3 in both the 45 and 9mil. The British and German SMG's are all 9mil and the Russian SMG's are 7.62 short. The Bren gun is the original .303."

"All that time I spent training you about handguns and silencers and you knew what I was saying all along. Your are one hell of an actor Lad, I truly thought you were learning new information." Sean thought for a second. "I though these guns were illegal in Canada? Does anyone know you have these?"

"They are illegal and no one knows about these. They haven't seen the light of day since this bunker was built. This is my ace in the hole, what I knew I had to come back to after I escaped. If your organization comes after me they will be in for one big surprise."

"Charley my boy they will have SMG's as well. And the ones they have will be new. I wouldn't want to match your ww2 vintage pieces up against the modern MP-5's that our opponents will be carrying."

Charley shrugged, "Let them. I'll put any of these old timers up against the HK any day of the week. All they're getting is a higher rate of fire, the calibers are the same so I figure it's even."

Sean shook his head. "Lad you have a lot to learn. The men hunting us will be well trained and used to using their SMG's. I'm trained on the MP-5, it's the only SMG I've ever worked with. I could learn to use one of yours but I won't be as good as the organizations men. It's the training that will make the difference."

Charley laughed and picked up one of the Sten guns and two magazines. He loaded the first mag, cocked the weapon and dry fired it to simulate running out of ammo. His magazine change was a blur of motion and ended with the snap of the firing pin hitting the empty chamber at the same time the first magazine hit the floor. It was one of the fastest magazine changes Sean had ever seen in his life, far faster then he could do with an MP-5, or any other member of the organization that he knew was capable of

"How did you learn to do that?"

"I've been practicing with these guns since I was a ten, that was the first time granddad let me. I know each and every one of them like an old friend. I've fired them all, stripped and cleaned all of them too. And I don't know about you but I wouldn't want to be running into the fire that an MG-34 can lay down. As for them coming after us, I wouldn't worry about it, no one will ever find us here. I've got water and unlimited power, food for several months and we are very well armed. We can relax for a bit and figure out what we need to do."

Sean shook his head. "Tell me honestly, what did you learn in the last six months of training? You certainly know far more then you pretended."

Charley laughed softly. "Well I learned to live off the land, Granddad never showed me that. I learned hand-to-hand combat; I never had to fight before. I learned a lot about alarms and electronics along with a lot about human nature. And I never had used a handgun before you showed me; I had just used the same cartridges, that's all. I've played a lot of war games with granddad and he taught me strategy and shooting, but actual fighting I've never had to do before. All this was just to give Granddad something to do and me something to play with. Even dad didn't know what was going here, granddad didn't think he would have approved of it. So aside from me, you are now the only other person that knows this place exists."

"I'm glad you feel so safe here. The only problem I foresee is running out of food. I would like to point out that I am not looking forward to spending the rest of my life down here. No offense but I don't find the idea of underground dwellings all that appealing."

"Sean I'm not planning on staying down here forever. I want my life back and I intend to get it. My idea is to find out who is behind the organization. That's what I need your help for. If all I wanted to do was escape and hide out here I could have done that anytime since we moved to Vermont. No, I want to be a free man again, will you help me do that?"

Sean shook his head. "Lad you have no idea what you are getting into.

These people will kill you the first time they see you. They have been around a long time and no one has ever gotten to the three wise-men before, unless they wanted them to. You really think you can do that? And if you do what makes you think that you can talk them into letting you walk away with the information you have. These people stay hidden because no one outside the organization knows about them. I know how they work, remember."

"Sean I'm asking for your help, you can give it if you want, or you can run away and hide. I'll give you a rifle and lots of ammo for it, and you can leave whenever you want. But I'm going to find these guys. Right now I'm a little tired so I'm going to get some sleep."

Charley locked up the gun cases, went into the main room and crawled into one of the bunk beds and was asleep with minutes. Sean wandered around the bunker checking out the different rooms. In the gunsmith workshop he saw all the tools to work on the guns and reload bullets. It was the best-equipped shop he had seen outside of an armory. It looked as if Charley could even build a gun from scratch if he wanted to; he had the lathes and steel blanks to do so. Sean eventually tired of his exploring and lay down to get some rest as well.

Sean woke up and had a moment of disorientation until he remembered where he was. Charley's bed was already empty, so he got up and headed for the bathroom. Charley was cooking something and Sean's mouth instantly began watering when the scent hit him. He grabbed a quick shower and headed back to the main room

"So what's on the agenda today, lad?"

Charley was dishing out two plates of food. "Well I was hoping you and I could reach an agreement for getting out from under the organization."

"You certainly do have a one track mind Charley. Would it dissuade you at all if I tell you that it's impossible?"

"I disagree, Sean. We got away from them, we're here and safe…"

"Well it remains to be seen if we are safe or not. We are in hiding which is far from safe."

"Well that's why we need to find out a way to get our self free, Sean. I don't want to stay in hiding for the rest of my life, I want my freedom back. So what do you say we work together to get out of this?" Charley placed the food on the table and the two men sat down to eat.

Sean ate several forkfuls before saying anything. "If I don't help you, are you going to try it anyway?"

"Yes I am."

Sean took a sip of his coffee. "Then I'm in lad, only because there is no way I can spend the rest of my life living in a hole drinking this swill you make for coffee. My god this is awful."

Charley laughed. "Well you can make lunch then."

"It's a deal lad. So have you though out what our first move will be?"

Charley thought for a moment. "We need information first. We have to have a plan and then a fall back, in case of problems. Granddad always said never do anything without a fall back plan. But the key to this is going to be information. Since they framed us we need to have information that will force them to forget about us and leave us alone. Since you've worked for them for a long time you must know some secrets that they wouldn't want out in the open, we can start there."

Sean shook his head. "That won't work lad. All the work I've done for the organization cannot be tied to them. Remember you and I are wanted men; anything we say is going to be suspect. We can't just give ourselves up and tell the police that we work for a secret organization that goes around breaking the laws, and oh, by the way, all this stuff we've done has been while working for the organization. They'd toss us in a mental ward and forget about us. No, we can't rely only on the work I've done. We need more than that."

Charley nodded his head. "I see your point. This morning why don't we check out the rest of the property to get you familiar with the layout of our new home, show you all the doors and where everything is. We can do some brainstorming this afternoon."

Sean nodded and got up to put his dishes in the sink. "We should also do some scouting around the local area, see if anyone is looking for us."

The two cleaned up the dishes then Charley lead Sean around showing him the tunnels and the hidden exits for them. Sean was impressed with the detail that had gone into the underground shelter. All the tunnel doors could only be unlocked from the inside and the only door that unlocked from both sides swung inward and could be barred with two solid metal bars to lock it, If they had to stay in hiding this would be a very comfortable place to do so. Aside from food it was self sustaining and totally hidden. Sean wasn't sure that the organization could find them, even if they knew they were in Nova Scotia. Sean also noticed that as well as being well hidden it was also set up for excellent defense. Anyone attacking them would have to come at them from a known access point.

Sean cooked lunch making coffee before anything else. He sipped the brew as he opened a can of stew and tossed it in a pot. After lunch, again the two cleaned up the dishes and then sat down at the table to draw up a plan.

"Before we begin anything I need to know how far you are willing to go to get your self free," Sean said. "What will you not do?"

"I'm not sure I understand Sean? What are you asking?"

"Lad if we do this, try to free ourselves, the organization will try to kill us. They will not settle for our being just tossed in prison, they will want us dead and will try to do it in a way that can be used as an example to others that try to leave. This will become a war. I need to know that you are prepared to fight a war, I need to know that you can kill if you have to."

Charley was quiet for several moments. "Sean I understand your concern. I have thought about that since I began planning to get free. I truly believe that you and I can do this without having to kill anyone. We need information and if we kill people then we can't get any information from them. This is going to be straight detective work, not search and destroy. Once we have our info we can use it as protection, they won't dare come after us if they know it will expose them."

Sean just shook his head. "Lad you have a lot more to learn that you think. These people are used to manipulating anything they want. But for now we'll try it your way. So how do you propose to get the information you're looking for?"

"First, I'll need to get onto a computer with net access. I'll start searching online and gathering information. I mean this is a big organization, they have to have public records somewhere, and it's just a matter of finding them. Walter said that they used online bulletin boards to leave messages for field agents sometimes, so I'll look for those as well."

Sean smiled at his young friends enthusiasm. "And where do we find a computer with net access?"

"The local library will have them. I'll hike into town and spend some time on the net and see what I can find. It's only about five miles away. "

"Do you think that's wise, Lad? The organization is still going to be looking for you. I can assure you that they will have agents in your home town."

Charley smiled. "That's the best part, this isn't my home, that's Port Williams where my house is. This is Kingston, it's about thirty miles away from my house. It's the nearest one to the woodlot. Since there is no house on the lot I don't actually live here there is no reason to look for me in this town. The best part is that there is a nearby military airbase so there's a lot of people coming and going, but the town it's self is not that big. No one is going to think much of me spending a few days at the library, they will just assume that I'm passing through the base on an exercise or something."

"I don't know lad, it all sounds risky to me. We've only been hiding for a couple weeks, not nearly enough time for the hunt to have tapered down yet. I suggest we wait a few more weeks before making a move. Give the agents watching more time to get bored. The hunt is still too new."

"That's why we need to start looking now, before they have more time to plant more evidence against us. Start searching before they suspect what we are doing"

"Lad they would never expect us to do what you're planning. No one has ever even left the organization, never mind try to expose them. No matter what we do, we'll be breaking new ground here. Just wait a little while longer. I know it's boring here but it's safe, and that's more important."

"I appreciate your concern but the risk is minimal. They can't cover every place at the same time. I'll be in town for a couple hours at most and all of that at the library. I'll go in an indirect route, keep to the back roads, cut across the fields, and come home the same way. Relax Sean, I'll be careful."

Knowing that further arguing was senseless Sean nodded and headed in to the armory. No matter how much Charley tried to convince him that they could fight back without having to use guns, he knew it was going to come down to a firefight at some point. With that in mind he knew that getting as comfortable with Charlie's WW2 relics as possible would only serve him well in the future. He spent the next two hours stripping a reassembling the variety of SMG's in the collection. He was becoming more and more comfortable with the Thompson. It was similar in layout of the MP5 that he was used to so it didn't take him long to become familiar with it's workings. He liked the option of the stick clip or the drum and best of all it was chambered for his beloved .45 ACP round. After the Thompson he preferred the German MP-40, again for it's similar layout to the modern SMG's. He also practiced with the MG34, he had never used a squad machine gun before. The option of having that much firepower really appealed to him.

Charley shouted that he was heading into town and left using one of the tunnels. Sean hesitated a moment and then he opened a box of, 45's and began loading two clips and a drum. Once completed he grabbed a set of webbing, stuffed the clips in the ammo pouch and put the webbing on. His instincts were telling him that Charlie's little trip into town was a bad idea. He picked up the Thompson and headed through the tunnel that Charley had taken. Knowing that the lad's skills were much better now than the last time he had followed him Sean knew he would need to be far more careful. The young man would be upset at being followed so he couldn't know. The problem was that this time Charley was on home ground and Sean did not know the ground he was to cover.

He hurried down the tunnel and got the trapdoor at the end that would let him outside. Next to the opening was a periscope that could scan the area in a full circle so that you could see if there was anything out there before opening the door. Sean did two full circles and saw nothing to alarm him. Slapping one of the clips into the Thompson he pulled the charging handle to load a round in the chamber, placed the safety on and climbed up and out the tunnel entrance. As soon as he was out he squatted down beside it. The tunnel entrance was concealed in a dead tree stump, the periscope beside it was also part of the dead hollowed out stump. Even sitting right next to it Sean could not tell there was a tunnel underneath, so carefully had it been built. He took a good look at the surrounding area, marking the location in his mind so that he would be able to find the place when he came.

Knowing that he'd be able to find the spot again Sean took off at a slow jog toward the south. He moved efficiently through the trees making almost no noise even though he was rushing. It took him 5 minutes to get to the edge of a field of hay and he was just in time to see Charley going into the tree line on the other side of the field. He counted a slow sixty and then ran across the field and into the trees where he had seen Charley go. Ten feet into the trees he was slammed into the ground as something fell on him. His reaction was swift and instinctive, he rolled to his left trying to get out from under what ever had hit him only to discover that it was a person holding tight to his back with their legs locked around his mid section and a choke hold around his throat. Knowing he had only seconds before the lack of air would begin to affect him Sean stopped rolling and concentrated on looking for a weakness in the attack. He was about to try slamming his head back into his attacker when the arm loosened around his neck and familiar voice spoke to him.

"What the hell do you think you're doing, Sean?"

"I was fighting for my life," he replied, rolling over into a sitting position.

"I can't believe this. You still don't trust me. Following me, and with my own Thompson? What the hell are you thinking?" Charley was almost yelling by now.

"Quiet lad and let me explain. I do trust you, but I have a bad feeling about your going into town. It's too soon, so I thought I'd just tag along and sort of watch your back. You go in and do your searching and I'll watch out for trouble. Believe me Lad I know these people a lot better then you do. If they know you own something they'll have it staked out somehow."

"Fine, if it makes you fell better you tag along and watch my back. But for christ sake don't get caught with the SMG. They are highly illegal in Canada and if you get caught you're going to jail."

"Lad I have no intention of being seen let alone caught. Shall we get going then?" he asked, picking up the Thompson and checking the action to make sure it was clear and free.

The two men got to their feet and continued heading south in silence. Charley walked with a sure measured pace confident of his surroundings. Sean continually looked around taking note of everything in view and looking for trouble. In a straight line it was about five miles to town and this was the route Charley tried to follow as closely as possible. They crossed several fields and went through groves of trees, never seeing any other people around. Sean was just beginning to think that this area of Canada was totally devoid of people when he heard the faint sound of a car.

Charley slowed down and whispered, "We're getting close to town, we need to cross the highway and from there it's going to get a bit tricky. Lots of houses around on the other side."

Sean simply nodded and followed Charley towards the sound of traffic. There was a final stand of trees to go through then about 100 yards of open area to the highway. On the other side of the highway Sean could see more open area and then houses. This was going to be tricky as the traffic wasn't heavy but it was steady with cars spaced a few hundred yards apart. They sat there watching the road for a few minutes and the largest break in the traffic was just over a minute. Sean searched the far side of the road looking for a place to go once they crossed. There was a vacant lot with brush and debris scattered around it and this would be the best spot to head for once they crossed the road. The hard part was going to be concealing the SMG and the web gear he was carrying. Charley was wearing a backpack so he took it off and gave it to Sean. Field stripping the SMG he put the parts in the backpack and then took off the web gear and hid it at the base of tree, covering it with some loose leaves and grass. It wasn't perfect but it would have to do. The two stood, and hurrying as quickly as they could with out looking suspicious headed to the highway. As soon as the next car went by, they ran across the road and headed to the vacant lot. The whole way Sean felt as if he was being watched and was expecting the shock of a bullet hitting him at any time. Making it to the lot unscathed was huge relief to him.

"Okay from here on it gets a little tough. We're on the outskirts of the town and there are lots of houses around. We'll have to just stroll along as if we belong here and head to the Library. There is one more major road to cross then it's all side roads to the library. There's an abandoned railway line that is used as a hiking trail and we can use that to get close to town. Why don't you hang back about 100 yards or so and just follow that way it won't look as if we are together. There's water and food in the pack so hide across the road from the library and I'll be out in a couple of hours and we can head home. It shouldn't take anymore than another thirty minutes to get there, ready?"

Sean paused. "Let me once again say how stupid I think this is. Now hurry up."

Charley headed off followed a few minutes later by Sean. It took twenty-five minutes to make the circuitous way to the town library but they did with out meeting anyone walking. The cars that passed paid them little notice and Sean began to relax. Maybe Charley was right after all and no one was watching this town for them. It didn't seem likely but if their luck held out they could get to the library and home without incident. He watched Charley walk into a brick building and he looked across the street for a suitable place to hide. He found a clump of shrubs that looked as if it might offer concealment and even be comfortable. He ducked into the clump and made himself as comfortable as he could. His view was mostly obscured by leaves and branches, which meant he was also hidden from view. Once he settled into wait he opened the pack and re-assembled the Thompson and took a sip of water.

The day was nice, warm but not to hot with a few clouds in the sky. Sean was lying on his stomach using the backpack to prop himself up so that he could see the library. He settled his body and mind getting ready for a long wait. He had long ago learned the patience needed for this, lying still for hours on end. The human body, even when sleeping tends to move a lot. No one really understood how much effort it took to lie completely still for even an hour. Sean could lie immobile for days if he needed to, but he hoped today the time would be short. As he got older the effort to get moving again after being still for so long was becoming harder. He suspected that he was getting the beginnings of arthritis as he was feeling more joint pains in the mornings and when ever it rained. Not that this was strange, he was sixty and even though he was in great shape age did bring certain limitations.

In the library Charley settled into one of the computer terminals and began running internet searches. He started with newsgroups, checking bulletin boards looking for posts that made no sense to the topic thread. After an hour of this he realized that unless he got very lucky he was never going to find any information. He switched to searching for information about the attempt on the President and the Pope to see what he could find there. This topic yielded lots of information including the name of the agent he had shot. With her name he began looking into her background. The time with Walter had taught him how to get into places he really shouldn't go, such as government databases. He started looking for her birth record and hometown hoping to find something that didn't fit. Thirty minutes later he had it. Her life history was all faked. Her records listed her town of birth as a Los Angeles, but when he hacked into the database holding the records her name wasn't there. He then hacked into the Secret Service website looking for a back door into their system. It took an hour to find but eventually he was able to get in and dug up her service file. Her file contained the same record of birth that he had already seen. He thought that was strange as the Secret Service would have done a complete background check on her and found the same thing he did. On a hunch he did a web search on just her last name, looking for newspaper articles. He found a newspaper report of a fatal car accident in an obscure newspaper in Alberta, Canada. The report listed that a car had been involved in an accident with a truck and two people had been killed. It also listed the survivor of the truck and stated that a girl in the car had also survived the crash. The occupants of the car had been on vacation and the article listed the hometown. As search of the hometown listed only one hospital, which boasted it's own website. He checked the website and it appeared that some eager beaver administrator was trying to show off the hospitals commitment to the 21st century and was advertising that they now had online searchable databases for many of the hospitals records, one of which was births. Several seconds later he had a listing for the agent showing that not only had she not been born in Los Angeles, she wasn't even a US citizen. She had been born in Canada, in a small town close to the US border. Once again the organization had recruited someone from another country to do its dirty work.

Charley checked the time on his computer screen and saw that he had been at it for over two hours. Considering the walk home he thought that was enough time to put in for today and logged off. He took a look around to see if any one was watching him and headed for the door he had came in through. He stepped through the exit, and in that instance broke one of the cardinal rules for people on the run, never use the same door twice. He should have gone out the other side, but he really didn't think that anyone would be looking for him here so he felt safe. He was wrong.

At the same second he saw Charley leave the library, Sean heard another door bang open. Moving the leaves aside he saw two men running across the lawn two houses up from where he lay hidden, both men were carrying guns. Charley had turned to his right to retrace his steps and so did not see the men as they were behind him. His first hint of trouble was a bullet hitting the brick of the library next to him and peppering him with stone chips. At the same time he hear the roar of a car engine and looked back to see two men firing guns at him and a car rocketing out of a driveway. He immediately ran across the street trying to get between the houses on that side. He was almost to the sidewalk when he felt the slam of a bullet hitting him in the side. The shock of it knocked him off his feet. As he hit the ground he heard the unmistakable sound of a Thompson machine gun opening up on full auto.

Sean jumped to his feet, tracking the two running men with his SMG. In his peripheral vision he saw Charley cross the street then go down, and he opened up on the two men. The SMG bucked hard in his hands causing his first rounds to miss but as he adjusted to the recoil of the heavy rounds he was able to get on target. He dropped the two men before they even had time to react to the new threat. He fired a burst into each man to make sure they were dead then turned his attention to the car that had stopped next to where Charley was lying half on the sidewalk half on the street. The driver was leaning through the window trying to level his gun at Charley when Sean opened up on him. He walked the rounds into the driver's door and window watching them hit the driver making him drop the gun and throwing him back inside the car. Suddenly the Thompson ran dry and the bolt locked opened, Sean dropped and grabbed the drum out of the backpack and swapped it for the now empty clip. He cocked and loaded the SMG, swung the backpack onto his shoulders and carefully stepped out from concealment.

Scanning the street he could see people coming out of homes and offices wondering what was going on, drawn out by the sound of gunfire. Sean went to the first two men he had dropped and checked them over. Both were dead having been hit by several of the heavy .45 slugs. He checked them over fast for ID and took what he found, also scooping up their silenced pistols as well. He ran over to the car next and verified that the driver was dead as well. The bullet hole in his forehead left no doubts at all. Tossing the backpack, pistols and the ID from the other two into the car he then checked on Charley. By this time there were several curious onlookers getting close enough to begin asking questions. A cursory examination showed bleeding on Charley's left side. He was awake and in obvious pain. Sean picked the Lad up and put him in the back seat of the car, then, pushing the dead driver aside, Sean got in behind the wheel and put the car in gear. People were yelling at him now to wait and getting close to the car. He took off just as one man was reaching for the back door to open it. As he sped down the street he could hear sirens in the distance.

"Charley! Can you hear me lad? Are you awake back there?" he yelled.

There was a groggy answer from the back seat and he heard the lad moving around trying to sit up. Sean ripped the shirt off the dead man with one hand and tossed it in the back seat.

"If you can hear me wrap that around your middle to try to stop the bleeding. I need your help Son, I have no idea where I am or how to get home. And I can't take you to a doctor so it's you and me lad, we're on our own."

"Pull over. I have to get in front or I'll be sick." Came the weak order from the back seat.

"I don't think it's a good idea to stop right now lad."

"I need to sit in the front seat so pull over."

Reluctantly Sean stopped on the shoulder of the road, far too many houses around for his comfort, as they hadn't left town yet. He could hear more sirens and he knew that the people on the street would quickly direct the police in the direction he had driven off.

Charley opened the back door and tried to move to the front seat, Sean jumped out as well and moved the dean man to the back seat allowing Charley to sit in front. Sean took an extra minute to wrap the wound and try to slow down the bleeding, and then got back behind the wheel. As he headed off again he passed the Thompson to Charley.

"Think you can use that if you have to?" he asked.

"No I don't," came the reply through gritted teeth.

"Shit! On the floor are the pistols from the shooters, think you can use one of those?"

Charley gingerly reached down and picked up the two pistols checking them over. They were both Beretta .380's with silencers screwed into the barrel. He popped the clips out of both and checked the rounds left. Between the three there was fourteen rounds, the capacity of two clips. He reloaded one clip so it was full, and chambered a round.

"Okay, this I can handle. But I need to see a doctor to get the bullet out Sean. I'm bleeding to death."

"How well do you know the town, Lad?"

"Pretty well." Came the pained reply. "If you turn right up hear we can get to the nearest hospital."

"Lad you and I are on our own. If I take you to a hospital, the Doc will call the police and you'll be in jail by the end of the day, then dead once the organization finds out where you are. Incase you didn't notice they had at least three people just watching the library in a town that happens to be only near where you own an apparently empty woodlot. When are you going to understand that you are dealing with people that have unlimited resources and they never give up. Now forget about a doc, I'm all you've got and at this point I'd say we have another ten minutes before the police are on our tail. No matter what, we cannot be arrested, do you understand? Now where is the nearest Drug store?"

Charley directed him around the outskirts of the town to a drugstore and they parked in the back. Sean left the car running headed into the store with the Thompson to get the things he needed for Charley. As soon as he walked through the door he began herding everyone to the prescription counter keeping them where he could see them. He told the pharmacist what he needed and gave him two minutes to get it ready or else. With shaking hands, the man loaded syringes, bandages, anesthetics, antibiotics, painkillers, surgical instruments, iodine and rubbing alcohol into a bag. Sean forced everyone to lie on the floor and headed out the back delivery entrance grabbing paper towels and cotton swabs along the way. He also grabbed some candy bars as well.

Back in the car he tossed the supplies on the seat next to Charley and hopped back behind the wheel, "The fastest way out of town, if you please. And if you feel up to it stuff that bag in the backpack." He said putting the car in gear and heading back onto the road.

It took fifteen minutes to cover the five miles to Charley's lot, staying mostly on the secondary roads. Sean parked the car on the side of the road and helped Charley out and across the ditch.

"Can you make it from here on your own, lad?" he asked Charley receiving a grim nod in response. "I'll go and ditch the car and then hike back here. I'll try to be back in an hour. In the meantime you go and lie down, take two of the painkillers and we'll get you fixed up as soon as I'm back.

"The road leads up the mountain and to the Bay of Fundy," Charley said through gritted teeth. "Shove it over the side about halfway up, that's only a couple miles from here. Should hide the car for a bit. I'm not sure I can get down the ladder on my own, I'll wait for you by the stump."

Sean nodded and tried to give Charley the Thompson. "You keep it, I couldn't shoot it anyway."

With that Charley headed towards the tunnel entrance and Sean took off to ditch the car. He followed the road halfway up the mountain and then stopped just after a curve. Getting out he looked things over and decided it was as good a spot as any. He cleaned the car of his and Charley's fingerprints as best he could then propped the dead man up in the drivers seat. Making sure the wheel was straight he put the car in neutral and gave a small shove, gravity quickly took over and the car rolled backwards toward the edge of the road. The shoulder here was very wide and as a result there was no guardrail. The car bumped across the grass and then toppled over the edge. Unlike the movies there was no explosion as there was nothing to ignite the gas in the tank. The car simply crashed its way down the side coming to rest on its roof in a stand of trees. It wasn't the best hiding job in the world but it would take an aerial search effort to find it so it would buy them a little time.

With the car disposed of Sean headed back to the bunker as fast as he could. Fortunately the road he was on was not well traveled and as a result he only had to hide for nine cars in the hour it took him to get back. The hiding was in part instinctive, but mostly because he was carrying an SMG and he didn't want anyone to report this to the police and possibly lead them to this area. As he neared the stump he began looking for Charley and making some noise. The last thing he needed was to be shot by his own partner.

"I'm over here Sean" came a small voice from behind a large oak tree.

Sean checked the wound and then helped the young man up. Together the got down into the tunnel and back into the sleeping area. As soon as Charley was lying down Sean started the stove and put some water on boil and tossed the surgical instruments in it. As it was boiling he went back outside and covered their tracks from the road to the tunnel entrance, taking care to erase any evidence of blood that Charley had left. Done with that he reentered the tunnel and locked the entrance so no one could enter after him and went back to his young partner.

"How are you making it lad?" He asked in a quiet voice.

"Not so good Sean. I feel cold and I'm dizzy."

"That's the shock and the blood loss hitting you. I want you to eat this candy bar to get some sugar in you. Then I'm going to give you a local and take out the bullet. After that I'll stitch you up, give you a shot of antibiotics and Mother Nature will have to do the rest." He sat Charley up and fed him the candy bar.

"Have you ever taken a bullet out of anyone before?" asked a concerned Charley.

"Yes I have, and on more than one occasion it was myself. So you can relax, I'm an old pro at this sort of thing. The good news is when I checked the wound it looked as it the bullet had hit a rib and slid around the back. It's just under the skin so it'll be easy to get out. The bad news is that most of the pain is from your rib being broken. Once I get the bullet out I'll wrap your rib to keep it still and then the only thing left is rest."

As soon as the boiled water had cooled to a safe temperature Sean took out the tools and laid them on a clean towel. He opened one of the syringes and the cotton balls. He soaked several cotton balls in the rubbing alcohol and cleaned the area around both the wound and where he could feel the bullet under the skin. Filling the syringe with the anesthetic he inject Charley next to the wound and the bullet and gave it a few minutes to take effect. Using the iodine he swabbed around the bullet and then held it still with his left hand, cutting the skin over it with the scalpel. Once the incision was made he pushed down with his fingers and the bullet popped through the skin and fell onto the bed. He swapped the area with a little more iodine, then threaded a needle with a suture and used two stitches to close the incision. Once he was done that, he rolled Charley over and worked on the entrance hole, swabbing it down and then sewing it closed as well. With the stitches in place, Sean swapped the wounds down with more alcohol and then bandaged them. As a final measure he sat Charley up and, using two roles of gauze, taped up his chest to help with the broken rib. The last thing he did was give Charley a shot of antibiotic to avoid the risk of infection from the wound.

Leaving the lad to rest and recover, Sean took the Thompson back to the amour and cleaned it before putting it away. He unloaded the clips as well to save wear on the springs. He had been impressed by the Thompson, completely changing his view of the old SMG. It had a much heavier kick than he had thought it would have but due to a slower rate of fire than he was used to it was more controllable than he would have thought. Another benefit of the lower rate of fire was that the clips lasted longer. The modern SMG's that he was used to had a rate of fire at least double the old Thompson and he had come to believe that this was necessary. His action this afternoon had completely disproved that theory. With the other SMG's in Charley's collection, they would be able to mount a very effective defense against the organization. He knew they would need it.

Charley slept until noon the next day but the instant use of the antibiotics avoided any infection. The young man was already starting to feel stronger and was hobbling around the bunker, bored with lying down. Sean checked the wounds and they were healing fine, the broken rib was causing more pain than the bullet wound was. The fact that he had been shot enraged Charley and was a clear indication that the organization wanted him dead. He was now filled with doubts about being able to get Sean and himself free of the organization. It had been weeks since they had run and yet the organization had still had 3 men hiding in an obscure little town on the random chance that he would show up there. The fact that it had worked was worse. The organization now knew he and Sean were in Nova Svotia so they had to leave as soon as they could. The real problem was where to go from here. As long as they stayed in the bunker they were safe, or so Charley thought, although he was now beginning to have his doubts about even that. If they tore apart the wood shed they would find the trapdoor and even though that route was protected by the bunkers steel door it could be blown open with enough explosives. Suddenly he had a bad feeling about the wood shed. It wouldn't protect hem from a determined search which he was sure was already on its way.

"Hey Sean, have you got a second?" he yelled as loudly as his damaged rib would allow.

Sean pocked his head out of the armory. "What's up lad?"

"I've been thinking about the shed and the trapdoor. If they poke around too much we'll be in trouble."

Sean came into the main room and sat down at the table with Charley. "That's true, we will be. If they get under the wood shed they can blow the bunker door. But what about the tunnel doors?"

"Those can be locked from the inside and unless you know where they are, it's unlikely they'll be found. I'm really afraid that the woodshed is our weak spot here."

Sean nodded in agreement. "Since they know we are in the area they will be coming to search this lot. We need to move on and as soon as we can. How are you feeling, think you're up to some travel?"

Charley chuckled, "That depends on what you mean by travel? If you mean hiking through the woods carrying everything we need, then no I'm not. If you mean a nice relaxing car ride, then I'm good to go."

"I was thinking of the nice relaxing car ride Charley. But even without a car we have to go, and soon. If possible I'd like to be able to keep this place in reserve, however to do that we need to let the organization know we've left without getting caught. If not this place will be found and your ace in the hole is gone for good. So any ideas lad?"

A big grin crossed Charley's face. "Let go to my house and see what we find there. I'm sure they'll have a car we can borrow."

Sean shook his head. "Sorry lad that place will be even more heavily watched then Kigston was. I don't want to get into another shoot out again; I got lucky the last time. We can't risk either one of us getting shot again. And unless you've changed your mind about killing, that would leave me to do all the dirty work"

"We don't have to kill anyone and there doesn't have to be a shootout. There is a way into the house with out being seen."

"I should have guessed by this place that you'd have some hidden entrance. What is it, another tunnel?"

"You guessed it Sean. There's a tunnel that leads to a hidden room in the basement. We can get into the house that way. Trust me it'll work. Let's pack what we need and get going. We'll need to creatively borrow a car or truck to get there. Do you know how to hotwire a car old man?"

"Yes I can hotwire a car. Okay so we head to your house and take a look around. Now tell me, are you up to moving?"

"As long as I don't have to do any heavy lifting or fight anyone, I'll be fine. Let's start packing."

The two packed up what little clothes they had and then went to the armory to load up there. Sean chose the Thompson with four stick and four drum magazines. He filled all the magazines and then packed up several extra boxes of cartridges. He also picked out a .308 rifle and five boxes of shells for it. Charley took the Silenced Sten gun along with the M3 grease gun and ten magazines for each. The sten was a 9mm and the M3 used the same .45's as Sean's Thompson so they would be able to share the bullets. He also took a 30-06 Sniper rifle. He wanted to pack the MG34 but knew that it was too much weight to carry for any distance. Along with this they also had the three silenced pistols Sean had taken from the organizations hit men but as they were .380 caliber the only ammo for them was what was in the pistols at the time, which amounted to just two full clips of seven rounds each.

Along with the firearms they also packed an assortment of combat knives and some food. With this done they were ready to go. Sean led the way to the south tunnel with each man carrying one of the .380's ready to fire. The sten and the Thompson were also loaded and ready to fire. As he got to the tunnel entrance Sean carefully looked around, making sure it was clear before climbing out. He helped Charley out and they headed through the woods toward the nearest road. They were almost to the road when they heard the sound of someone talking.

The firefight in Kingston made headlines in Canada because of the machine gun that Sean had used to kill the 3 men. The police started a manhunt looking for one man with an automatic weapon and a companion that was wounded. The two dead men were fingerprinted to try and determine their identities; as well, the house they were living in was thoroughly searched to find a clue as to what was behind the gunfight. None of the witnesses that saw the firefight were able to identify any of the men involved. It was discovered that one of the dead men had rented the house through a real estate company for a year and had paid with a credit card. A search of the credit card turned up nothing other then the fact that the man had an excellent credit record. All the bills were paid on a personal checking account from a bank in Oregon. The money to cover the checks seemed to come from an overseas bank account registered to a numbered company in Liechtenstein, which also turned out to be a dead end. After twenty-four hours the police were no further ahead in the investigation then when they started, and with no solid clues it looked as if they never would find out what happened.

Meanwhile the news of the fight made it on TV in the US where one of the organizations people happened to see it. He reported this to the three stooges, who immediately attempted to contact their men in Kingston. After four hours of no response they contacted the team watching Charley's house and dispatched one of the men there to Kingston to find out what had happened. Several hours later they were informed that two agents were dead and one was missing. There were two men involved with in the shootout aside from their own men and one of the other two men, was armed with an SMG, type unknown. It was assumed that the two unknown men were the two renegades, Sean and Charley. The fact that they were in Nova Scotia was bad enough, but coupled with the fact that they were now armed with automatic weapons and had eliminated one of the teams in a firefight, it was disastrous. They needed to meet with the three wise men to receive orders on a plan of action.

Carter was just sitting down to his supper when he heard the faint sound of a phone ringing. The tone was different and it took him a moment to realize the significance of the ringing, for his personal organization phone had only rung four times in the past. Each time signified a very important event. Getting up from the table he hurried as quickly as his overweight body would carry him to the study. He paused to close and lock the study door and was slightly out of breath when he answered the call.

"Yes?" he panted into the receiver.

"Sir it's James. There has been an incident with three officers and the two AWOL men. I would like to brief you and your colleagues and quickly as possible," said one of the three stooges in a rapid-fire voice. Even though the phones were scrambled he spoke in generalities.

"That will be decidedly inconvenient James. Has anyone else been notified?"

"It is being done now sir. We felt it best to notify all parties concerned ASAP. We will remain here until we receive directions to the contrary." With that the connection was broken.

Carter put the phone down and opened his desk drawer to take out a cell phone. He dialed a number as he walked back to his dinner table and was grateful that tonight he was eating alone.

His call was answered on the second ring. "Hello?"

"Have you received a call from your junior?" Carter asked without saying any names.

"Yes I did," answered the voice. "He requested a conference as I'm sure you've heard. Do you feel this would be a good idea?"

"Yes I do, the question is where?"

There was several seconds of silence before the voice replied "Would it be possible to do it at your weekend retreat?"

Carter paused for a moment. "That would be fine. Can you notify our colleague and I'll notify the juniors. Let's make it for tomorrow at 6 AM. I'll head out tonight and prepare things. See you in the morning." Carter disconnected without waiting for a reply and then went back to his dinner.

As soon as he was done eating he called his maid in and explained that he would be spending the night out and she would not need to prepare breakfast and could retire early.

He left her to clear the dinning table and went back to his study. After closing and locking the door he went to his desk and picked the phone, it was answered on the first ring.

"Sir?"

"The briefing will take place at my weekend retreat at 6 AM. All parties concerned will be there." Carter hung us as he finished without waiting for any response. The juniors were used to following orders and never needed clarification. After all, they had been chosen for their ability to follow orders to the letter.

Carter packed his clothes for tomorrow and went into his garage. Starting his car he left his townhouse and headed south towards the Virginia shore. His weekend retreat was a cabin on the Chesapeake Bay surrounded by eight acres of woods. It was very quiet and private ensuring that the meeting would be undisturbed. Arriving shortly after nine he went around the side of the cabin and started a small gas generator that supplied the place with electricity. Even though the cabin was only 400 yards off the highway, Carter had not had the power run into the cabin. This insured that he was self-sufficient and the noise of the generator made listening in with parabolic microphones next to impossible. Communications were all done by means of either cell phones or a satellite uplink for a laptop computer. The retreat also had a boathouse with a large cabin cruiser. The boat was seldom used but kept in ready condition at all times as an emergency measure and for the rare time that Carter felt like spending time on the water relaxing.

Turning on the heat to ward off the chill of the bay, Carter locked the doors and set his portable alarm for 5:30 AM then went to bed. When the alarm went off it felt as if he had just gone to bed. He rose and dressed quickly in a sweat suit, then went outside to check the generator. He topped it up with fuel and went back into his cabin to make coffee and wait for his guests. Ten minutes later the first colleague arrived followed a few moments later by the third one. The three wise men were together sipping coffee and making small talk when the juniors arrived at 5:57 AM.

All six men went into the room of the cabin that was right next to the outside generator. There were no windows and the door was locked. In the room was a plain table with three chairs on each side. In the middle of the table was a small electronic box that generated white noise to further protect them from electronic eavesdropping; it was turned on by Carter.

"You may begin your briefing," he told the three stooges.

One of the men opened his brief case and removed some papers and began reading off of them. "Following the failed attempt on the president the two agents assigned to the job, Charles Watkins and Sean Miller, disappeared. Despite an all out search engaged by all field agents, the two men have remained at large. No information regarding either man has been forthcoming from any of our information sources. Our agent in place within the presidential detail has also not reported any information concerning the still ongoing Secret Service investigation. A search was conducted of the building that was used as the shooting platform but no indication of the two was ever located. The building was placed under surveillance but no sign of the agents were sighted. The men were subsequently listed as fugitives and orders to terminate on sight were issued. As well full dossiers regarding the two, along with other crimes they are wanted for, were quietly leaked to law enforcement agencies by agents in place, and APB's have been issued. The FBI has also issued warrants for their arrest and they have been listed on the watch list for Customs and immigration."

The briefing was continued by another of the three stooges at this point. "As per standard procedure, any place that the fugitives were known to frequent were placed under surveillance by agents. Charles Watkins was listed as the owner of a house and a woodlot in Canada. One team was stationed at his house with a second team placed in the town nearest his woodlot with orders to perform periodic sweeps of the lot. Knowing that Mr Watkins has an affection for the internet, the team watching the woodlot was placed near the towns library, as this has public internet access. At random intervals they swept the woodlot, which is five miles outside of the town, with sensors and on foot to determine if anyone was there. Both teams were in place two days after the failed shooting and have not reported sighting either fugitive since this time. As Sean Miller has been with the organization for nearly forty years and was originally from Great Britain he has no locations he is known to frequent other than organization safe houses. These are all being monitored for activity.

The last stooge took up the briefing at this point. "Yesterday there was a firefight in the town of Kingston, which as stated previously, is located near the woodlot owned by Charles Watkins. The firefight involved our surveillance team and two other unknown persons, which we assume to be the fugitives but are not naming them so at this time. An agent from the house surveillance team was sent to investigate and was able to learn that two of our operatives were killed and one is missing. Also the authorities believe one of the two unknown men was wounded, although this can not be proven and if true the extent of the wound is not known. Both other men fled the scene by stealing the car being driven by the missing agent and have not been seen since. Neither the car nor the agent has turned up to this point. No weapons were recovered after the fight, indicating that the two men fleeing the scene policed up our agents weapons. However spent casing recovered from the scene indicate two separate calibers of weapons in use. The casings are for a

.380 and a .45. The .380 is the caliber of the pistols being used by our agents so that leaves the assumption that the unknown subjects were using .45's. Eyewitnesses have also indicated that the pistols were using sound suppressors and the unknown subjects were using an automatic weapon of an unknown type. Our agent was investigated the scene and was unable to obtain any of the casings. No police reports have been released and the bodies are being held pending identification. At this time we have not leaked the identity of the dead agents and are taking no action, pending your orders."

The stooges sat quietly waiting for their masters to speak. The silence was broken by Carter. "Would you three wait outside the cabin please?" It was an order, not a question.

They filed out in silence leaving the three wise men to plan the future.

Carter started off the discussion. "I propose we send a special action team in to do a through recon of the area. It seems that the two renegades are staying on this woodlot in some sort of hideout. Do you concur?"

"I do," replied the second man.

The third man paused for a moment. "I also feel we should manufacture some evidence pointing to these two as the people that attempted to kill the president. It was them, after all so the rest of the world should know it too. Have the juniors set something in motion and then call in a tip to the FBI and the news media. If the special action team misses then we can let the law enforcement arm do some of our work for us. It will be an easy matter to exterminate these renegades once they are in custody."

"That may not be wise," replied the second man. "If apprehended by the authorities the renegades will undoubtedly be interrogated. This could lead to the discovery of our organization. That we can't allow to happen."

"If they are captured we will know within hours of their capture. As I mentioned before it will be a simple matter to have these two terminated once that happens. As they are wanted for the attempted murder of the president I seriously doubt anyone will believe anything they say. And we can control it if they do say anything. The risk is acceptable and can be managed. These two need to be eliminated at all costs," countered the third man.

"Then we are agreed on our plan and I'll tell the juniors. We may as well leave, I know you gentleman have important business to attend to and it would not do to have the three of us seen together. Shall we adjourn?" Carter summed up.

With no further discussion two men left the cabin, going directly to their cars and heading back to Washington. Carter tidied up the kitchen then locked the cabin and went around to the generator motioning for the juniors to follow him.

"Send an action team up right away and search that damn woodlot. Also put together some evidence matching those two to the assassination attempt and tip off the FBI. Have it done in five days. You're dismissed." With that done he shut down the generator and went to his car. The juniors followed him out the driveway and both cars headed back to Washington to begin their respective days.

Carter traveled slowly so that the juniors would pass him and put some distance between the two cars. Even though no one would know that they were together he preferred not to risk the chance of even being seen. The juniors had already stared the planning to carry out their orders. The house in Vermont that Charley and Sean had been living in was still in the possession of the organization. They would use this as the tie in for leaking the evidence. They knew the bullet used was a 30-caliber even though all the parts for the rifle were for a 50-caliber. They had no idea how the two managed to change the rifle but it didn't matter; they would have one of the organization armories plant suitable evidence that could be matched to the bullet. Add in some maps and drawings and the photos Sean had taken of the area where the event took place, and the evidence would be enough to have the FBI start a manhunt for them. The order to send the action team had already been given by cell phone as soon as they began driving. The team would meet with the agents in place at the Watkins house by the end of the day. By 9 AM all the participants of the meeting were back at their respective offices as if it had never taken place, and they had all moved on to other matters, confident that the steps put in motion would resolve the minor crises that had resulted in the desertion of two of their number. They could not have been more wrong.

The action team flew into a small municipal airstrip in a small village called Waterville that was within twenty minutes of the Watkins house, around three in the afternoon. The falsified flight plan showed then as coming from another city in Canada so that they could avoid customs. With the weapons they carried on board they could not take the risk of getting searched. The pilot had in fact not filed a flight plan at all, flying the long-range twin turboprop plan on a long circuitous route that had begun at 10 AM that morning. The pilot flew towards Montreal first, descending to 300 feet to get below radar after he had crossed the boarder. His supposed destination was the municipal airport north of the city, however ten miles out he turned on an easterly heading and began climbing. To anyone looking at the radar it appeared as if he had just taken off and there was a flight plan on file to show that he was on route to Nova Scotia so no one would think to ask any questions over the radio of the blip flying eastwards on an approved flightplan. The organization had an agent call the local customs office and tell them that the flight supposed to land in Montreal had turned back and since no plane landed there was no reason to be suspicious.

When the plane landed in Waterville the team was met by one of the agents staying at the Watkins house. He introduced himself simply as Jim to the team leader and pointed to the Van he was using and headed back to it to leave the team to unpack. There were five men in the team and each man carried a duffel bag and a large hard-sided briefcase. They piled the gear in the backseat of the van and everyone climbed in, with the team leader getting in the front with the driver.

"I'm Mike," he said without mentioning the men in the back.

"Hi Mike, is there anything I can do to help?" replied Jim.

"We've been well briefed but have no knowledge of the local area so any maps or first hand information you can supply would be great. Has anyone scouted the area?"

"No one from my team has scouted the area, that was up to the team in Kingston. But we do have some topographical maps and a survey map of the area as well, they're back at the house. We got coffee and some sandwiches ready for you and your team and there is room to rest and prep in private. The house its self is set back off the road and has no close neighbors so you don't have to worry about being seen. This van is clean and at your disposal, the only thing I ask is when you are done with it, get rid of it. I'll be wiping it down when we get back to the house and no one but your team will be in it after that. The woodlot is about thirty miles from here and the route is already marked out on a map in the glove box."

"Thanks, we appreciate that."

The rest of the trip went in silence and they arrived back at the house in about half an hour. The team grabbed their gear and headed inside without saying a word. It was a two-story house and the team went right upstairs to two bedrooms that had been cleared out for them. They immediately opened their bags and began taking out the items they would need. They all wore black jumpsuits with flak vests and webgear to carry the weapons and ammo. Heavy black boots, black balaclavas and black, skintight, calfskin gloves completed the outfit. Each man stripped off his traveling cloths and put on the jumpsuit, boots and gloves. Then they opened the briefcases and took out their weapons. Each man was equipped with a silenced MP5 submachine gun chambered for 9mm, and a silenced pistol. Three of the team were using a Beretta 9mm to match the ammo with their SMG, but Mike was using a silenced 22 Ruger and the last man was using a silenced .45 M1911. One man was equipped with a .308 sniper rifle and another had a 12-gauge shotgun loaded with buckshot.

The five men had operated as a team for four years now and were so finely integrated that they could tell what the other members of the team were going to do before they did it. They communicated with grunts and slang, each attuned to the others on the team. Talking was kept to what was absolutely necessary. As soon as they were dressed, and their weapons loaded and ready, they assembled in one bedroom to plan the op.

The team leader had the maps spread out on the bed showing the layout and orientation of the woodlot. "Okay guys, here's the way we'll do this. We will be making a sweep through the area from the southeast to the northwest. We're doing this tonight so everyone make sure your Night vision gear has fresh batteries and everyone carry extras. There is no evidence that the renegades are there but as always we will assume they are and act accordingly. This is a search and destroy mission so anyone we see is to be terminated. We'll do the standard five-meter separation sweep and keep our fire zones to 45 degree arcs with the exception of the two outside sweepers. They will have a fire arc of 180 degrees. From this point on we will be using team numbers. I'm 1 and I will be in the middle with 2 and 4 on my right and 3 and 5 on my left. 4 and 5 you will be the outside flankers. Anyone have any questions? No, then let's get some rest and we'll move out at 22:00."

The five men split up and all lay down to get a few hours rest before heading out. At 21:30 hours they all once again checked over their gear and weapons and then finished dressing, putting on the vests and webgear. Once ready to go, the team went into the kitchen for coffee and some sandwiches. They ate in silence, each man thinking of the mission and sure it was a waste of time. There were no buildings on the lot, no sign of any people and no litter that would be associated with two men camping out. In fact the only thing on the entire property was a small lean-to that was said to contain some firewood. Even though this information came from the team that was now dead, the men had been reliable and so there was no need to doubt them. More than likely the two renegades were staying with an unknown friend somewhere. One of the men had been with the organization for forty years so he would know standard operating procedures and as such would have avoided the younger one's house. It was probable that Watkins had friends around here that he could stay with that the organization was unaware of.

Rested and fed the team piled into the van and headed to the wood lot. The team reached the search area around 10:40 PM and parked near the southeast corner of the lot to begin the sweep.

"Okay team listen up, we'll sweep the lot then double back and take a look at that lean-to to see if there has been anyone around. Use your NVG's and remember your free fire arcs and assigned areas. Any questions? Good let's move out," the team leader ordered.

Upon hearing the voice Sean grabbed the silenced Sten from Charley and checked to make sure a round was chambered. He motioned his young partner to sit behind a tree and he moved forward, alert and ready to fire. If it was, as he feared, an action team getting ready to search the lot he had only a few seconds to catch them together. Once they spread out and got organized with the search he and Charley were dead. As he stepped out from behind a tree he saw five men, all with slung weapons, putting on what looked like head mounted binoculars. He recognized these as night vision glasses and without hesitation opened fire on the five men. Sweeping his SMG from left to right he let the recoil of the gun track his rounds across his targets. He emptied the clip and dropped the SMG pulling his pistol as he moved toward the men now lying on the ground. He had hit all five, killing two instantly. One of the remaining team was trying to bring his own weapon around for a shot when Sean hit him in the head with one round from his .380. Then deciding that mercy was a liability he killed the remaining two with heads shots as well.

"Charley, get up here," he said in his loudest whisper.

The Lad joined him looking at the five dead and again wondered what had gone wrong. Sean was already stripping the men of their gear and piling it up to see what they could take. Help me search the bodies. I can see a Van near the road, they must have come in that, so if we find the keys we have a ride out of here."

Charley was in a state of mild shock. "Why did you kill them?"

Sean looked hard at the boy. "Because they were going to kill us and I don't feel like dieing yet. Now snap out of it and get moving. You wanted to get your life back and you'd better start realizing that to have that things are going to be messy sometimes. Now move your ass!" He finished harshly, going back to his own search.

Charley dropped down next to one of the bodies and started going through the pockets, finding the keys in the first one he checked. "Got them," he said in a quiet voice holding up the keys.

"Great, get your gear and head to the van. Start the thing up while I load up this gear and we'll get out of here."

Charley got in the van and started it waiting for Sean to finish up. The team's guns and gear were loaded up the Sean began dragging the bodies over and putting them in the van.

"What the hell are you doing?" asked a horrified Charley.

"Do you really want five bodies to be found on your property Lad? I don't think it will help your case with the police in Canada. I'm sure they will want to know why there are five dead men on your woodlot. That's exactly the type of question you don't want people asking if you are the number one suspect in an assassination attempt, so we'll move them somewhere else and throw the suspicion off of you."

Charley said nothing for the rest of the time it took Sean to load the van. When the bodies were in and the door closed Sean got in and told the lad to drive. He put the van in gear and headed down the road trying hard not to think of the dead men in the back. This was impossible to do, as the stench of death filled the van as a constant reminder to their presence. He drove carefully so as not to get stopped for any reason by the police, and after twenty minutes realized he was heading home out of habit.

"What are we going to do with the bodies?" he asked Sean in a quiet voice. "If we get caught with them and all these weapons in the Van we're screwed."

"How close can you get us to your house?" Sean asked ignoring the question.

"About a five minute walk. The tunnel entrance is in the trees behind the house."

"Okay get us as close as you can and then show me the tunnel. I'll go into the house and take care of the team there, then we can head out of here."

Charley thought for a second. "I have a better idea. Let's forget my place. I say we dump the bodies near my place then call the police and tip them off. Saying we heard gunfire and saw some men dumping bodies. Give them the general location and get out of here. If we stop in Halifax I can get some money transferred from my trust fund and then we get out of here."

"Stop for a moment and think lad. Do you honestly believe that you will be able to get money from any of your accounts? The organization would have frozen everything to ensure you had no money except what they allowed you to have."

Charley shook his head vigorously. "No, this is money that even the organization can't touch. It's not in my name and the only way to get at it is with the authorization code through a specific person that controls the trust. Granddad set it up as a backup in case anything happened and we needed an untraceable source of money, he was a very paranoid man."

Sean smiled. "If he could think that far ahead, then he was paranoid. Are you sure it will still be there though?"

"Yes I am. The money was never designed to be touched by me, it was supposed to go to my children when I had them. The trust fund is in my Grandmothers maiden name and you have to know the name Granddad called her to unlock it. How much do you think we'll need?"

"I don't know lad, I guess it depends on what we do. If we stay together and fight the organization, as you want to, we'll need a lot of cash. If we do as I'd like to do and find some quiet small town to hide out in we can get jobs and live pretty well. After what's happened the last week are you still sure you want to try and clear your name and get your life back? After all, these people have shown they want you dead and no hesitation to try and kill you."

Charley drove for a moment in silence. "I think we should fight them. If we run there will always be a chance that they will find us. And as we've seen if they do find us they're going to start shooting right away. I don't think we have a choice but to fight."

"Fine, then we fight. I will try to keep you out of any gunfights, but Lad, if you do have to shoot, make sure you aren't trying to wound them. We are going up against some very tough men who will not go down easy. For now let's leave your trust fund. I have a better idea on how to finance our war. We take the credit cards of the agents we run into and get cash advances. This will create a trail and we can lead them to where we make a stand against them. Do you have any moral issues with stealing from the organization?"

Charley's face lit up with a huge smile. "Now that, I have no problem with. And it saves me money too."

"How soon before we get to your house?"

"We're a few minutes from it. There is a field just up here that I can turn into then we can walk to the tunnel and get into the basement. Since you are the experienced one here, how do you want to handle it?"

Sean thought for a second. "Once I'm in the basement how hard is it to get to the first floor?"

"Up the stairs and you come out in the kitchen, but I'll show you the way."

"No lad you are going to create a diversion for me. I want you to drive the Van up to the house. When you get just close enough to see the place stop and get out of the van and hide somewhere. Take your silenced weapons with you but don't shoot unless you have to. Use one of the NVG's too, that will help. Now explain the layout to me and give me twenty minutes to get into position then drive up near the house. Blow the horn when you get there, then run. Have you got that?"

"Sean can we try taking these guys alive? Do they have to be killed?"

"Oh I want them alive, that's why I need you to drive the van up there. I'm going to shoot them in the legs with one of our dead friends MP5's then call the police. It's going to be difficult to explained five dead men in a van, your legs full of bullets and all these automatic weapons around. Now tell me how to find the tunnel and then give me twenty minutes."

Charley gave him directions then watched his friend take the MP5 and several clips and head off across the field wearing NVG's. He waited the twenty minutes then drove to his house and up the driveway to within site of the house. He left the lights on, then opened the van door grabbed his sten, a .380 and a set of NVG's, blew the horn, and moved as quick as he could into the woods. After several hundred yards he sat down behind a tree and waited. In the distance he could hear the commotion he had caused, then screams of pain.

With the NVG's Sean was able to move at a fast clip through the trees and towards the back of the house. Following Charley's instructions he was able to find the tunnel within four minutes of leaving the van. Opening the hidden door he went into the tunnel and jogged along it until he got to a little alcove in front of a brick wall. To the left of the wall was a shelf with a lamp on it and a key lying there. Sean took off his NVG's, turned on the lamp and picked up the key. Checking his watch he saw he still had a few minutes so he went over the layout Charley had described to him one more time in his mind. Then he used the key to open the lock and pushed on the wall, surprised at how easy it opened to form a door in the basement wall. He turned off the lamp, slipped through the opening into the house, and closed the door behind him. Once the door was closed he could not see any seams to even indicate that it existed.

Moving to the stairs he stood still and held his breath to listen for movement. Checking his watch he saw that twenty minutes had passed. He started up the stairs when he heard loud voices and the sound of running feet on stairs. The sound of a door banging open along with the fading of the footsteps was all he needed to rush into the kitchen and follow the direction the footsteps went. He moved far quieter then the others had and no one heard him come out onto the porch. A fast scan of the area showed three men, all with drawn guns, advancing on the van sitting in the middle of the driveway. Knowing he could not give then any warning Sean moved to the edge of the veranda to use the railing as a support for his MP5 and took careful aim at the three men. He took up the slack on the trigger feeling it tighten then break and the gun started bucking. Using a full clip he hit all three men several times each in the legs. He slammed in a new clip then moved off the veranda toward the downed men. All the men were down on the ground and in a lot of pain, even so they began trying to bring their own pistols around to fight back against the unknown attacker. Sean fired a few more bursts to let the men know he could kill them any time he wanted and to encourage them to lie still. As the rounds kicked up dirt around the heads of the three, they stopped moving and waited to see what would happen. Each man now knew he was alive only because the shooter wanted it that way.

They were ordered to toss their pistols toward the house and all did so. Sean kicked the pistols even further away from the fallen men noticing that these were all Beretta's. One of the watchers noticed him as he moved into the line of view to kick away the guns

"You!" he yelled. "I should have known it would be you. So how's it feel to be a traitor?"

"I don't know, you tell me." Sean replied quietly to the man on the ground then turned his head briefly and yelled. "All clear Lad, come in!"

Charley appeared in a few minutes, Sten gun in hand. "Excellent lad! I'm glad to see you taking this seriously. Now let's ask these fine gentleman if they are alone of if there are other vermin about. Please keep a look out and I'll ask the questions. So what is your name?" he asked to the man that had spoken to him.

"Haywood Jablowme, you stupid bastard!"

"Well Haywood, that's not exactly polite but I'll let you off this time with a minor warning." Sean calmly shot him in the left knee. "Now is there anyone else in the house?"

Charley flinched as the man was hit and had to bite his tongue to keep from saying something to Sean.

"Ahhhhh!" the man screamed at the fresh assault of pain. "Fuck you, asshole!"

"Now Haywood, do we have to do this the hard way? We can if you like, but it takes a while and tends to leave you a little more messed up than you otherwise would be. Now one more time, is there anyone in the house?" Sean asked as he pointed the MP5 at Haywood's other knee.

Knowing he could be crippled for life he chose to answer. "No, it's just the three of us."

"Excellent Haywood, see how easy that is?"

"My name isn't Haywood, it's Sam."

"I see, well then Sam we're almost done. How and when do you report to the three stooges?

"We call a blind number every second day at rotating times. There are different codes we use depending on the status. I'm not going to give you the all clear code no matter what you do to me."

"Well Sam I don't really want you to give me the codes. As a matter of fact I was wondering if you could call and let them know Charley and I are doing fine. So far we've managed to stay one step ahead but we are getting rather tired of the chase. You have eight dead agents so far, oh yes the action team you sent after us didn't make it. So tell the stooges if they leave us alone we'll go away and live a nice quiet life. If they come after us again we'll bring the war to them. Have you got that?"

"You two are dead, no matter what you think. You know the rules, no one runs away, ever! You better kill me now cause when I can walk again I'm coming after you. And next time I'll be ready."

"Like you were this time?" Sean asked with a chuckle. "If you are the caliber of people they have hunting me I don't know why I ever went into hiding. Charley go and search the house and get what ever you need while I make sure these gentleman behave, oh and call someone to get these boys some medical attention."

Charley searched the house making sure no one else was there and gathering up items he thought he would need. The watchers had a lot of gear with them and he picked through this as well, taking some and leaving others. He took all their ID, credit cards, weapons, and anything that they could use to hunt he and Sean with. When he was finished he went to the garage looking for a car. His was there along with his pickup and another car he had never seen before. the keys were actually in the ignition of the strange car so he got in started it up, backed it out and began loading the gear he had taken from the house in it.

He slowly walked up to Sean starting to feel pain from his wound "Okay I got everything I could that was useful and I found their car too, and disabled it. I'm all loaded up and ready to go."

"Watch these fellows for a bit, I'll load the weapons and we can be on our way. Did you call any one yet?"

"No, but I picked up one of their cell phones so as soon as we're ready to go we can make the call and then get out of here."

"Okay make the call lad, and we'll be on our way. These gentlemen need medical attention."

Charley started the car again and moved it around the van so that he was ready to leave and then called 911 to report a gunfight and people being killed. Sean rounded up all the firearms and those he didn't take he wiped down to remove any prints and then locked them in the van with the dead men. He checked one more time to make sure there was no danger from the men he was leaving alive and then got in the car with Charley and the two left. As they neared town they saw two police cars, being followed by an ambulance, go rocketing by, toward the house.

Sam heard the sirens in the distance and started swearing. "Do either of you have your cell phone?"

One did and he tossed it over to Sam who called in his report. He finished up just as the police pulled up the driveway, and to avoid reveling the organization he cleared the phone's memory so no one could find the number he dialed. The policemen advanced toward the 3 men on the ground with drawn guns. As soon as the lead officer looked in the van and saw the five men slumped over and the blood on the floor of the van he radioed for backup and screamed at the watchers to lie face down with their hands over their heads.

"I can't let go of my knee or I'll bleed to death," Sam calmly told the agitated officer "We have all been shot and the men in the van are dead. We have no weapons and we need medical help."

Shining their flashlights on the three, the police saw that the men were indeed hurt and bleeding. As soon as the paramedics arrived they moved forward and put handcuffs on the wounded men so that the medics could treat them. Once the safety of the emergency crew was looked after, one officer watched over them while the rest began searching the area and the house. As the medics worked, the police watched without words allowing them to get the wounded stabilized. The medics bandaged the wounds and then hung an IV on each to treat them for shock. With that done they announced the men were ready to be taken to hospital.

The senior police officer on the scene stopped them at this point. "They need to answer a few questions first." He turned to the wounded men. "Who wants to tell me what happened here?"

Sam answered for all of them. "We want a lawyer."

The officer issued a deep sigh. "Come on give me something. There was a major gunfight here and we've got five dead, you three wounded and machine guns that somehow were locked in the van with the dead folks. So since it couldn't have been you, where are the guys that did the shooting?"

The three were silent, saying nothing at all. Sam had made the demand for a lawyer and no one would talk until they had one. After a few futile minutes of trying to get something from the men the officer finally nodded to the medics to take them to the hospital. Each man was handcuffed to his stretcher and had a police officer with them as they were taken in. After the wounded had been taken to the hospital the police began the slow methodical search of the area to try and find out what had happened. By sunrise there were over twenty investigators on site desperately looking for clues, while the wounded men, now under police guard in the hospital, had all met with a lawyer and refused to talk. The lawyer informed the police that his clients would be making no comments and that they were to only talk to him then left the hospital.

An organization team was sent to the house in Vermont to plant evidence that could be used to link the two fugitives to the attempted presidential assignation. When they arrived they found a lot of equipment that Sean and Charley had left there. All the photos Sean had taken of the area and even used some of the original building plans that the organization had obtained for Sean along with the plans that listed the times and possible motorcade routes throughout Boston were still there. A gunsmith was consulted to find out how Charley fired a .30-06 round when the organization new he was using a .50 rifle. As soon as they knew of saboting they checked the house to see if the gear was there to do this and found it all. This along with the extra brass and reloading gear that Charley had left in the house was more then enough. The only thing that the team didn't have was a rifle, but they didn't need one with all the other evidence. Once done they went through the house and wiped it clear of fingerprints, using an alcohol solution that left a residue trace so that investigators would know it was cleaned. All that was left was to come up with descriptions and witnesses that would identify the two renegades as the shooters, and the job was finished.

The organization managed to find a local gun shop that dealt in bulk shooting powder and bought the store. Once done they forged receipts to show that Charley had purchased powder there, and even put some of it at the house so there would be a chemical match. The entire staff was replaced with organization personal that would all be able to identify both Sean and Charley. Once this last step was completed an anonymous call was placed to the FBI and with in an hour the house was raided and the long process of gathering evidence began, but the end result was the one the organization had wanted. Within twenty-four hours of raiding the house the FBI put out an alert on nationwide TV with pictures of Sean Miller and Charley Watkins naming them as suspects in the attempted assassination of the President and issuing a warrant for their arrest.

After leaving his house Charley drove steadily for a few hours and then was suddenly overcome with drowsiness. At the same time he realized he was almost out of the province. He had been traveling blindly, the throbbing in his side keeping him awake, with out thinking of what he was doing. Sean was napping in the passenger seat unaware of where they were going. Charley pulled off at the next exit and parked on the shoulder of the off ramp. As soon as the car stopped his companion was awake and alert.

"Why did we stop?" Sean asked with no trace of sleepiness in his voice.

"We stopped because I don't know what to do next. I just realized we are almost out of Nova Scotia and I don't know what we are doing or where we are going, my side is killing me and I'm tired"

"Well I think we should get into the US as fast as we can. Before too much longer the organization will have managed to get our names and pictures released to the media and everyone will be looking for us. When that happens, crossing the border will be impossible. I suggest we head for Maine."

"In a rental car full of machine guns? Have you lost your mind Sean?"

"Of course not, lad. I'll think of a way to get them across, after all we need them.

"We'll need a four wheel drive to get across though, have to get one soon."

Charley just shook his head. "And where do we get a four wheel drive?"

"Why we buy one lad, we buy one," Sean said, holding up the credit cards he had taken from the watchers at the house. "I'm sure these gold cards will get us what we need. Let's go see what used vehicles are available in the area, shall we."

Charley crossed into New Brunswick and headed for the city of Moncton to see what they could find. They spent the morning looking all over town checking for 4x4 trucks until they found an older model Ford that fit the bill. It was a full size king cab model giving them lots of room behind the seat. Sean bought it using one of the Gold Cards and then followed Charley off the lot to the nearest shopping mall. There he went in and bought a large roll of packing wrap and several rolls of duct tape along with a box of condoms. The next stop was at a hardware store where a grappling hook and several hundred feet of rope were added to the pile of purchases. Through all of this Charley merely followed his friend and wondered what was going on. Finally done with his shopping Sean headed back out on the highway turning south for the US/ Canada border and Maine, with Charley still following him.

As he drove Sean was looking for a secluded spot off the road that they could pull into. He found what he was looking for twenty minutes later and slowed the truck to pull off the road. Charley still with no idea what was going on, shrugged and followed, pulling in behind some bushes that shielded them from the road.

"Okay, can you tell me what the hell is going on now?" asked a frustrated Charley.

"Patience Lad, patience, all in good time."

"And you know, I'm a little tired of all this lad stuff, Old Man," Charley said sarcastically.

"I didn't know that my nickname offended you Charley, I'm truly sorry or I wouldn't have been calling you Lad all this time," replied a surprised Sean.

Charley shrugged. "It doesn't really, I'm just tired and edgy. We've been on the move since yesterday without a real nights rest and I need to sleep soon."

"Make a deal with you Charley, you give me four more hours then we'll rest for a solid twelve. Is that okay with you?"

"We don't have much of a choice do we? We need to hide this car and the guns. I'm a little pissed that I'm going to lose my SMG's but it's better then being tossed in jail for crossing the border with them."

Sean smiled at his tired companion. "But we are going to cross the border with them. Well not exactly with them but we'll have them in the US so you won't be losing your SMG's."

"Now how do you plan to get them across with us?"

"That's what we need the 4x4 for. Help me waterproof these and I'll explain it all."

Sean handed Charley a box of condoms and one of the silenced pistols. "Unroll the condom over the silencer and tape it in place. We need to do this with all the weapons. Once we're done we wrap them up in the plastic and tape everything shut. With everything all wrapped up, we drive down by they river between Maine and New Brunswick and I toss the grapple across into some bushes with a rope tied to it. On the other end are the guns. Toss that into the river, cross the border, and then once safely on the other side we use the rope to pull them in. Simple but effective."

The weapons were all wrapped and sealed in an hour. The two got in the

4x4 leaving the car there, and got back on the highway going south. Within two hours they were at the border and headed west following the river. As the road turned away from the river, Sean put the truck in four-wheel drive and headed off the road. The bumped and bounced their way along the shore looking for a suitable place and found one with in five miles. Sean used pieces of duct tape on the trees to mark the spot, and then tossed the grapple across the river. He needed four tries to get it good and solid against the far bank so that the current wouldn't wash the guns downstream. With the grapple in place the other end was secured to the bundle of guns and tossed into the river where it sank out of site. Getting back in the truck they were at the boarder crossing twenty minutes later Crossing was a formality as both said they were Canadian citizens and both had ID to show this. The ID was fake, but of such high quality that it would take an expert to prove that it wasn't real. The ID's were part of the legends that had been supplied by the organization and showed both men as Canadian. Sean didn't think that they would have been flagged by the US authorities as there was no real way for the organization to explain their existence so that information most likely would not have been leaked to the authorities. It was a risk, but a small one, and they had to get into the US. After stating that they were only visiting Maine for a few days, and verifying that they weren't looking for jobs they were waved through and were in the town of Calais Maine.

Sean headed up the river again staying with the highway until it no longer paralleled the river, then going off road again. It took longer than he expected to find the spot and they had to backtrack twice, but eventually Charley spotted the tape on the tree across the river. Sean searched the bank until he found the grapple and then slowly pulled on the rope to retrieve their guns. When the package was on shore he unwrapped everything and then with a rag wiped each and every weapon down, checking the actions to make sure they were fine. Loading everything back up in the truck and covering it all with a blanket, the two headed back to the road and then south. Sean pulled into the first motel he found and booked them a room using cash from the money Charley had taken from the bank in Boston. As soon as they had their gear in the room Charley fell on one of the beds and was asleep without even taking off his shoes.

Sean bothered to unpack and tidy up a bit first and when that was done he turned on the TV to catch the news. As with every other motel or hotel in the US this one offered CNN with its cable line up. Sean watched for thirty minutes looking for any news of him and his partner. With nothing on the national media he shut it off and went to bed. For now it was still just the organization hunting them, he had a feeling that would change.

The credit cards records were set to alert the organization of their use whenever any item was purchased. The truck bought by Sean set off the notification and this alarm was followed only minutes later by a call from the Lawyer called by Sam notifying the organization of the situation in Nova Scotia. With in minutes these two pieces of information were forwarded to the three stooges. They now had a confirmed sighting of the two renegades and it looked as if they were heading back to the US. As the FBI was due to release the information regarding the two men a decision was made not to alert the boarder patrol or customs. It was assumed that the FBI would have already alerted these agencies to be on the look out for the two men. The alert was a few hours two late but Carter had no way of knowing that.

As the extent of the events became known an emergency brief was prepared for the directors and the calls were made to inform the members that an update was ready. In all cases the update was done over the phone using code phrases to inform the three wise men of recent events and receive directions as to what to do. In each case the answer was to track and identify the renegades and when their location was assured report them to the FBI to allow the authorities to apprehend them. Once in custody they could be dealt with in a permanent matter but at this time no more organization resources to be used to deal directly with them. Another bloodbath like the one in Nova Scotia could cause more exposure than they could hide.

The three stooges left the stolen credit cards active and set up a team in a safe house with internet access to monitor and track the credit card use. They didn't expect any more information from this source, as they were sure that the two would assume the cards had been cut off and would stop using them. However stranger things had happened and the two may make a mistake, so every scrap of information that could be gathered would be a help.

The two men slowly moved south down the coast of Maine spending two days in Bar Harbor. Planning to head into Bangor the next day they got ready to hit the sack with Charley, as usual falling asleep the second his head touched the pillow. Repeating his nightly ritual, Sean turned on CNN for a last news fix and saw the breaking story just as the anchor was starting at the top to repeat what was known so far. The FBI was reporting that it had received and anonymous tip with regard to the attempted assassination of the president. Sean watched in horror as CNN displayed a shot of the house he and Charley had lived in. Sean sat in stunned silence as the news anchor went over the evidence that had been reported so far. Investigators had uncovered plans and pictures, reloading supplies and bullets and other materials that could all be linked to the attempted shooting, also the news report stated that there were two suspects rather than one and showed a picture of each. The pictures appeared to be driver's license photos although Sean was not sure. The only thing he could tell was that he and Charley were in far more trouble than they had been before. Now both the organization and the US government were hunting them, and their pictures were on TV. They were suddenly in danger from every person they could meet.

Sean turned the TV off and sat in the now quiet room thinking, and listening to Charley snore softly. This changed things drastically, Sean fully expected that at some point the authorities would stumble on either he or the lad in the investigation, they were too good not to. However, in all his time with the organization they had never given an agent up to the authorities, they had always dealt with problems internally. And the detail of information released to the media could only mean that the organization had released the information to the FBI. This indicated a level of angry that he had never seen before in his time with them. The missed hit must have been far more important than he thought it was for the organization to want them caught so badly that they would give them up to the FBI. He undressed and crawled into bed to get some sleep so he could think the problem over with a clear mind.

Charley awoke first and after his shower told Sean he was going out to get some breakfast.

"Don't do that, you need to turn on the news first," Sean ordered him gruffly.

Charley gave him a puzzled look but switched on the TV and tuned it to CNN. The lead story was still about him and Sean and it was still showing a picture of the house with reporters commenting on the information being slowly released by the FBI. The item that really caught Charley attention was the picture of he and Sean being displayed in the upper left corner of the screen for the world to see. Charley sat down on the bed his mind filled with the consequences of this. The organization had taken away his best protection, the fact that he was unknown, now everyone would be looking for his face.

"Are you okay lad?" Sean asked getting out of bed. "It's a setback not the end of the world, this just makes it harder for us not impossible. We'll need to be more careful but the most dangerous part is past us, we are already back in the US, we are on the enemies home ground so we don't have to try infiltrating. If this news had broken while we were still in Canada our task would be twice as hard, but we are here now."

"Yeah here now and trapped!" Charley replied bitterly. "What can we do now, the second we go outside someone is going to notice us and call the cops. And there is no way we can fight those odds."

"Stop being so pessimistic Charley. We simply disguise ourselves and keep on the move. When we travel we do it at night when it's dark and that will help."

Charley thought for a second about the new turn of events "Sean I have a few ideas, do you think those credit cards are still good?"

"I doubt it. By now the organization would have cut them off, why do you ask?"

"Because we need to go shopping. If we can't move as freely as we want that means we will need to be more self-sufficient. I was thinking that staying in motels is going to be very risky now so why don't we trade the truck in on a van and gear it up to camp in. I also need to get access to the internet so that we can do some more research and I don't think I want to risk any more libraries, I still remember the last one. That means I'll need to get the gear to remote connect, and I'll need a laptop."

"Lad what is this obsession you have with the internet?"

"Sean when you were with the organization how did you report?"

"Dead drops and voice mail, why?"

"Well when I was going through the factory they were teaching me to use newsgroups and bulletin boards to report in. So I need to be able to get online to access those. Then I can start looking for information that will help us out. If they were teaching me that it stands to reason that a lot of other agents use the same method. Maybe I can use this to our advantage."

Sean shook his head. "If you say so, I won't even pretend to understand it. But the van idea has merit so let's get working on it. First things first though, you stay here and I'll go out and get some stuff to help us disguise ourselves. Once that's done then we can go shopping."

"Cool, but can you get some food too? I'm starved."

"Glad to see your appetite is healthy, it means you're healing up fine. I'll get some first aid supplies too, it's past time we changed your bandage."

Sean went into the bathroom and had a shower but didn't shave, leaving his stubble to help hide his face. He also cut up one of the shower caps and took pieces and stuffed them between his lower cheek and jaw to fill out his lower face and make him look fatter. He combed his hair different and then put on his baggiest clothes, again to give the illusion of being overweight. Having done all he could do he took the silenced .45 and shoved behind his belt in the small of his back and left the motel. Charley took out his Sten and one of the silenced .380's and loaded them both, placing them close at hand in case anything went wrong. With that done he packed up the rest of their gear and started wiping down the room to remove their fingerprints. When he was finished everything he could do he sat near the window with the blinds closed peaking out to watch the parking lot, waiting for his partner to come back.

Sean drove slowly around the town scouting out stores, finding places to buy what he needed. After getting the layout of the town in his head he began making quick stops at drug stores and small convenience stores buying the items he needed a few at a time, spreading it out. At the last store he decided to take a risk and try one of the stolen credit cards to see what would happen. He was shocked when the transaction went through with no problems. He couldn't believe that the organization hadn't killed the cards yet. Still wondering what was going on he took his purchases and made his way back to the motel using a round about route to get there. When he entered the room he noticed Charley sitting by the window with the blinds closed and his sten close at hand. He smiled to himself realizing how far his young protégé had come in the last few weeks. He was starting to take precautions without having to be told what to do.

Sean dumped the bags out on the bed and motioned to Charley. "Come here lad and let's take a look at your wound, see how it's doing then well see about changing those boyish good looks of yours into something more forgettable."

After checking Charley's wound Sean declared it almost completely healed, swabbed it with alcohol and re-bandaged it using gauze and tape. Once done with that chore the two went into the bathroom and Charley stood in the shower while the older man cut and died his hair, as well they reshaped and died the eyebrows to match the hair color. Using plastic pads placed between the cheek and jaw his face was reshaped to look squarer. The last touch was changing his eye color with colored contact lenses. Charley surveyed himself in the mirror when it was all done and was surprised at how different he looked. Sean wasn't finished yet, he took one of the pillow cases and filled it with some cotton batten he had bought and then with a roll of gauze bandages he tied the contraption to the young man's waist, padding him up to make him look heavier than he was. As a last touch, Sean put a brace on his left leg to make him walk stiffly, and then pronounced the job finished.

It was now Seans turn and rather than die the hair he shaved it all off and then with a safety pin pierced his ear and put a gold stud in it. He replaced the pieces of shower cap with proper plastic pads to keep his face looking fuller. He was also going to grow a beard. To further help with his disguise he put an inflatable cast on his left arm and then put it in a sling. Once this was done he placed one of the silenced .380's in the sling.

"Now that's a good idea old man, and easy way to carry it but keep it hidden. I like that."

"Thank you lad, once in a while the old man has a good idea. It will also keep people from looking to closely at our faces when we walk down the street. If you are hurt or injured people always look at the injury not the face. In your case they'll be looking at your limp and in my case it will be my arm. And the police are looking for two armed and dangerous men not two guys that are hurt. In their minds, hurt people aren't dangerous. Now let's go see about getting rid of that truck and getting something else to drive around in."

During his shopping spree Sean had also picked up some hard side suitcases and the two men loaded the weapons into these. Charley placed them in the truck while Sean took a final look around the room and wiped everything down one more time. Leaving the key on the dresser they left and went looking for used car lots. Bar Harbor was a small town with not much in the way to choose from on the car lots they visited. With nothing else to do they headed towards Bangor, it being one of the larger cities they were sure they would be able to find something there.

The drive took a little over an hour but was through the countryside and was a very relaxing and enjoyable drive. Sean told Charley to stop at the first payphone he came to so that they could look up the car dealers in the area. The yellow pages had six pages of listings for the Bangor Brewer area and one caught Charley's attention right away.

"Sean look at this one, they sell campers and trailers as well as cars. Let's go take a look and see if we can find anything to in the way of a camper van."

Sean nodded in agreement and the two headed for the dealership, which was only a few blocks away. Once there, they took cruise around the lot and saw several vans that looked as if they would be suitable. Some were fully decked out as campers, while others had only the basics such as a bed or a sofa that converted to a bed. After a quick look through the lot they went back through at a slower pace taking a closer look. A couple of times a salesman offered to help them out, but Sean declined saying they were only looking for now. After few minutes they had it narrowed down to 2 Vans on the lot. One was a simple panel van with nothing on the outside to show it was set up for camping. Inside it had been set up with a settee that converted into a set of bunk beds along the left side of the Van. Along the right side was built a counter top with shelves that contained a sink and a two burner stove for cooking. Under the counter top there was storage for luggage or water jugs and a built in 12-volt electric cooler. Right at the back was a propane space heater. There were also two sunroofs with screens that could be removed if needed. One was over the driving compartment the other was in the middle of the van over the cooking area and was used for ventilation when preparing meals.

The second van was fully decked out as a camper. It had a raised roof to give standing headroom, contained a full kitchen area with stove, oven, sink and fridge. There was also a built in furnace and the dining area folded down into a double bed. At night another double bed could be set up in the raised roof so that the van could sleep four adults comfortably. To round it out the van even had a toilet so that it was truly a self contained unit.

With the choice down to two, Sean went and found a sales agent and in his best Canadian accented voice discussed the trade of the pickup truck for one of the two vans. Both vans were of late 80's vintage but were in excellent shape and had surprisingly low mileage. The truck was an early 90's model and the sales agent was eager to make a on the plain panel van camper as it was the cheaper of the two by a considerable margin. The salesman wanted the 4x4 plus $2,000. Sean and Charley talked it over and the idea of an even trade appealed to them. The truck was worth the same as the van so they talked with the salesman, bargaining him down to the truck plus $500. Sean made the deal using money from the hidden account, and forty-five minutes later they transferred their luggage and plates to the camper and drove off the lot. The best part of the exchange was that there were no electronic records of the purchase as it was a trade plus cash and they were using their Canadian plates from the rental car. The sales agent didn't even bother to send in the normal registration papers to the state motor vehicle office as he assumed they van was heading to Canada with the new owners.

After a stop for gas, groceries, and another one of Sean's shopping sprees at a hardware store, they were on their way with Charley driving. The old man sat in the back and unpacked and stowed the weapons and food in the various cupboards and storage areas. With the items he had purchased at the hardware store he began to fashion holders for several of the SMG's and handguns around various areas of the camper so that, while out of site, it was less than a seconds work to get them out and into action. When he was finished with his work he moved up front with Charley and handed him a soda from the groceries that had stocked up on.

"So, Lad where to next?" Sean asked in a satisfied voice.

"I need to get internet access but I need to be mobile as well. Do you think those cards are good for one more big purchase?"

"Yes I do, I think the organization is trying to use them to track us. What do you need?"

"I need a laptop computer, and a satellite setup. The speed won't be the same as I had in Vermont but it will still be better then dial-up and best of all I can use it anywhere."

"Okay lad if you say so, I'll leave the internet and computers to you. So what do you need and where do we get it?"

"I think we should head to Connecticut, there will be lots of electronics stores close to New York with all the commuters. I'll ask around and someone is bound to know of a place that sells what I want. Once we get the gear I can set it all up and we're mobile. Oh, just one thing, we'll probably have to by a portable generator to run the stuff off of. We can get that anywhere."

Sean looked at him with a quizzical expression. "You do understand lad that we have to cart all this gear of yours around and that we will be living in this van, right? How big is all this stuff going to be?"

Charley shrugged. "No idea, but it shouldn't be that big. We'll find out when we get it."

Sean shook his head. "Well you're driving lad so go where you like. Take it easy and don't get us pulled over now, I'm going to hop in back and take a nap." With that Sean crawled back and lay down on the settee and was asleep before a mile had passed.

Charley drove steadily obeying the speed limit at all times and trying to blend in with traffic. He was actually starting to enjoy himself and could almost forget the danger he was in. At one of the rest areas he pulled over and picked up a map and noticed that they would encounter toll roads at the southern end of Maine, but he could bypass these by getting off the interstate and traveling along the old number one route, which he did. Sean stayed in the back the entire time as the authorities were on the look out for two men so a lone driver would mostly be ignored. As he neared Portland he spied a strip mall with a satellite store and on an impulse he pulled into the parking lot to take a closer look.

Parking in front of the store he saw several banners advertising two way satellite internet service. He though for a moment then headed out of the parking lot heading north. Sean, alerted by the stop joined Charley up front and noticed the turn north.

"What's up lad?" he asked, his voice showing sudden caution.

"I found a place that sells satellites for internet connection and I remembered seeing a Staples store back up the road a bit. I'll go there and get a laptop and then pick up the satellite set. After that we find a place to get a portable generator and we're all set, we can stay in New England and do some research."

Sean thought for a second. "Okay, we'll get the gear you need but we won't be staying in New England. We'll hit a bunch of ATMs for cash advances until we've got a few hundred dollars then we head south. I don't want to stay in the area after all this shopping, the organization will be sending agents to search for us. We've used those cards as much as is safe for now and we've set up a pattern heading south which they will assume is a false trail so we will keep going that way

Charley nodded. "I know they'll know we're here, but think about it, we do a lot of spending and then we stop using the cards after a bunch of cash advances. They'll think we left using the cash we got to go somewhere else. We go into the woods camping for a bit and in a couple of weeks they stop looking thinking we left. The don't know that we have this camper yet so we should be okay."

Sean liked the logic of it and contemplated it for a second. "No lad we'll leave the area, get down south someplace and then do some camping. Now let's get your gear, where was that Staples store?"

Twenty minutes later they were in the staples store discussing laptops with a sales clerk. When Charley explained his needs were mostly internet related the clerk tried his best to sell him a desktop model as it would be cheaper and more powerful for that application. Charley, however explained his need for compactness and portability and insisted on a laptop. In the end they settled on a mid-level model that had all the features Charley was looking for, although he declined the extended warranty. Adding a spindle of recordable CDs to the purchase, Sean paid with one of the organization's gold cards and they left the store.

On the way back to the satellite shop Sean drove so that Charley could set up the laptop and get it ready to run, setting up all his preferences. When they arrived at the satellite shop, Charley took the laptop into the store with him so that they could be sure they bought a compatible system. The sales agent assured them that al the systems would work just fine but suggested going with Direct Star as it was the cheaper of the systems with a better monthly rate on the internet access charges. He also convinced them to take the basic TV plan as well, as the bundled price was the same as the internet alone price. Even though they had no TV at the time Sean took the deal as it might turn out useful down the road. They settled up, paying for the system, and the monthly fees three years in advance, all in one lump sum. Sean used his old Vermont address for billing purposes and the only snag came when the sales agent insisted that for the warranty the company had to install it. Sean and Charley simply wanted to walk out of the store with the gear as they were putting it in the van and not installing it in a house. It took a little time to make the sales agent understand why they did not need an installation as they were traveling. The sales agent wanted his technician to install it in the camper but the last thing the two wanted was for the salesman to know what they were driving. In the end the salesman agreed that under the circumstances they could simply take the equipment. Charley did have the sale agent set up the satellite in the store and hook it up to his computer so that they could ensure it was working and get the internet account created. This also served to satisfy the sales agent that the gear was in working order and had the young man sign the slip saying that before he left the store.

Once the equipment was all packed up in the van the two continued south with Charley behind the wheel. "Where to Sean? Do you have a place in mind or should I just start driving?"

"Let's go to Tennessee lad. I hear it's nice there. We can go to the Great Smokey National Park and I can spend a few days communing with nature while you do what ever it is you do with those new gadgets of yours."

Charley chucked at Sean's comments. "As you command oh ancient one," he said jokingly, poking fun at his friends dislike for computers.

"Ancient one is it? That's the problem with today's youth, no respect for their elders," Sean retorted with mock indignation.

Charley laughed. "So how do we get to Tennessee and this park of yours?"

Sean opened the map book of New England he had purchased and began scanning the route they would need to take. "For now keep heading south on Route One until we get into New Hampshire, but if you see a Wal-Mart along the way pull in and we'll get a US atlas. Then we can plan the fastest route."

"Sounds like a plan to me."

Chapter 10

Immediately after the attempted assassination Holly spent every working minute of her day tracking the posts on bulletin boards. After a couple of days she had come across several hundred posts that kept mentioning two renegades. She and her immediate supervisor had gone to see General Donavan soon after she had found the posts, thinking it might be related to the attempt on the president's life, however the general was skeptical as it was dealing with two people and not one. All the official reports to date mentioned one assassin and that was the presumption the Secret Service and FBI were working under. The lone gunman theory was once again popular in DC and the general didn't want to upset the apple cart so he didn't pass along the information to the Secret Service or FBI. He did ask that he be briefed regularly on the data that was gathered as it might be another domestic terrorist issue that the FBI would need to check out, but until further notice this was a low priority matter and they should concentrate on looking for information relating to a single person.

Holly had set spock to work on finding the people posting but in every single case the trace ended in public locations, most often libraries. She was unable to find a single instance of one of the postings coming from an IP that had been assigned to a personal account. It seemed strange that all of the posts she was now monitoring seemed to be coming from public computers. After a week she had isolated all the different postings. There were occasionally posts that were random but for the most part they seemed to be almost regular reports originating from libraries clustered in regions or towns. Using a map she had plotted 200 cities and towns whose public internet access points showed as originating postings. All but two of these were in the US, the remaining two both came from small towns in the Canadian province of Nova Scotia.

Now knowing where the posts were being made on a regular basis, she set spock to monitor the sites and let her know when a new post was made. The posts clearly indicated a dedicated network of people that were actively searching for two people. No reference had ever been made to a name other then the two renegades, and no information was posted that would give her a clue as to who the two renegades might be or why they were being searched for.

One morning spock popped up with a report of a post in the New York City area that made reference to something termed the "attempt in Boston". Holly rushed the information to her boss and the two spent the rest of the day cross-referencing the database of posts they now had to look for some type of pattern. At the end of the day a report was drafted and sent up the chain of command with the stated opinion that there was another group of people, so far unknown to the government, that were looking for two people they blamed for the assassination attempt on the President of the United States. The report noted the lack of positive information on who the group consisted of or how many members it had, and also it lacked any detail on the two people in question. It was assumed the two were both male but even this could not be confirmed. The report created more questions than it answered and still didn't prove that the group or the two renegades were in any way related to the president's assassination attempt.

Holly went back to her desk and logged off her system to head home for the night. Another long exhausting day with nothing to show for it other then more questions. The frustration was beginning to get to her and she was considering asking to be put on another case. It looked as if this one was going nowhere fast. If the two renegades mentioned in all the web posts were indeed the men responsible for the assassination attempt, they had disappeared from site, and it didn't look as if any one was going to be able to find them anytime soon. She shut off her desk lamp and headed for the door. She had no idea that her work was suddenly about to become very important.

To the south of Fort Meade, in the treasury building of Washington, DC, another woman was ending her working day as well. Andrea was back at her desk after being cleared by the doctors to work. Her leg was still stiff but was healing nicely, the surgeons had been as careful as they could when removing the bullet and the scaring was minimal. She had consulted a plastic surgeon but nothing more could be done and her leg would forever carry the scar of the bullet wound.

The bullet its self was in the FBI evidence room at the Hoover Building waiting for the time when it would be used in a trial against whoever was eventually indicted for attempting to assassinate the President of the United States. That they would eventually catch the person was not in something anyone doubted as no assassin in the history of the US had ever taken a shot at a president and gotten away. They would eventually catch the man, it was just a matter of time As to how useful the bullet would be that was still up in the air as there were no rifling marks at all on it so it would be almost impossible to match it to a rifle barrel. As they still hadn't found the rifle yet even that was a moot point.

A panel of experts had gone over the bullet and all had agreed that the round had been saboted, it was the only explanation for no rifling marks on the round. Tests were performed to prove the theory and the results were close enough that they were added to the case file and would remain there until positive information as to how the bullet had no marks, surfaced. Everyone hoped that the perpetrator would be caught alive so that they could confirm the theory.

All of this information was also in the secret service file on the case to which Andrea had access, as she was assigned to the case. On the way home from work she used a dead drop to leave a copy of her notes from the investigation so far. The case had gone cold and it looked to the FBI and Secret Service as if the shooter had simply dropped of the face of the earth, even the release of the information from Vermont hadn't helped the search

After dropping the notes she went to the supermarket to pick up some items for supper, using the time to check for a tail. This was now an instinctive habit for her after her time working for the organization, she could not afford for anyone to find out she lead a double life. With her shopping done she headed home to supper and a hot bath.

At 1 AM a homeless man shuffled down the sidewalk stopping every few yards to inspect the ground for cigarette butts or any other useful items that other might have thrown away. During one of these frequent inspections he expertly emptied the dead drop that Andrea had filled the day before. With the information in his pocket he shuffled on a few more yards then ambled to the bus stop at the corner to catch a ride into DC. He had six more drops to service before 6 AM and then make sure he had all the packages at the secure mail drop before 7.

He had been doing this for the past five years and had never once come even close to being caught. There was a large population of homeless in the DC area and it was the perfect way to move around. His disguise was perfect, homeless people were ignored, even by the police. If anyone did suspect him of anything he only had to begin begging for change and the person would hurry off. The biggest danger he faced was the prospect of being mugged by another homeless person which was attempted several times a year as his clothing while well worn and shabby was cleaner then the average street persons and this was enough of a reason to try and take it from him. His training, and the fact that while he looked like a bum he was far from being one, and in excellent shape, allowed him to always fight off the attackers. He actually enjoyed these fights as they gave him a work out and served to help keep his senses sharp and alert.

The 3 stogies stopped at the secure mailbox and picked up the nights drops. With the information in hand they headed to the facility to begin the days work. After checking with the on duty supervisor of the facility and getting an update on the last days happenings they retired to their office and began going over the gathered information. The first package the opened was from Andrea as she was working on the most important investigation. They slowly worked through all the packages and then opened their laptops to download the electronic information gathered at home into the facilities main frame. Another typical Saturday was underway, updating ongoing operation files and seeing to the planning of new operations.

Holly was sitting at her desk as usual, surfing the news sites when she was first saw the breaking news story regarding the presidential assassination attempt. She went to the CNN streaming news site and watched the new report that the FBI was now stating there were two men involved in the assassination attempt on the president. The news reporters were showing pictures of a house in Vermont and saying that the FBI had confirmed the two men had lived and planned the attempted in the house, which was now being searched for clues. There were two men involved in the plot; it suddenly hit her that she had been right all along about the posts. The two renegades were indeed the men that had attempted to kill the President of the United States.

On a hunch she began reviewed the data from spock and was troubled by something that she couldn't quite put her finger on. After a few minute she realized that there were no new posts from Canada. They had been sending in daily posts and then today nothing had shown up, or the day before for that matter. On a hunch she did a websearch for news media in Nova Scotia and found reports of the gunfight in Kinston. A quick use of spock regarding the gunfight revealed it was a national story in Canada but due to the recent FBI release it had not drawn a lot of coverage in the US. Such an event in a relatively quiet community, in a country with very strict gun laws, was bound to be national news and checking the websites of the major papers she found reports concerning the shootout. The details were sketchy and limited but from eyewitness accounts there were a total of five people involved all men. One young man, three people in their late 20's or early 30's, and one middle-aged man. Everyone agreed that the young man was unarmed, the middle-aged man had a machine gun, and the other three all had handguns that may or may not have had silencers on them. Here the details began differ. Some stated that everyone was shooting at the young man while others stated that the three with handguns were shooting at the young man while the older man was shooting at the three with handguns. What was confirmed for sure was that two were dead and the other three had left the scene in one car. It was speculated that all but the middle-aged man were wounded in some way but there was no way to prove this. After reading a few more news reports Holly was sure that the young man and middle aged man were both the two renegades mentioned in the posts and the two the FBI were searching for.

She was euphoric that she had been right and her search engine had found the information long before anyone else. It was a validation of her work and in government service that was important. As she was mentally patting herself on the back and getting her notes together to pass on to the higher ups, her phone rang, it was her boss telling her that the General wanted her in his conference room ASAP. She smiled thinking that he wanted an update on her search data in light of the new information released by the FBI. She locked her terminal, gathered her notes and headed for the elevator humming to herself.

Her boss was waiting for her at the door to the conference room when she arrived, with a concerned look on his face. He opened the door for her and as she entered, she was suddenly struck that the room was full and the people there were all department heads or their direct assistants. And they were all starring at her. She froze in the doorway until the Major nudged her from behind moving her into the room. He guided her to the last two available seats holding her chair for her as she sat down, then sitting down him self and apologizing to the assembled people for being late. Everyone was still starring at Holly.

The General brought the meeting to order and quickly recapped the information that the FBI had released to the media adding in those items that had been withheld such as the saboting of the 30-caliber round to fit in a 50-caliber rifle. It was deemed by the FBI that this data should not be made public. There were also a few other minuet details that were held back and were used to identity anyone calling in claiming information about the case or even responsibility for the crime. This was standard procedure in all cases to avoid anyone simply reading about the crime and then claiming responsibility to gain notoriety. Looking up from his notes he looked around the table and then starred directly at Holly. "I'm sure everyone is wondering why a junior staffer such as Miss McClare is doing at a meeting of this nature." Heads around the table nodded. "I'm going to let her tell you. Miss McClare would you fill everyone in with the information you have given me, along with anything new you've obtained in the last twenty-four hours?"

Holly cleared her throat, looked at her boss, who smiled at her and gave a barely perceptible nod indicating he was confident of her ability to pull off the briefing and then shuffled her papers into order and began reading directly from her notes avoiding eye contact with everyone. It took several minutes for her to covert he material to date, ending with the news of the firefight in Canada.

"Why am I just hearing about this now, Miss McClare?" the General demanded.

"I found this data just before you called the meeting sir."

The general nodded then looked around the room and asked for input concerning the information given by Holly. There was a lively discussion for a few minutes, focused mostly on Miss McLares speculation that there was a non government group that was previously unknown by anyone, hunting the two men. Most found the very idea that any group that was the size that her information indicated it to be could escape the notice of the United States federal enforcement agencies. However the data could not be explained any other way, there was a group of people in over 200 cities posting information to the internet concerning the two men the FBI were looking for. In the end a consensus was reached that they were dealing with a domestic terrorist group but until they had more proof then internet posts they were going to proceed slowly and with caution. The General directed that a working group be put together to prove or disproof the existence of this group and what, if anything they had to do with the prime suspects in the assassination attempt. After it could simple be individual conspiracy theorists passing ideas around to each other, stranger things had happened. To the surprise of everyone The general placed Holly in charge of the working group.

"With all due respect sir," Interjected Sam Watson, the deputy director of the NSA, and a career civil servant. "I don't think she has the experience to lead such a group. I would suggest she be second in command and some one more senior run the group."

"Someone like you Sam?" Asked the general quietly.

"Well no not me, I am too busy but I could offer one of my senior aides to give some guidance to Young Miss McClare."

"I'm sure you could Sam." The General replied dryly. "But not this time. Miss McClare is in charge and everyone will assist her in anyway she requires. Miss McClare I want to be briefed daily at 16:30 hours on your efforts. I want you to set up a working group, pick whomever you need and I like you and the Major to me at 16:30 today. I want this done and done soon. One further thing Ladies and Gentleman, the information concerning a possible domestic terrorist group does not leave this room. Miss McClare I want all of your data secured on hard disk with no paper copies to anyone until we confirm or deny the existence of this group of yours. Is everyone clear on that? Fine then, any other business people?"

When no one responded the General adjourned the meeting and everyone began filing out. Holly was stunned with her new responsibility and had no idea what to do next. The General was not known for tolerating failure very well. It did please her to have the job and he felt she could handle it, so she began thinking how to handle the job. She was determined to have a plan in place by 4:30 so that the general would not be disappointed with her.

Heading back to her desk she was stopped by the deputy director. "Miss McClare I'm sure you have no idea of the immensity of the job ahead of you," He began condescendingly "so I'd like to suggest that you take one of my assistants on board to help you out and offer some guidance. Jason is not too busy and he would be able to work with you on a daily basis, you would of course be in charge, he would merely offer his guidance. I'll send him over to give you a hand."

Holly had heard the rumors about Sam Watson since the day she started at the NSA. He had been a civil servant his entire life and was always taking the credit for other people's successes and deflecting his failures on to others. No matter what operation was going on it seemed that he managed to insinuate one of seemingly endless supply of personal assistants into the group and end up controlling it in the end. Suddenly she was determined that that would not happen to her.

"Thank you sir that is really kind of you. What is Jason's background with computers?"

The question threw Watson. "I'm not sure Miss McClare, but you can ask him when you see him."

"That's' great but if he doesn't have computer expertise he won't be any use to me at all. Send him down anyway and I'll see if the group can use him."

"Miss McClare I was thinking more of you using Jason's administrative abilities to help you guide the working group. He'll prove to be invaluable in helping you recruit the people you will need."

Holly was sure his help would be focused on making sure his bosses favorites get involved in the working group, so that in the end, Sam Watson was in charge and got the credit, if there was any. She was also sure that if they failed Sam's people would have fully documented prove of her incompetence. "I'm afraid, Mr Watson, I don't have use for anyone without computer skills but if Jason has them, I can use him."

Sam smiled. "I'll send him over to you directly, have a good day."

As she stepped off the elevator her boss was waiting for her. "So how does it feel to be in charge of your own team?"

"Feels pretty good."

"Well you proved you can get the job done, but you'll need some help on this one. Please pick a team of people from the duty roster and submit it to me to get them cleared to work with spock. You can pick anyone you want, but before they can work here we have to make sure they get cleared, that will be my job not yours, okay? I'll let you get to work on you plan and your briefing for the General"

"Sure thing boss," Holly said and headed to her desk to get to work on her new project. She started by making a list of what needed to be done and then writing down various ways to carry out the tasks. As she was checking the staff directory to find the people that she needed Jason showed up. He pulled up a chair from another desk and sat down next to her and immediately began to read over what she was working on.

"Hello Miss McClare, Mr Watson says you and I will be working together for a while. Do you mind if I call you Holly?"

"Go right ahead, is it all right if I call you Jason?"

Jason smiled at her. "Of course it is. So what are we working on right now?"

Holly noticed the 'we' remark in the question and decided that there was no time like the present to find out how long Jason was going to be with her group or if was going to be in the group at all.

"So what is your computer background Jason?" She asked throwing him off balance.

"Computer background? I'm not sure I understand."

"Well every member of the team will be working with a computer to try and find this group and assist the FBI in the search for the two suspects, so I need to know what your background is to slot you into the group."

"I don't see what relevance my computer skills have to so with administering the group, Holly."

Holly looked at him. "Administering the group? No one will be doing any administering of the group Jason. Everyone working with me will be doing computer searches trying to track down whoever is making these posts on the net and looking for clues to the two fugitives. There really isn't going to be anything to administer. I'm sorry if Mr Watson gave you the wrong impression before he sent you down, but there is nothing for you to administer here."

Jason was shocked at this. "Well, surely you agree that someone has to lead the group, and I have the experience to do just that. My help will be invaluable to you. Why don't I just look over the information you have so far."

Holly smiled and opened a page of computer code on her screen then turned the monitor so that Jason could see it. He sat there for thirty seconds staring blankly at the screen full of computer code. "Holly, what is this?"

"This is what the group will be working on of course." She answered in a voice so sweet sugar wouldn't melt in it.

Jason shook his head. "But how is this related to the group? Where is the information that we are supposed to be tracking down?"

"There is no information yet Jason. We have to write a computer program to find the information we are looking for. As I said everyone working in the group needs to have computer skills."

"What about when you start to find information, who will be collating it?"

"Again that will be something we will program the computers to do Jason, this group will be working together, no one is going to be leading or administering anything at all. And if there is to be an administrator it will be me."

"With all due respect Holly, it's clear that you lack administrative experience. Someone needs to be in charge of the group otherwise its chaos. People will do as they please unless given clear, concise, directions to work under. I feel that you should allow me to guide the group and help you manage things."

"Jason I appreciate your offer, but unless you can write a computer program you are no use to the group. We will be working on code here and we will have no time to answer questions. I don't have the time to teach you and I don't have time to answer any more questions. Thank you for the offer but you can go back to your office now I have to get to work finding the staff I need to get this program written."

Jason sat there stunned as Holly began working on the computer again. "What do I tell Mr Watson?"

"I don't know and I don't have time to help you come up with a creative answer Jason, I really have to get to work. Thanks for stopping by," she said dismissing him.

Jason shook his head and headed back to his office. Once he was out of site, Holly shut down the program she had open and went back to the staff directory to find the people she needed to help her with her task. There was no way she was letting Jason in, he would take over and she would spend too much time answering stupid questions and briefing other people. The team had to be kept small and closely knit so that they could all work together. She needed specialists, of which the NSA had in abundance. A few more minutes of going over the staff directory and she had a list of possible names, some military some civilians which was the mix in the NSA anyway so it shouldn't present a problem. Most of the military people were used to working closely with civilians at the NSA, so she didn't see any problems with mixing them on her team, as she now thought of it.

She wrote out the list of names and walked to her boss' office to have him make the arrangements to get the people temporarily transferred to her section. It took a little over an hour for a background check and the approval to clear them for spock. Matt let Holly know the new people were on their way down. With that done she went to the mini boardroom that her section had for meetings and waited for the people to arrive. The new team began assembling fifteen minutes later with the military members showing up first as she expected would happen. One good thing about the military was that when you gave them an order they followed it and got on with the job. The civilians being a little more relaxed showed up about five minutes later, having stopped to go to the bathroom and get a fresh cup of coffee on the way. Holly had set up a very small team with the mix being two civilians, and two military personal.

The military people had reported to her boss first, coming to attention as they did so. He redirected them to Holly, explaining that she was in charge of the group. They again reported to Holly snapping to attention once again. Holly wasn't used to this and simply asked them to have a seat and relax, the meeting would start in a few minutes. As soon as she had all the people together with the Military on one side of the table and the civilians on the other, with each person wondering why they had been called to the meeting. The military personal were from the communications and security sections, while the civilians were from computer services and operations sections. She had picked the people based on two criteria, their computer skills and what they did in their respective sections. Every person at the table had a master's degree with one holding a PhD. There was a lot of brainpower sitting at the table right now and all of them waiting for Holly to tell them why there were sitting in a conference room in the basement of the NSA.

She looked over her new team one at a time trying to get a feel for them. On the civilian side she had Doris Mayweather, a 31-year-old programmer with a double masters in Mathematics and Computer Science. She was the perfect picture of a '70's urban housewife, hair up in a bun, glasses, and a floral pattern dress. One look at her and you would never guess she worked at the NSA. Next to her was John Atkinson, from operations, another double major, this time in psychology and computer science. He was what could best be described as average. He was around 5'10" with brown hair; wearing black pants a polo shirt and a sport coat. There were no distinguishing marks at all and he seemed to be totally relaxed. Holly got the impression that he could stand in a room full of people and never be noticed once. Across the table from them were Marine Corp Gunnery Sergeant William Ortega, and Air Force Sergeant Mary Erwin. The Gunny was a fireplug of a man with the obvious look of a weight lifter to him. At 5'7' he wasn't very tall but he would stand out in a crowd just from the width of his shoulders. His specialty was computer security and spent his days trying to create and then break computer security programs; he had a PhD in computer science. Mary was a very pretty woman in her early forties with shoulder length hair worn loose in a very unmilitary fashion. She had a masters engineering degree in computer systems with a minor in mathematics. She worked in the cryptography department running and programming the supercomputers that the NSA used to break codes. It was a very diverse team, but one that she thought would be able to do the job very nicely.

"Hello, I'm Holly McClare and we will be working together for the next little while." She began with a trace of nervousness in her voice. "As we are all wearing our ID badges I think we can dispense with the name exchanges and move on to what the project is that you will be working on. We have been tasked with tracking and find information regarding to the Presidential assassination attempt. Preliminary reports indicate that there is another, as yet, unknown group also looking for the two suspects and it would appear they are ahead of us in the search. What we will be doing is searching the internet looking for data to either find this other group or prove that it doesn't exist. Each of you has your specialties and we will need all of them. From the military side we have communications and security experts. If I read your files right you are good at cracking codes and breaking into secure systems, correct?" The two military people nodded in unison. "And on the other side we have a computer expert and an operations man, so I think we have a balanced group here and we should be able to work well together. Before we all start does anyone have any questions?

Sergeant Erwin raised her hand "Yes Sergeant Erwin?"

"Ma'am, who will we be reporting to?"

"Well I guess to me, but I'd rather that you didn't report to me, just work with me."

"Yes ma'am, how should we address you, ma'am?"

"Please call me Holly. I'd like this to be an informal working group."

The two military people looked at her as if she had just told them to strip naked and run around the room. They were both sergeants, and they had spent their careers addressing people by rank or title. The thought of a working relationship being informal was an alien concept to them.

"Ma'am, I feel that I speak for those of us present when I say that a well established chain of command helps the flow of information." The Gunny stated in one of the deepest voices she had ever heard with a decidedly southern drawl.

"Yes Sergeant I am aware of that, however I am more comfortable working with peers, we're all have an equal input. That's the way we are going to work this group, we all have an equal input and we will all help each other out. If it makes you fell better to call me Miss McClare then please do so. But ladies and gentlemen let me make this perfectly clear from the outset, this is a team effort. We all take the same share of the glory or blame on this one, there will be no grandstanding. The General has asked me to find something for him and I will do just that. Our reports will go directly to the general from this group and he will be briefed daily at 4:30. Any other questions?"

"Thank you Miss McClare and uh, it's Gunny if you don't mind ma'am."

"Sorry Gunny, we don't have any Marines down here in the pit," she said, referring to the pet name given to the basement. "So anyone have any questions?"

"Just one thing," asked John Atkinson from the operations group. "I know why these people are here but why am I here. I'm an ops guy."

"John if I'm right and there is another group out there, they may well be a paramilitary ro similar type of outfit and we need you to tell us how these people think. I'll have you reading over transcripts and giving your opinion of them. As I understand it you have a masters in psychology?"

John simply nodded his head.

"So how does someone with a masters in psychology and computer science get into the operation directorate of the NSA?"

"For some reason someone thought I could read minds and thought this would be a good talent to have in the NSA," John answered with a straight face.

"If you can read minds then you are going to be very useful to us John. So let's break this down into what everyone will be doing. I have been tracking online message traffic since shortly after the shooting. From the messages it appears to be a concentrated group effort to locate two people referred to only as renegades. I say this is a concentrated effort by a group and we need to find out if this is true or not. All the posts are coming from public access terminals, libraries, schools, places that are open to the public and free. John I want you to read over the information I've already got and what ever else comes in to give me a professional option on if this is a organized group effort behind this or not. Doris I'd like you to build us a database to put all the information in, I'll leave it up to you how best to do it. Sergeant Erwin I'd like you to help search the net and find information, you'll also be doing a little decoding work to decipher what these people are saying to each other. I'm not sure if there is a code or not but I'd like you to look into it. Gunny I'd like you to try and track down where the messages are being posted from and see if you can set up some computer security programs to track these people to actual computer stations.

Once we know where these people are logging in from maybe we can find some of them. Since there are only five of us on this project we will need to stay tight and communicate to make sure no one is missing anything so if anyone has an idea or notices anything that someone else missed please speak up. The general is expecting results and fast. We will have our own little section of the bullpen set up on this floor with five terminals, they are on their own network with secure VPN access to the NAS main frame and independent net access, so that we don't leave footprints as the NSA when we surf. Oh that reminds me, Gunny your first job it so secure our systems. When you're not doing anything else I'd like you to be searching the net and reading message posts. What information I do have is saved online and here are your access ID's and passwords to access the database. I want everything we do to be online and saved in the files I've created for security. Any questions?" Holly passed them all slips of paper with the log-in info on them.

Everyone shook their heads and headed out to the floor following Holly to their desks where they would be working until the project was completed or they were once again re-assigned. Everyone memorized their log in information them tore the papers to small pieces and put them in a waste can that was marked as a burn bag, meaning each night the contents of it were thrown into an onsite incinerator to destroy them. Holly nodded at this instinctive measure, knowing that she had a good team and they were security conscience already. Once everyone was logged in they brought up the folders Holly had created and were astounded at the amount of data already stored there.

"Ma'am, how long have you been working on this?" asked Gunny.

"I started working on it a couple of weeks or so after the assassination attempt, why do you ask?"

"Ma'am there is an awful lot of data here," he said with a note of new found respect in his voice.

Holly chuckled. "I can't take all the credit, most of the work was done by a search program I call spock and it works pretty well. Since you've all been cleared for it, I'll show you the program."

She spent the next few minutes showing her new team her program and how it ran. She set it to do a fresh search for the word renegades on news groups and came up with several new references. The group was stunned at the speed of the program and how easy it worked.

The Gunny looked up with a shocked expression on his face. "You!" he exclaimed in a voice loud enough to make everyone jump. "We've been trying to find you for over a year!"

"Excuse me?" asked a shaken Holly.

"I'm sorry ma'am I spoke out of turn," the Gunny stated flatly.

"No Gunny I don't think you did. Say what's on your mind," Holly said in an even voice, but left no doubt that this was not a request.

"Yes ma'am. My section commander has tasked us with finding out who or what was raiding the secure government databases. This program has been in everything on the net and we haven't even come close to finding a way to stopping it. I've spent the last eight months trying to build a firewall that this thing couldn't get through and failing everytime. I couldn't even trace it back to where it was coming from. And all this time it's been coming from this room. My section commander is going to pitch a fit over this."

"Well Gunny the name of the program you were trying to find is Spock. However, you can't tell anyone about this program. It's classified even within this building. You will all be surprised to hear that your security clearances have all be moved up so you can work with this program. And under no circumstances are you to mention the existence of this program to anyone."

"Any other little surprises for us?" John asked.

"If there is it's all in the data in the files. Right now those files are all stored on the computer in the corner there." Holly pointed to the back wall of the cubical they were in. "That system is a stand alone and not connected to anything. Once Gunny has our security up and running we'll get it on the network here so more than one person can access it at a time.

"Who wrote this program?" Doris asked. "And are they on our side?"

"I built it and yes I am on your side." She was suddenly looking into four sets of eyes that regarded her in a new light. Everyone now knew why she was leading them and agreed with the choice. All doubts were now gone and they would get on with the job at hand, completely confident of the skills of their new boss.

Charley and Sean pulled into the campground, tired after the marathon drive from New England to Tennessee. They were staying in a National park in the mountains that had very little to offer in the way of amenities. As a result the people that were there were hardcore campers, or people with self contained RV's, out to live in the quiet of the wilderness. They were friendly but everyone stayed to themselves, after all, the solitude is why every one was staying in a wilderness campground. Because of this Sean and Charley hoped to spend time her unnoticed and un-recognized.

Charley had set up the satellite on the roof of the van spent the first two days reading posts of the bulletin boards of the Yahoo! news groups. He was fairly sure he had remembered the correct boards from his short time with the organization, and there were many posts discussing what the posts called 'two renegades'. No names were ever mentioned or used in the posts; everyone had an online user ID. This would make it harder to track down people but not impossible, or so Charley thought. The more he dug to find a name the less information he got. User accounts on the networks were protected by firewalls and encrypted databases. Charley soon found himself stuck and unable to get any further. He realized that he needed the services of a first class hacker if he was ever going to get any information from the user ID's so he changed tactics and went in a different direction.

He created his own account using a fake name and address and began making posts of his own trying to get information from some of the other posters. He dredged his memory for the procedures to be used in making reports online and then drafted a post hoping to get some reaction. If he remembered the code correctly he was telling the organization that he had sighted the two renegades in Maine and gave a description of the car they were in. He checked the board the next day and there was a response to his post. It was in the shorthand code used by the organization of course and if he had read it right it was asking for his current location and an update on the renegades.

Charley created his fictitious report detailing information the new information asked for. He put the location of this sighting in New Hampshire, in the White Mountains, and added in that he thought he had been sighted by the two renegades and his cover was blown. He requested immediate assistance to be dispatched. It took less than an hour for the answer to come back and it was a simply request for him to phone home. Charley called Sean from his endless wanderings around the campground to look at the posts.

"I've got them old buddy. They think we are in New Hampshire and being followed by one of the organization. I've asked for help and left it vague and they want me to call home. It should drive them nuts looking for us. I think I can string them along and get them to believe we are on the west coast in about a week or so. After that I'll stop making the posts and we'll see about finding some information that we can use against them."

"Charley you're playing with fire here, Lad. Is there anyway they can trace this back to you."

Charley shook his head, "No way. I couldn't break into the databases to find out who they were so there's no way they can do it either. And even if they did all they'll get is a fake name. I didn't use any information that could be traced back to us."

"Lad you be careful, the last thing we need is to be attacked by the Organization or the FBI in a national park."

"Don't worry Sean, it's all under control. Relax we're as safe as we're going to get in the US, right here."

"Fine lad, you keep playing with the computer I'm going to look around some more." With that Sean left to resume his endless wondering, looking for signs that they were in danger.

The posts Charley had sent had not gone unnoticed by Spock and were dutifully added to the building database, and an alert sent to Holly. The team had been together for two days and these were the first new posts to come in, she alerted Sergeant Erwin and John so as to get their input on them. Erwin had checked the database of posts looking for a code and it turned out that there was no code used, as such. The people writing the messages were using private shorthand to exchange messages. No names were ever used to name anyone at all, rather, obscure references were used to let people now what was being discussed. It took her less than two hours to figure out how to read the posts and get the right information out of them, and after that she spent her days simply surfing the net looking for similar messages to find other sources of information.

The two read over the messages and came up with very different reports for Holly

The Sergeant was excited as the reports indicated that the two suspects were in New Hampshire, while John viewed the messages as a false trail. She asked everyone to stop what they were doing for a second to concentrate on the new posts.

All of them crowded around Holly's desk. "Okay, the sergeant thinks we should send some people up to check this out and try to find these two before our competition does. John on the other hand thinks these messages are fake, so John why don't you tell us why."

"Well first of all these posts are different from the rest. These are new posts; I can't find any others coming from that user ID. I think it's someone trying to lay a false trail. Why, I have no idea."

"If you're right John, it adds a new dimension to the case," added Gunny.

"Why is that?" Holly asked.

"If John is right then it could mean a few different things It could be either the two suspects have done the same thing Holly did, found the posts of some shadowy group trying to find them and are trying to throw them off. Or they are part of the group it's self and have gone rogue. Or it could simply be someone that has nothing to do with either the two renegades or the group and really thinks this is all some kind of game and are joining in?"

John was intrigued by this line of reasoning. "Gunny I think you have stumbled onto something there, but deeper then you think. If they are, or were part of the group that's hunting them, and they took a shot at the President, it may be that now the rest of the group is pissed and wants them dead so they don't tell anyone about the existence of the group. Holly did you say there was a shootout in Canada near where some of the posts were coming from?"

"Yes there was, why?"

"That makes sense if it was a fight between our two guys and this group," the Gunny added in.

"So it looks as if Holly has been right all along about a group hunting the two suspects," added Erwin. "They want them dead for taking a shot at the president and exposing the group."

"Okay, but Gunny also mentioned that it might be someone that has nothing to do with any of this and thinks it's all just a game. What if that is what's really going on here?" Holly asked to make sure they discussed every possible scenario.

John shook his head. "I don't think this is random or accidental. I thing this is the two guys on the run, or at least one of them, and he's laying a false trail."

Doris jumped in. "Wait a second let's get it straight here, did the two suspects take a shot at the President on their own and upset the apple cart, or were they ordered to take a shot and missed, and now the group is pissed about that?" adding yet another level of complexity to the discussion.

This new thought shut everyone up for a second while they thought over the implications of an organization that had tried to have the President of the United States assassinated. It was a conspiracy theorists nightmare come true. If it was true what could be the motivation? Killing a head of state was a dangerous thing and killing the head of the worlds only super power was more than dangerous, it was stupid. The search for those responsible would never stop until they were found.

Gunny spoke first "So which way did it happen; did they go rogue, take a shot and miss, or were they ordered to take a shot and they missed and now have to be eliminated for failure?"

"Ladies and gentleman that's what we need to find out. John you think the posts are a fake lead, will the opposition think so too?" Holly asked.

"At this point I don't think they can afford not to take it seriously, so no, I don't think they think they are fake, I think they'll follow up on it."

"Okay I want you to head up to New England and look around. I don't expect our two suspects to be there but someone will be looking for them so see who shows up."

John nodded his head. "What action do you want me to take?"

Then question stopped Holly for a second. "When you say action, could you define what you mean, and please remember I'm really new at this so I won't be insulted by you explaining things to me?"

John chuckled admiring her honesty. "Thanks Miss McClare, do you know how long I have waited to hear someone tell me they didn't understand what I was saying." Holly's face turned red "What I'm asking is if the opportunity presents itself, do you want me to do anything at all, such as have a chat with someone, maybe bring someone back to talk to the general? And if I'm wrong and the suspects are there what do you want done about that?"

Holly nodded. "First can every one please call me Holly? To answer your questions I'd rather you didn't do anything other then just watch. If the suspects are there call the FBI and let them handle it. I don't want you to risk harm to yourself at, in fact if you think there's a chance that you could get hurt you should take someone else with you."

Her interest in his well being took John totally by surprise, it was the first time in his life that any supervisor had ever asked him to place his well being above the job. "Ma'am I assure that no harm will come to me. I never take unnecessary risks. If all you want is for me to take a look around then that's all I'll do. Just for the record though I'd like to point out I am very used to field operations and I am quite good at them so you really don't need to worry about me."

"John I sit in front of a computer and the most danger I've ever been in my life is from my own government wanting to arrest me and put me in jail. They gave me a job instead. If the information from Canada is correct these guys don't have much of a problem with shooting first and worrying about the clean up later. If the Gunny is agreeable would it be better to take him along?"

"If the Gunny is agreeable, yes it would be better to have him along. This is just a look and see job and a second set of eyes is always good to have. How about it Gunny, want to go for a drive in the country?"

The gunny smiled at the thought of getting away from a computer for a while. He was marine after all and he craved the outdoors. "I'd love to."

"Good, it's settled then. You two head up and take a look around to see who or what shows up. John, since you are the expert I'll leave it up to you to set up check in times. Just leave me some notes before you go so that I'll know what's going on. I'll include this in the brief to the General today and you can take off in the morning. You and the Gunny might as well get together and do whatever you need to do, or get what ever you need to get, to get ready for tomorrow.

The two headed to the armory for a sidearm planning as they went. Both agreed that even on a scouting mission like this being armed made sense. John signed out a Walther chambered for .32 caliber along with hollow point rounds, a sound suppressor, and two spare clips. Gunny got a Beretta 9MM, the same one issued to the marines on active duty, along with hollow points, a suppressor and two spare clips.

"Now why would you want to carry a little mouse gun like that, John?"

"Well Gunny, everyone has a preference and if you ask fifteen gun experts which is the best round to use I'm sure you'd get fifteen answers. Fact is that I like the small size of the Walther, it's easy to carry and easy to hide. The .32 round is slower than the 9 so it's easier to suppress the sound and as long as you can hit your target even a .22 can take down a man. One other thing I like is that because the .32 is a slower round it doesn't usually go through the target like a 9MM has a tendency to do."

"Yeah everyone has a differing opinion, even in the corps. My drill sergeant was always telling us about the old Colt .45's that they used to use, some still do, and how good they were for stopping a man. He said he had no use for the 9mil; it was too light to do the job right. But the range instructor said that the 9mil was better then the .45, more reliable and you could carry more rounds. Personally I'm not much for handguns at all, I'd rather have a good M16 with me, but it's kind of hard to carry one of those around with you, people tend to notice and point at you. I do like having the fifteen rounds though, sort of makes me feel safer."

"Gunny if we get into a situation where we need the fifteen rounds in your gun then we didn't do our job right. This is all about seeing, but not being seen. Most of the time I don't even carry a gun, but what Miss McClare said is true; these guys will have no problems with shooting first and finding our who we were later. That's the only reason for the side arms. By the way when was the last time you were on the range?"

"John I'm a marine, I'm on the range every week. How about you?"

"Yesterday," John answered heading toward the elevator to head back to his desk.

For the rest of the day everyone concentrated on searching the net or trying to find the people making the posts. Gunny had written a program to back track the IP address of the people making the posts hoping he could get some information from them. No one thought much about the chances of that working but you tried every thing and hoped something worked.

At 4:30 Holly briefed the general in his office with the information they had found so far and the actions she had taken, he agreed with the trip to New Hampshire and agreed with the orders the two men had been given. As he listened to the brief he noticed that the young lady always spoke of her team members and listed everything as a collaborative effort. She took no credit for anything and this was a very refreshing change. She even openly told him of her lack of success so far, which he mentally disagreed with. So far her group had given him more to work with on the assassination attempt than the rest of the NSA combined. It was a shame that the actual arrest would fall to the FBI and they would get the credit for the case after all the work this young lady had done. No one would or could ever know how much she had contributed, well he would place a letter of commendation in her file for the work, which was the least he could do.

John picked up a car from the motor pool as he left, asking the mechanic on duty for specific make and model of import, with a set of New Hampshire plates on it, and went straight to his place to pack. As soon as he was ready he called the Gunny to make sure he was ready to go, getting an affirmative he locked the door to his apartment and headed over to pick him up. The Gunny was waiting for him by the side of the road, standing ramrod straight looking every inch the military man, even wearing jeans, T-shirt and a denim jacket. He had put on a ball cap to cover his regulation marine haircut but there was nothing he could do to hide his military bearing.

"Gunny tossed his bag in the back and got in the passenger side, putting on his seat belt. "I thought the only cars the government owned were big Fords or Chevys. When did they start picking up sweet little imports like this one?"

Sam Watson was still angry that Jason had been so casually rejected by that slip of a girl. Thirty years in public service had taught him how the game was played and how easily it could be manipulated. This was one occasion when all that experience was completely useless simply because a mere girl that had no idea how the game was played. He had taken his concerns to the general the second Jason had reported back to him that he had been, in effect, tossed out, stating that Miss McClare was letting the group run wild with no one in control. He pointed out that Jason was a proven entity with years of administrative experience and he would be able to help the group make better use of the information they gathered so as to brief the general in a more timely fashion. For the first time since the General had taken command of the NSA he ignored his deputies advice, which was another shock for Watson. Having spent the last fifteen years at the NSA moving up the ranks, hitting the ceiling for a civilian in the deputies slot—the director of the NSA was always a military man—he had gotten very used to getting his way so that he was almost running the place. So far every director he had worked under had listened to his advice and taken it, until now. This was not something that he could allow to happen as it would weaken his standing and others would soon get the idea that projects could be run without one of his numerous assistants being involved in an administrative role.

He mulled over ideas in his head trying to come up with a way that would force the young lady to give in out of sheer frustration. He settled on one of his tried and true tactics, that of having the person brief him personally on a regular basis and asking endless questions. He would waste their time and then suggest that this would be much easier if one of his own staff were involved in the group so that they could deal with the daily brief. After two or three wasted days they normally broke down out of frustration and took one of his assistants into the group.

Sam wrote up a memo requiring Miss Watson to brief him personally every day and to bring a printout of all data to each briefing so that he could look it over and stay up to date. When he was finished he called his receptionist to find Jason and have him come in.

"Yes sir?" Jason asked entering the office.

"Take this memo to Miss McClare and wait for her to read it. When she's done offer your services in this capacity so as to spare her the drudgery. Let me know how it turns out." Sam ordered.

Jason took the paper from his bosses out stretched hand and left the office, reading it as he went. He broke into a big smile waiting for the elevator knowing how annoying his boss could be with briefers. Miss McClare was in for a rough time of it.

"Hello Miss McClare," Jason said approaching her desk. "I have a memo from Mr Watson and he has asked me to get confirmation from you that you understand it," he handed Holly the paper.

Holly read the memo with no expression on her face but cursing in her mind. She could see Jason out of the corner of her eye and noticed the smug look on his face. "The memo states that I am to brief Mr Watson Dailey at 11 AM, I assume that means today as well, correct?"

"Yes that's correct. It's already 10:30 so if you could get things together as quickly as possible and be ready for 11 that would be great. If I can help in anyway I would be glad to," Jason offered.

Holly knew this was Watson's way of getting his assistant into the group. He would waste her time and then suggest that Jason give the briefings to spare her time. She had heard the stories about his legendary abuse of staff briefers. This time however it would be different, she had been given a job to do and she was going to do it. No one was going to sabotage her work simply because they didn't believe her theory about the second secret group. Well she would take this one in stride and find a way to beat him at his own game.

"Please let Mr Watson Know I'll be there at 11 sharp, thank you." With that Holly turned back to her computer screen and continued working, effectively ignoring Jason.

"Is there anything that I can help with to get you ready for the briefing, Miss McClare?"

"No thank you," Holly replied with out even looking up from her keyboard, continuing to type away.

Finally realizing that he was not about to fluster the young lady Jason left the computer center and reported back to his boss letting him know that the memo had been delivered.

At 10:58 AM Holly reported to the receptionist for Mr Watson, stating she was there to give a briefing.

"Please have a seat Miss McClare, the deputy director is running a bit behind this morning and he will be with you as soon as possible."

Holly nodded and sat down in one of the hard plastic chairs in the room. So this was how it was going to start, keep her waiting and wasting her time. There was nothing she could do about it of course, he was her superior and she had to wait for him. She wondered what other tricks he had up his sleeve?

"Miss McClare please go in now." The receptionist told her 14 minutes later.

When Holly entered the office Watson was sitting at his massive oak desk with Jason hovering directly behind him. "Sorry for the wait Miss McClare, I'm running a bit behind to day. " The deputy director said without a trace of sincerity in his voice. "So let me have the briefing papers and we'll get started."

"I'm sorry Mr Watson but there are no briefing papers, I will be delivering it from memory." She stated trying her first trick to derail Watson's plan

Sam was stunned, he has stated clearly in his memo that he was to be given a set of the briefing papers. This was so that he could go through them and pick holes in the briefing, ask useless questions and generally drag things out. With no set of papers of his own he was unable to do this.

"Miss McClare, I believe I was very clear in the memo regarding the briefing papers, do you have a problem understanding my orders?" He asked in his official voice letting her know he was upset.

"Oh yes sir it was very clear in the memo." Holly said in a pleasant tone.

"Then please explain to me why you have no papers for me." He said his voice raising slightly at the end. The smirk on Jason face also grew with each word his boss spoke.

"Orders from the General sir. He was very clear when the group was set up that there were to be no paper copies of the data."

"I'm sure you will agree Miss McClare that I would be the exception to that rule." Watson said with an edge to his voice. He could not believe that this mere girl was standing up to him.

"With all due respect Mr Watson, the General doesn't get a paper copy of his briefing so I don't see how I could make an exception for you, sir."

Seeing that she wasn't going to budge Watson conceded this issue and moved on. "Fine Miss Watson I'll take notes to keep track, begin your briefing."

"I'm sorry sir but the general's orders are very clear on this, there is to be no paper on this. If you take notes I can't brief you."

"Miss McClare you are trying my patience, do not presume to tell me whether I can take notes or not. Now begin your briefing," Watson ordered, putting a pad of paper and a pen on his desk with a flourish. The smirk on Jason's face was now too large to hide.

Holly knew the next words out of her mouth would determine her future but she had been given an order, which now contradicted her orders from the director of the NSA. "Sir I wish to protest your actions and I must inform you that I will be notifying the Director of the NSA of your breach of security at my next briefing." With that she began her briefing, which only preceded a few sentences before the questions started.

"Miss McClare you just said that your group is searching newsgroups online; which newsgroups and how are you searching for them?"

"Mr Watson the list of newsgroups is very long and I did not memorize them. As to the method of searching we are using the internet."

"Yes I understand that you are using the internet but did you stumble across these when randomly surfing during company time?"

"How the information was obtained is classified sir and I am not allowed to discuss it," Holly stated flatly.

"Are you telling me that you are unable to inform the deputy director of the NSA how you perform your job young lady? My security clearance is higher than yours Miss McClare so you will answer my questions to the letter or I will have you fired! Now one more time, how did you find the information?"

Holly straightened up and drew a deep breath. "Sir that information is classified and I am not at liberty to discuss it."

Watson jumped to his feet and slammed his hand on the desk. "I have had enough of your grandstanding. You are relieved of your duties, my assistant will escort you to your desk where you will turn over all of your files to him and await security at your desk. Jason get this woman out of my site."

"Yes sir," Jason replied with a huge grin on his face. "Miss McClare, follow me please."

As soon as they stepped on the elevator Jason turned to Holly. "So how does it feel to be out of a job? All you had to do was play along and you would have been on the way up. I never get you prima donnas; you all think your special. Mr Watson is the one really running this place and you screwed yourself by not doing things his way, lady."

Holly smiled. "Jason, how do you breathe?"

"What? What do you mean?"

"With your head so far up Watson's ass, how do you breathe?"

Jason shook his head and chuckled. "Boy you are one dumb bitch. On your way out of a sweet government job and trying to piss of the one guy that can smooth things over for you. I was going to offer to make nice with Mr Watson for you, to keep you in the group but now, not a chance. I hope you learn from this lesson."

"Oh I have Jason, don't worry. I have," Holly told him as the elevator stopped and the doors opened.

Holly headed straight to her desk where she spotted a military police officer waiting for her and her two team members looking worried. Also waiting for her was her boss.

"Holly would you have a seat please, security has been ordered to come down and escort you from the building and I am just waiting for a confirmation of that order," Matt told her.

"Excuse me Major but my orders are from the deputy director himself and I am to personally make sure Miss McClare hands over her files to me and then leaves the building," Jason said. "I'll need her to open her system and give me the passwords and all her data to date."

"What is your name sir?" Matt asked.

"Jason Maxwell, I'm Mr Watson's personal assistant."

The major thought for a moment "I'm sorry Mr Maxwell but your name is not on the list of personnel cleared for the project so I can't allow you to view Miss McClare's work."

Jason chuckled "I assure you Major I have a higher security clearance than you and I have been authorized by Mr Watson himself."

"sir the very fact that you are not on the list of people cleared for this project tells me that your clearance is not high enough, even if your clearance is higher then mine. I'm afraid that I can not allow you access to the data."

"I don't have time for this, Mr Watson is waiting for this information." Jason said sat down at Holly's system. "Give me your password Miss McClare."

"Mr Maxwell step away from that terminal, Miss McClare do not give him that code."

"Major I have had enough of this foolishness, Miss McClare is in no position to do anything other than what I tell her to do, she no longer works here. And if you don't start co-operating I can assure you, you won't be here much longer either. Now give me that access code."

Matt walked over to the wall and hit the alarm instantly initiating a lock down of all the terminals in the room as well as the elevators and the doors to the stairwell. The alarm alerted the security section and instantly an armed reaction team was running for the elevators and the stairwells heading for the computer search division. Everyone was locked in until the security section removed the lock down and let them out. As soon as the alarm went off the attitude of the MP changed like a switch being thrown.

"Everyone, move toward the elevators and wait in a group in the entranceway please." He said in a command voice that told everyone the please was merely lip service to civility, it was an order to everyone in the room the Major included and all knew it.

Everyone but Jason stood up and moved carefully toward the elevators. "What the hell was that all about Major?" Jason almost yelled. "Have you lost your mind? I'm calling Mr Watson, I hope you like the cold Major because you're about to be reassigned to the South Pole."

"Put that phone down now!" Came the bellowed command from the MP freezing everyone in the room.

Jason had the phone halfway to his ear when he looked up to see a gun pointing right at his head. Slowly he replaced the receiver on the cradle and stood up watching the gun the whole time. "Do you know who I am soldier?" he asked, finally finding his voice.

"Sir I don't care if you are the Chairman of the Joint Chiefs, this room has been locked down and you WILL step away from that computer terminal and follow security procedure. This is your last warning, sir" The MP explained ominously.

Jason stepped away from the desk his face twisted with rage. "You will regret this." He muttered to the guard before joining the rest of the people by the elevator.

As they got there the elevator doors opened and more MPs in full combat gear stepped out. Barely seconds later the stairwell door opened to reveal more combat troops with a captain at the front. "Who's in command here?"

Jason stepped toward the captain before anyone had a chance to say anything. "I am and I want the major and this MP arrested immediately." He was pointing at the guard who still had his gun drawn.

Seeing one of his security staff the captain ignored Jason and moved over to the marine with a short. "Report!"

"Sir! This man," He pointed to Jason. "Accompanied by this woman," he pointed to Holly. "Arrived approximately six minutes ago. At that time the man ordered the woman to grant him access to her computer terminal. Upon giving this order, the Major intervened stating that the man was not on the cleared list of personal to view the materials on the computer. The man refused to listen to the Major and tried to gain access to the terminal. The Major sounded the alarm to initiate a lock down of the room. After the lock down this man," Again he pointed to Jason,. "attempted to use the telephone in violation of standing security orders. I drew my weapon and ordered him to step away from the computer and wait by the elevators, sir."

"Very good soldier, you are relieved." the captain told him turning to Jason. "Your name sir?"

"I'm Jason Maxwell, personal assistant to Deputy Director Watson. Why haven't you arrested those two?"

"Sir, everyone in this room is currently being detained except the MP, he was following the standing orders for a security lock down. You do understand that during a lock down all personal are to secure from what ever they are doing ensure all documents are locked up and move to the floor rally point correct?"

"Captain I don't see what your little lecture has to do with not arresting that MP for pointing his gun at me and failing to obey my authority," Jason said angrily.

"Sir, after the lock down was initiated did you attempt to make a call?"

Jason let out a large sigh before answering. "Yes, I was calling the deputy director to inform him of what was happening. Can we move along a little faster here Captain? I have work to do and Mr Watson is expecting me back soon."

"Sir how long have you been with the NSA?"

"Captain I am out of patience with you and this entire mess. Are you going to arrest those two men or not?"

"Well, sir at this time the only person that I can determine that has broken security protocol is you. I'm afraid I'm going to have to detain you."

The Captain motioned to one of the MPs to handcuff Jason who was stunned into immobility with the turn of events. As two marines bundled Jason on the elevator the captain turned to Holly. "As I understand it you were about to be escorted from the premises, is that correct?"

"Yes sir it is," Holly answered quietly still not sure what exactly was happening to her.

"Then I am afraid ma'am that I will need to detain you as well. I don't think handcuffs are needed if you will co-operate fully."

"Yes sir," Holly replied meekly and then followed the MP that the captain indicated to the elevator to wait to head up to the detention area.

"Excuse me Captain but I think that it would be better if Miss McClare remains here under my supervision until her status is cleared up. She is working on a highly classified project that is restricted to this department, specifically her team. I can place her in the meeting room and an MP can be stationed outside."

The captain thought for a second, the major did out rank him but this was a security matter and as such he was the sole authority in the matter so he decided to follow SOP. "For the moment sir I think it would be better for Miss McClare to accompany us to the detention center until the issue is cleared up. Would you like to come along sir?"

"Yes I would Captain, thank you."

"Is the situation under control here now Major?"

"Yes it is Captain."

"In that case the lock down is released and your people can go back to work. Thank you for your co-operation." With that command all the guards headed back upstairs to the security room followed by the two officers.

Jason and Holly we placed in separate detention rooms, each room had a table, two chairs and a window in the door covered with steel mesh. In the ceiling was a security camera covered with a Plexiglas bubble to keep watch on anyone in the room and prevent them from damaging the camera. Jason was pacing and cursing quietly while Holly simply sat and stared at the door. As soon as the major arrived he asked for a phone and was directed to an empty desk in the corner of the security office. He picked up the receiver and dialed the internal number for the director's private office line.

The general picked up the phone on the second ring. "Yes?"

"We have a situation with Miss McClare, she is in the detention center along with one of Mr Watson's people," Matt said without preamble.

"Shit, what the hell happened Major?"

"I'm not sure sir I haven't had a chance to speak with her. She went to brief Watson and came back with one of his little flunkies in tow. He tried to access her terminal and I punched the lock down alarm. The MPs have them both here waiting to sort this out."

"Okay you stand fast, I'll have my Chief of Staff down there ASAP and get this mess cleaned up. As soon as Miss McClare is cleared bring her up to see me."

"Yes sir," Matt replied, putting the receiver down and took a seat at the desk to wait.

Major Barkhouse had taken his third sip of coffee when the corporal at the front desk leaped to his feat and with a parade ground voice bellowed "Attention!" Every military person in the room stopped what they were doing and came to rigid attention, the major included, as a navy captain entered the room.

"As you were. Corporal where...never mind," he said, looking around and spotting Matt.

"Major I'm Captain Hamilton, General Hayes' Chief of Staff. He outlined the problem to me, where is the young lady?"

"She is in that room there, sir," Matt said, pointing.

"Okay, great." Just as Hamilton was looking around for the commanding officer of the MP detail the captain in charge appeared and came to attention.

"Sir, Captain Thomas reporting sir," he announced in true Marine fashion.

"Captain I understand there has been a security issue in the computer search department?"

"That is correct sir. I am just typing up my report now, would you care to see it sir?"

"That won't be necessary Captain, I have an order from the director to release Miss McClare back to her section. Please see that it's carried out ASAP." He said handing an envelope to the Thomas

"Yes sir," Thomas replied, did an about face and marched back to his office yelling at a Sergeant to report to him on the double.

Captain Hamilton smiled. "That's the best thing about Marine MP's, they snap to and follow an order fast. Miss McClare will be out in a few minutes, as soon as she is released could you accompany her to the general's office."

"Yes sir, will do." Matt replied and with that Hamilton turned and left.

Holly was free within two minutes and still wondering what was going on. "Am I leaving or staying Major?"

"I believe staying, Miss McClare but we have to go up and see the General, I think he'll be making the final decision, let's get going."

The two left the security offices and headed up to the top floor where the General had his office. As they entered the office the general's personal secretary motioned for them to go right in. Entering the office they saw the general sitting behind a large desk covered with folders and paper and four telephones. He was facing the door with another desk to his left that held a computer terminal. Behind him was a wall covered with the mementos of his career in the US Military. There were also photos of his various commands. On the right was a large window with a view off to the south and a credenza under it on which sat a coffee percolator. Built into the credenza was a small fridge and shelves, holding mugs and a sugar bowl.

"Major, Miss McClare, thanks for coming up. I won't take up too much time here. It would seem that there is a bit of confusion as to your current project. I had thought that I was clear on your reporting only to me but I see that message was not as firm as I had thought so I will reiterate. From this moment on you will be briefing me and only me, no one else. Sorry Matt but I'm even cutting you out of the loop. Miss McClare you and your team are on your own, whatever you want send the request to Captain Hamilton and he'll see it gets done for you. Here is his contact information on it and he can be reached night or day." The general held out his hand with a card in it. "You will stay in the computer section simply because you are already set up there and moving you would be a waste of time, again sorry Matt, you're losing some real estate, but it's only in the short term."

"No problem sir, I'll make sure everyone in the section stays clear of Miss McLare's group," Matt said, ever the team player and career military man.

"Thank you Matt. Miss McClare from this point on you work directly for me until your project is finished. If there are any problems or questions direct them to Captain Hamilton, or, if he isn't around then contact me. Captain Hamilton won't be asking any questions so you won't have to explain your requests to him. Just tell him what you need and it will get done. Do you have any questions?"

"Well sir to be honest I thought I was fired. What about Mr Watson and Jason? Are they still going to be involved with the team?"

"Miss McClare, I will say this one last time, you and you alone are in charge of the project. You will brief me and me only on this matter. If anyone and I mean anyone at all asks you about your current work you will direct them to this office. Forget everything that has happened today and let's get back to work, and let's skip today's briefing, I think that I'll have a full plate; we'll plan for tomorrow at the normal time. Anything else?"

Holly sensed that she was being dismissed so that the general could work on more important matters. "No sir, thank you very much." With that she and the major left the office and grabbed an elevator to head to the basement.

"Matt what the hell just happened?" Holly asked as soon as the doors closed.

"Holly I have no idea what happened, I'm not even sure what is going on right now. Whatever is going on, is way above my pay grade. But you still have your project so that's a good thing."

"But what do I do about Mr Watson? I mean he wants a briefing every day too."

"I would say at this point he isn't going to get one. The general's orders were very clear."

"What do I tell him if he demands one?"

"I believe that Mr Watson will be informed so you shouldn't have to worry about that, but if you do simply refer him to the general," Matt said as the doors opened "I've got to get back to work, you have a great day." With that he went back to his office.

Holly slowly headed back to her own desk to find the Sergeant and Doris waiting for her. "What is going on around here?" Doris asked in a loud whisper.

"Ladies I have no idea what is going on. I was just in the general's office and we are now reporting only to the general, other then that I have no idea. Even Major Barkhouse is out of the loop now. Anything we want or need, goes through the director's chief of staff, Captain Hamilton."

"So is it back to business as normal?" Sergeant Erwin asked

"I guess so," Holly said. "So let's get back to work and see what we can find in today's posts." with that she sat down at her desk, logged into her computer and opened up Spock.

"Captain can you come in here a moment please?" The General replaced the receiver and waited for his chief of staff who arrived thirty seconds later.

"Yes sir?"

The General handed the Captain a folder. "This is the info on the project that Miss McClare and her group are running. You and I are the only contacts on this and if she needs anything she will be calling you to get it. I have a feeling that the young lady is right on this one and if she is, the national security issues are huge. I want her given a free hand with this, no interference at all. You are going to make sure she gets the chance, so I need you to go to security and make sure that Sam's assistant ends up somewhere harmless. I don't care where or how but get that little shit out of here."

"Will do sir but that's going to upset Mr Watson some."

"Mr Watson is going to have other things to deal with," the general stated with a steely look in his eye. "Don't worry about fall out from him. Get right on it Captain and don't bother to tell me what you do, I no longer care."

"Aye sir." The captain left the office heading for the security office.

When Hamilton walked through the door, once again the MP's came to attention. "At ease," he replied offhand. "Where is the CO?" he asked the corporal at the front desk.

"I'll get him for you sir," the corporal said, picking up his phone.

Ten seconds later Captain Thomas arrived. "Sir how can I help you?" he asked, coming to attention.

"At ease, do you still have Jason Maxwell in custody?"

"Yes sir we do. One of my men is with him now getting a statement on the actions. He is demanding to speak with the deputy director sir."

"Okay Captain Thomas what I want you to do is call the FBI and turn him over to them. As of this moment his security clearance is revoked. He will be investigated for breach of security protocols. I want him gone ASAP."

Thomas snapped to attention and barked, "Yes sir," and headed back to his office to carry out his orders.

Hamilton returned to his office and went back to work the matter already marked in his mind as taken care of. With in the hour Jason was in the custody of two FBI agents on his way to Washington for interrogation. The only thing he was insisting on now was his right to a lawyer, and even this demand trailed off when he was informed that he was being investigated under a national security issue, and he wouldn't be taking to anyone soon.

As Jason was being escorted from the NSA the general was dealing with the deputy director, who had barged into the directors office "Just what in the hell do you mean by having one of my assistants arrested by the FBI? You call the Bureau and get this cleared up now!" Watson ranted.

The general was tired of Watson's antics and dirty tricks. He had been the director for just over two years and after this post he was looking to retirement. While the NSA was headed by a flag rank military officer the deputy was a civilian and a political appointee and as such he couldn't fire Watson with out a very good reason. If he gave his deputy enough rope maybe he would provide a reason for the General to fire him.

"Mr Watson I would remind you that while you are the deputy Director I am the Director. I run the NSA, not you, no matter what your self-important ego may tell you. Who the hell do you think you are barging into my office yelling like a petulant child about an assistant that violated security? Are you telling me that this man was acting under your direct orders?" The general asked in a quiet voice.

Watson stopped for second suddenly realizing that he had put himself in a dangerous situation. "What do you mean violated security?" he asked.

The general explained what had taken place not bothering to either offer his deputy a seat or stand up.

"I was unaware of that." Sam told him after the explanation.

"Glad to hear that Mr Watson, but I am curious as to why you ordered Miss McClare to brief you on an operation that I had told you to stay out of?"

"I must have mis-understood you sir, I assumed that you only wanted my assistants to stay out of the loop I wasn't aware that you would be keeping me out of the loop. This is a rather important operation and I am concerned that the young lady does not have the experience to manage a job of this magnitude."

"Then let me make this completely clear Mr Watson, Miss McClare will be reporting to me and only me. There will be absolutely no one else involved in the chain of command regarding her work. This includes you Mr. Watson, you will receive only that information that I deem you to require. If I have to repeat this order I will have you removed from the NSA pending a hearing for breach of security and your dismissal from government service. Are there any questions?"

Sam new that he was on thin ice here and the only option was to agree with the General and hope that he could get around it later. "Yes sir, perfectly clear."

"Thank you Mr Watson, you may go," the director said, dismissing the man.

Chapter 11

"So are we driving all the way up?" Gunny asked with a trace of curiosity in his voice as John pulled into traffic, leaving Gunny's apartment.

"It'll take to long to drive, we have to fly up."

"I'm confused John, you signed out a car that has New Hampshire plates on it. Why do that if we aren't going to be driving up."

"I need the plates off this car to put them on the rental car we will get when we arrive. That way if anyone does get our plate it'll be the ones off this car and when they trace them they'll hit a brick wall."

"You take this cloak and dagger shit seriously don't you. Why don't we just use a fake name for renting the car?"

"Forget the spy movies you've seen gunny, the real world is a whole lot different. If I rent a car in a fake name I need the whole legend to go with it, credit cards, history, address, everything. Takes time to make a legend that will hold up under scrutiny. It's easier to get a company car with New Hampshire plates and then borrow the plates to use on a rental. The plates on this car already have a legend that can't be traced back to me so if anyone sees them it makes no difference."

The gunny noticed that John wasn't heading for the interstate but was heading back to Fort Meade. "Ummm, you said we were flying up right?"

"That's right Gunny."

"Did you forget something at the office?"

"Nope, got everything we need."

"So shouldn't we be heading for BWI?" Gunny asked, using the acronym for Baltimore-Washington International airport.

"Nope, we're flying out of Tipton, the local municipal strip near the base. We aren't flying commercial, we'll be using a small twin-engine plane, and we're flying into another municipal airport near the town we're going to. It can only take small planes but it's still faster then flying commercial and more anonymous."

"So how long with it take us?"

"It's around 400 miles and the plane cruises at 145 miles an hour so the flight time is going to be around 3 hours."

"Did you say 145 miles an hour?"

"Yes, why?"

"John when you said a twin engine plane I was thinking a small Lear jet or whatever they have in the air force for twin engine jets. What kind of plane are we using?"

"We're using my own plane Gunny. I have a Gemini, it's a twin engine kit plane that I built myself. Great little thing to fly in."

"A kit plane!" Gunny said with alarm. "You mean one of those tiny cramped home built deathtraps?"

"Relax Gunny, I've got over a 500 hours on this plane; it's safe, stable, it's not cramped, and best of all it's untraceable. If we charter something it leaves a trail. This way I'm just off for a little trip and since I'm flying from one municipal airport to another I can get away with out filing a flight plan, even though technically I should as I'm crossing state lines."

Gunny stayed silent for the rest of the trip to the local airfield waiting to pass judgment on the plane when he saw it in person. John turned into the airport and parked his car in the terminal lot. The two men took their bags out of the car and then Atkinson removed the plates using a small multi-tool he had in his pocket. Locking the vehicle he turned and followed by gunny walked toward the tie-down area where several dozen private planes were parked. John walked up to a red twin engine job that sat about five and a half feet tall. He took a key out of his pocket, hopped up on the left wing and to unlock the cockpit and open it. Gunny hopped up beside John, careful to stand on the strip that was clearly marked for walking on, and looked through the bubble canopy covering the cockpit. What he saw was two comfortable looking bucket seats in an area that was about four feet across, an array of instruments that he did not recognize, and a storage area behind the two seats into which John tossed his bag on top of several other duffel bags already there, after he opened the canopy. The one thing he did not see was a control column or steering control with which to fly the plane.

"Have a seat, I'll pre-flight the bird and we'll be on our way," John said, moving aside so the Gunny could climb down into the cockpit and move to the right hand seat, John got into the plane and began flipping switches and turning knobs to turn on the instruments get the plane ready for flight.

John hopped back up out of the plane and proceeded to remove the tie-downs and wheel chocks, storing them in a small compartment near the tail. He then did, what seemed to Gunny as, a very though inspection of the plane, checking the tires, propellers, wings, airilons, rudder, and tail surfaces. He also checked the surface of the plane running his hand over it. The Gunny had no idea what this was for, but was very happy to see that it looked professional to his eyes.

John crawled back into the cockpit, pulled the canopy closed, and looked over the gauges before pushing a button on the instrument panel mark NO 1. There was a whirring sound of an electric starter turning over an engine and then the plane started to tremble as the left side engine came to life in an uneven idle. Once John was satisfied that the left engine was running, he hit the Button marked NO 2 and the right side engine started also, increasing the trembling of the plane only slightly.

The Gunny was surprised at the low level of noise in the plane. "Umm, John I hate to sound stupid but how do you steer this thing?" he said in just a little louder then a normal speaking voice

John smiled and reached into a pocket next to his knee and removed a padded rod that was threaded at one end. He screwed it into a socket on the floor between his knees and began moving it in a circle. He looked at the wings, watching the control surfaces respond to the movement of the stick. He looked over his shoulder and moved his feet on the rudder controls to check the movement there as well. Happy with his tests he reached behind the seats and grabbed two earphone headsets with boom microphones built in, handed one to the Gunny, plugged in his headset and pointed to the other jack so that the Gunny could plug in his headset.

"The volume control is built into the right ear-pad so you can adjust it to your comfort level. You can speak to me and hear the radio but your mic isn't wired to the radios so you will need to hit that switch there to talk over the radio. My headset is hot-wired to override yours and talk on the radio." John explained. "Have you done much flying with the corps?"

"Lots of riding in choppers and the large transports before transferring to NSA, but this is the first time I've been in a small plane. Not sure I like this that much, not used to seeing what's going on. The back of transports isn't much good for sight seeing."

"Well you should enjoy this then, we'll be flying around 5000 feet so it'll be a good view and the weather is clear the entire route. We should arrive just after sunset. All set?"

Gunny was buckled in and had his headset dialed to a comfortable listening level, nodded to John who then snapped on the radio. He got clearance to take off, taxied out onto the runway, lined up the plane and opened the throttles. The plane accelerated down the runway leaving the ground in less than 500 feet and climbing to 5,000 feet in less than five minutes. While the take off and climb out startled Gunny a bit the view was incredible. The air was crystal clear and the sun low on the western sky painting the ground in highlights and shadows. John set a course north and settled the plane into cruising speed.

"Wow, this is a great view John. Nothing at all like I thought it would be." Gunny said over the headset intercom. "It's a lot quieter than I thought it would be too."

"Well Gunny you're wearing headphones so that masks a lot of the noise, but for a twin engine it is fairly quiet. I test flew a plane a buddy of mine built with one of these engines and I loved it, responsive, reliable and low maintenance too. So when I decided to build my own I looked around and found this one. Not that there was a lot to chose from, not a lot of twin jobs in the home built market."

"John, isn't this plane metal skinned?"

Yes it is, another reason I went with it. Made out of aluminum, so it's strong but light."

"Well I don't know much about planes but I pictured something tiny, cramped, noisy and made from wood and canvas. How did you build it with metal?"

"You're right gunny a lot of home-builts are made from wood or canvas, but I wanted a solid body so I went with metal. Added a lot to the cost but the result is worth it. As for building the metal is riveted together and bolted to a welded tube frame. Again the construction makes for low maintenance."

"Is that why you were rubbing your hands all over it before we took off?"

"Yeah I was checking to make sure none of the panels were lose or seams split. Now don't get all worried, it's a habit I picked up from the days when I was flying wood and canvas planes and it just sort of carried over to this one. I haven't had anything come loose on her since I first took off."

"Well I have to admit it is a comfortable ride and I love the view."

"Relax and enjoy then Gunny, we've got three hours of this ahead of us and you'll be able to watch the sun set from 5,000 feet. That alone is worth the trip."

John tuned in a local radio station and piped the music into the headsets at a low comfortable volume and enjoyed the flight himself. Gunny never stopped turning his head, watching the ground pass below them. The sunset was spectacular and Gunny watched it till the sun was totally out of sight then resumed his ground watching marveling at the lights below. They arrived about twenty minutes after sunset and John called the tower requesting clearance to land and to have the runway lights turned on. Gunny had no idea how they were going to land until he saw the runway light up.

John circled the field once to get his bearings than lined up his approach, turned on his landing lights, dropped flaps and gear and set the plane down with a minor jolt and screech of the tires to signify they were once more on solid ground. He taxied to the transient tie down area, parked the plane and shut down both engines. Once the propellers stopped turning he killed the battery power and the cockpit lights went out leaving the two in the dark.

John opened the canopy, stepped out and jumped to the ground heading towards the tail of the plane. He removed the chocks and tie downs from their compartment and made his plane secure.

"Gunny do me a favor and toss out the bags would you, please. Also grab the three bags other bags as well, if you don't mind," he asked as he was finishing up with the tie-downs on the wings."

The gunny grabbed the bags, dropped them to the ground and jumped down beside them. "So what's the plan John?"

"Well for now I'm going to call a cab to come and get us and take us to the rental car, I had the agency leave it for after hours pickup. Once we get that we'll find a camp ground and get some sleep, that's what's in those other bags, a tent and sleeping bags."

"We're going to stay at a campground?"

"Around here they're more plentiful than motels and easier to find, they also offer anonymity."

"Sounds good to me." Gunny replied, watching his partner pull out his cell phone and dial the operator for the number for the nearest cab. It took forty minutes for a cab to arrive but they were at their rental car fifteen minutes after that. John switched the plates while Gunny put their bags in the trunk and then they were off, following the directions the cabby had given them to the nearest campground. When they arrived the office was already closed but there was a box nailed to the door that contained check in slips that doubled as an envelope, and map showing what sites were empty. John filled out one of the slips, put the posted amount payment in cash for two nights in and sealed it, then and dropped it through the mail slot picked up the chalk tied to the door with a string and put an X through the camp site he chose as the instructions told him to do. He would stop by the office tomorrow when it was open and get a receipt then. Parking the car at the chosen campsite the two began the process of setting up the four-man dome tent and inflating the air mattresses to sleep on. Both tasks were done in under ten minutes and the two crawled into the tent to get some sleep. John wanted to be in the town by 7AM.

Both men dropped of to sleep almost immediately as they were both accustomed to camping. John used campgrounds when ever possible on his field assignments, and the Gunny was a marine. Having been in an infantry company straight out of boot camp he had quickly become accustomed to the contact training and life in the field. He had spent many a night with a lot less then the tent he was now in. Both men enjoyed the chance to be out of the office for a while and back in the field, even though both thought this to be a wild goose chase.

At 6 AM John's tiny travel alarm went off, it was a waste of time as both men had awakened a few moments before, conditioned to early risings. Grabbing their shower and shaving kits they headed to the bathrooms for a quick shower. They were finished and leaving the campground at 6:30 for the short drive to Littleton.

Like most small New England towns Littleton was a community built around two main streets. There were several coffee and donut shops, a couple of drug stores, some hardware and sporting good stores and the usual collection of garages. The town was as unremarkable as the people were friendly. John parked the Car at the end of one of the main streets and he and the Gunny walked along until they saw a coffee shop and went inside.

Both ordered a coffee and muffin and then took a seat next to the large plate glass window looking out on the street. The Gunny was looking up the street at the intersection and had a very good view of several stores and two garages. He took note of all the vehicles on the street, and slowly crossed most of them off his mental list of being something to watch. In the end there were four trucks, two vans, and half a dozen mini vans that he would keep an eye on along with watching for people. John was looking down the street to where his car was parked and there wasn't a single thing along the stretch to be even slightly curious over.

"Gunny I'm going to poke around the town and see what's interesting, you watch the street and see if anyone shows interest in me. I'll stay in view of the window at all times so if I suddenly disappear, you come running," John told the Gunny in a quiet voice.

"Aye aye sir," Gunny said, falling back on training and instinctively addressing his superior in the approved marine corp manner.

John smiled, got up and ordered another coffee to go, then slowly wandered down the street towards the intersection looking in store windows, acting like any other tourist the world over. In reality he was using the storefront plate glass windows to survey the town around him. It was a very old trick used by intelligence agencies everywhere and still highly effective, even though it was known by everyone. Every person walking down the street looked in the windows and for that very reason you could never tell if a person was actually looking in or at the window. What John was looking for was himself, that is another person doing the same thing he was, wandering aimlessly around the town looking in windows.

The Gunny was sitting in the coffee shop with his coffee and muffin watching John and looking for anyone that seemed to watch his partner as well. This was his first time playing what he called a covert operative and he was surprised at the boredom of it. He had wrongly assumed that he would be wary and his adrenaline would be pumping just from the excitement of the chase. Every mystery novel he had read or movie he had watched had always shown the spy types to be highly intense and nervous. In truth this was ass-numbingly boring and only after, he glanced at his watch, seventeen minutes of it. He had been assured that he would be doing this, or something like it, all day. Gunny was starting to rethink his agreement to come along.

After an hour of wandering aimlessly around the small town, always with in site of the coffee shop window, John was sure of only two things: it was going to be a long day and he had to find a bathroom. He decided that the garage across the intersection would do just fine, pulled out his cell phone, called Gunny to tell him what he was doing, as he would be out of sight for a few moments, then headed across the street. As he was crossing the street his peripheral vision caught something out of the ordinary and his mind was suddenly alert. Even though his stride never changed and his head never once turned he was looking for danger and ready to run. Something was very wrong on the street and he had to find out what fast. John went into the garage, asked for and received the restroom key, and went around the side to the restroom, which was in clear view of the coffee shop. After emptying his bladder he washed his hands in the sink while reviewing in his mind the things on the street, trying to find what it was that put him on alert.

As he was drying his hands the image of the panel van parked across the street popped into his head. It had moved as he walked past it, almost as if there was someone inside trying to get a look at him. He thought for a minute to see if he remembered the van parking while he was walking around. No it was already parked there when they arrived and he hadn't seen anyone get in or out of it. The meant that if there was someone inside they were there waiting. But for what?

John exited the restroom and went back into the garage proper to return the key. He thanked the mechanic and walked back out to the sidewalk pretending to look down the street. With his eyes he checked out the cars parked in the lot and there he saw a black pickup truck parked next to the building adjacent the garage. A black pickup identical to the one described in the posts he had said were fake. From down the street the truck was unseen but from just across the road it was as plain as day. The perfect vantage point to watch from in a vehicle such as a panel van.

John walked straight back to the coffee shop moving with the rest of the people on the street thinking the truck and van and what they represented over in his mind. The more he thought the more convinced he was there was someone in the van and they were watching the pick up truck. Did the truck mean that the posts weren't fake that the two really were in town? He suddenly realized that Miss McClare was right on the money with everything she had said to date, there was another group trying to find the two men that had taken the shot at the President. He knew that whoever was in the van was not with the government. If they were, they wouldn't be parked a cross the street in a van, they would be all over the town. Hundreds of people trying to blend in and standing out because of it. But there were no people in the town that didn't belong except for him, Gunny, and whoever was in that Van. Miss McClare had told him that if he found the two men to call the FBI, she said nothing about what to do if he found the other team, as he was now thinking of the other people hunting for the two shooters. An interesting idea formed in his head and the more he thought about it the more he liked it. By the time he reached the coffee shop the only thing left to do was talk Gunny into it.

John ordered two more coffees, took them to Gunny's table, and sat down across from him. "Did you see anything at all strange or out of place? Anyone looking at me or watching me?" He asked hunched over in the chair his face low to the table close to the cup.

"John the only thing at all I noticed, and to be honest I'm still not sure I really saw anything, but when you walked by that van up there to go to the Garage I thought I saw it rock back and forth an little bit. It was almost as if there was someone in it, but I haven't seen it move since then and it's been there since we got here."

"Well if you are imagining things, then I am too because I thought I saw it move as well. I think someone is in it and I'm not sure what they are doing but I'd bet they are watching the black pickup in the garage parking lot that you can't see from here."

"A black pickup truck? Like the one in the online post?"

"Yup, just like it."

"Well, son-of-a-bitch! They are here, the post was right. So did you use the garage to call the FBI?" The Gunny asked with a small trace of excitement in his voice.

"Nope, and I'm not going to either," John replied quietly.

"Are you insane? We have orders to notify the FBI as soon as we have evidence of the two wanted suspects, John. That means we have to call the FBI."

"That's the problem Gunny, we don't have any evidence."

"What the hell do you mean? You just told me that you saw the Truck that was described in the internet post, doesn't that qualify as evidence?"

"No Gunny it doesn't. The post mentioned a black pickup truck but didn't give too much in the way of details. There isn't enough to call the FBI with. But I am curious about something though."

"What's that?"

"Who is in that van and are they watching the black pickup truck?. If they are then it means they also read the internet posts and potentially, that Miss McClare was dead on about everything. Gunny we have a problem here, that truck could belong to the suspects or it could belong to a local. We can't call the FBI because they will ask questions we can't answer. The other issue is that we need to know who and how many people are in that van. I don't like the fact that someone beat us here and are already in place."

"You got a point there, John. You are the spook here, so how do we find out who is in the van?"

"Gunny if this was a straight up recon job how would you deal with this?"

Gunny thought for a minute. "I'd create a situation that would require me to speak with the driver. Something like an auto accident, maybe bumping the car when I was parking it, something like that."

"Then you and I are on the same wavelength because that's what I would do to. In fact that's the way we will do it. I'm going to walk back up and hang around the garage; you get the car and back into the front of the van. Not hard but enough to bump it so you need to talk to the driver."

"What are my rules of engagement if the person in the van has friends and turns violent?

"Use your own discretion, Gunny, I'll back you." With that John left the coffee shop and walked casually back to the Garage.

The two left with Gunny heading back to the car. As he hopped in he looked up the street to see John arrive at the garage. He pulled the car into the street and drove up the street to where the van was, stopping just in front of it and then parallel parking in front of it. In his rear-view mirror he could see someone slouched behind the steering wheel of the van and in the back, shadows that looked like other people. Across the street John was looking in the window of the pickup truck and the person in the van was watching him rather than the car parking in front of him. Gunny got to within two feet of the van and then acting as if his foot slipped; he moved it from the brake pedal to the gas pedal and stepped down hard. The car lurched back and hit the van causing both vehicles to rock but the actual damage done was minimal. The surprise of the driver of the van was obvious as he was suddenly sitting straight up in his seat.

Gunny got out of his car, swearing and shaking his head as if he couldn't believe what had just happened. "Oh man I am so sorry, my foot slipped off the brake and hit the gas. I'll pay for the damage of course," he said to the van driver, while looking at the damage to the two vehicles.

Unseen from the outside were several men in the back of the van, all members of the organization and expertly trained para-military fighters "What the fuck happened?" one of the men asked.

"Some local just backed into us." The team leader said quietly from the drivers seat. He's checking things over now so everyone stay loose and I'll deal with this. No one gets out or makes a move, just stay cool," he ordered getting out and looking at the damage himself.

"It doesn't look too bad I don't think I hit you that hard. How are you feeling yourself?" Gunny asked in his best concerned voice.

"I'm fine sir, you didn't hit me that hard at all, just a mild jolt. I don't even really see that much to worry about here. Certainly nothing to worry the insurance or police about," the van driver said, wanting to get this done with as fast as possible and avoid drawing attention to him and his men.

Gunny pulled out his wallet and dug out his driver's license. "Mister you are being too kind to me, but we really should exchange information, just in case. See I'm not from here, just up visiting my sister. I'm headin' home day after tomorrow. I really want to pay for the damage so you take it to a garage and then call me collect and I'll send you a money order to get it fixed up. My name is Andy Stevens, from Atlanta. I'll write all this down soon as I find a pen and paper, 'scuse me for a sec," Gunny said, using the fake ID the NSA had set up for him, as he was patting his pockets, then went back to his car reached in and grabbed a pen and one of the travel brochures in the car to write on.

The van driver seeing that his quickest way out was to simply trade info, also dug out his wallet and pulled out his driver's license. "Hi Andy I'm James Hanley." He didn't volunteer any more information.

Gunny tore the brochure in two and wrote his info on one half and James info on the other. He handed over his info and pocketed James info. "I'm really very sorry about all this. It's not my car you see, not used to it at all. And please send me the bill, I'll take care of everything."

"I'm not even going to fix it Andy, all that happened was a bent bumper. I couldn't care about that at all. Don't be concerned and enjoy the rest of your vacation." The entire time he was talking he was glancing over at John watching him check out the pickup truck. "Excuse me would you I think I see a friend of mine, Hey Jimmy let's go, okay?" he yelled at the van, and then headed across the street.

Another man got out of the passenger side of the van carrying a gym bag in his left hand and jogged across the street to catch up with James. Gunny watched them go, crossing his arms and sliding his right hand under his coat to grab the butt of his pistol in the shoulder holster. The two men from the van were together now and slowly walked toward John, who suddenly acted as if he just noticed them and headed towards the garage to go inside it.

"Excuse me sir? Can we talk to you for a second?" James yelled out to John, who ignored him and kept going toward the door to the garage.

"Sir? Hold on we need to talk to you." The two walked a little fasted and Jimmy pushed his hand inside the gym bag.

"Sir stop!" James yelled while Jimmy suddenly pulled an MP5 Machine gun from the gym bag.

Gunny's reaction was automatic, he pulled his pistol out leveled it and was aiming it at Jimmy when he saw the man jerk, drop the MP5, and start to turn around. He jerked a couple more times then crumpled to the ground. Gunny looked past the downed man and saw John with his pistol leveled at James, who was standing next to his fallen partner with a look of shock. What seemed like an hour passed, which was in reality, less than five seconds.

James found his voice, screamed for help and dove for the MP5 lying on the ground. Gunny had no idea who he was yelling to, but could not believe the mans quickness. James actually managed to get the MP5 off the ground and up into a firing position before he was hit with bullets from both John and Gunny. As the man was falling he reflexively pulled the trigger letting off a burst of automatic fire that filled the air with noise. The bullets went into the garage, thudding into the wall and making the people inside duck and run. Luckily no one was hit by the random fire. The noise of the MP5 and Gunny's pistol, drove the other men in the van into action. They opened the side and back doors exploding from the van with weapons at the ready. Every single man was armed with an MP5 and concussion grenades. They were also wearing body armor.

John yelled for gunny to get away from the van, noticing it rocking and the back door opening. He changed clips then began shooting at the men coming out of the back of the van. He noticed they had vests on and assumed that were Kevlar so he took aim at their legs. He nailed three men, all of who hit the ground, cursing in pain at the bullet wounds, but they weren't out of the fight. From the ground they twisted to get their MP5's around to shooting position and take out John. Seeing this he sprinted for the open garage work doors, ducking inside just as bullets began peppering the building.

Across the street Gunny had watched John change clips than shoot at the van. He spun around, saw the armed men, and switched his brain to automatic letting his training take over and control the flow of his fight. Automatically he began cataloging things, noticing that he was on the street side of the car, putting it and the van between him and anyone on the sidewalk. Moving toward the front of the car he crouched down to get the engine block between him and anyone moving from the van. He was just in position when he again heard the sound of automatic weapons fire, his mind telling him that it was from MP5's and there were three separate weapons firing. Half a second later two men appeared on the sidewalk moving forward from the van to get a clear shot at the garage and whoever was shooting at them. As the first man moved into his sights Gunny saw the vest and moved his aim from center body to head and squeezed off a shot, instantly tracking on the next man in line knowing that his round and hit the mark dead center of the forehead and his target was already dead. Gunny's second round was also on the mark, taking off the top of the next man's skull and dropping him before he had a chance to react. The wounded men at the back of the van hear the pistol shots coming from the front and two of them rolled up onto the sidewalk to get a shot at whoever was there. Adrenaline had overcome the shock and pain of being shot and this along with the small caliber of the bullets allowed both to get to their feet and open fire on the car that had bumped into the van. It was also the car Gunny was hiding behind. The glass exploded from the rental car and Gunny hit the ground just in time to avoid having his head blow off in a rain of fire.

John noticed the opposition trying to take out Gunny. He removed the silencer to get better range from his pistol and to let them know there were still two people to worry about. Taking careful aim he could see part of a head through the vans windows and tossed a round at it. He was surprised to see the man grab the top of his head and drop from sight. Thinking the window would deflect the bullet and miss his target, he was only hoping to make the shooters duck and give them something else to worry about. Gunny was back on his feet moving, doing his best to use the car as a shield. John had to think of someway to get him out of there fast, there were two many bullets flying around and his luck would run out eventually.

As he was looking around the garage for a way to help Gunny, John heard the police sirens. He emptied his clip into the Van and reloaded, hoping Gunny could hold out till the police arrived. He looked out and saw someone trying to come around the back of the van on the street side to get at Gunny. John put three rounds into the man's legs and watched him drop, but keep rolling out into the street to get a shot off at Gunny. John stepped out of the garage and carefully aimed, firing four timed shots, two hit the man's body armor one, passed through his upper arm going into his chest cavity through the opening in the vest just below the mans arm and the last shot grazed the back of his head spinning him over and back toward the sidewalk. As he fired his last shot John felt something slam into his right side and spin him around. This saved his life as several bullets cut through the air he had just been standing in. John hit the ground and rolled back into the safety of the garage propping himself up against the wall. He grabbed his side and felt a wet stickiness, knowing he had been hit, but not how bad. He applied pressure to where he felt the blood coming from and pushed himself back to his feet. The shock of the wound was keeping him from feeling the pain but this would wear off soon, until then he had to help his partner. He moved back to the open garage door and looked out to see two police cars pull up and officers jump out with shotguns.

Gunny glanced over his shoulder and saw John standing in the open firing at the back of the van. He checked and saw the man trying to get a shot at him just as John hit him in the head. Turning back he saw John spin fall and scramble back into the garage. He knew things were getting bad fast but there was nothing he could do about. He was caught almost in the open with nowhere to run to. The second he tried he would be cut down and he knew it. His only option was the old standby motto of: The best defense is a good offense. He would attack and hope that the very audacity of this would shock his opponents long enough for him to take them out. He changed clips to get a full magazine and was gathering himself for a charge when the sound of the sirens came to him.

The two cruisers screeched to a stop in front of what looked like a scene from the Middle East, not rural New England. There was a gunman hunched down behind a car that had almost been shot to pieces. Behind the car was a van that was in no better shape and scattered around the van were three more gunmen, all wounded, but all holding automatic weapons. There were four officers between the two cars and when they jumped out every one of them was ready to shoot first and ask why later. Gunny laid down his pistol and stretched out flat on the road with out having to be told, seeing the jumpy nature of the officers. One of the men behind the Van made the mistake of firing at the officers and was almost blown in two by shotgun blasts. Not even body amour would stop a 12-gauge shotgun blast from less then twenty feet and he was hit by at least three of them. As soon as this happened the last two gunmen still alive laid down their MP5's and then spread out face down on the ground in silence. The officers carefully moved from man to man and used plastic riot cuffs to restrain everyone, even those not moving, and pick up the weapons.

Just as the police were about to cuff him Gunny spoke up. "I'm a federal officer and my ID is in my right hand back pocket," he said slowly and clearly.

Gunny lay completely still while he was frisked and his ID removed from his pocket to be checked out. As this was going on there were more sirens in the background getting louder by the second signifying more emergency vehicles were arriving. From across the street John holstered his gun, took out his ID, and with both hands held up at shoulder level he slowly walked towards the police calling out to them to get their attention.

"Hold it right there pal!" an officer yelled as he noticed John for the first time.

John stopped, still holding his hands up to show he was no threat. "I'm a federal officer and the man by the car is my partner. I've been shot and I need medical attention."

One officer moved across the street with his gun in hand not pointing it at John but letting him know he was ready for trouble. "Sir please show me your ID." He also saw blood, staining Johns shirt under his open jacket.

John opened the folder containing his NSA identification and held it out to the officer who moved forward and carefully read it with out taking it from John. Seeing that the ID appeared genuine he radioed it in asking for verification on the name on the ID and then holstered his gun. The verification came back almost immediately and the officer visibly relaxed.

"Thank you sir please sit down the paramedics should be here soon, I'll grab the first aid kit from the car." The officer turned to head to his cruiser but was stopped by John.

"It's not that bad officer it can wait a few more minutes. I really need to contact my office to let them know what's going on here, and I assume you will want statements from myself and my partner."

Just then Gunny sauntered up, a huge smile on his face relieved to still be alive. He was about to make a smart-assed remark when he saw the blood. Instantly he was all business and asked the office for a first aide kit. At that point an ambulance arrived and the paramedics jumped out grabbing gear and heading to the wounded. Gunny told them to attend to the prisoners as he would look after his partner, assuring them he was a trained field medic. The paramedic tossed him a first aid kit and went to help with the other wounded. Of the seven men from the van only two were still alive.

John peeled his jacket off and unbuttoned his shirt to look at the wound. The bullet had just nicked his side hitting a rib and digging a small furrow in the skin, the bleeding had already slowed to just seeping. Gunny declared the wound minor, by gunshot standards, swabbed it clean, applied antiseptic gel and then bandaged it with gauze and tape

"So John, do all your field assignments turn out this fun, or was all this just for me?"

John burst out laughing, a result of Gunny's remark and the draining of the tension in his body. "No this is very unusual. And to think I had this written off as a wild goose chase."

"Well we did manage to catch some wild geese, I just wonder if it's going to be worth the effort."

"Oh shit, we have to call this in and get these guys transferred to federal custody. Have you got your phone on you Gunny?"

Gunny pulled his phone out of his pocket and turned it on. The phone was a dual mode system that used both cell access and secure satellite as well. As he was about to dial John had him switch to the sat system for security.

Gunny started to dial then stopped. "Who do I call man?"

"Call McClare, she's the boss and she was right on this one so she can clean up the mess we made."

Gunny chuckled. "I wonder how happy she's going to be to hear from us?"

Holly noticed her private line flashing on her phone and picked it up assuming it was either the General or Matt, as they were the only two that ever called this line. "Yes sir?" she answered automatically.

"No ma'am, you out rank me, it's Gunny calling in."

"Hi Gunny how are things? Find anything out?"

Gunny spent the nest few minutes explaining what they had found and had what had happened, including John's getting wounded. He then asked what there orders were.

Holly sat stunned. "Excuse me, ma'am? Are you still there?" Came Gunny's voice from the phone in her hand.

"Uh, yeah, I mean yes Gunny I'm still here."

"Ma'am what do you want us to do?"

"Gunny we need to talk to those men. I'll get something going on this end but for now you stay with those men, where they go you go, understand?"

"Yes ma'am."

"How is John?"

"Just a scratch ma'am he'll be fine."

"I want him checked out at the nearest hospital. You two hang in there, I'll get help there soon.

"Yes ma'am, will do."

Gunny disconnected and turned back to John. "Boss lady wants us to stick with the prisoners until someone comes to get them."

"Good idea, what else?"

Gunny broke into a huge smile. "You are to get checked out at the nearest hospital, bosses orders."

"For this?" John asked in a shocked voice "I've been hurt worse skiing. Let's go see who we've caught, okay?"

"No sir. I have my orders and you are to get checked out at the hospital so that is where you are going. I'm to stick with the prisoners until the boss sends someone to take over," Gunny said his voice dropping into a serious tone.

"I can't believe you are serious about this Gunny? We've got a bunch of bad guys here and you really expect me to go get this...this SCRATCH looked at? Come on Gunny, you've seen worse than this in training accidents."

"Yes sir I have, and those men always went to sick bay to get treated. Boss lady says you go get checked out, then as far as I'm concerned, you go get checked out." With that Gunny waved to one of the paramedics to come over.

As they were walking towards one of the ambulances the senior officer on the scene walked up to get their statements. John relayed his orders from Holly and explained that they were waiting for confirmation to take the unknown assailants into federal custody. There were only two men left alive and one of those had a head wound, however he was conscience but was asking for a lawyer. John and Gunny had no idea why they were attacked and stated that their reason for being in New Hampshire was classified. They quickly and concisely explained what happened from their side of events which did little to shed light on why seven men armed with automatic weapons opened fire on them. All of the police were extremely impressed with the fact that the two men had managed to take on a group armed with machine guns and win, especially with one of the guns being a small caliber .32. No matter why they were there the police were very grateful for the fact that they had been or who knows how many could have died.

News media was on the scene and was quickly describing it as a terrorist act with plenty of eyewitnesses to point out the two heroes of the hour. John explained that he and his partner needed to remain away from the public eye so the police keep reports back. Done with the questions they continued to an ambulance so John could go get checked out.

"Gunny what's with this new Boss Lady thing anyway?"

Gunny smiled again. "Well I'm used to having a title or rank to address people by. They put Miss McClare in charge and she keeps telling us to call her by her first name. I can't do that and she doesn't really have a title so I kinda came up with boss lady as a substitute."

John shook his head. "Marines, gotta have a title on everything. Well what ever works for you Gunny. Now go check on the prisoners, I see the medic coming with the stretcher so I'll be out of here and on the way to the hospital. As soon as I'm cleared I'll call you."

As soon as Holly was off the phone she called the direct line to the director.

"Hello sir, I have an update from the two men in New Hampshire, John Atkinson, and Gunnery Sergeant William Ortega. It seems they have been in a gunfight with seven men, identities unknown. The local and state police are at the scene now. John was hit but the wound is described as light and he was moving around and talking. He is on the way to the hospital now. I have ordered the second man to stay on the scene until further notice. Of the seven others, five are confirmed dead, and two are wounded. That's all the information I have at this time, sir."

"How bad is our man hit?" the general asked.

"Gunny called and reported in and described it as a grazing wound that glanced off a rib. The bleeding was under control and he was talking as the report was being made. Gunny is cross-trained as a medic and his opinion is that the wound is minor sir. John was actually not even going to go to the hospital."

"Very well Miss McClare, good to hear the men are okay. It looks as if you are once again right and we do have another team in the play here. One part of me was hoping you would be wrong this time."

"Yes sir," Holly answered automatically. "Sir what would you like me to do?"

"We need to get those men transferred to federal custody. I'll take care of that. Get your men bake her ASAP and keep digging for the other team. I'll have a team of interrogators work on the prisoners to see if we can get anything from them. Anything else to report?"

"No sir."

"Good work McClare, and I want to see the paperwork for commendations for your two men, I think they earned it. When you talk to them again, please give them a well done from me." With that the general disconnected and dialed his phone to get an outside line.

He contacted the federal marshals service and filled them in on what was going on in New Hampshire, letting them know that this was a national security issue and he wanted the men transferred to federal custody for interrogation by the NSA. As soon as the General hung up, six marshals were dispatched to take over custody of the assailants and move them to Fort Meade. Once they were there the NSA and FBI would begin interrogation of the prisoners.

Holly called back Gunny to let him know that US marshals were on the way to take custody, but to keep an eye on the men until the marshals arrived.

Charley logged into the internet and uploaded a new message to the bulletin board indicating that he and Sean were now in New York state and heading west. Once he had done that he began searching the news services to find out what was going on. Totally by accident he stumbled across the story of the gunfight in New Hampshire where five men were confirmed dead and two others wounded and in custody. It was being described as a terrorist attack and crediting two unknown but suspected federal agents, for foiling the event, which was still unclear at this time. He spent the next hour searching for more information but found nothing at all. Logging off he went looking for Sean who was just coming back from his morning jog.

"Lad you need to get more exercise, you're spending too much time in front of that computer," Sean chided his young partner.

"I know Sean, I know, but I have some news. There was a shootout in New Hampshire between federal agents and several unknown gunmen." Charley let his statement hang in the air for a second. "I was wondering if you think we should move farther south?"

"Let's pack," Sean said simply and began grabbing items and storing them in the camper. With in fifteen minutes they were ready for the road. Sean stopped at the washrooms on the way out of the campground so that they could shower and clean up before hitting the road.

As they pulled onto the interstate heading south Sean searched the radio for a news update on the events in New Hampshire but was unable to find anything more than what Charley had found on the internet. They decided on traveling to Florida so that they could get lost in the crowd of tourists in that state.

The dead and wounded men were all taken under heavy police guard, to the same hospital as John, Gunny went along keeping an eye on the prisoners, telling the local authorities that the matter was being taken over at the federal level and they could expect marshals to arrive to take custody. No one was surprised by this, so the prisoners were handcuffed to their gurneys with police officers stationed near by to watch until such time as they were the feds problem. Anytime an officer asked a question of the two wounded men, he was simply met with the demand for a lawyer. The prisoners were sedated to keep them quiet after their wounds were treated. John was released after a cursory inspection by the doctor who admired the first aid job done by Gunny. The wound was clean and did not need stitches, simply requiring bandaging. With a parting admonition to change the dressing every day and avoid exercise for a while the doc let John go.

John shortly found Gunny. "Hey Gunny how are the prisoners doing?"

"They're handcuffed to their beds, we're just waiting on the Marshals to move them. How are you making out?"

"All patched up and ready to go. Doc gave me a clean bill of health, just doesn't want me playing any sports too soon. He didn't even stitch me up, just changed the bandage you put on it. He admired your handy work too."

Gunny's voice was suddenly very serious. "John I owe you my life. That bullet you took was meant for me. Thank you."

"You're welcome Gunny." John said simply and emotionally.

"And you are one hell of a shot man. I can't believe you dropped all those guys with a .32 and that fast." Gunny said with a touch of awe. "I've never seen anyone that fast in my life."

"I don't know Gunny, you reacted pretty quick there yourself. You took those second two down before they even knew you were there."

The two spent the rest of the morning being congratulated by everyone they met.

The US marshals showed up about three hours later with a bus that was converted for carrying prisoners. The bus was nothing like was shown on TV, where they always had the old beat up school buses strung with chicken wire. This was a modern 48-passenger bus with a lot of modifications done to it. The back of the bus was laid out to carry stretchers and came with two medics and medical equipment on board. There were also seats for the guards, although one of them was always walking the length of the bus to keep an eye on the prisoners. The front half of the bus was the same way it had been when it was originally built with the exception that in front of every seat a post had been welded to the floor. At the top and bottom of the post was a stainless steel ring and the prisoners were secured to this with both leg irons and handcuffs. As a further security and safety measure, each seat had a five-point harness that secured to a buckle in the front that could only be opened with a key. Even if a prisoner did get loose from the post they could not get up out of the seat. The straps were made from Kevlar and lined with stainless steel threads to make them almost impossible to cut with a knife. In addition to the features inside the bus the windows were all replaced with bullet-resistant lexan, the sides lined with Kevlar, and the tires were all mounted on run flat rims. An air conditioning system was installed on the roof and was a closed system so that gas could not be introduced into the bus. As a last precaution the engine compartment was armored against anything other than an anti-tank rocket. The bus was outfitted similar to an armored car, the guards were all carrying automatic weapons, and it was tracked by GPS monitoring so that if it stopped an alarm would ring. If the driver did not respond to a radio call an emergency response team was dispatched right away.

The bus pulled up to the emergency entrance which had been cordoned off by the state police. Under the watchful eye of 6 US marshals and ten local and state police officers the two wounded men were moved into the bus one at a time. The back of the bus was built with stretcher racks that had steel rails down the sides to secure the prisoners to and more Kevlar-steel belts to lock people down to the stretchers. As a second precaution any prisoner transported on a stretcher was also sedated. Once both men were loaded and locked in place the bodies of the other five were loaded on as well. The driver radioed in that they were on the move to Baltimore and the GPS tracking was turned on.

With the bus gone, and no car to drive, John and Gunny called a cab to take them back to their campground. They paid the driver to wait while the packed up so he could take them to the plane. As John was wounded, most of the packing fell to Gunny who joked good-naturedly about John just getting hurt to avoid working. They got a receipt for the camping fees and with the bags in the trunk the cabbie took them to the airport where once again most of the work fell to Gunny.

While Gunny loaded the plane, John preflighted it and checked it all over making sure it was ready to fly. Once the bags were stored Gunny climbed in and waited for John to finish his preflight. Once satisfied everything was good to go, John gingerly climbed aboard and started the engines.

Both men donned their headsets and plugged into to the intercom and radios. "Gunny I know it's kind of late to ask, but did you remember to switch the plates on the car again?"

"That bullet slowed you down a bit John, I've been waiting for you to ask that since the hospital. And yes I got them switched back. I did it while the cops were loading up the bad guys. The car has been impounded as evidence so I didn't even have to worry about contacting the rental company; the police did that for us so we are good to go. Just one thing John, you sure you're fit to fly."

John smiled at Gunny. "Only one way to find out." With that he hit the throttles and the plane jumped forward heading down the runway and into the sky.

Chapter 12

Charley saw the rest area sign and began slowing down to pull in. He parked at the far end of the lot closest to the exit leading back on to the interstate, with the van ready to drive out in case they needed to leave in a hurry. Sean, woken by the change in speed, moved into the front seeing that they were at a rest area, Charley got out of the van and stretched, trying to work the soreness out of his back from hours of driving. He went into the restrooms and then into the information booth to get some local brochures of the area. Picking up some info on campgrounds he grabbed a coke from the vending machine and headed back to the van.

Sean opened the side door and stepped out as Charley approached. "Where are we lad?"

"Just crossed the Mississippi state line. I got some info on campgrounds, do you feel like stopping or do you want to keep driving?" At the last minute as they were heading south, the two decided to head southwest instead.

"Let's keep driving, I'll take over for a while. I'm going to hit the restroom and then we'll get back on the road."

Five minutes later they were back on the interstate heading west with Sean driving and Charley sound asleep in the back. He turned on the radio just before the top of the hour to catch the news. The top story was still the shootout in New Hampshire between federal agents and unknown assailants. The government was not commenting on the story however there were rumors that it had to do with the attempted Presidential assassination. Reports indicated that the two prime suspects had been seen in upstate New York. The newscast went on to another story and Sean turned the radio off to think in quiet. If the government thought they were in New York then they were safe. No one would be looking for them this far south so soon. This offered a window of opportunity that he needed to talk to Charley about. He saw a sign saying it was another thirty miles before the next rest area where he could pull over, so he spent the driving time planning things in his head to have a coherent plan to talk over with his young partner. When he finally got to the rest stop most of the details were already worked out in his mind.

"Lad wake up, we need to talk," he said, pulling into the parking area.

Charley was up instantly noticing the change in speed, thinking something was wrong. "What it is?" he asked reaching for the SMG he had laid on the floor close to him.

"Relax lad, I just need to discuss and idea with you."

"Old man, don't do things like that, I almost had a heart attack."

Sean chuckled. "You're too young for a heart attack. Listen, the news reports think we're in upstate New York right now, so I was thinking that this gives us a window to get the information you want. The only problem is we need to head back north to DC and it will require some rough stuff, are you interested?"

Charley thought for a second. "How rough?"

"I was thinking we snatch the three stooges. They run things after all, so if the info exists they'll know where to find it. The down side is we may have to torture them to get it."

"Where do we snatch them at?" Charley asked, for the moment ignoring the torture comment

"We take them as they are entering the factory." Sean quickly outlined his idea and for the next few minutes they went over it to look for flaws. The plan was to take the three by surprise and drug them. Once unconscious they could be taken to a quiet place and questioned. Charley already knew where to buy tranquilizer guns off the internet, as his partner had found out the hard way, complete with darts, and sedatives to fill them. The decision was made to go up and at least look around to see if it was possible. Charley set up the satellite so he could connect to the net and once online he searched for rental mailboxes near DC finding several in Virginia. He rented a box using the credit card he had created for Sean; he was given the address as soon as the order was processed. With that done he ordered the tranquilizer guns from the same company as the last time complete with darts, to be shipped to the mailbox. As an afterthought he checked the bulletin boards for new information. Seeing nothing he uploaded a post giving the name of a small town in New York near the Canadian border saying that the renegades had been spotted, still heading west.

Holly came in to work to see John and Gunny already at their desks. "Guys how are you two?" She asked happy to see them both back.

"I'm fine, Gunny how bout you?" John said casually.

"Never better," came Gunny's reply.

"John, you were shot, shouldn't you take a few days off work?" Holly asked with concern in her voice.

"Miss McClare," Gunny said before John could reply. "I've seen worse cuts from saving. He doesn't need time off."

"Well thank you Gunny, for that concise medical report, but I believe the lady was speaking to me. And Miss McClare I'm fine, the doc in New Hampshire cleared me. I just need to be careful lifting things, and change the bandage every day. It'll heal up in a week or so. What's on the agenda for today ma'am?"

As Holly was sitting down at her desk, Sergeant Erwin and Doris came in, they also expressed concern over John not taking a couple of days off, but were reassured when he stated he was cleared by the doctor. The two men related their adventure for the women filling them in on all the details. John also offered his opinion that he thought the tips fake, and that the two men were no where near upstate New York. One thing was perfectly clear though, there was definitely another group of people out there also searching for the two, and it was well funded and highly trained judging by the actions of the men in New Hampshire. They were being interrogated but had so far refused to say anything other then to ask for a lawyer. Even after it was explained to them that they were being held under national security rules, and as such didn't get a lawyer, they only repeated the demand for one. The captives were in being held in the hospital and when not being questioned the doctors kept them semi-sedated. Tape recorders were placed near and left running in the hope that one of them may say something in their drugged state. So far nothing useful had been learned.

The team went back to work checking through the take from Spock. Gunny finished working on a trace program and set it up on the bulletin board that they had gotten the tip from. Sooner or later someone would post again and they would try to find the IP address to back track the user with. Gunny finished it and uploaded to the server that he had had hacked into, now all they had to do was hope that it worked.

When Charley posted his message both Gunny's program and Spock saw it and did as they were programmed to do. Spock downloaded it to the database set up for that purpose while Gunny's program started the trace route to find the IP. In terms of human time it was blazingly fast, however in computer time, it was agonizingly slow. The trace took 1.6 seconds to complete but came up with the IP address of the computer that had posted the message and matched it to a service provider. It put this information in an email and sent it to Gunny, who had his system sent to monitor the email and pop up a notice anytime he received a new email. The notice of new email popped up and Gunny checked the message to find the IP address showing there.

"Miss McClare, I have an IP address from a poster, getting the info on the trace now," Gunny said, opening programs on his system.

He checked the IP address to find out which company controlled it and discovered it was a satellite internet provider. By now the rest of the team had stopped working to follow what Gunny was doing. When he announced who controlled the IP, everyone began trying to break into that company's database with the tools at their disposal. Holly was the first one to get in and get the list of assigned IP addresses, using Spock. Luckily for her the company used a static IP system that assigned an IP to a customer and never changed it. She gave the IP to Gunny and had him check to see if it was still online and hack into the system is possible. In less than a minute Gunny had discovered that the customer was still online and was running Windows XP. He exploited a security hole in the open socket connection and had the system grant him access to the hard drive.

"I'm in! I'll do a data search and then download what I can get. Do we have a location on this guy yet?"

"You guys aren't going to believe this but I think this is one of the men we're looking for," Holly told her team. "According to the records the address on file is the same house that the FBI announced as belonging to Sean Miller and Charles Watkins. The name is different but the address is the same."

"You mean they're at the house in Vermont?" John asked.

"I don't know, probably not, they have a satellite connection so they could be anywhere in North America. The address they have on the account is the Vermont one but account is prepaid for at least a year, unlimited access and bandwidth. Gunny, anything yet?"

"Getting some data now, looks like they did some online ordering. They ordered four tranquilizer guns and darts to go with them. Damn I lost the connection, he must have logged off."

"Did you get a location of where they are?" Holly asked.

Gunny searched through the records. "No but he's been doing some online banking. Smart boy though no account numbers or passwords saved on his hard drive. I did get the figures and the institutions they have their accounts at. Bingo, they have credit cards, I can hack into their bank and see where the last time they used the card was."

Charley suddenly noticed his internet connection lagging and the hard drive light was on showing data transfer. He began checking over his system to see what was going on and then noticed that he was being hacked. He quickly tried to do a back trace and hit a firewall that stopped him cold. Knowing that he was losing data with no idea who he was losing it too, he did the only thing he could think of, he shut off the power to the satellite.

"Shit! I just got hacked," Charley told Sean.

"What does that mean lad?"

"I'm not sure yet, I'm still checking to see what they got."

Charley pounded the keys searching the computer and trying to determine what if any damage had been done. After twenty minutes he knew that they were in trouble.

"Sean, they got my online banking info, all of it with the exception of two credit cards, those were the ones I set up for you, the ones that were secured with prepayments on them."

"What does that mean for us lad?"

"It means we can't use any of my cards anymore and they are going to know where we've been and everything we've bought. The only thing they didn't get was the new post office box I just ordered, I used your card for that. From now on we have to use cash and your cards only. They also know about the tranquilizer guns."

"The last few times you bought gas did you use cash or plastic?"

"I used the cards so they're going to have a clear trail right to us Sean."

"Okay we already decided to head back north so we are already changing direction. Let's get going, we need to get out of the state ASAP."

Sean started the van and got back on the highway while Charley packed up the gear. Checking his map he saw an exit a few miles up the road that got them to a state highway, heading north. Sean decided that would be the route they would take.

Gunny gave the banking information he got from the hard drive to Holly who had Spock crack the banks database and give then a printout of the transactions on the account. Scanning down the list it showed the last purchase as being for gas in Mississippi. Working backwards the credit card activity started in Maine and showed a path south with a stay in Tennessee at a national park.

"John you were right the post in New Hampshire was a fake and it was the suspects who posted it. I looks as if they are in the south headed west and trying to cover their tracks by laying a false trail in the north, question is what do we do about it?"

"What do you mean 'do about it' ma'am?" Gunny asked. "We alert the FBI and let them catch these guys, they are wanted criminals."

"They are not criminals yet, Gunny. They are wanted for questioning and the number one suspects in the shooting attempt on the President but they are still innocent until proven guilty. I shouldn't have to tell a Marine that."

"Yes ma'am, but we still need to tell the FBI what information we have."

"Does anyone else have a thought on this?" Holly asked the group.

Doris was the first to answer. "I don't think we should tell the FBI, I think we should track them ourselves and see what happens with regard to the posts. These two seem to know there is someone other then the FBI hunting them and are trying to lay a false trail. I'm wondering why?"

"I agree with Gunny, they are wanted for questioning so we are obligated to inform the FBI," Sergeant Erwin said flatly.

Holly noticed John sitting there looking thoughtful but not saying anything at all. "Do you have any input John?"

"Here's the problem as I see it. The FBI is looking for these two so we are required to hand over any information that will speed in their apprehension. The other side of the coin is that once they are in jail this mystery group that is looking for them will also know where they are, as it will be national news. I think that the chances of these two suffering a fatal accident shortly after their arrest is extremely high, very much like Oswald and Ruby. If that happens we are never going to find these other people that we suspect are also hunting the two suspects. In my mind this is a national security issue and as such, we can keep investigating this ourselves. Of course that decision has to be made by the general."

"I never thought about it that way John," Gunny said. "Miss McClare I think this one should go to the general and John's got a point. I think maybe we do need to know who the other team is more than we need to talk to those two men. But I'd like to suggest we get as much info on them as possible so that when the time comes to bring them in we can do it quickly."

"Agreed, Gunny," Holly told the team. "I'll take it to the general and see about letting us keep working on this mystery group at the same time we track the suspects."

Holly picked up her phone and dialed the Generals assistant to see about meeting with him. She got a time for later that morning and with that done went back to work.

Too much was happening at once for the three stooges. The remaining team members from the New Hampshire action were in federal custody, but they didn't have a location yet, and one of their star agents was missing. As well it appeared that an agent was following the two renegades across the North East heading west. From the look of the posts it was a fairly new recruit as he was sending dis-jointed and hurried messages, but had failed to answer requests for direct communication. There was the possibility that the posts were fakes but they could not be sure. If the posts were fakes then it hinted at a far more troubling possibility; that someone knew of the existence of the organization and was setting up a false trail to lead agents into a trap to capture them. This information required direct and immediate input from the wise men. There was a procedure for such an eventuality, albeit one seldom used. It was time to use in now.

A time was set and a suite rented at one of the numerous upscale hotels in the city. The stooges ordered a lunch buffet for six to be set up on warming trays prior to the meeting so that all the men could eat without any waiters being in the room. They could not risk anyone seeing the board members together in the same place. The three wise men would all take a different route to the Hotel and arrive at staggered times to reduce the danger of being seen together. The three juniors would arrive early to set up the room for the meeting and scan it for listening devices.

In three different offices three very influential men juggled their schedules, not telling anyone why. The meeting would not be on any listed schedule anywhere, and for a portion of the afternoon no one would be able to contact the three men. This was rare but had happened enough in the positions these men occupied, that it was not questioned by any of their staff. It was assumed that they would be secretly meeting with politicians.

The meeting began as soon as the last board member arrived. The juniors briefed their superiors on the events in New Hampshire and the sudden disappearance of one of their star agents. All options were weighed and then plans laid. It was agreed that the organization was in danger of exposure, but not how this was happening. None of the agents from New Hampshire had been heard from so they were not able to get any information from them as to what happened. Second hand reports indicated that agents from the NSA were involved in the shootout but that could not be proven, all that was know was that federal agents had been involved. They were trying to confirm this and find out were their own agents were being held. One of the board members answered these questions for them and confirmed that the agents were in federal custody, being held as threats to national security. The FBI was interrogating them but so far none of the agents had talked. This was good news to the board as they knew that the agents were highly trained and motivated so there was little risk of them giving up any information. As the meeting wore on and more information was revealed, the name Holly McClare came up. The reports mentioned her as the person that had first reported the existence of the organization but no one knew how she had found them. Plans were made to find out what she knew, and if necessary, remove her as a threat.

The stooges were ordered to begin looking into Holly McClare and how the NSA came to suspect that the organization exists. As well they were to contact the agent reporting on the two renegades and get him linked up with another action team. The board wanted this matter cleared up ASAP. Since they were meeting anyway, and it needed to be done they wrapped up the meeting by discussing preliminary plans for another attempt on the president.

With the meeting over the board member left each taking a different route out of the hotel, leaving the juniors to clean up and sanitize the room. They wiped down all the surfaces ensuring that no fingerprints were left in the room. They also sprayed an ammonia compound over the carpet to destroy and DNA in the form or skin cells or hair follicles that may have been left. The dishes that were used by the three wise men were put into a sack and taken with them when they left, they would simply pay extra to replace the dishes that were missing. With the room completely sanitized, they left to carry out the orders they had been given.

Sean pulled into the rest area again following his usual procedure of parking at the closest spot to the exit, ready to leave at a moments notice. Getting out he stretched, working out the kinks, as he looked around checking the rest area for signs of danger. Satisfied that everything was normal he reached under the seat for the silenced .380 he had strapped there and tucked it behind his belt at the small of his back, closed the door and walked toward the restrooms to empty his bladder.

Coming out of the restroom he stopped at the vending machines to get a couple of sodas for him and Charley before heading back to the truck. As he left the vending machines he saw two men staring at him from a car in the parking lot. The man behind the wheel looked familiar to him. He saw recognition light up the man's eyes just as he himself realized that he was looking at one of the organizations top killers, a man he had trained himself. The car engine roared with power as it leaped forward headed straight at Sean all the while the driver motioning to his partner in the passenger seat and pointing forward.

Sean dropped the cans of soda and ran toward the van screaming for Charley. Knowing he would never make it he leaped behind a parked car pulling out his pistol and ducking down for protection. His pursuers screeched to a stop and both erupted from the car carrying guns and looking for Sean. Charley opened the door of the van to see what was going on and saw two men with guns moving forward in the classic military approach method of cover and rush, he also spotted the head of partner poking up from behind a parked car. Everyone, with the exception of the three armed men, was screaming and running away from the parking lot. Without thinking about it Charley reached back into the van and grabbed a rifle. Sighting on the far man he squeezed off a shot and watched the bullet blow the gun out of the man's hand. The sound of the shot and the sight of the gun disintegrating made both turn their attention from the man they were hunting to see who was now hunting them This cost them, as Sean, already knowing where the shot came from stood up and fired four times, hitting each man with two shots in the head. Knowing both men were dead, he calmly tucked the gun out of sight and walked back to the van which was now running with his partner behind the wheel and ready to go.

Sean motioned the young man to move over as he opened the driver's door to get in. Gratefully Charley hopped in the back to let the old man drive and as they left the rest area he took the bolt out of his rifle and started to clean it, more from habit than any real need to do so.

"Charley, lad, are you okay?"

"What the hell happened Sean? Who were those guys?" Charley asked suddenly starting to shake as the adrenaline began draining from his system.

"Just bad luck Lad, that's all. Those were two organization assassins and they recognized me. There was no choice in what I did, they would have gladly killed us both. We're only a few miles from the state line so hopefully we can get across before the police get a description of our van from witnesses. For safety sake lad I think you should break out the SMG's and load everything up. We could be in for some trouble and we should be ready for anything. By the way that was a hell of a shot you just made."

With something to occupy his mind and hands Charley started to relaxed and loaded up all their weapons as Sean drove the van with a calmness that belied the fear eating at his stomach. They crossed back into Tennessee and got off the interstate to drive on the secondary roads pushing north the entire time. Sean had tuned the radio to an all news station as soon as they left the rest area but so far nothing had been reported about their incident. They were almost into Kentucky before they hear a news report concerning a shootout that killed two men in Mississippi. The radio reported that one man was wanted in connection with the incident and he had fled the scene, heading west in a blue two door car.

Sean couldn't believe it, no one had identified their van and they were only looking for one man. Charley had also heard the news report and was confused. "Is that us they are talking about?"

"I think so lad, but they have their facts all screwed up it would seem. It sounds as if we are safe for now. I think we are still a go for grabbing the 3 stooges as soon as we get the tranquilizer guns, this won't give them any indication that we are a threat to them. Did you get any idea when they would be there delivered?"

"It was supposed to be an overnight delivery so they should be there tomorrow, we can go the morning after in that case."

"Okay we'll head for DC right now and do the snatch as soon as we can."

They drove through the night taking turns behind the wheel, and napping while the other drove. The postal outlet where Charley had rented the box was just west of Washington CD in northern Virginia and was open 24 hours. They stopped there and Charley went in with the fake ID he had used to rent the box. There were two packages there waiting for him, and when he opened them in the van they contained the guns, darts and sedatives he had ordered.

"You got to love the internet!" he exclaimed. "We have everything we need Sean. It's only 1 AM do you think we can do the snatch this morning or do we need more prep time."

Sean thought for a second. "We need to park the van someplace and steal a car that we can dump later. If we can get a car in the next twenty minutes we can go this morning."

With the decision made Sean began driving around looking for a car that they could steal. Ideally he wanted something that would not be missed for a few hours and not attract attention to them. He found a Toyota parked behind a garage about ten minutes later and pulled up to it. Peering through the window he saw a note taped to the steering wheel indicating repairs that needed to be done to the car. It looked as if someone had dropped the car off after hours to be fixed in the morning. It was mere seconds of work to get into the car and hotwire it. Sean drove the stolen car out of the garage lot two minutes after he had pulled into it. Charley followed him in the van and the two cars headed into Washington.

They left the van at a long-term secure parking garage, transferred the weapons they would need, and a duffel bag that Charley had packed, to the car. Sean drove heading to the outskirts of the city into a rather seedy section of town that contained the only industrial section of Washington. And to even call it this part industrial was stretching the limits of the word. It was more an area of warehouses used to store goods for businesses in the city area. Washington didn't have any true industry because it was the nations capitol and the major business here was the government. Parking the car on a side street the two men prepared themselves, then locked the car up and left it.

Two shadows detached themselves from the surrounding darkness and crawled their way to the fence. A slit was cut in the chain link and two men slipped through it making sure that the fence looked undisturbed by their passing. It required an hour to cover the distance from the fence to the seemingly abandoned warehouse and then another half hour to make the way to the front to gain entrance. Their movements so slow that anyone glancing at them would not notice anything, only by focusing on them could you see them moving at all. The two were conscience of every sound and movement, careful to move in complete harmony, timing everything perfectly. They were sure and confident and totally alert. It was as if they belonged in the night, their movements were precise and economical, no wasted motion even though each one wore a backpack.

When they reached the front, one worked on the simple door lock to gain entry while the other watched making sure they remained unseen. A car approached and with a simple touch the order to drop and cover was communicated; the two, as one, laying against the base of the wall faces pressed to the ground so no shine of skin would reflect light. Their clothes were all natural fibers and flat black in color so they blended into the shadows perfectly. The car, a police cruiser on a routine patrol of the area, passed by without even slowing down. This part of the city was all industrial and quiet after dark. Most of the companies using private guards and attack dogs rather then alarms, making the job of the police that much easier. With the police out of sight the door was opened in another few seconds, the two moving through it softly then locking the door behind them.

They stopped at the door and wrapped cotton rags around their boots to avoid leaving any solid footprints in the dust and dirt of the floor. The inside of the building showed tire tracks from the large bay door to one of the small side offices, with nothing else in sight at all. No furniture or equipment of any type was inside the main part of the building. All the windows were covered over in plastic and the place was strangely empty of birds, which always seemed to take up residence in abandoned structures. The only thing to see at all were the tire tracks. The intruders moved along the wall stepping as close to the wall as they could, until the reached the tire tracks in the dust. They followed the tracks careful not to step outside them and leave tracks in the dust to mark their passing. Where the tire tracks stopped footprints began, leading into one of the empty offices. Following the in the path of the footprints the two entered the office to find the floor swept clean and a mat to wipe their feet on. The only furniture in the office was a large metal filing cabinet in the far corner and the mat just inside the door.

"Where's the elevator?" a puzzled Charley asked.

Sean pilled on one of the draw handles of the filing cabinet and it swung open to reveal an elevator car. "Let's get set up, we've got some time if they adhere to their schedule and I'm sure those anal retentive pricks will," Sean replied, looking at his watch. "Let's eat and then get settled. And let's keep an eye on this elevator car, we don't want anyone coming up behind us.

After their breakfast the two moved back to the door of the office and each took out a tranquilizer gun from their packs along with a blackjack as a back up. Once they checked the guns over and had the darts loaded and ready the tossed the packs into the corner and each took one side of the door, settling down to wait for their quarry. Exactly on time they heard the warehouse bay door open and a car drive through inside. A few seconds later the engine was shut off and the sound of people opening car doors and getting out was audible.

At the sound of three car doors closing Sean counted to ten, signaled Charley and jumped into the left side of the office doorway, while Charley filled the right side. They fired almost at the same time each one shooting the three men walking toward them once in the chest. One of the men had time to pull a pistol halfway out of his holster before the fast acting drug knocked him out. Dropping the Tranquilizer guns Sean and Charley moved to the three stooges and tied them up using duct tape. The three were immobilized by wrapping tape from the wrists to elbows and ankles to knees, and also putting tape over the mouth to keep them quiet when they woke up. With the men secure they dragged the unconscious bodies into the office and propped them against the wall near the filing cabinet.

"I wish we could have some coffee," he commented to the empty office. Charley chuckled at his friends obsession with coffee.

"How do you think it will take for them to wake up?" he asked Sean.

"Lad you should know better than me, you've been unconscious more than I have," he chuckled. "I would think about 3 hours or so, it's fast acting but we didn't give them that big a dose. The hard part comes when they wake up, we'll most likely need to use some form of persuasion to get any information from them you know."

Charley had thought about that since he and Sean had started on their little crusade. To get his life back from these people he would need to be as ruthless as they had tried to make him in the first place, but he didn't want to do that. Suddenly he had the answer to his moral dilemma. He remembered a story his Grandfather had once told him about questioning people without resorting to brutality. He moved to the three men and searched them until he found the keys to the car.

"I have the answer but we can't do it here, we need to take these guys with us and question them somewhere else. Somewhere secluded, with lots of water."

"What have you got up your sleeve lad?"

"An old trick I heard about a long time ago. We've got nothing to lose so let's give it a try. Help me load these guys into the trunk and we'll get out of here."

They quickly loaded the three men into the trunk of the car, extremely glad it was a full size ford with a trunk large enough to hold them. Charley tossed the keys to his partner and hoped in the passenger side. Sean started the car and drove to the door, searching above the sun visor for some type of remote to open the door. Suddenly he shut off the car and looked at Charley.

"They are going to know that these men are missing and directly below us are more men that used to be stooges. We have to try and keep the organization from knowing that these men are missing as long as possible."

"We can set fire to the building, that way they might think that the stooges are dead. It also has the added benefit of the fire department maybe finding the elevator shaft and exposing the place

"That won't work Lad, there will be no bodies which there would be if they died in a fire. We need something else or we need a way to let the organization know that the stooges have been taken." Sean thought for a minute coming up with the answer. "We have to blow up the shaft then. We have enough explosive to do the job. It will take a while to clear the rubble and after an explosion it would certainly take time to confirm that there are no bodies. It also has the benefit of shutting this place down, for a little while at least and possibly exposing it to the world."

"What's the best way to do that?"

"Well Lad, they built it using a hydraulic lifting arm on the bottom so there are no cables and even if their were the car brakes would stop it from falling. Our best bet is to line the joint of wall and floor with explosive and blow the bottom out of the car. The rest of the car should drop to the bottom of the shaft.

Out of their backpacks came two blocks of C4 that were rolled out into the shape of a rope. Once it was an even thickness and length they put it along the floor of the cage where it met the sides, covering all four walls. Once in place Sean set up a thirty second pencil fuse and the two ran from the office after pushing the cabinet back into place. It seemed much longer than thirty seconds, but eventually they were rewarded with a loud bang and the sound of the filing cabinet falling over. They went back in and saw the elevator gone, lying at the bottom of a wrecked shaft with the lift arm mangled beyond repair. The filing cabinet was on it's side in the middle of the floor so the two men picked it up and moved it back in place to hide the shattered elevator shaft. They returned to the car, took a quick look outside to see if the explosion had drawn any attention, and exited the building into the morning light after seeing that no one seemed to be aware anything was wrong. At the gate Charley got out and simply smashed the lock off, after Sean had driven the car through he replaced it with a similar lock to give the place back its normal appearance. If all went well they would be clear of the area before anyone knew there was a problem.

The explosion rocked the shaft at the bottom and the Guard on duty heard the screech of metal and the bang of the elevator cage hitting the bottom of the shaft. He hit the alarm to bring the security detail to the elevator shaft and to call the on duty supervisor. In less than ten seconds the alert security team was there followed less than a minute later by the supervisor.

"Report!" he ordered the sentry.

"Sir, less than two minutes ago there was a topside explosion and then the sound of something hitting the bottom of the elevator shaft. Fearing a breach may be in progress I sounded the alarm."

The supervisor approached the shaft door and listened intently for any sounds of movement on the other side. The guards all stood pointing their weapons at the entranceway, with two men behind the lexan shield. Hearing no noise he held his hand near the metal door feeling for the heat of fire. The door was not giving off any heat so he placed his hand directly on it feeling for any vibration. Everything seemed normal, could the guard have been hearing things?

"Soldier open this door." He ordered one of the security team.

The ordered man moved forward and entered the security code on the keypad. The door slid open to revel the wrecked elevator car blocking the shaft, the supervisor moved forward to get a closer look as the smell of the explosive reached him.

"Shit! Go get the maintenance team, right now. And get another security team up here to guard against possible attack, someone used explosives on the elevator." He checked his watch and realized that the juniors normally arrived at this time and suddenly wondering if they were in danger. Until the elevator was cleared there was nothing he could do. Having been a junior himself he know the emergency contact procedures and numbers, once the shaft was clear he would send out an alert and try to contact the juniors to ensure they were okay and knew about the attach.

Working with cutting torches and crowbars several men from the maintenance team had an opening cleared into the shaft proper in thirty minutes. Two guards checked out the shaft noticing that the hydraulic arm that lifted and lowered the elevator car was still in the raised position but bent and would be impossible to lower. Using a pair of binoculars, one of the men checked out the top of the shaft noticing that the top of the shaft was still mostly obscured with light showing around the edges of what once would have been the actual elevator car. Most of the car now lay shattered on the floor of the shaft. With the door now clear they again called the supervisor for instructions.

Chapter 13

Sean drove west at the flow of traffic, careful not to draw attention to himself. He was a wanted criminal with three kidnapped men tied up and drugged in the trunk of the car. If they were stopped he and Charley would be immediately arrested and tossed in jail. If that happened they were both dead and he knew it. Even though he wanted to speed up and get there faster he knew that safety lay in patience. Charley tilted the seat back and tried to relax as if catching a nap on the morning commute. Both men were far from relaxed.

Sean turned off the interstate heading for one of the farms that the organization owned in the area. As he neared the farm Sean pulled of the road and took his pistol from the holster in the small of his back. Charley checked one of the guns taken from one of the stooges and checked it over to make sure it was ready to fire. He then crawled into the back seat and opened the duffel bag lying on the floor. He pulled out his sten, checked the action before loading it with a clip chambering a round and lying down on the seat to be out of view. Sean was hoping that the farm was not being used right now but was prepared to fight his way onto the property. With both men ready, Sean headed to the farm.

He pulled up in front of the house and shut the car off. He put his gun in his waistband got out of the car, walked up to the door and knocked, there was no answer. Sean looked at the car and noticed Charley just peering over the seat at him, he motioned with his head to indicate he was going behind the house to check the barn. Charley nodded his understanding and as quietly as he could, opened his door and crawled out of the car to cover Sean. As Sean circled around the house to the barn Charley shadowed him staying tight to the side of the house. When the barn was in sight Charley pointed the sten at the door and stopped, allowing Sean to check it out. He opened the large door and called out to see if there was anyone there. After thirty seconds of silence Sean moved inside to search.

Charley waited what seemed like an hour but was only a very tense minute, and when Sean re-appeared he joined him in front of the barn.

"Well Lad, it looks like we have the place to ourselves. Let's move the car into the barn for some privacy and then have a chat with our friends." Sean headed back toward the car.

"Wait, shouldn't we check the house?" Charley asked.

"No, it's alarmed and if anyone were here they would have come out by now. If all goes well we can be out of here in an hour."

Sean walked to the car and then moved it into the barn, once inside Charley closed the door, plunging them into shadows. As he was about to turn on the lights Sean stopped him with a shout.

"Don't, we don't need them anyway. Let's get these guys out of the trunk and see how talkative they are."

They dragged the three stooges out of the trunk and moved them further back into the barn. Sean climbed into the hayloft and tossed a few bales down to the main floor where Charley made a little wall out of them and leaned the stooges against them. Sean rejoined him on the floor and the two men took a duffel out of the back seat of the car. Then waited for the stooges to regain consciousness, which took a couple more hours but eventually they were opening their eyes and shaking their heads.

Sean sat down on floor in front of the three. "Good morning Gentleman. Do you know who we are?" none of the men moved at all. "Allow me to introduce myself, I am Sean Miller and this young man is my associate Charles Watkins. Until recently we were employed, a word I use euphemistically, by your organization. Together we decided that the terms of our employment were not to our liking and attempted to resign. For some strange reason you gentleman objected and ordered that we be terminated. Charles and I, understandably, object to this harsh treatment, and in light of your latest actions we thought it would be best to talk to you in person and see if we could come to some accommodation. So with that in mind I believe that my associate would like to ask a few questions. Charles?"

"Thank you Sean. I apologize for the way we brought you here but I was afraid that you may not want to come willingly and to be honest I was anxious to get this whole issue between us resolved. I was a confirmed pacifist right up until the moment your thugs shot me, to say I didn't like that would be a huge understatement. I can see by the look in your eyes that you are surprised by the news. You had no knowledge that I was injured? That was probably because Sean killed your agents and they couldn't report back to you. Now the end result of this is that my moral qualms about harming other people underwent some changes as Sean was digging a bullet out of me. Do you know how much that hurts? Add in the fact that I couldn't go to a hospital because I'm wanted for a crime that you framed me for and, well, I have a little unresolved anger towards you folks. Just so you know, I don't bluff, not at all, you men will talk to me. So I'm going to take off your gags one at a time and ask you some questions. Unfortunately we don't have a lot of time, I'm sure someone will miss you soon. As a result let me say I'm sorry in advance if some times we seem to be a little rough in the way we ask our questions."

Charley took the gag off the stooge on the right. "What's your name?"

"Fuck you" was the reply.

Charley shook his head. "Sean can you believe this guy? He has me framed, kidnaps me, and then tried to have me killed and when I ask him for his name he replies with profanities."

"Some people have no manners at all," Sean commented. "Would you like me to educate him?"

"Thank you, but no. I believe I can handle this one."

"You pussy, you couldn't even perform the task we asked you to after we recruited you. You think I'm going to be frightened of someone like you? Think again shithead," the man said defiantly.

"You should be," the young man said flatly.

Sean and Charley grabbed the man hauled him on top of the hay bales and laid him out on his back. They then took a canteen out of the duffel filled it at a water tap in the barn and went back to the man on the hay bales. With Sean holding him Charley pinched his nose closed and slowly started pouring water into his mouth forcing him to drink or drown. Charley was sure that this would work but didn't take into account the dedication of the man he was dealing with. Rather then try to avoid the water or swallow it, he started to breathe in deeply pulling the water into his lungs and choking. Sean quickly flipped him over and pounded on his back to get the water out of his lungs and breathing air again. He was fine in a few minutes, but it was obvious that Charley's idea wasn't going to work. They dropped the stooge back on the floor next to his comrades and moved away to confer.

"Lad we are going to have to be brutal here, there is no other way. Your idea was a good one and on normal people it would have worked. But on these fanatics we need to use pain. You go on outside and keep watch, I'll deal with them." Charley just nodded and headed toward the door.

As he passed the hay bale wall the stooge began taunting him asking him if that's all he had and laughing at him, calling him names, which was a huge mistake on his part. He thought he knew the young man however he was very wrong.

Charley suddenly turned, an evil look in his eyes, smiled at the man and went over to the duffel bag and opened it. He removed a .22 pistol and a silencer and screwed them together. Cambering a round he turned and shot the man in the left knee. The stooge screamed and fell on his side drawing his legs up and curling into a fetal position. Calmly Charley grabbed the mans right foot and pulled his leg out then shot him in the right knee. Placing the gun on the floor he re-gagged the man and moved on to the stooge in the middle and removed his gag. Sean was stunned at the sudden brutality of his young partner but wisely stayed quiet letting the stooges think this was normal behavior

"So what's your name?" Charley asked quietly, casually picking up the gun.

The stooge looked at the first man rolling on the ground in pain. He stared at Charley, his eyes narrowed down to slits trying to think of his options. Charley let him go for about a minute then quickly put a bullet through the man's right foot. Placing the gun on the ground again he re-gagged the second stooge who was now also curled up in the fetal position. He un-gagged the third stooge and picked up the gun

"By now you know that I'm not bluffing and I don't really care about any of you. I'll ask a question and I'm only going to wait so long for an answer before I shoot you. So one more time, what's your name?"

"I go by John, but I've changed my name so often I'm not sure what it really is anymore"

The middle stooge made muffled noises through his gag and tried to kick John. Charley casually shot him in the calf to stop the kicking. "Now see how easy that was?" he said to the two bleeding sobbing men. "I asked and he answered truthfully and I didn't shoot him. That's how this works."

"Sean, since John here is so co-operative, do you think we could simply dispense with the other two and discuss things with him?"

"I'm feeling lenient today, why don't we give them a second chance later on, after they've had some time to think. We'll take John into the other room so his friends don't get too upset with him and talk to him there." With that Sean got up and helped John to his feet then moved him to the other side of the barn.

Charley looked at the other two angrier then he had ever been before in his life. "You have no idea how lucky you assholes are. If it were up to me I'd kill you like you tried to kill me. But my partner feels you still have some use, I just hope he's wrong."

Once on the other side of the barn John changed his mind and once again refused to say anything. Charley picked up the gun but Sean stopped him. He smiled at the stooge, calmly reached out and broke the little finger of the mans left hand. A few moments of moving the broken finger around and John once again became co-operative. They took turns asking John questions and the longer they talked the more shocked they became. The scope of the organization was massive. It had agents in almost all the fortune 500 companies, every branch of the government, all the Federal police agencies, the armed forces; several judges were members as well. Both Sean and Charley were surprised to learn that the US government had nothing to do with the organization, it was private, but the largest shock was the three men who controlled the organization. For several seconds neither man spoke.

It was Sean who broke the silence. "Those bastards!" he said with feeling. "All this time I was working for the very people I was told I was fighting against."

Charley smiled. "I knew there was something fishy about these people. So now that we know, what do we do?"

"There's nothing you can do," John answered. "We're too big. If you come back we'll forget this whole little incident. We can pick up where we left off. The organization is right, we are fulfilling a destiny. You kill the president and all will be forgiven."

Sean calmly pulled the pistol out of his partner's hand and shot the stooge in the forehead while muttering "shut up". Charley jumped at the action and quickly turned away.

"We're going to have to fight a war against these people aren't we?" Charley asked, his face pale.

"You realize that if you fight you'll have to kill someone or you'll end up dead. You are an expert shot but you cannot shoot to wound people like you did here. In the real world that just won't play."

"I know," he replied quietly.

"Charley if you hesitate, even for a second against these people you'll die. I can't fight them and protect you at the same time. If we do this you'll be on your own in a firefight. Until I know you can pull the trigger I can't trust you to watch my back, which means I won't be watching yours. I don't like to be hard about this but that's the way it has to be."

Charley nodded his head making his decision and walked back to the other two men and removed the gags from both. "So you are a private group, nothing to do with the government? I really shouldn't be surprised by that considering what you tried to have me do."

"You tell that traitorous shit that he's dead," one of the stooges said.

"Well you're too late, my friend Sean has already taken care of that. But what you should be worried about is yourself. You see John told us some great stories but I'm the skeptical type, I like to have things confirmed. So let's try the question and answer again and see what happens this time."

"You can still go fuck yourself asshole!" the defiant one answered.

Charley shot him in the stomach, the silenced .22 hardly making a sound. "Hurts don't it. You lay there and bleed for a bit, I'll talk to your friend here. As you can see I don't really have an issue with shooting you. So here's the rules, I ask and you answer. Hesitate or swear at me and I shoot you. So let's begin, what's your name?"

"Sam," came the one word reply.

"Excellent, Sam. See that wasn't so hard. Do you work for the US government?"

"I know you're going to kill me anyway so why should I give you anymore information?"

"You've got a point there," Charley said and shot Sam in the head twice. "You get to bleed to death in pain." Charley said to the remaining stooge, and he shot him two more times in the stomach.

Charley dropped the gun back in the duffel bag and then walked to the door and went outside. Sean looked at the third stooge and then shot him in the head to end his suffering, he didn't see the need to be cruel. He followed Charley outside to check on the Lad and found him kneeling against the barn, throwing up, tears streaming down his face.

Sean patted him on the back and helped him to sit. "That was a hard thing you did in there Charley, are you going to be all right?"

Charley took a couple of deep breaths and wiped his face. "Yeah, I'll be okay. I'm sorry I doubted you Sean, you told me this would be a war and until now I had the idea that we could just expose these people, prove our innocence and go back to our lives. That's never going to happen is it?"

Sean sat down next to the young man. "No, no it isn't. Even I didn't know how entrenched the organization was. We can't just turn this information over to the FBI and claim we were framed, no one would believe it for a start and no one would want us alive with what we know. It would seem we are at a crossroad here, Charley. We can use what information we have to run and hide, and thanks to you, there's now a better then even chance we'll get away. Or we can try to destroy the organization. I'll leave it up to you and we'll do whatever you want."

Charley paused, thinking about what he just did. "I'm a killer; I never wanted to be a killer Sean, I just wanted to shoot my rifles at targets and be a better shot then anyone else. I never ever wanted to kill anyone."

"Charley lad, let me tell you one thing here. You are not a killer. A killer is someone that commits murder for no good reason other then he wants to. You may not believe this but you are a warrior. You became a warrior the second you decided to defy the organization. And now you and I are in a battle to stop these people from committing evil acts. That's something I should have done but never had the courage to do. You did it instinctively and did it extremely well. Better then I ever could have in fact, and if you still want to fight I'm with you, all the way. I've got your back."

"A warrior huh?" Charley laughed bitterly. "Some warrior I am, sitting here crying, wiping puke off my chin."

"Lad the day you can end a life and not be bothered by it is the day you do become a killer. Taking a life is something that should bother you, however if it is just or necessary you do it and worry about it later. And for the record I still have nightmares about the work I've done and the people I've killed."

"So what do we do now Sean?"

"Lad, I've been following your lead since we got the van in Maine. Whether you know it or not, you are in charge so we do what you want to do. You've proven all you ever have to prove to me. Do we run or fight? So far you've made all the right decisions and I'm more then willing to keep following you Charley."

This admission startled the young man; especially coming from so experienced a person as Sean. He thought for a second. "No matter what we do this information has to get out to the proper people. We can't allow the organization go on unchallenged. For now I think we should take what we've learned here and keep hiding for a little while longer until we have some kind of plan other then stumbling blindly around. Also we have the three stooges computers with all their records, I'll need to go over that and see what info I can find there too. Let's clean up here and get back to the van and head somewhere quiet to do some thinking. Does that sound good to you?"

"Lead on my young warrior prince, your humble servant will obey," Sean answered in a light tone to try and cheer his young friend up.

Feeling better about himself Charley got to his feet and with Sean in tow headed to the stolen car. They drove carefully back to where they had left the van and while Charley moved their gear and the stooges computers to the van Sean carefully wiped down the car. With everything in the van and the car clean the two left. Twenty minutes later he and Sean were on the interstate heading south enjoying the sunny morning and trying very hard to forget what had happened at the farm.

The shaft was finally empty of the elevator car wreckage, an exercise that had taken 4 hours to complete. Once that had been done, two men had climbed to the top of the shaft on the maintenance ladder built into the shaft side and cut away in the remaining floor of the elevator car. A security team now stood watch at the top of the shaft and ropes had been rigged down the shaft it's self to allow others to be lifted or lowered by ropes and pulleys, which was much easier than climbing the ladder. With this done and a second security team set up at the bottom of the shaft the supervisor climbed up to the top and used a cell phone to call the emergency number to alert the three stooges of the attack. To his surprise his call was unanswered. He tried four more times before finally dialing another emergency number and leaving a voice message that the factory had been attacked and his calls to the stooges had been unanswered, although he didn't call them the three stooges in his message, instead he referred to them as the juniors

It was 12:32 PM when the message was left. At 1 PM when the message was heard, there was disbelief and shock. No one had ever believed the factory could be attacked, it had been kept hidden and no one other then a very trusted member of the organization was allowed to know its location. The person that had checked the voice mail had been Carter's personal assistant, a man that had been with Carter for more then a decade. He tried at first to contact the juniors and when he couldn't he panicked and picked up the intercom phone, completely forgetting that his boss was in a meeting with the Secretary of the Treasury.

The intercom buzzed and at first Carter ignored it, continuing on with the secretary. Eventually the constant buzzing bothered the Secretary who told Cater to answer the damn thing to make it stop.

Carter picked it up angry at being disturbed and used the tone of his voice to convey his anger. "What is the problem? I told you no interruptions!" he barked into the phone.

"Sir the training facility has been attacked and I can't find the juniors anywhere," he blurted out.

Carter had spent a lifetime learning how to not react to bad news; all that training was put to the test at that second in time. Aside from a minor tightening of his jaw line he showed no reaction at all to the news that frightened him to his very core. This was an attack on the heart of the organization and who knew what damage could come from this. His mind processed the information and he debated what action to take, completing this mental exercise between heartbeats. First he would need to finish his meeting with the secretary and then contact his peers and see if they had the information as well.

"Thank you for the update. Please hold onto the note and I'll see you after the Secretary has left. No further calls please," he stated calmly to his stunned assistant, then hung up the phone.

He turned to the secretary and chuckled. "Young people today, they can get so flustered. A minor disagreement and they assume it has world ending consequences. I apologize for the interruption sir, where were we?" Sitting back down he resumed his meeting, forcing his mind to concentrate on the information in front of him and get through it as quickly as possible.

The meeting lasted another agonizing ninety minutes and then the secretary left, satisfied that all was in order. Carter took a few moments to clean up from the meeting and clear his mind to focus on the disaster then paged his assistant to come in.

"Cancel all appointments for the rest of the day then call the cleaners and have them come up here ASAP." He started without preamble, using the slang for the men that swept for listening devices. "Have you been able to contact the juniors yet?"

"No sir," came the barked reply.

Carter hesitated for a moment, then his over-riding need to contain the problem over-rode his concern about possible listening devices. "Then we must assume they are compromised. Call the ready action team yourself and tell them to get out to the factory and assess the damage and report back. If the local authorities are on site everything must be cleaned up, nothing is to be left untidied no matter what measures they have to use, explain that to them, now go."

His assistant left the room without another word to carry out his orders. Carter sat down at the desk and logged into his computer terminal to access the server. Once in he ran a system wide security scan to see if anyone had tried to log in without proper identification. When the scan came back with no reports he breathed a sigh of relief. Even though he kept no organization records on the server, if anyone suspected him they would try to hack into the network to see if there was anything there that could be used against him. As he was setting up a remote access through a proxy server to access the organization bulletin boards the cleaner came into the office with his equipment.

Carter shut off the computer monitor so that nothing would be displayed and stood up. "There has been a security problem so I want the entire office swept for bugs with particular attention paid to the phone lines. I must know if they are secure."

The man simply nodded and began setting up his gear and proceeded to sweep the room. He moved slowly, scanning every square inch of surface space making sure he missed nothing. Switching equipment he then checked all the light fixtures and electrical outlets and switches, with nothing showing up at all. He checked the windows looking for invisible laser beams that might be trying to read the vibrations in the window glass but there was nothing there either. The windows themselves were inlaid with a fine copper mesh that was electrified to create white noise and make it impossible to penetrate the room with a directional microphone or other listening device. In theory it was supposed to stop laser penetration as well but Carter didn't trust it to do that. Once the scan was done he had the heavy sound deadening curtains closed in front of the windows to add to his peace of mind.

Once finished the cleaner packed up his gear and moved to the outer office to scan that area as well. As soon as he was out of the office Carter turned his monitor back on and went back to the internet to check the boards for updates. Nothing had been posted since the previous afternoon and there was no indication that anything was out of the ordinary. With that task completed he opened the bottom drawer of his desk and pulled out his private cell to call his peers and update them as to events. Neither of the two had any indication that anything had happened as they had not accessed the voice mail that day yet. As soon as everyone was free a conference call was set up and options were discussed.

The three men decided that Carter would act as a point man and would select a team of juniors from the staff left at the facility if they were still alive. If there were not enough retired juniors they would select three new ones from the ranks of senior agents. He assured the men he would have this taken care of with in twenty-four hours and keep them updated. They agreed on his actions so far with regard to the action team being dispatched and the orders given to them. With matters taken care of the three went back to their government jobs to complete the working day.

With nothing left to do but wait until the action team reported in with their findings on the factory Carter called his assistant back in and resumed his day with the instructions to inform him the second the action team reported in.

Charley had been driving for half an hour when exhaustion hit him. "Sean, buddy, I can't drive anymore can you take over?" he asked, the weariness evident in his voice.

"Sure lad, pull over at the next rest area and we'll swap places."

A few miles later a rest area appeared and they pulled in. Sean got behind the wheel and Charley crawled in back and was asleep before Sean got back on the highway. Sean was tired too but was used to the after action shock effects and could cope with them better, He wanted to rest but he wanted to be out of the area more then he wanted sleep. He drove steadily south getting farther and farther away from the Washington, DC area. He had the radio on switching from one news station to another listening for reports of their adventures. So far he had not heard any reports of murdered men being found at a farm in Virginia. Every second the stooges remained undiscovered was one more second that put them further away from the crime scene. As he crossed into North Carolina he actually felt himself relax a little bit and decided that he could find a place to stop and relax. His first thought was to stop at a rest area then he decided to look for someplace more secluded. He continued on the interstate until he saw a sign for one of the many parks that dotted the countryside and followed the exit to get to it. As he slowed to exit the interstate Charley awoke responding to the change in speed of the van.

"Where are we?" he asked, his voice still heavy with sleep.

"North Carolina, I'm just pulling off to rest in one of the state parks. We'll lay up for a day and see what happens with regard to the news."

"What do you mean Sean?" Charley asked, too groggy to make his mind work properly.

"If the FBI finds out what happened or the organization leaks info about us then the news will broadcast a warning to be on the lookout for us in the DC and surrounding areas. But for now I think we can rest for a bit. The state park will be a better place than a campground, fewer people because the facilities are a bit more rustic. We should be there in under half an hour so you may as well go back to sleep."

Charley lay back down and did as he was told while Sean carefully drove on fighting the exhaustion that was threatening to consume him. He finally came to the entrance of the park and saw that it was simply a picnic area and not a true camping park but it was open 24 hours. It was about 4 acres in size with shaded parking spots that had a barbeque pit and a picnic table at each site. Trees separated all the spots and gave a nice quiet private feeling to the place. The signs all said no pitching of tents but did not forbid overnight parking. Sean scouted the area finally picking a spot halfway between the entrance and the back of the park. He stopped the van trying to get it as level as possible on the grassy ground. Happy with his location he stopped the van, opened both sunroofs and made sure the bug screens where in place. With a gun close at hand he locked all the doors and fell into his bunk, dropping into a sound sleep in seconds.

The supervisor had not heard from anyone at all and it was now 1 PM. He briefly thought about sending another message then decided against it. He thought over his actions to this point, he had the shaft cleared and security team top and bottom, he had alerted his superiors to the events to date and he was waiting for the juniors to show up. That they were several hours late played heavily on his mind and caused him a great deal of concern. He called the security team at the bottom of the shaft on a secure two-way radio and instructed them to mine the shaft and then rig a remote detonator and send it up to the top of the shaft. If they had been attacked once, it could happen again and he wanted to be able to seal the shaft if he needed to. He didn't think this would be likely, as the first attack did not do this it merely blew up the elevator to seal them in but not completely seal off the shaft. It appeared as if they just wanted to make sure people couldn't get in or out of the factory with ease not shut it down for good. Still, if another attack occurred he wanted to be able ensure the security of the organization, and blowing the shaft was the only way he could be sure of doing that.

He had a relief team sent up along with water and rotated the current team back down to the factory and set up a four hour rotation of the security men allowing them time to rest so that he would always have fresh men on guard. Shortly after 1 PM the security team on watch in the warehouse reported a cube van pulling up to the gate. The supervisor ran to the window and watched the van pull through and then a man relock the gate behind them. He ordered the team back to the office at the top of the shaft and called down to prepare the team at the bottom that there could be a problem. He had a feeling that the men were with the organization but at this point he was taking no risks.

The action team opened the door, drove into the warehouse then closed and locked the door behind them. In the dust of the floor the team leader could see dozens of footprints between the windows by the door and the office that held the elevator. He ordered his men to stand fast in the van just in case it was an ambush.

Stepping clear of the van and holding his arms clear of his sides to show he was unarmed he called out. "If you are from the factory we are an action team sent in response to the mayday call. If you are intruders please be advised we are heavily armed and prepared to do anything necessary to make sure you don't leave here alive. You have twenty seconds to respond before we fill the place with gas, starting now."

"I'll go out and talk to them, if anything happens to me you men have the shaft blown and take as many as you can then get out of here to report what's happened, got it?" the supervisor ordered in a whisper.

The security men simply nodded and got ready to fight as the supervisor stepped out of the office.

"If you are the action team whose office dispatched you?" he asked as he cleared the office doorway.

"Carter," came the one-word answer.

"Stand down, relief is here." The supervisor called to the men near the shaft as he put his arms down and walked toward the van. As he did four more men climbed out of the back of the van, all carrying automatic weapons and wearing body armor. "Glad to see you men, have the board members and juniors been alerted to our situation?"

"I have no idea, we were simply told that the factory had been attacked and to either retake it or neutralize it completely. What is your status?"

The supervisor filled the team leader in on events as the rest of the team met with the factory security agents and began moving gear out of the van to beef up the security at the shaft. Two heavy machine guns were set up, and rocket propelled grenades were laid out with in easy reach. Once the weapons were in place they began removing sand bags from the van and used them to build emplacements around the machine guns to offer some protection from small rounds. Once everything was done the team leader sent two of his men to the bottom of the shaft to take over there and had two, facility security agents sent up as replacements. He also ordered food, blankets and more water to be sent up as well. Until further notice he was in charge of security for the factory and he would stay were they were the most vulnerable. He also had the maintenance people begin working on creating a more stable lifting system out of ropes, pulleys, some steel plating and a couple of electric motors. This would speed up the movement up and down the shaft. Once done, he settled in to wait until the juniors or their replacements relieved him.

Chapter 14

It was late morning when Charley finally woke up. He could hear the even rhythmic breathing of Sean telling him his partner was still asleep. Knowing that if he got up it would wake his old friend Charley stayed in bed and used the time to think. He had killed, something he had promised himself he would never do. Having done so, he was now committed to a different path, one he hated, but knew he had to travel anyway. Sean had been right, they were fighting people that had no regard for life and would not hesitate to take a life. The information they had gotten from the stooge that had talked had proven to him that he might be forced to kill again to stop what was going on. It was no longer even about clearing his name anymore; the organization was planning to murder the President and to use his death to bring about oppressive changes. He was still hoping that he could report this to the FBI at some point and hand over the evidence he and Sean had gathered so that their names would be clear, but until that time he had some other ideas about what to do. He had lots of things to talk over with his sleeping friend when he woke up. Suddenly the urge to pee became overwhelming and he had to get up. As he opened the door the slight noise woke Sean who came out of his bunk with a gun in hand looking for trouble.

"Easy old man, relax. I'm just going to the can," Charley said in a low voice.

"Take a gun with you and knock five times before you open the door," Sean said in a voice that was a command not a request.

Charley tucked a .380 behind his belt at the small of his back and pulled his shirt down over it then left for the rest rooms. He didn't take long and when he got back the van tapped five times on the door then pulled it open to see Sean sitting on the lower bunk loosely pointing the Thompson at the door.

"For someone that complained about my antique weapons you sure seem to be attached to that Thompson." Charley said as he climbed into the van

Sean looked at the gun in his hands as if it was the first time he noticed what he was carrying. "You know something, I never even thought about which SMG I picked up I just grabbed this one. I must have gotten used to it over the last little while. It does have a nice feel to it and it can certainly shoot straight."

"Yup, that's true. I was thinking it might be time to look over the computers we took from the stooges." Charley said changing the subject. "Do feel safe enough here to spend some time, or do you think we should keep moving?"

"I think we're safe enough for a couple hours. I'll look around for a bit and you see what you can find."

While Sean did his usual scout of the park, Charley started looking over one of the laptop computers they had taken off the three stooges. On booting it up the computer prompted him for a user ID and password. The security took less than fifteen minutes to crack and then he was able to read the contents of the hard drive. The information was stored in folders that were labeled according to their function. He opened the one marked as ongoing operations and saw several sub-folders. He had just scratched the surface when Sean arrived back at the van.

"Anything interesting in there, lad?"

"Yes, the entire history of the organization and its activities. All I've had a chance to look at is a few folders but they are fascinating. I have to find a way to get this information to the FBI. There are dozens of criminal activities going on that the organization uses to finance it's self. I've only seen drugs and blackmail so far, but they are making a ton of money just from those. I spent some time thinking after I woke up and reading this I now think my idea is doable but I want to see what you think. How would you like to go into the crime fighting business? It would mean getting rid of this van and getting something newer but I know how we can pay for it."

"What did you say?"

"Crime fighting. If you agree we are going to shut some of these operations down. I think we should start with the Drug smuggling going on in the Florida Keys. According to the files there is a five-man team down there that is bringing in two tons of cocaine a month. They always have cash on hand so that will be where we get out expense money. What do you say, sound like a plan?"

Sean couldn't believe the change in Charley. At first all the boy had wanted to do was gather evidence and turn it over to the police, insisting that that would be all they needed to do, they could avoid a fight altogether. Now he wanted to start shutting down the organization. "Lad what turned you around all of a sudden? I thought you wanted to get the proof you were framed and clear your name. You've got the proof right there. Go to the FBI, hand over the computers and turn yourself in. They will probably give you a medal."

"I can't do that. The Organization has a lot of men in the FBI. The second I turn myself in I'll be killed. The order is in the file to terminate us on sight, no matter what. Any agent spotting us is to shoot on sight regardless of when or where. If we spend even one hour in custody we are dead."

"I see," Sean said quietly. "So now you think we can bring them down ourselves if we hit them where it hurts, in the wallet? Well even if it doesn't stop them it will sure piss them off and we can use their own money to fight them with. I like the poetic justice of that. But lad, this will mean more shooting, and the potential for more killing will be very high. If you are ready for that I'm in."

"Then let's head south old man," Charley said with a smile.

Sean hopped behind the wheel started the van and headed towards the highway and south. As Sean drove Charley spent the time pouring over the laptop reading the information. As he skimmed over file after file he began to truly realize the information he now had access to. The entire history of the organization was contained on the computer. Who started it and when, all the members since it's creation and the names of all the agents who were being forced to work for them. When he stumbled across the file that contained the names of the people in charge of the organization he almost stopped breathing. Along with the file of names was the outline of what the organization was founded to do. The magnitude of the planning was enormous. The organization had been around since the 1930's and their goal was manipulate the government of the United States until such time as they had enough of their own members in the White House, congress and senate to control the country. Charley could not believe how many of the top officials in important government posts were already organization members or being blackmailed by the organization. Charley had to find some way to get this information out to the FBI but the more he read the more he wondered if he had any chance at all, so powerful the organization seemed to be.

They stopped for the night at an interstate rest area at the bottom end of Georgia breaking the night up into two-hour shifts. While one slept the other watched, ready to leave the rest area fast. And even though the neither man got a truly good night sleep they were refreshed and alert the next morning. As a further measure to try and ensure enough rest, against the time when Sean assumed they would need to go with out rest for an extended period of time, while one drove the other slept. The end of the day saw them forty miles from their objective parked next to a small sandy beach on the ocean. According to the information contained on the computer the five-man team had received a shipment two days ago. It took three days to convert the large bundles of cocaine in to smaller amounts and get them ready for shipment north. To process the drugs the five men used a boathouse that was owned by the organization. They planned to hit the team that night, before they were ready to ship the drugs.

The two organized their plan so that they would be in complete harmony when the action started. They dressed all in black and got ready for another night raid. The only difference this time was that there were no tranquilizer guns being used, this time the guns were real. They drove to a spot a mile north of the boathouse and parked the van on the shoulder of the road as if it was out of gas. They headed onto the beach staying near the trees and started walking the last mile. Every few yards they stopped while Sean scanned the area with night vision goggles, looking for signs of alarms, traps, or other people. When they were within 200 yards of the boathouse both men donned night vision goggles for the actual work ahead. It took better then an hour to cover the last stretch of land between them and the boathouse. But so skillfully did the two do this that not a whisper of sound was made.

Charley had used some of his organization training on the van ride down to make up a few homemade bombs from ingredients they picked up a grocery store. Taking two out of the pack on Sean's back, Charley attached them with tape to the top and bottom of the door. That done he then took out one more homemade bomb. Lighting the bombs was the trickiest part as they were using fuse that they had bought that was meant to be used in replica toy cannons. As a result the fuse was noisy and smelled when it was burning. And even though Sean had cut the fuse to two seconds on the door bombs, and three on the one in Charley's hand, that time seemed like an eternity to the two men waiting for the door to explode inwards allowing them access to the building. One second after lighting the two on the door Charley lit the one in his hand.

The bombs went off and the door was blown inside in a hail of splinters, followed closely by the third bomb and then the flare. The noise of the door being blown up woke the organization men in a panic. Before they had time to react to the door blowing in, the bomb tossed inside afterwards and going off inside the building assaulted their eardrums and nasal passage with its concussion in the enclosed space. When Sean and Charley entered the building there was no resistance at all from the five inhabitants, the concussion having momentarily stunned them.

Forcing them to the floor with their hands clasped behind their heads and feet and elbows held off the floor Sean was able to watch them while Charley bound them with duct tape one at a time. Once all five were secured they split up to search the building. The drug processing was easy to find; it was a section of the open boathouse that was surrounded by sheets of clear plastic tapped together. The concussion had ripped the plastic down and knocked over the table inside the sheets but there was still clearly a large quantity of white powder under the plastic. Debating what to do with the piles of white powder they could see they finally decided to leave it alone and call the police after they left. That way the organization agents would be arrested as drug dealers.

From the outside it looked like every other boathouse in southern Florida. From inside the view was quite different. The five men had been sleeping in cots arranged along the far wall of the building. The slip that would normally have held a boat was covered over to use as floor space with the large garage type door facing the ocean was barred shut. Next to the wall holding the door that no longer existed were a kitchenette area, a desk, and several locking metal cabinets. Sean looked the cabinets over picking the locks open and searching the contents. One cabinet was filled with weapons. Handguns, shotguns, high-powered rifles, machine guns and even an old Soviet Union RPG-7 model rocket launcher. There were also three crates of rockets for the launcher so Sean pulled it out of the cabinet and signaled Charley to put it outside.

Another cabinet held food and clothes while the last two held nothing put bundles of cash. Grabbing one of the sleeping bags from a cot Sean began filling it. At the end they had two full sleeping bags of money each weighing about thirty pounds. Tossing those by the door as well, Sean turned his attention to the desk looking for any papers that might contain information. Everything he found was in some sort of personal shorthand, but it was similar to those Sean had used himself in his time with the organization. It was something they trained every agent to do, use some form of personal shorthand when keeping a paper trail. This made it harder for others to figure out what you were up to but not impossible.

After a few minutes of reading it became clear what the papers documented, it was the delivery times of the drug shipments and the values of them. It also listed several boats which Sean assumed were being used for bringing the drugs to shore. Grabbing a pair of binoculars sitting on the desk Sean stepped outside to check out the boats he could see anchored near the boathouse. Four were very close and three of those were fast looking cigarette type boats, perfect for smuggling drugs. The fourth one resembled a fishing boat about forty feet long.

Going back inside Sean motioned to Charley to join him at the desk. In whispered tones he described his finding and the boats outside. "Do you think they own them lad?" he gestured to the men bound on the floor.

Charley shrugged. "Only way to find out is to ask."

Grabbing one of the men they drug him outside and down to the water's edge. Sean ripped off the tape covering the man's mouth making him grunt in pain. "Who owns those boats out there?" Sean asked him.

"Fuck you," the man spat back.

Charley kicked him lightly in the head and rolled him over so he was lying face down. "We don't have time to do this the nice way so it has to be the hard way. You are going to tell us what we ask; it's only a matter of time. Unfortunately I lack the time to do a proper job so this is going to be nasty and fast," Charley said quietly in the mans ear then grabbed a handful of hair and pushed his face into the water holding it there as he fought to get his head up to breathe.

It took almost ten minutes of Charley dunking the man's face in the water until he stopped struggling then letting him breath while he asked the same question over and over again, before the man broke. Finally, near drowning, he admitted that all the boats belonged to the organization. Sean asked a few more questions about procedures and reporting in, getting answers from the now broken man. With nothing more to learn from him the dragged him back inside laid him on the floor next to his comrades making sure he was gagged again.

While Charley carried the money and weapons out to the van Sean watched over the captured men. "All done old man, time to go," Charley reported.

"We're not quite done Lad, there is still the matter of these gentleman," Sean said, an evil look in his eye.

"Oh yeah, I had forgotten about them. What did you have in mind?" Charley replied not sure what his friend was talking about but curious to find out.

"You know how much I abhor drug dealing and the people who deal them, so I was thinking we simply torch the place with them still inside."

"That sounds a little harsh don't you think? If we have to kill them let's just shoot them and go."

By now the five were squirming on the floor and trying to shout through their gags.

"And why shouldn't we be cruel to them? They deal poison to people, they don't deserve any compassion," Sean stated with an edge in his voice.

"That may be true, but if we do that we are no better then they are and I don't think I like that. How about this, we dump the drugs all over them, toss the weapons next to them, torch the boats and then call the cops. Their prints are all over this place, the papers document their activities, so the cops are going to bust then for intent to traffic. I think it would do them good to spend a few years in prison."

"Lad that's a good idea in theory but you and I both now that there is no guarantee they will see prison time with this country's legal system. I don't want to take the chance that they will be selling drugs again. The only way to make sure is to kill them." By now Sean was getting into the act and had a hard edge to his voice. It was the classic good cop-bad cop routine and Charley was actually surprised to see it work.

Charley knew at some point people would have to die but killing the five in cold blood wasn't something he was going to let happen if it could be avoided at all. "I've got an idea. We break their left knees before we leave. That way even if they do avoid jail they limp for the rest of their life. Pretty hard to run drugs if you can't run.

Sean looked at the lad and saw that he was serious about kneecapping the men. He had to admit it was a great idea and he liked it. "Okay you talked me into it. We kneecap them, torch the boats, and call the cops. But let's at least be civil about the process. I'll be right back."

Sean ran out to the van and grabbed the tranquilizer guns, came back into the boathouse and shot the five men, knocking them out. Once unconscious, Sean and Charley went from man to man methodically shattering their left knee. With that done they made sure the weapons and drugs were in plain sight, turned out all the lights and closed the door.

Sean took the RPG-7 out of the van and opened one of the crates of rockets and loaded one into the launcher. Sighting on the farthest boat, Sean fired the rocket, which took off with a whooshing sound and a flash of flame. It traveled the several hundred yards to the boat in seconds and slammed into the stern near the waterline. The explosion was ear shatteringly loud in the still night air, tossing the boat half out of the water. Sean had a second rocket loaded and was firing it even before the first boat had settled back into the water, flames pouring out of the gapping hole where the rocket had hit. In less than a minute all the boats were on fire and sinking. Tossing the launcher back into the van the two men made sure everything was secure got in the van and left the area as if nothing was going on. Charley had also taken a cell phone from one of the men and used this now to call 911 and report the boat fires and tell the operator that he thought that it was fight between drug smugglers. Giving the location of the boathouse he told the woman taking the information that he was traveling to key west on business and didn't want anything to do with druggies and hung up refusing to give his name or phone number. Crossing the next bridge he tossed the cell in the ocean disposing of it.

"Where to next?" Sean asked.

"Well let's boot up the old laptop here and see if there is anything else in Florida worth taking a shot at," Charley said, booting up the computer and checking the files.

"There is an illegal gambling operation in Miami that we could hit. And there is also a black-market pawnshop near the everglades. Going further north there's a couple of prostitution rings; some more gambling places and they have a place that runs guns. I think we should hit one of the gambling houses, say this one just north of Orlando. It's near Disney world, I think we should take it."

"Well let's take a look at it first and see what it looks like, okay lad?"

They timed their arrival shortly after sunset and drove past the place mentioned to a vacant lot a street beyond it that looked like it was used as a parking lot. The gambling shop was set up in the basement of a small sporting goods store that was just outside the Orlando city limits. The road was one long parade of gift shops, fast-food outlets, and strip malls.

Sean wanted to watch the building for a few days to establish a pattern of movement, see how many people worked there and determine the number of guards. Charley didn't feel they had the time, and had to hit it right away. By now the organization would know that their drug team in the keys was out of action but may not know for sure it was Sean and Charley that were responsible. Charley wanted to keep the element of surprise on his side, if they waited two long the organization could flood the area with men and they would have to leave just to avoid being caught. With not quite twenty-four hours between the attacks they could leave Florida with a large amount of the Organization's cash. Some anonymous tips would take care of the rest of the activities going on in the state and leave a hole in the organizations cash flow. Sean, seeing a new and aggressive side to his young partner, finally overcame his cautious nature and agreed with reservations.

"Lad I know these people are evil and they need to be stopped. I also know that we can't just go to the FBI and hand over our evidence but we need more of a plan that we've had in the past. You haven't finished going over all the files on those computers, who knows what else they have planned? After we take down this place we go somewhere quiet, hole up while you look over their files then we start planning this right, like I trained you to do. This is the last half cocked job we do."

"Agreed old man. From now on we plan it just like the Boston job," Charley told him, referring to the moment both their lives had changed.

Sean smiled at that. "Well not exactly the same as the Boston job, I want us to both be using the same plan."

"Deal."

Sean demanded one other concession from the lad and that was to use only firearms that they had taken from the organization. They would use guns taken from the boathouse leave them at the scene after they left to avoid having them in their possession if they got caught. Both men readied an MP5 and Berretta 92F, each chambered in 9MM and fitted with silencers. Both had put on Kevlar vests with military surplus web gear over them that they had taken from the drug runners, stuffing extra magazines in the pouches designed for that purpose.

"At least we now have the proper gear for the work now," Sean said quietly, settling the last of his gear.

Charley said nothing, looking over his weapons. He knew his older friend was right, he was acting on emotion and that would get them both killed. He thought on his recent change of heart with regard to fighting and having to kill. He had started this sure that he would be able to go back to his old life simply by using the rule of law to prove he was an innocent man. He now knew that for that to work both sides had to use the same rules and the organization had shown time and again that they made up their own rules. The only way he was going to win his fight for his life was to make up his own rules as well. The problem with that was that when he was finished with the organization, the quiet peaceful life he had known before would be gone forever. He would have to live with the knowledge that he had killed other men and already that was starting to affect his sleep, causing him nightmares.

Sean had parked the van in a vacant lot behind the illegal gambling house with a clear view of the back door. This was the primary entrance for the gambling area and for over an hour now they had watched a steady stream of people come and go through this door. There was no real sign of security other then two men waiting just inside the door checking people when they opened it. There were no signs of cameras watching the area or of peepholes with armed men behind them. This told Sean that the place had been in business for a while and the workers were very relaxed. Perhaps they paid off the police or the organizations influence protected them. No matter what the reason, it was not a well-guarded place. That would probably change after tonight.

Sean slid the side door open and the two men stepped out, Charley locking the van behind them. They walked toward the gambling house with a sure measured pace, looking as if they belonged there. It was dark and the lighting bad, so their features were hard to see as well as the fact that they were heavily armed. In fact only one person did see them, a drunken gambler that was leaning against the side of the building trying to sober up so he could go inside and win back the money he had already lost.

Sean opened the door with his left hand holding his Berretta in his right. Charley had his MP5 cradled in both hands with his thumb on the safety ready to go. Stepping through the door into a short hallway, Sean was met by the bouncers who were shocked to see a man in combat gear holding a gun. The shock lasted only a second as one man lunged for a button on the wall near the doorway and the other reached under his jacket. Sean shot both twice through the chest, dropping then to the floor instantly. Sean moved through the door stepping to the right letting Charley inside. Sean holstered his Berretta and unslung his MP5, snapping the safety off as he did so, both men moving purposefully down the hallway to the well light area at the end of it.

As they cleared the hallway they were in a large room with a bar at the back, tables filling the room, and slot machines along the sides. There was a large mirror across the back of the bar that Sean assumed was one way so people could sit behind it and watch the room. Around the tables and bar were about 100 people drinking and gambling. Sean fired at the mirror exploding it into tiny glass fragments, showing five men sitting in a room watching the gamblers. Even with the silencer the sound of the MP5 was audible in the room, mixed with the sound of breaking glass it cause everyone in the room to duck. Charley and Sean headed to opposite corners of the room to get distance between them making it harder for one person to shoot at both men. It also allowed them to know where the other was and gave them cross fire on the men behind the bar.

The organization men finally reacted each reaching for a weapon Sean and Charley opened up with controlled bursts from their SMG's walking rounds from the outside in towards the center. Seconds later three men were down and two shooting back into the crowded room heedless of the innocent bystanders there. Charley flipped a table on its side and ducked down behind it to change the magazine on his MP5. In other corner Sean did the same thing and when both we reloaded the two jumped up and on full automatic sprayed the area behind the bar taking out the remaining gunmen. With all five down, Sean and Charley once again changed mags and surveyed the room looking for resistance. No one moved and the only sound was the crying of some of the gamblers.

"No one move and you'll be fine," Sean yelled into the room. He pointed at Charley and motioned to go and check out the back room to make sure all the gunmen were down.

With his MP5 up and at the ready Charley moved across to the bar taking a quick look behind it before moving around to the other side. He quickly flashed his head through the open space for a glance then ducked back out in case someone was laying in wait to sneak a shot off. His fast glance had detected no movement so he risked another longer look. All five men were on the floor bleeding, and no one was holding a gun.

"All clear," he yelled, snapping the safety on his weapon and slinging it over his shoulder to climb through the hole were the mirror once was.

"Ladies and gentleman, please bear with us for a few moments longer, we'll be on our way shortly and this will all be over. No harm will come to you as long as you remain calm and lie still," Sean told the room.

Charley checked the men over finding three alive and two dead; he searched them for weapons, kicking the guns into a far corner of the room. Looking around he saw six canvas bags loaded on hand carts. Checking them he found them full of cash. One at a time he tossed them over the bar and into the room then grabbed the hand cart and tossed that over the bar as well. Once back into the main room himself he loaded four of the bags onto the cart. Opening the other two he stuffed his hands inside the bags and tossed the money into the air letting it rain down on the floor. He headed to the door pushing the remaining money on the cart. As soon as he disappeared into the hallway Sean backed towards the door still watching the room like a hawk. A quick glance over his shoulder showed Charley out of the building, he began counting to 100 to give his partner time to reach the van and load the money. By this time everyone in the room was eyeing the money that had been dumped on the floor and only the threat of Sean's machine gun kept people from making a grab for it.

As the count reached eighty-seven Sean heard the sound of a horn letting him know his partner was ready. "Now listen carefully people. The money on the floor is yours, however no one is to leave this building for two minutes. Anyone trying to leave before that time will be shot." With that said he ducked into the hallway and saw Charley's weapons lying on the floor near the door. He dumped his with them and bolted through the door, sprinting back to the van.

Charley was standing next to the open side door of the van with his rifle trained on the doorway, the bags of cash already loaded into the van and it was running. Sean dumped his webgear in the van jumped behind the drivers seat and yelled to Charley to get in. Just as he was about to hop in the door of the gambling house opened and the bartender emerged holding a shotgun. Charley fired, the bullet smacking into the wall next to the door causing the would-be gunman to flee back inside. With no one else showing themselves Charley stepped into the van and slid the door closed. Sean stepped on the gas the second the door clicked shut heading north.

Out of habit Charley started stripping the rifle down to clean it. He had the rifle apart and was working on swabbing the barrel when the shaking started. At first it was his hands then quickly spread through his entire body until he was shivering uncontrollably, lying on the floor of the van. Sean glanced over his shoulder and noticed this and immediately pulled over to check on his young partner.

"What's wrong lad?"

"I....I...d-d-don't know." He stuttered. "I....I...c-c-can't-t st-st-stop sh-sh-sh-aking"

"It's okay lad this is normal. What's happening is the adrenaline in your system is burning off. It's just a little post fight thing. You'll be fine in a few minutes," Sean explained reassuringly.

"Open the door I'm going to be sick!"

Sean opened the door just in time for Charley to stick his head out and throw up. Sean got a bottle of water out of the cooler and handed it to the young man to rinse his mouth out with.

"I hate to do this to you Lad, but we have to keep driving. Lay down on the bunk and rest for while."

"How do you do it Sean?"

"Do what, lad?"

"You're calm and collected, killing those men didn't bother you at all."

"It does bother me, a great deal, that I have killed people, and the fact that I have learned to live with it does not mean I am used to it or that I like it. In fact I hate it," Sean told the lad quietly with eyes that looked older than time.

Charley crawled into the bunk while Sean restarted the van and pulled back onto the road to continue their drive north.

Jason was finally freed from FBI custody and allowed to go home. He was however out of a job as his security clearance had been revoked for a breach of regulations. His apartment was in Baltimore and he was stranded in Washington with no car, the FBI had driven him down. He was faced with the unattractive prospect of paying for a cab to get home, a ride that would not be cheap. He could always take a shuttle or a bus, there were several that ran between the two cities on a regular basis but that would mean being surrounded by other people, not something he wanted to do right now. With nothing better to do he began walking heading towards the White House, drawn to it as any other tourist would be.

From the White House he walked over to the Washington monument and stood starring at it for a while. It was pleasant day and there were a lot of people out doing the same thing he was doing, taking in the historical sights of the nations Capitol. For the first time in years he had nothing to do and no place to go and the feeling was an alien one to him. Used to being in a rush with important things to do, the realization was hitting him that he was no longer an important person; he no longer had any power. This more than anything else was what he would miss.

Deciding to head home he began looking for a cab. As he was about to hail one, two men in a car stopped next to him. "Can we offer you a lift sir?" the one in the passenger seat asked

Jason looked at the two men, both wearing dark blue suits and driving a dark blue four-door sedan with the mark of federal agents all over them.

"I thought the FBI was done with me?" he asked cautiously.

"I wouldn't know about that sir, we received a directive from the board members to find you and bring you in for a meeting sir."

Jason got in the back seat without another word and the car pulled away from the curb and into traffic. He was worried about what would happen to him now that his usefulness to the organization was gone and had been putting off contacting them to inform them of what had taken place. It seemed as if they already knew and wanted to speak with him about it. He was afraid he would be sent to the factory as a trainer and left there until he was old enough to retire, that he would no longer be able to contribute to the cause that he had dedicated his life to. As he was thinking about his past and his uncertain future he failed to pay attention to the passing scenery. The car stopped, jolting him from his revere, in front of the Madison Hotel and the two men in front simply sat there making no attempt to get out.

"Please go to the desk and give them your name," the nameless man in the passenger seat instructed Jason.

Getting out of the car without a word he did as he was told, presenting himself at the front desk and stating his name. The desk clerk greeted him warmly and handed him a key, telling him to enjoy his stay. Jason went to the third floor and opened his room to find two other men in the room. It was a standard room with twin beds, a small table, two chairs, a dresser with built in desk and the obligatory TV. The two men were sitting in the two chairs and Jason noticed three brief cases on the desk with envelopes taped to them. Closing the door he stopped just inside the room waiting for someone to speak. No one did, the other two stared expectantly at Jason.

"My name is Jason, I was told there was a meeting here?" he said, finally breaking the silence.

"I'm Sam, I was told the same thing." said the man in the right seat.

"I'm Brian and that's what I was told as well." chimed in the last man.

"So who called the meeting?" Jason asked

"No idea." Sam and Brian answered almost in unison.

Jason walked to the desk and looked at the envelopes on the briefcases. They were number 1, 2 and 3, with nothing else being written on them at all. With nothing else to do he sat on the bed to wait until someone showed up that knew what the meeting was about. The phone rang just as he got settled.

Brian answered it. "Hello.... Yes sir....I see sir...very well sir....thank you." The other two heard from the one sided conversation.

Brian hung up them looked at the other two. "We're supposed to open the envelopes and brief cases. I'm 1 Jason is 2 and Sam is 3. Everything we are supposed to know is in the letters."

The three opened the letters each being to read the letter number for them. Slowly the realization came over them that they were to be the new Juniors for the organization. All three were stunned at the news. The letters outlined their duties, listed contact numbers and briefing times for the board members, gave the important contacts and listed the directions to the organizations training facility where their offices would be. The letter also listed the problems that had recently happened and informed the men that each had a laptop in the brief cases that held a record of the organizations activities and agents.

Jason was elated; he went from being a disgraced agent to co-coordinating the day-to-day activities of the organization. When he first joined he had never dreamed he would make it this far. He greatest hope was only to be a successful field agent and that he had been for five years. He took this as a sign of his value to the organization, a sign of his dedication and intelligence. That the organization did not view him in this way was something he would never know. The juniors were chosen from the ranks of volunteers, recruits could never be juniors as their loyalty would always be in question. Juniors we also picked based on their obedience to orders, abilities to carry out assignments, and the ability to think on their feet. However the organization was facing a crisis, never in it's history had it ever lost all three juniors at once. They had to be replaced immediately, there could be no waiting, the organization had to have juniors to look after it. For this reason they picked 3 men who's only attributes where their blind obedience to orders and success at fulfilling tasks. All three were viewed as very average in their mental abilities and this was the perfect attribute for the emergency at hand. The board could rest easy knowing that the three would simply do as they were told with out trying to do things on their own or plan new operations. Once the crisis was over they would move the three to the factory to fill in as trainers, but that information was understandably kept from them. Let them think that they were truly important for now.

The orders for the three were all on the notebook computers in the brief cases and the men took their time going over the information, adjusting to their new responsibilities. When all had absorbed the information and were clear on their tasks the put the laptops away picked up the brief cases and wiped down the room to clean it of fingerprints before leaving. Brian stopped at the front desk to pick up an envelope in his name that had a set of car keys in it, as his instructions had told him to do. Heading to the parking garage they got in the car and headed out to the facility.

Arriving at the factory was done with great care, they knocked on the door before entering and all three men went inside with their arms in the air, Jason holding a white envelope in his right hand. The action team leader searched them then took the envelope and read the letter it contained which ordered him to obey the three men as the new juniors. Once the action team cleared them and verified the orders, the facility supervisor was called and he was also informed of the new appointments The formalities of the new stooges taking over were gone through quickly and the first order was to get a proper elevator constructed so that the factory could get back to normal. The new juniors also announced that the abandoned warehouse front they had been using was going to be changed. The organization owned a diaper service that was very popular in the DC area and they would be moving that operation, along with its fleet of panel trucks to the warehouse so that it would always have people in it to avoid a repeat of the attack that had crippled it. Part of the makeup of the maintenance staff would be an action team with weapons stored on site at all times. The juniors wanted the operation up and running out of the warehouse with in seventy-three hours, and sent the site supervisor on his way to make it happen.

The new juniors rode the makeshift lift down to the facility and looked everything over to make sure it was still working as it should. Going into their offices for the first time, they logged into the onsite computer system and began going over all the files getting themselves up to date on the organizations activities, downloading the files to their new laptops. The rest of the day was spent reading and discussing the information to get the organization back on track. They did not yet have the news of what had happened in Florida, that information would find it's way to them later that night.

Holly was a loss to figure out what had happened. The posts had slowed dramatically over the last few days with no reason for it. There was nothing to indicate that they suspected they were being monitored, none of the posts looked like warnings and even the false trail posts were no longer showing up. Along with that, the IP address that Gunny had hacked into had not come on-line again, so either the IP had been changed or they hadn't logged on since the hack attempt.

She had everyone scanning news reports looking for any incidents that mentioned two men, one young, one middle age, involved. She broke the country up into four regions and had split them up among her team to keep a watch on. Spock was running full time on the police databases trying to see what they could come up with and found possible two matches in Florida, of all places, that had happened twenty-four hours apart. In both cases it was reported that two men with automatic weapons were behind the robbery of a group of drug dealers and an illegal gambling house. So far they had no descriptions other then there were two men, one moving much quicker then the other nothing about their looks at all, but it was the closest she had gotten. One other interesting thing to note was that the police had arrested men at the drug site and two men at the gambling house and all of them had demanded a lawyer and said nothing to the authorities. In both case a very successful, high-powered lawyer had shown up demanding an immediate bail hearing. The men in the drug case had been denied bail due to the volume of drugs found, it was assumed they would skip bail and run. The men running the gambling house made bail hours after being arrested. She marked these as something to look into a little deeper.

The van was getting a little crowded with all the gear and money they had taken off the organization. Charley was having problems sleeping; the shootouts were giving him nightmares. It was time to stop and rest somewhere, count the money up to find out exactly how much they had, do some laundry and start working on a detailed plan. Both men were starting to get a little ripe in their odor and it was way past time to fix that. They redid their respective disguises and checked over the maps for a place to stop. After some careful consideration Sean picked Myrtle Beach in South Carolina. It was primarily a tourist and golf spot, famous for the challenging links that people came from all over the world to play. There were several large campgrounds and the beach was lined with Motels and Hotels. Stopping at one of the many rest areas on the interstate, they had picked up several brochures on Myrtle Beach explaining all the things it had to offer the weary traveler. After much debate, and the fact that they really needed a place to count the cash, and get out of the cramped van, they chose a Motel right on the beach that offered units with kitchenettes. This would allow them to cook their own food, and minimize the amount of time they had to be out in public.

Sean used his Credit Card to book the room but paid cash in advance so that the transaction would not go through on the card leaving an electronic trail. Paying for a week in advance they took the last room on the end with a patio door over looking the beach. Parking the van so that the room door was blocked from the road the two moved the money, dirty clothes, weapons and their food into the room as quickly as they could. Charley also moved the computers and satellite gear into the room as well. With the gear moved in they sorted everything out and flipped to see who showered first, Sean won, and headed into the bathroom while Charley looked over their weapons and out of habit began stripping and cleaning one of the SMG's.

Sean came out of the bathroom thirty min later and flopped on one of the two beds in the room with a loud sigh. "It feels good to be clean again, lad. Your turn." And with that Charley headed in to clean up.

While Charley was enjoying his shower Sean sorted clothes that desperately needed cleaning as well. He looked through the phone book on the nightstand and discovered that the motel offered a laundry pick up service. He called the number and told them he would leave the clothes outside the door, then gave his room number. Using two clear garbage bags he put the clothes outside and then lay back down on the bed to relax. A few minutes later he heard the sound of a cart being wheeled down the walkway in front of the rooms then the sound of the bags being tossed in it. As a random thought he noticed that he could hear outside sounds fairly well which was good as it would make it hard for anyone to sneak up on them. Sighing deeply again he got up and opened one of the bags of money then dumped it on the bed to begin the long task of sorting and counting it all. When Charley came out of the bathroom he dumped one of the other bags on his bed and joined in on the counting.

The knock on the door caught both men by surprise and had them diving for their weapons. The familiar word 'housekeeping' came through the door and they relaxed feeling foolish for their actions. Sean creaked the door just enough to see standing outside was a lady with their laundry.

"How much do I own you ma'am?" he asked blocking the view of the room and the money on the beds with his body.

"Twenty dollars sir."

Sean paid her and took the bags waiting until she began to walk away before going back inside the room. Tossing Charley's clothes to him, Sean dropped his bag on the floor and went back to counting. It was dark outside when they were done and the total was over six million dollars. They had bundled them up into 5,000 dollar bundles using twine to tie the bundles up. Rubber bands would have been faster and better but twine was all they had. The bundles were rebagged and then stuffed in the closet for the time being.

"Wow that's a lot of cash," Charley remarked.

"It's certainly more then I thought we had, lad. Looks like we are well financed so what do you want to do next?" Sean had thought they would need to hit several organization places to get enough money to keep them going. Two jobs and they had more cash than they knew what to do with.

"I need to spend more time with the stooges laptops to find out what's going on. Why don't you take one of the laptops and look it over and see what information you can get from it."

"Lad I know nothing about computers and I'm too old to learn. I'm going to sort through our weapons collection and thin it out a bit. We are carrying around too much hardware.

The two men started on the respective tasks, each becoming engrossed in what they were doing. Sean finished up a few hours later and had everything sorted into to piles, the gear he was keeping and the gear he was throwing away. The keep pile contained all the hardware they had started with along with two MP5's, two .45's with silencers, and the RPG. Even though it was dangerous to keep it had shown that it could come in very handy. He took the other weapons and stacked them in a pile near the door. He had stripped them of the magazines that could be used in the guns he was keeping and all the bullets. Next he inventoried the bullets and found that they were almost out of .380 and .22 bullets, they had a couple of boxes of .45's and were well stocked with 9MM rounds. Taking out the phone book he checked for sporting good stores and found several including a firing range that carried the rounds he was looking for. A glance at his watch surprised him with the time of 10:12 PM. He had no idea it was so late or that they had skipped supper.

"Time to eat lad, I was thinking of ordering pizza, sound good to you?"

Charley's stomach suddenly came awake at that. "Yeah that would be great!"

Sean checked the phone book, found an ad for gourmet pizza that looked good and placed an order to have it delivered. With dinner taken care of he finished up sorting the excess guns and wrapped them up in sleeping bags to dispose of later. Charley was still working on the computers, he had all three unlocked now and discovered that the files were identical on all of them. This made it easier to concentrate on working on just one leaving the other two as backups in case something happened to the first one he was working on. When he originally unlocked the system he had noticed one file encrypted, but had been leaving that alone, as the other files were readable. He now concentrated on opening that file and this had, so far, consumed his entire evening. While waiting for the pizza to arrive he went back to the file still working on breaking the encryption. Charley was so engrossed in this that the knock on the door thirty minutes later startled him, it was the pizza. Sean slipped into the bathroom with one of the SMG's as a precaution while Charley paid for the pizza.

The two men wolfed down their food, then Sean crashed for the night while Charley went back to cracking the encryption on the file. He finally cracked the file encryption shortly after 3 AM and started to read the file. The heading caused him to sit bolt upright and yell "Holy Shit!" which woke Sean up, making him reach for a gun.

Sure that there was nothing immediately wrong, he gruffly asked Charley "What the hell is the matter with you?"

"The organization has another plan to kill the President and it's going to happen soon."

Sean was not overly impressed with this news. "Well lad, you and I failed so of course they are going to have another plan, they want the man dead. I hope you weren't naive enough to think that with out us it couldn't be done, were you?"

"Sean you don't understand. This plan is better then the one we used and harder to protect against. It's going to happen at sea while the president is sailing, I guess he has his own boat and insists on sailing it himself. He has planned to have his yacht sent down to Puerto Rico then fly down and spend a week onboard. The organization is going to hit him then."

Sean rolled over to go back to sleep. "Lad, that's not a workable plan. When the President sails, he is surrounded by US navy ships. I don't think even the organization can get past the US navy so don't worry about it. The plan was probably just some preliminary report that never got tossed out."

"No Sean it isn't," Charley said in a quiet voice "This one is going to work."

Sean rolled back over. "Lad, when the man sails he is surrounded by the US navy. There is an aircraft carrier around just to provide air cover for his one little boat. The secret service has chase boats in the water with Navy Destroyers to back them up and I'd bet there's a sub or two in the area as well. So tell me, what could the organization possibly do to get past that security?"

"Ever hear of a captor mine? That's what they're going to use. The fishing boat we destroyed in Florida was supposed to carry it out to the area the President is going to sail in and drop it off."

Sean was fully awake now and listening. "What is a captor mine?"

"Basically it's a sealed tube that has a sonar set and a torpedo in it. The sonar picks up the sounds of the ship or boat and fires the torpedo at it when it's close enough. They use them mostly in sub hunting from aircraft but it would be a perfect weapon against the president. They can plant it weeks or months before; the sonar battery is good for a couple of years. It also has remote activation capabilities. The Organization can drop this and then simply wait until the president sails by to blow him up. The report states that they are using an old soviet designed homing torpedo they bought from Cuba through an arms dealer in South America. Sean we have to tell someone about this."

Sean shook his head. "No one would believe us, they think we tried to kill the man once already, remember? Do you have information on how or where the mine is to be laid?"

"Not specific co-ordinates no, at this point this plan is just an outline with the weapon en route to the US. It was supposed to be picked up by the fishing boat in four days time. I'm sure that's been changed by now."

"I'm sure the stooges have been replaced by now, so yes that would be one of the first things they would change. They must be waiting until the sailing dates are firm before they set the mine after all they wouldn't want another boat to set it off."

"That's the beauty of this plan Sean. They can program the mine to respond only to the sound of the president's boat. Apparently every boat has a unique sound signature because of the machinery on it, the type of engine, and the actual hull it's self. All they have to do is program the mine and pre place it near where the president sails. He seems to like the same places and keeps going back there."

"But how will they get a recording of the boat sound?"

"I think that would be the easiest thing for them to do, they have agents in the secret service so one of them can just record it when the boat is being checked over for explosives or just having maintenance done to it."

"I never thought of that lad, you're right. But how do we stop it, I mean we need to tell someone that will believe us and has access to the president. We can't tell the Secret Service or the FBI, so who does that leave?"

Charley thought for a second. "I'll need to get online again and check the government sites to find someone."

"Can we set up the satellite in here? Is there a direct line of sight for it?" Sean asked.

"I don't know, I'll need to check it with a compass," Charley said heading to the van.

Taking out a compass he took a bearing and found that the motel was sited to give the window a line of site to the satellite. Taking the gear into the room he plugged everything in and booted up his laptop. Remembering the last time he was online and had been hacked, Charley now had a firewall installed, and had also removed all his financial information. He was taking no more chances. Once all the equipment was up and running Charley logged into the server and connected to the net, bringing up Google to do a search of government sites.

After a couple of days of nothing there was once more activity on the bulletin boards. Gunny had his spyware program running in auto mode continuously searching for the IP address of the renegade, as they had taken to calling him. Most of the new posts seemed to deal with business matters and requests for information as to if this place was open or that place was open. The posts were using nicknames of course but based on inquires some of the establishments had to be illegal. The information was all being saved for later investigation and if it turned out to be an illegal setup they would forward it on to the FBI. The tracking of the two renegades across the northeast had stopped and no new posts were being named in regard to this. In fact no one was even talking about the renegades anymore, it was almost as if the people making the posts knew someone from outside their group was reading them.

The program Gunny had set up to watch for the IP address started the second it noticed the IP active. It directed Spock to download all the information from the other system but slowly so as to avoid making it clear that any information was being lost to the other user. The last time Gunny had hacked the system it had been so obvious that it had scared off the suspect from using the Credit Card that he had found, making it impossible to follow the electronic trail it would leave. The program also put a pop up on Gunny's screen letting him know that there was new information in the database to look at.

The new stooges had made the decision to stop using the bulletin boards for information about the two rogue agents; it made sense that the young one was reading the posts as he had been trained to use them himself. It may even have been him that started the whole disaster in Vermont and they wanted to avoid that happening again. The loss of the group in the Florida Keys was of grave concern considering the upcoming operation and the wise men had ordered a team from the west coast in to take over that operation. They wanted people unknown to the area as the weapon was enroute and needed to be picked up in four days time. A new boat had already been found and was being refitted for the pick up in an organization boatyard. The action team would have a couple of days to familiarize themselves with the boat before making the pickup.

The factory now had a new working elevator, and the warehouse was now operating under its new cover. One of the action teams had been released with the second one being permanently assigned as security to augment the security on-site already. As a result there were now two men always on duty in the warehouse and another two at the bottom of the shaft. The machine gun had been sited at the top of the shaft as well as new intruder alarms being installed around the perimeter fence. If the place were attacked again they would get a warning of it and be ready to fight back.

After the two Florida attacks the stooges had dispatched action teams to the area to both beef up security to their operations there and search for the two renegades. It was believed that the same two men had carried out the two robberies and the most likely candidates were the renegades. Jason thought this a waste of time, but as part of the stooges he agreed with the decision. The two men had shown themselves to be extremely smart and cautious, avoiding all intentional contact, and the organization had gotten close twice only by accident. He had no illusions about the renegades being in Florida or that the two jobs were done by the same team. But whoever was really responsible was certainly gone from the area. For now the search was to be placed on the back burner while the operation against the president was prepped and executed. They could return to the two renegades once the operation was done with out the worry of splitting their assets. The organization didn't hold the renegades as a threat to the operation so there was no worry from that quarter. If the FBI or police did actually manage to catch them, the two could always be eliminated while in custody.

The stooges had fallen into a routine after only a few days on the job and already the organizations assets were almost all back on track. The information flow had been restored and was even now being gone over by the analysts getting all operations back up to speed. The two attacks in Florida had been a set back but only a very minor one.

Charley felt more then saw his system slow down. He wondered if whoever had hit him the first time was back for more. Opening up his DOS prompt he did a netstat and saw that there were more connections open to his system then he had started, someone was hacking his hard drive. Rather then do anything about it he ignored it going back to his search. He had found the White House website and was scanning through the pages when he saw one listing the people that worked at the White House, including the National Security Advisor and the Chief of Staff. The pages contained short biographies of the people and pictures of them as well. He was amazed that the government would put information like this on the web available for all to read and see. Just in case his surfing was being monitored he moved on to other pages, checking out other government websites, again amazed at the information contained on them. Once done with his surfing he opened google again and began random searches just to make his system appear busy. At the same time he began a back trace to find out who was hacking his system. Whoever it was they were very, very good.

After fifteen minutes of effort Charley still had no idea who was hacking his computer. His experience with hacking on his own was limited to what he had learned at the Organization's facility and while it made him very good in comparison to the normal user of the internet he was by no means skilled at it. The only thing he could state for sure was that whoever had attacked his computer was either a software genius or worked someplace that had access to really powerful computers. With no other way to find out who it was Charley created a text file with his email address and a request to talk to him and placed it on a part of the hard drive that was sure to be copied. With that done he surfed news sites for a few more minutes then logged off.

When he had first set up his account one of the options he had signed up for was a dial up back up connection in case anything happened to the satellite. It was only good for ten hours usage per month but it would no come in handy in giving him another IP address. He was fairly sure that's how they were getting into his system, so by changing the IP address he used they would need to start all over again. Plugging in the dial up modem to the phone jack he connected to the internet again. This time the access was much slower but he noticed that his computer showed no signs of being hacked. Not having to worry about his surfing being watched he first used an online virus scanner to look for viruses and Trojans on his hard drive. When that was done he began searching information directories to find the phone numbers and address of the two people he was looking for, as expected one was relatively easy and the other extremely difficult. He had to hack into the telephone company of Maryland's database to get the number he was looking for. The address was much easier to find. Once he had what he needed he wrote it down on paper and deleted it from his hard drive. Charley also cleared the temporary files and memory from the system deleting the record of the sites he had been to.

It was 4:30 in the morning and well past time for sleep when he crawled into bed with a smile on his face. Knowing for the first time how he was going to get the information on the organization's laptop out to the government.

Arriving at 7AM Gunny was going over the information he had hacked when he saw the text file with the email address. He called Holly over as soon as she arrived at 7:30 to take a look at it.

"What do you think Gunny, worth emailing him to see what he has to say?"

"That's your call ma'am. But there's no information of use on his system now. He learned from the last time and deleted anything that might lead us to him or give us a way to track their location. I don't think we have anything to lose by sending out an email."

"Okay so next question what message do we send? Do we ask him to call us?"

John arrived at that point "Ask who to call us?"

"Morning John." Holly greeted him "Gunny's program found our renegade last night and it turns out he knew we were hacking him and he left us a message with an email address. Gunny and I are wondering what kind of a message to send him."

"Gunny, what does it look like he's using for an operating system?"

Gunny checked his computer for a second. "Looks like windows, why?"

"Well if it's windows let's exploit some of those security holes to our advantage on this one. How about we email him and ask him to log on with his firewall turned off. At that point Gunny can hack into the windows messaging and we can talk to this guy live. But be sure we tell him we are going to do that as a way to communicate in real time. He already knows we can't trace his location that way so he might go for it. He's way too smart to go for a phone call."

Holly liked the idea. "Okay Gunny that's what we'll do, ask him to log on sometime this afternoon and we'll see if we can talk to whoever it is out there. Great idea John."

Gunny drafted up the email and sent it to the address in the text file then resumed his daily surfing for information, as did the rest of the group, who all heard about it as they came in to work. Everyone was waiting impatiently for 3 PM to see if the mystery person would talk to them.

It had been almost daybreak when Charley had finally gotten to sleep and Sean had been careful and quiet when he woke up giving his partner time to sleep. It was 11 AM when Charley woke up, not fully rested but ready to start the day anyway.

"Morning sunshine." Sean greeted him.

Charley grumbled a low good morning back and logged onto his computer and then connecting to the net using the dial up to check the email address he had given the hackers. Finding one message waiting for him he downloaded it and disconnected from the internet. Opening the message he read: Please log on at 3 PM and turn off your firewall. We would like to talk with you and would prefer to use windows messaging to do this in real time.

Calling Sean over he showed him the message. "What do you think?"

"Is there anyway to trace our location this way?"

"No, it's over the net and we're using a satellite which gives them our IP but not our physical location. Because it's line of sight we could be anywhere in the US or lower part of Canada and there is no way for them to find out where. I already know they can hack my system and steal information but there's nothing important on the system anymore."

"In that case Lad, let's get something to eat and then find out who our new friends are."

Sean used the kitchenette to make brunch while Charley had a shower. Once they had both eaten Charley cleaned up and did the dishes while Sean took his normal stroll around outside looking for any indication of trouble. To kill time after doing the dishes Charley stripped and cleaned his SMG and the silenced .22. At 3 PM both men were in the room and Charley logged onto the net, shutting down the firewall.

Several hundred miles away Holly and her team were crowded around her desk where Gunny had set up his monitoring program. As soon as it detected the correct IP it opened up a windows messaging session and searched for the security hole to enable a chat session on the other system.

Less than a minute after Charley connected a message popped up on his screen: "Who is this?" it asked him.

"You contacted me, who are you?" Charley wrote back.

"My name is Holly McClare, I work for the National Security Agency."

Charley looked at Sean. "Figures it would be some sort of spy agency. What do you think?"

"Find out who is in the room with her," Sean said.

Charley typed in "Who is in the room with you?"

"Now that's an interesting question."

Gunny commented, "Why do you supposed he wants to know that?"

"Let's find out," Holly replied, then typed in the names of her team

Charley read over the list of names he received the asked them to wait a moment. He opened up the stooges laptop and did a search of the names in the organization agent database. If the list was real, none of the names came back with a match. As satisfied as he could be that he wasn't dealing with any organization agents that had penetrated the NSA he went back to the messaging. "Thank you, why did you hack my system?"

"We are searching for the two suspects that tried to assassinate the president and your system showed evidence that you may have been involved with that. Are you Sean Miller or Charles Watkins?"

"I'm Charles Watkins and I did not try to assassinate the president. You are looking for the wrong person."

"There is a warrant out for your arrest. If you are innocent then turn yourself in to the police or tell me where you are and we will have someone come and pick you. There are questions that need to be answered."

"There is far more to the story that you know, I can't turn myself in," Charley typed.

"Can you tell us were to find Sean Miller?"

"No, I can't."

Holly decided to take a different tack., typing in that he was under arrest, spelling out his miranda rights and ordering him to surrender himself to the nearest law authorities.

Charley laughed at the message "Well she's gutsy I'll give her that," he said to Sean, then typed in; "I've been chased for the last several months and you really think a message over the internet is going to cause me to worry. I've got far more to bother me that your ineffective threats. The FBI hasn't even come close yet and I know there is no way for you to trace this. What's to stop me from simply disconnecting and never logging back on. You'd have no idea where I was. So cut the crap. The fact that you sent me an email means you want to talk to me so talk. Ask your questions but I'm not giving anything away for free here. If you want to know something specific ask it, don't beat around or threaten me. You don't scare me."

"Wow, he's awful sure of himself isn't he," Doris said to the group.

"Well he's right," John told the group. "He has managed to stay ahead of all of us so far. And if we are right and there is a second group hunting him then I'm sure that death is a much stronger motivation then prison and we still have to convict the man first. The other people will simply shoot first and worry about it later, as Gunny and I found out."

"Well might as well ask him if he's being hunted by anyone else and see what he says," Holly said before typing in: "Are you being chased by anyone other then the police?"

"Before I answer any questions I need to know your chain of command. Who do you report to and who sees the information you generate?" Charley typed back.

"I report only to the director of the NSA, there is no one other then him in my chain of command. The only people that see the information we gather are the names on the list I gave you and the director. Why do you ask?"

Charley looked at his partner "Well old man, I think we may be able to use these people to get the info about the organization out to the proper people. None of the names she gave me is on the organization lists and she reports to the director."

"Only one way to find out isn't there. Tell her everything and see what she says," Sean told Charley.

The next twenty minutes Charley spent typing in his ordeal with the organization, from the original framing up to the training with Sean and their escape to Canada to try and live quietly. He left out the part about the shooting, not being ready to admit to shooting the secret service agent for two reasons; first he didn't want anyone to know about her, and second, even shooting at the stage holding the President was a federal crime that would land him in prison. He then explained how the organization had chased the two of them and admitted to being the one that posted the fake message on the bulletin boards. He revealed the depth of the organization but didn't mention any names or give specifics of their members or businesses. He would do that only when he was sure they were dealing with someone that could help them.

"Holy shit!" Holly yelped at the end of the message. "If this guy has proof of anything he is saying the FBI is going to busy for a long time," Holly typed back, asking why she should believe him.

Charley told her he had proof of everything he was claiming and more. Hinting that the organization had highly placed government members in its ranks. He explained that he needed someone that could be trusted to hand over the information to. He was worried that the organization might get the information back using one of it's agents and then cover everything up.

Holly insisted that she could take the information straight to the head of the NSA and he in turn would ensure that it got to the right people. There would be no cover up attempt. She told him to wait online and she would report it now.

"WAIT." The message appeared on the screen. "THE NSA HAS AGENTS OF THE ORGANIZATION WORKING IN IT. DO NOT TELL ANYONE YET! I am trying to contact someone that can help get the information out but I need time."

The message in bold frightened Holly and shook the other people in the room. "That's bullshit." Gunny stated flatly.

"I wouldn't be so sure Gunny. Other intelligence agencies have gotten spies in the US, this is a group that is made up of US citizens so for them it would be even easier to get spies in place. After all the people aren't working for a foreign power so technically it's not treason. I think he's telling the truth. Okay so we take him at his word for now but let's remember he is still a wanted suspect and we should try to bring him in." Holly started typing again. "If you are right then we are going to need your help to find these people. Please turn yourself into me and I'll see that you are safe and protected while we work to clear this up?"

"What about mine and Sean's freedom? Can you promise me that we won't be tossed in jail?"

"That's not in my power to promise." Holly told him truthfully. "But I'm sure that as long as you haven't committed any major crime the attorney general would give you immunity in exchange for you testifying against these people."

It was the wrong thing to say.

Charley said he would think about it and get back to them, then logged off before Holly had a chance to write anything back.

"Shit he's gone. Holly you should have promised him no jail," John stated flatly.

Holly shook here head. "The last thing I'm going to do with these guys is lie to them. If they did take a shot at the president there is no way they are going to walk free. He'll be back, I know it. He really doesn't have anywhere else to go, this is the only safe way for him to talk with anyone with out being traced. We can be patient. In the mean time let's see what else we can find out about this organization he was talking about, and I have to brief the director on this."

"Why did you turn it off, lad?" a confused Sean asked.

"I need time to think this one over. We want this information to get to the right people and make sure that the organization gets caught. We know they are going to try and kill the president again and we have to make sure that that doesn't happen. The problem is that they think we tried to kill the president so they aren't probably going to be reluctant to believe us about another attempt."

"So what do we do?"

Charley smiled at his friend. "That's why I need time to think this over. I have to do this in a way that clears our names as well as saves the president. It's just going to take a little time but I think we can do it. I've got a couple ideas but we need to head north again. What do we do with all this extra hardware?"

"Just before we check out I'll break into one of the empty rooms and leave it all there then we call 911 and warn the cops when we leave."

Charley nodded at the plan and for the rest of the day the two relaxed and enjoyed some down time. Supper was Chinese take out and as they ate Charley began discussing an idea to get the government to believe them about the organization and get it out into the open. This would be proof positive of its existence and no way for the organization to bury the information. They would head out in the morning and set the alarm for an early rising.

In the morning after showering and getting ready to go in the morning Sean broke into an empty room two down from them and dumped the guns on the floor as Charley was checking out. Leaving the motel they stopped at a payphone and called 911 reporting the guns and telling them which room it was in, then headed north.

Andrea noticed the pick up signal for her dead drop and took the usual precautions to ensure she wasn't being watched before she picked up the message. Taking a long way home, it was after seven when she finally parked her car. She headed straight for the bathroom to read the message, then memorizing it she burned the paper and flushed the ashes. Her chore done, she cooked supper while thinking over her change in orders and how she would carry them out. The change seemed both simpler and harder than before but she was sure the organization had it figured out. This time she would do the job right, erasing her earlier failure, although no one blamed her personally for the failed hit on the president.

After dinner she changed into a loose fitting jogging outfit and ball cap with a low brim that hid her face in shadows and headed out to the car. Remembering her orders she drove a circuitous route to where there was a drop waiting for her. Andrea parked a block away and began jogging a brisk clip towards the dead-drop. She breezed past it going another block them turning left towards a deli. She stopped at the deli and bought a fruit juice then walked back to her car. As she walked past a waste bin she dropped her juice bottle into it, missing the can. Bending down to pick it up she palmed the package taped to the bottom of the bin as she stood up and dropped the bottle in the can. Her hand dropped the package into a pocket in her jogging pants and she walked casually back to her car. As she slid behind the wheel she transferred the package to the floor beneath her seat. She would need it tomorrow when she took the advance team to check out the president's sailboat.

The next day Andrea and the rest of the advance team went over the president's sailboat with explosive and chemical sniffers, along with a metal detector. Divers checked out the bottom as well. These procedures were followed even thought he boat was moored at the US Navy's Norfolk naval base and guarded around the clock. Before the boss went on board the boat was checked top to bottom. Once the inspection was finished a team of agents would be with the boat until the President came on board. The sailboat would be prepared for the trip and then loaded onto the deck of the USS Wasp, an Amphibious Assault Ship that would carry it to the Caribbean. The Wasp and her escorts were slated for training off the Puerto Rican island of Vieques. The assault group would provide the security for the president while he enjoyed a week of sailing in the area. As it was a live fire training area, it was listed as off limits to all normal traffic, which made it an excellent location for the president to enjoy a vacation. The wasp carried Harrier attack jets, assault helicopters and over 1,500 marines. There were other ships as well that would be in the area, including at least one submarine, and the secret service had small fast boats that would be near the President at all times.

The president understood how hard it was on his protection detail to ensure his security while he was sailing which was why he only used his boat when it coincided with training schedules of the navy. Using the navy ships to provide security was a cost effect way for him to enjoy a vacation and the Navy was always glad to help out. It provided a real training aid and sailors were on their toes keeping an eye on the President. It was also a huge moral booster, as the president was known to occasionally eat lunch or dinner in the crew's mess on some of the ships. The men loved that the commander in chief would dine with them rather than be catered to in the officer's mess. It was hard on the captain of the ship of course due to protocol but when it came to the president's wishes navy protocol played a back seat. The president was of course always careful to ask permission to come aboard in line with tradition and was always gracious in his praise for the men and the officers. His entire reason for springing the surprise visits was to allow the men to see him as a real person, one of them. And he hated the pomp and ceremony of the job. Eating in the crew's mess always ensured him a regular meal as he took whatever everyone else was eating and he got to talk to the everyday sailor. The first few minutes was always awkward as the men were a little stiff around him but they always loosened up after a bit and the banter was about ship life and looking forward to home. It helped the president realize that everyone had pressures that were as real to them, as the affairs of state were to him.

With the boat checked and signed off on Andrea ducked below for one last look around. From her pocket she removed an ordinary mini-cassette recorder that had been in the package in the dead-drop. Opening it she took out a slim card that was a quarter of the size of a credit card and placed it on the bottom of the auxiliary engine. The device was back in the dark confines of the tiny engine housing and undetectable. Her task completed she went back on deck, closed the cabin door and sealed it with tape. No one would enter the vessel until it was opened to be stocked for the president when the ship arrived in the Caribbean.

A crane lifted the boat from the water under the careful gaze the agents and lowered onto a cradle directly aft of the island on the wasp's deck. Deck hands rushed in to unhook the crane and secure the boat to the cradle again under the watchful eyes of the secret service. Next to the boat was what looked like a travel trailer. It was the mobile command center for the secret service and contained a communications consol that allowed them to talk to anyone, anywhere in the world, along with bunks that gave the detail agents watching the boat a place to sleep. From this point on until the boat was lowered back in the water a agent would be standing with in visual sight of the boat at all times. It would be checked over one more time of course before being lowered into the water.

As head of the advance detail Andrea had the option of staying with the boat until the president flew down to meet up with it but chose not to. She turned the detail over to her second in command and left the base to head back to her temporary office in the treasury building, content that her job was done. On the way back to her office she stopped at the proper place and made the proper mark to indicate that she had completed her task.

Later that evening another organization agent drove by noticing the mark and filing his report stating that the job had been done, not knowing what it even was he was reporting.

Sean and Charley drove straight through to Boston retracing their steps to the building that Charley had left the BMG in. Security in the city had long since returned to normal so the danger to the two men was no higher than in other locations in the US. Both experienced a sense of deja vu as they once again made their way through the sewer system and into the high-rise building. The two had worked out a plan of action for the coming weeks. Sean had argued against coming here to get the rifle thinking it an un-necessary adventure, but Charley was insistent that it would be a very useful tool, and had won the debate. Retrieving the gear took four hours and they were on their way south again.

Sean stopped in Connecticut to pick up some ammo for their weapons, including some more rounds for the BMG. This was dangerous, as the 50-caliber rounds were rare, so he had to stop at one of the larger sporting goods stores in an urban area. There was also a chance that sales of the ammo were monitored by the police and would be reported, but as it was only ball ammunition he thought this unlikely. Still, Sean only got twenty of them just in case the sale was monitored and hoped this would be seen as a normal purchase for a sport shooter that was shooting on weekends for fun. He did this in New York and New Jersey as well, giving them sixty rounds in addition to what had been cached with the rifle. Sean had also picked up a ten round clip at the last stop that would fit their rifle. Charley had stripped and cleaned the rifle and was now checking over all the rounds they had purchased making sure everything looked fine. He now had four clips, two in six round and two in ten rounds. He loaded a ten round mag with the last nine sabot rounds he had made himself, then filled all the other clips with the normal BMG rounds mixing his handloads with the factory loads until only the factory loads were left. He hoped he wouldn't need the firepower the big rifle gave him but he wanted to be prepared for anything.

The two men again alternated driving straight through to Virginia just south of Washington, DC. Sean disguised himself again and went into the first tourist rest stop on I-95 to get maps of the surrounding area. Finding the information he wanted he got back into the Van and headed south for another sixty miles stopping for the night at the first campground the found. They would need to set this up fast and then get out of town in a hurry.

The planning was completed the next day as there really wasn't that much planning to do aside from the route in and out of the areas they were going to. They would drive through the area tomorrow scouting the streets and looking for signs of surveillance or security. After that they would decide when and if, to pull off the operation. With nothing more to plan the two dropped off to sleep.

"So Adam what's on my plate today?" the president asked as his chief of staff walked into the president's private dining room

Adam gave the boss a brief rundown of the morning, mostly filled with meetings from members of congress. There was only one photo op slated, making it a light morning. Adam was trying to get all the important work wrapped up in the next week, preparing for the president's sailing vacation. The president would have some long days this week but all the business of state would be addressed. It was one the biggest challenges Adam faced, as his boss would not miss his sailing time for anything less that a national or international crisis.

The stooges briefed the board one at a time on what was happening in the organization and how they had developed contingency plans to work around the recent disruptions in the organization. The hunt for the renegades had been slowed momentarily to concentrate on the operation ongoing against the President. As a result of the loss of the fishing boat and team that was slated to make the pickup of the torpedo the stooges now were late taking delivery. Because of this the sound of acoustic signature of the presidents boat could not be programmed into it. The stooges had instructed agent Drake to plant a beacon on the Presidents boat instead. The beacon had a range of twenty-five miles and would be remote activated from a small plane that would fly near the off limits area. Once active, if the beacon came with in 4,000 yards of the captor mine the torpedo would be fired, home in on the boat, and destroy it and everyone on it.

The torpedo had been picked up that morning on the Bahamian island of Cay Santo Domingo, itself not far from Cuba. They pick up was being made by an action team rushed in from the west coast using a fishing boat that had been stolen from Haiti, repainted to match a Bahamian fishing boat. The fishing boat would move in over night to the area the President would sail, and drop the captor mine. Since the area was used a naval training fire zone there was lots of used un-recovered practice ordinance littering the bottom. The captor mine would lie inert until it was activated by the same small plane that would activate the beacon on the president's boat. In this way if it was discovered it would look like any other piece of expended equipment on the bottom of the sea. The stooges had taken care to ensure no one knew what was happening this time around. The operation was being carried out in three carefully separated steps. No one other then the stooges and the board members knew what was going on. They would not make the same mistake of trusting an agent to kill the President this time. It would be done by remote control with no way for a human to interfere once the beacon and torpedo were activated. All agreed, this time it would work with in a week there would be a new president in the Oval Office.

"So how do we get to them, Lad?" Sean asked as he made his morning coffee

"I think we should play this one fast and lose, Sean. Let's get in and out fast, but we need to get a car and a place to work from in Washington, for that we need a disguise."

"That's gutsy Lad, you sure you want to run that kind of a risk?"

"It will be unexpected of us and we do have a lot of cash to work with, the only thing that will be a problem is, paying cash for everything may get us noticed. That's the only part that concerns me. The other option is to use the last two credit cards we have."

Sean thought for a second. "There is one way we can use the cash and not have anyone think twice about it. We pose as diplomats from the Middle East. They usually pay cash so they don't have any paper trails to what they do or where they go. After all, most are from Muslim countries and it would be hard to explain credit card bills from nightclubs now wouldn't it. First thing we'll need to do is get suits and some headdresses."

"Headdresses?" asked a puzzled Charley.

"That's right lad, headdresses, trust me on this one. We also need a drug store, let's get going."

With the decision made Sean dumped his coffee, the first time Charley had seen him do this, and he two packed up heading north to Washington, DC. Sean stopped at every exit checking phone booths along the way looking for men's stores that carried expensive suits. Sean also looked for a drug store and found one at the first exit. He purchased hair dye and chemical tanning solution along with some colored contact lenses used only to alter the eye color. Back in the van each took turns darkening their skin with the tanning solution and dying their hair black. The contacts turned their eyes brown and Sean added pads inside his cheeks to fill out his face.

They had to go to Alexandria to find what they were looking for and each bought a suit several shirts and ties and a pair of Italian leather shoes, spending over $7000. The clerk looked at them a little strange when they passed over that much cash. Sean said something in Arabic to Charley and the foreign language really got the attention of the clerk.

"Are you gentleman from out of town?" he asked suspiciously.

"Yes sir," Charley answered deferentially. "We have just arrived from Qatar, we are to work in the embassy. We thought that everyone in America wore jeans so this is what we brought with us. The ambassador was displeased, as there is an official function tonight so my father and I needed to properly attire ourselves. We chose your establishment as we heard it was very discreet so our embarrassment would not become known." Sean merely stood trying to hide what he thought looked like shame.

The clerk smiled and nodded, living so close to Washington this story was one that was believable and he did occasionally get diplomats in here. "I understand gentleman and you can be assured that we are indeed the very sole of discretion." He said to the two men while thinking to himself the hilarious story he would tell his buddies about the two foreigners that were so backwards they thought fashion was blue jeans.

The two changed their clothes while the clerk wrapped up what they had wore into the store. Once back in the van Charley looked at Sean. "What did you say back there?"

"I asked where the men's room was. It's one of the few phrases I know in Arabic. But hey it worked. We need to make a couple more stops, let's go.

Now looking like two Middle Eastern businessmen the headed into Washington with Sean again stopping to check the phone booths for the yellow pages. Eventually he found what he was looking for and using a map guided Charley to a store in an upscale part of the city.

"Just drive around the block until you see me waiting on the sidewalk again. " Sean ordered then hopped out of the van at a red light.

Charley circled the block seven times before he saw his partner waiting at the same intersection he got out at. He slowed the van timing it so that he hit the next red light and Sean opened the side door and tossed in two expensive looking leather travel cases and climbed in after them. They made one more stop at an army surplus store where Sean bought an oversized duffel bag, then he ordered Charley to the airport, short term parking.

After parking the van Sean opened the cases and took out two traditional Arab Headdresses that the each man donned. Next they each stripped down an SMG, Charley choosing his silenced sten and Sean choosing the Thompson as it used the same ammo as the handgun he had chosen to carry, and placed them in the cases along with a silencer and several boxes of .45 ammo. Charley also packed his .22 in his case. They both had $9,000 in cash and a tranquilizer gun in the case as well and Sean somehow managed to stuff the duffel bag in his case as well. The cases looked similar to the kind a businessman would use on a short trip and made the two look like travelers. Locking the van they walked over to the terminal, found the cab stand and hopped in a cab asking for the Grand Hyatt Washington.

Sean paid the driver when they arrived tipping generously and with Charley in tow walked into the hotel straight to the check in desk. "I will need a room for myself and my servant please. They must be adjoining rooms," he ordered the young lady at the desk.

Used to people from all over the world and different cultures the young woman smiled and checked her computer looking for what the gentleman requested. "Yes sir, will you require smoking or non smoking?"

"Non smoking please."

"Yes sir I have adjoining rooms available on the 6th floor. How long will you be staying sir?"

"We will need the rooms only for two nights and I will pay you with cash."

Again used to such business transactions the young lady only smiled. "Certainly sir."

Sean used a made up Arabic sounding name and handed over $2,000 which more then covered the bill. When the desk clerk attempted to make change Sean shook her off. "Keep it all, I may wish to make use of room service. If I incur more expenses I will settle with you when I leave."

"Thank you sir. Do you need a porter to carry up your luggage?"

"No we have only these cases." Sean gestured to the ones he and Charley were holding.

She handed Sean both room keys. "Thank you and enjoy your stay sir."

Sean left heading for the elevator with out saying another word, Charley following behind. They rode to the 6th floor in silence and both went into the first room they came to.

"What the hell was that about servant old man?" Charley asked as soon as the door was closed

"Relax Lad it's expected. Arab business men never travel without someone to help them out." Sean grinned at the young man.

"So how come you aren't the servant?"

"Because I was the one talking and you weren't. Let's get to work shall we?" Sean picked up the phone and ordered a car specifying a Lincoln Town Car to be picked up at the front entrance in twenty minutes. Both men took the pistols out of the cases and made sure they were loaded, stuffing them behind their belts at the small of the back. Each dropped several spare loaded clips in their pockets along with cash and headed down to get the car. Charley carried his case with his SMG, both tranquilizer guns, and the duffel bag in it.

Sean sat in the back with Charley driving to keep up the façade that they were master and servant and headed towards Georgetown. They appeared to be just one of thousands of the people that dotted the city. Removing the headdresses to avoid drawing too much attention to themselves, they scouted the first area with one quick drive by then headed north of the city to the second destination. They took more time scouting this one as it was the middle of the day and their quarry was at work, or so they hoped.

With the scout work done there was nothing to do but wait until dark. Once back in the city proper they donned the headdresses again and Charley drove aimlessly around seeing the sights. After wasting the majority of the day, Charley stopped to fill the car with gas and headed back to Georgetown. Sometimes luck is better then planning and this was one such time. As he turned the corner he spotted their quarry getting into the back of a taxi. Taking care he followed the cab, which went in a direct route to a restaurant where the man they were interested in got out and went inside. Charley was able to park the car on the next block and the two men took off the headdresses and walked back to the restaurant.

"What do you think, lad?"

"Well, if he's alone I think we should try sitting down and talking to him Sean. After all if we want someone to believe us then that's the best way about it. And this is a lot safer than knocking on his door at home. Here we can use the other people as a shield if we need to. Did you notice any bodyguards around him?"

"No I didn't, which I find strange. I would have thought someone in his position would have secret service around him. Let's it play it the way we planned. You talk to him and I'll watch your back. As you said, doing it here is better then doing it at his house. Okay, if he's by himself just walk up to him and sit down as if you're an old friend."

As they entered Sean went straight to the bar and ordered a whisky while

Charley went into the dinning area where he was met by a maitre d. Trained to scan a room fast Charley was able to spot his man sitting alone near the far end of the room, simply smiled at the maitre d and said he was meeting a friend as he walked past without giving the man a chance to stop him.

In seconds he was across the room and next to the table that Adam Miles was sitting at, without saying a word he pulled out a the only other chair and sat down. "Good evening Mr Miles. I know you were not expecting me but I really do need to speak to you. It is extremely urgent and I promise you it will not be a waste of your time."

As the chief of staff for the President of the United States, Adam was used to people doing this all the time. It seemed that everyone thought interrupting him at dinner was a new and untried idea. "Whatever it is, I do not talk business when I'm eating unless it has been prearranged first." He told the man raising his hand to get the maitre d's attention and have the intruder removed.

"Before you have me thrown out you should know I'm the man that they say shot at your boss and everyone is hunting me. I have some news about another plan to kill the president and you may want to listen to me."

That caught Adam's attention right away, however the maitre d was already coming over with another larger man, having seen this signal before and prepared to forcibly remove the newcomer.

"Is this man bothering you Mr Miles?" he asked when he arrived.

"No Jerry, he's actually joining me for dinner and I completely forgot, I'm very sorry. Can you have someone bring another setting for him."

"Absolutely sir, right away." He motioned one of the busboys and made a rapid motion with his hand to alert them to the second guest. "I'll bring you a menu straight away."

"Actually Jerry I bragged about how good you were to my friend and I've made a bet with him that you could stun him with a meal. Why don't you surprise us with something, I'll let you choose everything including the wine and dessert."

Pleased with the high praise from so powerful a man in Washington, he nodded and his face beamed with a huge smile. "Of course, I will speak with the chef and we will create something wonderful for you both." With that he hurried to the kitchen and another bus boy came up with the place setting and laid everything out for Charley. Right behind him was the wine steward who uncorked a bottle and set it on the table to breath informing them that he would be back shortly to pour.

"I think you've helped make Jerry's year. One of the things he likes best is to be in charge and order for people. This will be the first time I've let him do that and I'm afraid of what he has in store for us. By the looks of the wine bottle it will be something expensive and spectacular, so you really better be who you say you are. Just one question though, how did you know I would listen and not just yell for help?"

"I didn't which is why my partner is in the bar watching my back. But the truth is I need to speak with someone that will get the information I have to the president. If I don't get it to him he's going to be killed."

"Then call the Secret Service they are in charge of protecting the president."

"I can't, at least one agent that I know of on his detail is involved in the plot, and there could be others. Telling them would be a waste of my time."

Adam frowned I in disbelief at that. "You don't need to be theatrical I said I would listen. First things first, who are you?"

"My name is Charles Watkins, please call me Charley, and my partner is Sean Miller."

"That proves nothing sir, all that information was in the news."

"Have you seen the reports on what the police found and the evidence from the shooting in Boston?"

Adam nodded "Yes I have."

"Then this will be easy. In Boston the only person shot was Andrea Drake and she was shot with a 168-grain boat tail 30-06 caliber bullet. The strange thing about the bullet was that there were no markings on it at all from the rifle barrel. No weapon was ever found and the shooting site was never identified. Correct so far?"

Adam simply nodded and Charley went on to describe the house in Vermont in extreme detail including many things that had never been released to the news. Charley also listed all the photos and weapons found in the house, along with other information that could only have come from someone that had either been there or read the police reports, a fact that Adam brought up.

"I could have read the police reports," Charley admitted. "But do the police reports mention that the bullet was fired from a .50 caliber rifle over 2,000 yards away? I'm sure they also don't mention that the suspects evaded capture by hiding in a ventilation shaft for several days and then left the county by boat? Which is what we did. What they also don't mention is that while the target was supposed to be both the Pope and the president, the bullet fired hit the target that it was shot at."

"Excuse me?" Adam asked sharply just as the waiter appeared with a salad for the two men.

"It is a lobster salad with a spicy lemon dressing sir. I can ask the chef for something different if you prefer," the waiter said, thinking Adam was speaking to him

"No no," Adam replied to the waiter. "Please, it looks delicious."

The salad was served and the wine poured. Both men tasted it, surprised by the mix of flavors and textures. As he enjoyed the salad Charley continued with his story. "I was the one that pulled the trigger and I hit exactly what I aimed at. I was afraid I would break her leg but the news reports said that didn't happen, can you confirm that?"

"It was a nice clean shot, according the doctors, no broken bones and about as little damage as can be expected from a large bore bullet wound. Forgetting for the moment that you have just admitted to a felony can you tell me why you shot a secret service agent?

"I had to. If I didn't shoot her she would have shot the president."

Adam put his fork down anger beginning to show on his face for the first time. "That is preposterous. I've met that agent in person, as a matter of fact I recommended her for the job. This is load of crap."

"Mr Miles it gets even better. If you think that's hard to believe wait till you hear the whole story. Oops I think the waiter has something else for us."

At that moment the waiter did indeed appear carrying a small tray. "Compliments of the chef, Alsatian Onion and Bacon Tartlets," he said placing them on the table with a flourish then leaving.

Charley picked one up and popped it into his mouth savoring the taste. "WOW! These are great. Do you mind if I take one for my partner. He's not really getting anything to eat."

Adam signaled to Jerry again, who was at the table in seconds. "Jerry, we have a mutual acquaintance in the bar and I was wondering if you could have a few of these tartlets sent over to him? They are incredible."

Pleased with the praise for the food Jerry said it would be done at once and asked who the gentleman was. Charley looked over his shoulder and could see his partner at the bar seemingly looking around aimlessly, but in reality checking the room for danger every few seconds. Charley pointed him out and made a motion to Sean to let him know they were sending something over to the bar for him.

"Thanks Jerry and put his tab on my bill please, what ever he wants."

"Of course sir." Jerry said to one of his favorite customers.

The tartlets were sent to Sean who upon tasting them immediately signaled his approval and enjoyed the plate with gusto nodding to Charley and Adam as a thank you.

"I hope your friend isn't a heavy drinker, this meal just keeps getting more and more expensive."

"I would be surprised if he even finishes one drink Mr Miles. You see he's on duty, so to speak. As a matter of fact so am I, which is a shame because that wine is out of this world."

"Please call me Adam. Do you mind if I call you Charles?"

"Charley is what I go by, I don't mind at all. I'm sorry that I upset you but you have to believe me, I know what I'm talking about. We will have proof later tonight and I'm sure it will convince even you."

"Why don't you invite your partner to join us? I'm sure it will be okay."

"Thank you but no. Sean doesn't even want to be where he is right now and the fact that I pointed him out to you is something I'll be hearing about later. You see we have only stayed alive for so long by being paranoid and avoiding situations that could potentially be a trap. Both of us at this table with no ready escape route would be foolish."

Adam chuckled at that. "I am hardly a threat to either of you. Your friend looks very fit as do you and I'm sure that either one of you could subdue me with out very much effort. I don't exercise often."

Charley smiled back at his host. "It's not just you Adam. What if someone in the crowd recognizes us, an off duty FBI agent for example? We are wanted men after all. No it's better this way. Although I have to admit Sean sure got the bad end of the bargain tonight."

Just then Jerry showed up with the main dish. It was pancetta-studded beef tenderloin and a vegetable medley that consisted of small new potatoes, carrots, radishes, green beans, white onions, and peas in the pod, cooked in extra-virgin olive oil with basil, chives, savory, anise, hyssop, tarragon and sea salt. He also brought another bottle of wine, which was already open and had been allowed to breath. "Bon appetite gentlemen."

Charley and Adam were silent for several moments as they enjoyed the meal. It truly was the best meal Charley had ever eaten, even Adam found it to be superb, and he was used to gourmet food. "So tell me about this proof of yours," Adam prompted.

"I can't do that right yet. But I will tell you a story that you are really not going to believe." With that Charley began to tell him about the organization and what it had done to him. He detailed the plan for the President he personally had been involved in and what was supposed to happen, then outlined the plan that was going to happen next. Adam was shocked that Charley knew about the Presidents sailing trip and was even more shocked to hear about the captor mine. Charley explained that they did not yet have all the details on that but should have them tomorrow at which point he would try to get them to Adam somehow.

"You have to tell the authorities, I have to tell the authorities. Why haven't you turned yourself into the FBI with this information?"

"Because the organization has the US government penetrated. If I were to turn myself in the information would be lost, destroyed or discredited and if it could not be, the plan would be scrapped and then the organization would try again. They would also have me killed, not something I'm in a rush to have happen. And if you tell this to anyone, they will scrap the plan and start all over. To be honest I'm not sure I can get the information I have now, a second time."

"But you could be placed in protective custody," Adam protested.

"I was in prison when I was 'recruited' the first time, so to speak. I have no faith in the ability of the authorities to protect me in jail a second time. I'm better off taking my changes on the street."

"But we have to stop this attack," Adam insisted.

"And we will. Right now there is no proof of what I'm saying. Nothing that I could take to the police and show them. I need to get the proof, something that no one will deny. See I'm not in this to just save the President I'm in this to destroy the organization and clear my name. I don't want the President to die but if this attempt doesn't succeed they will just try again until they do succeed. The organization wants the president dead and they are going to keep at it until it happens."

"Okay so let's say you get proof will you come to me with it?"

"I'm not sure yet. You seem like an honest man but I'm still a wanted fugitive and you have no idea how powerful the organization is. Right now I don't know who to turn to. The problem is I know how deep the organization goes so I know where I can't go with the info. I can say it will be you or someone at the NSA though," Charley paused. "Maybe both of you."

Adam took a card out of his pocket and passed it to Charley. "Please contact me no matter what. If you know something is going to happen to the boss on his boat I have to stop him from going."

"I agree, but what ever you do don't announce that his vacation has been canceled or they will start another plan to kill him right away. If they still think he is going sailing then they will stay with the plan they have in place."

Jerry showed up with desert, chocolate raspberry almond torte, before Adam could respond. The two finished the meal in silence as both thought out what they had to do next.

Adam ordered a coffee and the bill. "Okay you have to get your proof in the next four days, I'll stay quiet for that long. After that I cancel the president's trip. Thank you for trusting me and coming to see me. If you are right I will see about getting your name cleared as well."

"Thank you, I appreciate that. And I promise we will get proof to you, but you can't say anything to anyone until that time. You truly do not know how high the organization goes in the government. By the way how much do you think this meal is going to cost you?"

Adam looked at the two bottles of wine and the empty plates mentally calculating it in his head. "Probably a thousand dollars or so. The wine was very expensive."

Charley reached in his pocket and took out $2,000 and placed it on the table. "This is money we took from the organization. Let's let them pay for the meal. Leave it all, the left over can be a tip, it was worth every penny."

Charley got up and without a backward glance left the restaurant. Sean followed a few seconds later scanning the room to see whom, if anyone was watching. No one seemed to be. Meeting up with Charley on the street they walked back to the car alert for danger, If anyone tried to take them here it would be a difficult thing to get away from. The walk to the car was uneventful and both sat in front this time with Sean driving. He immediately headed north out of the city toward the second target of the night, this one sure to be much less friendly than Adam had been.

Driving by, they saw lights on, indicating that someone was home. They were lucky to find a parking spot right out front and as they left the car each man took a tranquilizer gun and tucked it behind his waistband. This was a little uncomfortable but the suit coats hid the weapons well. Charley knocked on the door and then pulled out his tranquilizer holding it low and close to his leg shielding it from view. As Andrea opened the door Charley shot her then simply stepped in, as any guest would do upon being invited. Sean followed, and as soon as the door was closed, helped Charley move the now unconscious women into the kitchen. Getting in had been the easy part, now the danger began. How to get the woman out of her own place and into the car with them?

Sean tied her up using strips torn from a towel making sure that she was immobile also securing her at the elbows and knees. The towel would leave very little in the way of marks but would be as secure as using rope. Charley had also found a roll of duct tape in the kitchen and they wound that around the towel a few times just as an added measure of security.

"Okay we wait a few more hours then I'll get the duffel bag and we can get her out of here. Might as well relax and watch some TV. I'm going to look and see if she has any coffee, would you like some?" Sean said casually.

Charley shook his head, He was keyed up and tense, waiting for something to go wrong, and his partner was making himself at home. "You are unbelievable pal. I don't know how you can be so relaxed at a time like this."

"Who says I'm relaxed lad?"

Charley turned on the TV to CNN and spent the rest of the evening listening to the news. There was a brief update on the manhunt still ongoing for the two of them, but that was all. The search had been relegated to filler because it was taking so long. The attention span of the news media was not that long and it reflected that fact in the reporting of events. As usual the reports were quick with facts being reported and very little background information given. No wonder people had such poor knowledge as to why the rest of the world hated America.

At 1 AM Sean stood up and quietly said, "Let's go." The two men packed the still unconscious woman into the duffel bag then out to the car. Rather then put her in the trunk Sean put her in the back seat on the floor, where they could keep an eye on her. If she regained consciousness in the trunk and began making noise they would have to stop the car and open the trunk to sedate her again. This way all they needed to do was reach over the back seat. As they neared the hotel Sean heard stirring in the back and calmly reached over the seat and shot the bag with another tranquilizer dart. The stirring stopped almost immediately and they came to a halt in front of the hotel. Charley got out and took the bag out of the back and slung the carry strap over his shoulder, carrying it calmly as he followed Sean to the elevator. This late at night the lobby was almost deserted and only the bell captain asked if they needed help. Waving him off they got into the elevator and went straight to their floor. Both men relaxed when they shut the room door behind them.

Changing back into his jeans Sean tucked his pistol back behind his belt and went back out for the most dangerous part of the job, he needed to find drugs so that they could make the woman talk. As distasteful as it was, drugging her was much better that torturing her and they needed to get information. Taking the car he headed into the seedier part of Washington, the part no one talks about, and tries to pretend doesn't exist. Standing on a street corner was exactly what Sean was looking for: a young drug dealer. Rolling down his window Sean asked for a price. The young man named a figure and Sean took the cash out of his pocket careful to hide it below the window of the car and counted off the amount mentioned. With his gun hidden out of sight in his right hand he stuck his left out the window with the money in it. The dealer palmed the money and slipped a plastic envelope of powder into Sean's hand in a motion so smooth that it could have been taught at any of the better intelligence agencies as a brush pass.

An all night drug store provided him with a disposable diabetic syringe on his way back to the hotel, his nights shopping trip over.

Both men were exhausted from the long day, and they dropped fully clothed onto the king sized bed. Even though they had separate rooms both slept in the same room for safety reasons. Their guns were within easy reach and the duffel bag still containing their kidnap victim was on the floor at the foot of the bed.

The boat motored through the night its engine compartment heavily insulated to muffle the noise. Four men lounged on the deck admiring the stars in the incredibly clear night. With no moon and no lights to interfere, the view was breathtaking. The boat was running blacked out using an autopilot linked to a GPS plotter to steer it to the proper spot. There was a man sitting at the wheel with his hands in his lap, letting the electronics guide them but ready top take over at a seconds notice. The area they were in was off limits but fishing boats were known to transit it all the time. The navy kept a presence in the area and the men were alert for any sign of another vessel. If they were stopped there was nothing on the boat to identify them as anything other that what they appeared to be, a fishing boat. There were no weapons of any type on the boat. Their mission was to deliver a captor mine and to do this they were relying on stealth and deception.

The mine itself was slung under the boat and could be released from the wheelhouse by the man on duty there. When they reached the proper place, according to the GPS, a small buzzer sounded alerting all on the boat and the man in the wheelhouse pulled on a lever beneath his seat causing the mine to drop to the ocean floor. The boat lurched a tiny bit from the release of several thousand pounds of weight but never showed any other signs of having performed a highly illegal act. Continuing through the night they cleared the area twenty minutes later and everyone visibly relaxed at having gotten in and out of the restricted zone without notice.

When they docked six hours later the team leader would send a coded message to indicate the job was done, never even knowing what the mine was for, but as he dropped it in a navy training area he assumed it would be used against a navy ship.

The rustle of cloth woke Sean who lay still, assessing the room waiting for whatever it was that had disturbed him to repeat itself. It did, and this time it woke Charley. Sean calmed him by motioning to the bottom of the bed and the bundle resting on the floor there. They had managed three hours of sleep, not enough to rest the two men but they couldn't go back to sleep leaving their guest by herself. Getting up, first Sean then Charley paid a quick visit to the bathroom then sat down to deal with the squirming bundle on the floor.

Charley opened the bag and pulled it down to free Andrea's head and shoulders. "Good morning Miss, how are you feeling this morning?"

The hatred in her eyes blazed at the two but the tape on her mouth kept her from screaming at them.

"Now little lady," Sean began. "We are going to remove the tape on your mouth. Please don't scream. You seem to be an intelligent woman so I'm sure I don't need to go through the theatrics of threatening you." With that he reached forward and in one quick motion yanked the tape off.

A small squeal slipped out then she quietly sat there opening and closing her jaw to work it loose. "Are you…." She began her voice coming out as a croak. Clearing her throat she started again. "Are you two insane? Kidnapping a federal agent is a really dumb career move. The US government does not negotiate, so I'm worth nothing to you. If you let me go know I can promise I'll put in a good word for you at the trial."

"What makes you think we are kidnapping you?" Sean asked.

Andrea snorted "Let's see, I'm tied up, I was knocked out and I have no idea where I am but I know I'm not at home. What would you call it?"

"It could be called a citizen's arrest. You are, after all, working for a criminal organization that is attempting to assassinate the President of the United States, and you personally have actively assisted in this," Charley said quietly.

"I am a federal agent in the treasury department and you two are under arrest." Andrea defiantly began reading the two men their rights.

Charley left the room and came back carrying a small bag. Opening the bag he took out a syringe, a spoon, and a bag of white powder. Scooping some of the powder onto the spoon he removed a lighter from his pocket it light it and held it carefully under the spoon. Shortly the sound of bubbling was heard at which point he closed the lighter and used the needle to draw up the now liquid substance in the spoon. Making sure there were no air bubbles he took out an alcohol swap and wiped it on Andrea's arm. Up to this point she had watched the young man fascinated, thinking he was going to shoot himself up on heroin right in front of her. Realizing he was going to inject her she began to thrash and drew in a large breath to scream. Sean grabbed her and slapped the tape back on her mouth holding her still for his partner.

"Now we both know who you work for and what you have done. What we don't know is what you are doing now. We don't have the time to be nice and I can't stand the thought of torturing a woman, so the alternative is chemicals. Sorry that I couldn't get the right stuff but in a pinch I've heard heroin will do. I guess we'll find out. Oh yeah just for the record I'm the guy that shot you in Boston." With that Charley jabbed the needle in her arm and pushed the plunger.

The powerful narcotic took effect in seconds making her head droop and eyes glaze over. Charley hadn't been sure of the dosage and hoped he hadn't gotten it wrong and given her too much. He wanted her calm and relaxed with her inhibitions broken down but not too stoned to answer any questions, or worse, dead of an overdose. Slowly he and Sean began talking to the woman. He had gotten the dose right, she was barely coherent but she could speck clearly enough for them to understand and better still she didn't appear to know she was talking. Charley turned on one of the laptops and plugged in a mini microphone to the computer. Then starting a program he had downloaded off the net, began recording the conversation. There was enough hard drive space for about two hours of recording time but he didn't think this would be necessary. He was right, it took less than ten minutes to find out that she had planted something on the boat under the engine but had not recorded any sounds from the boat. After another thirty minutes it was apparent that that was her entire part of the operation, she wasn't even on the detail slated to go with the president. They also learned that the boat was on an assault ship that was heading down to the area and guarded around the clock by the Secret Service and a squad of Marines. There was no way to get near it to recover what she had planted without the organization hearing about it. Having gotten all the information they could regarding the new attempt on the president, Sean re-taped her mouth and put a pillow under her head to make her comfortable while the heroin worked its way out of her system. She would be relaxed for several more hours and would pose no problem during that time.

"Well lad we have our proof. We have the plan on the laptop and we have her. I say we drop her off with a copy of the recoding you made to the FBI and leave it up to them."

"I dunno Sean, the FBI has a lot of organization agents in it. There is a small chance they will get to her first and cover everything up. We need to get this information to people we know aren't in the organizations grip."

Sean thought for a moment. "You know, we could use the people at the NSA and the president's chief of staff. We contact them both and see if they are interested. If so we set up a meet somewhere and give them just enough time to get there but not enough time to set up a trap for us. We drop of the girl and the computer and get the hell out. All we need is someplace remote yet with an easy escape route and a fast car to get us out of it."

Charley liked the idea, so Sean called room service and asked for some maps of the area to be sent up. The request was actually a normal one for a hotel that catered to international guests and kept a large selection of maps on hand. Maps covering the DC area and the states of Virginia and Maryland were sent up an hour later. After pouring over them Charley was struck with an idea. Several areas of the shoreline were set aside for wildlife sanctuaries with the only way to reach them being boat, helicopter, or on foot. A quick check of the phone book listed several boat dealers in the area. Charley started calling them looking for a fast boat using jet drive that had a small cuddy cabin. He found one on his fifth phone call at a dealer in Annapolis that had everything he was looking for. A sport fisher with a cuddy cabin, twenty-four feet long powered by a large V-6 using jet stern drive. Perfect for shallow water and sand bars.

Sean took a cab to the airport to retrieve the van while Charley cleaned up the room and got ready to leave. He loaded the tranquilizer drug from one of the darts into a syringe and knocked out Andrea again so that she could be moved. As soon as Sean was back he took Andrea out the back using the duffel to carry her to the van. As he was doing that Charley went to the front desk and checked out.

Two hours later they finished up the paperwork on the boat, paying with the organizations cash, to the joy of the sales agent. Moving the boat to a public berth to transfer the gear from the van to the boat was a huge risk but had to be done. Everything was done in less than 5 minutes, with the weapons computer gear and Andrea stored in the small and now cramped cabin. The boat was fully fueled and ready to go and had a complete set of charts of the Chesapeake Bay and Potomac River. It was also equipped with a GPS, radio, and fish finder that doubled as a depth sounder.

For the first time in several months the pair were traveling separately. Sean drove the van to BWI to park it in long term parking while Sean motored the boat from the dealer in Annapolis to Baltimore. After making a call from a payphone Sean took a cab from the airport to the water front with one stop along the way. By the time he arrived at the waterfront Charley had been waiting for thirty minutes growing more and more alarmed as time went by. He felt enormous relieve to see his partner, mentor and friend step out of the cab when it pulled up on the dock. Sean was carrying a bag and apologized for being late simply stating that he needed to pick something up. Charley just nodded, happy that his friend was okay.

"Something I'll need," Sean said, motioning to the bag as he climbed onto the boat. "Ready to go?"

"Before we go let's chat with our friend at the NSA." Charley said.

Charley set up his computer and satellite praying that the boat would be calm enough for him to maintain a connection with it. Five minutes later he was online hoping that Holly was waiting to talk with him. He shut down the firewall and waited.

At the NSA they had a system set up full time, waiting for Charley to connect to the net again. In fact Holly had one person always on rotation at the computer waiting for the IP address they had placed a watch on, to show active. At this time of day it was Doris on duty. "Holly he's back," she announced as the computer alerted her that the watched IP was active.

Holly knew whom she was talking about and moved into the seat Doris vacated and started typing.

"Hello." The message popped up on Charley's screen. "Are you and your friend okay?"

"Yes we are. How are you?" Charley typed back

"I was becoming anxious that I wouldn't hear from you again. I was afraid I had upset you last time we talked."

"I didn't see the sense of talking to you anymore until I had something worth saying."

"I hope you don't mind but I told my boss about you, I had to. No one else knows though and he was wondering if we could meet sometime? He said that the time and place would be of your choosing and promises no tricks."

Charley glanced at Sean. "This wil be easy to set up, she already wants to meet us, her nad her boss."

Sean scowled. "I'm not sure I like that lad. It sounds like a trap, tell her to forget her boss, just her and Adam.

Charley nodded and began typing his reply. "Okay, but not your boss. We don't want him along. And we have something for you but I will be inviting someone else to the meeting, it's someone on your side and I'll make sure you meet him before you meet us. I need a phone number that gets only to you and someone will be calling you soon."

It took her a second to get him a number that would ring right through to her and then gave it to him. "When and where do we meet you? Who is the other person?" she typed in.

"Not right now, I'll contact you tomorrow at 9 AM and you will have two hours to get to the location I give you. I'll be using co-ordinates from a GPS unit along with highway routes so you will have an exact location. Is that clear?"

"Perfectly clear," Holly told him. "I'll wait for your contact at 9 AM."

With that Charley logged off and shut down the computer. Packing everything back up in the cuddy cabin they cast off the lines and headed away from Baltimore back towards Annapolis. Charley drove the boat fast to get the feel of it, sliding it back and forth across the waves speeding up and slowing down as well as playing with the trim tabs. After a few minutes of this he had the rhythm of the vessel and was piloting it across the bay smiling widely, wind blowing through his hair. A sudden thump from the cabin reminded him that they had a guest on board and she was apparently awake.

Sean opened the cabin to see Andrea on the floor rocking back and forth. He had removed her from the duffel as soon as he had her onboard. The torn cloth and duct tape had been replaced with prison issue leg irons and handcuffs that attached to a belt around her waist locking in the back. She could move around more than before, but there was no way she could move fast or gracefully. The hatred in her eyes when she looked at him was intense and violent. Knowing how long it had been since she had food or water he knew what kind of discomfort she was in but didn't feel the least bit of pity for the woman. If the positions were ever reversed she would kill him without a seconds hesitation. No, the fact that she was a woman was secondary to the fact that she was a dangerous operative of the organization. Still there was no reason to be cruel to her.

Sean removed the tape from her mouth and held a canteen of water to it. Andrea sucked greedily on the canteen trying to get some moisture into her parched lips and tongue. "Careful girl, not too much or you'll be sick, Sean said, taking the canteen away. "I'll give you some more in a few more minutes. Do you need to use the toilet?"

With the mention of it, the urge to pee became overpowering. "Yes I do," she replied urgently.

The boat had come equipped with a marine head and Sean now opened the door to it allowing Andrea to hobble painfully in. He closed the door for her to allow her some measure of privacy. A few minutes later a knock sounded and he opened the door again; careful to stay to the side just in case she tried something stupid. Andrea looked at him then struggled out into the main cabin falling back onto the V berth.

"Can I have some more water?"

"Of course, here you are. Sean handed her the canteen this time allowing her to slake her thirst totally.

The motion of the speeding boat along with the limited mobility of her arms made it hard to drink. "Any chance you can remove these things?" She motioned to her restraints.

"None at all. In fact I'm afraid I'm going to have to restrain you into the bunk. I wouldn't want you trying to do something dangerous and we have a lot of delicate gear here." With that Sean used another pair of handcuffs to lock her leg irons to the birth preventing her from getting up.

He went outside but left the door open so he could watch Andrea. "How are we doing for time Lad?"

"We'll make it with time to spare. I'll go and do the shopping if you'd like to stay and keep our guest company?"

"That sounds fine."

The rest of the trip back to Annapolis passed in silence as both men enjoyed the feeling of freedom on the open water. It was cold but not that bad sitting behind the sport fisher's windscreen. There was a canopy to sit under as well and they could have used the dodger on the boat to enclose the driving area for further weather proofing but both men preferred the open visibility not using the dodger gave them. Charley pulled back into the marina in Annapolis and the two tied up again.

Charley went up the street to the local sporting goods store to pick as few things up, intending to go to a grocery store as well for food, while Sean went into the cabin and closed the door. He pulled out the .22 pistol and pointed it at Andrea. "Please be quiet until my partner gets back and everything will be fine. You'll be released in the morning."

Charley was back in half an hour and a few minutes later they were heading back down the bay towards the Potomac River. The trip took several hours and they had to stop and put up some of the dodger, as the air was getting colder. They reached their destination after dark and had to use the bow-mounted spotlight to check things out with. In the darkness it looked fine but only daylight would tell for sure. Still it looked good and should fill in nicely. At this point the river was about a mile wide and there were deserted stretches of river back scattered all along the area. They had picked a spot from a map but had gotten lucky to find only one abandoned boathouse along a two-mile stretch of the river. The boathouse was on the Virginia side of the river while directly across from it on the Maryland side there was a road less than 100 hundred yards from the river. Charley looked at Sean with a huge grin on his face then went forward to toss the anchor overboard for the night.

The two moved all their gear into the cockpit, then Sean went below to cook supper on the small one burner stove. Charley had picked up several cans of Chunky soup and some rolls for supper along with some instant coffee and a carton of orange juice. Sean cooked enough for all three of them undoing one of Andrea's hands so she could eat her supper. He set the bowl and spoon with in reach after freeing her hand then backed up. When she was done eating he ordered her to put the handcuff back on before picking up her bowl and spoon.

Charley washed the dishes and then rolled out two sleeping bags for him and his partner in the cockpit. They locked the cabin door after saying goodnight to their guest then went to sleep, each enjoying the starry night and the gentle rolling of the boat. All too fast the rising sun woke the pair telling them the new day had arrived.

While Sean went below to see to the needs of Andrea, Charley began laying out the gear he would need. Taking an empty backpack Charley began to pack it. Placing in it, his silenced sten gun, wedging it to one side, then he placing five magazine clips in beside it. Next went one of the beretta's along with the silencer and five magazines for it. Last went a sponge mat to lie on. The other bag he needed was already packed and in it was the BMG with all its clips and available ammo. Ready to go he knocked once on the cabin door to let Sean know he was done.

Sean came back on deck to go over the plan one more time. As they devised the plan it had finally been decided that Sean would be the one to do the actual meet. Charley would land by the boathouse enter it and open the river door halfway. One he had a clear fire of the opposite shore he would let Sean know exactly where to land the boat so that he had the best field of fire. Sean would then cross the river, and he and Andrea, along with one the stooge's laptops would wait on the beach at the location they had chosen. But before Charley could leave the boat he had to pass along his directions to Holly and Adam.

He did this by using the VHF radio on the boat to place a marine ship to shore call to Adam Miles.

"Hello," answered a groggy voice on the second ring.

"Hello Adam, this is the gentleman that bought you dinner the other night. I was just wondering if you had some time free this morning?"

The recognition of who was on the phone jolted him awake. "Not really, but for you I think I can make the time. What did you have in mind?"

"Well at around 8:45 you'll get another call and a set of directions, then you'll need to call someone I know and tell them that you need a lift and where to. You come out and meet my friend from the restaurant and he'll have something for you. It'll take all morning though and it has to be done today. You should be back in the office by 1."

"Okay I got it. I'll make the time. Anything else?"

"Yes, I won't be making the next call and I need the number where you'll be at 8:45."

Adam gave Charley his direct office line and then hung up and got out of bed. He had a lot to do so he could get out of the White House for the morning.

Sean motored close to the shore, with in yards of the boathouse and Charley jumped to the bank. Getting into the boathouse was no harder then prying a rusty padlock off the backdoor and he was inside. Opening the river door halfway he lay down on the deck and took stock of his view of the other side. Communicating with Sean on a handheld VHF he was able to tell him how the set up would be arranged. It took less then twenty minutes for everything to get set up and then came the hard part, the waiting.

At 8:45 Sean, this time, used the VHF to call Adam and gave him a detailed series of directions explaining that they were both highway numbers and GPS co-ordinates. Lastly he gave Adam Holly's number and explained that he was to bring the person that answered the phone. Adam was curious as to what this was all about but was sure it wasn't a hoax so he dialed the number and heard a woman's voice answer

"Who is this?" he asked.

"You called me sir, who are you?" came the woman's reply.

"My is Adam Myles and I'm the White House Chief of staff."

"I'm Holly McClare with the NSA, why are you calling me, sir?"

"The NSA? Do you mean the National Security Agency?"

"Yes sir I do. I hate to rush you but I'm expecting a very important communication and I have to get off the line. How can I help you?"

"Were you expecting to hear from a certain young man that is being looked for by the FBI?"

Holly couldn't believe that the Chief of Staff was talking about Charley; it had to be someone else. Before she could say anything Adam continued talking. "He had his older friend just call me and give me a set of directions then call your number. I was told that whoever answered could give me a ride out to pick something up."

It had to be Charley nothing else made sense. "Please forgive my surprise, I am a little shocked that someone else is contacting me and absolutely stunned that it would be you. But yes I was expecting some directions this morning."

Adam gave her the direction Sean had given, and then they made arrangements to meet on the road towards the final destination. Adam would be alone while Holly would have two other men from the NSA with her. With plans made, both hung up and headed for their cars, a deadline to meet.

As Holly was leaving one Sam's assistants was stopping by the basement to have a programmer check something for him. The deputy director was looking for constant updates on the woman's whereabouts since he was no longer in the loop for the information she gathered and a day didn't go by that one assistant or another was in the basement to check and see the young lady was still there. The second the programmer was finished the assistant hurried back to the deputy director's office to tell his boss what he had seen. Holly was always in the building during business hours and her leaving at that hour with the two men of her team made his sense of danger tingle. Always a man to trust his instincts he headed down to the basement to see if he could find out anything. When he arrived he saw just the two ladies and decided on the spur of the moment to try and coerce information from them, thinking that his position as deputy director would intimidate them. Knowing military members respond to rank better he picked her as his target.

"Good morning Sergeant, where will I find Miss McClare?"

"She's out at the moment sir," Sergeant Mayweather answered coming to attention as she would with any superior officer.

"Yes I can see that. What I am asking is, where is she? I need to speak with her."

"I'm not at liberty to say sir," came the cautious response.

Sam sensed uneasiness in the women and immediately went on the attack. "Sergeant as I understand it, your assignment to Miss McClare is temporary. At the conclusion of her work you will be reassigned. If you do not tell me what I want to know I will make sure that your reassignment is somewhere out of this building and decidedly less pleasant. Now I understand that your project is classified and I respect that. However I am not asking for information on what you are doing I am asking where Miss McClare is, which is not classified information. You will answer the question and do it right now," he ordered.

Stiffening the Sergeant hesitated for another few seconds before caving in and answering. "She went out to meeting sir. She received a call and looked very surprised, she wrote something down then she John and the Gunny left."

"What did she write down?"

I have no idea sir, she took the paper with her."

"And she left no information on where she was going or when she would be back? I find that very difficult to believe Sergeant."

"I'm sorry sir but she said she needed to keep the information confidential. She indicated that she would be back this afternoon but did not give a specific time sir."

"I see. Well thank you Sergeant, I'll track down Miss McClare tomorrow as it appears she is gone for today." With that Sam picked up the notepad that was sitting on Holly's desk and left the room.

Mayweather was so relieved she failed to notice that he had taken the notepad at all. She simply sat down and returned to work making a mental note to tell Holly about the visit when she got back.

As soon as Sam returned to his office he place the notepad in the center of his desk and took a pencil out of the drawer. Lightly rubbing it back and forth on the page produced an image of the indentation from the page that was above it when someone wrote on it. Three careful minutes later and he had the complete set up coordinates and directions, which puzzled him at first. The notation at the bottom suddenly jumped off the page at him. In the margin at the bottom was a notation to meat Adam Miles before seeing Charley and had a question mark after it. The implication caused him to break out in a cold sweat. If the pad was to be believed, Miss McClare and the White

House chief of Staff were meeting with one of the suspects in the attempted shooting of the President.

He grabbed his phone and dialed the FBI. It took less than five minutes to inform the FBI that there was a possible location of one of the most wanted men in the US. As he was making the tip anonymously he deliberately left out the fact the chief of staff or members of the NSA would be there as well. He only mentioned that the tip came from reliable sources and hung up. As the phone system the NSA used was secure, he was confident that not even the FBI would be able to trace his call. He just hoped that he was in time to capture the suspects.

At the FBI his tip caused an uproar. The director was notified and he immediately called the stand by Quick response team. Trained as a counter terrorist unit they were also highly capable of capturing wanted suspects as well. Two helicopters were already warming up and would be the way to collect them. Used to short notice, the team leader took his orders in stride and walked over to a secure fax to retrieve the directions that had been sent over to him. The same directions were being sent to the chopper pilots so they would already know where to take the team after the pickup.

Reading the information he noticed it was on the Potomac River on the Maryland shore. The formula dictated that the teams split and approach from two sides in a pincer movement. In this case he decided to land one of the teams on the road near the shore line and give them a few minutes to move into place, then have the other chopper come up the river fast to try and trap the suspect between his two teams. If there was a boat he could follow it in the chopper while contacting the Coast Guard to move in and detain the suspects. All in all it looked like a straightforward assignment. He took for granted that the suspects would be armed and dangerous, they always were when his team was called in.

Waiting was the hard part. Charley and Sean kept in contact using the VHF radios but kept conversation to a minimum. Even though they were on a seldom-used channel someone might over hear them and they didn't want to risk blowing the meet. Sean had kept Andrea confined in the cabin so that she would not know he was alone. They had thought about drugging her but the need to have her coherent at the meeting, outweighed the need to have her docile. Sean would keep her handcuffed and though he wanted to keep the prison chains on her there was no way to get her off the boat wearing them.

With no dock to tie up to Sean got as close to the shore as possible then dropped the anchor. The water was about three feet deep and with no other way off he simply jumped into the water and waded to shore carrying a rope. He secured the rope to a tree at the rivers edge then waded back to the boat and tied off the rope as a security measure in case the anchor slipped in the river mud. With the boat secure he packed his gear up in two duffel bags and carried them to shore then went back for Andrea. Both waded to shore and once on dry land Sean used the prison chains to secure her to a tree out of reach of his two bags, while he headed back to the boat a final time. Opening the bag he had picked up in Baltimore he pulled out a bulky pair of coveralls and what looked like an antique football helmet. Sean clipped his portable VHF radio to his belt and tucked the earpiece into his ear then ran the cord over is shoulder and down his back to the radio. With that done he put on the coveralls and helmet then strapped on a holster for the berretta and dropped some extra mags in the pocket.

Adam met Holly and two other men half an hour from the final destination. Introductions were made between the Chief of staff and John and Gunny so that everyone knew how the other person fit into the group. They all got into Adam's car and proceeded toward the rendezvous. During the drive Adam explained how he had gotten involved and began asking questions of Holly. She explained that she was under strict orders not to discuss anything without permission and so could not give him very much detail. Adam, in a move that was uncharacteristic for a political appointee in Washington, understood and didn't pressure her. As they got closer to the meeting point the two men sitting in the back of Adams car took out pistols and checked them over. The mere sight of the guns increased Adam's anxiety level

"Are those really necessary, gentleman?" he asked looking in the mirror at John.

"I hope not, but after what happened in New England I'm not counting them out either."

Adam simply nodded and continued to drive.

"I'm going to shore now, watch my back lad," he said them hopped into the river for the final wade to shore. The radio clicked twice in his ear to signify that Charley was on the rifle and watching now.

Sean unchained Andrea from the tree and moved her down the beach, chaining her to another tree out of view from where he had stashed the bags.

He went back to his gear and took out the Thompson, a couple of MP5's, the RPG, spare mags and rockets, and the last of the carefully hoarded grenades, placing them around the area close at hand, but far enough apart, that moving from one to the other gave him different cover. He had a nagging feeling he was going to need them and it worried at his mind. With everything laid out for easy use he grabbed the bag containing the laptop walked back to Andrea and unchained her from the tree, still leaving the handcuffs on her. With nothing other to do than wait Sean moved fifty feet down the beach and simply sat down.

Andrea watched him for a moment; eyeing the bag next to him then followed his example. "So what happens next?" she asked.

"We wait for some people to show up and then you and the laptop I have in the case, leave with them."

At the word laptop her instincts perked up but she made no outward show that she had even heard him mention a computer "As soon as I report in I'm going to give away your location. You should let me go and surrender to me now. You won't get away with kidnapping a federal officer."

Sean smiled at her. "Now want makes you think I'm all that worried about you telling the world I kidnapped you. I've been hunted by the police, FBI and Secret service; along with the animals you belong to and so far I'm still here and free. Lady you don't scare me worth a damn."

Andrea had noticed on the boat that Sean was alone but hadn't said anything as she thought Charley was just out of site at the bow or something. Now with just the two of them on the beach she tired to play him off against his partner. "Listen I know Charley was the one that shot me, but no one knows you were with him. All you have to do is let me go and I can help you. It's clear he is in charge. He coerced you and forced you to go along. At least that's what we can tell people." She smiled at Sean and turned on her charm hoping to sway the older man to listening to her. She had to get her hands free and see what was in the bag near Sean.

"Now why would you want to help me?"

"I think you're a kind and gentle man," she replied, turning up the smile a notch, trying to look innocent and charming at the same time.

"Well little lady I'll admit your are a pretty girl but I'm too old for your looks and smile to work on. I think we'll sit right here and wait."

Adam pulled to a stop at the side of the road on Holly's command. "Are we there?" he asked nervously.

"The GPS says we are with in 100 yards, but we have to go that way now and there's no road." She answered pointing to the right at the river.

Everyone got out of the car and looked around. The stretch of road was in a rural area with a house in view a few hundred yards up the road; the rest was grass, fields, and trees. It looked like farming country but this time of year everything had been harvested. John and Gunny checked their pistols then headed toward the river with Holly and Adam bringing up the rear.

As soon as he reached the riverbank John spotted a boat anchored just upstream and two people sitting on the beach. He pointed them out to the rest of the group them everyone climbed down the riverbank to the beach along side the water and slowly started walking toward the two people sitting. Gunny heard what he though was a helicopter in the distance but when he glanced around he didn't see anything so he brushed off the sound and concentrated on what was in front of him.

Mike Little was the agent in charge of the helicopter detailed to land and let off the team away from the river to go overland. He had the pilot stay on the far side of the road and land in one of the grass fields to let him and his men off. As soon as the chopper was within six inches of the ground everyone bailed out with their gear and the chopper pulled up and away to circle a mile away from the river, downwind and out of hearing range.

Every agent got his gear ready for action, then they jogged toward the road and the river on the far side. They passed Adams parked car taking the same route to the river that Holly and her group had. As soon as they were with in ten yards of the river the team spread out and began approaching very slowly so as to remain undetected to anyone on the beach. One of the team saw Holly and her group then noticed Sean and Andrea and motioned to everyone that he had contacts. He did everything with hand gestures, total silence was maintained. The team moved upriver to flank the people on the beach. They would be in place and set, in a couple of minutes.

Sean stood up and pulled Andrea to her feet. "That's about far enough please. Who are you folks?"

Adam spoke first. "I'm Adam Miles, we didn't meet but you must remember me."

"Your face is familiar sir, and I assume the young lady with you is Miss McClare but what I'm most concerned with is who the two men carrying pistols are?"

Holly was both irritated and surprised at the same time. How did he know that Gunny and John were armed?

"You look like a military man." Sean said pointing to Gunny "But you have the look of a spook." He pointed to John. "I don't like spooks, they can't be trusted."

Holly spoke up. "The two men are with my team and we all work at the NSA. Are you Sean Miller?"

"Yes I am," he answered, never taking his eyes off the two men.

"Can I ask where Charley is?"

"You can ask but it will be a waste of your breath. Look I'm here to give you this woman and a laptop taken from one of the men that ran the organization on a day-to-day basis. That will give you all the proof you need, so if you please, take them I'll be on my way."

When Andrea had heard the letters NSA she had begun to worry but had maintained a calm face showing no emotion. At the mention of the laptop she had nearly blown her composure and it was now taking an incredible force of will to show no reaction. She had to do something and soon, that laptop could not be allowed to fall into the NSA's hands.

"Excuse me but if you people are from the NSA, arrest this man. He is a wanted in connection with the shooting attempt on the President and he kidnapped a federal agent, me. So get these handcuffs off me and on him, right now!" Andrea demanded.

Charley was across the river watching the whole scene and even though he could only hear what Sean said he had a good idea what was going on. It was at that moment that his radio heard something else. "Team one in position and ready for your go."

The VHF radio he had was a top of the line model with a scanning feature that covered all the marine and commercial bands. What he had heard was the team at the river telling the airborne team a mile upriver they were in place. He didn't know they were FBI but Charley new Sean was in an ambush. That he had heard anything at all was a testament to the bureaucracy of the US government. The HRT rescue teams had the latest and best, scrambled radios, however the funds to supply the counter terrorist teams had been spent on other things than radios. As a result they were not using scrambled signals and even though they didn't know it yet this cost them their surprise.

Charley grabbed the radio and hit the send key speaking in a low level voice so as not to startle his partner. "Sean it's a setup, get back on the boat now."

Sean dropped to one knee and pulled out his berretta in one fluid motion. John saw the man reach for his gun and did the same thing himself. His gun was out almost at the same time Sean's was. The rest of the group, including Gunny, were caught by surprise.

"Put the gun down," Sean ordered.

"I don't think that's a good idea," John calmly replied.

"Were are your teams?"

"What? What teams are you talking about?"

"My Partner overheard a radio transmission. They have to be close for him to overhear radio chatter so that makes this a setup. I promise you the first person I shoot is going to be you, you spook sun of a bitch. Now drop that damn gun."

Holly watched the exchange between the two men stunned at the sudden turn of events. She had to do something and fast. "John, drop your gun."

"Excuse me?"

"Do it, that's an order," John complied and his gun fell to the sand.

Sean stood up slowly keeping an eye on everyone. "The laptop is in the bag and you've got the woman, she's an organization agent. I'll be leaving now." He tossed the handcuff keys beside the bag and began backing toward the tree.

At that second the FBI helicopter came screaming down the river ten feet off the water. The scene before them was Sean holding a gun on everyone else. "Execute now," came the order through everyone's radio.

"FBI, everyone on the ground with your hands over your head now!" The loudspeaker in the helicopter boomed. While on the beach men popped up along river banks edge all screaming "FBI, DOWN, DOWN, DOWN, ON THE GROUND!"

Sean turned and ran for his gear while everyone else was looking at the chopper or the men on the riverbank. Everyone but Andrea that is. She dove for the pistol John had dropped, scooped it up turned and shot Sean in the back twice, just as he reached the tree, the force of the shots slamming him to the ground. Andrea then emptied the clip at the pack containing the laptop. John was about to grab for her when she suddenly flew backwards turning in the air to land on her face in the sand, a red stain blossoming from under her. Shots started going off at that point with the men on the bank shooting toward the tree. John looked over and was stunned to see Sean still alive, behind the tree shooting at the FBI agents, he had watched the man take two shots in the back.

Holly, Adam, John, and Gunny were now in the middle of a firefight with nowhere to go. They all lay tight to the sand and watched Sean fight back. Knowing that he didn't have any hope of winning against the overwhelming odds against him. As the helicopter was about to land and drop off the second team smoke started pouting from it and it began wobbling in the air. Sean had completely ignored the chopper and the threat it posed to his back concentrating on the men on the bank. Holly suddenly knew that Charley was out there somewhere and was dealing with the chopper.

Gunny now had his pistol out and was about to take a shot at Sean when John put his hand over the gun and pushed it down to the sand. "Gunny he hasn't taken a shot at us yet so let's not give him a reason to, okay? And to be honest if we did try to help out the FBI I think we'd be on the losing side."

Holly looked at John. "What do you mean?"

"If I'm right, Sean's young friend is out there some where with a very high powered rifle and he's going to be shooting anyone that even looks like a threat to that man down the beach. I don't know about you but I don't think I want to end up shot like the lady." John indicated Andrea.

Just then the group heard the whooshing sound of a rocket and saw Sean firing the RPG at the agents on the riverbank, the explosion cart wheeled several men in the air. Next they saw Sean toss a black object and the explosion identified it as a grenade. Picking up one of the SMG's he had hidden near the tree, Sean started firing short controlled bursts at the FBI agents. A glance at the group huddled on the beach laying in the sand showed they were no threat, so he concentrated his fire on the agents shooting at him.

"Besides that Miss McClare, I think he is much better armed then the bureau at this point. I don't know about you but I'm going to just lie hear and hope that Charley isn't angry about this and decides we lied to him. If that happens we could all be dead in a few more minutes," John speculated to the others face down in the sand.

"But we had nothing to do with the FBI showing up, why would he shoot us?" Adam asked. Not used to gunfire he was more frightened than he had ever been in his life and knew it couldn't possible feel worse.

"The problem is he doesn't know we had nothing to do with this," John replied.

Just then a geyser of sand erupted in front of the group making all of them flinch. "No one move." John yelled. "That's just Charley letting us know he hasn't forgotten about us."

Across the river Charley had watched Andrea kill his friend and then shoot at the bag with the laptop. All his plans were coming undone. Adam and Holly had betrayed him and because of it Sean was dead. With out thinking he laid the scope on Andrea and squeezed the trigger. The clip was loaded with the sabot rounds and the .30 caliber bullet nearly tore her shoulder off. He should have gone for a center mass shot but he was hopping that she would live and at least something from this disaster would be salvaged. Next he turned his sights to the helicopter and fired two rounds into the engine nacelle. The results were immediate and it began smoking and wobbling in the air. At the same time he hear the distinct sound of his Thompson firing on full auto. A glance across the river showed Sean behind the tree in a firefight with the FBI. Charley had no idea how he was still alive but he needed help. He tossed another round at the chopper putting this one through the windscreen, and it took off heading inland trailing smoke.

He saw Sean fire the RPG and toss a grenade then pick up a MP5 and start firing again. With out thinking about it Charley tossed a round into the sand in front of the group on the beach to let them know he hadn't forgotten about them, then began to look for shooters along the bank. He still didn't want to kill an officer of the law but he had to get his partner out of there. He shot one and the saw him go down but the body armor the agent was wearing stopped the bullet. The FBI agent struggled to his feet, the wind knocked out of him, and resumed firing at the man behind the tree, not knowing that he was in far more danger from much further away.

Agent Little was totally unprepared for what was happening. He saw the man running, watched the woman on the beach shoot him, and knock him down. His getting back up had been a minor surprise, after all if the wounds weren't serious many people could get up after being shot twice, especially if the gun was a small caliber. The sudden firing of a machine gun startled him and made him wonder if the man had been hit at all? Then he thought it had to be the man's partner; they were looking for two men after all. But the second teams chopper being hit and having to abort their landing worried him. Followed by the RPG and the grenades, he began to wonder what he was facing here. The man next to him was suddenly knocked off his feet but the bullet was stopped by the man's vest and he got back up, slowly, showing a lot of pain, and resumed firing at the suspect taking cover behind the tree.

A part of his mind told him that with the firepower he was facing, he should fall back and wait for the other team to join up, but another part told him it was only two men and refused to believe that he and his team could lose. The agent next to him again was knocked down but this time it was much different, there was a large gaping wound in his upper leg and he was out of the fight screaming for help. What the hell was that guy shooting at them?

When the agent he shot got back up Charley swore. They were wearing body armor and the sabot rounds had to travel to far to punch through it, they lacked the power or weight after the trip across the river. His first shot had been on instinct, now with time to think about it he lowered his aim and squeezed the trigger again. This time the round tore through the man's thigh taking him out of the fight. Taking a shot at another agent, he put his last sabot round in the man's leg as well and saw him go down. The fire from the bank was slackening as there were no only a few men left standing to fight; Charley thought it was time for Sean to get out of there before the other team got back from the damaged chopper to help out the remaining men on the river bank.

"Sean cease fire, cease fire," he called into the VHF. "I'm going to try and contact the people shooting at you, I think I can get onto their frequency."

"Understood Lad, let me know how you make out and keep an eye I'm going to reload." Sean ducked behind the tree and slammed a fresh clip into the SMG's and reloaded the RPG waiting for Charley to get back to him.

Charley slapped in a new clip of 50 caliber rounds, switched to the channel he had heard the other radio message on and started calling. "Attention, attention, anyone on this channel, please respond."

Little heard the call on the radio and was pissed at the distraction. "Whoever is calling get off this channel it is reserved for government use only. I repeat get off this channel."

"If you are the man on the bank of the Potomac shooting at the beach you really want to talk to me." Charley said then looked through his scope and fired a shot at a small tree next to one of the agents. "The next shot hits someone if you don't talk to me."

Little was showered by splinters from the tree next him being blown in half. What the hell was that guy shooting? Then he realized that voice on the radio was the one shooting at him. "This is Special Agent Little of the FBI, identify yourself."

Charley saw the man next to the tree he had just shot at speak into his shoulder-mounted mic. "Stop shooting right now or I promise you the next bullet has your name on it Agent Little."

Little looked at his remaining men, "Cease fire, cease fire. Everyone stand down," he ordered his team. "Okay now who is this?"

"Who I am isn't all that important. What is important is that the man on the beach be allowed to leave."

"That's never going to happen. You are under arrest for the murder of federal agents, throw down your weapons and come out behind the tree with your hands over your head."

Charley swore under his breath at the announcement that agents were dead, but it was too late to change that now "I'm not behind the tree you idiot. I'm looking at you through a scope sitting on top of a 50-caliber rifle. I haven't tried it yet, but I think your body armor is a little light for that kind of a round, so here's how it's going to work. The guy on the beach is going to get on the boat anchored in the river and leave. If you do anything and I mean anything to try and stop him you are the first person that dies. Do we understand each other?"

Knowing he was outflanked Little tried to buy time for the second team to show up. "Why don't we discuss this?"

His answer was a bullet hitting the ground in next to him showering him with dirt. A second later the unmistakable boom a very large rifle was heard. Whoever was shooting was across the river and he was good, too good. "Okay tell the guy to get in the boat and leave." He said in the radio. "Listen up men. We have wounded and we are under the scope of an expert sniper. We have to let this one go so stand down. Is everyone clear on that?"

A chorus of yes sirs was the reply. "Okay, tell your man to move."

Charley switch back to the channel Sean was on and told him to pack up and head for the boat. Sean was packed and wading out just seconds later. As soon as he was on the boat he fired it up and used a knife to cut both the line to shore and the anchor line than headed full throttle to the boat house where Charley was, taking care to stay out of the line of fire. At the boathouse, Charley started to pack his gear up as soon as the boat was in motion. By the time Sean got to there he was almost ready. Leaving the pad he tossed his gear to Sean and jumped into the boat. Sean picked up the 50 cal and cradled it in his arms as Charley took the controls and fire walled the throttle heading down the river toward the ocean.

Holly and Adam got up when they saw the boat leaving and started walking toward the bag on the sand. John and Gunny rushed to Andrea and found her still breathing but bleeding badly. Taking off his belt John made a tourniquet and used it to slow down the bleeding. From the river bank they heard "FBI no one move." John ignored the voice and continued trying to help Andrea.

"My name is Holly McClare, National Security Agency, who the hell are you?" she asked the first man down the bank.

"Special Agent Little, you're all under arrest."

"Well Special Agent Little I hope you have an excellent explanation because I'm sure the president is going to want one," Adam said.

"Who are you?" Little asked warily, hearing the man invoke the president.

"I'm Adam Miles, the Presidents Chief of Staff. Now what the hell are you doing here?"

The information that the Chief of Staff and an NSA agent were on a beach meeting with the suspect wanted in the attempted presidential assassination made his head spin. "Just what the fuck is going on here?"

"Well Agent Little what is going on is that you screwed up an information drop, that's what is going on. One with national security implications."

The sound of a helicopter approaching could be heard and at that John spoke up. "Miss McClare we need to get this woman to a hospital, NOW!. She's still alive but won't be for long."

Holly turned to the FBI man. "Agent Little we need your helicopter to get the wounded to a doctor."

"I'm sorry ma'am but we have fugitives to chase. We'll radio for another chopper to medevac the wounded but we have to chase after those men."

Adam stepped forward. "Agent Little listen very closely, that woman over there is vital to the security of the United States. She is more important that those two men and her welfare comes first. If she doesn't get help right now she will die. That can't be allowed to happen. You will take this woman to Bethesda Naval Hospital and stay with her until you are relieved do you understand?"

Knowing he was outranked, Little did what he was trained to do and followed orders. If the director got upset about this he could take it out on the president's Chief of Staff. Little acknowledged the order and told the pilot to land the chopper on the beach to pick up wounded. The Second team ran up just the pilot was setting down, their chopper having emergency landed in a field up the road. A check of the men showed that none of them were dead, but several were severally wounded, the agents hit by the blast from the RPG were all suffering shrapnel wounds but were still alive. The agents got the wounded stabilized as best they could then loaded them on the chopper for the trip to the hospital.

"John, Gunny, go with her and don't let her out of your sight. She's all we have now," Holly ordered, thinking of the shot up laptop.

The two simply nodded and got on the helicopter.

Once it was gone the agents that couldn't fit on the chopper went and sat in the shade to wait for another chopper to come pick them up. Holly looked at Adam, picked up the surprisingly heavy bullet shredded bag and started walking back to the car.

"Well that was a total screw up," Holly said tiredly. "And we were so close. If Andrea dies we'll never know what's going on. You have to stop the president from going on his vacation now."

"How? I have no proof and from what Charley says the secret service is in on it. I believe him too because Andrea is on the presidents detail and she shot up the laptop. Whatever was on it she didn't want us to know."

"Speaking of that could I ask a huge favor? Can you carry this thing? It weighs a ton."

Adam took the bag from Holly and almost dropped it not being ready for the weight. "Whoa, this is way too heavy for a laptop computer."

He set it on the ground and opened the bag to find a black bundle tied with rope. Untying the rope he removed what turned out to be bulletproof vests covering a laptop, which was rolled up bubble wrap. Unrolling that he found the laptop, without a mark on it. Excitedly, sitting in the field he and Holly opened it to find a note from Charley with the password to log into the computer and a list of which files to read over. They had their proof after all. The two ran back to the road and Adams car so she could get back to the NSA and Adam could get to the White House.

Charley raced down the Potomac, then into Chesapeake Bay heading up toward Baltimore. After covering about twenty miles he knew he had to find someplace to hide. The FBI would have issued a report with the description of his boat and he needed to get it under cover. He was looking for another boathouse to hide in but so far hadn't seen anything useful. Suddenly ahead he saw a boathouse that was huge with a cottage nestled in the trees behind it. It was more then large enough to hide in. He turned towards it and a few minutes later they were alongside the door facing the water. It was locked from the inside so Sean waded to the bank to look for another door. Finding one opposite the river he saw it was locked with a deadbolt and had it picked in no time at all. Opening the door revealed a boat already inside but enough empty space to also hide theirs. He unbarred the river door and Charley slowly motored inside with his partner closing the door again shielding them from view.

Sean instantly picked up the Thompson and went back outside to begin looking around while Charley tied the boat up. Looking through all the windows in the cottage he saw no movement at all, the cabin and surrounding area looked deserted. He tried the door finding it too, locked with a deadbolt. Leaving it for a moment he briskly circled the area taking stock of the surroundings and looking for signs that they were not alone. Finding nothing he went back to the boathouse, closed and locked the door.

After they were settled and sure they were alone, Charley's curiosity got the better of him, and he started checking over the other boat. It was a fully loaded ocean going cabin cruiser with a diesel engine. After twenty minutes of going over it Charley knew he was looking at a boat with a more than thousand mile range and stocked for a long trip. There was a lot of canned and freeze-dried food on board along with a water maker. Whoever had bought this boat had planned to be able to take a long trip with it. If they needed to, he and Sean could take it, and head for Bermuda. The island country was only about 800 miles away.

It was only a short time later that they heard the sound of a powerful jet engine screaming overhead. Looking out the window they saw a pair of US fighters about 500 feet off the water flying down the bay.

"Think they're looking for us?" Charley asked quietly.

"I'm sure they're looking for us lad. Good thing you found this nice cozy little place to hide in. We could be here for a few days, so let's make the most of it and set up a proper defense just in case we need it."

The pair spent the next hour getting set up and comfortable in the boathouse; setting out the RPG and the last grenades they had left. They also set out the SMG's and made sure all the magazines they had were loaded and ready for use. When they had done all they could Charley began making something to eat more out of habit then hunger.

On the ride to the hospital Agent Little called in his report. The FBI sent out an APB for the boat and listed it as carrying two men heavily armed and very dangerous. An hour later they requested assistance from the Navy and Coast Guard to search for the boat. The Navy sent out fighters while the coast guard sent out helicopters to begin looking for the vessel. The search would continue for two days, but no sign of the boat or the two men ever showed up. Once again they had disappeared.

At the arrival of the helicopter at the hospital a bureaucracy fight over who was in charge broke out. Concerning Andrea Drake the NSA won simply by invoking national security. Shortly after arriving, an agent representing the Secret service showed up and tried to take charge stating that the agent had been reported missing. Again national security was invoked and John refused to release her from the NSA's custody. When a detachment of federal marshals showed up everyone waited to see whose side they would be on. When it came to people in federal custody the US Marshal service was the ultimate authority. The lead agent deferred to John and said he would be working under the NSA and that ended all jurisdictional fighting.

Holly and Adam split up when the arrived where her car had been left, each going their separate ways. By the time Holly arrived back at the NSA, everyone had heard of the meet and the firefight that had followed it. There was a message for Holly to report to the Director as soon as she arrived. Sergeant Mayweather was also waiting for her. "Ma'am I need to speak with you."

"Can it wait sergeant? I have to report to the director."

"No ma'am, it can't wait. After you left Mr. Watson came down and ordered me to tell him where you were. All I told him was that you had gone out to meet some one and had written the instructions down but had not told anyone. It was only later that I noticed your message pad was gone. He must have taken the pad that you had written your directions on. I think he was able to read the indentations and find out where you had gone."

"Oh shit!" Holly exclaimed. "Thank you for the information Sergeant. Can you look after this, please?" Holly handed her the laptop. "Don't let that out of your sight until I get back."

Holly headed to the top floor wondering what she was going to find. The Secretary motioned her to go right into the general's office when she got there.

"Miss McClare, what the hell happened this morning? The FBI is up in arms, the Secret Service is raising hell about one of their agents and to top it all off the two most wanted suspects in the US are still at large after meeting with you and having a shootout with the FBI. Just what the hell are you doing?"

Holly was taken aback by the sudden outburst. "Well sir I was meeting with persons that had information pertinent to the case. They would only meet under specific conditions and I honored that request to get the information they were offering. How the FBI found out about it I have no idea, but you may want to check with your deputy. Apparently he was speaking with Sergeant Mayweather this morning wondering where I was. It would seem he found out and let the information slip."

"Okay I want a straight answer, did you or did you not meet with a man wanted on a federal warrant?"

"Yes sir I did."

"So why the hell is that man not in custody? Why did you not arrest him, why did you not assist the FBI in arresting him, what the hell are you doing? What are you thinking? Do you realize you added and abetted a fugitive?"

"Yes sir I did, and if the information he gave us is what I think it is then it was worth it."

"And what information might that be?"

"Plans to assassinate the President of the US," Holly said calmly

"Excuse me? Are you serious? Have you reported this to the secret service and FBI yet?

Holly shook her head. "No I haven't reported it to anyone other then you. The reason is that I don't have the details yet; they are on the computer that we were given this morning. As soon as I examine the files I'll have all the details. There is another development as well. We have reason to believe that the plot to assassinate the President involves members of the Secret service. The woman we picked up this morning is with the secret service and we have been told she is also a member of a group known simply as the organization. This is the group we have been looking for. Once I go over the files on the computer I'll have more information. The woman was injured in the shooting and she's at Bethesda now, I have John and Gunny with her to keep an eye on her. I would suggest sending some people over to relieve them sir."

The general thought over all the information he had received and before he had a chance to say anything more his private line rang interrupting him. Normally he would have ignored it to concentrate on the information Holly had just given him, but less than a handful of people knew about or had the number to his private line, so when it rang he always answered it. "Hello?" He suddenly stood up, almost at attention. "Mr President, how can I help you?"

As soon as Adam returned to the White House he headed straight to the Oval Office to speak with the president. He found him in the middle of a meeting with two junior congressmen discussing a bill that they were trying to sponsor and looking for presidential backing on it. "Excuse me sir I need a few minutes of your time," he said, interrupting the meeting. "Gentlemen I'm sorry but this is national security, however it will only take a few minutes," he said to the congressmen who then stood up to leave.

"No actually we'll go into my office for this; you gentleman can stay seated. sir, please?" He motioned to the door adjoining his office with the Oval Office and waited for his boss to go through.

His Chief of staff interrupting him was not at all unusual but asking him to leave the Oval Office to speak with him was. His curiosity peaked he walked through the adjoining door with Adam following him. Once in Adam's office the door was closed to give them privacy.

"So what's up Adam? Where have you been? More important, are you okay?" The president suddenly noticed dirt on Adam's clothes.

"I'm fine sir but I have bad news. There is a plan underway to assassinate you. I was..."

"What? What are you talking about? Why are you telling me this instead of Corey? I thought the Secret Service handled all assassination threats?"

Adam spent five minutes explaining all that had happened to him that morning and what he had found out. He left nothing out, explained that he didn't have all the information, but there was a laptop with all the details on it at the NSA. There was also a member of his secret service detail in the hospital and it looked as if she was in on the attempt to kill the president. At the moment Adam didn't want to tell the Secret Service until they were sure who could and couldn't be trusted.

The President thought for a minute. "Why are we in your office?"

"I didn't want the tape recorders in your office catching any of this. My office is clean. If the report about the secret service being involved is true I don't want anyone to know about this threat. The problem is I don't know who we can trust and who we can't until Holly gets the information from the laptop we were given. Supposedly there is a full list of agents that the organization controls."

"Holly? Is that the woman you were with this morning? Do you trust her?"

"Yes sir I do, I also trust the two men who supposedly took a shot at you." Adam said quietly

The President was shocked at what the Chief of Staff had just said "The two men that tried to kill me? Are you insane? How can you trust them?"

"Sir I have spoken with the man that actually pulled the trigger on the rifle and he didn't shoot at you. Until this morning I wasn't sure he was telling me the truth but now I believe him. This man is an incredible shot."

"The who was he shooting at?"

"He was shooting at Andrea. She was the organization agent that they were turning over to us this morning, but he had to shoot her again. As a matter of fact he shot several people but it looks as if he was careful not to actually kill any of them."

The president shook his head. "Andrea got shot again? By the same man? I'm confused here, we are searching for two men for trying to kill me but they were actually trying to save me by shooting a secret service agent that was in on the plot to kill me? That sounds like a bad plot from a B movie. Do you actually expect me to swallow any of this? And how can you be so sure this man is telling you the truth when all the evidence points to him trying to kill me. This could be his way of trying to escape life in prison."

"I'm sure because he didn't kill any of us sir. When the FBI showed up he could have slaughtered us all and didn't. Of course he probably thinks we set him up so I don't think he's going to be in such a trusting mood when it comes to talking to anyone from this administration again."

"Do you mean you intend to try talking to him again? No never mind we don't have time to get into this right now I have to get back soon. I will need a full report on this as soon as you can but for now tell me what do you think we should do."

Adam quickly outlined what he was thinking and the best way to accomplish it. He stressed the danger and the need for absolute silence.

The president shook his head. "This sounds more and more like a bad movie script. Things like this aren't supposed to happen you know. If anyone were to hear you talking this way they would think you were some conspiracy theory nut. Okay Adam, I don't really like the idea, but I trust you, so for now so let's run with it, but I think I should have a chat with this woman at the NSA and see what's on this computer you were given. Also call the marshal's office and see to it that Andrea is under the watch of the NSA for now.

"Yes sir and I'll call the NSA and request that Holly come down and brief us when she has some information from the laptop."

The president stopped for a second "Let's do this right Adam, do you have a private line here?

"Yes sir I have a private line and it also has a scrambler built in, provided the other person you're talking to has one too, the conversation is secure, no one can overhear you."

"I don't suppose you have the number of the NSA just lying around do you?"

Adam smiled. "Even better sir I have the directors private line, and he also has a scrambler."

The President picked up the phone Adam pointed to and dialed the number. "Hello General this is the President speaking." He was sure he heard a chair move as if the man who answered had stood up as he answer the phone. "Have you got a minute to speak with me General?"

"Of course sir," the general answered wondering why the commander in chief would even ask.

"I'm told your phone has a scrambler on it could you activate it now please?"

The general and Adam turned on the scramblers and after half a second of static the line was quiet and secure. And they were now free to speak without fear of being overheard.

"General I'm told that an analyst that works for you spent the morning with my Chief of Staff, do you have any information on this?"

"Yes sir, I have Miss McClare in my office right now briefing me. If she was out of line I apologize sir and it won't happen again I can assure you of that." The general glared at Holly, whose face turned scarlet.

"Well actually General it turns out that if she is right, I own her much more than a huge debt of gratitude, I may owe her my life. From what I understand she is in possession of a laptop, do you know if she has had a chance to look at any of the information on it yet?"

"No sir she hasn't. Should I turn it over to the secret service sir?"

"No General, from what I understand the young lady started this thing so I think we should let her finish. My chief of staff tells me she is on to something important and there are security issues at stake. Can you tell me how many people are in the loop on this thing?"

"As of right now sir Miss McClare is working directly for me on another project that has developed this information."

"Would this project she is working on be anyway related to the attempt on my life in Boston awhile back?"

"Yes sir it would," answered the general, extremely surprised that the president was so well informed.

"Well that is good news General, as of this moment by National Command Authority Miss McClare is to be relieved of all duties not pertaining to the current investigation. Her sole job is to track down what appears to be a conspiracy, and to find any and all parties involved. She is to be given any and all assistance with her investigation and any thing she needs is hers for the asking. Her project is now the NSA's top priority and she will brief not only you but this office as well. Adam will contact you later today to set up the contact procedures. Make sure she has everything she needs General and thank you for your help."

"Yes sir," the general answered automatically.

The president hung up the phone. "Adam you heard what I just said so do some planning and set up times for you to get briefed when you need, and call the general back later. Update me as soon as there is something new. One other thing, I don't want anyone to know about this so you will be the only one in the building to work on this."

The general hung up the phone and looked up at Holly. "It appears Miss McClare that this has become a bigger problem than we had thought. The president has ordered that this be given top priority."

Holly felt her heart stop with those words. "sir, is the President turning the investigation over to the FBI?" she asked in a shaky voice, seeing the several months of work disappearing before her eyes.

"No Miss McClare, you are still working on the case however you are now also to brief the President's office with new information as well as me. You have the resources of the United States at your fingertips all you need to do is ask. I won't hold you any longer, please get to work on the laptop, and let me know the second you have anything. I'll be sending you the contact procedures later for the White House."

Holly headed back to desk, completely oblivious to the huge responsibility that was now hers, her mind focused on the laptop and what information it might contain.

The new stooges arrived at the factory at their usual time of 7AM and went through the familiar security check to get to their office. Once there they all took out their laptops and plugged them into the central network to start the workday. Jason logged into the system to download the morning's intelligence updates, as did the other two members of the group. The news of Andrea was read by all three men within moments of each other however they finished reading all the new information gathered over night before saying anything. Once done the three discussed the situation and then an agreement was reached on a plan of action. An agent would be dispatched to the hospital first thing to confirm the reports and gather any new information. As well the board members would need to be notified at once as to what had happened.

The next hour was a blur as the three updated information on ongoing operations, as well as plans for future operations. Finally finished with the office work they logged off, packed up the computers and headed for the surface. Though they were anxious to get more information about their agent, security could not be compromised and procedures had to be followed. The men made their way to one of the many upscale hotels in the city and went inside to use payphones chosen at random. Jason was chosen to contact an agent and give him the details of Andrea and orders to find out what was going on and to terminate her if she was a threat. That done all three called their immediate senior and reported on the situation asking for further instructions. The decision was unanimous, if Andrea was in any way compromised she was to be removed, the security of the organization was more important.

Wanting to be sure the job was accomplished, Jason placed a call on his cell phone to another agent, also asking the agent to look in on giving him the same orders as the first agent had been given. The agent hung up without saying a word. He was a second-generation member, brought up believing by his father and totally loyal to the organization in every way. Understanding that Andrea might be under guard in the hospital, he could well die ensuring the authorities did not find out anything about the organization, and as with most fanatics he was prepared to do just that.

Parking three blocks from Bethesda the agent walked into the main entrance looking for all the world like another visitor. With no idea where to go he simply walked up to the information desk and flashed a Treasury Department ID. "Where can I find Agent Drake?" The woman behind the desk had not been told to withhold any information, and the man had a proper federal ID so she gave him the room number and smiled as she was thanked for this. The man walked away heading in the direction of the room he had been given.

Several minutes later he rounded a corner and saw several men standing in the hallway. With out even slowing down he walked straight towards them.

"Excuse me sir but this area is off limits, you'll have to leave," one of the men told him while he was still a good fifty feet from the room has was told held Andrea.

That gave him all the information he needed and in one smooth fluid motion his hand snaked under his coat and snatched a 9MM pistol from behind his belt. Without slowing his pace he brought his weapon up and fired at the man that had spoken. The recoil pushed his arm up several inches and he used the momentum to shift aim to the right firing at another man how was now trying to draw his own firearm. His marksmanship was impressive and in less than four seconds he was the only man still standing in the hallway, everyone else on the floor either dead or dying. He walked forward casually shooting everyone once more in the head as he went, ensuring that they were all dead.

The sound of the gunfire echoed through out the hospital alerting everyone in earshot. Three of the people alerted were John and Gunny, who had just finished eating and were on their way back to the room, and Andrea, who had just woken up and was still groggy from the anesthetic. John drew his sidearm and began running toward Andrea's room followed closely by Gunny.

Andrea was still trying to make sense of what she had heard when the door to her room was pushed open and a man in uniform came rushing in. She had no idea who he was and looked at him with confusion, about to ask who he was when the door banged open again and two more men came in. These two she recognized from the beach.

She finally found her voice "What's going on?" she asked quietly.

John looked at her for a second then at the guard. "Get her into the bathroom and lock the door. Nothing is to happen to her, do you understand?"

"Yes sir," he answered, scooping Andrea out of the bed and carrying her into the small bathroom, locking the door behind them.

In the hallway they could hear the sound of doors being banged open, slowly moving in their direction. Gunny quickly pulled open the door and stepped into the hallway before John could stop him. Two gunshots rang out almost as one and John saw Gunny punched back and down to the floor as he was hit.

The organization's assassin opened the door next to the men he had just shot and stepped in scanning the room with his gun first then looking at the hospital bed, it was empty. He reversed direction and opened the room on the other side of the hall, thinking he had just opened the wrong door. That room too was empty. Checking the number on the wall next to the door he confirmed he had the room given him by the woman in the lobby. He silently swore to himself, too much time was passing; his chance to escape was fast running out. He walked up the hallway checking rooms as he went, looking for Andrea, she had to be somewhere on this floor, there wouldn't be security men guarding nothing at all. Their presence guarantied he had the right floor. The sudden appearance of the man with the gun told him where his quarry was and his shot was just a hair quicker and a bit better aimed, as a result his shot hit true while his opponents bullet merely burned the left side of his rib cage.

He erred on the side of caution and assumed there would be other people in the room guarding his target. He moved the side of the corridor closest to the room forcing anyone else in the room to move their head all the way into the corridor to see him and moved toward the open door as quietly as he could. He reached the door without seeing anyone else, but in the distance he could hear running footsteps. He knew he was out of time.

John put Gunny out of his mind and stepped behind the open door looking through the small gap between the door and the wall. Kneeling down he extended his arm and carefully aimed at the doorway. He assumed that the next person through the door would be the killer but he did not know that for sure, as a result he couldn't just blindly fire with out knowing he was shooting at the right person. He was going to have to break one of his cardinal rules and shoot to wound.

The killer had changed clips right after shooting Gunny and now fired two rounds into the ceiling. He then called out saying that it was all clear. He was trying to get anyone else in the room to believe that he was a security guard and it was now safe.

John heard the two shots but didn't hear the sound of a body falling. He ignored the all clear and concentrated on the tiny opening he had to aim through. Suddenly a flash of movement filled his vision and he fired reflexively at the shape. As the person fell they fired several times driving rounds through the door trying to kill John. That answered the question of who it was in the doorway and John fired a second and third time into the mass he could see through the slim crack then waited to see if the person moved. The sounds of running feet reached him behind the door and then he heard someone yelling if everything was all right. The body suddenly moved with deceptive quickness rolling back into the hallway and the sound of more shots rang out.

John moved out from behind the door with out thinking about his actions and stepped into the open doorway, gun hand up and ready. He saw the killer lying on the floor bleeding, his pistol pointing down the hall. John shot him in the head as the man tried to bring his own gun to bear. Kicking the gun from the now dead hand John shouted an all clear down the hall and looked for Gunny. His partner was lying flat on his back unmoving on the cold tile floor, blood beginning to pool under him, but his chest was rising and falling in a regular pattern.

John checked the man he had shot for a pulse out of habit and found none. Suddenly the hallway was filled with people with guns. John carefully holstered his then went back to gunny. The wound was high on his right side, the bullet has passed straight through so there was a lot a bleeding. Before John had a chance to ask for one, a doctor was at his side and began caring for the wounded man. The next few minutes passed in a blur and suddenly he was aware of someone asking what had happened to the prisoner. John went into the room and knocked on the bathroom door telling the guard to come out. There was no answer.

Opening the door he saw Andrea slumped on the toilet a bullet hole in her forehead. Turning wildly around he rushed from the room looking for the security guard he had ordered to look after her. He had to be the killer as he was the only person to get close to Andrea and John cursed himself for his stupidity. The organization had once again shown its ruthless efficiency.

Adam hung up the phone after receiving the latest news about the murder of Andrea. John had been debriefed and along with a sketch artist he had provided a composite drawing of the guard he had last seen with Andrea. No one in the hospital recognized the man and a federal warrant was issued for his arrest.

Adam stood up from his desk and walked into the Oval Office, the President was there with another group of freshmen congressmen for a photo op. He nodded to his boss with out saying a word, the silent message conveyed as well as words. Less than five minutes later the president wrapped up the meeting and did it so skillfully that no one noticed it was concluded early.

Once alone the two moved back to Adams office and he briefed his boss on the murder of Andrea. The President was aghast at the audacity of the action and angered at the same time. That they could be both so bold and cold-blooded at the same time shocked him and made him fear for his own safety. As a politician he was not trained for this type of thing and not having the ability to even trust his own security agents left him with a cold chill running down his spine.

"What do we do Adam? I'm out of my depth here and I need help. Are you sure we can't bring Corey in on this?"

"Sir I feel that we should set up a private briefing with the Director of the NSA and the woman running the operation. They may have some insight as to what to do next. At the very least they will be able to give you the full scope of the problem you are facing."

"Fine, set it up, but cover it. Let's do it in the private dining room so no one knows what's going on, and use the tunnel to get them in the house." He ordered, referring to the tunnel from the treasury building.

As soon as he was alone Adam picked up his phone and dialed the direct line to the head of the NSA. "General? It's Adam Myles sir. The President would like you and Miss McClare to come to the White House. I'll have someone on my staff pick you up and bring you down. We want your visit to go unnoticed."

Adam called one of his aids and gave him instructions to drive to the NSA headquarters and pick up two people then bring them back through the tunnel. He went back to work until they arrived.

Holly opened the laptop and followed the sheet of instructions that Charley had taped to the screen to log in. Once she was in she created a LAN connection and plugged the computer into the network her group had set up in their office, then downloaded the entire contents of the hard drive onto her computer under the groups shared directory. That done she shut down the laptop, secured it in a shielded box that locked with a combination only she knew and called someone from the records storage department to come pick it up. The laptop would be stored in the records vault with all the other highly classified files to keep it safe, this way if anything happened to Holly's system the original files would still be safe on the laptop in the records vault. The person from records labeled the locked box as eyes only for Holly McClare and NSA director then took it, giving Holly a receipt for the box.

With the original now safe, Holly Doris and the sergeant opened the shared files and began working on them. Holly worked on the file Charley had marked as the one associated with the president's assassination while the sergeant and Doris looked into other parts. Doris took the section marked as Investigations while the sergeant took the section marked as personal. Holly skimmed quickly over the report them went back to re-read it in detail making notes on a legal pad as she went. When finished, she read through it a third time making more notes on the legal pad. With the report systematically read over she closed the file and looked over her notes. Once she was done she called the directors office to request a meeting and was told to come right up. She told the other two ladies she was going to talk to the director and picked up her legal pad to leave when the sergeant stopped her.

"Miss McClare I believe the general will need to see this as well," she said, pointing to her computer screen.

"What is it?"

"Ma'am it's the breakdown of the personnel working for the organization along with the people in charge. This has to be a fake ma'am. Some of these names are people that work in this building

Holly sat back down to let the news sink in. If the files were true they were in trouble. The NSA had access to most of the secrets of the nation.

"That's not all ma'am it gets worse."

"How can it possible get worse, Sergeant?"

"Ma'am the organization is extremely large, this is a list of personnel on their payroll and where they work. According to this they have every federal agency of the US penetrated, including the Secret Service. There was also a note added at the bottom of the list signed by Charley. It says that he has the names of the men in charge of the organization and will trade that information for immunity."

Holly picked up the phone and hit redial. "Could you please ask the general to come down to see me please?" she asked the general's administrative assistant. "I have some files that he needs to see right away and I'm afraid I can't bring them up."

The general stepped off the elevator four minutes later his face a barely controlled mask of rage at being ordered, even if it was in the form of a request, to come see Holly rather then her come to his office. Maybe she had let the importance of the mission override her good judgment, he had seen it happen in the past and on those occasions let the person know that no matter how important their job he was still in overall command and his time was not to be wasted.

Holly noticed his building anger and headed him off before he could say anything. "I apologize for asking you down here sir but the information is too sensitive to print off or copy, I can't risk anyone other than you seeing this," she told him, pointing to the computer screen with the data displayed on it.

The general sat down and began reading, the red slowly leaving his face, then building back up again. "Those traitorous bastards," he said lowly to himself, as he recognized the names of people that worked for the NSA then in a louder voice. "Miss McClare please contact the captain of the guard detachment and tell him to come down right now."

"General if I may speak to you in the board room for a moment before we do anything?"

"We can talk as soon as I have those people arrested," the general said coldly.

"Please, General, let's talk in private for a moment," Holly, insisted leading him to the boardroom and closing the door. "I think it would be a mistake to arrest them, we don't have enough proof to hold any of them let alone convict anyone for anything. All we will be doing is letting the organization know that their secret is out."

"Miss McClare those men are traitors to the nation and I will not stand by for one second while they remain free to cause more harm to this country."

"That's the problem General, aside form this data, which by the way cannot be confirmed, and was given to us by a man wanted for attempting to assassinate the President, we have no concrete proof of wrong doing. These people have insulated themselves extremely well. If we arrest them all we are doing is tipping them off that we know what they are doing. If that happens then they will destroy all evidence and we have no chance of catching them, ever."

"Are you suggesting that we allow them to try and kill the president again? You are very mistaken if you think I'm going to stand idly by an allow an attempt on the life of my commander in chief young lady."

"Sir can we at least discuss this with Adam before we do anything? He'll take it to the president and we can let him make the decision," Holly pleaded with him.

At that moment the general's personal cell phone rang. He answered with his usual curt "Yes?"

Several seconds of silence was followed and "Thank you" and he shut the phone off putting it back in his pocket. "It seems Miss McClare you'll get your chance to let the president make the decision after all. We have been ordered to the White House a car will be here to pick us up shortly. Please prepare the notes you need and you'll be called as soon as the driver is here."

Holly simply nodded as the General started to leave and his phone rang again. The call was longer this time punctuated by questions from the General asking for clarification. At the end of the call he turned back to Holly and told her that the call was informing him of the attack at the hospital. Andrea was dead and Gunny was in surgery, although he was expected to pull through fine. There was some question as to the extent of the wound and it had done serious damage to his shoulder. An orthopedic surgeon was working on him now. They would have more information after he was out of the OR.

As the two exited the boardroom they were met by Doris "Excuse me, General, Holly, you both need to see this." She told them motioning toward her desk and heading back to it.

"What is it Doris?" Holly asked walking over to look at the computer screen Doris was pointing to.

It took only moments to read the file but the enormity of it hit her like a ton of bricks. It was a plan to abduct or kill her. The organization knew about her and was prepared to murder her. Suddenly her work took on a new and personal role. As she was thinking of why this could be happening the General read the information on the screen and when done immediately picked the phone on Doris' desk and dialed the extension for security. "Send a three-man team to Miss McClare's desk on the double." He ordered then hung up.

The room was silent until the door to the stair well burst open and three armed MP's ran into the room carrying rifles and jerked to a stop looking for trouble. With no obvious danger in sight they did what all well trained military personal do, came to attention saluted the highest ranking person in the room and in unison loudly stated. "Security detail reporting as ordered sir!"

"At ease men. One of you take position at the stairwell the other two by the elevators. No one comes in without my authorization."

The trio shouted "YES sir!" and took their assigned positions.

The General turned to Holly and in a voice almost a whisper asked. "You said we now have the names of all the agents in the organization, correct?"

"Yes sir we do," she answered in a similar soft voice.

Turning back to the security detail the general ordered then to sound off with their names while Doris checked the men against the list of organization agents in the database. None of the three were listed which brought a sigh of relief to the general.

"Miss McClare you will have a security detail with you from now on until this mess is sorted out. It would appear that you have become a thorn in the organizations side, and if they are willing to kill you then you are obviously on the right track. I'll call you when it's time to leave." With that the general went back to his office, explaining to the soldiers that they were to protect Miss McClare with any force necessary and only those currently present were allowed access. He would send down a list of approved personal later and he then left for his office.

After sitting in the boathouse for the day Sean was becoming restless. Charley had cooked and cleaned up afterwards, then spent the rest of the time going over the two boats taking a careful inventory of what was on hand. Towards evening Sean slipped out of the boathouse and went over to the cabin. He picked the lock and thoroughly searched it looking for some clue as to who owned the place. As with the boat, there nothing to indicate who the place belonged to. There was a great deal of food and fuel on hand but no phone and no electricity, instead just a portable generator that appeared to be the sole source of power for the cabin. Whoever did own it had taken care to make it as self sufficient as possible.

There was a dirt road that presumably ran to a main road somewhere, but Sean resisted walking along it to find out where it went. Instead he satisfied his curiosity by looking at the charts and maps of the area. The GPS gave them the exact location and by comparing it to the maps they had he could tell they weren't that far from a main road, however the trees around the area covered any noise of traffic. In fact, aside from the sound of boats on the water and the occasional aircraft flying over the place was very peaceful. With the GPS and charts he had a good feel for the layout of the land around the cabin and boathouse but studying a map was no substitute for walking the ground.

"Charley, how long do you plan on staying here?" he asked noticing the obvious comfort Charley was in.

Charley thought for a second, amused at his old friends just as obvious discomfort. "I thought a week or two would be nice, it's quiet and seems unused so I don't think there is much chance someone will come here," he answered deciding to have a little fun with Sean.

"Lad if you think we're staying here for a couple of weeks you're insane. The search will have scaled way back within three or four days so that's as long as I feel comfortable staying here. And no matter the look of the place, someone owns it and there is no way to predict when they might decide to drop by and check things over."

"I was only kidding Sean, I don't want to stay here any longer than we have to. The president is supposed to start his vacation in about four days and if we haven't heard anything by then we'll bug out. Thank you for sticking with me through this, I'm just sorry it turned out to be a waste of time."

"Now why do you say it's a waste of time lad?"

"Well before I handed over the computer I put a file on it saying that we had the names of the men in charge of the organization. I told them we'd trade the info for immunity but since then we've killed FBI agents in that shootout, so there is no way they are going to let us go free after that. We can't even claim self defense because we were technically resisting arrest. The best we can do now is run and hide. I'm sorry I failed, I really wanted to give you the freedom to retire and enjoy it."

Sean chuckled lightly. "Well now lad I don't think we did so bad after all.

If nothing else there is too much evidence out now about the organization for them to stay secret anymore even, if the NSA doesn't have the names of the leaders. You and I may not be free, but I'm sure they will be a little too busy running themselves to worry a lot about us. Not only that, but we're millionaires too, courtesy of the organization. At least if we have to run we can do it in style."

Charley was happy to see his friend looking at things in a positive light. He himself wasn't feeling happy about the way things had turned out but they had tried their best. It wasn't their fault that no one had believed them. "Sean do you think the President will still go on his sailing trip or will they believe us and call it off?"

"No idea lad and I don't really care. It's his neck on the line and we've done all we can. I say for now we worry about us and figure out how to get out of here."

Charley smiled at his friend. "Why we'll simply trade boats and head out to sea. I hear Bermuda is lovely this time of year. We still have our fake passports and no one is looking for this boat after all." Charley pointed to the large cabin cruiser tied up next to their own boat.

Sean nodded his head in agreement. "Sounds like a good idea. We'll need to check the weather though, a storm at sea could ruin the whole thing."

"I still have the satellite so that will be no problem at all. We'll check it in the morning, right now I think it's time for supper, let's check out the menu from our new vessel."

Chapter 15

Adam's assistant showed up at the NSA and was surprised to see that MP's with automatic weapons intended on joining them for the trip to the White House. The car was a Ford Crown Victoria, and the driver was relieved to find out that only one armed person would be traveling with them, the other two would follow in a SUV. The drive was less than an hour and went by in silence, everyone in deep thought over what was going on. They parked at the treasury building and the security detail followed as far as the tunnel then the Secret Service took over. The General ignored the questions when asked about the armed MP's muttering national Security and leaving it at that. As the soldiers would not be coming into the White House proper the Secret Service agents let the question drop, realizing that the Director of the NSA had no intention of telling them.

Once in the White House, the agent lead them into the Presidents Private dining room where Adam was waiting. With a nod to the agent he motioned everyone to sit down. "The President will be along shortly, he has taken the liberty of ordering a light supper for everyone I hope this is fine." Adam said sitting down

Both the General and Holly sat down in silence simply nodding, as if anyone would object to the President ordering supper for them in his own house. For the General it was simply a case of being ordered to appear by his commander in chief, eating with the man was not something he had even considered. For Holly it was even simpler, an order from the Director was all she needed, eating at the White House in the Presidents private dining room was an event she would never have even dreamed about.

The steward came in and asked if anyone wished coffee, Adam being the only one comfortable enough to accept. The general and Holly both merely gave a polite no and resumed sitting quietly with their thoughts.

"Relax please," Adam said. "The president just wants an update on what you have found so far."

Before either of them had a chance to reply the door opened and the President, flanked by secret service agents, entered the room. All three people stood up. The president smiled and motioned everyone to sit as he peeled off his suit jacket and draped it over the back of the chair. Regardless of his motion to sit no did until he did and he smiled to himself, still in awe of the power of his office and the deference people paid to him because of it.

The secret service agents had taken up stations next to the door, as was their custom, used to not leaving the president alone with visitors. Normally the president ignored the agents used to them being around, but he surprised the two this evening by asking them to leave the room. They did as ordered going outside and taking up stations just outside the door. Almost every room in the house had hidden cameras so that the president was under observation at all times by an agent, his personal dining room was no exception. The only time he was truly alone was in the residence with his family and even then, there were agents in the halls waiting should their presence be required. Anytime the president wanted to discuss anything in private he either used the private dinning room or invited them up to the residence.

"We can talk in private here, we'll just wait until the steward sets everything up then we can eat and you can bring me up to date on things."

At that moment the steward came back into the room with a serving cart and began setting up the room for a light buffet style dinner. Holly looked over and was shocked at the food she saw being laid out. There was meatloaf with gravy and mashed potatoes along with carrots and rolls. Once done the steward smiled at the president, announced it was ready, and left. He was already well trained as to the likes and dislikes of his boss. The President had grown up on simple food and still held a great love for it. He also enjoyed serving himself and during his first few weeks on the job had actually been known to go down to the kitchen to fix himself something to eat. This peculiar habit had caused a minor mutiny with the White House cooks and staff. It was their job to serve the president and anything less would be undignified. So a compromise was made to sooth everyone's feelings. The president sent down his favorite recipes to be used when dinning in private or with close friends and it was set up buffet style. Any other time the staff took care of everything and were allowed to surprise the president with their choices. The plan worked perfectly allowing the cooks to be totally creative and having a free hand during state dinners. If there was anything that could not be served the protocol office notified them but other wise they were on their own. This freedom more than made up for cooking the simple foods and allowing the man to fill his own plate when it was a small affair. At one point the head chef had even asked the president if he would show him the way he liked the meatloaf prepared so as to get it perfect. It was this rapport that made the current resident of the Oval Office a very well liked man.

As soon as the steward was out of the room the president grabbed a plate and began helping himself. "Dig in please, I don't allow the staff to serve in this room so it's everyone for themselves."

Adam followed his bosses example and got up to get a plate, Holly and the general followed unsure of the protocol but assuming that if the chief of staff and the President were serving themselves then that was the way things would be done.

Once everyone was seated again the president smiled and scooped up a forkful of meatloaf. "I only get this about once a month. Too bad really because the cook does it perfect. I sure hope you folks like it." With that he spent the next few minutes making the contented eating sounds of a man totally enjoying his meal. To their collective surprise everyone else enjoyed the simple but extremely good meal as well.

Noticing that everyone was nearly finished the president sat back and sipped his coffee. He had quickly noticed during even these private dinners that as soon as he was finished everyone else stopped eating as well. Not wanting to spoil anyone's dinner he had learned to eat slowly so as to give people a chance to actually eat their food. All to often a dinner at the White House meant a lot of talking and not much eating. This president had changed that simply because he enjoyed good food as much as any other person. Just because he was the most powerful man in the world was no excuse to display poor hospitality. So during his administration it became common practice that the actual meal was eaten in near silence and the conversation was done at the end. This was an alien concept in Washington but one that was observed simply by the fact that the president refused to talk while he was eating.

As usual once everyone noticed the president sitting back enjoying his coffee they all pushed their plates away and stopped. The president noticed that the plates were nearly clean so he hoped everyone had eaten enough and he know from experience that if he asked the answer would be yes no matter what the reality was.

"So did everyone enjoy the meatloaf?" the president asked getting a chorus of headshakes accompanied by affirmative replies from the three around the table. "I'll pass that along to the chef. He enjoys compliments especially when it's from something he considers so simple like this. General, Miss McClare, I'm sure by now you are dying to know why I asked you here. First because you two have done a great job, I wanted to thank you in person and show my appreciation. One of the perks of this office is that I can have people over for a meal once in a while and thank them in person. I would love to publicly recognize your efforts but I do understand the needs for secrecy so I hope this will do."

"Mr President, sir, I am a soldier first and last, doing my duty for my country is all the reward I require, or deserve, for that matter. Having dinner with you is an honor I shall cherish sir, but I did my job out of duty and nothing more," the general said quietly. "However I must confess that I do not deserve the honor you have shown me today. I have failed in my duty by not finding this organization sooner. By allowing this group to exist we have placed your life in danger not once but twice. They are planning a second attempt on your life."

"A second attempt? Is this information you got from the laptop Adam told me about?" the president asked.

"Yes sir it is. We haven't had time to complete a formal report but at this time we assess the information as reliable and we are ready to issue the proper warning to the FBI and secret service."

"We'll need to discuss that, but General no one even heard rumors of this group before you reported it," Adam told him. "And the news of a second attempt is a warning I would not have had without you, so you have not failed in any way."

"Adam is right General. From what I understand we were lucky to find them even now. But now that we know about them we can go after them," the president added.

"Sir the credit belongs solely to Miss McClare. I have to confess that I didn't believe her initial reports and it was only her perseverance that brought this threat to light."

"Has that laptop turned up any other information?" asked the president.

"Miss McClare is the one to brief you on that sir. Miss McClare would you tell us all what you have found?" the general asked the young lady.

Holly started to speak and her voice cracked causing her to cough lightly. The president chuckled. "Relax Miss McClare, you're among friends here. I need to know what you have found so that we can plan what to do next."

Holly spent the next several minutes going over the information they had found out about the organization from the laptop. Then she spent several minutes detailing the current plan to assassinate the President concluding with what had happened to John and Gunny in the hospital with Andrea. She added in, that her own conclusion was that the threat was very real and all precautions should be taken. Holly stopped short of actually recommending that the President cancel his planned vacation but the implication was obvious to every one in the room. After a pause of a few seconds Holly went on to detail the information they had learned up to that point about the organization itself. She explained the sheer size of the group and the fact that the computer held a detailed list of members and people acting as agents. There were also contact arrangements and times, with listings of dead drops and online chat rooms and bulletin boards for communicating with agents. All-in-all the group was very sophisticated. She closed her brief with the power structure of the organization using the terms that they used themselves, board members and administrators to describe the three man set up. She also admitted that they did not at this time know the names of the men in charge of the group or those running the day-to-day operations. She paused and was about to tell them about the offer to trade the names of the men in charge for immunity but before she could the president asked her a question

"Adam tells me that this laptop was provided to you by the men we are hunting for trying to kill me in Boston. Is this true?"

"Yes sir it is. That entire operation is detailed on the laptop as well. Along with the plan to frame them and release the information to the FBI which has already happened. The organization has been trying to kill these two, they do not want them captured, as this would expose the organization. There was also a note attached to the laptop from the two, it says that they have the names of the board members and are willing to give them to us in exchange for immunity."

"Are you serious?" asked the president. "Young lady how do you know that this isn't a plot to misdirect you planned out by these two men?"

"We have other evidence that supports their claims sir, independent evidence that was collected by my team. Also sir I have spoken with these men and I believe them. They have both said they were blackmailed to try and kill you and when they failed they were set up themselves and then hunted by their own organization. I've seen some of the evidence and I believe them."

"That's fine Miss McClare, but that doesn't prove they are right. I'm not inclined to grant immunity to two men that stand accused of trying to kill me. The political aspect alone is enough to deny their request. General what do you think?"

"Sir, if these two truly can give us the leaders of this rogue group then I think we must seriously consider the idea of immunity. As I understand it they are both foreign nationals so we could deport them as soon as we have the information. No one would have to know about the immunity, sir."

"It would leak out at some point and I would need proof that they are innocent before I grant them immunity. If they contact you again tell them to turn themselves in and if the information they provide helps us prosecute the men behind this group I will consider immunity for them, but not before."

"Sir I have also spoken with them and I believe them as well," Adam chimed in. "And from the depth of this organization it's safe to assume that if they did try and turn themselves in, they would be dead in a matter of hours."

"Okay just to play devils advocate let's assume they are right and can give us the leaders of this organization. The information you have, will it hold up in a court of law?"

The general answered this one. "Yes sir, at least for a conspiracy charge. We can also get them on espionage. Both of those will hold up under legal scrutiny."

"Sir I disagree," Holly said quietly. "A good lawyer would argue that the evidence was made up. The laptop would be tossed out simply because it's not verifiable. And the information my team gathered can't be used simply because I can't tell the court how it was obtained."

"She has a point sir," Adam said. "She would have to testify and we can't let that happen. The methods she used are classified, but even in a closed court we can't deny the methods used to the defense, by law they are entitled to know that information. And we certainly can't reveal those methods."

"Interesting, the head of the NSA and the person he tasked to head the group hunting this organization disagree completely. So we seem to be at an impasse here, is that what you are telling me?" the president asked.

"Well sir once we know who the people we can give over the names to the FBI and set up surveillance on them. Eventually we will catch them breaking the law and then we can arrest them." said the general.

Adam shook his head "That won't work either. The second we hand over the list of names someone will leak it and within hours the organization will find out. Once they know they are being hunted they will take steps to cover themselves and we will be worse off then we are now. We can not afford to lose the element of surprise here."

"How can you be sure they will find out Adam?"

Adam looked at Holly and she quietly answered the question for him. "According to the list of members the organization has the FBI penetrated along with most other federal agencies. Including the secret service sir."

To the surprise of the group the president nodded and sat back in his chair silent. Everyone had expected a different, more vocal reaction from the man. Not knowing his mood they sat silently waiting for the man's lead. "General Donovan, Miss McClare, thank you for joining me for dinner, it was a pleasure. I'd like you to continue with your investigation and submit a formal report by end of day tomorrow to Adam. However I do not want this matter to go beyond this group for the moment."

With that the president stood and left the room leaving Adam to show their guest out. Once the General and Holly had left the building Adam headed to the Oval Office to see what his boss was thinking.

"Adam what do you say to game of chess upstairs?" the president asked.

Knowing that he wanted to discuss this in private Adam nodded and the both headed up to the residence. Once the board was set up and each man had a drink next to him they quietly studied the board between them and the President made the first move. This was a ritual between them now, using the game of chess to talk over important issues. Adam always won simply because he played at a masters level while the president's skill level was that of an amateur. Adam played while focusing on the problem they were discussing while his boss focused almost entirely on the game. And even distracted as he was he could still handily beat his boss. Also his pride in the game would not allow him to play a losing game, even to the President of the United States. It was the only way the president could get a decent game in as any one else he played always allowed him to win. It also allowed him to use the gift of Adam's intellect while he himself relaxed and enjoyed his leisure time. The president doubted that Adam even knew how valuable these chess games were. With out really thinking about anything other then the game at hand, two hours later the president had both, lost the game, and had a strategy in mind to catch the ringleaders behind the shadowy organization. The truly amazing thing was that Adam didn't know that it was he that was solely responsible for the decision his boss had just made.

The General and Holly headed back to the NSA, both remaining silent in the car all the way back. When the car dropped them off the security team formed up on Holly and the General nodded his approval. He followed her back to her desk and then asked her to speak with him in the boardroom for a moment.

"I would like you to create a list of the Secret Service agents in the organization and FBI and get it to the White House ASAP. Once that's done write up a report and have it sent up to my office. I'd like you to remain on site for the night as a security precaution, if you don't have any objections?"

"Yes sir that will be fine. I'll get the lists ready and start on the report right away."

With that taken care of Holly returned to her desk and the general returned to his office.

The next day dawned sunny and bright and Adam was already in his office when the President entered from the Oval Office. "Morning Adam, did you sleep well?"

"No sir I didn't. Our dinner quests sent over a list last night by courier, I was just leaving when it arrived. The list is on your desk and the headings should be self explanatory," Adam told him.

The president sat down at his desk and went over the list quickly noticing that some of the names were people he knew personally and in more than one case was on a detail in the White House. "I think we should let this sit for a bit Adam, it will wait until after my vacation." He said as he was writing a note in the margin.

Handing the papers back to his chief of staff he nodded to the notes and then with a cheery voice asked what was up first on his day. The two spent the next few minutes going over the day's agenda and then Adam headed to his office to allow the president to begin his day. As soon as he was at his desk he read the note his boss had written then picked up his secure line and dialed a now familiar number.

Sean had become extremely restless and wanted to leave now. Not one to wait around he was used to mobility and viewed it as the key to his survival to date. Charley however wanted to wait until the president was out of the country. The plan was to take the large boat and head to Bermuda. Once the president was in the Caribbean the majority of the Coast Guard and Navy search craft would be sent down to ensure his safety. That wasn't to say that there would be no coast guard or navy ships around but there would be fewer than normal. Sean had even suggested forgetting the boat idea entirely and simply picking up their van again and driving back to Canada. In his mind they had done all they could. No one wanted to listen to them; the actions on the riverbank had proven that, so they should leave as soon as possible. It was time to hide for good in his mind. Sean shot that idea down right away. They had been planning on getting rid of the van after the Florida ops and hadn't yet, so in his mind now was good time to forget it for good. If they did leave by car it would be something new.

"Relax Sean and trust me. Once the man is out of the country we can slip out with a lot less risk."

"I know that Lad but something doesn't feel right. We need to leave now."

You're just getting antsy Sean. No one knows where we are, we are as safe here as anywhere."

"And what happens should the owners of this place decide to come and check on things?"

"Well in that case you were right and I was wrong."

"Stop joking around Charley. I have a bad feeling about this place. I think we should we go now."

Charley knew his old friend was serious and he had learned to trust the man's feelings. They had served the pair well so far. If something was bothering him Charley could not just dismiss it. "Okay Old man, let's do a scout around and I'll check the internet to see if there have been any news reports in the last few days. If everything looks fine we bug out tonight."

Sean nodded and picked up the Thompson. "I'm going to check around outside, you do your computer magic." And with that he was gone.

Charley set everything up and logged in to the web. A check of the major news sites turned up nothing out of the ordinary and just as he was checking his mail the instant messenger he had used with the NSA popped up. He was shocked by that, they were the last people he had expected to hear from after what had taken place.

Holly had been going over the list of people working for the organization and was thought she saw a pattern but was too tired to think it out clearly. She was getting ready to leave when she heard the alarm on Gunny's computer signal that an IP he was tracking had come online. A check of the system showed it to be Charley and she immediately tried to trace him but the result was the same as always, there was no location listed and nothing they could do to find one. Finally she tried to message him not sure if he would respond or not, After all he probably held her responsible for the attack at the river.

"We need to talk," she typed in.

"I don't think so," came the reply back

"WAIT! It wasn't me that set up the attack at the river. That was done without my or Adam's knowledge. Please believe me."

"It doesn't matter who set it up, it happened. Besides you have the laptop and Andrea, You don't need me."

"Andrea is dead."

Charley stopped at that news. "Damn I didn't think I had hit her that bad. I'm sorry that you lost her but she was trying to destroy the laptop. That by itself should tell you something. I am assuming that the vests protected it and you got the information from it?"

"You didn't kill her Charley, in fact you and Sean didn't kill anyone. You wounded a few of the FBI people and of course you did shoot Andrea but she was murdered in the hospital after we got her stabilized. She would have lived if someone else hadn't shot her. At this point we can only assume it was the organization that did it."

"WHAT? Who let that happen?" Charley was outraged. The best source of information they had on the organization, one that would hold up in court, and the NSA let someone kill her. Maybe they weren't as powerful as he thought they were. "What about the laptop? Is that okay? Did you get the info from it?"

"Yes we did, thank you very much. I took your request for immunity to the President and he is thinking about it."

Charley was stunned once more at what he was being told. He had tossed in the note as an after thought not really thinking anyone would seriously entertain the idea of immunity but he figured there was no harm in trying. He wasn't sure if he should believe her or not. Maybe it was a trick to force them to meet again and this time with better planning on their part to catch he and Sean. Well that wasn't going to happen, he was done meeting people. Anything else they wanted to do could be done over the internet, or not at all. "So what did you want to talk about?"

"I was going over the list and I have a question about the membership, are there any minorities in the group?"

That was a strange question to ask, Charley thought about it, but then realized that it wasn't that strange after all. As far as he could remember he had never seen any minorities in the organization at all. He would need to check with Sean to be sure. "Hang on for a sec," he typed on the computer.

It took him a few minutes to find Sean. "I'm talking to the NSA and they asked a strange question that now doesn't seem so strange, are there any minorities in the organization?"

"What the hell are you talking to them for? Leave well enough alone lad and let's just concentrate on getting out of here," Sean said, completely ignoring the question.

"Stop being so paranoid for a second and answer the question. Is it a whites only group or not?"

Sean frowned but thought for a second. "Now that you mention it, I can't ever remember seeing any minorities in the organization. Not that it's a big deal lad. They are after all working in the US. It's the old boys club rule here."

"Okay thanks, that makes sense."

Charley went back and told Holly what Sean had said about it being an old boys club mentality.

Holly had never though about that but it made sense. Washington was the ultimate old boys club, but her mind was still nagging about something. She would think about it tomorrow when she was better rested. For now she needed to keep Charley at least communicating with her so she had a chance of getting the names of the ringleaders.

"I want you to contact me in a couple of days, I should have news about the pardon by then."

"No promises. If we talk then we talk. I don't think you can help me so I don't see the benefit in staying in contact, but I can see all the risks. Even if you didn't plan the trap for us someone you know did, and they could only have found out from your side. Talking to you is dangerous. I'm done for now." With that Charley logged off the net.

Holly also signed off and headed to bed for some much needed sleep.

Sean had come back into the boathouse to see what was going on and after Charley logged off he looked at his young partner. "What was that all about?"

"I don't know for sure, but they are probably working on some conspiracy angle. You know how spooks love those."

"True enough lad. So what did you find out?"

"Two things, first off you and I didn't kill anyone at the river. We wounded a few but no one died."

"Well I suppose that's good news, at least they won't be adding any murder charges to the list for killing a federal officer. What's the second thing?"

"Someone got into the hospital and killed Andrea. I can only assume it was the organization that did it, but she's dead."

"Well no big loss as far as I'm concerned," Sean said lately.

"But she was the link to the organization Sean. She was the one that was going to clear our names."

"Lad to be honest I never really thought your plan had a chance. The organization has been around for longer then you know. There is no way to bring them down and you better get used to that idea. The best we can do is run and hide and I am really sorry about that but that is the hard reality."

Charley was silent for a moment thinking over what his friend was saying, and began to see that he may be right. "There is always the chance they will trade immunity for the names of the board members," he added hopefully.

"Lad, to do that they would want us to surrender and then testify at a trial. How long do you think we would live after surrendering? We need to think about running now and the farther the better. The good news is that the organization doesn't care very much about anything outside the US and I have never ever heard of anyone operating outside of the Americas. We could head to Europe and find a nice quiet place to live there. With six million dollars we don't have to worry about work."

"But I want my life back Sean. The took it from me and I want it back!"

"And if I could get it back for you I would Lad, but I just don't see that happening. Now we should pack up and head for Bermuda. From there we can get to anywhere in the world."

Charley was starting to feel guilty, his partner had followed his lead on every plan so far and now all he wanted to do was get away before their luck ran out. And if they stayed and fought much longer, it would at some point. The law of averages was against them now. "Okay Old Man let me check the weather and see when a good time to leave is."

Charley logged back on to the net and checked all the satellite pictures of the Atlantic and downloaded the latest weather reports to get a clear idea of how things were between the US and Bermuda. There was a low-pressure system moving offshore creating a small gale and lots of rain that was expected to be gone in two days. After that there was a predicted five-day window for the trip. Charley got out his charts and looked everything over doing the math in his head.

"Okay Sean, we can leave in two days time, right now the weather is a bit rough out there. This boat could handle it but no sense making us sick if we don't have to."

Happy to have a plan in place Sean smiled widely. "Two days it is, thanks Lad, it will feel good when we finally leave. Think I'll take a walk around, I'll be back in a while." Going out once more even though he had just come in

Charley went below to once again check over their new boat even though he knew it was as ready to go as he could make it. But like Sean's patrolling, the actions of going over the things relaxed him. In two days he would be starting a new life and that made him very sad. He would miss all the things he was leaving behind in Canada, he had hoped that his plan to clear their names would have worked and that Sean would come and live with him. The old man had become like a second father to him. It was time now to do something for him, and giving him a place to live out the rest of his life would be Charley's gift, not that he would ever tell his friend that. If Sean knew that he was quitting the fight only for him he would insist they keep fighting and the old man deserved some peace and quiet after the decades of work he had done for the organization.

The only thing was where to settle down? Anywhere around the Mediterranean would be nice. Moderate climate and they could use the boat to get there if they planned it right and were careful. The only snag was getting it registered in their name so they wouldn't get arrested for possessing stolen property. Charley figured he could track down the registered owner and then use the computer to forge the papers and fake a sales receipt. If he did it enough and changed the name a few times he should be able to muddy the trail enough that no one could find them. He would discuss it on the trip over with Sean and see what he thought about living on a boat in the Med

Sean came back from his walk and the two decided it was time to bed down for the night. After rigging a few traps for anyone trying to break in, they set their weapons within easy reach, rolled up in their sleeping bags on the deck of their new home, and quickly fell asleep.

Chapter 16

Holly woke at her usual time, and after a shower, headed to the kitchen for a cup of coffee. One of her security detail was posted at the bottom of the stairs looking as alert as when she headed up to bed. He preceded her into the kitchen but refused her offer of coffee. After the coffee the two headed outside where they meet the second member of the team who was seated in the car that would take her to work. As Holly got into the back the driver started the engine and pulled out of the driveway and as soon as he was on the road the third member of the team materialized next to the car seemingly from nowhere. Five minutes later they arrived at the NSA office and the three men were relieved by another team that looked just like them and were also deadly serious about their work. Once she was comfortably at her desk the security team took up stations at the entrances and everyone arriving for their job was checked as soon as they came in to ensure that they were who they said they were and that they belonged there. Several people were refused entry simply for not being on the list of people stationed on that floor. The people refused entry were angry and frustrated but had enough sense not to argue with the security troops, so they left until they could procure proof that they belonged there.

After logging on to her computer Holly checked the database to see what new information Spock had come up with while she was sleeping. Nothing new was showing but she was actually expecting this. It seemed as if the organization had stopped using the internet for communication, they were catching on. Holly knew that they needed to get the leaders very soon or they would lose the chance. Some how the President had to be convinced to grant immunity to Charley and Sean so that they could get the names of leaders. She looked for the number of Adam and once she had it she dialed the number. The phone rang through to his voice mail and she left a message asking him if the President was considering granting the immunity. She asked him to call her back if there was any news so that she could contact the two men and pass it on.

John came in just as she was hanging up the phone. "Morning John, how is Gunny doing?" she asked

"He's going to be fine Miss McClare. I spoke with him late last night and he was anxious to get back to work to help put an end to the organization. I told him to stay in the hospital a few days and heal. He said he would think about it. He is one stubborn man. In the end I had to get the doc to order him to stay in the hospital for at least three days for observation."

"John I'm new at this but I get the feeling that everyone is missing something. I'm trying to figure out what the organization is up to with trying to kill the President and I have no idea. Do you have any theories at all?"

John sat down and leaned back in his chair. "I'll say this to you because you're my boss, but not to anyone else. And if you ask me to repeat this to anyone I'll deny it. I think that the people in charge of the organization work in the government."

Holly smiled at him. "Why do you say that?"

"Because it's something we would do, that's why. Let me ask you, why are there so many conspiracy theorists around all spouting off about how the government is always conspiring against someone or other?"

"Because it happens?" Holly asked in response to his question only being half serious.

"Sounds like you don't really believe that but it's the truth. It happens and you should know it. Look at what happened to you after you created Spock. Tell me that there wasn't a conspiracy to get you working for the government."

Holly nodded at this. "So what do you think is going on? Why are they trying to kill the president?"

"I don't know, but I do know one thing, whatever the reason I'd bet money that it's something that is going to surprise everyone and also something that is most likely a narrow minded ideal."

Holly was puzzled by his reply. "Why would you say a narrow minded ideal?"

"It has been my experience that any time a group of people gets together and tries to change things using violent means they are doing it for a reason that is hard to defend and narrow in it's thinking."

"That's rather a cynical statement isn't it? I mean this country was founded through a revolution which was violent but the reason it was done would hardly be called narrow minded."

"Do you really believe that? The leaders of the revolution were a small group of rich land owners that were upset about unfair taxes. They wrote a constitution publicly declaring all men to be free while at the same time the majority were slave owners. Add in the fact that only landowners could vote and you have a small group of men with a narrow view of their world. What we are looking at here is an organization that is run by a small group of people and is being used to further their own beliefs. They feel that they are in the right, doesn't sound that much different from the revolution does it? It is of course but they feel that they too are patriots acting for the good of the country," John told her.

At that point the other two members of Holly's team came in to work and Holly greeted them, then went back to her computer trying to figure out what the organization was up to. No matter what it was she had to help stop them, permanently.

Adam was waiting for the President in the Oval Office for their morning ritual of going over the day's agenda. Once they were finished Adam headed back to office but was stopped by his boss. "About what we discussed last night, I want to discuss that later today. Can we squeeze that in sometime? I'd also like the young lady and someone she trusts. You know the type I'm looking for?"

"Yes sir." Adam said going into his office and figuring out when he could fit the meeting into the day's schedule. It took some juggling but finally he found 20 minutes around 2PM. He picked up the phone and dialed the number.

"Hello, Holly McClare speaking" came the voice after the second ring.

"Hello Miss McClare, the president was wondering if you could come over at 2PM today."

"Absolutely Mr Miles. I'll let the General know right away."

"That won't be necessary Miss McClare, his presence isn't required, however I was wondering if the two men that were with us at the river were available to come as well?"

"Gunny is in the hospital, he was shot when Agent Drake was killed but…"

Adam cut her off. "Is he going to be okay? Is there anything I can do to help him?" he asked with genuine concern in his voice.

"The doctors say he is going to be fine, thank you for asking. John is available though and I'm sure he would be happy to come along."

"That's great Miss McClare, can you bring him along please?"

"Yes sir I will."

"One other thing Miss McClare, I'll be sending a driver for you again and you'll be coming in a different way. I'll let the General know what's going on as well."

"Okay we'll be waiting." With that she hung up and asked John to meet her in the boardroom.

Once the door was closed she explained that the two of them would be going to the White House for a meeting with the president after lunch. John was surprised by the news and asked what it was about. Holly told him she didn't know but to be ready for anything. They headed back to their desks and went to work until it was time for their meeting.

In the meantime Adam had called the general and told him about the meeting but that his presence wasn't required assuring him that the president was only looking for an update from the young lady and wanted it in person, it had nothing to do with going behind the general's back. Used to the ways of politicians the general understood and took no offense at it. Adam left out the part about the request for the paramilitary person, wanting to keep that secret.

At the sound of the ringing Carter opened his desk drawer and picked up the phone that very seldom rang knowing it could only be one of a dozen people. "Hello?" he answered simply.

"We need to meet in person." The voice on the other end said with out preamble. "Can we use your place again?"

"Yes, what time?" Carter replied.

"Tomorrow at 6AM. It will be brief but I feel it's necessary. I'll contact our counterpart as well, the juniors don't need to be there."

"Fine, I'll see you then." Carter hung up the phone and went back to work putting the meeting out of his mind.

Knowing that they had a time line to leave Sean was far more relaxed. He still went out to scout around as the sun was coming up, old habits die hard. Charley once again went over the boat checking that everything was stowed correctly and that they were ready to leave at a seconds notice. His biggest worry was that he would lose his weapons. The guns that his grandfather had spent time collecting and left to him would be gone. The ones he had with him he would have to toss overboard once they were close to Bermuda. They could not risk getting caught with illegal arms on board. It was illegal to take any firearm into the Bermuda, automatic weapons would get them thrown right into jail. And he could never go home again, not while he was still a wanted man.

Sean came back into the boathouse as Charley came up from below deck. "Lad did you put some coffee on?"

"Just for you, old man," Charley said, smiling at his friend.

"How's the weather looking?"

"Same as yesterday, it'll be clear day after tomorrow so just relax. We'll pull out nice and early, around 4 AM. That will get us clear of the coast before sun-up. I was thinking about trying my hand at fishing, see if I can catch our supper, sound good to you?"

Sean nodded at the Lad and simply nodded his agreement to the idea. Grabbing the fishing tackle the two headed outside and down the river to see what would bite.

The driver showed up at 12:45 to pick up Holly and John. They got into the car and one of the security detail hopped n the front seat beside the driver while the other two followed in their own vehicle. The drive as usual, took about an hour, once again parking in the basement of the treasury building. The security detail stayed behind as they had before while Holly and John followed the driver through the tunnel into the White House.

John set off the metal detector and was forced to leave his pistol at the security desk before he was allowed to enter the house. If it hadn't been for Adam's assistant it was unlikely that he would have been allowed in at all, even though he was a carded NSA agent and licensed to carry a firearm. The Secret Service was very wary of letting anyone that carried a firearm into the home of the president. The security agent that escorted them kept a closer eye on John out of habit, marking him as a dangerous man.

Holly was surprised to be lead upstairs to the president's residence, she hadn't really thought much about where she would speak with the President but she had imagined it would have been in the Oval Office. The driver left Holly and John in a sitting room with the secret service agent watching them. With nothing other to do than wait the two simply sat on the couch in silence, it wasn't a long wait.

"Hello Miss McClare, I'm glad you could make it," the president said, walking into the sitting room.

Holly and John sprang to their feet. "Thank you for inviting me back, Mr President. This is my associate John."

The President stuck out his hand and grabbed John's. "Good to meet you. Would you both follow me please? That will be all David, Adam and I would like to be alone with our guests," he told the Secret Service agent standing behind him as he turned and lead everyone into his personal study. The agent did not like this at all and eyed John the until the door was closed.

Once the door was closed he motioned Holly, John and Adam to sit down and took a seat in a rocking chair himself. "I've been thinking things over and I need someone to bounce some ideas off of. I need someone that is unbiased and will give me an honest answer. Miss McClare you strike me as being that type of person but before we start I'd like to know a little bit about your friend here. I'm not sure if Adam was clear, he can sometimes be a little obtuse in his wording of things. Did you understand his meaning?"

"Adam didn't really explain anything sir he simply asked if Gunny or John was available to join us."

"Okay Miss McClare, do you trust him?" the president asked, pointing to John. "I mean would you trust him with your life?"

"I already have," came her instant reply. "John please tell him a little about yourself

For the next couple of minutes John gave the president a rundown of his past and what he had been up to. Suitably impressed with his qualifications the president nodded and smiled.

"Perfect, Miss McClare. Now let me ask you a hypothetical question: if you wanted to catch the leaders behind this organization you found how would you do it? And for the purposes of this discussion you can use any means necessary, that includes using me."

Holly thought for a second not sure of what she was hearing but then started. "First I would grant immunity to the two men accused of trying to kill you so I could have the names. Then I would fake your death using the plan that they have already set in motion, and follow those men to see what they did next. Once they have acted on whatever plans they have I'd arrest them."

"Okay so you have given me an outline, now flesh it out; how would you do all that. Remember you can't tell anyone in the government about your plan, the organization would find out about it and it would be game over."

Holly smiled. "I'd ask John to help," she said simply.

The president nodded and looked at John. "Okay so she's asked you for help, how would you help her?"

John jumped into the conversation with no hesitation at all, explain how he would tackle the job First off Holly could handle getting the names leaving him free to set up the manpower end of the job. Planning the death of a president, even a fake one using the organizations plan to assist, will require manpower. He would need contact people that he trusted implicitly and once the names of the leaders are known, set up surveillance on them. Now the truly hard part, the actual assassination attempt could be done without military people if it had to be but would be much more doable with the military in on it. With the military involved and the job taking place at sea it was completely possible to pull it off. The military is used to taking orders and once the plan is set up you only need to involve people you can trust and the rest never have to know, they will simply follow orders. First you assemble a team that is outside the chain of command with one person in charge so that everyone else involved only takes orders from that person. Have the team flown to the WASP where they wait for the president. The team takes the secret service agents into protective custody and assumes their identities. They ready the sailboat then the president appears, sails it out and let the organization actually do the hard part, blow it up and appear to kill the President of the United States. The real sacrifice is the sailboat, it will have to be blown up to appear realistic and have any chance of the masquerade succeeding. Once the boat is destroyed, the news of the president's death is released by the press is always present. After the news breaks the admiral in charge is ordered to radio silence and a through search is started. The team quietly gets the president back to Washington while the fleet is doing a search and recovery for a body. Hopefully by then the organization leaders have tipped their hand and are in custody with their final plans known."

The president nodded his understanding and began to ask a few follow up questions "Let's start at the beginning with the surveillance. You said we need men you trust implicitly. Do you know such men?" the president asked.

"Yes I do."

"I see. Let me think for a moment please." He told the three then leaned back in his chair and relaxed. Four minutes passed and he sat up straight again. "Okay people I'll need all your help. We are going to end this hunt if we can. Miss McClare can you contact the two men?"

"I think so yes sir."

"Good please do so and tell them that immunity is out of the question, but I can give them a Presidential pardon, if the information they give us helps take down this organization. I'll sign it and give it to you before you go back to your office. That should get us the names we are looking for. Do you two mind if I call you by your first names?" he suddenly asked. When both nodded he went on "Holly you said that you had a list of all the traitors names so every person we recruit gets checked against that list. John I'll need the names of the men you can trust before morning. I assume they are in government service?" He received a nod and continued. "Get the list to Adam and he will get the orders cut placing them under the command of Holly, so once you have the names of the leaders and the men are ready to go, get the surveillance set up right away. John I want you to lead the men taking over security for me on the WASP. For that I want to go with Marines but I need to have them picked from people that are loyal. Can you do that?" Again John nodded his assent thinking of Gunny and knowing he would be able to call on a people of unquestioning loyalty.

"Excellent get those names together and send them to Adam as well and we'll get the men sent out to the WASP ASAP." The President continued before anyone had a chance to say anything. "This has to be kept absolutely silent, no one can learn of this. I'll call General Donovan and tell him that you to are working out of the White House for a few days while I'm on vacation. Let me be clear on this people, if I am going to let my boat be blown up this plan damn well better work. I would truly hate to go all through this only to come up empty handed at the end of it all. So let's get to work."

"Excuse me sir but there is one last problem that Holly has neglected to mention to you," John said.

"What's that?"

Holly tried to stop John but he spoke up ignoring her warning glare. "The general has ordered round the clock security for Holly. It seems that the organization wants her out of the way. On the laptop were plans to kidnap or kill her."

"Why didn't you tell me this earlier Holly?" asked the president harshly.

"Sir I didn't think it important enough to bother you with. Your safety is more important than mine."

"I disagree young lady," he said forcefully. "Since my safety relies on your actions it would seem that the two are on an equal footing. The security team the General placed on you, are they all military?"

"Yes sir."

"Get their names to Adam as well and we'll have them placed on the temporary duty roster for the White House. They can work here with you and keep you safe. Anything else we forgot to cover? No? Great then I'll let you two get to work." With that the President stood and left the room.

Adam had one of his assistants escort Holly and John back to the treasury Building and drive them back to the NSA. Not wanting to discuss anything in the car they were silent all the way back each going over the next few days in their minds. The two could not have been farther apart emotionally. John was happy to be back in the field working on a job that held an element of disaster, while Holly was terrified for exactly the same reason. If either of them failed the President of the United States could be dead by the end of the week.

Chapter 17

The morning they were slated to leave started off the same as the one before it had; Sean rose before daybreak and left the boathouse to scout the area, making sure they were still alone. While he was gone Charley started coffee so that it would be ready for his partner when he returned. Sean always carried one of the radios for communication and was still carrying his now beloved Thompson. As he was on the opposite side of the cabin, scouting the driveway, he heard the sound of a car getting closer. Sean ducked behind a tree and radioed Charley to let him know something could be happening. Peeking out from behind the tree Sean watched a car pull up and a portly man get out of it. The newcomer disappeared behind the Cabin and a few moments later the sound of a generator starting could be heard then the man walked back around to the front, unlocked the cabin and went inside.

Sean faded back into the trees, radioed his young partner to get everything ready but not start the boat yet. He then started moving toward the water to get closer to the boathouse in case something happened and he and Charley had to leave in a hurry. He was about to break from cover and dash to the boathouse when two more cars came up the drive and parked in front of the cabin. The men got out and looked around briefly then went inside. Sean stared at the men, feeling that he knew them from somewhere, but not sure where. Rather then head to the boathouse Sean radioed Charley to sit tight, he was going to wait and see what happened.

The three were inside for about forty-five minutes then everyone came out together. Once again the first man to show up went around to the back and this time shut off the generator. Sean was absolutely positive he knew the three men he just couldn't place them. Then he had it, he knew who they were. Sean waited five minutes after the last car left to see if anyone would come back, then moved to the boathouse, sprinting the last few dozen yards to the door. He knocked and spoke through he door to let Charley know who it was and waited for the door to be unlocked. He heard the lock snap open but the door remained closed. He smiled to himself and opened the door carefully staying in plain sight as he stepped through. He spotted Charley next to the boat covering the door with his silenced Sten.

Sean smiled at his young friend and nodded, then stepped inside and closed the door, locking it behind him. "How much tranquilizer drug do we have left?" he asked.

Charley was surprised by the question but tried to remember. "I think enough for four or five darts, why? No never mind that now, you can tell me later. The boat is ready to go so help me with the door and I'll start the engines."

1 "Slow down Lad why the rush?"

"WHAT?" Charley shouted. "The rush is because you said to get ready to leave. The rush is because the guy that owns the place just showed up and we should get out of here before he comes back. That's why the rush. What the hell is wrong with you, Sean?"

"Now calm down Lad. It seems I may have been mistaken about my haste to leave. Did you have a chance to look at the men that were here?"

"Not really, I was getting the boat prepped most of the time. I checked the yard a couple of times but didn't really see anyone, Sean what is going on?" Charley asked not knowing what his friend was thinking.

"Well lad it appears by a stoke of very large luck that you and I have happened on the secure meeting location of the organizations board members."

Charley digested that bit of information and then abruptly sat down when it has sunk in. "The board members were HERE?"

"Yes lad they were. And I have a feeling that they will be back again, no idea when but they will be back."

"Then we should leave right now."

Sean shook his head. "No lad, think for a second. The one thing that will truly help us is if we were in a position to trade our freedom for the men that are behind the entire organization. If we have them we can contact the girl at the NSA and offer to give her the board members in return for our freedom. It's a deal they can't say no to."

"And if they still say no to immunity for us? Then we are stuck with the board members. Our only option then is to kill them, and while I don't think it would upset me all that much to kill those three men, it would mean that the last way to clear our names would be gone forever."

"True enough lad but here's the leverage, if they don't agree we tell them that we will simply turn the board members loose and leave. The government would have no way of knowing if we did or didn't."

Charley's face broke into a huge grin. "You know that's blackmail Sean. But I like it."

"Oh don't be so dramatic lad, it's not blackmail. It's just simple negotiation. Now let's plan this out and set it up."

The two got down to planning their trap and worked steadily through he rest of the day.

Holly showed up at the White House with her security team at 6:30 AM wondering what kind of a reception she would get. Adam had briefed the Secret Service on her arrival and the security team she would be bringing. It was against protocol for any person other then a secret service agent to carry a weapon in the White House but in this instance Adam had overruled protocol and the members of the security team would be wearing their sidearms while on duty and their duty area would never allow them near the West Wing or Oval Office, they would be restricted to the basement areas. When not on duty they would lock up their weapons with the watch officer. As well a secret service agent would also be posted with them at all times.

Her first order of business when she arrived was to get the name of the secret service agent assigned to her. She then found her desk and logged into her computer bringing up the list of known organization agents with in the secret service. As she suspected the man's name was on the list. She assumed that any agent she had assigned to her would be an organization man. She had tried to explain this to Adam and the president but they had cut her off and she never had the chance. At the NSA the general could control who had access to the floor she worked on and the security around her. Here in the White House no such luxury existed.

Since she was already logged in she began working, opening the active files and going over the data. She didn't have direct access to Spock, rather she had set up a secure virtual log in to the NSA and was accessing already saved files to review and go over. She also emailed Charley again asking him to contact her. She needed to let him know about the pardon and to get his help in stopping the organization.

John was right about Gunny knowing men who could get the job done, and with his help it had taken no time at all to get a team assembled. Now he and his team were landing on the assault carrier WASP after twelve hours of travel, the last few in a very large and loud helicopter. Like most pilots he loved to fly only as long as he was the one in the pilots seat. He had to admit though that the guy flying the chopper had done a superb job. As soon as they were on the deck he and his team were out the door and heading to the island, where they were met by the admiral's aide. He escorted them to their quarters with out any talking and as he left told John that the admiral had requested his presence in thirty minutes adding that a marine would be by to escort him up. With that he left closing the door behind him. The men all found a bunk and dropped their gear on it then looked around getting the lay of the land. Some had been on an assault carrier before while others had not. For those that had, it was all very familiar including the gentle role of the ship. The first timers were finding the maze of overhead pipes and small bunks difficult to get used to although no one found the ships role at all uncomfortable. John was happy that so far no one was showing symptoms of sea-sickness. He needed all his men to pull off the job. The quarters that had been given had their own head and showers so his team would be completely isolated form the rest of the crew with the exception of meal time. He was sure they could adjust that, so as to cause the minimum of interaction between his men and the rest of the ship. That there would be interaction was something he could not stop and the one bad thing about the navy was that now matter how big the ship, it was still a small place. By now the entire crew would know that they were on board and would be wondering why. They would follow orders though, so things should be fine until they had to arrest the secret service men.

John changed into the uniform he had been given which showed him to be a colonel in the marines and waited. Twenty minutes later a marine corporal showed up to take John to see the Admiral and brief him on what was going on. The walk to the admirals quarters was a series of turns and climbs up ladders until the point where John wasn't sure he would be able to find his way back with out the corporal to guide him. They arrived exactly on time and the corporal banged loudly on the door, which was followed by a bellowed

"COME" from the other side.

The marine opened the door and stepped aside to allow John to enter the room then closed the door after him. John took a quick glance around the room to see the admiral seated behind a large desk with a photo of the president on the wall behind him. Standing to his right was another man wearing the uniform of a captain. Both men were watching him intently. John came to attention and smiled.

"Colonel are you normally in the habit of smiling at a superior officer?" the admiral asked in a low but very menacing voice.

"Yes sir I am, my mother always taught me to be friendly and smile at people I met for the first time," John answered honestly. "No disrespect intended Admiral and I have a letter you need to read before we go any further." John opened his uniform coat and took out the letter the president had given him to hand deliver. "sir this is from the President of the United States and his instructions were that you were to read this alone." John reached forward and handed it to the admiral then stepped back and waited.

"Thank you colonel would you and the captain please wait here." With that he got up and went into his private cabin.

It was several minutes before he cam back into the room and when he did the look on his face was grim. "I'm not sure I like this," he said to John. "I have only one question for you, are you sure you can pull this off?"

"Absolutely admiral or I wouldn't be here."

"Well you have the president's personal backing and he is my commander in chief so I will of course follow my orders. However this ship belongs to Captain Haines here and he has the right to know what is going on. Colonel would you be so kind as to tell him?"

Even though he had orders directly from the president to tell no one other then the admiral what was going on John knew that the captain of a ship was the absolute ruler of it. If he were to get anything done he would need at the least consent from the captain. "First, please call me John, I work in the NSA and I'm not really a colonel…."

The admiral cut him off. "Son in my task force if you wear the uniform of a marine corp colonel then you are a marine corp colonel and don't you ever repeat to anyone else that you are not, is that understood. As to your real name I don't give a damn what it is I will address as your uniform indicates. If the President trusts you that's good enough for me so I will as well."

"Very well admiral. I'll be very brief. Captain there is a threat on the president's life that is being staged by a group of unknown persons that we believe may be working within the government. The plan was uncovered by the NSA and fully explained to the president. In short it is to take place at sea while he is on vacation on his sailboat. My orders are to take the secret service detail into protective custody and provide security for the president. After that we are going to have a double sail his boat to see if the information we received is real. If it is the president will decide the next course of action."

The captain read the name off John's uniform. "Colonel O'Neil, since the admiral is treating this seriously I can assume this is not a drill or a readiness exercise in preparation for the president's visit. So let's get to the point, are you able to outline your plan at this time?"

John nodded and began explaining what was going to happen and how. It was a simple plan and one that would severely limit the involvement of the ships crew. The actual arrest would be done by John and his team. They would need the Marine MP detachment and the brig to secure the men after they were arrested.

"I don't understand the need to toss these men in the brig Colonel O'Neil. Are you saying that the entire detail is in on the plot? If that is so how did these men ever pass a security check and get that close to the president to being with?"

"To be honest Captain I have no idea if any of these men are in on the plot," John told him. "And to be blunt sir I don't care. My mission is to ensure the safety of the President of the United States and assist him with the plan he has set in motion. If I have to detain innocent men to do this then I will. And please remember that these men are federal officers so the normal rules do not apply. I am not asking you or your men to do anything illegal, I am merely asking for the use of your brig and to have the men watched by your MP's."

"I understand your motives Colonel, I am just wondering if it is necessary to put them in the brig? I would prefer we confine them to their quarters. That happens all the time on ships for a variety of security reasons and avoids the entire matter of wrongfully imprisoning any innocent men."

"I wish we could just confine them to their quarters Captain. However if any of these men are in on the plot they may have the means of communicating with the others involved in the plot and alerting them to the fact that we know about it. They could then simply stop this attempt, wait until another opportunity presents itself in the future and make the attempt then. The only way to ensure there are no leaks is to put the men in the brig and watch them until the mission is over."

Up to this point the Admiral had simply watched the two men debate and kept quiet, he jumped in at this point to end the discussion. "Captain your concern of the men is noted. However I feel that it would be best if we followed the Colonel's plan. If we are wrong then the president will correct it when he arrives.

Still not happy but knowing when to go along the Captain simply nodded his agreement on that point and moved onto his next concern. "Colonel what happens when the President is about to arrive? Even though this is a US Navy ship the secret service agents on board with him will try to contact the agents here to confirm that everything is in order. And when they don't get any answer the president's helicopter will simply not land."

"One of my men will be on the radio when the chopper calls in. He will have the day codes to confirm that the landing is secure and all is well. As you say sir this is a US navy ship, surrounded by a US Navy battle group. As long as we have the proper day codes and answer the radio call I don't see them being suspicious at all. I'll have my men in civilian dress for the landing and it will seem to the men on board that the detail here is covering the deck. Once the chopper is down the detail will deplane and we will take them into custody at that time."

"Sir I hope that this goes as simply as you seem to think it will. Having watched the detail already on board for the last few weeks I seriously doubt that it will go anywhere nearly as smooth as you seem to think it will. But I will support you in the president's plan." The captain turned to the admiral. "If you will excuse me sir I need to get back to the bridge."

"Certainly Captain. Dismissed." Once he had left the room the admiral motioned John to sit which he did. "The captain's concern is justified, Colonel. He has a valid point, if things go wrong we could end up with a fire fight on the deck of this ship with the president in the middle of it."

"Sir we have thought out all the possibilities we could and the plan in place is the best that we could come up with. Believe me if there was anything better we would be using it."

The Admiral had a sly look on his face. "So you are aware that something could go wrong?"

"Yes sir I'm very aware that something could go wrong. However the President has accepted the risk involved."

"As have I Colonel. You go and get your men ready and let me know if you need anything at all. Dismissed."

John got up and stood to attention before turning and leaving the room. In the passage way outside the Admiral quarters was the same man that had escorted him up, waiting to take him back to his men. The trip back was just as confusing to John and he was glad to have the guide along to show him the way. Once back with his men they all went over the plan once more, then checked their weapons and hit the bunks for some sleep. It would be a long night no matter how well things went.

"Sean, I have to say that it's a little weird to see you wanting to wait here now after the huge rush you have been in to leave. Weird but nice."

"Lad when we started all this I never once imagined that we would have any chance at all to succeed. And to be honest unless we get our hands on those 3 I still don't see any chance at getting free. Even if the government does decide to leave us alone, the organization never will. And I have very little faith in the ability of the government to catch the boardmembers, but if we catch them ourselves then we have a chance."

Charley smiled at his mentor and friend. "Nice to see you think we can do this after all, old man. The gear is all ready it's just a matter of setting things up, then waiting for them to come back. I'm going to check and see if the people at the NSA are thinking of us."

Charley went and got the computer and satellite, and set everything up to connect to the internet. Once connected he opened his mail and downloaded the waiting messages. As the last email came in, his instant messaging program opened and up popped a message from the NSA asking him to check his email immediately. He thought it was strange that that happened but had no way of knowing that Holly had programmed one of her computers to monitor the net for his IP address and once detected as active to send the message asking him to check his email. With everything downloaded he logged off and started going through it. The majority was spam but there was a message there from Holly marked as urgent. He opened it and skimmed it, the information it contained hitting him like a ton of bricks. He slowly re-read the email and then read it a third time before asking Sean to read it over as well.

Sean read the email then looked as Charley. "They are offering us a presidential pardon, it's as good as immunity. I never thought they would let us off completely but that's what they are doing." he said in a stunned voice.

"Sean we need to think something through here. Do we simply give them the names and take the pardon and leave? Or do we wait here, hold off telling them anything, catch the board members ourselves and then call them? After all when we started this we were only trying to clear our names so we could live out a normal life. This pardon gives us that, but only if they shut down the organization. You have expressed doubts about that happening so I need to know what you want to do."

"Lad part of me wants to give them the names, take the pardon and run. But to be honest we have the element of surprise on our side right now. No one knows were we are, we know that the board members have been here once and will likely come back. I'm thinking that this boat was set up as a fail-safe plan so they are not going to abandon this place. I vote for catching them ourselves when they show up and then handing them over to the government."

Charley looked at his friend and could see the desire in his eyes to catch the board members himself. They were responsible for ruining the last four decades of his life. "Okay then let's catch these guys ourselves."

Sean's face broke into a huge smile. "Thank you lad," he said quietly. "I'm going to go have a look around." With that he grabbed up his SMG and quietly left the boathouse to go and check things over.

Doris noticed the computer screen flash out of the corner of her eye, and turned to see the alert on screen that the IP they were watching was active. She picked up the phone to call Holly and alert her that Charley was online. By the time Holly answered the phone the computer alert had shut down, signifying that he had logged off. Holly was disappointed that she had missed him and told Doris that the next time he came online to try and talk to him and get his answer to the email they had sent. She needed the names of the board members, time was running out.

John formed up his team and everyone checked over their weapons one last time. Every team member had a tranquilizer gun tucked into their waistband at the small of their back, and carried a P90 submachine gun at the ready. The plan was to take everyone alive however the mission objective came first and they had to remove the secret service agents before the president landed. Leading the way to the deck John headed towards the Van next to the Presidents boat where the agents were working and sleeping. At all times there were four agents on duty around the clock meaning there were twelve agents on the ship. One agent was always on the Presidents boat, two roving around both the boat and the van and one sitting inside monitoring a bank of cameras that were pointed at all access points to the van and the boat, which were directly behind the island with no easy access point to reach them. Anyone wanting to get to either of them had to cross open deck under the eyes of the agents and the cameras. There was a thirty-foot exclusion zone around the area that was off limits to all ship personal.

The wasp had a roving patrol of marines that constantly wandered around the ship while it was underway. John had his team now dressed up as the roving patrol and was moving across the flight deck towards the island. The agents were used to seeing this patrol and understood that it was a security feature of the ship and it actually helped them. The only area of the ship that they weren't allowed in was the secret service exclusion zone. As they walked to the island the team came very close to the exclusion zone but the agents did no more then take notice of them and watch to ensure they maintained the thirty-foot perimeter. They were no more or less alert then at any other time. John made it look as if he and his patrol were heading for the aft hatch on the island he waved at the agents to acknowledge their presence. None of the agents waved back but then they were trained not to so it was expected. As they neared the invisible thirty-foot line John reached to the small of his back pulled out the tranquilizer gun and shot the agent on the Presidents boat, hitting him in the upper leg. His shot was the signal for the rest of the men to take down the other two agents on deck, which they did with in seconds of John's shot. The drug they were using was fast acting, but the training of the agents and their reaction times allowed all three to pull out their weapons and fire a total of seven shots at John and his team. None of the bullets hit anyone as they were running toward the van and weaving at the same time making it too hard for the drugged agents to aim accurately at anyone. All three were unconscious in under ten seconds.

The team ran toward the van with two men pulling explosive charges from their pockets and two others pulling stun grenades. The agent on duty in the van saw all this on the surveillance cameras and pushed the panic button on his console to wake the other eight agents then grabbed the radio to alert the office in Washington and abort the president's arrival. As the other agents spilled into the watch room carrying weapons, the on duty agent was yelling into his radio getting nothing but static in return to his calls. The room was laid out to guard the door and there was no other way in. The agents took up stations situated around the room and aimed at the door getting ready to fight back.

The door of the van opened inward and was steel set in a steel frame, making it impossible to blow the hinges off to open the door. John had briefed the captain on the entire job and when it would be happening. At the same moment that John had begun taking the agents out the control center of the

Wasp had activated it's radio jamming equipment. This was the reason that the duty agent had been unable to contact Washington and what John was counting on to keep his activities a surprise from the organization. The team was using C4 and the two carrying it and rolled it out into long round strips and stuck it in place around the entire seam of the door. John then picked up a device that looked a lot like a giant ice pick and slammed the pointed end into the door. The point was needle sharp made from tungsten and coated with Teflon, which slid through the steel door as if it were soft bread. As soon as the tip was clear of the other side it fell open and reveled a spray nozzle, which began spewing a fine mist into the room. The agents farthest from the door were able to get gas masks but the other agents were too slow and the gas being released knocked them out.

The tank on the device was emptied into the room in under twenty seconds with enough gas released to push a fine fog throughout the entire van. John then attached a detonator to the C4, set it and stepped to the side. The C4 went off with a loud bang and blew the door into the van. A split second after the door disappeared the two men with the stun grenades tossed them in. The grenades were designed to produce a pressure wave that disoriented anyone in the room and they worked exactly as they should knocking all the agents in the room flat. It also smashed all the electronics in the room ensuring that no one was going to be calling out on the radios to raise an alarm. John and his team rushed the room, checked over the agents and removed all their weapons.

As soon as everything was secure the team handcuffed the agents then contacted the captain to inform him that all was secure. The captain ordered the radio jamming stopped and told the infirmary to check over the agents to make sure they were all right. The captain also called the admirals quarters to inform him that the operation was over and had been a success.

John immediately posted two men to cover the president's boat. Once the medics had cleared the agents John had them escorted to the brig and locked up. The agents were still stunned enough that no one even bothered to ask what was going on or why they had been attacked. With the secret service agents secure, John and his team began cleaning up the van and repairing the radios so that he could again contact the Secret Service headquarters in Washington in case they called. A search of the van turned up the list of day codes so they were all set to answer any inquires with the correct codes. The backup plan in place in case the codes weren't recovered was to contact Adam and he would supply then with the codes they needed.

By morning the team was fully in place and dressed in civilian cloths to complete the masquerade. They had been contacted by radio twice already, checks being done every four hours, and had passed using the proper code responses. As the President wasn't on board and it was a US carrier the checks were more for routine and formality then anything else. No really expected that anything would happen, which is exactly why John felt confident of his plan.

The president looked up at his chief of staff, caught the look in his eye and nodded slightly. He was in the middle of dictating a letter to one of his assistants so he quickly finished up and then headed to Adam's office.

Adam stood as his boss entered. "Sir, Miss McClare still hasn't heard back from the two men. With out those names we have nothing to work with, I feel that we should consider calling the whole thing off."

The President thought for a second. "We decided to do this to try and catch the people behind the organization, do you feel that we can't flush them out if we go through with it?"

"Sir I think we are needlessly exposing you to danger with out some idea of who the men are."

"Well Adam we still have time. John will meet us on the WASP and if Holly still hasn't heard anything by then we can call it off and come home. But I want to try."

"Yes sir, as soon as we have any information I will radio the WASP and let them know."

The President simply nodded then headed back to the Oval Office to finish up before leaving. The helicopter was slated to arrive in less than thirty minutes and he wanted to be ready to go by then.

Charley set up the satellite and booted up the computer. Once connected, he opened the messaging program and tried to contact Holly. At the NSA the computer set to monitor his IP beeped alerting Doris once again that it was active. She picked up the phone and immediately called Holly, who was now at the White House. While the phone was ringing the computer screen popped up the instant message program with the words "Holly are you there?" on the screen.

Doris was all set to answer when her boss came on the line. Holly told her to shut down the message program on the NSA computer so she could start it on her computer at the White House. Doris did so and once Holly had the message program open she typed in "Yes, did you get my email?" and hit send.

Charley, who had no idea he was now talking to a different computer, replied, "Got it tks, but things have changed, Sean and I will get the board members for you rather then just give you the names. Since I haven't heard his vacation canceled can you tell me if the president is still going through with his trip?"

Holly ignored the question concentrating on his statement to deliver the board members. "What do you mean deliver them? We need the names so that we can set up surveillance and catch them with evidence of a crime. The President has authorized a pardon for both of you the instant you turn over the names. I thought that's what you were looking for."

Holly's non-answer confirmed to Charley that the trip was still on. "You can't let the President go on that trip. Please tell him to cancel. Once he does it will upset the organizations plans and we will be able to capture the leaders for you and turn them over. Just get the president to cancel!!!!"

"Give me the names and let us handle this."

Charley swore loudly and logged off the computer. "That stupid bastard is going on his trip, can you believe that?"

"What do you mean Lad?" Sean asked, "Did she tell you that?"

"No but she wouldn't answer any questions about it and kept asking for the names of the men so they could put them under surveillance. They're going to kill him and there's nothing we can do. We might as well leave Sean. It's over."

"Not so fast lad, not so fast." Sean said with a half smile on his face. "Did she say they wanted to put the men under surveillance, exactly like that?"

"Yes."

"I think the president is playing the game too. The only way to force their hand is if they think he is dead. So if he allows them to think he is dead and they are being watched them he will have the evidence against them. It would also reveal why they want him dead so badly."

"So what do we do? Do we give them the names?"

"No I don't think so lad. If they screw it up and the board members catch on they are being watched they will disappear most likely coming back here. If the president does set up a fake assassination then when it is revealed that he is alive they will still think they are still safe and will come back here at some point for a meeting. Either way they come back here and we catch them and have a chat with them."

"Okay Sean what ever you want, old man."

"Sir we still don't have the names," Adam said over the secure line to the Presidents Helicopter.

"Don't worry about it Adam. I'm going to do a little relaxing and have some fun. You do the same and make sure you treat that young lady to dinner, use my dining room and have the meatloaf," the president said, not wanting to discuss it even over a secure channel. After all they were unsure of all the agents with him in the helicopter and there was no reason to risk letting the cat out of the bag at this point.

He disconnected to leave his chief of staff stewing with worry 100 miles behind him and looked out the window at the blue water below him. They were twenty minutes out from the Wasp flying in formation with two huge pavelow choppers, also with secret service aboard, as escorts. There was also a flight of navy fighters off one of the Nimitz class carriers orbiting 20,000 feet above keeping an eye on the president as well. The navy kept a close eye on it's commander in chief when he traveled with them.

As the chopper neared the Wasp the secret service agents onboard radioed the Van to let them know how far out they were and verify that it was safe to land. John himself replied that all was good using the correct day codes. A few minutes later the sound of the aircraft approaching could be heard. John and his half his team left the van looking exactly like secret service agents should and formed a circle in the vicinity of where the President would land. Farther out from John and his team were Marines from the Wasp's security detachment and everyone was looking away from where the helicopter would touchdown.

Once down the pilot kept the engines running at full speed using the collective to hold the chopper on the deck, in case they had to make an emergency take off. The two pavelows kept pace with the wasp just aft of the flight deck covering the Presidents bird. The lead agent opened the door and stepped out, taking a look around making sure all was well before speaking into his wrist mic. Two more agents stepped out then came the president himself followed by the rest of the team. The Captain and the Admiral were standing at attention by the Island waiting for the President who was hustled clear of the rotors by his security detail. The Marine guards had all been given direct orders from the Admiral that no matter what happened they were to stand fast and do absolutely nothing at all.

As the president and his team cleared the down wash area John and his men moved with them until every one of the president's agents was covered by one of John's team. The attack had been carefully choreographed so that all the agents were taken at exactly the same time. The signal to move was the admiral saluting the president. As soon as the admirals hand touched his hat brim John and his men moved as one, each drawing a tranquilizer gun from behind his waistband and shooting the agent nearest him. It was a testament to the training of the agents that even though hit they all reacted instantly to cover the president and begin running him back to the helicopter to get him airborne again headed to safety. Two of the agents drew weapons and tried to shoot but they were jumped by the man covering them and pulled to the deck. The drug used was the same as used on the other agents and with in seconds every agent was down and losing consciousness. The president was surrounded by John's men and once again they headed back to the island and then into the admirals day cabin.

John and two of his men took up the direct security of the president while the rest of the team with the help of the captain and the marine security detail moved the secret service agents to the brig to join the men already there. The captain, using a radio ordered the pilot of marine one to power down the engines and secure the aircraft. Unsure of what else to do and unable to radio a mayday due to jamming from the Wasp the pilot complied. The captain also ordered the pavelows to land and they being from the Wasp followed orders. The agents aboard new something was wrong but were powerless to do anything about it. Their radios were being jammed and they had been told to drop their weapons and exit the aircraft with hands on their heads. With no other option available to them they complied, also being taken to the brig and secured.

A few minutes later the captain arrived in the admirals day cabin. "Everything is secure sir," he told the president.

"How many injuries?" It was a measure of his leadership that even though he himself had ordered the attack, he was still concerned with the men getting hurt.

"None at all sir. And no radio messages were sent either sir. The pilots of Marine one have been assigned a cabin with the other flight crews and your aircraft has been tied up next to the security van and your boat, according to SOP. No one will know anything has happened until you say so sir."

From his tone it was clear that the captain still did not like what was going on but like the career sailor he was he followed orders.

"John how long before you are ready to go?"

"We're ready now sir. The equipment was installed last night. We have also checked over the ships personal records and there are several men that, from a distance, could be mistaken for you. The media pool is all onboard other ships and even with telephoto lenses they won't be able to get a good look at whoever boards your sailboat."

"Okay according to my press release I will have lunch with the Admiral and Captain and then go sailing. Is that timetable still in place?"

"Yes sir it is."

"That's great then what's for lunch?"

The admiral knowing the presidents love of low-key fare had ordered the cook to whip up a meatloaf for lunch that day. The president and everyone else would be having it for lunch simply because the president did not like it when the cooks went to, what he considered extra trouble, to make something just for him. "Your lucky day sir, cookie has meatloaf on the menu."

"Admiral why do I think that you ordered him to put it on the menu?" the president asked with a grin. "I hope the men like it as much as I do."

"To be honest sir we serve meatloaf once a month on the WASP. It does seem to be a dish the men like," the captain told him truthfully.

"With your permission sir I'll go and get everything ready," John said.

"Go ahead John I'll be down right after we eat."

"Thank you sir, two of my men and several marines will be right outside the door and will escort you to the flight deck when you are ready."

John headed to the flight deck and the Presidents boat. The WASP was ordered to heave to and the sailboat was lowered into the water. During this time the screening escorts were circling the Wasp lashing the water with sonar and scouring the skies with radar to make sure no one got close to the task force with out being noticed. Any ships or planes detected with in 150 miles were quickly looked over by one of the Wasps helos or Harriers to determine if they were a potential threat. There was a security exclusion zone that extended thirty miles around the ship and anyone coming close to that zone would be warned off, if ignored they would be fired upon. The security of the ship and her VIP guest was paramount.

John and his team had the boat in the water and ready to go when the President stepped out of the island onto the flight deck. He strode to the secret service van where John was waiting with the door held open for him. Once inside the door was closed and the President headed to the bedroom at the back of the van. Standing rigidly at attention was one of the Wasp's sailors who bore a remarkable resemblance to the president. Part of the similarity was due to makeup and a wig but still it the man could have been a brother.

"I'd like to thank you sailor, it's a brave thing you are doing," the president said quietly. The man simply saluted, and the president returned it then held his hand out grasped the sailor's hand and shook it warmly.

John then handed the sailor a hat and escorted him outside and down a gangplank to the waiting sailboat. "You remember what to do?"

"Yes sir I do. Count on me I'll get the job done right for you sir."

"Just stick to the plan, I don't want you getting hurt."

With that John cast of the lines and gave the boat a gentle nudge to move it away from the carrier. The man on board started the engine and pulled the tiller over putting distance between the huge ship and the small boat. John hopped into one of the wasps small patrol boats with four other men from his team and two sailors and began following the boat at a distance. Once the sailboat was 100 yards away the WASP put her engines to ahead slow and turned the opposite way from the small boat opening up the distance further for safety's sake.

The press corp were all on the escort ships and were never allowed with in five miles. The only boats allowed closer then that were the secret service chase boats and these were limited to two all staffed with agents and sailors from the wasp. The press had telephoto lenses and all were directed at the president's boat, taking picture after picture. The escorts had all been ordered to steam at twenty-five knots in a zig zag pattern to keep the press from getting a good look at the 'president'. This idea had come from the admiral and John heartily approved of it.

There was a submarine attached to the task force and at this time it was one mile to the east lying drifting at 200 feet of depth with a floating radio antenna deployed. In this way it could listen with its powerful passive sonar and talk to John. They were at the stage of the deception that most worried him. The sailor now had to quickly set up a dummy at the tiller, slip on his wet suit and scuba gear, set the remote control autopilot and then slide over the side with out getting caught. He would dive to ten feet and wait for the second chase boat to drive over him. Under the boat they had rigged a sling for him to grab onto and then he would be pulled into the boat and hidden under a tarp. It took the sailor eighteen minutes to set everything up and get into the water. John had been watching for it and had only barely seen the man go over the side. Unless the press was very lucky there was no way they could have seen it. And there, sitting in the stern of the boat steering for all to see was the President of the United States, or so it appeared.

Suddenly two Harriers went screaming overhead heading southwest. John radioed the Wasp and was informed that they were checking a contact that had appeared 100 miles away. Several minutes later the Harriers radio the WASP to inform them that the contact was a twin-engine private plane and this information was relayed to John. This could be what they were waiting for. The plan that that they had discovered originally called for the mine to be activated by another boat however a small plane would work equally well. He radioed the WASP and told them to have the fighters tail the plane from a distance to see where it went. The two harriers had already turned to return to the wasp when they received their instructions, rather then turn around and be seen by the plan they climbed to 30,000 feet and began flying in a slow race track pattern, following the plane on infrared by the heat from the engines. Now it was all up to the organization.

The pilot was flying the apache at 8,000 feet on the heading his passenger had given him. The charter had been set up a week ago and was to fly from Miami to Puerto Rico. Once they were in the air the passenger had asked the pilot to fly near the island of Viqeunes. He had explained that there was a no fly zone around the island so he could only get with in thirty miles of it. The passenger had informed him that the President was supposed to be vacationing there and he just wanted to get a picture of his sailboat. He showed a camera with a large telephoto lens on it to prove his point. The pilot warned him that there could be an extra charge due to the extra time in the air. The passenger agreed with out hesitation and the pilot shrugged and set the waypoints into his GPS. From 8,000 feet the view should be just fine and from the look of the lens on the camera the thirty-mile no fly zone wouldn't be a problem.

The passenger spent the first twenty minutes of the flight fiddling with the camera and the lenses. To the pilot it looked like any other photographer, but what was actually happening was that he was setting up the transmitter to signal the mine and activate it if he saw the president's sailboat anywhere in the water.

They were a couple hours into the flight when two fighters blew by less then 100 yards off the left side of the plane. The pilot was slightly startled but the passenger while also startled seemed relieved by the fly by. The lead Harrier radioed the apache informing them of the restricted airspace they were approaching and asking them their intentions. The pilot responded explaining they were heading to Puerto Rico but were planning on taking some photos of the islands around the area. The fighters again informed them of the no fly zone and that it would be vigorously enforcing the limit and the pilot would face a huge fine for violating it. The pilot thanked the fighters for the information and watched them fly by one more time then turn to the northeast. They did not see the planes return and had no idea that they were being followed, which would not have changed the passenger's immediate plans.

It took another forty minutes to reach the edge of the no fly zone and by this time the two men were able to see the navy ships to the north of the island, however they were to far away to see anything as small as a sailboat. The pilot began a slow turn to the left to allow the passenger a chance to take his pictures which might show the sailboat through the telephoto lens. Just as he started the turn two more fighters showed up again warning them of the no fly zone. As he began the turn the fighters informed him of the headings open to him and thanked the small plane for his immediate cooperation in turning away.

The passenger was indeed able to make out the president's sailboat through the big lens and began snapping away with his camera. The first click of the shutter sent a signal to the mine to activate it, while the second activated the homing device, the rest just burned up film taking shots of the sailboat and the carrier. He shot a whole role of thirty-six frames of the sailboat the chase boats and the task force. As he shot his last frame a small red light in the lower left of the viewfinder popped on. This was the indicator he was hopping to see telling him that the mine and boat had received the wake up signal and turned on. With a smile on his face he removed the telephoto lens and put it in his camera bag also putting away the camera as well. He settled in for the rest of the flight knowing that by the time he was eating supper the terrible news of the US president's death would be broadcast to the rest of the world.

John got on the radio to make sure that the small plane was being followed and was told it was. If the organization was really trying to kill the president with a mine that had to be activated by remote then the attempt would happen soon. The small plane was the only non-military craft that even come close.

The president had been smuggled back to the admiral's day cabin where he sat starring out the window watching his sailboat. He picked up the satellite phone and dialed his Chief of Staff who answered on the first ring.

"Please tell me you have the names Adam."

"No sir we don't."

"Did they make contact with them?"

"Yes they did sir but an interesting thing happened, rather then give up the names they are asking us to cancel the plan and they will hand over the men. How they will do this was not mentioned."

"Really? They will hand them over? I'll call you back." The president hung up and picked up the phone on the admirals desk. It rang on the bridge where both the captain and admiral presently were.

"Yes sir?" The Admiral said knowing that it could be only one person calling on the line that had rung.

"Call it off Admiral. Have them bring my boat back and ready my helicopter," the president ordered.

"Yes sir," the admiral answered and hung up. He relayed the orders to the captain, who in turn had his yeoman radio the chase boat and instruct them to return to the WASP.

John was surprised by his orders however they had come through the proper channel so they were valid. He motioned to the man controlling the president's boat via remote control to turn it around and move it back to the WASP. He spoke quietly to the helmsman telling the man to move along side the boat so that he could board it, then fall back again. He had planned for the eventuality that nothing happened and was going to put the dummy below decks as if he wasn't feeling good then steer the boat him self back to the WASP.

The helmsman pushed the throttle ahead just as the radio crackled alive. It was the submarine warning of a transient coming from the vicinity of the sea floor near the sailboat. John immediately knew what that meant, they were too late. The mine was active and was going after the sailboat. The radio crackled again to report a torpedo in the water. The helmsman jammed the throttle to the stops and the boat leapt ahead rapidly closing on the sailboat. The race was over before it really began. The torpedo was coming at the sailboat from below at a speed of seventy knots while the chase boat was coming from behind at a speed of only forty knots. The torpedo won the race and slammed into the stern of the boat right under the engine. The torpedo, designed to cripple warships, obliterated the wooden boat throwing small pieces of wood high into the air. The shock wave nearly swamped the chase boat throwing everyone on it to the floor. The helmsman broke his arm and everyone else ended up with cuts and bruises of varying degrees.

John had one of his team tend to the helmsman while he took over the helm and began circling through the pool of wreckage. The radioman followed standard procedure and radioed a mayday even though everyone on all the navy ships watching had seen the explosion. The press pool was going wild with frenzy taking pictures and asking every sailor in sight what had just happened. Those with satellite phones were own them calling their news offices to report the explosion. It was nearly ten minutes before the captain of the destroyer found out that the news people were filing reports via sat phone and once he did he immediately had them confiscated. He told all the reporters that all news stories were to be filed through the public relations officer on board the WASP. The Damage however was done, exactly as John had thought it would be. The media was already reporting the explosion and asking the Pentagon and White House for comments. The standard answer was no comment so with nothing to go on CNN was the first to air the unsubstantiated report of and explosion on the president's sailboat. A total of seventeen minutes had passed since the torpedo had blown up the boat.

The WASP had launched four helos and six rescue boats to search the area. Due to the violence of the explosion it was being called a search and recover effort rather then search and rescue. The Admiral was on the radio to both the Pentagon and the White House every two minutes explaining that nothing was known yet.

The president had the admiral radio John and tell him to return to the Wasp. Once he was back on board a marine guard escorted him to the Admirals cabin and waited outside the door while he went in. Once the door was closed the door to the admirals private quarters opened and the president stepped out.

"Is everyone okay John?"

"One sailor had a broken arm and some cuts and bruises but nothing serious sir."

"Thanks John I appreciate all your efforts but I think it might have been a waste. We never got the names we needed. Admiral, tell the Pentagon and White House I'm fine. I'm sure they are screaming for information by now."

"Sir wait," John said. "Let's keep it up a little longer just to see what plays out. I'll call Miss McClare and see what's going on, but please let's give it a bit longer."

"What did you have in mind?" the admiral asked.

"Mr President I think you should take one of the pavelows to Camp David on the quiet. We can have it refueled in the air and no one has to know. Stay out of Washington for now. Give us another six hours just to see if anything breaks. If not, we announce that you are fine and the reason for the delay was doctors orders."

"Okay I'll give you six hours but why do you want me to use one of the pavelows? My helicopter is still here."

The Admiral answered that question. "Yes sir and until you are reported as either missing or alive your helo needs to be seen to stay right where it is. The second it lifts off the news media will be all over that. We have already had requests to allow over flights from the major networks. I've refused everything but why take a chance. We put you on a pavelow and send you that way. We don't even tell your flight crew or the one on the pavelow. I figure we put you in a flight suit with a helmet and no one will know."

The president nodded. "Okay let's do it that way. John you and your team will provide me with security."

"One man will need to stay on board to keep radio contact with the secret service office sir." John reminded him.

"Yes that's right. Can't we let the agents out of the brig now?"

"No sir not until we let the world know about you. The second they are free they will radio their superiors and with in minutes of that the organization will know something fishy is going on."

The president nodded his understanding and the admiral issued the orders to get things moving. A pavelow was moved into position on the flight deck and orders were cut to give it a mid-air refueling so that it could fly all the way to Camp David with out landing anywhere. The flight plan was filed but the destination was listed as Pax River, the navel test flight area. The pilot would get his new orders after the refueling. This would keep the final destination secret until the last possible moment. John did however contact Adam to let him in on what was going on.

The president, John and the team minus one, all dressed in flight suits and helmets that covered their faces, made their way to the flight deck as soon as the helo was ready. Everyone including the president was carrying a shoulder slung weapon and web gear making it look as if it was a training exercise. They boarded the helo and John personally strapped in the president as this aircraft was considerably different inside then the one he was used to flying on. There was no soundproofing of any kind and the seats were all fold down canvas bolted to the walls and floors. The helmets were necessary just to keep from going deaf.

They were in the air less then a minute after strapping in and the ride was a bumpy one as they kept the bird to under 1,500 feet to get away from the fleet without drawing too much attention. Once they are twenty miles away they slowly began climbing and the ride smoothed out. It would take most of the six hours the president had given to get to Camp David and the ride would be boring with nothing to do. They couldn't even plug into the intercom as the second they did the flight crew would know who was on board. The president desperately wanted to talk to Adam for an update, but knew trying to use his sat phone in the noisy chopper would be futile so he sat back and tried to sleep. After thirty minutes he gave up trying to get comfortable and looked around amazed to find most of the men around him sleeping like they were in a five-star hotel. He wondered how they did it.

Charley had the radio playing an all news station listing to the weather reports that cycled through every thirty minutes. The announcer cut into a commercial suddenly with a live report of the explosion on the President's yacht. At this time there was no information other then the reported explosion and no comment was coming from the White House or Pentagon.

"Sean, news is reporting an explosion on the president's boat. I think they got him. We should get out of here." Charley got up to open the boathouse doors but Sean stopped him.

"What did the news report say?"

"Not much other then there was an explosion and no one is commenting on it. But we both know what happened, everyone ignored us and now the man is dead."

"Wait a sec lad. Try getting in touch with the young lady and see if they are still hot for the names. If they are then he's alive and a trick is being played on someone." The smile on Sean's face showed what he thought was going on.

"You really think he's still alive?" Charley asked.

"Lad I think any politician that had the balls to put his own life on the line wouldn't do so unless he had a plan to save his own skin."

Charley booted up the computer and logged onto the internet. Almost instantly there was an inquiry from the NSA via email asking again for the names. He ignored that and started the message program and tried to contact Holly.

Adam was in the basement talking with Holly when his private secure sat phone rang. He answered and listened quietly not saying anything but a small smile played across his face. He hung and was still chatting with Holly when the news of the explosion broke. Instantly there was pandemonium in the office. The watch officer contacted the secret service asking for information from the president's detail, while his second in command contacted the WASP directly looking for information. In both cases the information was sketchy and the only thing known at this time was that the president's yacht had blown up and a search was underway. Instantly everyone was looking tot he Chief of Staff for direction. Adam called the secret service and told them to secure the vice-president and return him to the White House. He then contacted the Pentagon and told them to update the White House on the search every five minutes until the president was safe.

With that done he quietly moved over to Holly. "Did we get the names we were looking for yet?"

"No we didn't," was the flat reply. Holly had a look of abject failure on her face while Adam didn't seem at all upset.

"Don't worry all is not lost yet," Adam told her cryptically.

Just as she was about to question him on this her phone rang. "Holly McClare," she said as she picked it up.

"Miss McClare it's Doris. Your chat program just came on and they are asking for you. What do I tell them?"

Holly thought quickly, she needed to speak with them but she wasn't at her secure computer. "Doris, tell them I'm at the White House and to contact you back in five minutes. I'll have something set up then."

Doris relayed the message and Holly logged onto the internet then logged into a free proxy server. She knew this wouldn't hide her completely but it would make a trace harder. She quickly navigated her way to a chat room and created an identity and set up a room that required a password to log into. She then called Doris back and gave her the information needed to let someone joining her chat room and waited for the information to be relayed.

It took four more minutes before she was joined. "Hello how have you been?" she asked cautiously.

"I'm fine, how are you and your boss?"

"Everyone here is fine. Did you still have the names of your friends that you wanted us to contact?"

Charley ignored the question "Are you sure everyone is fine? I heard a rumor that your boss wasn't feeling well."

"You know how rumors are, once started they are hard to stop. Everyone here is fine. We really would like to look up your friends though."

"Brb," flashed on the screen, internet shorthand for be right back.

Charley looked up from the computer at his old friend. "She says everyone is fine. They still want the names."

Sean smiled. "I thought so. Well lad we can give them the names or keep them secret a while longer. Once they announce the President is fine then the board members will be beside themselves and want to meet. That means they will come back here and we can catch them ourselves. It's up to you."

Charley nodded and turned back to the screen. "We'll round them up and call you when we are all together," he typed in. "I have to run, you take care." And with that he logged out of the chat room.

"Damn, he logged off already," Holly said. "And with out giving me any names. He said that he would call us later when they are all together. I think he intends to capture them himself."

"You could be right, but since there is nothing we can do, speculating is a waste of time. Sit tight and have your team keep an eye out for anything out of the ordinary."

With that Adam went to talk to one of the military advisors for a news updates as to what was happening on the Wasp. He wasn't worried about the president, as he hadn't heard from John or the admiral, which was the pre-arranged signal for a problem. He did want to know where they were but he couldn't call as the channels were all being monitored. He would have to wait like everyone else.

Carter picked up the phone knowing it could be only one person after what he had heard on the news report. "Yes sir?"

"It would seem as if our plans have finally come to fruition."

"Yes sir I believe so. I haven't heard from our agent in place so it is safe to assume that the President is dead. I am going to activate our network and start the process."

"Let's wait on that for a few more hours. I want it confirmed by the White House that the President is dead. Once you hear that then activate the networks. In the meantime please call your peers and ask them to be ready to gather in town on short notice. Until then everyone is to keep working at their respective desks."

"Yes sir. I will let the others know."

Carter called his fellow board members and informed them of what the immediate plan was. They also settled on a course of action for the organization and agreed that each would contact their respective junior and issue the necessary orders. Carter called his junior and instructed him to head back to the factory and be ready to activate the networks, then hung up the phone and went back to work. The smile on his face would not go away. More then half a century of planning was about to end with success after so many failures. It was enough to make a man sing.

The Admiral was being hounded for answers. It had been thirty minutes since the explosion and the White House and pentagon wanted to know where the president was and his condition. There were fighters now flying top cover and the Chairman of the Joint Chiefs was on the line waiting for an update. The Navy and coast guard had ordered every ship in the area to assist in the search and were bringing in more assets to help out. A Navy three star was being sent down to take command of the search and rescue operation along with a team from the FBI to begin an investigation as to what happened. The admiral was hoping that he could hold on a little longer. The only ace he had was that he was following orders directly from the president.

He checked his watch for the fifth time in the last thirty seconds; he only had to bluff for another five hours and twenty-eight minutes. Then the President would announce he was safe at Camp David. It would be very long day.

For the next four hours very little happened. The president was flying, Holly and Adam were desperately hoping that they would be told who the board members were so they could catch them, Charley, Sean, and the rest of the world were waiting for news of the president. The only people really busy were the military men and women involved in the search which none of them knew was useless.

Once refueled the pilot was told by John to head for Camp David. The pilot, used to such changes of flight plan simply nodded and adjusted his heading to the new destination. The co-pilot recalculated the flight time and fuel consumption and nodded to the pilot that there was no problem with the new destination. John pulled out a pad and pencil and wrote a note to the President letting him know that the pilot had been given the new destination and the ETA on arrival. It would be another hour until he was on the ground.

Charley had discovered that in the middle of the day he could catch fish right in the boathouse. The fish were attracted by the shade offered and would drift in during the bright part of the day. It was easy for him to bait a hook, drop in a line and pull out two or three fish. He never tried for more then that so as not to spook the fish and ruin the easy meals this offered.

He also had the radio playing on the news station and the dominating story was the explosion of the Presidents boat. There had been nothing new to add to it since the original story had aired; yet they somehow managed to keep talking about it. One expert after another was called and questioned to get their take on what was going to happen. There were now discussing the eventually that would occur if the president was indeed dead. The vice president had been seen at the White House and it was assumed that he was now in the situation room waiting to be sworn in, although this could not be confirmed.

Sean became annoyed with the incessant guessing and speculation and went for a walk around to make sure no one was around. As normal he had an SMG with him but he now also carried a tranq gun and darts. He could feel that the board members would show up, it was a matter of when, not if, to him.

The president stepped down from the chopper and headed directly to his cabin. The Marines on duty stopped him, not knowing who he was, but having standing orders that no one went into the president's personal cabin with out prior approval. He pulled off his helmet and smiled at the marine who immediately came to attention. One reached for his radio to inform the guard that the president was on site, when John stopped him with a curt command. The rest of John's team fanned out and covered the area with one member going to the pilot and copilot to order them to shut down the engines and get out of the aircraft. Once the flight crew and marines were all assembled the president himself addressed them all and explained that until he directly ordered it his presence was to be kept a complete secret. The flight crew would be housed in a guest cabin and were free to move around but could not leave the area. The marines on duty would remain on duty to augment John and his team. No one was allowed in or out until the president authorized it. He thanked the men and then went inside.

The Marines and the rest of John's team gathered together briefly to set up a chain of command with John at the top and the rest to worked out among the marines and went into the presidents cabin. They were all military and all marines so it was settled very quickly by seniority and then every one split into pairs and a duty list was draw up. Until further notice they were to be eight hours on, eight hours off around the clock. John took care of notifying the camp commander once he was inside the president's cabin and referred him to Adam for confirmation of the orders. The camp commander knew the name of the Chief of Staff and so accepted the orders at face value. He would simply log the order and follow it until it was countermanded by a higher authority.

The sudden ringing in his pocket startled and relieved him. He knew it could be only one person. He answered the phone to hear the voice of the president. "Hello?"

As John was issuing was talking to the camp commander the president called Adam on his sat phone. "Hello Adam, how are things back the house?" came the casual greeting.

"Well to be honest things are a little hectic right now," Adam replied with out addressing his boss. "How can I help?"

"Well you can give me some good news and tell me that we got the names we needed."

"Sorry, but that hasn't happened yet. We have a call out for that info but at the last minute they have offered to bring them in themselves. I'm not sure how interested you are in that so I haven't bothered with a reply yet?" Adam said trying to be a vague as possible in the crowded situation room.

"Really? Did they elaborate on how they were going to do that?"

"Well they first wanted some travel plans canceled, after that they didn't explain but they did say they could definitely deliver. Our lady friend has talked with them since the news broke and they still seem to think they can deliver. To be honest I think if they say they can then they can."

"What do they need me to do?"

"I'm not completely sure but if I were to guess I think that they need a public failure without a lot of information."

The president thought for a second. "At the top of the hour I want the press secretary to announce that I am safe at Camp David. No other comment is to be made."

"Okay, will do." With that Adam headed up to the pressroom to pass on his bosses' orders.

The President then had John contact the Admiral on the Wasp and give him a heads up as to what was happening and when the official announcement was going to be. When reassured the admiral was to simply state he was following presidential orders and direct all further questions to the Oval Office. John made it very clear that the admiral would have full Presidential protection for his part in the slight of hand. It was very relieved voice on the other end of the phone that agreed when John was done. It would also be a very close thing as a three-star admiral was forty minutes out and would be taking over command of the task force on arrival. The admiral thanked John and hung up satisfied that it would all be over in a little while.

Sean came back into the boathouse just as the radio was going live to the White House for a special announcement. The press secretary announced that the president was at Camp David, he was fine, in good health and that a full briefing would be held at a later date. The press pool instantly began yelling, asking for details. The press secretary spoke over the room stating again that there was no further information at this time, another statement would be issued later. The radio announcer came back on then and repeated everything that had just been said. Another so called expert joined the announcer and they began discussing the news release going over the various implications of the news release and speculating like mad as to what may or may not have happened.

"Crafty bastard the president. I would bet that if he had those names we would still be wondering if he was alive or dead." Sean said with a chuckle.

"So do you think the board members will be back soon," Charley asked.

"I would be money on it lad. Contact the NSA lady and see if you can get a phone number to call her direct. Once the board members show we will have a very short window to capture them and deliver them. I want this exchange to go much smoother then the last time so let's go over the maps and see what we can find for a meeting place."

The two poured over the maps for the next hour until they found a piece of coastline that fit their purpose. Then they perfected their plans and prepped everything to be ready at a seconds notice. Sean had placed one of the tranq guns outside, just inside the tree line on the other side of the cabin, and one in the boathouse, as well, both men always carried darts at all times. With no other preparations to make the two settled down to wait, keeping to the routine that they had fallen into since their arrival.

Carter called his fellow board members as soon as he heard the news. He felt that they needed to meet to plan what to do next, there was a lot of information that needed to be gathered. He suggested the usual place and that the juniors be there was well to answer for the failure. His peers agreed; the juniors were contacted to notify them when and where to be and that extra security was to be arranged as a precaution.

The juniors sent out two security teams to scan the area and then arrived themselves an hour before the board members were set to show up.

Charley was watching out the window when the first security team showed up. Sean had just left to take one of his walks around and was on the other side of the property at the time. During the planning they had both been worried about the best way to capture the board members. Sean wanted one of them outside and one in the boathouse so as to cover all sides of the cabin. Charley didn't want to split themselves up so that they could cover each other. They knew they were going to be outnumbered they just didn't know how badly.

They had finally agreed that they would deal with it however it happened, if Sean was out scouting they would attack separately, if he was in the boathouse they would attack together.

Hearing the car arrive, Sean moved to where he had left the tranq gun and loaded it. He then checked over his SMG and mentally marked off the steps to where he had stashed extra ammo and clips. In the boathouse Charley was doing the same thing. Both were as ready as they could be and each hoped that the security teams did not bother to open the boathouse but just check the lock on the door. Sean had made sure that the lock was in place and looked undisturbed so that no one would feel that they had to go inside to check things over.

A Mini van pulled up beside the cabin and five men stepped out, all heavily armed. They split up and began checking over the area looking at the locked doors of the cabin and boathouse, but no one entered either. Satisfied that the buildings were secure they began looking over the grounds.

In the boathouse Charley was lying directly under the window in such a position that he was impossible to see. Outside Sean slid backwards into the trees so he wouldn't be seen. They communicated via their portable radios, letting each other know they were okay. A few minutes after the first van arrived a second one showed up and five more men got out, again heavily armed. The second team paired off with the first team and now there were five two man teams patrolling around the cabin. Twenty minutes later a third vehicle arrived and three men got out and walked around the cabin talking with each of the patrolling teams. Once satisfied that everything was fine they went back to the front of the cabin and waited.

It took another hour for the first board member showed up and with in ten minutes the other two had arrived. The first man to arrive walked to the back of the cabin and started the generator to get power going in the cabin, then unlocked the door and went inside. The juniors waited until all the board members arrived before they also went inside, the security men took up stations at the four corners of the cabin with one team patrolling around the perimeter.

The boathouse was covered on the outside with cedar shingles. One of the preparations Charley had made after the decision to try and capture the board members was to cut a hole on the wall of the boathouse that faced the cabin. They had removed one of the shingles very carefully so as not to break it then cut a hole through the rest of the wall and tacked the shingle back in place. The hole was just big enough to shoot through with his rifle and low on the wall to allow him to shoot from the prone position. All he had to do was poke the barrel of the rifle into the hole and knock the shingle off and he was clear to shoot. His vantage point allowed him to take out the two teams at the back corners of the cabin and, if timed right, the roving team as well. Since Sean was outside he would take out the two teams at the front and would also be ready to take out the roving team if Charley couldn't.

Sean radioed Charley and told him he was in position. The roving team was on his side so he would take them out at the same time he took out the two teams at the front of the cabin. Charley moved into position with his rifle and knocked the shingle out with the barrel. His SMG and tranq gun were lying next to him but for now he was more comfortable with the rifle. He had five shots and four targets. The two had decided that they would have to take out the guards as they didn't have enough darts to get everyone and there was no way they could get close enough to shoot them with a tranq gun.

Charley sighted in on the first guard and settled into a breathing pattern locking the gun to his shoulder. When the two radio clicks sounded in his ear he was ready to shoot and his brain sent the message to his finger with out any thought at all. The rifle went off almost as a surprise and the first guard was down, a 165-grain bullet having torn into his right shoulder at the spot where it met his arm, producing massive trauma and nearly severing his arm. Charley threw the bolt and sighted on the second man who was looking for where the shot had come from. He still had no idea when he too was thrown to the ground with a bullet tearing through his shoulder at the same spot. Charley had the third guard down before his location was spotted. The fourth guard started shooting at the boathouse as the same time he tried moving to cover, but all his rounds were slamming into the wall above Charley's head. Charley lead the guard a little and then squeezed off another shot taking down the last man on his side with a shot in the throat.

He jumped to his feet grabbing up his SMG and the tranq gun then headed to the door. He was suddenly aware of the sound of gunfire as he kicked open the flimsy door and rolled outside moving quickly away from the structure. Before heading around the cabin to help Sean he emptied a clip into the generator and had the satisfaction of seeing it burst into flames.

On the other side of the clearing just inside the trees, Sean clicked the mic twice then sighted down the barrel of the Thompson at the roving patrol. As soon as he heard the first shot he aimed low and squeezed the trigger sending a stream of lead into the legs of the guards mowing them down. He had warned Charley that the men would most likely be wearing vests so to shoot at an unprotected part of their body. He was taking out their legs, which was why he had chosen the big .45 Thompson slug for the job. The shock of the bullet hit would help to immobilize the wounded men. Once they were down he changed clips and fired on the team at the corner nearest him. In his case the guards quickly located where the fire was coming from and they started shooting back. He had three men down and one wounded before he was forced to duck under cover from bullets coming his way. He again changed clips and rolled to a new location.

Popping up he opened up on the far team emptying half the clip before again ducking under cover and moving to yet another location. Popping up again he emptied the rest of the clip and was about to duck behind the tree when he was slammed to the ground. He had been hit. He changed clips and took a second to check himself. No blood just a lot of pain and what would become yet another good-sized bruise in the morning. The bulletproof coveralls had saved his life again. Moving to another location he popped back up and was about to shoot at the first team when he saw the remaining man go down. He didn't hear anything, but a quick check showed Charley with his silenced SMG moving up the side of he cabin taking the man under fire.

Sean moved again and then opened fire on the two remaining guards. Suddenly the cabin door popped open.

The board members were deep in discussion when the sound of a rifle shot silenced the talking. It was followed by automatic fire and three more rifle shots. Everyone jumped up yelling and accusing each other of not taking proper precautions when the lights died and the sound of the generator stopped. The gun fire continued and Carter was the first to order his junior to find out what was going on. This was echoed by the other two men in the room and all three juniors drew their weapons and headed for the door.

Throwing the door open the three men raced through it heading to their car. They all carried handguns but in the car they had automatic weapons and from the sounds of the firefight they wanted to be as heavily armed as possible.

Both Charley and Sean saw them at the same time and each emptied a clip at them then reloaded and concentrated on the remaining guards. The training of the guards was their downfall. Trained to never abandon a post they were left in the open with no where to go and were cut down by the fire from two SMGs. Reloading again Sean moved from the tree line toward the cabin while Charley tossed two and three round bursts towards the cars. They had no idea if the three men that had run from the cabin were still in the fight or not. Until they new for sure they would act as if they were still a threat.

Once joined up they covered each other and moved to the cars making sure to watch the cabin door as well. They sprinted the distance to the first vehicle then Sean dropped to the earth and peered under it. He saw the three men all lying on the ground not moving and blood staining the dirt next to them. Moving around the car he confirmed the three were out of the fight then motioned to Charley, slung his SMG, drew his tranq gun, moving to the cabin next to the open door. Charley rolled onto the ground in front of the door and holding his weapon high sprayed bullets into the ceiling of the cabin.

Sean used the distraction to roll through the door and search for targets. As soon as he sighted a person he fired and with in seconds he had all three board members darted and losing consciousness fast. Even though shot with the fast acting drug, at least one of them managed to get off a few shots at Sean but none hit him. Checking the pulse of the three men Sean made sure they were alive but asleep then joined Charley back outside to check on the guards. Of the thirteen wounded men two had died the rest were alive but in bad shape. Normally Sean would have seen to their wounds immediately however these were men that had tried to kill and they included the new stooges, all of whom were among the living.

Even Charley didn't protest Sean's decision to not help but simply gathered up the guns and checked everyone over for other weapons. Once they were sure there was no possible way any of the wounded could be a threat the two men went back inside the cabin. Sean used nylon zip ties to bind the hands of the board members behind their backs. Just in case any of the three were double jointed he tied their elbows together as well so they wouldn't be able to slip their hands to the front.

Once their arms were secured they carried the men one at a time to the boathouse to load them onto the boat. What they did not know and could not have known was that Carter had tripped an emergency beacon once the shooting had started. Even as they were getting ready to leave the organization had two choppers full of armed men on the way to the cabin. Not only were the men armed, but so were the helicopters.

As Sean and Charley were carrying the last and heaviest of the men to the boathouse the two choppers suddenly roared into view and opened fire on them spraying the ground next to them with bullets but being careful not to actually hit them or the man they carried. Dropping their burden the two dove the opposite way, Charley toward the boathouse and Sean toward the Cabin.

As one chopper kept up a stream of bullets driving Sean away from the fallen board member and toward the cabin, the other landed and dropped off the organization troops. Once safe inside the doorway of the boathouse Charley emptied his clip at the chopper offloading the men and had the satisfaction of seeing smoke spill out of the back end of the bird and the sound of the engine start to die down. The pilot and co-pilot jumped clear, joining the troops they had just offloaded. The organization men started laying down fire to both the cabin and boathouse. Sean radioed Charley and told him to start the boat and leave he would try for the woods and meet along the riverbank. Charley was about to argue when he saw a grenade go off next to Sean throwing him into the air and slamming him into the earth. His partner and friend didn't move.

Charley screamed and grabbed up his rifle and began picking the men off one by one. He had five down and was reloading when the volume of fire toward the boathouse became so intense that he was unable to stand near a door or window with out risking getting killed. The men had all found cover to shoot from and were using it to keep him pinned down while they leap-frogged forward. Knowing the cause was lost, Charley picked up his weapons and crawled to the boat sliding on board with out standing up.

There were two of the board members lying in the cockpit and Charley had no time to move them into the cabin. They were lying right over the engine compartment so they would act as shields he hoped, to keep the remaining helicopter from firing at him and disabling the boat. Starting the engine he rammed the throttle to the stop as soon as it caught not bothering to allow it to warm up or opening the doors to the river. The powerful boat smashed the doors off and accelerated away from the shore in a zig zag to throw off the aim of anyone shooting at him.

The shooting tapered off rapidly as the distance opened up. The men were armed with SMG's, great in combat but with not a lot of range to them. The chopper was a different story though. It wheeled in the sky and came after the boat 100-feet off the water. It briefly opened fire then stopped as the pilot saw the two unconscious men in the cockpit. Racing ahead of the boat the door opened and a gunner with a machine gun appeared in the doorway. He sent a stream of lead into the water directly in front of the speeding boat trying to make it turn back to shore.

Charley set the GPS and autopilot giving it a course to take the boat out to sea. Once set he picked up his rifle and kneeled in the cockpit wrapping his left arm in the sling to get a better grip on it. The sighting as carefully as he could while on the deck of a moving boat, he fired at the back of the chopper. He was trying to hit the engine or fuel tanks and after four shots he got lucky and clipped the hydraulic line for the rotor control assembly and the chopper immediately began losing altitude and crashed into the river. There was no explosion but the chopper began to sink rapidly because of the open door.

Charley picked up his sten gun and kept it pointed to where the chopper had crashed. A body floated up but stayed face down in the water and didn't move. Within minutes the wreckage was out of range and fast falling behind. Charley left the throttle wide open trying to put as much distance between him and the cabin as he could just in case more air support was called up.

Two hours later with land behind him out of sight and the men tied up in the cockpit beginning to stir Charley slowed the boat down setting the throttle at ten knots. He also updated the GPS setting a course to take him out past the two hundred mile limit. With that done he went into the cabin got his .22 pistol along with a few items from the galley and tool room. In the cockpit the two men were groggy but awake. Charley tied them to deck chairs at the stern then crouched in front of them not pointing the gun at either one of them directly but letting it waver in their direction.

"Gentlemen it would seem that I have managed to escape yet again, This time though my partner got killed buying time for me to do that. That means trouble for both of you because right at this point I'm very tempted to just shoot you both in the legs and then drag you behind the boat until you become shark bait. Before you people screwed up my life I was a normal guy. I wanted to find a girl, get married, and settle down. I wanted the same things that all other people my age are looking for, but thanks to you I won't have it. A year ago I couldn't have even contemplated shooting you let alone torturing you for information. That was one year and a different lifetime ago. Sean is dead and I want to know why he died and why you bastards felt that you could ruin my life and use me any way you wanted. So it will be a long night for one of you because you get to watch me work on your friend and if he tells me nothing then I get to work on you. And just so you know I got a lot of information out of you three stooges so I'll have a great idea of when you are lying. So to keep things interesting, and you clowns honest, I'll be tossing in a question to which I already know the answer every once in awhile."

With his speech out of the way Charley untied one of the men form his chair, keeping his arms bound, and shoved him down onto the deck. As the man started to struggle Charley calmly leaned over and shot him through the knee with the .22. The man screamed, curled up into a ball, and stopped moving. Charley set down the pistol picked up a small pot and began asking the man questions. Each time he failed to answer or Charley felt he lied, the pot was slammed into the shattered knee. This went on for a while until Charley, concerned about blood loss put a tourniquet on the leg, to slow down the bleeding. He also wrapped the knee in a pressure bandage. Even after this the man still had not given up all the information Charley was looking for. The names and covers of the board members had been confirmed along with some background on the organization and the plans, also information he had gotten from the stooges. But Charley still did not know how they were going to take over after the president was dead.

Knowing that this was taking to long the young man picked up the empty cartridge case and a hammer he walked over to the second board member, and without any warning, hammered it into the kneecap of the man that had been watching his friend get tortured. His scream was long and loud, with no one to hear it outside of the boat. Letting the man stew in pain Charley went back to his first victim and broke the two outside fingers on his left hand than began to work the bones back and forth grating the jagged edges against each other. Another scream rent the air and Charley began asking his questions again, totally detached from the agony of his captives. It took a total of four hours for him to get all the information out of the two men but in the end he was sure he had everything. The men were spent and would have done anything to stop the pain Charley was inflicting on them. Once finished he took two tranquilizer darts and jabbed one into each mans thigh knocking them both out.

Charley shut off the engines, rigged a sea anchor and went to the bow to drop it overboard. In a few minutes the boat was bow onto the wind and waves and had settled down into a gentle two-degree roll. Hoping it was stable enough, he set up the satellite and computer and turned everything on praying for a signal.

The organization men secured the area and collected all the brass they could find. There was nothing they could do about the bullet holes in the cabin and boathouse but they did remove the shattered and hanging doors and put them inside the boathouse so they wouldn't attract attention. The crew covered the damaged helicopter with camouflage netting that they carried with them and, at least from the air, it was partially hidden. Several of the men checked over their comrades finding most of them had already died from their wounds. The few still alive were treated by a medic and they would live if they could get to proper medical attention soon. All the vehicles were fine and drivable. They loaded the dead and wounded into the vans and placed the lone board member in the back seat of one of the cars. Sean went into another car and when everything was as clean as they could make it they all headed back to D.C. and the factory. There was an operating room there with a surgical staff on standby. Once again there was a command vacuum. The juniors were all dead and two of the three board members were gone with the remaining one unconscious. Not knowing what he had been drugged with there was nothing to do but wait until the drug wore off.

The president had Adam and Holly flown out to Camp David, as he didn't want to be seen at the White House just yet. Once there they went over everything that had happened. Before anyone knew it, it was suppertime and a navy steward discretely entered and asked what the president would like for supper and if he would be having guests. John and his team along with the on duty Marines were still the only security men near the president and so he ordered supper for everyone and told the steward to do his best to see that everyone was fed as quickly as possible so that they had a hot meal.

It was during supper that Adam's cell went off. Pulling it out of his pocket he looked at the small screen and read the text message scrolling across it. He mouth dropped open in shock at the information he read. "Sir I have the names of the men who ran the organization. You aren't going to believe this but they are, the deputy director of the FBI, James Bolton, the deputy director of the NSA Sam Watson and the head of the secret service, Jack Carter."

"WHAT?" exclaimed the president. "Are you sure?"

"Well sir according to the message Bolton and Watson are currently captives of Charles Watkins while the whereabouts of Carter are currently unknown. Miss McClare he has been trying to contact you online and has asked me to check on you and tell you that he will be online at the top of every hour until dawn then he will again be online after dark at the top of every hour. That's all the message says."

The president was stunned by the news while Holly checked her watch and saw that it would be the top of the hour in nine minutes. "Adam where can we find a computer with internet access?"

"In my study," the president said woodenly still trying to absorb the information that three men that he thought he had known well were behind the attempts on his life.

Holly and Adam went into the study and she quickly logged on to the internet. She downloaded the instant message program she needed, grateful that the connection was a fast broadband one and not dial up. With forty seconds to spare she had the program configured and was logged in waiting for Charley to come online.

Several hundred miles away and well out to sea Charley logged onto the internet and opened his message program. He was happy to see Holly online, Adam must have gotten his message to her. He sent her a smiley face and waited. She wrote back that she was with Adam and the President at Camp David and thanked him for the names he had sent; She asked him how he and Sean were doing and was stunned at the news that Sean was dead. She didn't respond for almost a minute and when she did she told Charley that she was very sorry. Not knowing what else to say she left it at that and waited for him to resume the conversation.

Charley began to choke up but fought back the feeling and concentrated on his job at hand. He began typing in the information he had learned from the two men, even admitting that he had used torture to get what he was telling them. The president eventually made his way in and asked what was happening. Rather then explain it all Holly copied the messages received so far and began printing them off on the laser printer sitting next to the desk. The president was a fast reader and was quickly caught up then began following the messages on the screen. The breadth and depth of the organization was staggering. They were planning nothing less then the complete takeover of the United States government. It would be just the same as a military coup only more cunningly engineered. If they had succeeded in assassinating the president before a year was out they would have controlled enough members of the government, either through blackmail or outright memberships, to effectively control everything. Charley didn't give them everything holding the most important piece back.

"So what do we do now?" the president asked looking at Adam. We know what's going on but the young man has obtained the information through torture so we can't use it in court."

Before he could answer a question popped up on the screen from Charley. "sir you should read this," Holly told the president.

She moved over so he could read the computer screen, which read: "I know that this information is useless in a court because of how I got it. However to be honest I don't think this should ever make it into a courtroom. If this got out to the public they would never trust the government again. It also might cause Carter to do something rash. Tell the President I will take care of the two I have and go after Carter myself if he can clear my name and stop the search going on for me. It should be easy to confirm that the men I have named are involved simply by trying to find them. Think it over before you put out an APB on Carter or anyone else. I'll give you time to think it over and contact you at the top of the hour."

By the time the President had finished reading the message Charley had logged off. He turned to Adam. "He is offering to take care of the two he has, does that mean what I think it means?"

"I believe so sir. He is offering to kill them."

"Can you ask John to join us for a moment? I want his thoughts on this."

Adam found John and had him join them just as dinner was about to be served. The president asked the steward to set the table for four and they all went into the dinning room. Over a simple but tasty dinner they talked over the information Charley had supplied and what he was offering. John believed him and advised the president to take the offer. Holly was against the killing of the two men as was the president, until Adam and John explained the full ramifications of the two staying alive. None of the information could be used, no matter how true it was. If they lived the rule of law had to apply. John's argument was the simplest; the organization didn't operate by rule of law so the board members had given up all recourse to the law themselves. Adams was a bit more sophisticated but he agreed on the course of action. The two should die and simply disappear. A cover story could be made up later to explain where they had gone.

The president asked them to hold their talking through desert so he could think it over. By the time they had to log back online to speak with Charley the president still hadn't said anything. He just stood up and motioned to the study and left the dining table. The other three followed him into the study and Holly connected to the net and opened the chat program waiting for Charley. The president motioned to her and she got up so he could take her place.

The chat program popped open on screen when Charley typed in "You there?"

The president began typing the message that would forever change him as a leader and the way he looked at the world. "Mister Watkins this is the President of the United States. I would first like to thank you for the job you have done for the country and myself. It has been an immense act of courage and dedication to fight on behalf of a country that has been doing it's best to capture or kill you. I sincerely apologize for what you have been through. I will gratefully grant you a full pardon and will instruct the Attorney General to begin proceedings to clear both your name and that of Sean Miller, first thing in the morning. I only regret that Mr Miller is not alive to enjoy his freedom. If you will accept it I would like to have you sworn in as a member of the NSA. As an active officer in the NSA you would fall under the jurisdiction of the federal government and as such subject to national security orders. If you accept your first act would be to eliminate the threat to national security offered by the persons of Sam Watson and James Bolten. These individuals represent a clear and present danger to the United States and their death is authorized by national command authority."

Adam looked at his boss with wonder in his eyes. "Sir what are you doing?"

The president looked at his young chief of staff with a face suddenly ten years older. "After all this courageous young man has done for me I am not going to let him have the murder of two men on his head. If they have to die then I am the one to order it and live with that decision."

After he had typed the message in he looked at Holly. "Miss McClare I need two things, how do I send this and how do I print it off." He wanted a permanent record of his personally ordering the death of two men he had known for years.

Holly sent the message then printed it off for him while they waited for the reply.

"Thank you sir but I don't feel that it is in my best interest to be a member of the government. After all I'm about to kill two high-ranking members and start hunting down a third. These men had friends that won't believe what happened and may want justice of their own. Also I don't feel that you should officially have anything to do with what is going to happen. It is best if I act alone. Just having a pardon and my own clear name will be enough. One question, do you need Carter for anything?"

"A rather ambiguous question," the president muttered. "Do you think he is asking it that way to give me plausible deniability?"

"I doubt it sir, he has been more then willing to let you know what he is doing and taking on his own head. I think he is asking in case you need remains for a funeral." Adam told his boss hiding what he really felt was behind the question. He was thinking that if they did not need a body Carter was going to die in a very painful and slow way.

The president typed "NO" in capital letters and hit the send key then stood up and walked into the living room.

Holly sat down and finished the conversation with Charley while Adam took the print out that his boss had asked for, ripped it into strips and burned it in an astray. Charley explained that he was going to disappear for a few days to rest and prep and then he would start tracking down Carter. With the conversation finished Holly logged off and shut down the computer. When she went back into the living room the president was sitting in his chair staring at the ceiling. She found Adam in the kitchen; John had gone back out to join his security team. The two stayed in the kitchen quietly talking and waiting for the President to call for them, leaving him alone with his thoughts.

Out at sea Charley also logged off and shut down the computer. He then picked up the .22 and shot each man twice in the back of the head. Feeling for a pulse he got none from either man. He next took the spare anchor and attached a chain rode to it. He wrapped the chain around the two bodies making sure it was secure and that there was no chance that either body would slip free. The next thing he did bothered him a lot but he knew it had to be done. He took a large filleting knife and slashed a deep would into the abdomens of both bodies. This would ensure that intestinal gases would not form and cause the bodies to float to the surface in a few days time. After all, the anchor was only a thirty-five pound one. Done with his grisly task he dumped the bodies and anchor over the side then restarted the engine and set a heading for Nova Scotia. He had to go home for a few days before he started the hunt for Carter. It would also take time for the paperwork to filter through to clear his name and he wanted to be some place safe while that was going on.

Chapter 18

When Carter regained consciousness he was in the infirmary at the factory. As he tried to sit up, he was noticed by the on duty nurse, who called for the doctor, then rushed to his side. After checking his reflexes, taking temperature, blood pressure, and pulse, the doctor pronounced him fit to get out of bed. After finding out from the doctor where he was an why Carter thanked the man and left the infirmary heading to the administrators office to get an update on what was happening. The head of the security detachment that had rescued him was also there and between the two men they brought carter up to speed on what was going on, the little that they knew. What they didn't know was where the other two board members were. The agents in the police and federal law enforcement agencies were not reporting anything unusual. No APB's or arrest warrants had been reported and the radio had not reported the shoot out at the cabin, so that was still under wraps.

"I need access to the internet and to an all news radio station," Carter told the factory administrator.

"You will need to go to the surface sir, there is no connection between here and the surface at all," came the reply.

Carter simply nodded his understanding headed for the elevator. The administrator jumped to follow as soon as he realized where Carter was heading. The ride up was one of silence and as soon as they were on the surface, Carter walked to the desk in the room and sat down.

"Bring me a radio and a computer with net access," he ordered.

The administrator rushed out to comply with his orders and with in minutes a laptop was set up and plugged into the phone line to connect it to the internet. A radio was found in the lunchroom and brought in as well, then tuned to one of the many all news networks in the city. Carter searched and listened for the next several hours, finding nothing at all about himself, the organization, or his two missing peers. He sat back and pondered for a moment then opened his email and composed a letter taking care to make it seem completely harmless yet still get across the message he needed to. When he was done he hit the send key and shut down the computer.

"No one is to touch any of this," he ordered motioning to the desk and then heading to the elevator. He went back down to the factory and made his way to the cafeteria for something to eat.

The President woke up refreshed, but with a feeling of dread hanging over him. He had a full day of planning in store and needed to do all of it from Camp David. His schedule was clear as he was still officially on vacation. After a shower and a shave he walked out of the bathroom to find a steward waiting to take his breakfast order. He asked for coffee and a bagel and to have John, Adam, and Holly join him in thirty minutes. The steward left to carry out the instructions while the President returned to his bedroom to find clothes all laid out for him. One thing he hated about the office was the constant attention from servants seeking to fulfill his every need. There were some things a man just enjoyed doing for himself and picking out clothes was one of them. Ignoring the clothes on the bed he walked to his dresser and pulled out a pair of jeans and a polo shirt. Grabbing socks and underwear he sat in the edge of the bed and dressed, still thinking about all he had to do today.

Entering the dining room he saw the other three already there waiting for him. As one they stood to their feet and he waved them to sit down. As per his standing orders the coffee was in a pot on the table and the toaster and bagels were on a sideboard waiting to be toasted. It was a small thing to make his own breakfast but something he enjoyed doing all the same. Since he became president the only time he got to do his own cooking anymore was when he was on his boat. The thought of that reminded him that his boat was now destroyed and a wave of sadness washed over him.

With his bagel toasted and cream cheese smeared all over it he sat down at the table and poured himself a cup of coffee. The steward was hovering in the corner in case something else was need and the president told him that everything was fine which was the signal for him to leave. As soon as the steward left the president looked at Adam and raised his eyebrows while taking a sip of coffee.

Adam recognized the signal and began filling his boss in on the information he had gotten overnight. "Sir we have been able to quietly confirm that the three men named as the leaders of the organization are indeed missing. All three left their offices shortly after it was announced that you were alive and have not been seen since. They did not go home last night and no one seems to be able to explain where they are. Other than an unexplained helicopter crash on the Potomac close to the Chesapeake nothing of interest happened at all yesterday. I had a call placed to the NTSB agent investigating the crash and there was no flight plan. The aircraft has been recovered and is registered to a numbered offshore account, so far no luck in tracing it back to a person in the US. All the bodies recovered so far have been armed with automatic weapons and a search of dental records and finger prints has revealed no information at this time."

Chewing on his bagel the president thought for a few moments. "Adam what are the consequences of letting this young man hunt for Carter?"

"To your administration, none at all sir."

"What about the risks to him?"

"Well as a civilian and a foreign national he is not allowed to carry weapons on US soil. If he gets caught he would be arrested and jailed," Adam explained

The president shook his head. "The more I think about it the less I like letting this young man do my dirty work for me. He could get killed and after all he has done for me I don't want that to happen."

"Sir I've seen this boy shoot," John said quietly. "He was in a position to kill you and the Pope, two of the most heavily protected men on the planet. I don't really see Carter being much of a problem once he finds the man."

The president looked John square in the eye. "Would we be able to find and take out Carter without the info getting leaked to the media?"

"Yes sir," answered John truthfully. "The NSA is very capable of doing the job quietly and effectively. Assuming we find him before Charley does."

"What do you mean?" asked Adam.

It's become personal now with Charley. His friend and partner is dead. This is no longer the innocent young man of a year ago. He wants Carter dead and he isn't going to wait for anyone else to do it. He will start hunting the second he is ready and nothing we say or do is going to stop him. Remember he has been successfully evading both the combined might of the US government and the organization since he went on the run. One more hunt on his own terms won't be a problem for him. I truly think our best option is to stay out of his way and let him do the job giving him as much help as we can."

"Okay John how do we do this?"

John spent several minutes outlining how it could be done. They would first create a complete ID for him and slip it into all the national databases in the various enforcement services. They could make him any one of a dozen federal agents however the best bet would be a US marshal. Next they would need to hack all the databases and replace his fingerprints with fake ones. When asked if her program could do this she nodded that it would. The next step was to let Charley know what they had done, don't ask if he wanted it simply do it and let him make the choice to use it or not. With the legend already in place if he was caught and his prints checked the ID that would pop up would be the one the NSA had created. They would flag the ID and if anyone did search for it they would know that Charley was in trouble and could help him out. If he actually accepted their help it would be a simple matter to get the ID to him and he could use it to legally carry his weapons.

The president nodded his agreement with the idea "Even though he doesn't care about it I want this boy protected, at least legally. And as distasteful as this is to me I agree that we need to eliminate Carter. If I am going to let this young man to kill for me then I want as much of the rule of law to cover his actions as much as can possibly make it. Holly, do whatever you can to make contact and tell him I am making him a special US marshal whether he likes it or not. We will have a complete set of ID for him and would like him to use it. Given the last time he met a member of the government I will completely understand if is unwilling to met with anyone again. Ask him how we can get the ID to him and follow whatever instructions he gives you. If he says that I have to hand it to him personally then that's what I will do. But make it happen."

Holly arrived back at the NSA by one o'clock and headed straight for her desk. The men assigned as security had been alerted that she would be heading back to the NSA and were waiting for her there to resume their duties. The sergeant and Doris welcomed her back with hugs and she had barely logged onto her computer when the general showed up.

"Miss McClare, glad to see you are all right." He nodded to the security men noting that they were alert and on duty.

"Thank you sir. Would you like an update on what is happening?" Before she had left Camp David the president had given her the okay to brief the general in fully on what was going on and getting his help to set up the ID for Charley.

"Only if I am cleared to know everything. If not then I'll wait until it's official" He answered, the complete soldier following his commander in chiefs orders even though he was dying to know what was going on.

"Yes sir the president has cleared me to talk about it. I will actually need your assistance on something he has ordered me to do. I can brief you in your office at your convenience."

Catching the hint that what she had to say was not for everyone the general looked around and noticed the boardroom was empty. "Well there's no sense making you go all the way up to my office when I'm already here. Why don't we use the boardroom and you can brief me in there."

The two went into the boardroom, the general telling the security team to make sure they were not interrupted and closed the door. Holly told him everything that had happened, leaving nothing out. After she was done the general smiled. "That is one ballsy man risking his own life that way. So all we need to do is create a persona and ID for this Charley Watkins to use, clear out all the databases of his real fingerprints, insert fake ones, add his new ID to all the law enforcement databases, contact the young man and then get the ID to him anyway he tells us to?"

Holly smiled "Yes sir that's all. I've never done anything like this before but John said to use a name close to the one Charley already has. That way it's easier for him to remember it."

The general nodded. "He's right, it is. I think that Chris Wilson is a nice close name for the young man to use. Can you set everything up in the database from here?"

"Yes I can."

They discussed the specifics of the identity for a moment then the general got up to leave "I'll have the documents section create everything he needs, drivers license, social security card, credit cards, the works. To keep this secure you will need to create a background for him and upload it to the proper databases and clear his old prints. Is that something you can do with spock?"

Holly nodded and the meeting was over. The general went back to his office to get the wheels in motion while she went back to her desk and started creating the information to load into the databases. With in an hour she had created a completely new person by the name of Christopher James Wilson. She had just uploaded his data to the last database when a courier came by with the ID cards for her. Once everything was ready she called Adam on his direct line and gave him the information. Now for the really hard part, she opened her email and started writing Charley letting him know what they had done and why. Now it was back to a waiting game for everyone, including the organization and the ironic part was that both sides were waiting on the same person, Charley.

It took five days for Charley to make his way to the coast of Nova Scotia. He made his way up the Bay of Fundy under the cover of darkness, running with no lights or radar. He was taking a risk of running into something in the dark but it was less of a risk then having lights or radar going. He had set the GPS to a waypoint as close to his home as he could get by water and turned on the alarm to let him know when he had arrived. By running at slow speeds he had been able to conserve fuel at the cost of a much longer trip but at the end there was still half a tank left.

Charley loaded his weapons, satellite, computer and personal gear into the tender at the back of the boat and prepared to abandon ship. Before he did, he reset the autopilot and GPS, programming the yacht to head out to sea aiming for the Azores but knowing there was not enough fuel to get that far. Hopefully by the time it was found, too much time would have passed to tie it to him.

Stepping into the tender he started the outboard and slowly moved toward shore glancing back once in a while to watch the yacht turn and head back the way it had come. Soon it was lost in the darkness and he concentrated on getting to shore. With the worlds highest tides the biggest danger in the Bay of Fundy could be the walk to shore. He had lucked out by arriving as the tide was almost full and was able to get close to the tree line at the shore. Tying the boat to a tree he began unloading the gear and hiding it under brush which too took several trips.

Once done he set the tender adrift hoping that the tide would take it out to sea, but not really concerned as the tender didn't seem to have any distinguishing marks on it and it certainly couldn't be linked to him. Marking the area around where he had cached his weapons so he could find them again he hiked inland to find a car. The one good thing about Nova Scotia was that the province was small and you never had to walk far from the ocean to come across a house or road. He had barely covered two miles when he saw a garage that had a payphone.

Charley had plenty of cash on him, all of it in US currency. That wouldn't be a huge problem as most people would take US dollars, there were worth more then Canadian dollars and if he had to he would pay at par. The phone booth had a yellow pages, listing several cab companies. He called the one with the largest ad and got an answer right away. Charley gave the name of the Garage he was standing next to and asked if they would be able to take him to his house, giving the address. He also explained that he had only US money on him asking if that would be a problem, they readily agreed and said a car would be there with in thirty minutes.

The cab showed up and Charley hopped in front next to the driver, truly headed home for the first time in a long while. The drive took a while as the driver was being paid a flat rate already agreed to and was in no hurry. Besides it was the middle of the night so fares were few and far between. Charley had the cabby drop him off at the house next to his own and paid the fair along with a decent tip but not enough that he would be overly remembered for long. He waited until the cab was out of sight before slipping off to the side of the house and heading across the field to the tunnel entrance to his own house. He had risked carrying a .380 hidden behind his waistband at the small of his back which he pulled out now the and entered the tunnel.

The walk to the house went quickly and he saw no signs that anyone else had come through the tunnel since the last time he had been through it. Entering the house quietly he heard no sounds to indicate anyone was there. Taking his time he searched the place top to bottom and discovered he was alone. Going into he study he got the keys to his car from his desk and went out to the garage to see if it would start up after being idle for so long.

It took a while to get his car running but eventually he did. It was just after sunrise before he finally left the house and he needed to get to a service station and fill it up with gas. Once that was done he headed back to the shore where he had left his weapons and driving through a field got as close as he could to the shoreline. He was still a good hike away and working as fast as he could it was still close to noon by the time he was done and back home.

Charley locked the car in the garage with all the gear still in it and headed for a shower. He spent a long time soaking under the hot spray letting it relax him and help massage away the aches of his labors. He had not let him self think of Sean during the trip home and he did so now. The grief was nearly overpowering as he thought of the man that had taught him so much in such a short period of time.

Stepping out of the shower he went to his room, placed the gun under his pillow and curled up for some sleep, still missing his old friend. He stopped short of promising himself that he would destroy the organization, he was now out and that had been the goal all along. He was not a soldier, not a warrior, no matter how much Sean had taught him. Soldiers trained constantly and still died in battle all the time. He was alone and there was nothing he could do to avenge his friend and mentor. It was up to the government to dismantle the organization. All he was going to do was hunt for Carter and make sure he didn't escape justice again.

Charley woke up in the early evening and pulled himself out of bed to go make coffee. He smiled as he perked the coffee thinking of how much Sean enjoyed that first cup of the day. Even when they had been in the woods and the coffee had been a disgusting strong brew that burned all the way down to the stomach, Sean had relished the first cup of the day. In memory of him Charley brewed the coffee strong and drank it black nearly gagging on the taste. There were only canned goods in the house and all the fresh food had long since spoiled and the freezer was empty as well. Picking through the cupboards he found a can of chicken stew that he opened and dumped into a pot. The power was still on because it was paid automatically out of a trust fund set up after his parents had died. He had been too young at the time to have power billed in his own name so it had been set up this way. Once he had become of age he left it alone for the simplicity of the set up. While the stew was heating up he searched for some crackers to go with it and finally found an un-opened package. He ate slowly mixing crackers with the stew to fill it out. Once done he washed up the dishes and put everything away erasing all evidence he had been there save for the empty can, which he washed out before dumping it in a recycle bin under the sink.

Going out to the garage he took out the satellite gear and computer carried it all into the house and set them up in his bedroom as it faced south. It took a few minutes of fiddling for him to get a signal from the satellite, but eventually he did. Booting up his computer he logged on and checked his email. There were several from Holly, a few spam emails, and one inviting him to a chat room that sounded vaguely familiar. He opened the ones from Holly and glanced quickly over them. He couldn't believe it, they had set up a cover ID for him and everything was ready. They were leaving the choice of pick up method entirely up to him and even stated that the president was ready to personally deliver the papers to him if that's the way he wanted it. The rest were all pleas for him to answer or call them. Holly had included her direct number and that of Adam as well.

Suddenly the chat program popped up with Holly's user name asking if he was there. He briefly debated ignoring her but the tones of the emails had been sincere so he answered her. Charley didn't tell her were he was just that he was fine and safe. That was enough, she didn't pry just asked him to consider letting them help him in his hunt for Carter, outlining what the help was and what she had done so far. He told her that he would think it over and get back to her in the morning. He signed off and closed the program. Charley spent a few hours surfing the net catching up on news and what had been going on over the last week. There was something tugging at the edge of his mind but he couldn't seem to get a handle on it. The more he thought, the father away it seemed to get. Finally he gave up and went to bed.

It was two days before Carter got a response to his email. He read it twice when he finally got it, relishing the message, and relieved that it was the one he had been looking for. While the government was looking for both him and his two missing compatriots it was doing so in a very secret and quiet manor. All three had officially been listed as a missing person with no other information being available at this time, however it was being speculated that a terrorist cell was behind the disappearance. It meant that the organization was still safe, or so he thought. He was sure that if security had been compromised one of his agents would have found out and reported it by now. But that had not happened and the email confirmed it was so.

But he could not return to his government job, not after being gone for two days. He would never be able to come up with a rational explanation, and so would be forever suspect. No, it was better to remain missing for the time being. He would run the organization directly and continue on with the plan to kill the president. They still had all their agents in place and a vast network of informers. He thought it strange that he still hadn't heard from his agents on the Presidents detail as to what had gone wrong, but he had too many other things on his mind to dwell on it. He sent out routine requests for information from his field agents and left it at that.

He sat for a while formulating a plan and finally came up with the supreme irony. He would try and coerce young Charley into doing the job anyway, there was nothing to lose. He called for one of the security men and sent him down to the factory for the items he requested then started drafting an email. The one thing he was afraid of was that the contact email address was no longer being used. That was a chance he would have to take. Once done, he sent the email and then uploaded some files onto one of the bulletin boards that the organization used for field agent contacts. Now the only thing he could do was wait to see if the bait was taken.

Charley woke up from a sound sleep completely alert. He suddenly realized what it was that had been tugging at his memory; it was one of the emails he had discounted as spam. It had been advertising a chat room and it was this that had been skirting the edge of his memory. The chat room was a secure, online organization meeting place. He jumped out of bed and ran to his computer, cursing at the slowness as it booted it. Once up and running he opened his mail, glad that he hadn't emptied his trash yet. The email was offering him a free membership to an exclusive chat room and included a user ID and a password. There was also an expiry time included in the email, which was four hours away. The hair on the back of his neck stood up and an eerie feeling came over him, the email he had at first discounted could only have come from the organization. He had assumed that with two board members dead and the third in hiding they would no longer be a threat to him, yet here they were emailing him.

Standing up and silently cursing himself for his complete and total stupidity, he strolled out to the car, casually looking around and pulled the duffel bag containing his weapons from the back seat where he had left them. After a year living constantly with a gun at his side the first thing he had done on returning home was leave them in his car. True he had assumed that the organization was no longer any danger, but the email showed him the flaw in that thinking. The young man promised himself that from that moment on until the organization was truly destroyed he would never again be unarmed. He spent an hour prepping his guns and secreting them around the house so that one would always be close at hand no matter where he was. Tucking a .380 into his waistband at his hip he headed back to his computer

Back in his bedroom he checked his firewall to make sure it was updated and running properly. He then burned off all the data on his hard drive to a CD and deleted it. Running a check he made sure that anything that could possibly identify him was gone including deleting his email account setup. Once he was sure that his computer was as clean as it could be short of formatting it, he logged into the chat room with the ID and password provided.

There was only one other user in the room and the user name was showing as Sean. Charley was outraged at this and nearly logged out. However he had come this far so he decided to see what the organization had to say. He might be able to use it to his advantage in hunting down Carter. "Too afraid to use your real name, so you are using that of a dead man?" Charley typed in.

"We wanted to get your attention. We needed you to know your friend is very much alive and back where he belongs, with his old friends at the training facility that you were a student of. We are also wondering what happened to our colleagues?"

Charley starred at the message on his screen. Could his mentor really be alive?

He decided to get the dirty work out of the way up front. "If you mean the two traitors that you used to work with, they are dead. I killed them and dumped them at sea in response to your goons killing Sean."

"There was no need to do that, as I said Sean isn't dead."

"I saw him die," Charley typed in, tears welling in his eyes.

"I assure you he is alive and well. Why don't you come and visit him?"

Charley realized it was simply another organization trick. Since informing the man that he had killed the two board members he hadn't mentioned them. They were already forgotten as far as the organization was concerned. But Sean was dead; he had seen him blown up with his own eyes. "Why should I believe you?" he asked, side stepping the invitation for a moment.

"I will send you a picture of him taken just a few hours ago. He is holding today's newspaper to prove that the picture is real."

Just then a request to transfer a file popped up on his screen. He clicked on it and the file downloaded to his hard drive in seconds. Charley opened the file and two things happened, a picture of Sean holding a newspaper appeared and his hard drive started to spin. His firewall popped up an alert telling him that an unauthorized connection to the internet had been established then it shut off. He smiled; they had given him a virus just as he suspected they would. He disconnected the computer from the net then rebooted and ran a virus scan on the system. It identified the virus, which also contained a trojan. It was the work of a few minutes to kill both, and clean the system. Once done he opened the picture and saw is friend holding a newspaper with the date circled. He couldn't believe it, Sean really was alive! But he had seen him blown up. Charley looked harder at the picture and something about the circle bothered him, it was then he saw that the circle had been drawn with computer graphics. The organization had screwed up; the picture was a fake, done with a photo-retouching program. For now the young man decided to play along with them and no let them know he knew the picture was faked. It might actually help him in his hunt. He erased the file then reconnected to the net.

Once back in the chat room he typed in, "That was a stupid thing to try, do it again and we're done talking."

The person he was chatting with ignored this completely. "So should we expect you soon?"

"I don't think so. As I recall the security was a little slack last time I was there. I don't think I would feel all that safe."

"I assure you it's more secure now, and completely safe for you. If you like we can even have someone pick you up and drive you here, all you need to do it tell us where you are."

Charley got his first piece of information for this exchange. They had beefed up security, which was something good to know. "If I change my mind I'll let you know. Now what did you want to talk to me about?"

"We would prefer to discuss the matter in person. We will guaranty your safety. Please come and see us."

"Thanks but that's not an option right now. Tell me what you want or I'm logging off for good." Charley knew that the threats would start now.

"Sean is in good health now but he is old and something tragic could happen. Why don't you reconsider and come and see him. He is asking for you."

"I don't believe that for a second. He would want me to stay away from you no matter what. Who am I talking to?"

"That doesn't matter, I have the full authority of the organization to speak on their behalf."

"Fine, I'm not coming and that's final. Last time, say what you have to say or I'm gone."

It was nearly a minute before another message began scrolling across the screen. "You didn't finish the job we asked you to do. We are still anxious to see that job carried out and urge you to consider doing so in a timely manner."

Charley almost laughed out loud at the message. Even in a secure chat room they could not bring themselves to speak plainly. The absurdity of the situation was comical.

"You mean you want the president dead and you want me to kill him? Is that the job you are referring to?"

"If you must be so crude Charley, then yes that is the job to which we are referring. We are very eager for this to take place and as quickly as possible. We need your answer right away. Please keep in mind your friend Sean. I don't wish to be blunt but his continued good health hinges on your decision."

Charley did laugh out loud at this threat. It was based on the assumption that he believed that they had Sean and he was alive. If he didn't believe that then it was an empty threat. It was a measure of their desperation that they were even trying it.

He would need to buy some time so that they didn't try to kill the president another way. If he agreed and they thought he was going to do the job for them then for the time being the president was reasonably safe. "So if I do this then you will let Sean go and leave both of us alone?"

"Yes," came the one-word answer.

Charley didn't believe them for a second but he played along. "For our freedom I'll think about it. How long do I have?"

"Twenty four hours. We will extend the user ID and password until this time tomorrow for you. If we don't hear from you we will assume that your answer is no, and that you no longer value the life of your friend."

With that Charley logged out of the chat room but stayed connected to the internet. He had pulled it off; they actually believed he was thinking about doing the job. He needed to contact Holly or Adam and let them know what was going on as soon as possible. Using the internet he used a voice over IP program to dial the number for Holly hoping it would ring, as it was still very early in the morning.

It was picked up on the second ring and a groggy woman's voice answered. "Hello?"

"Hi," Charley said conversationally. "Sorry to call you so early in the morning but I have decided to take you up on your offer if you are still willing to help me that is."

Holly had no idea who was on the phone or what offer he was referring to. It was a few seconds before she realized what line it was that she had answered. It was a secure line that had been installed by the NSA and only a few people had the number. Of the people that had the number only one person would be asking about the help she had offered. "Charley?"

"Yes. So how about it, still willing to help?"

She was wide-awake now. "Yes we are. We have…"

"Not we, you." Charley cut her off.

"Excuse me?"

"I said, not we, you. I don't want to deal with other people, just you. I will do all the dirty work and take care of Carter for you but I only want to speak with you on this.

"But everyone wants to help you Charley. The orders come directly from the President himself."

"Doesn't matter to me who they come from. Let's just say that I feel safer this way."

"Okay Charley whatever you want. So how can I help you?"

"You mentioned that you had a new identity set up for me, I can use that."

Holly explained the identity they had set up for him and gave him all the specifics of his cover. She explained that he had a driver's license and credit cards as well. All he needed to do was pick them up. The NSA would be paying his credit card bills so he didn't need to worry about money. He laughed at that and explained that he had plenty of money stolen from the organization so he didn't need the credit cards. He also knew that using credit cards was an easy way to be tracked. He would stick with using cash but he didn't reveal that to Holly. He told her to send the papers to general delivery in Kentville, Nova Scotia, Canada, and he would pick them up there. Holly didn't bother asking him if that's where he was, he probably wouldn't tell her anyway.

Holly wanted to set up a contact schedule but Charley would have no part of that. She argued that it was the only way to know that things were okay.

"Lady I've been running from both the US government and the organization and stayed ahead of everybody by doing things my own way. Do you really see a need for me to change what is working?"

Her silence was all the answer he needed. "Okay you keep this number next to you at all times and I will make sure to call once in a while to let you know how I'm doing."

She agreed and Charley disconnected the call. Next he logged back onto the internet and entered the chat room. His message was short and simple; "I'll do it but I want your word that Sean will be released unharmed." He didn't wait for a reply but logged off and shut down the computer then went into the kitchen and made coffee, thinking over what he needed to do. He had enough weapons with him but he wanted to head back to his bunker and sort out the load to carry. Right now he had too much gear and need to drop some of it off. He also wanted to pick something up. Once at the bunker he spent a few days there enjoying the quiet and privacy. Most of his time was spent in the armory but a little time was spent on his range fine-tuning his shooting skills.

After a few days had past Charley packed up the gear he wanted and left he bunker. His time there had given him a chance to reflect on what he was about to do, In the beginning it had been all about clearing his and Sean's name and returning to the life he had known before. That life was lost forever to him now. He had never really known why his grandfather had collected weapons of war and built a bunker until now. They were a remembrance of the time he had made the same choice to fight evil and go to war. Charley had grown up with the stories told to him by his grandfather. They did not glorify combat, as did movies and TV, but explained the harsh realities of death and destruction. The rifles, SMG's and machine guns were mementos of a deadly conflict that his grandfather had shared with others, and hoped Charley would never have to go through. Charley had grown up using them as tools, the same as he would have a hammer or saw, now he would once again use them for the deadly purpose they had been built for. As much as he wanted to go back to his quiet life he could not. To sit by and do nothing after all he and Sean had been through would be a waste. The organization had to be stopped and he would have to be the one to do it. Not only that but the one piece of real information he had learned from the two board members was not something he could reveal to anyone, let alone the President of the United States.

Charley took his time getting to Kentville, making sure he was not being followed or watched. The reason he had chosen the town was for its size. There was no place for an outsider to sit unnoticed and wait for him to show up. When he arrived at the post office there was a package waiting for him. It was the papers Holly had promised, everything from a drivers license to credit cards, and most important of all the ID and badge of a US federal marshal. He left as carefully as he had arrived taking a circuitous route home checking constantly for anyone following him. He realized that with the technology available to the NSA they could have simply bugged any of the papers he had been given and follow him via satellite. If that was the case there was nothing he could do until he got home.

He parked in the barn and checked the telltales he had left to make sure no one had opened the doors while he had been gone. Nothing was disturbed but he still checked the entire house as a precaution. Taking everything out of the package he tossed it all in the microwave for fifteen seconds. When he took them out they were slightly warm but otherwise fine. If there had been anything in side them to track him with they would be useless now.

Several thousand miles away an Army technician had been watching a monitor that was tracking a signal. What the signal was and who it belonged to where unknown to him. He simply knew where it was and that it was a solid signal being relayed to a geosynchronous satellite in a polar orbit. He had been watching it travel up the coast for two days then sit in one location for several more until it had moved several miles then suddenly with out warning stopped. He turned up the gain on the equipment to try and pick it up again but nothing worked. He called the duty officer and reported the signal loss then waited for orders.

Holly called the general for her afternoon brief. He had decided that have her come up to his office was unnecessary and she could update him over the phone. Most of the time there was nothing to report. Today however she had to report the loss of the tracking signal from the ID papers that they had sent Charley. It was not unexpected, as Holly had explained that the young man was extremely suspicious and would assume that the NSA would try to track him somehow. She had argued against bugging the package sent to Charley, but had lost.

Now the only thing they could do was wait for him to call. She had not told anyone what Charley had said about only talking to her as she didn't want anyone to think that she was trying to make her self indispensable. If it became and issue she was sure Charley would make it clear to whomever took over from her.

Crossing the border this time was simple; he just drove up to the customs agent and showed his badge. He stated that he had been in Canada on a federal matter and was waved through after declaring that he had purchased no alcohol or tobacco. Hidden under the back seat were his weapons, but that was more to keep them out of sight of the casual observer them really hide them. He knew that both the organization and the government wanted him back in the US. No one was going to try and stop him from entering; leaving would be another story entirely.

He had the satellite and computer in the trunk and if asked about them would have just said that he used them to communicate with head office. It was not entirely a lie as he did use them to contact Holly and Carter. Once in across the border he went as far as Portland, Maine, checked into a hotel making sure he got a room with a southern view, set up his computer and satellite and logged onto the internet to check his email. There was one from the organization instructing him to log into a website that they used for a drop and pick up his orders there. Anyone reading the email would not have known what it meant, but to Charley it was crystal clear. He did so and got the itinerary for the President for the next month. He smiled to himself as he found out where they wanted the assassination to take place. He would be heading back to Boston again.

It was time to Call Holly. He used the online phone program to call her, knowing that it would be impossible to trace and she answered on the first ring. "Hello Miss McClare, how are things at the NSA."

"Charley it's good to hear your voice. Everything is fine here how are you doing?"

"Just great, thanks for asking. Just wanted to let you know that I got your package and I'm on the case. I'm back in the US and I've started the hunt. Something I wanted to pass on with regard to the president, have him use only minorities on his security team until I find Carter. I'll give you a call once I have more information."

He hung up before she could say anything else and the remark about minorities really puzzled her. With that out of the way Charley shut down the computer and went to bed. He would have a long day tomorrow.

Carter had taken over running the organization directly. He could not go back to his job so there was no need for a junior. Also as he was the only one still alive he was the natural choice to lead, besides everyone was already looking to him for orders.

Once Charley had accepted the job he moved from the factory to a safe house that had been set up. It was a location that the young man could not possibly know about, but he did know about the factory. The factory had been attacked once, he was not going to take the chance that Charley wouldn't try it again. It would be in his character to try it to rescue his old friend. He had given orders upon leaving the factory that if an attack did occur, not to kill the young man if it was him. They needed him alive to kill the president, he could be disposed of after that.

Once settled into the new location he began setting up a computer network to track the daily operations. Slowly but surely the day-to-day activities of the organization returned to normal. He was still looking for information as to how the President had escaped death in the Caribbean but several of his agents were still among the missing. He sent out inquires to find these men and get their reports, then put the thoughts out of his mind to focus on other matters, it was clear by now that his men had been compromised in some way.

The president was still at Camp David even though his official vacation had ended. As he was about to have the navy release the Secret Service Agents that had been detained he contacted the Captain and asked to speak to his detail head, Corey. Over a secure line he explained the situation as best he knew it then requested that Corey keep the agents on the WASP for a few more days. He assured his detail chief that he was safe and well protected by men from the NSA and US marines. Corey was stunned to learn that men on his detail could betray the oath they had taken to protect the president. He understood the man reluctance to trust the secret service at the moment and assured him he would follow the president's orders to the letter. For now he was asking that the agents simply stay on the carrier and out of communication with the rest of the world, Corey readily agreed.

Waking up to a new day the president had Adam net at his cabin for breakfast. "So do we have an update?"

"Yes sir we do. Charley has accepted our help in a limited way. He took the ID and we think he is in the US again but can't be sure at this time."

"What do you base that on?"

"Miss McClare said that she received a call from him stating he was in the US and had started looking for Carter. He also passed along the message that you should use minorities on your security detail until he caught Carter."

"Did he give any reason for this?" the president asked.

"No sir he didn't. But everything he has given us so far has been right; I see no reason to think he would start playing games with us now. We need to get back to work sir, and I think that this will allow you to get back to the White House. The media and congress are all howling to know what is going on and how you are doing. Everyone things you are hiding injuries sustained in the explosion."

"Okay, let's get a team in place made up of minorities. I also want John and his men on the job so get them transferred to Treasury and assigned as agents as quick as you can. Do we have a replacement for Carter yet?"

"Actually I was thinking of giving that to John temporarily until we can find Carter and prove or disprove that he is behind the organization."

"Excellent idea, make it happen. Back to Charley, aside from the ID how are we helping him?"

"He has refused any other help, he is doing this on his own."

"Damn it Adam he is just a kid, we need to get some people out there helping him."

"At this point sir we don't even know where he is. It is impossible to help someone that won't let us. The best we could do is send out a notice letting the federal and state agencies know that we have a man in the field and to assist him with what ever he needs. The problem with that is the organization might hear it and it could put Charley at risk. For right now we need to trust that he will be fine, and to be honest we didn't catch him when we were hunting him"

"Okay, get Corey off the WASP, get everything in place and I'll be heading back to the White House this afternoon."

Adam met with John after breakfast and informed him of his new duties and what Charley had said about minorities. Between the two of them they hashed out a temporary plan to protect the President and get him back to the Oval Office and back to work, it was time now to get back to running the country. They would try to keep what they had done secret for as long as possible, but at some point the story would leak and the organization would learn the truth. Hopefully Charley would be finished what he was doing before that happened.

Charley drove south to Boston and found a bed and breakfast place booking a room for a week. He spent the time wandering the city, watching TV and surfing the net. He was looking for anything that would indicate that the organization knew where he was. Nothing he saw alerted him to anything out of the ordinary. The lack of anything suspicious made him think that the organization actually believed he was going to kill the president.

According to the time line he had a little over a month before the date given to him by Carter. At the end of the week he was satisfied that he could do everything he wanted to and so packed up once again and headed south. As he traveled he stayed at out of the way places, using back roads. He started and ended every day running at least five miles. When he went out to run he always had a .45 tucked into the small of his back, just in case. The last year had taught him to be cautious if nothing else. Some would call it paranoia but Charley now just called it being careful. He also did martial arts each night in his room keeping his body limber and in top condition, ready for anything.

When he got to Maryland he parked his car in long term parking at the airport and rented a minivan with tinted windows. He used one of the credit cards that he had set up when on the run with Sean, as security, but paid for a month's rental with cash. He quickly transferred all his gear to the Van and headed to Washington, DC.

The first time he drove by the factory he was sure he had the wrong place, there was a thriving laundry service in place with vans coming and going. He checked the map he had picked up with the van and confirmed that he did indeed have the right area. He risked driving by one more time and was sure that he had the right building. The fencing was all-new and looked electrified and alarmed along with video cameras mounted on the corner of the building. He also thought he spotted a security guard letting one of the vans out of the building.

Charley drove south into Virginia booked into a small motel and paid cash for a week. As always he insisted on a room with a southern view and once in the room set up his computer and satellite to log onto the net. He checked out the name of the laundry service that had been written on the side of the vans, and got as much information about it as he could. There was a website up for it and according to the information posted they serviced the DC area only, specializing in diapers. There was also information on rates and how to contact them for pickup. As with any commercial site they carried quotes from customers to be used as testimonials. He found out that several of the upscale hotels in DC used their service for the hotel guests.

On the drive south he didn't really have a concrete idea as to what he was going to do and even now wasn't sure why he had come to DC. In the back of his mind was the thought that just maybe Carter would be hiding in the Factory and he could check it out to see. Seeing the laundry service threw him off for a while but now the beginnings of a plan were starting to form. He doubted that Carter was there but it was obvious that the organization still believed themselves secure and were operating there. The building would have required far too much of an investment to be turned into a laundry service for anyone other then the organization. It also made a great cover; no one would look under dirty diapers for criminals.

He next morning he headed into DC proper looking over the hotels he had seen listed on the website. Sure enough, as advertised, they all used the laundry service and there were early morning pickups and deliveries. He watched for a few days and noticed that the schedule never varied, a hallmark of a well-run company. Finally he selected the gear he needed and called ahead to book a room. Tossing his duffel in the van he went into DC and checked into the hotel he had selected.

Once in his room he unpacked and assembled the STG44 he had brought with him from the bunker. For this trip he had decided on an assault rifle rather then an SMG. He needed a combination of firepower and range and the STG44 gave him that. Once together and loaded he dressed in the Kevlar overalls and hat that Sean had given him, padding himself under it with layers of sweat pants and shirts. The overalls would stop a bullet but the shock of impact could still knock him out. Hopefully the padding would soften any blows, should he get hit. He put the rifle in a kit bag along with spare clips, gloves and a balaclava and a few other items. He tucked the .45 into the small of his back and left the hotel the back way. Checking his watch he saw that he had seven minutes until the laundry truck arrived. It always made its pick up and delivery's in the back using an alleyway.

Dressed in his coveralls Charley was just another worker amount thousands in the city. He waited at the back behind one of the dumpsters until the truck arrived. This was the part of the plan that would be totally ad-libbed. He would hop in the back and look for a place to hide; if he couldn't find one then there was no way for him to get into the factory unseen.

The driver left the van running as he went into drop off and pick up laundry bags. The second he was out of sight Charley was in the van searching for a place to hide out. There were bags of laundry piled into cages and he took a chance diving into one and covering himself with the bags of laundry. Now was the dangerous part, if the driver discovered him it was all over. He heard the back door slide open and felt the van rock as someone climbed in, the light sound of laundry bags being tossed into one of the cadges could just be heard over the idle of the van then the door slammed closed and the driver got behind the wheel and headed into traffic.

Charley had picked this hotel because it was the last one on the drivers route and he headed back to the factory right afterward. The drive in traffic was longer then he would have guessed but that also could have been the driver trying to pad his working hours a bit as well. Once at the factory the driver simply drove in the building, shut off the van and left it for another crew to deal with.

Charley climbed out of the pile of laundry put on his gloves and balaclava, loaded the STG and chambered a round quietly. He then pulled two stun grenades from the bag and pulled the pins on them. He opened the back door, stepped out of the van and took a second to orient himself to where he was and what he remembered of the layout of the building. He picked out the office where the elevator had been, assumed that it was still there, and lobbed the grenades into it. They went off with an eardrum-shattering roar and he rushed into the room rifle at the ready.

There were guards in the room but all were unconscious from the concussion of the grenades, on the floor with blood dripping from noses and ears. A quick glance told him that none of the men was an immediate threat however he knew there were more just below him and he need to make sure they stayed there. Pulling open the filing cabinet he saw that the elevator car was at the bottom. As he was starring at it he saw it being to rise. He pulled a homemade bomb from his kitbag, lit the fuse and dropped it down the shaft. Moving away from the opening he covered his ears and opened his mouth to counter any concussion. The explosion shot a gout of flame up the shaft along with smoke then everything quieted down. A glance down the shaft showed him a destroyed elevator car with several dead bodies in it. More importantly, everyone down below was still trapped there.

That there had been no counter attack yet worried the young man, this was going a little too easy. Done with the shaft it was the work of a few seconds for Charley to disarm the unconscious men. He flipped a desk on it's side and pushed it to face the door, acting as a shield should anyone try to attack him. Using nylon zip ties he secured all the men and began searching the room for anything of value. This time around he would make sure that the organization didn't have the option of reopening the factory. He dragged the men, now starting to wake up, to a delivery van and loaded them all in the back. He was still surprised that there was no counterattack yet, but he wasn't wasting time waiting for one either. He had no idea that at the sound of his grenades going off everyone in the building had run out, several using cell phones to call the numbers they had been given in case of an emergency. Even now there were organization action teams racing to the warehouse but they would be too late.

With the men loaded he took out a homemade Molotov cocktail, lit it and tossed against the side of another parked van. Using the van he had loaded the tied up men in as a battering ram, he broke down the door, then stopped long enough to throw two more Molotov cocktails into the building before driving off.

As the first action team was arriving he was pulling onto the I95 south merging with the rushing traffic in the afternoon sunshine. Behind him he could see flames from the fire he had set shooting into the sky. This time there would be no way to hide the organizations training factory hidden below the building. And if Carter were there he would be caught by the authorities. Charley would question the guards later to see if they knew where he was however he seriously doubted if Carter was in the factory or if the guards knew where he was.

It was dusk when Charley dumped the van south of Arlington, Virginia, in a woods road. He left he guards tied up in the back after making sure they knew nothing of value. It took most of the night to hike back to where he left his car. Once back at his motel he took a shower and checked the morning news. The big story was the fire in Washington that ended up being investigated by the FBI. The TV talking head was reporting tales of an underground bunker, but that all questions to the fire department, police or FBI were not being answered at this time. Charley resisted the temptation to check his email and instead went to bed.

The first action team was trying to put out the fire when the fire department showed up. They tried to keep the firemen out but the effort was futile as the police were called in to clear the way. As soon as the first automatic weapon was found by a fireman the FBI and ATF were notified. With in minutes the place was crawling with federal agents. The building was gutted and it was several hours before the investigators could start combing through the rubble. Shortly after that the elevator shaft was discovered. A man was lowered down the shaft to check it over and promptly shot by the guards below. Not knowing what they were facing, the FBI called in an HRT team and dropped a phone to the bottom of the shaft. A hostage negotiator shouted down to try and get someone to pick up the phone to no avail.

By morning they still had no idea exactly what they were facing other then an underground bunker and men armed with automatic weapons. No one had picked up the phone to talk to them and when they lowered a camera to take a look it was destroyed by gunfire. It was finally decided that they would need to take the place by force. With out knowing what they were facing the agent in charge was unwilling to allow an assault by the HRT even though they were eager to try. He ordered them to drop gas down the shaft to clear the way first.

The first canisters were a fast acting paralyzing agent that was designed to incapacitate people with out permanent harm. It was non-persistent agent that would last only for 15 minutes. After that they dumped in CS gas and the HRT officers followed it down the shaft. They made it into the main area where they were met with a barrage of gunfire. Everyone in the factory was armed and had taken up a position facing the elevator shaft to put up as much of a fight as possible.

More gas was used until the entire factory was fogged, making visibility impossible past a few yards. The rate of fire slackened and finally died out altogether. The HRT men swept the building looking for pockets of resistance and rounding up the weapons as they went. Once it was declared all clear, fans were lowered to blow the gas back up the shaft and clear the place out. It took over an hour to secure all the people in the bunker and by that time they were beginning to recover from the gas.

The debriefing of the people in the underground bunker took several days and was conducted by the FBI and ATF on site rather then risk transporting any of the prisoners. In the end however, they came up with very little in the way of useful information. As soon as the security tem had announced the shaft breach the factory administrator ordered all documents and computers destroyed. During questioning any of the people that would actually have relevant information simply asked for a lawyer and sat silently ignoring the FBI agents questioning them. Even without discovering any real information. it was a major blow to the organization, one that would severely cripple their ability to recruit and train new people, and it put them in the open for the first time. The President was extremely happy about it and allowed the FBI to take complete credit for the discovery even though no one had any idea who had actually started the fire that had lead to the discovery of the bunker. When it was actually reported to the public the size and scope of the facility was severely underplayed, saying it was nothing more then a money laundering and weapons storage area. The FBI announced that the place was discovered as a result of a fire and was the work of a criminal group that was all American in its make up. They stressed that there were no foreign nationals found at the site at all, so as to avoid any panic that might have occurred. It was still a black eye to the law enforcement community as a whole that the place had existed at all. There was large public outcry to find out how this had happened, a question that was being asked by a lot of politicians, even those that had been compromised by the organization were making a lot of noise. Some saw this as their ticket to freedom and were jumping on the bandwagon.

While the organization was now out in the open as far as the President was concerned, the extent of their influence, and the fact that the three men that had headed had been high-ranking members of the government itself, was kept a very closely guarded secret. The number of people that actually knew about the board members and who they had been was still under twenty, the White House intended to keep it that way. If congress ever found out, every agency in the government would be subject to a congressional investigation and this was something the President wanted to avoid at all costs.

The list from the laptop was cleaned up a bit and released to other agencies to begin the task of rounding up organization members very quietly. It was a slow process, which would take a long time to complete, but it had at least been started. It would effectively cripple the organization if not wipe it out all together. Charley was sent an email telling him this and asking if it had been him that set the fire. He didn't reply and anytime Holly tried to chat with him online he simply disconnected. He would talk with them when he was ready, not before. He had too much to plan and didn't want any distractions at all. Carter still had not been found, Holly had told him that he wasn't at the factory, and the deadline given him was approaching. Life for most seemed to be getting back to normal. Even Adam had sent him an email thanking Charley for all the hard work and letting him know that if he needed help he only had to ask. Charley wished it was just that simple.

Carter was furious; the loss of the factory could not begin to be calculated. Add in that he had finally gotten some information back about the president's trip and he felt that the organization was under siege, which was very true. He was losing members to arrests daily and sources of information were drying up. If this continued for long all that he had spent his life building up would be lost forever. He warned off the older agents, gaining some satisfaction that some managed to escape hours before they would have been arrested. He was also informed that the president had replaced all of the White House secret service officers and had someone from the NSA temporarily in charge. Carter looked into this but had lost all his assets in place and as a result could not find out anything of value.

He typed out an email to Charley chiding him on the raid and the fire. He had no proof that it was the young man however the logical assumption was that it had indeed been Charley, so he blamed the young man. He stressed in the email what needed to be done and what was at stake not even bothering to hide his meaning in any type of code.

To be on the safe side, Carter and his entourage moved again. This time to a location that he purchased through one of the dummy companies that the Organization had set up in the Cayman Islands. It was a small farm in Kentucky that raised sheep and paid for from an offshore account controlled directly by Carter. There would be no way to link it with the organization at all so it would be safe for him to live there until the president was dead.

Charley checked his email and as expected there was an email from carter. He didn't even try to hide who he was anymore now that the organization was out in the open. His message was short and specific; the president was to be killed. Charley was even given the time and place and the irony of it was that it would be exactly the same location as the last attempt, Boston. The email stated very clearly that if the President was not killed Sean would be tortured to death and the whole thing would be taped then emailed to Charley. To prove Sean was still alive there was yet another photo attached of him holding that morning's newspaper.

Charley read the email and laughed. The man was desperate to convince him that Sean was alive. Of course as Carter was using that as his leverage he would need to act as if he believed it. He typed up a reply to Carter returning the threats reminding the board member that his life was also on the line if he failed to live up to his end. Sean was to be released the second the job was done and the two were never to be bothered again.

Carter had been checking his email every two minutes since sending off the message and was relieved when he got a reply back. He hadn't even been sure Charley would get his email let alone respond to it. He was actually shocked a little when he read it then he chuckled to himself pretending that he did not feel the cold shiver run down his spine. This young man, really a boy, had ruined over half a century's work. He was not someone to underestimate. Suddenly things were not as clear as Carter had first thought. His intention had been to blackmail Charley with the threat to kill Sean and once the job was over use the emails as proof that the lad had killed the President to shift the blame from the organization. He would sit back and let the government hunt the boy down while he had Sean removed. Now he wasn't so sure that the lad be left alive after the hit. The thought of that young man hunting him was not something he was comfortable with, even if the young man was being hunted for killing the president. He would need to have Charley killed immediately after the hit, he assumed the same building would be used so he knew where to place his own agents. He typed in his own reply to the threat and sent it off then shut down the computer and headed off for some sleep.

Charley received the reply, read it then began composing another email taking his time over it and getting the wording just right. He also spent considerable time with a photo-editing program until he had the effect he was looking for. Once he was done he read it over one last time to make sure it was perfect and attached the photo with the email. He then programmed the computer to send the email to the server and hold it there until the time he specified, the email would be automatically sent at the exact time he had set it for, he just hoped that he was right with his timing. With that done he shut down his computer and began packing. He had a long road ahead of him.

Heading back north to Boston he found a bed and breakfast south of the city. He scouted the area briefly but there wasn't much he needed to know. The President was giving a speech there in a couple weeks, using exactly the same venue as he had used before. As a result Charley would also use the same venue as before, hoping that no one had found out how he had done it the first time.

The danger here was that Carter also knew the venue as Sean had submitted regular reports to the organization on the plans. Charley knew it was stupid to use the same building as before, Carter would surely have men waiting for him to kill him after he did the job. However the job had to be done in Boston, that was the way the organization wanted it. Charley didn't have time to scout a new shooting perch he would simply be extra careful when he used the old and he had another card up his sleeve that the organization didn't know about.

He scouted the building only once and would move in a couple days before the job. He stopped by radio shack and picked up a few items that he was sure he would have need of. In the city the Secret service was out in force. Charley had moved close to the venue twice and both times was asked for ID before being allowed to pass any point that was with in 500 yards of the platform being set up. On both occasions once his ID was checked he was allowed to move on.

Charley packed all his gear and headed into the building making his way confidently to the same location he and Sean had hide after the first job, the gear they had left there was still serviceable. He had brought the .50 with him and also had some new sabot rounds that he had made while at his bunker. Now was the boring part the wait, and this time he was alone.

"Morning Adam, what's on my plate today?" the president greeted his chief of staff as he entered the Oval Office for the morning briefing. It had taken a week to get things running smoothly after they had returned to the White House. The changing of all the secret service agents had turned out to be a bigger problem than at first thought. Eventually though it was set up and running, with John acting as the director for the time being, until the organization was finished. Then it had been the media demanding to know what had happened on board the president's yacht and not leaving it alone until they were told a concocted a story of a propane explosion that had thrown the president clear but destroyed the boat. The reason for the length of stay at Camp David was assigned to a concussion from the propane explosion. This mollified the press and the White House was allowed to get on with business.

Adam went over the day's schedule with his boss, then at the end mentioned that nothing had been heard from Charley.

"Are you concerned about that?" the president asked.

"Yes sir I am. Miss McClare has a watch on his IP address and has reported that he was until recently still logging on daily. However all attempts to communicate with him have been ignored."

"Do we know where he is from this IP address thing?"

"No sir, he is using a satellite to log on with so we can't get a physical location on him."

"Is there any reason to believe that he has been captured by the organization?"

"No sir however you are slated to speak in Boston tomorrow. Remembering what happened the last time you were there I was wondering if you could be persuaded to cancel the trip."

The president laughed at the suggestion. "No Adam I'm going and that's final, besides we have Charley on our side this time, he isn't going to let the organization try anything in Boston this time around. The vice president will be there as well, so I can't miss it."

Adam didn't have his bosses positive feeling about the event but simply nodded in agreement anyway. "If that's all sir I'll be in my office."

The president nodded as his chief of staff left, picked up the papers on his desk to begin reading them to prep for his next meeting.

The night before the hit Charley scouted the buildings elevator shafts using a hand held child's toy called the bionic ear. It was a crude directional microphone set into a parabolic plastic dish. Surprisingly it was very effective even though it was a child's toy. With in minutes he picked up voices of people talking in low tones in a place that they shouldn't have been, the bottom of the elevator shaft. It would be organization agents setting up to wait until after the job then kill him and leave his body to be found. Typical of the way they thought and a very predictable move on their part, one that was easy to counter now that he was aware of it.

And then finally the morning was here, Charley moved into position on the roof as the sun was breaking over the horizon tossing shadows everywhere and making night vision gear useless. This was the second time he had done this and did it without having to think about it this time. He was also calmer then the last time as he knew exactly what he was going to do and why, he also agreed with it this time and knew it had to be done. He made himself as comfortable as he could it would be a long wait until noon.

The silent alarm on his wrist woke him up at 11:30. He was a little surprised that he had been able to sleep. He put the rifle together and loaded it with his sabot rounds getting ready to shoot. Looking through the scope he saw nothing but agents and local politicians on the podium. But that's as it should have been, the speech wasn't slated until noon. He truly hopped that the man was on time, this time it was critical.

He put the rifle down waited the seconds taking an eternity to tick by. Then the roar of the crowd made him pick up the rifle again. He sighted on the podium and saw the senior senator from the state of Massachusetts at the microphone speaking. What ever he said it had a positive result as the cheering could be heard all the way to where Charley lay. Suddenly there was movement at the back of the stage and the President of the United States bounded up the stairs and into view.

Charley laid the cross hairs on him and tracked him all the way to the microphone. He could see the man gesturing but was too far away to hear any of his speech. He could however hear the cheering of several hundred thousand people and guessed that the speech was going as planned. As he was looking through the scope the vice president also moved onto the podium and took a stand to the right of the President. Charley checked the positioning of the two men to make sure his shot would go where it was intended to and not veer off killing the wrong man.

As he settled the cross hairs of his rifle he was almost overcome with nausea. He would be killing in cold blood and even though he thought the cause worthy it still bothered him greatly. There would be no disabling shots this time, he would shoot to kill. The fact that the reason behind the murder was an excellent one, did not ease his conscience at all. Checking his watch showed it was almost time. He had a specific time line to follow, one that would coincide with his email being sent out. The time he had marked in his mind arrived and he went into an automatic mode. Sighting through the scope he put the crosshairs on the center of the targets chest, telling his mind he was no longer aiming at a man, just a target.

Charley took up the slack in the trigger without thinking about it. Suddenly the gun bucked in his hands as the bullet was fired. He watched the target take the round just to the right of the center of the chest, exactly where the heart would be. The round was a 30-06 coated with Teflon and sabot into a .50 caliber cartridge. When it struck it was traveling around 3000 feet per second. The Kevlar vest slowed it considerably but had no chance at all to stop it. The bullet ripped the mans heart in two killing him instantly.

Charley bolted for the door to the top of the elevator shaft as the platform erupted in pandemonium. The president and vice president had been standing side by side on the stage holding each other's hand, lifted in triumph when Charley had pulled the trigger. The bullet had hit with enough force to drag both men to the floor. However the vest contained what little blood there was so no one knew immediately which man had been hit. It made no difference; the secret service agents grabbed both men and dragged them from the stage.

The news media went into a frenzy commenting on how Boston was again a city of tragedy. There was a lot of speculation but very little in the way of facts being reported. Whenever any reporter asked and official for information they were met with a steel curtain of no comments.

Carter was watching the news and saw it happen on live TV. The lad really had done it this time. He had seen the president knocked down from the bullet with his own eyes. He could see his destiny coming true. All he had worked for had arrived.

His computer beeped from the corner indicating that he had received an email. He got up as crossed the room to check who it was from. Strangely it was showing as being from Charley but that couldn't be, he had just killed the president, live on TV, there was no way he could be sending an email this fast. Carter was unaware that emails could be set to auto deliver. Sure that it was important he opened it and quickly scanned through it. The horror of what it contained left him holding his breath. He read it over again and then a third time praying that this was all some horrible hoax. He checked the address it had come from and recognized the one Charley was using. Then he noticed two very important things, far more important then the content of the email it's self. He saw the addresses in the carbon copy row, and that it had a picture attached it had been sent to the White House Chief of Staff and to the NSA.

He opened the attached picture to see Sean smiling up at him with his arm around the President and holding a copy of a newspaper dated for tomorrow. The caption read 'I can fake a picture too.' Carter realized that at that second he had failed. He read the email on more time.

> "Dear Mr. Carter.
>
> Something I should have told you was, that before your colleagues died, I had a chance to ask them a few questions. I put all the talents your organization trained me with, to good use and it was ironic that it was the board members themselves that received the results of my tutelage. But enough about that, let's get down to what I learned.
>
> I was indeed shocked to learn that you and your two peers were not the actual power behind the organization. I must admit that had I

not had two men to question and hearing them both agree on the same story I would never have believed it myself. After all it isn't every day that you find out the Vice President of the United States is a leader of a white supremacy group. Add in one that is about to make him the President, and I think you'll agree the premise belongs more in the movies than real life.

I wondered how anyone could ever get passed the screening to make it as high as the vice president but them I remembered the golden rule: "Whoever has the gold, makes the rules.' It took me a while to verify the information but eventually I did find the connection. I must say that the founders of the KKK were very forward thinking men to build a secret arm that far back, then have it sever all ties to the public KKK. That the vice president's direct ancestor was the man in charge was something that took me a long time to find out. The evidence has been very carefully buried and the history glossed over, but if you know where to start it can be found.

And it only makes sense for each leader of the secret organization to recruit their own son and groom them to take over the reigns one day. But the true genius of the plan was to insinuate members into places of power with in the government until you have in place the ability to take it over. You had enough members in place to control the congress and the senate; either through direct association or blackmail to pass any law you wanted. All that was waiting was the man to take up the presidency to start the ball rolling. And in today's climate of ethnic mistrust it would have been so easy to get those laws passes. What you people had planned would make apartide look like a mild social program in comparison.

So when I found out, I couldn't sit by and do nothing, I had to act. And with the power you people have in the government I couldn't rely on passing on the information and not having it suppressed so that meant I had to take matters into my own hands. If you haven't heard from the news already you will soon. The man that was shot was not the president, but the vice president. The sick, twisted, demented leader of your organization.

Right now I'm sure you are wondering how this could have happened. You were sure you had me over a barrel and that I was young and stupid enough to follow along with your plan. Well I saw my friend die, killed by your agents at your cottage. You had no hold over me at all but I couldn't let you know that or you would have gotten someone else to assassinate the president. I played along and even though I will hate myself for it, I decided to kill your leader and destroy this plot of yours. I knew that as long as he was alive, the president would never be safe. Well now he is dead, and with him any danger to the president, the government, or the country.

Just to let you know, I am coming for you too. Your only chance is to turn yourself in to the FBI and hope they put you someplace I can never find you.

Until then keep looking over your shoulder, I'll see you soon.

Regards

Charles Watkins"

Carter pounded on the desk screaming at the top of his voice. His bodyguards burst into the room with drawn guns ready for action. There was no one other then Carter in the room, but even still they checked everything over to be safe. It was at that moment that the TV newscaster announced to the world that the president was fine and on his way back to the White House. Tragically though the vice president had been killed in what was apparently an attempt on the president gone awry.

Carter threw an ashtray at the TV smashing it to pieces all the while screaming "no" over and over again.

Holly had been at work when the vice president was killed so she got the email that had been CC'd to her right away. Adam was with the president and as a result did not receive the email until he returned to his office, where a copy was waiting for him on his computer.

Holly called him on his private number as soon as she read the email over once and was relieved that he answered. After all things would be extremely hectic where he was.

"Hello? Who is this?" Adam asked in a harried voice.

"It's Holly McClare, I have some information you need to know right now."

"Miss McClare you must not have been watching the news but there was another attempt on the president I can't talk right now."

"Adam the attempt wasn't on the president, the intended target was the vice president."

There was several seconds of silence then Holly read the email to Adam letting him know that he was copied on the email as well so he would get to read it when he got back to his office.

"Since it was Charley that pulled the trigger I can only assume that the VP is dead?"

Adam, still stunned at what he had just heard simply replied. "Yes."

"I'll let you go for now but be sure to tell the president when you get a moment, he'll want to know that his life should be safe now."

"Thank you," Adam said, then hung up the phone to go and find his boss and let him know that the person behind the attempt on his life had been his own vice president.

Charley once again stashed his gear where he and Sean had hidden the last time. This time however Charley had no intention of hiding out or going down the shaft to the waiting organization killers. He crawled out of the air duct in one of the bathrooms and changed into the clean clothes he had brought with him, sealed in plastic bags. Washing up in a sink he wiped off the grime of the ventilation system and then covered his wet hair with a ball hat and walked out to the hallway, taking an elevator to the lobby. On the ground he exited the building and melted into the crowed doing the one thing the organization would never expect, heading toward the site of the shooting. He knew that there were organization agents waiting for him in the sewer assuming that that was how he would leave the building as that was what he had done the last time. This time however was different; he was a US marshal now.

As soon as he hit the street he was surrounded by mass confusion, people milling around trying to get closer to the podium area but being turned back by police as the area was sealed off and a search begun. Walked a few blocks encountering two cops who, seeing a man alone asked for ID. He flipped them his badge stating that he was in town on vacation and on his way to his hotel to check in, in case extra manpower was being requested. The two officers nodded and let him go immediately, knowing he was most likely going to be helping with the investigation in a short while.

Taking a cab back to his room he showered and then crawled into bed. He picked up the phone to call Holly but quickly put it down. It was one thing to call over the internet but another all together to call from a land line. They would trace him the second the call was connected and he could not risk that right now. Even though what he had done was, in his own mind, justified, he had still murdered the vice president of the United States. Worse he had sent an email admitting to the act. Before he called anyone and let them know where he was he would need to get a feel for how the government viewed his actions.

Once back at the White House Adam checked his email. He could not believe that what he was reading was true. At this point the only thing he could be sure of was that it had indeed been Charley that had killed the VP. He sent an email to the young man asking him to call as soon as possible. That done he headed to the residence to see the president and brief him what he had learned.

The President sat in total silence shaking is slowly side-to-side. His eyes were unfocused and starring across the room out a window into nothingness. Adam let him have a few minutes to absorb the news then asked if he needed a drink.

"Damn it yes I do, and so do you," the president said emphatically.

Adam mixed them both a scotch and handed a glass to his boss. "At least we know what happened sir, there is no wondering if it was another attempt on your life that simply went wrong."

"I almost wish it was Adam. It would be better then learning that the man I trusted all these years, the man I picked as my running mate to help me run this country, is a traitor to the very oath he swore on taking office."

"Sir none of that has been proven. We only have the word of the man that shot the vice president to go on at this point."

"Adam do you believe he was telling the truth in that message he sent?"

Adam hesitated for a moment, looking at the floor then raised his head "Yes I do sir," he answered with conviction.

"Well so do I. As deplorable as this sounds I think we may owe that young man a debt of gratitude we can never repay. We have to bury this whole thing, as quickly and deeply as we can. The country can never know that a traitor got elected as VP. That would shock the country to its core and destroy the entire political system."

"Worse than that sir, it would give every lunatic fringe organization out there the idea to try it themselves."

"How many people know about this?"

"The email was sent to Carter, Miss McClare and myself. It was Miss McClare that alerted me to it in the first place."

"Please ensure that miss McClare knows not to breath a word of this to anyone."

"Yes sir," Adam replied leaving to carry out his orders. The president gulped back the rest of the drink and thought about what he had just learned.

Carter was in the study storming around the room in anger, throwing things and cursing at anyone that came into his sight. He had been that way all afternoon, since the shooting of the vice president. The guards were concerned that he would have a heart attack and considered restraining him. Just as the head of security was about to call for a doctor Carter slammed open the door and lurched out holding a pistol in his hand. His eyes were bloodshot and his clothing was disheveled but when he spoke he sounded calm and back in control.

"Take me to see our guest, I want to let him know what that little shit he trained has done before I kill him." Sarcasm dripped off the word guest.

Two guards lead Carter to the basement where they had Sean chained to a post in the middle of the room. A measure of how dangerous they thought the man to be showed in the fact that there were always four men guarding him.

Carter stopped in front of the figure on the floor. "I just wanted you to know that you young protégé has managed to destroy the plan we spent a century trying to bring to fruition. I have ordered his death and once he is gone you will join him. Until that time you will remain tied up here like an animal and if needed used as bait to lure him here."

The figure on the floor began to chuckle in a low voice at this news. "He really did it? The lad really stopped you? I'll be damned." Sean Miller looked up at Carter, staring into his eyes. "How did he do it?"

"How he did it is immaterial, but I assure you he will pay for it with his life."

Sean just laughed at the statement. "Fools like you never change do you. That must be some deluded world you live in. You only came close once before and that was because Charley didn't think you were as ruthless as you are. Now that he knows, you haven't got a chance against that lad."

"But this time he doesn't have your traitorous help to run from us."

"Now this is one piece of news I'm actually going to enjoy telling you. The entire time we were 'on the run' as you term it, I wanted to do just that, run. But that lad would have no part of it. He wanted to bring you people down, and no matter what I said he wouldn't give up the idea of exposing you slimly thugs. We weren't running sunshine, we were trying to find you and your friends. We finally did and it was all because of Charley. I had nothing to do with it other then back him up with a gun. And here's some advice for free, because you're going to need it. When, not if, but when, that young man catches you, he is going to be extremely upset so the best you can hope for is that he kills you quick and clean."

Carter snapped and began kicking Sean and screaming at him. "You lie, you lie you lie. It was all your doing you filthy traitor. Without you the president would be dead and we would be in charge. All our plans are ruined because of your treachery."

Sean curled into a ball to protect himself. The kicks were mostly ineffective, as they weren't properly aimed. Carter was fat, old and out of shape so the fury of the assault died rapidly and the kicks slowed down until the man was standing over him panting like a dog. Even though it wasn't smart Sean goaded him more. "You know he's going to come after you don't you? He personally blames you for ruining his life and he wants revenge. It isn't about just stopping you, it's about ruining your life like you did his."

Carter took one more weak kick at Sean then headed to the door, but he slipped up and let out something he shouldn't have. "He thinks you are dead and nothing I say will convince him otherwise."

"If you let me go I'll try and talk the lad into letting you live. Once he knows I'm alive he'll be happy to go home. As long as you leave us alone we will leave you alone."

Carter turned to look at Sean with hatred burning in his eyes. "You will both die and by my hand. You took an oath to the organization and betrayed it. I would not trust you to keep your word again. Your very existence is a stain on my honor and I will not allow that. We will catch the impudent boy and once we have him you will be reunited so you can watch each other die in agony cursing the day your mothers bore you."

With that he was gone and Sean was left alone to think over what he had just learned. It was obvious that Carter was on the edge of insanity, but then anyone that would devote his entire life to trying to being down the country he was living in, wasn't to tightly wrapped to begin with. The thing that disturbed him most was that Charley thought he was dead. That could make the lad reckless and could kill them both.

The paperwork clearing both Sean and Charley was done and Adam sent an email to Charley to let him know that he was free man with a clear name. He also told the young man that the president had invited him to the White House to formally thank him for his efforts on behalf of the United States. He ended the email asking Charley to contact him at his earliest convenience.

Adam wanted to let him know that it had been decided to put a lid on the entire vice presidential assassination but was leery of putting anything in writing that could later leave a clue that anyone in the administration knew what had really happened.

The president had ordered that the Secret Service and FBI to investigate the matter and find the person that was responsible for the murder. In the Oval Office he had ordered that all traces of the email from Charley be deleted and that no one was to mention it again. He also ordered that the NSA do the same thing. Holly was tasked with this and within moments of getting the order had the systems purged of any trace of the email. She was sure that at some point a conspiracy theory would surface that blamed the government, they would never know how right they were.

Adam called Holly to find out if she had heard from Charley, the president was getting anxious to hear from the young man. Charley had been detected online several times but all attempts to talk to him were ignored. At this time no one knew exactly where he was but it was assumed that he was searching for Carter.

Charley had started his hunt for Carter as soon as he was clear of Boston. With no idea where the man was hiding, the only option available to him was to begin hunting known agents of the organization in an effort to locate one that knew where Carter was. He started in New York City with the list of agents he had found on the stooges laptop. Most of the agents were gone either having been arrested by the FBI or running to avoid being arrested, but he was able to find some of them along with several organization safe houses and business fronts. In all cases he broke the knees of the agents and set fire to the business fronts and safe houses. He searched everything he found, desperately trying to get a hint as to where his quarry was, but no matter what threats or tactics he used no one had any information on where Carter was.

He logged in to several of the bulletin boards used as information drops by the organization and left clear massages that he was looking for Carter. He offered a reward for information and his email address where he could be contacted should anyone want to contact him.

Each morning he checked his email and was bombarded with emails filled with promises of torture and death. There were also attempts to infect his computer with viruses. He simply ignored all this and kept searching for Carter, leaving a new message on the bulletin boards each day. He hated the methods he was forced to use but with nothing else to go on he was left very little in the way of options. He had ignored the emails from Adam and Holly promising him help. He knew that his methods would not be approved and if they tried to get information from these agents relying on legal means the men would simply demand a lawyer and say nothing. In this hunt he was on his own, there would be no one to help him out or watch his back.

From New York Charley headed to Washington to continue his hunt. He assumed that it would become both more dangerous and more difficult to find agents and capture them for questioning but he was wrong. The agents still in place in Washington seemed oblivious to the fact that Charley was on the hunt, and in most instances were taking no precautions at all. Charley had no idea it was because the people he found were all men that had been recruited in a manner similar to his own, and the president had ordered them left alone, going after only the true believers who had joined voluntarily. This didn't mean he relaxed his guard; on the contrary he became more cautious then ever.

To find an agent he took a name from the list and then did a web search for a phone number, which he was usually successful in finding. Once he had a number he hacked into the phone company computers and got the address for then scouted the place to see what type of security there was. In most cases there was no security at all. These agents had spent their lives operating in the country they had been born in, for an organization that no one knew even existed. For them the secrecy of who and what they were was their greatest security, and as a result none had felt the need to secure their homes. After all they were the hunters not the hunted. It was the organization that went after information and people not the other way around.

Charley had picked up more drugs for his tranquilizer guns. It was easy for him to pop a lock and gain entry and then wait until the owner arrived home. He waited till they entered and closed the door behind them then darted them with the fast acting drug. By the time they woke up they would be gagged and tied to a chair with Charley looming over them. In every case it was the same questions; where was Carter? Who did they report to? What was their mission?

As a result of the tranquilizer drug very little physical force had to be used, which made Charley happy. He didn't like the thought of torture but would resort to it only if he had to. So far no one knew where Carter was but he did get a few more names to add to the list and the addresses of organization businesses and safe houses. Once done the questioning he would knock the person out again then break both knees. Charley wanted them out of commission but he didn't feel there was any need to be cruel about it.

Charley used the names to move up the list and torched the businesses and safe houses. In every case he made it look like a robbery by ransacking the place and taking anything of value that could be pawned or fenced. In one case the organization owned a pawnshop that was being used to fence stolen goods. Charley walked in carrying all the stolen goods he had to pawn and looked over the security. It was about average for a pawnshop relying more on the man behind the counter being armed then anything else. Charley went back that night and robbed the place then as he did every other time he called the police and gave an anonymous tip. That way the agents would get hospital care and his movements were written off to a home invasion turned violent.

It had been three weeks since the vice president had died and while Charley had talked to a lot of agents no one had any idea where Carter was. He was getting a lot of emails from Holly and Adam wondering where he was and what he was doing, he had even gotten an email from the president requesting he visit the White House. His name was clear and no one was looking for him. He should be happy, he should feel great that he had a clear name again, but all he could think of was his dead friend and mentor. Sean should have lived out a good retirement, with peace and honor, after the horror of serving the organization for most of his life.

Sean was getting strange looks from the guards now when they came to drop off his food. Since the first visit from Carter he had not seen the man since, but had heard the guards talking in low voices. It seemed that Charley was hunting down agents and kneecapping them as well as setting fire to any organization business or safe house he found. And to add insult to injury the Lad was posting messages on the internet telling everyone he wanted Carter and that if the organization gave him up the hunting would stop. Carter was becoming more and more paranoid each day and now only those most trusted people were allowed to see him. He had locked himself in house and wouldn't leave. The guards were also restricted to the grounds and food was being dropped off at the front of the house with access restricted to only those personally authorized by Carter.

Sean could see the panic in Carter trickling down to the men. He was not a leader, he was a manager. He had never been in any personal danger before in his life always having worked in the shadows using go betweens with his identity kept hidden. Now that he was out in the open he was feeling what it was like to be a marked man. He was feeling the terror he had inflicted on so many others. All because of Charley. Sean smiled at the thought of what the Lad was doing and silently wished him good luck.

For his own welfare Sean was not optimistic. He was actually surprised that Carter had kept him alive this long. If Charley believed him dead then he was useless as bait and just another mouth to feed, someone to waste manpower guarding. Initially he had tried to talk to the guards but they had orders to ignore him and followed them to the letter. They watched him but never spoke to him. He was fed twice a day and given water whenever he asked for it. There was a sleeping pad and chemical toilet placed with in reach but that was all. He wasn't allowed to bath although he tried his best to wash with some of the water he was given. As a result of being chained to a post with limited movement Sean spent most of the day sleeping. When he was awake he tried to keep in shape with sit ups and push ups being careful to not break a sweat, just keep the muscles toned, but it was not the same as regular activity.

The worst part for him was living in the same clothes day after day. He could feel the grime building up on his body. The only good part was that because he didn't move much he hadn't built up an overpowering body odor. He still asked the guards for soap and clean clothes so he could wash and change but no one was listening.

One morning he heard movement but ignored it until a gruff voice ordered him to his feet. Opening his eyes he realized the reason for the sudden compassion he had been shown, Carter had come to visit him.

"That little bastard you trained is creating havoc among my agents." Carter yelled spit flying from his mouth.

Sean could not believe the sight of the man. He had aged ten years, smelled terrible, and was wearing filthy clothes. His eyes were red rimmed and looked as if he hadn't slept in a long time. He was also carrying a large pistol that he clutched so tightly his knuckles were white.

"What is he up to?" Carter demanded to know.

"I have no idea, I've been locked up in this basement."

"You're lying, I can smell the treachery on you. Tell me what he is up to or I'll kill you here and now." Carter pointed the gun at Sean's stomach.

Sean was at a loss for words, if he didn't say something he was a dead man, but he had no information to give the deranged man. With nothing more to lose, he decided to push the man even further "He is coming for you. His entire goal was to get the man that ruined his life. As you said, he thinks I'm dead so he wants revenge, he wants you dead now too," Sean explained with no idea that he had hit the nail on the head.

"Are you saying that when you were with him all he wanted was to stop me, not kill me?"

"He wanted you in prison to suffer for what you did to him. That was all he was trying to do." This wasn't exactly the truth but Carter had no way of knowing. When Sean and Charley had been hunting the organization they had only wanted to clear their names. After that, whatever happened would have been up to the government, they really didn't care one way or the other

"If I let you go do you think he would leave me alone?"

Sean realized that the strain on the man had been too great; he was coming apart and grasping at straws. "I'm sure of it. If I can talk to him I can convince him that you have suffered enough and to leave you alone."

Carter thought to himself for a moment then his eyes glassed over again and he began yelling again. "LIAR, LIAR, LIAR!!!! You are just trying to save your own worthless life. Once you are free you would help that spawn of Satan kill me. I will see you both dead, BOTH OF YOU!"

Carter almost ran from the room heading back up to the study to lock himself in and go over more reports from the agents he had looking for Charley.

"That man has gone nuts and is going to get everyone killed," Sean said to himself. Then added for the guards benefit, "Of course it doesn't matter to me much, I was already marked for death, but I feel sorry for you lot." Then he laid down again.

The next morning the head of the security force allowed Sean to go upstairs for a shower and told everyone to leave the room, remaining as the only guard to watch the prisoner.

"I need to ask you a question."

Sean was surprised by this but didn't let it show simply grateful for the chance to be clean once again. "Sure, go ahead."

"You trained Charley, just how good is he?"

"What I told your boss before, the entire war against you people, that was all Charley's planning. I was along for the ride. And if you'll remember he got away, I was the one that was caught."

The guard ignored the comment "But you helped him escape after he missed the first try at the President. Why did you do that?"

"I helped him? Who told you that? The truth is that Charley knocked me out before the hit ever took place. And for the record, that boy hit exactly what he was aiming at. He meant to shoot that woman in the leg and he did. But what do you mean by first try? He only tried once." Sean said confused at the reference to more then one shooting

The guard narrowed his eyes at that. "He didn't miss? Are you sure?"

"Positive. What ever that boy aims at he hits. He was using a .50 cal that he had put together himself. He is a scary shot with a rifle."

"So if Charley was to try a second time and miss that time too, then it would not be an accident?"

"I can promise you that the last thing on earth Charley would do is try to kill the president. He wouldn't do it even to save my life."

"Sean the vice president was assassinated. The FBI is saying that the real target was the president but that the shooter missed and hit the vice president who was standing next to him. Would Charley do something like that?"

A light popped on in Sean's head. The screaming of Carter and the statement that Charley had ruined everything. Could it be that the vice president had been controlled by the organization? It would make sense for that to be the case considering how much effort they put into trying to kill the president. Sean realized that he was taking to long to answer the question. "No he wouldn't, if the VP is dead and it was Charley that pulled the trigger then he meant to kill the VP and no one else."

"Has anyone told you what he is doing now?"

"The only information I have been given is what your boss has told me. And I tend not to believe that too much."

The Guard checked his watch and motioned for Sean to dry off and get dressed. "Your young friend has been kneecapping our agents and burning down our safe houses and businesses when ever he finds them in an attempt to find my boss. He is posting this on the web and telling everyone that all he wants is our boss and the rest of us are free to do what ever we want, as long as we leave him alone. He was in New York for a while but we think he is now in Washington. We sent an action team after him but we never came close. He eventually got all the members of the team one at a time. The reports from the agents he talks to all say he only asking for information about the board member and where he is, nothing else."

Sean smiled as he slipped on his shirt. "That sounds like Charley. Too kind to kill them."

"I'm glad you think his crippling people is kind."

"Look at it this way, at least they are alive. He could be leaving a trail of dead bodies behind him."

"You mean he is deliberately not killing anyone?"

"That's right. The Lad only kills when he feels it's absolutely needed. If he is kneecapping it's only to make sure that they don't come after him anytime soon."

The guard seemed to think for a moment then came to some decision of his own. "If we were to free you and hand the remaining board member over to the police would you stop Charley?"

Sean was stunned and it showed. The guard smiled at the look on his face then asked him the question again.

"Yes I would. After all, the Lad wants revenge on the man who is responsible for trying to ruin his life. If that man is in jail then I think Charley would settle for that. But to be honest I don't think you want that to happen. If that man thinks that he is being betrayed then he will fight back like a cornered rat. That could be trouble for all of us. I think it better if he retired completely, if you understand what I mean?"

The guard nodded then opened the door and motioned the others inside to put the chains back on Sean. They lead him back to the basement and tied him to the post with out anyone saying another word. Then he was left alone for the first time since he had been captured.

A few minutes later one guard came back and tossed a set of keys at Sean's feet, turned around and left. Sean cautiously picked up the keys and removed his locks. Not sure what to do he approached the stairs slowly, being as quiet as he could, went up one at a time, pressing himself close to the wall so as to keep his weight as much to the side as he could. This eliminated most of the sound but not all. There was the odd squeak at which Sean froze then resumed when no one showed in the stairwell to investigate the noise.

At the top the door was open and the place sounded deserted, there was no noise at all that he could hear. Peeking around the doorway he spied no one at all in his line of site. He made his way to the door and looked into the yard. He saw a van leaving the driveway that looked full of men. Glancing around the yard there was no one in site and no vehicles in site either. Sean could see a barn but the door was wide open and he couldn't see anything inside it.

Looking down the hallway he spied the kitchen and moved towards it carefully checking for any sound that would indicate another presence. The kitchen was empty and he looked through the drawers finding several knives, picking one that felt like a suitable weapon he picked it up and continued his search of the house. The doors to rooms were open, nothing was in disarray. It looked very much like when they left they had planned this, taking time to clean the place down. It had probably been wiped for fingerprints as well.

Moving upstairs Sean began checking out the bedrooms and got a major shock when he saw Carter tied up lying in the middle of a bed in one of the rooms. There was a pulse but the man was obviously out cold as he did not stir when Sean nudged him. The bindings on his hands and feet were secure but not tight enough to cut off circulation so it was safe to conclude that he wasn't going anywhere until he was released by someone else.

The rest of the house was empty, not even any personal items were left behind. Sean checked out the outside as well, there, also finding that the place had been well cleaned. Not knowing what else to do he picked up the phone and got a dial tone. Charley had made him memorize the number that Adam had given them just in case he ever had to call the man. With no one else to call he dialed the number now, hoping that he was not making the wrong move.

Adams personal phone rang as he was trying to write a memo. He pulled the phone out of his pocket and looked at the call display but did not recognize the number. "Hello? Who is this?" Adam asked very annoyed at the interruption.

"Hello I'm looking for Adam," Sean said simply

"Who is this?" Adam demanded again.

"I don't expect you to remember me but we met on a beach a while ago. My name is Sean."

"WHAT? But you're dead! I mean it was reported that you had died. Charley said that you had died" Adam nearly shouted into the phone.

Sean chuckled. "To borrow a line from Mark Twain 'reports of my death have been greatly exaggerated'. I'm very much alive."

"How.... where...I mean where are you now. How can I help?"

"I hope you can, I don't know how to contact Charley to let him know I'm all right. The other problem is that I have no idea where I am."

"I can have a trace run on your number if you hold on for just a moment," Adam told him.

"Sure thing but before you call anyone else, get back to me please?" Sean asked him.

"I will, just hold on." Adam hit the mute button and picked up his office line to have a trace run on the number that had come up on his cell when Sean had called. In less then a minute Adam had the address of the number Sean was at and gave it to him.

"I can have someone out there to pick you up in a couple of hours," Adam told Sean.

"Is there anyway you can contact Charley and let him know where I am? I have his email address but no computer to contact him with."

"He gave me an email address to use as well. I can send him your number and ask him to call you but to be honest Charley isn't really talking to us these days. Are you aware of what had happened over the last few days?"

"Well I know the major stuff but I'll let the lad fill me in on the details when I see him. I have some news for him as well. If you'll send the email I'll wait for him. But please don't tell anyone else that I called."

Adam agreed and as soon as he was off the phone sent an email to Charley informing him that Sean was alive and the number to call him at.

Charley did not check his email until late that night and when he did read Adam's email he thought it was a hoax. He thought about calling Adam to see if he had sent an email then decided to just call the number listed. If it was a hoax he would be able to tell when he spoke with whoever answered the phone.

It was dark and Carter was awake when the phone finally rang. Sean had known it would take time to reach Charley so he was prepared for a long wait. He had made sure Carter was secure but that his binds would not restrict blood flow. "Hello?" he answered.

Charley heard his old friends voice and tears welled in his eyes. "Is that really you Sean?"

"Hey Lad, how have you been? I heard you were causing a bit of a ruckus lately."

"Old man I thought you were dead. Are you okay? Where are you?" The questions piled on top of one another.

"I'm fine lad, just fine, but I have a problem that I need to talk to you about. By the way what happened to the two board members you had?"

"They're dead. And when I see Carter he will be too. I'll explain it all when I see you, tell me where you are and I'll be on my way."

Sean gave the young man the address and then explained that the grenade that Charley thought had killed him had only stunned him and knocked him out. He had been captured and used as bait but for some reason the organization guards had taken off leaving him free. Sean wasn't sure if they would be back was fairly sure that they were gone for good. It looked like the organization was falling apart, and when Charley asked how he knew that it was then that he explained he had Carter.

Charley was shocked at that news and told his old mentor that he was on his way, then disconnected and packed up. Putting away the computer he then started thinking over the call. In his excitement over hearing Sean's voice he hadn't even tried to verify that this wasn't a trick. He knew it was his friends voice but how did he know it hadn't been recorded and washed through filters to make it sound the way someone else wanted it to. He had no evidence that Sean was free and that he wasn't walking into a trap. Things were now not adding up, how did Sean have Carter? How was it that he was alive and free now after so long a time? There were a lot of questions that he should have asked, but it was too late now. He would simply head in as if it was a trap and see what happened next. Even if it was a trap Carter would be close. He wanted Charley too badly to not be around somewhere.

About the same time Charley was having doubts Sean started realizing that the lad hadn't been suspicious enough on the phone. He knew he would show up but by the time he did he would think that he was walking into a trap. That was an easy way to get shot so Sean decided that he would make sure Charley saw nothing that would make him nervous or edgy. The lad hadn't given him an arrival time but he assumed it would be the next day. He would get a good night's sleep then spend the day sitting on the front step in plan site with carter on the ground in front of him.

Charley took his time driving planning on getting there at noon the next day. He drove past the property once with out slowing or looking too closely and saw no cars or people around. The house it's self was a way off the road and had a barn next to it. The trees had been cleared all around to a distance of several hundred yards giving it a commanding filed of fire. There were trees in the back of the property but none at all in the front. It looked deserted from the road but that didn't mean that there wasn't someone hiding in the upstairs window with a sniper rifle. A look at a map showed a road ran near the back of the property as well so he circled around to come up from the rear through what tree cover there was there.

Parking a mile down the road, he opened the back of the van and took out his gear, wrapped in a duffel bag so no one could see it. He stepped down into the ditch and began walking back to where the house was located. Moving through the trees he was careful to look for trip wires and snares or anything that was man made. Once he was a few yards away from the road and sheltered by some trees he opened the duffel and took out the MG34 and assembled it. Once assembled, he clipped a fifty round drum to the breech and cycled a round. He took out a set of web gear, clipped spare drums of ammo to it, then removed a silenced .22 and holstered that on the web gear as well. Dropping the duffel he slung the MG over his shoulder and headed toward the house, this time prepared for anything that the organization would have waiting for him.

Sean had moved a chair out onto the porch and found a book to read in the house. He was enjoying the nice weather and the book was actually very good. It was a mystery by a writer he had never heard of, but was very well done. Carter lay at his feet tied up. The old man had spent a large portion of the morning cursing at Sean and thrashing around trying in vain to get free. The resiliency and hatred of Carter was amazing. Sean had thought he would be exhausted from his exertions before an hour went by but here it was nearing 1 in the afternoon and he hadn't stopped since 10 AM. Carter was bathed in sweat and his skin had an unhealthy gray color to it, Sean figured him for a heart attack if he didn't start relaxing. Of course his dying of natural causes would end the dilemma of what to do with him.

Sean caught a flash of movement and looked up to see Charley standing at a corner of the barn pointing a machine gun at the house. Slowly putting the book down he lifted his hands chest high and stood up.

"It's damn good to see you Lad. Even if you are pointing that at me," Sean said, his voice husky with emotion.

Charley lowered the barrel but didn't point his weapon away from the house. "I still can't believe you're alive Sean."

As soon as he heard Charley's voice Carter rolled over and started screaming at the top of his voice. He told both men that they were dead and described horrific ways that they would be tortured and killed. Sean kicked him hard and told him to shut up.

"I promise you that we are the only two here Lad, but if you like I'll drag the old windbag over there to you."

"I'd like that a lot Sean, thanks."

Sean stood and grabbed carter by the feet, then hauled him across the yard to where Charley was. The lad motioned for Sean to keep going around the back of the barn, following them. Once out of site of the house and road Charley felt easier about being out of sight but was still nervous that it was still a trap.

Sean noticed this and tried again to reassure the lad that everything was okay. "Lad I know it makes no sense, but the security guards bugged out leaving me and the fat man here alone. I have checked the place over from top to bottom and there is nothing and no one around."

"What about aerial surveillance?"

"Good point but why risk leaving him here." Sean pointed to Carter. "I don't think they would risk his life for a trap, he's too valuable."

"So why would the security men leave him trussed up for you and take off?"

"I do believe that you would be the reason for that lad. Some of the men were getting nervous that you would catch up with them eventually and they didn't like that thought. But it doesn't matter now; you're here so let's get the hell out of here. We can drop this guy off at the first police station we come to."

Charley pulled out his .22 and pointed it at Carter's head. "We aren't dropping him anywhere old man. The president doesn't think that it would be good for the country for him to stand trial. Before Sean could say anything Charley put five bullets into Carter's head. Changing clips to reload, he holstered the pistol and hitched the MG a little higher on his shoulder getting ready to leave.

"Well that answers the problem of what to do with him," Sean said casually. "Which way to your ride?"

Charley handed Sean a loaded 9 MM and began retracing his steps back to his car with Sean following behind. There were a lot of questions that each had for the other but they would wait until they were away from the place and felt much safer. The hike back went quicker as they were not concerned that they were walking into a trap so they moved fast, making good time.

Once in the van and on the move Sean asked Charley what he had been up to. Charley explained everything starting from the moment he had seen Sean go down. The story took a while to tell and as he was telling it Charley was constantly watching for a tail. The Lad explained what the organization really was all about and who had been the actual leader. He related the blackmail attempt and how he had simply cut the head off by killing the VP. He also told Sean that the only reason he was able to do what he did was that he figured Sean was dead so the threat to kill him was an empty one, as far as Charley was concerned. Once he knew why they wanted the President dead he knew the only way to stop them was to kill the head. At this point Sean now understood why Carter had said that the young man had ruined everything.

"So with the leader and all the board members and juniors now dead, what happens to the organization?" Sean asked.

"Don't know and don't care. You and I are out of it. We have our names cleared and we can live a normal life again."

Sean chuckled. "After the last year are you sure you could ever live a normal life again lad?"

"Well old man I sure want the chance to try. I'm glad this nightmare is over. But the big question is what are you going to do?"

"I don't know lad. I never really thought about any kind of a life away from the organization. They are all I've really known. I can say this though; it feels great to have the chance to make my own choices and maybe even plan for retirement. I was hoping I could spend some time at your place, if you don't mind of course."

Charley looked at his friend. "My house is your house, for as long as you want."

"Well that's a relief, I haven't got anywhere else to go and no job or money to go with."

"What do you mean no money? The cash we took from the organization is half yours and I've gotten a little more in the last couple weeks. How does it feel to be rich?"

The two started laughing and didn't stop for miles. Life was looking up for both men.

The trip back to Nova Scotia went without incident, the only stop was to get back the young man's car and then the two traveled straight through with one driving while the other slept. Charley wanted to be out of the country as soon as possible and Sean agreed.

Once in Nova Scotia the two put the weapons back in the bunker keeping a couple of rifles and pistols out as personal protection, then went to the house. Charley set up the satellite and computer and logged onto the net to talk to Holly one last time. It was the middle of the afternoon so he knew she would be around. The conversation was short and to the point, he told her where Carter's body was and that he was home with Sean, both of them were fine. He thanked her for the help and wished her well adding that he was done and home for good, then signed off and shut down the computer.

Satisfied that all the loose ends were tied up Charley went into the kitchen to start making something to eat. Just as he was finished Sean appeared in the doorway having smelled what was cooking and the phone rang. The two looked at each other with raised eyebrows both wondering who would be calling, the old suspicions instantly raised after the past year.

Charley picked up the phone. "Hello?"

"Hello Mr Watkins, this is the President of the united states. I wanted to speak with you in person and thank you for the great service you have done for our country. May I call you Charley?"

Charley wasn't sure that he had heard right and simply said yes.

"Charley, I understand that Sean Miller is with you and he is doing fine as well, is that correct?"

"Yes sir it is."

"Would it be possible to get him on the line as well?"

"Just one moment sir and I'll do that." Charley had Sean pick up the extension phone telling him that it was the President of the US.

Once they were both on the line the president continued. "First I want to personally thank you for saving my life. I would also like to thank you for the great service you have done for my country. You both have done an outstanding job and we, myself included treated you extremely poorly. My chief of staff Adam has suggested that in light of your service we award you the Freedom Medal, it's our countries highest civilian award, and I agree. I would like to invite you to the White House for a visit and so that this nation can properly thank you for what you have done for us."

Charley answered first. "Thank you for your offer sir but to be truthful I'm not sure that is such a good idea. After all we were federal fugitives for a long time and I don't think the public ever needs to know about us. If we show up at the White House there will be questions asked and eventually what happened might come out. It was my pleasure to help bring down the organization and I did it as much for me as for you."

Sean joined in, in declining. "I agree with Charley, Mr President. Just being free of the organization is reward enough for me sir."

The president smiled at his Chief of Staff having just won a bet that they would decline the offer. "I understand gentleman. There is one other thing I'd like to offer. You are a very effective team and we can always use men like yourselves. I'd like to offer you a job with the NSA, don't answer me now, think it over and get back to me. If I don't hear from you I'll take that as no."

The conversation went on for several more minutes with out Sean or Charley answering the president on his offer of employment. Then it was time for him to hang up and he again thanked the two leaving them his personal number should the ever need to call him.

After hanging up Sean came back into the kitchen and sat down at the table. "Are you interested in his offer lad?"

"Not really Sean, I think I've had my share of action for my lifetime, besides I don't think I could get used to dragging your sorry butt out of trouble all the time. But what about you? After working for the organization for all these years are you sure you can get used to the slow life here?"

Sean leaned back in his chair. "Lad I've never had anyone in my life look out for me before you. I've sort of gotten used to it over the last few months. If it's all the same to you I think I'd like to retire here, don't worry, I can pay for my room and board, my last employer gave me a generous retirement package. Now, what's to eat?"

Charley laughed at the old man and put the food on the table, relaxed and finally home.

Printed in the United States
64000LVS00003B/13-21

9 781424 143535